MW00606397

KINGS OF THE HIGH FRONTIER

by

Victor Koman

Book One
of
The High Pilgrimage

Final Frontier
Books

Kings of the High Frontier is a work of Fiction. All names, places, and institutions (both public and private) are either completely imaginary or used fictitiously. There have been, are, and will be many attempts — some high profile, some clandestine — to break the bonds of Earth. Any resemblance to actual people — living or dead — or to actual events, locales, secret projects, or high-level conspiracies is entirely coincidental. Any resemblance to actual governments and their institutions is purely malicious.

Published by Final Frontier Books, a subsidiary of Bereshith Publishing. Printed and bound in the United States of America.

First Limited Edition 1998
ISBN 0-9665662-0-3

Library of Congress Catalog Card Number: 98-86467

Final Frontier Books
a subsidiary of Bereshith Publishing
PO Box 2366
Centreville, VA 20120
(703) 815-0600
tempus@mindspring.com
www.bereshith.com

Kings of the High Frontier

Victor Koman

Victor Koman

This first edition of KINGS of the HIGH FRONTIER is limited to 1250 signed and numbered copies of which this is number 807.

Other Books by Victor Koman

Solomon's Knife

MILLENNIUM: Weeds

The Jehovah Contract

Jonuta Rising! (with Andrew J. Offutt)

The Carnadyne Horde (with Andrew J. Offutt)

DEDICATED TO A
WHO BURN WITH THE

Dramatis Personae

Tamara Reis	Space Shuttle Pilot
Gerald Cooper	President, CEO, Freespace Orbital Launch Vehicle Company
Sherry Cooper	CFO, Freespace Orbital, Gerald Cooper's Wife
Thom Brodsky	Freespace Orbital engineer; Editor, *Private Space Journal*
Dr. Barry Gibbon	Founder, *National Organization of Space Supporters*
Evangeline Gibbon	His spinster sister
Joseph Lester	Reporter
Hillary Kaye	Photographer
Laurence Norman Poubelle	President & CEO, American Atomic
Chemar D'Asaro	Poubelle's co-pilot
William David Crockett IV	Physics grad student, New York University
Bernadette Wyzykowski	Engineering grad student, New York University
Samuel Friedman	Chemistry grad student, New York University
Marcus Aurelius Grant	Smuggler & Black Marketeer
Joscelyn Donahue	Grant's aide
Montgomery Barron	National Security Agency, Project *Stark Fist*
Jack Lundy	NASA SRB engineer
Melissa Lundy	NASA environmental engineer
Alan Shepard Lundy	Col., U.S. Space Command
Chad Haley	Virtual Proselytizer
Paul Volnos	Tammy Reis' childhood friend
"Ace" Roberts	Aging rocket tinker
Col. Vladimir Tuchapski	Commander, Space Force (Russia)
Ludlow Woolsey III	U.S. Senator (Utah)
Ludlow Woolsey IV	U.S. Representative (Oregon)
Cdr. Scott Boyd	NASA Shuttle Commander
Jon Franck	Astronaut
Samantha Madison	Astronaut
Federico Kayanja	Astronaut
Bryan Kirk	Manager, NASA Astronaut Corps
Rex Iverson	Aging writer
Grace Iverson	His wife
William Braverman	Satellite media mogul
Steven James Milton Jr.	National Security Advisor
Nolan Crane	President, United States
Ed Laird	Ex-astronaut; owner and barkeep of The Heat Shield

It is the heretic that makes the fire,
Not she which burns in't.

—William Shakespeare
A Winter's Tale

PROLOGUE

I dreamed of falling out of the sky, of burning up, of feeling intense pain, then blackness, then nothing.
— **Brian O'Leary**
The Making of an Ex-Astronaut

Falling…
Falling…
Nine miles and more.

The ocean and sky merged into one seamless blue-grey blur as she dropped in free fall for a terrifying eternity. Hands that must have been hers reached for the helmet behind and above her head, but fear-clenched fingers refused to obey her commands.

A whistling sound outside intensified until it swelled into a banshee howl of death. The crew cabin shifted about with a gut-wrenching jolt. Wires and control cables trailing behind the shattered orbiter gripped the thickening atmosphere, acting like vanes to stabilize the cabin's descent. Now she clearly saw where they were doomed to die.

No one could save them. Something had gone terribly wrong and nothing could stop their horrible plunge into the Atlantic.

It had happened at throttleup. The shuttle started to oscillate. Then the explosion. Then an awful lurch as the crew cabin broke free and — no longer aerodynamically streamlined — hit the thin atmosphere and began to tumble wildly.

One of them screamed. That she heard it at all meant that the compartment still held pressure. Atmospheric forces acted upon the cabin, slowing the huge piece of the demolished orbiter, shoving them forward against their restraining straps. As if a giant's hand dragged them toward the earth, she felt a mighty force in front of her pull them down, down, downward to the sea.

She wanted to scream but no breath escaped her frozen lungs. The orbiter contained no ejection seats, the controls of the ruined crew cabin connected to nothing, the wings and rudder and elevons trailed somewhere far away, fluttering slowly in pieces toward the ocean.

Her tortured mind frantically sought some way to survive, but only one horrifying realization seized her terror-consumed thoughts.

They lied!

The screaming outside grew louder than even the thundering roar of liftoff. They plummeted straight toward a delicate mosaic of waves in the wall of water below.

It couldn't be much longer, could it? Did Houston know they were alive?

Her family watched from the Cape. Watched this!

The looser cables ripped away from the cabin with the shattering crack of gunshots.

Ahead of her — below her — glittered the tiny white splashes of a frolicking pod of dolphins.

"Oh, God!"

Tammy Reis awakened an instant before impact. She always did.

Heart racing, sweat-soaked, she ran a pale, trembling hand through her neck-length sable hair, then reached toward the night stand. The cool condensation on the water glass sent a chill through her fingers and palm. She shuddered and took a long drink.

The explosion of the space shuttle *Challenger* years before still haunted her dreams. For a space shuttle commander, such nightmares constituted a betrayal by that most intimate of enemies, her subconscious mind.

She refused to submit. After every night of terror in which she fell to her death, Tammy Reis seized the dawn with an angry fervor, a renewed conviction that she would not permit the spectre of death to wrap its dark claws once more around the Shuttle. She possessed the power — the *will* — to steer NASA toward its destiny. Death, even her own death, served a higher cause if it came while reaching, not cowering. And in every morning light that pierced the darkness of her private hell, she clenched her fist up at Fate and swore anew that she would triumph.

Part One

The Velvet Glove

CHAPTER 1

All pioneers throughout history have reached their destinations either in spite of or because of interference from others. They either willingly departed intolerable social conditions (the Plymouth settlers) or were forcibly deported (the Botany Bay colony). While we see no agency that would exile us to Space (we should be so lucky), we plainly see many that would forcibly prevent us from leaving Earth. These agencies, groups, or individuals are demonstrably the enemies of peace, progress, and human evolution. Their names shall become known to you.

— Preface to *The Orbital Settlers' Guide*

14 January, First Year

A warm gulf breeze caressed Tammy's face as she ran through the humid Houston morning. She exercised despite the billowing rain clouds, as she did every day at dawn after her arrival at the Lyndon B. Johnson Space Center. Rainy days soothed her. IFR days she called them, because she would use instrument flight rules when piloting a jet on such a day. Constant drizzle or intermittent downpour, wet weather calmed her in a way no sunny day could. When it rained, the spirit surrounding the Space Center mirrored the stark greyness in her heart.

Houston was home to the Johnson Space Center not because it was intended to be the source of any manned spaceflights, but because President John Kennedy, nearly four decades before, required the cooperation of his running mate to win votes in the south and west during the hotly contested 1960 election. The price of such cooperation was for Texas to control spacecraft launched from Florida — from Cape Canaveral, 900 miles away. The deal set the tenor of all subsequent space projects.

The Johnson Space Center and its Floridian counterpart shared one unfortunate similarity: both endured frequent encounters with hurricanes. One was due this morning.

Tammy ran amid evidence of the power of the National Aeronautics and Space Administration and felt like a child among giants: rockets permanently affixed to pedestals towered over her head; spacecraft flown by her heroes long before she was born arced toward the slate sky, frozen in flight; flags snapped loudly in the wind. She took a deep breath and savored the warm, wet smells released by the approaching low-pressure weather system. The smacking sound her running shoes made against the wet pavement put her in a runner's trance with its steady beat. She had to psych herself up for one of her most loathsome duties as an astronaut: another session of Meet The Crank.

▼ ▲ ▼

Tammy sat in the cramped conference room waiting for the arrival of her nine o'clock appointment. The clean, dry shuttle astronaut jump suit felt crisp and businesslike against her skin. She glanced at her calculator watch beneath the cobalt-blue sleeve: nine-fifteen. Only mildly annoyed, she resumed reading the tech manual for the new flight software required by the new advanced shuttle rocket motors that would soon be used on *Constitution*, the fifth orbiter Congress had seen fit to fund to maintain employment in key districts an election ago.

A moment later, she heard a knock on the open door. Glancing up, she saw a tall, gaunt man dressed impeccably in a dark blue suit, white shirt, and narrow black tie. He could have been an executive for a major computer company, but behind his deep brown eyes glowed a fire which the forces of corporate evolution generally selected against.

"Gerald Cooper?" she asked.

"Dr. Reis." His voice was level, authoritative, something she had not expected from someone who fancied himself a spacecraft designer.

"Call me Tammy," she said. "That's what the press corps wants."

"And what do you want?"

"A five-minute meeting," she said with curt politeness. NASA arranged these disagreeable affairs, and Reis and the other astronauts unlucky enough to pull such public-relations duty resented the time lost.

Cooper sat on one side of the minor axis of the elliptical table, slid a black leather portfolio onto its polished surface, and immediately pulled drawings from inside. One by one, he quickly slid them in front of her. She sat back and watched.

He had obviously rehearsed his spiel to be quick and simple. Simple, that is, to someone as intimately involved with spacecraft as Tamara Reis.

"Vertical takeoff and landing, single-stage-to-orbit rocket using a super-cooled liquid hydrogen slurry for fuel. Reentry using low-cost ablation rather than tiles for atmospheric braking. Off-the-shelf components where possible. Hull made of aircraft-grade aluminum. Can be manned or unmanned." He looked at her. "Or should I say 'crewed or uncrewed'?"

She smiled for the first time that morning, a sardonic curl to her lips. "Be as crude as you want to anything but the language."

He grinned back at her, then promptly continued: "Payload for this small version is two thousand pounds to low Earth orbit, fourteen thousand for the larger. If the engines, airframe, and avionics meet their minimum design lifetime of one hundred flights, cost per flight could be between a few hundred thousand and a million dollars."

All Reis said was: "Spreadsheets." He produced them instantly.

She looked them over for a moment, then said, "You estimate the cost of construction to be one hundred million dollars?"

"For the large version. The small one should be around twenty million."

She frowned. "You're talking about routine access to Space in craft only a little more costly than airliners."

Cooper nodded.

"You realize that the capabilities of this..." — she glanced at the name on the designs — "Starblazer of yours are similar to the promises initially made for the Shuttle: low cost, fast turnaround time, small ground crew for launch."

Cooper nodded and said nothing. She watched him for a moment, realizing that he must have been through this many times before, must have reached this point with others, and now he sat patiently, as if expecting the head-shake to come, followed by a condescending smile at the dreamer and a hundred reasons why he was wrong. Instead, Astronaut Reis turned her attention back at the spreadsheets.

The five-minute mark came and went.

After ten minutes, Reis raised her head to gaze at her visitor. In her eyes glimmered something beyond mere approval, something approaching near reverence. Yet her first question belied the look: "Do you know why this spacecraft will never fly?"

Cooper remained silent.

"Neither do I." She let the papers slide back to the surface of the table. "Whom have you shown these to?"

"Everyone I can. People at Stratodyne, General Aerospace, MacArthur-Truitt. You're the first one at NASA to grant me an interview."

Her smile came back; just a tilt on the right side of her mouth. "I didn't grant it. You were sloughed off to me. I'm supposed to let you talk for a few minutes, awe you with my presence, give you an autograph, and hustle you out. We receive hundreds of requests for meetings every day, Mr. Cooper. People who want to tell NASA that we're going about it all wrong, or that God is angry at our attempts to breach Heaven, or that they have evidence the Apollo moon landings never happened. Add to them the malcontents and half-wits who want to be astronauts, and we endure a flood of requests. We even get a few spacecraft designers a month. I've met some of them. They're all very sincere. And their designs are trash, lead buckets that could never fly." She laid her hands upon the diagrams and figures, strong hands with trim, clean, unpolished nails that she suddenly realized were the kind of hands into which such a miracle should be delivered. "These could work. These *would* work. And at the costs you estimate. Why?"

"Because," he answered slowly and carefully, "Freespace Orbital does not labor under NASA's technological imperative to create new systems. Everything in Starblazer is based on currently available technology."

Reis nodded grimly, feeling suddenly very old, like a mother who had watched too many of her children die young. "And that is why your attempt to interest NASA is futile. You'll never procure a contract to build something this cheap, this simple, this... *effective*."

Cooper looked mystified. Not at the truth of her words, she suspected, but at the fact she uttered them at all. She watched as, slowly, an awareness took hold of him. She had told him as directly as she could that NASA was uninterested in Starblazer not because it wouldn't work, but because it *would*. His gaze hardened, his voice cooled. "Dr. Reis, I'm afraid there's been some sort of awful misunderstanding."

She looked at him with a premonition of danger, as if she had just lit a fuse to something uncontainably explosive.

"I never intended," Cooper said, "to ask for NASA's help with Starblazer."

"Then what do you want of us?"

"I want NASA to stay out of my way."

Reis stared at the man, stunned. After a moment, she asked a question in a cautious voice.

"Do you know a man named Paul Volnos?" Above all things, she feared an affirmative answer.

"Who is Paul Volnos?"

Tammy Reis said nothing, but the terrible pounding in her heart lessened. With an imperceptible sigh, she gathered up Cooper's presentation and handed the papers to him without a word.

Cooper accepted them. "Thank you for your time, Dr. Reis." He zipped up his portfolio. It sounded to her like the rending of flesh. He rose with a cool dignity and turned toward the door.

"Mr. Cooper!" she said suddenly to his retreating back. The anguish in her voice caused him to stop and turn, alarmed.

In that instant, her composure returned. "Mr. Cooper, it is both noble and futile to stand in the path of Juggernaut."

"I won't stand," he said coolly. "I'll fly beyond its reach."

The door closed behind him. Astronaut Tamara Reis stared at the mahogany oval for a long while afterward. Then she noticed one sheet of paper had fallen to the floor. She picked it up. It was a sketch of Starblazer. Carefully, reverently, she slipped it into her binder and stole away with it.

▼ ▲ ▼

The meeting both disappointed and yet somehow exhilarated the rocket designer. Gerald Cooper felt like a force of nature as he strode off the grounds of the Center. Everywhere around him stood the evidence of NASA's waning power: rockets towered overhead, unusable relics corroding in the ocean air; spacecraft bolted to pedestals arced toward the grey sky, never to touch the heavens again; flags trembled in the wind. Amid all this fading grandeur, he knew that he possessed a greater power: the power of an idea.

The spaceflight center stood as a monument, Cooper thought, to a dinosaur. Big and lumbering, it had once stumbled its way to a great summit — the Moon — and shortly thereafter collapsed under its own weight. Cooper, with his tiny, elegant spaceship, emulated the quick, darting mammals that would someday grow to become the dominant force on — and off — the planet. Starblazer, the spacecraft he had designed, was to the Saturn rocket what man was to Tyrannosaurus Rex: smaller and weaker, surely, but in the end more versatile, more adaptable, more able to perform the variety of functions necessary to put people into Space.

And now Gerald Cooper, the next stage of evolution, departed the lair of the gigantic beast he sought to supplant. And he smiled. He had met the beast, and saw that it was toothless.

▼ ▲ ▼

At his hotel room, he switched on his computer and over the next half-hour created a press release. It would go to only one publication: *The Private Space Journal*, a monthly eight-page newsletter published by Thom Brodsky as an adjunct to the mission of Freespace Orbital.

The fact that Cooper paid Brodsky's salary never guaranteed publication of his press releases. Though a partner in Freespace Orbital, Brodsky held his own high editorial standards. Cooper worked hard to craft the article. When finished, he read it over.

> In a meeting with Space Shuttle astronaut and possible first female Shuttle pilot Tamara Reis, Freespace Orbital founder Gerry Cooper made his case for the cost-effectiveness of the Starblazer class of VTOL/SSTO spacecraft. Dr. Reis was very receptive to the presentation, expressing her opinion that, indeed, Starblazer could and would operate as envisioned.
>
> Though Dr. Reis broached the subject of NASA support for the Starblazer concept, Cooper explicitly stated his desire not to have Freespace involved with NASA in any way. His vision of the future foresees private enterprise, not tax subsidies, as the main engine of progress in Space.
>
> Overall, the meeting was cordial and encouraging, with Dr. Reis contributing a safety tip (of which Mr. Cooper was already aware). While there may be some at NASA who are openly hostile to outside competition, Dr. Reis was charming, witty, and enthusiastic. NASA has chosen a fine representative to interface with the alternative launch system enterprise.

That ought to do it, he thought.

▼▲▼

Everything she had learned in her eight years at NASA told her to forget about Gerald Cooper. The National Aeronautics and Space Administration had one single goal, one solitary path to Space, and that was the Shuttle Transportation System. Its development consumed billions of dollars. Hundreds of millions of man-hours had been spent already, with no end in sight. Cost overruns and constant delays had been part of the atmosphere of the project long before she had joined up in the days after the destruction of *Challenger*. She knew nothing different. She was trained to pilot a movable pyramid, a gargantuan monument to NASA. No other systems could be afforded or permitted.

She remembered, though. She remembered a man — a boy, actually. A boy with a mind and a drive most men did not even have the capacity to *wish* they possessed. Where was he now? Where was the man who had reached so high to touch the stars? Had she — more than a decade ago, a child of fifteen — truly destroyed him? Where was Paul Volnos?

Paul was gone. Of that much she felt certain. Otherwise, he would have made his presence known in some way. His dreams — had he pursued them — would have shaken the world by now.

Here, though, came another one such as he: Gerald Cooper. Maybe there was a chance to do for Cooper what she could never have done for Paul.

Tamara Reis made her decision. She would help Gerald Cooper. The thought of the possibilities thrilled and terrified her. After eight years in the NASA bureaucracy, she knew that only an indirect method would work. She needed an outsider. Someone with connections in aerospace, but unaffiliated with NASA. She needed Barry Gibbon's help.

The thought of *that* made her guts tighten.

▼ ▲ ▼

Barry Gibbon was her mentor, if he could be called that. Many people considered him their mentor. He certainly acted as her patron; the Robertson Barrett Gibbon Space Scholarship paid her way through college, the National Organization of Space Supporters championed her astronaut career, and Gibbon himself had become nearly a friend, which made her growing discomfort at the meeting all the more disturbing.

She flew a T-38 jet trainer from Houston to Washington DC. Jon Franck, a friend and fellow astronaut, flew with her. Instead of landing at Andrews Air Force Base, they touched down at Washington Naval Air Station — Franck was a Naval aviator — and took a pool car to Gibbon's home in Langley. Franck dropped her off and drove away to sightsee, his flaxen hair a splash of gold between the Navy blue car and the battleship grey of the winter sky.

Gibbon's home made a statement by making no statement at all. Of moderate size, it sat quietly and without ostentation at the end of a cul de sac of equally expensive and tasteful homes in an older part of Langley that had not lost its colonial charm to the metastatic growth of government buildings. Tamara walked briskly up the steps to ring the doorbell.

After a moment, the door unlocked and swung wide. A small, grey-haired woman in a high-necked, ankle-length dress from another era gazed warmly at the visitor.

"Tammy, dear," she said with gentle lilt. "What brings you here?"

Reis smiled with equal warmth. "Hello, Evangeline. I have an appointment with Barry. How are you?"

A pair of cats — a Persian and a tabby — padded through the

dimly-lit, wood-paneled foyer to rub their heads against the old woman's ankles and gaze haughtily up at Tammy.

"Oh, I'm simply grand." Her voice possessed an other-worldly tone. She had always been that way, ever since Tammy knew her. According to her brother, she behaved that way even as a teenager.

Gibbon appeared at the door, portable phone in one hand. His receding, thin grey hair reflected the hue of the dense cloud cover. A dark brown paisley silk robe and matching slippers blended into the deep chestnut hue of the woodwork in the hallway. He seemed a part of this place as if he had been carefully painted in.

"Lud," he said to the handset, "I have a lovely guest and must ring off immediately." He smiled cordially at Tammy. "No, you old dog, one of my protégés. An astronaut." He pronounced the title with a verbal flourish that would have sounded sarcastic coming from anyone else. This, though, was the resonant voice of Barry Gibbon, the man who had made space exploration commonplace.

With an imperious tap, he switched off the phone and set it on the foyer table. He brushed past his sister to say, "Come in, Tammy, my dear. I haven't seen you in months! Angie — bring us some tea."

A dry heat filled the home, repelling the cool humidity outside. Tammy smelled tea in the air, and, faintly, the scent of their half-dozen cats. She sat in his office in a comfy, antique leather chair, gazing at the photographs and awards on the walls: Gibbon shaking hands and smiling at the most powerful, influential people in the world, with presidents, kings, actors, and baseball legends. One wall he devoted entirely to astronauts. She saw herself standing at her graduation, receiving the National Student Space Award from Gibbon. She looked so young in that picture, so enthusiastic, so… unstoppable.

"Well, Tammy," Gibbon's sonorous tone filled the room as he took the tea tray from his sister and set it on a small table made exclusively for the purpose. Evangeline left the room without a word. "How has NASA been treating you lately?"

She shrugged. "Very busy, what with *Endeavour* prepping for another flight. The delays have been unbelievable."

Gibbon dismissed it with a wave of one hand while the other passed her a teacup. "Space travel itself is unbelievable, hence such delays are to be expected. Exploring space is as complex an undertaking as—"

"As the invasion of Normandy in World War Two."

Gibbon smiled. "I suppose I must come up with a new simile. As complicated as Desert Storm?"

Reis put her teacup down without taking a sip. "Barry, why *does* space travel have to be complex? Why is the Shuttle so expensive, so intricate? The Russians dragged way behind us technologically, but *Mir* was a legitimate space station. And Skylab took just one launch. Why are—"

Gibbon waved a finger at her. "Now Tammy, what have I told you all these years? What have I been telling everyone? Space exploration is humanity's greatest adventure, and its most dangerous. One can't just pop up there and set up housekeeping. The Shuttle is our workhorse, our space truck, our Conestoga. Unlike trucks and wagons, though, it can't break down halfway through the trip. We learned that from *Challenger*. Slow caution must be the watchword." His grey eyebrows rose a minute degree. "With you I seldom have to lapse into bits from my speeches. What's troubling you?"

"This." She handed him the sketch of Starblazer.

Gibbon glanced at it quickly and handed it back to her. "Gerry Cooper."

"You know him?"

Gibbon eased back in his chair. "Of course I know *of* him. I keep track of many of these… private efforts."

"You never speak of them. I haven't seen articles about them in the club journals."

"Does a medical journal deal seriously with every crackpot cure for cancer that crops up? The National Organization of Space Supporters can't waste time with such people. We'd be up to our ears in space cadets."

"Isn't that what you want?" Something in the way he spoke made the nervous knot in her stomach grow tighter and tighter.

"I want people who are sober and solemn about space, Tammy. People such as you. People who are in it for the long haul, who will work with NASA and the United Nations for as long as it takes to bring about a permanent presence in space. Look at what happened with Apollo. A headlong rush to make it to the Moon, then what? The first American in space becomes the first man to play golf on another planet. After that, nothing. I wouldn't call that a victory. The progression into space is something we have to take slowly. It may be thirty years before we see people regularly living in space or on the Moon. We can't expect — and we must not allow — NASA to make short-range compromises just to satisfy the wanderlust of a few hopeless romantics such as Cooper."

Reis took a sip of the tea. It tasted too sweet, went down too easily. "Don't you think I know that?"

"I'm sorry, my dear. Of course you do. Your devotion to NASA is something I would never question."

“Then you understand why I would like to find some way to involve Mr. Cooper with NASA.”

A thin smile slowly grew on Gibbon’s lips. “I think I’m beginning to. You realize, of course, that such assistance on my part must be purely *sub rosa*. This is a personal favor I would not grant to just anyone.”

“I understand.”

Gibbon relaxed into his chair, as if some great battle had just been won. His gaze never strayed from his guest. “I’ll help you with Mr. Cooper, Tammy. You have my promise on that. I’ll see to it that NASA takes care of him.”

▼▲▼

Reis left Gibbon’s home feeling weak and confused. She felt the same way, she realized, as when she told Paul Volnos of her intent to join NASA. She squelched the memory and refused to consider why every time she defended the greatness of her agency she felt as if she betrayed something even greater.

CHAPTER 2

The State is waste. Being wasteful is its nature, since it neither creates wealth nor earns it and hence has no reason to practice thrift. In a perverse way, though, this can — in the short run — play to our advantage through the wonderful world of government surplus. Many aerospace items are available from the government since — as soon as a technology becomes perfected — the State dumps it in order to buy newer toys, all at taxvictim expense. Don't think of purchasing surplus as profiting from this plunderous arrangement. Think of it as restoring goods to the private sector.

—The Orbital Settlers' Guide

10 April

The old man bumped along the back road in a battered Ford truck that dropped flakes of rust-stained white paint almost as fast as the ancient finish picked up dust. The road was wide, but filled with potholes and gullies that larger trucks and semis easily ignored. The dust kicked up behind him like a rocket trail, blowing across the New Mexico landscape, red in the morning sun.

"Ace" Roberts maneuvered through the obstacle course with slow care. His blue-grey eyes peered at the horizon from beneath craggy folds of lined flesh. He remembered the land well, though the last time he rode this trail Eisenhower resided in the White House. The land lay unchanged, paying no heed to presidents or other ephemerae.

The proving ground at White Sands had seen better days. He knew that — he had lived the better days. Now, with a sad nostalgia and nervous anticipation, he approached both his past and his future.

The shuddering truck ached over one more dusty hillock. The road, such as it was, dropped away from his sight beneath the peeling hood. He stopped, tottering on the brink.

Before him spread the desert, pinkish yellow in the dawn's light, just as he had seen it so many times in the distant past. The hills hadn't changed at all. Maybe the morning air held more haze — smog drifting north from El Paso. *For the most part, though,* Roberts mused, *Man hasn't affected this part of Earth in much of any way.*

The thought comforted him as it would any other traveler returning homeward. White Sands had been his home for nearly eight years back in the 'fifties. And now he intended to bring a piece of it home with him.

With a grind of gears, he set the truck into low and lumbered warily down the road, steering nearly by Braille. Less than a mile away spread a complex of unkempt buildings — Quonset huts, T-hangers, and rusty rectangular hovels — and open-air bins, stacks of dusty, rusting metal and faded plastic.

Ace Roberts gazed at the horn of plenty.

Somewhere in that acres-broad jungle of neglected hardware lay a trio of pearls beyond price. To him, that is. To the sergeant on duty, it represented mere surplus, more junk with a very definite price.

Roberts swerved to avoid a fissure in the road that could have swallowed his front end, then hit the brakes and skidded fifty feet down the slope.

There had to be an easier way to build a rocket ship.

The old man grinned. *Not at this price*, he thought.

The Ford hit bottom; he shifted into second and sped up across the flatter, though still thoroughly pockmarked, terrain. At long last he braked to a stop at the loading dock. A pair of flatbed trailers squatted quietly, loaded with what looked like industrial air conditioning units, plus some rusty machine tools and jigs. A Kenworth sat off to one side, a pair of feet sticking lazily out the driver's window. Music drifted through the still desert air: The Sons of the Pioneers. Roberts cut the engine and listened for a moment, gazing around at the perfection of it all. For a brief moment, he was forty years younger.

Suddenly, a rumble pierced the morning quiet. Roberts fumbled with the door, shoved it open, and jumped out, scanning the horizon. Then he saw it.

A thin column of fire arced up from behind a hill miles away. Crackling and sputtering, it shot skyward with impressive speed. After a few seconds the bright flame died out. For a brief moment the metal bird kept flying upward, straining against gravity. Then — in defiance of the ballistic behavior of other rockets — the engines fired up again and the contraption *hovered*. Shaped like an elongated pyramid, the rocket ship further impressed the old man by moving *sideways* for several seconds.

A thrill of excitement shot through Roberts. He remembered feeling the same way four decades before, watching captured V-2's blast up over the unchanging sandy terrain.

"Easy for you guys," he muttered after a moment.

The bizarre vehicle, dropping stern-first, settled out of sight below a hill. An instant later, a small cloud of smoke and dust puffed upward.

Roberts backhanded some sweat from his forehead. Seven in the morning and already the sun began to blister the countryside. The low humidity, though, moderated the oppressive heat.

Roberts seized a well-worn black briefcase from the cab and walked over to the office, whistling along to *Cool Water* on the truck driver's CD deck.

The door opened on a cramped reception area consisting of a grey desk, green chairs, and walls covered with paperwork. Behind the desk sat an army sergeant studiously involved in a crossword puzzle. In his late thirties, he stood lean and gangly, with tan, leathery skin and sandy hair laced with a premature frost.

Nipping the cigarette from his lips, he said, "Yessir?"

The other put out his hand. "Ace Roberts. I'm here to pick up some engines."

"Where're you from?"

"Saratoga, California."

"Long ride for old motors," the sergeant said, rising to shake the offered hand.

"They're pretty special motors," Roberts said with a thin smile. Closer now, he could read the sergeant's name tag. "Sergeant Wells," he added. Pulling a sheaf of papers from his briefcase, he handed them to the man behind the desk.

After a moment of flipping through the stack, the military man smiled.

"Oh, yeah. Pretty special. Three Aerobee Three-Five-Oh's." He looked across at the man and grinned. "Goin' somewhere?"

Roberts smiled. "Just local."

Wells tore a few pages off the bottom of the stack, ran them through the timer stamp, and dropped them into an empty tray on the desktop. "You're that rocket guy, right? From California?"

Roberts nodded.

"How long you been working on that thing?"

"Nineteen years."

The sergeant shook his head. "I've got a friend," he said, "who's been working on a kit airplane for ten. Hasn't even got the wings on the fuselage yet." He picked up a clipboard and stepped out from behind the desk. "Let's grab a forklift and find these babies."

▼ ▲ ▼

Sgt. Wells maneuvered the forklift between lines of rusting trucks that seemed to have been carved out of the red desert earth. Roberts followed in his truck, which looked right at home in the graveyard. They turned left at a stack of drive shafts and bounced eastward toward a grey line of Quonset huts.

Wells stopped the forklift at the sliding doors on one end of the nearest hut. Hopping out, he fumbled with a huge set of keys, trying this one and that, until at last the rusty padlock clunked open. Roberts stepped up to help. The doors rumbled apart like distant thunder to release a dry, dusty smell from inside.

Light pierced the hut through holes in the curved roof, filling the space inside with parallel lances of gold. Roberts let his eyes adjust to the partial darkness, then gazed around like Carter in King Tut's tomb.

"Over there, I think." The sergeant pointed toward a pallet halfway down the length of the building.

They hopped aboard the forklift and lumbered in, slowly gliding past stacks of aluminum and magnesium tubing, fins, vanes, and nose cones. Smaller pallets here and there supported cases of guidance equipment, telemetry devices, and vacuum tubes.

"Yep," Sgt. Wells drawled. "Here're your babies."

Ace slid out and stepped over to the pallet. On it, wrapped in thick plastic sheeting, lay a trio of identical objects about five feet long and two feet in diameter. Through the translucent plastic, Roberts saw tantalizing glimpses of tubing, superlative welds, and the graceful bell curves of the exhaust nozzles.

"Guaranteed prime surplus," Wells said with a grin.

Roberts smiled. "Let's do it."

▼ ▲ ▼

Ace watched with boyish excitement as the forklift slowly lowered the pallet onto the back of his truck. The pickup groaned under the weight, but took the load without further protest. He climbed into the bed to lash the precious cargo tightly.

"Thank you, sergeant," he said, climbing into the cab when he had finished.

"Have fun with 'em," Wells said. "But be careful." He smiled. "I guess I don't have to say that to someone who's taken nineteen years to build something."

Roberts smiled, nodding. "I'll be careful. I'll be sitting on top of these babies. I'll be *very* careful."

Wells leaned against the side of the forklift and lit a cigarette. His smile turned wistful. "Hell," he said, "punch a hole in the sky for us, then."

The sergeant watched the old man pull slowly out of the junkyard. For a long while he leaned against the forklift. When he finally finished his cigarette, he flicked it to a bare patch of ground, put his hands in his pockets, and spent a long time staring up at the clear blue desert sky.

▼ ▲ ▼

The trip back to California would be long and dull for Roberts. He appreciated the view of New Mexico, Arizona, and the Mojave, but they could not rival the excitement that pulsated within him. Three rocket engines, covered with an olive-drab tarp, lay strapped to the bed of his pickup, and they were all his. It had taken years to save up the money to buy them, years of paperwork shuffled back and forth to gain authorization to possess the small motors. Now they were his to use.

An Aerobee 350 engine can lift a six hundred pound payload two hundred miles into Space. Roberts' design called for two of the Aerobees to constitute the first stage of his rocket. The third engine would propel the second stage into orbit. The payload would consist of Ace Roberts, telemetry, life support, and whatever else he needed to ferry himself up to an orbital rendezvous if all worked as it should. Roberts spent his life making sure things worked as they should.

Born in Iowa to farming parents, Roberts was the only one of seven brothers and sisters who spent any time looking upward at the sky instead of downward to the earth. He could not explain his early fascination with airplanes and flight, nor the reason that he alone of his family was so profoundly affected by the sight of a skyrocket screaming upward on Independence Day. His family and friends watched such annual displays and saw only brilliant colors; Ace felt drawn into the sky with each ascent, experienced an explosion of heavenly glory with each air burst.

At age sixteen, he enlisted in the Army. By the time of the Second World War, he was a lieutenant in the European theater of operations. When Operation Paperclip successfully rescued Wernher von Braun and his team of rocket scientists from the encroaching Soviets, Ace Roberts helped smuggle out V-2 parts and cartons of documents from Peenemünde to Fort Bliss, Texas. He followed von Braun to Huntsville, Alabama — nicknamed Hunsville after the arrival of the Germans — and eventually settled in White Sands, New Mexico, to work as a design safety officer.

The captured V-2 missiles inspired him. Test launches, whether modest successes or spectacular failures, never ceased to excite him in a way he found to be inexplicable to his fellow workers. Rockets awed them, certainly, but Ace could tell that the reactions of most of them did not rise from any deeper well than did the oohs and ahhs of his family at the fireworks displays. They possessed no sense of the religious about rockets. Ace did. He ached with a reverence for the sanctity of a rocket's flight, he yearned to rise up with it, to feel the comforting weight of acceleration, to see with his own eyes the Sun alight in the black night beyond Earth. A glimpse at the Moon filled him with an awe impossible to communicate to his friends and co-workers. Nor did he wish to. These were his dreams and innermost thoughts. As might a pilgrim in a foreign land, he kept his worship secret and spoke not of his goddess. He did not proselytize to the unconverted. To others, he was just an old prairie boy with no formal education beyond the tenth grade, who happened to build rockets, who sometimes looked up at a rocket's trail with a mist in his eyes that was no doubt an effect of the desert heat and nothing more.

Ace Roberts had met someone once who also worshipped at the altar of the stars. A man — a boy, at first — who burned with the dream of Space and struggled with him to get there. He could still remember the eager, hungry look in the boy's eyes as he watched Ace launch a twenty-foot test rocket. He wondered about Paul Volnos, where he was and what had become of him over the past few years.

The broad, flat interstate highway spread about him, narrowing like a sword point toward the west. *Man has always moved westward*, Roberts thought, *always chasing the setting sun, never able to catch it. Now, just as we've reached the end of our westward journey around the planet, we must turn and head toward the east in order to leave Earth, launching into the rising sun.*

His thoughts followed that line for a long while, and he forgot again about Paul Volnos and the past. Ace Roberts contemplated the future.

▼ ▲ ▼

Marcus Aurelius Grant contemplated the future, too; a far different future. The evening of that same day, he sat behind the wheel of a luxury Jeep overlooking the gloaming darkness of the New Mexico desert less than a hundred miles from where Roberts had purchased the surplus Aerobees. Marcus Grant dabbled in surplus, too. He specialized, though, in import and export. The violet sky fading to black occulted his features, and the craggy bluff on which he parked hid most of his vehicle from view.

He gazed down at a truck and trailer rig parked incongruously in the middle of the rocky wasteland. Its lights were off, its engine as silent as the still air around it. From inside the cab came the muted sound of Gogi Grant singing *The Wayward Wind*. A coyote howled somewhere amid the boulders. The call received an answer, then spread to other hideaways. Grant lit a cigarette while keeping his gaze focused on the southern sky. His wristwatch chimed; it broke the calm as surely as a siren. Without a word, he flicked the cigarette to the ground, the red ember following one parabolic trajectory while Marcus Grant watched another.

The red dot in the southern sky would have been invisible over even the smallest populated area. Here in the wilderness, where no city light shone for thousands of square miles, its meager glow was just barely noticeable. The point of crimson appeared to rise upward, like a minor planet racing the stars. Long before it reached the zenith, though, its glow flickered and died. Grant's eyes moved slowly, their gaze following the remainder of the trajectory of the invisible object. It would hit a mile or so northeast of their position. He raised a pair of night vision binoculars to his eyes.

In the smeared green glow of the instrument, he saw the desert below illuminated by amplified starlight. It could have been the surface of Mars but for the occasional bold movement of nocturnal creatures unaware of their observation by man. This man was a hunter, but his quarry was not a living thing. His target appeared as a blinding, lime-hued cloud in the binoculars. A few seconds later, the sound of the crash reached him, followed by a curious crack and whistling sound that rose backward up the tone scale. The coyotes ceased their calls and scrambled for cover.

He adjusted the rangefinder on the binocs, lowered them, and gunned the Jeep into life. The truck diesel engine below roared simultaneously.

▼ ▲ ▼

The dust still hovered around the impact crater, not completely settled yet, when the Jeep skidded to a halt, the truck still half a mile away. Grant jumped out, ran to the rim of the hundred-foot-wide hole and switched on his flashlight. In the glow, his triumphant grin revealed a line of straight, white teeth; his eyes glimmered with excitement; dark, wavy hair, tied back loosely in a queue, fell to one side of his neck. He gazed down at a billion dollars.

Actually, the two-by-eight-foot cylinder with rounded ends that looked so much like a giant drug capsule had a street value of only fifty million dollars. Marcus Grant simply liked to contemplate the future. For now, though, the immediate future depended on the prompt recovery of the missile payload and an equally prompt escape from the desert.

With a groan of air brakes, the truck stopped, turned, and backed up to the crater. Rear doors clattered open. Two muscular men jumped out and — pulling two lines behind them — joined Grant in a slide down the crater slope.

Grant looked quickly at the scattered remains of the rocket: only the thick payload canister had survived intact; Grant had designed the rest of the vehicle to absorb a major portion of the impact forces by crumpling. No part of the forward payload shroud was visible. The tail section that comprised engine, fuel tanks, guidance systems, and control surfaces lay all about the sides of the crater in twisted pieces of aluminum and steel.

Grant found the recessed attach points on the rear of the cylinder; they had survived the landing. The two men clipped hooks to the rings and ran back up the slope. They worked wordlessly, as though the desert possessed ears to hear what transpired in the dusty pit.

A motor squealed into life, winching in the cables to hoist the capsule out of the crater. Grant cleared a few large boulders from the path of the cargo to avoid entanglements and watched it ascend to the rim of the crater. Stars glowed sharply in the black sky.

He looked away, back toward the earth. Marcus Grant never looked at the stars. Furthermore, he had planned this operation for a moonless night. He refused to confront Moon or stars, even with a glance.

He concentrated on climbing out of the pit. Eyes focused on the cylinder, he felt a thrill of triumph surge through him, a sense both of vindication and of vengeance. He had won his first battle. He knew now that he could win the war.

3 May

The news was two months old when it landed on Joseph Lester's desk. The woman who tossed it there, Hillary Kaye, worked as a photographer for the Fort Collins Sentinel, the city's newspaper. Lester, their science reporter, stood tall — and wide — with dark curly hair and a broad, brooding face that did nothing to disguise a deep, ever-present anger. At twenty-eight years old, he looked much older. Few people liked him. He liked even fewer, if any.

He stared at the curling fax paper and said, "What's that?"

"There's this new fad, Joe. It's called 'reading.' " Hillary kept moving.

He glanced at the slug line, then shouted: "Hey! Did this just come over the wire?"

Hillary turned. Younger than Lester, slimmer, shorter, lighter-haired, and considerably more attractive by any criterion, her mood struck a similarly sour note.

"No, Joe, I've been hiding it, waiting for just this moment to spring it on you. The whole office is in on it."

Lester snorted and read the wire story.

> LAS CRUCES, NEW MEXICO — Military officials confirmed today that a small ballistic rocket crash-landed two months ago in the desert halfway between the town of Deming and the Mexican border. NORAD/Space Command tracking equipment could not pinpoint the launch site, but sources suggest that the rocket may have been launched from as far south as the central Mexican desert.
>
> NORAD refuses to speculate on the mysterious missile, but insists it was too small to have had any military purpose, suggesting that a sounding rocket may have gone off course.
>
> An unidentified source within the Drug Enforcement Agency gave credence to the view that the missile might have been a sophisticated attempt to smuggle cocaine into the United States. "These drug lords control billions of dollars, and rockets would simply be the latest toy in their deadly game," the source said.
>
> Investigators found a crater, missile debris, and tire tracks. There are no suspects, though the rocket fragments will be examined for any clues they might yield.

Lester's heartbeat quickened. Purely out of habit, he hid his excitement. "Who's covering this?" he asked.

Hillary shrugged. "No one. It's old news. There's nothing out there but a hole in the ground. Why get so worked up?"

"I'm not worked up. Don't you see this is news? Drug-smuggling missiles raining down on America? Who could have devised such an idea? How did they build it? Where? Why?"

Hillary shook her head of wispy blond hair. "You forgot *what* and *when*."

He ignored her attempt at humor. "There are cheaper and more reliable ways to smuggle drugs. Why go for something as bizarre as a rocket?"

"You expect sanity from coke fiends?"

"Drugs are a business, not an art form. The successful smugglers are the most level-headed and ingenious."

"Maybe this guy's not successful."

"Maybe he won't be. Maybe I'll want to be there when he screws up."

Lester slid the New Mexico article into a manila folder and put the folder into his tickler file.

CHAPTER 3

Everything in space obeys the laws of physics. If you know these laws and obey them, space will treat you kindly.

— Wernher von Braun

10 May

Astronaut Reis gazed at the two white solid rocket boosters that stood like Greek pillars propping the fat, rust-brown external tank between them. Attached to the ET by only three bolts, the shuttle orbiter hung like a stuffed, corpulent sea gull, its white, black, and grey wings outstretched in the spring sunshine.

She hated the sight of it.

She also knew that it constituted humanity's only path to Space. Not because it was the best. Not because it was the cheapest or most efficient. Simply because NASA was stuck with it and permitted no competition. So Tamara Reis served NASA with a fierce devotion, because she worshipped Space as one would a god, and NASA stood between the two as the priest she must entreat for passage to Heaven. She strove to repress the memory of a time before NASA, but the fresh ocean breeze and the sight of the towering rocket awakened a remembrance of youth, of many springs earlier, and of the first time she saw a flame leap into the sky.

3 May, 1975

She was eight, with dark, long hair braided into a ponytail that flew in the breeze as she raced through the park. Her blouse rivaled the few clouds in the sky for purity of white, her blue denim overalls rubbed crisp and new against her legs.

Cool air, descending from the Santa Cruz mountains, carried with it the scent of pine trees and of the ocean beyond the hills. The sun warmed her skin, the verdant grass tickled the soles of her bare feet. She never felt as fully alive as when she ran beneath the great blue vault of the sky. Up and over the small hills she sped, tumbling down the slopes to the bottom then leaping up to ascend the next peak.

She breathed great ferocious bites of air and drank in the view of grass, oak trees, and mountains.

Los Gatos — a small California town straddling a freeway — possessed all the traits of a more rural community: a vital main street comprising a drug store, movie theater, barber shop, five-and-dime, and radio shop; a town hall, library, and community center; and townspeople who knew one another and shouted greetings across the street without hesitation. People still rode horses down unpaved University Avenue and old men could still sit on their front porches cleaning shotguns without police swarming the area.

In such a Norman Rockwell world of near-perfection just on the border of adolescent freedom, no thought of past or future entered young Tammy's mind, just the glorious joy of unbridled existence. She crossed the final hill of Oak Meadow Park, the one that stood just before the marshland of Vasona Creek.

At the shore of the tiny wetland she saw two groups: a small cluster of boys, five in all, gathered around something that momentarily held their interest. A few hundred feet away to the right sat a dozen or so of the few remaining pure-bred hippies, colorful people from up in the Santa Cruz mountains that sometimes still gathered in the park. With them sat a few of the first wave of punkers, dressed in black leather, razored t-shirts, and safety-pinned flesh. Though Los Gatos fit the image of an almost rural town, it lay just a few miles from San Jose, a growingly cosmopolitan city.

A cloud of smoke drifted from the center of the cross-generational gathering. It blew Tammy's way, carrying a sweet, burnt-rope smell that nonetheless made her sneeze. They laughed and reeled, swaying to the music on a portable radio. They seemed ferociously, monomaniacally happy, as if they could not force out any more laughter without rupturing vital organs.

The knot of boys laughed, too. Mean-spirited laughter, the sort that might be elicited from bullies vivisecting one of the frogs that lived in the marsh. They backed away and Tammy saw the object of their amusement. On a small metal launching pad sat an eight-inch-tall model rocket of very simple design, nothing more than a tube half an inch in diameter standing on three triangular fins and surmounted by an unpainted balsa nose cone. Wires ran out of its rear end and into a small control box twenty feet away. The boys now clustered about it and began to argue.

"Me!" one shouted. "My turn!"

"You did the last one!"

"Did not!"

"Well, you did one and I ain't done any!"

"Me neither! Gimme that!"

The argument continued for a few more turns until the biggest boy, who had a large belly and walked with it shoved forward like the prow of a ship, grabbed the control box and stabbed a finger at the switches. "Fire!" he shouted with a belch.

The rocket sat on the pad for a second or two. Then, much to Tammy's startlement, it simply exploded with a bang that knocked over the launcher. Rather than disappointing the boys, this event prompted a round of gleeful howls. They lost interest in the box and ran back to the pad to investigate the damage. Tammy realized that their desire had not been in launching the rocket, only in arguing about who would. And their subsequent argument now centered about who would get to blow up the next one.

Off to her left, she heard a strange whooshing sound that dropped in pitch as it dropped in volume. She turned her head to see a thin column of white smoke arc into the blue morning sky. At the top of the column she caught the barest glimpse of a black and red rocket. Suddenly, before it lost too much speed, a second blast of smoke erupted from beneath it, propelling it higher into the air with a hiss that reached her ears a second later. When the vehicle achieved the apex of its flight and nearly vanished from sight, she saw it break in half to release a red-and-white parachute.

She followed the dissipating smoke trail back to its source. There, on a hillock near the marsh and far from those clustered around the remains of the demolished rocket, stood a boy alone. Not too tall for his age, which looked to be about twelve or thirteen, he nonetheless watched the sky as if surveying his personal property, like the young master of a vast estate. His fists rested on his belt, from which hung bulging army surplus ammo pouches. He stood straight as the rod atop the carbon-seared launch pad a few feet beyond him. The breeze tousled his restless blond hair and rustled his khaki shirt and matching corduroys.

To Tammy, he looked as if he could easily fly upward to touch the rocket as it soared.

He watched it, though, quietly, with some internal calculation apparent. Ignoring the boisterous knot of other boys, he picked up his launch pad and walked toward the descending parachute. Tammy followed, never letting her vision stray from the scene she witnessed. Her gaze encompassed the slowly falling parachute, the halves of the rocket dangling beneath its lines, and the moving figure of the golden boy. They seemed connected somehow, as if they moved as one, as if he could control even the law of gravity. The two approached each other. The boy picked up speed as he neared the touchdown zone.

The parachute hung just twenty feet above the ground as he was ten feet down range. It continued to fall; his hand reached up. In one smooth motion, he plucked the missile out of the air and let the parachute drape around it. He turned, grinning.

Finally aware of Tammy's existence, he held the split rocket aloft as if in salute. Tammy ran up to him without introduction, without any social qualms. For her, no society existed in that moment. The entire universe consisted only of the two of them, and the rocket.

"How high did it go?" she asked.

He shook his head into the breeze to remove a few wild strands of flaxen hair from his eyes. "About seven hundred feet. The first stage takes it up to three hundred, then the second stage takes it up the other four hundred." He handed her the crimson and ebony halves of the rocket, detaching and keeping the parachute.

"Is the second stage more powerful?"

He shook his head. "No. But by the time it fires, the first stage rocket has burned up and ejected, so the same-rated motor pushes less mass and can provide greater acceleration." He sat down on the grass. Tammy followed.

"I could put a larger motor in this design," he said. "Would you like to see that?"

Tammy nodded eagerly.

They spent the rest of the day launching the rocket over and over. The pouches on his belt contained a seemingly limitless supply of rocket motors, little cardboard tubes that looked more than anything else like big firecrackers, yet contained a controlled power to burn, not explode. He showed her how to reassemble the rocket, fold and load the parachute, insert the motors with all the necessary packing, and connect the electric ignition wires to the solid rocket fuel. Tammy watched this last operation with near awe. She had always been fascinated by fireworks, the way they lit up the night with color and sound. Fireworks, though, were something that her father controlled. He would light them and then back nervously away. Her mother would tell Tammy to cover her ears and shield her eyes. Tammy never obeyed. She stood brazenly unprotected to watch the roaring, whistling, shrieking fires, wanting desperately to control — just once — the joyous power they released.

"Put the wire in there," the boy said, pointing. With a mixture of excitement and anticipation, she placed the thin heating element inside a narrow, tapering hole in the black, tarry rocket fuel. He handed her the wadding to place in after it. "Now mount it on the rod." Gently she cradled the foot-long spacecraft, carrying it to the launch pad. She raised it up above the yard-long stainless-steel wire.

"The rod stabilizes the attitude of the rocket," he said, as if he were teaching an important skill, as any other boy might talk about one's grip on a baseball bat. "The first three feet of flight are critical. That's when the rocket gains enough velocity for the fins to become effective. After that, it's all aerodynamics. If the rocket is built badly, it's going to fail in flight. If it's built well, you can punch a hole in the sky."

Tammy placed the guiding tube, glued precisely straight on the side of the rocket, over the tip of the rod and mated the two, then carefully lowered the rocket to the launch pad, a six-inch-wide stainless steel disc. The missile rested on its three shark fins to point toward the Heavens. She took a moment to gaze closely at it.

It was nothing more than a pair of cardboard tubes with balsa fins on the lower half and a nose cone on the upper, yet the boy had constructed it flawlessly. The tube and nose cone fitted together without an apparent seam, though she knew there had to be one. The fins had been attached with the same precision, each exactly one hundred twenty degrees away from the other two. Though the balsa had received some dents and scratches from multiple launches and landings, she could tell that it had been pristine when first created. She rose and stepped back.

He handed her the control box and walked away without saying a word. She knew that this was the highest honor he could grant her. He had permitted her to fold the parachute and pack it, assemble the rocket, load the motors, wire them, and place the entire spacecraft on the launch pad. After this solemn ritual of preparation, she held in her hands the power of flight.

The fire control looked like a toy. Perhaps it was, to minds more wizened. It consisted of a black plastic box with a doorbell button, a plastic keyhole, and a light; the keyhole, marked ARM, had the red light; the button was marked FIRE. She inserted the plastic key hanging from a red ribbon into the ARM switch and turned it. The light glowed. She looked up at the boy one hundred eighty feet behind her. He smiled and nodded, holding up a protractor with a string kept taut by a small fishing weight at the other end. He sighted along the flat end toward the rocket.

"*Fire in the hole!*" she yelled at the top of her lungs, and pressed and held down the button marked FIRE.

The rocket did nothing for an agonizing moment as the batteries in the control box poured electricity into the heating wire tamped inside the motor. Unseen, the wire grew hotter and hotter until an unstoppable chemical reaction took hold. The propellant ignited furiously, with a pop and a hiss that spewed smoke and fire across the steel disc. Instantly, the red-black missile screamed along the steel rail, the fins biting air to stabilize the flight.

Faster nearly than sight, the rocket shot upward to become a part of the sky, trailing a straight, narrow cloud that could only have been made by human intent. Tammy watched gleefully, her hands tightly gripping the control box. Her heart pounded as it had at every launch that day. This time, though, she felt an even greater thrill, the powerful emotion of ownership. This launch belonged to her. He made her a gift of his power, and she made it hers by exercising it. She had not abused it by sloppy preparation, she had not defamed it with false humility, she claimed it by the only right that made it hers: she launched a perfect flight.

The boy followed the ascent with the edge of the protractor. The hanging string ticked off degrees. When the second stage reached its apogee and the parachute blossomed, he pinched his thumb over the string and lowered the protractor to read the angle and ran back to Tammy.

"Eleven-hundred twenty feet. A new record!"

Face flushed with excitement, she raced toward where the rocket descended. Her feet flew over the grass, her gaze locked solidly on the wind-borne missile. Every muscle in her body responded to her command, concentrating upon only one goal: to pluck the rocket out of the sky. She ran faster than the wind, laughing with an infinite joy that drank in the entire sweet sky and thirsted for more. Closer now, closer — the red and white checkered hemisphere of thin plastic drifted down toward her. She maneuvered to keep pace with it. Over her now, it dropped gently into her hands just as her toe rammed against an exposed root, tripping her. Panicked, she twisted about so that her back would take the brunt of the fall. The rocket lay cradled in her hands.

She hit. The earth knocked the wind from her and streaked the back of her blouse with emerald grass stains and deep chocolate smears of mud. She ground to a halt and hoisted the rocket aloft in triumph.

Its creator arrived laughing. "You're a mess," he said.

Tammy smiled and stood to hand over the precious cargo. "Not a scratch."

He did not take the rocket back. "You rescued it. It's yours."

Her eyes widened. "But it's so pretty, so perfect…"

"I know you'll treat it well." He brushed dirt and grass off her back. "Look at that. Your mom'll kill you."

She shrugged and held the rocket close to her, feeling a warmth greater than the sun provided. "Are you sure you want to give this to me?"

He headed back toward the launch pad. "Sure. I'm working on a three-stage model. Want to see it?"

She nodded, walking beside him, but said, "It's almost sundown. I've got to get home."

"What's your name?"

"Tammy Reis."

"Like wild rice?"

"Spelled differently. What's yours?"

"Paul Volnos."

"Are you with them?" she asked, pointing toward the cluster of boys busily setting fire to a rocket they had stomped flat. She realized the instant she said it that he could not possibly be. The darkening sky hid her flush of embarrassment.

Paul shook his head. "The fire department won't let us launch unless we're part of a supervised group."

"Where's your supervisor?"

Paul pointed toward the circle of hippies and punkers. "There."

A man — probably not more than twenty-two, though short hair and glasses made him look older — rose from the giggling, beclouded group. He wore the only white shirt with a button-down collar, though he staggered a bit as he walked toward them, hollering.

"Paul! Where the hell were you? You know we have to stay in a group if we're going to—" He squinted. "Hey, who you got there?" Off to his right, the flaming rocket exploded with a sickly pop and fizzle. He turned and stumbled toward the other boys, cursing in a most unteacherly manner.

"I'll be over in a second, Mr. Woolsey!" Paul brushed a strand of blond hair from his eyes and looked at Tammy with a smile. "Mr. Woolsey's a senator's son. Lives out here with his mom while he teaches Civics at junior high. He doesn't give a spit about the club, but he needs brownie points for his college degree." He shook his head in amusement. "Robert Goddard had to deal with idiots, too."

"Who's Robert Goddard?"

"The father of American rocketry. Don't you know?"

She shook her head. "But I want to learn. I want to learn everything!"

▼ ▲ ▼

That evening she walked home by way of the library and checked out as many books on rocketry as she could carry, plus a novel entitled *Space Ship "Goddard"* by someone named Rex Ivarson. Night had fallen, and she walked under a canopy of stars. A crescent moon hung over the west like an encouraging smile. For the first time she thought about the Moon as more than just something that lit up the sky. She thought of it as a planet, as a place that could be reached, touched, walked upon. The idea evoked in her a strange emotion, something that tightened her throat as if she were about to cry or shout; as if some great pain urged to explode outward and only with its release would come true happiness. She walked faster, the Moon keeping pace with her stride.

Tammy was intensely aware of the space program, as were most people her age. She dutifully raised her hand whenever teachers asked who would like to live there. Now, though, she read through the books and began to ponder the question. What *were* her chances of living on the Moon or in Space? Only one woman, she noticed immediately, had ever made it into Space: a Soviet named Valentina Tereshkova, and she had not exactly made a career of it. The books about Your Future In Space, she thought, should be titled Boys' Future In Space, for most lacked any illustrations of women.

She lay in bed that night, frowning at the books arranged around her on the comforter. Then she gazed up at the red and black rocket perched atop her dresser and remembered the ease with which Paul admitted her to his world. That was the way it should be. She thought about Paul and saw only the image of him standing on the hillock, fists on his hips, gazing into the blue at a rocket's trail. To her, it became the symbol of everything good and right, something she wanted to experience every day: the heady emotion of continual triumph.

▼ ▲ ▼

Tammy knew her choice involved risk. She redoubled her effort to be worthy and prepared. Fighting the nausea that threatened to engulf her, she stumbled out of the stainless steel enclosure and staggered to the exit.

The sharp tang of ocean air hit her, restoring her stamina. One more time; she could endure one more time. This had been her mantra for the past five trials. She strode to the entryway and presented another ticket to the operator.

"Hey, hey, little girl," the craggy old man said. "You're startin' to look green."

"I can take it," she said, climbing into the roller coaster seat and yanking the lap bar down with both hands.

The Giant Dipper, on the boardwalk at Santa Cruz Beach, was the wildest ride within an hour of Los Gatos, at least ever since Playland-at-the-Beach closed down in San Francisco years before. At her pestering, her older brother Spence drove her there when he went to spend the day surfing. She would join him in the water later, when the time came to practice splashdown drills. For now, Tammy worked on pulling gees.

Slowly the train pulled out of the station. Climbing the initial hill, Tammy looked around from the blue-grey Pacific on her right to the pine-green Santa Cruz mountains on her left. The cars paused at the top. For an instant, Tammy — in the front seat — thrilled to hang over the precipice. Then the rear caught up and shoved her forward and downward with delicious acceleration.

The roller coaster, an ancient beast built of whitewashed wood and rust-dripping steel bolts, creaked and shuddered every time the cars took a curve or pulled out of a dive. Tammy screamed, then realized that astronauts never screamed, and clamped her mouth shut. She shrieked inside, though, with exhilaration and terror and pure riotous joy.

The Tilt-A-Whirl came next. To train for tumbling space capsules.

▼ ▲ ▼

Not all her weekends centered around the Boardwalk. Most she spent in the park with Paul, launching rockets without supervision until the park ranger galloped over to them to threaten mayhem if they did not scram immediately. Tammy suspected that the old man with the handlebar moustache and the Smoky Bear hat — a World War One veteran, she later learned — actually liked to watch the rocket flights and only shooed them away when his own superiors insisted.

On the weekends that she neither launched rockets nor suppressed launching lunch, she ventured by bicycle to tiny Reid-Hillview Airport on the southeast edge of San Jose. It was a fourteen mile trip that took her over an hour. And when she got there, almost nothing ever happened.

She leaned her red Murray bike against the corrugated steel of a Quonset hut and sat on a rough wooden bench from which colorful layers of paint curled and flaked away. For hours she watched aircraft come and go: Common Cessnas, Pipers, Beeches, the occasional Taylorcraft. Now and then, a Stearman biplane or some older vintage airplane flew in and out again.

The pilots fascinated her: young men only a few years older than Paul, acne-spotted and grinning; grizzled old men in worn leather A-2 flying jackets; middle-aged professionals of her father's generation, dressed in suits and flying their planes on business trips. Women, too. The wives of pilots, some looking annoyed at another Sunday squandered watching their husbands tinker with spruce spars, clecoes, sheet aluminum, and recalcitrant engines, others appearing to enjoy the outings. No girls her age, though. And no women pilots.

Then, one summer Saturday, the air above Reid-Hillview vibrated with an odd buzz unlike the throaty cough of a radial engine or the steady drone of a Lycoming, more like an angry hornet than an aircraft engine. She looked toward the Eastridge Mall, a huge enclosed shopping center under the glide path to Reid-Hillview that she loved to walk around in because it evoked in her a feeling of living on the Moon. Above it soared a swift white shape that looked for all the world as if it flew backward.

Tammy jumped to her feet and ran to the flight line to get a better look. It could not be flying backward, yet it was! The propeller sprouted from the rear of the plane, as did its wings. On the front, two short, slender extensions looked like the elevators one would see on a normal plane's empennage. It had no rudder anywhere, though the two large wings bent up at the outer edges. Tammy stared in wonderment. The backward little plane was simply the most astounding thing she had ever seen outside a rocketry book.

It buzzed downward at a high rate and touched the runway on two fixed landing gear positioned under the rear-swept wings. She could see now that it was not flying backward; the pilot faced forward and the wings were obviously designed for flight in that direction. But what a design!

After a very short roll-out, the nose of the plane descended to the runway. In a moment of terror, Tammy thought that the nosegear had not dropped and that disaster was imminent. The aircraft, though, continued to roll forward. Only then did she notice the smallest of wheels making contact between the runway and the underside of the plane.

It taxied to the tie-down area by the airport café. Tammy was not the only one rushing out to inspect the strange contraption. Half the airport bustled over to surround the visitor as if a flying saucer had just landed.

The bubble canopy popped open, hinged at the front. The pilot stood and stretched. Tammy's jaw dropped. The pilot of the bizarre, futuristic airplane was a woman!

She knew about Amelia Earhart and Jacqueline Cochran and Harriet Quimby and a dozen other historical aviatrices. Here, though, stood a *real* one.

Her dusky auburn hair curled down past her shoulders. She wore a flight suit of Nile green that clung to her figure and whose color only made her hair appear redder. All the men watched as she bent over to tie down the wings. The older woman's body exuded as much youthful vigor as Tammy's.

"Hi, boys!" the pilot called out to the mostly male cluster. "Who wants to buy a Coke for a thirsty gal?"

Tammy followed the airport wolves into the café, enthralled. Most everyone else stayed outside, ogling the airplane.

"Whose little girl are you?"

Tammy stared upward, surprised at being addressed by the woman when a dozen attentive men surrounded her. She simply shrugged.

"Well, come and sit with me. I'm sure one of these handsome pilots'll buy you a soda. Won't you, boys?"

The drinks appeared almost instantly. The two sat down in one of the burgundy vinyl booths. The pilot smiled at the young woman across from her. "What's your name again?"

"Tammy." She thought that the woman purposely ignored the men around her, as though far more interested in Tammy's company than in theirs.

"My name's Winnie Mae. My daddy named me after an airplane. Isn't that silly?"

Tammy shook her head. "Winnie Mae's a pretty name."

"Well, you can just call me Winnie. Everyone else does. What are you doing here?"

"Watching the planes."

"Is your mama a pilot?"

Tammy shook her head.

"Your daddy?"

"No."

Winnie sipped at the Coke. "Out here on your own?" She winked up at the waitress, a stout woman with a weary smile and her hair in a bun.

"Yes, ma'am."

"Ooh, and polite, too. You like airplanes?" Seeing Tammy's eager nod, she downed the rest of her drink and pounded the table. "Then let's go take a check flight."

"Huh?"

"It's built for two. Think your folks would mind?"

Tammy's eyes nearly bugged out of her head. "*Who cares*?"

Winnie strode through the café crowd, which parted like the waters before Moses. "Hey!" she hollered to the people around her plane. "Look but don't touch!"

"What the hell is it?" somebody asked.

Winnie grinned. "It's called a Vari-Eze. Pusher prop, forward canard with a higher angle-of-attack so it stalls out first, drops the nose, increases the airspeed. Stallproof. Well, almost." Her grin grew wicked as she pulled a few business cards from her breast pocket. "Built it myself from plans. Guy named Burt sells 'em. Here's the address."

Everyone tried for the five she held out, then gathered in a knot around the lucky ones, pens clicking into action to copy the information. She undid the tie-down chains.

"Pudknockers," she muttered under her breath to Tammy as she lifted the girl into the rear tandem seat. "Pardon my Anglo-Saxon. Half of them'll write or call Burt, a tenth of them will order plans, and maybe two or three'll actually start to build one. Maybe one will finish it."

"Why's that?" Tammy asked, strapping the five-point harness where Winnie pointed, then tightening the belts down to her size.

"Just lazy. Just dreamers. Dreams without action ain't nothin' but happy sleep. You know what happy sleep is?"

Tammy shook her head. Winnie slid catlike into the pilot's seat and strapped in.

"Happy sleep is how most people live until they die. They're content, even if they gripe about day-to-day stuff."

She reached down to remove her slip-on deck shoes. "I fly barefoot. Know why?"

Tammy shook her head.

"Better contact with the pedals. I can feel the plane better. Gets cold sometimes, though. That's why I like warm weather." She turned her head to the right to shout "Clear!" Everyone backed away. The engine buzzed into life, the bubble top lowered and locked. They taxied to the run-up area.

Tammy could not believe what was happening to her. First the worry that she had broken the parental taboo against speaking to strangers, let alone the one about going anywhere with anyone at all. Then the fear of the unknown. Then, warming through her like a stolen sip of New Year's champagne, the thrill of sudden and utterly spontaneous adventure. She had run off to join the aerial circus!

"Okay, honey, now I have to talk to the tower and concentrate on takeoff, so keep quiet till I tell you."

Tammy nodded silently. The pilot went through her checklist, testing all the control surfaces, running up the engine, checking the radio, magnetos, oil pressure, compass, and more. Tammy tried to see all of this over the woman's shoulder, but was too low in the seat.

"Niner five four eight Sierra, requesting clearance for takeoff."

"Roger, four eight Sierra," a voice over the loudspeaker said. *"What sort of a weird bug is that?"*

"Ask the boys in the diner, tower, over."

"Roger, four eight Sierra. Clear for takeoff."

"Hang on back there!" Winnie slid the throttle forward and the plane bounced down the runway, picking up speed until the nose suddenly lifted off the ground. They rolled for a few more yards that way and then suddenly the bouncing ended and Tammy knew they were airborne.

Her stomach dropped giddily away. This was better than the Giant Dipper! The Vari-Eze climbed steadily, swiftly, yet Tammy — staring out of the canopy in reverent awe — had little visual clue to their speed. The urban sprawl of San Jose spread beneath them, yet their movement over it seemed slow and majestic, totally unlike roller coasters or even cars, where telephone poles whipped past at a blurry rate.

A sea gull sculled air above and ahead of them. They tore past it at a velocity that made it look like a backward-flying missile. Now *that* was speed! The airplane banked and turned toward the golden hills to the north.

"I'm gonna level off at three thousand, Tammy, then you can take the controls." She said it so matter-of-factly that Tammy was not quite sure she heard correctly over the constant buzz of the engine.

"The controls?"

"Sure. Fly her a bit. I never saw a kid hanging around a little gimcrack airport who didn't want to be a pilot. Am I right?"

Tammy, without even thinking, blurted out the secret she had only shared with Paul: "I also want to be an astronaut."

Winnie craned her head around. Her smile, broad and genuine, revealed twin curves of perfect teeth glinting pure white.

"That's fantastic, honey! If I weren't so old, I'd be trying out for a seat on that new Space Shuttle thing they're building." She turned her attention back to the instrument panel but continued to speak. "I'm a forty-plus semi-rich widow, though, so I'll probably just keep tooling around airports like yours, flying low and clipping treetops or flying high and teasing warbirds…

"You know why I picked you up?" Her voice turned from wistful to serious.

"No, ma'am."

"Because I can read people. That's my best quality. All those guys clustered about me and the plane? There's only three kinds of pilots. One's gotta touch every plane he sees and one's gotta touch every woman. And then there's you and me and a few others. We've just gotta fly. I saw that in you. Stay away from the ones who want to touch you or your plane. They'll be gone the next morning and you'll just have to clean pawprints off your fuselage. Find someone who wants to fly with you because flying's something in the blood. You gettin' this?"

Tammy shook her head.

"Don't worry. It'll come back to you when you need it. I fly across the country dispensing priceless wisdom from a woman who's seen it all and done most of it at altitude. Here. Keep her straight and level. There's less turbulence over water."

They passed over the hills and flew above the Calaveras Reservoir. Tammy took the side-mounted stick in her small left hand and gripped it. Her short legs strained to reach the pedals that controlled the winglet rudders. She knew the instant Winnie let go because the controls suddenly ceased to move and were now under her command.

"The trick to flying is easy movements. Never jerk the stick or pound the pedals. You're moving tons of air mass. Sudden movements are as ineffective as slamming a board against a mound of clay. Do it fast enough and the board breaks. Press slowly, and the clay moves."

Winnie put her through the paces of straight-and-level flight, then a few easy turns. When the plane banked, Tammy looked out of the canopy to see the sparkling blue water below her. For only an instant she wondered what would happen if the airplane failed her, if she were to fall toward that shimmering surface into the cold depths below. Then Winnie brought the plane slowly out of the turn and the fear dissipated.

Heading back to Reid-Hillview, Winnie put the Vari-Eze through some very mild aerobatics. For the first time in her life, Tammy felt two seconds of genuine weightlessness as the plane performed a parabolic dive. Then she felt the crush of g-force as the plane pulled gently out.

The landing thrilled her with the suddenly renewed impression of speed. The runway tarmac blurred past as they touched down on the rear wheels. When the nose lost its lift and descended firmly to earth, she saw the end of the runway with the tower and diner rushing up toward them. Then the aircraft turned and they slowed to a halt in the tie-down circle.

"Hop out, honey," Winnie said as she cut the engine and flipped a few switches. "The first one's free, then your hooked."

"Huh?"

"Do you want to be an astronaut? Then learn to fly as soon as you can. Don't waste a minute. You can't solo until you're fourteen, but the next five or six years you should start saving for lessons, read all you can, and find someone trustworthy who'll ignore the dumb laws and teach you on the sly. That's the way to make it in this world. Ignore the dumb laws. And follow the common-sense laws because they're common sense, not because they're laws. Now give your Aunt

Winnie a kiss; I've gotta go refuel and fly home."

"Where's home?"

"The desert, honey. The deep desert where nobody bothers me and I can fly whenever I want." She unclipped the fob from her keychain. "Here — 'A' is for Astronaut." She handed Tammy the metal trinket, a white letter A with white wings sprouting from either side, on a circle of red. "It was a gas station giveaway, but it fits, doesn't it?"

Tammy grasped the medallion tightly as if it were the greatest honor she had ever received and kissed Winnie Mae on the cheek. Her nostrils caught the scent of jasmine and baby powder and magnolias amid the surrounding aroma of av-gas and vinyl. She pulled back; Winnie yelled "Clear," lowered the canopy, waved, and gunned the engine into life.

Tammy watched her taxi over and fuel up at the pump, hop back in, and fly away into the clear blue.

She never saw Winnie Mae again, but Tammy knew that the feeling that day of excitement and camaraderie and future triumph would carry her through adversity for the rest of her life.

▼ ▲ ▼

Nearly two decades later, astronaut Tamara Reis stood staring at the Space Shuttle feeling nothing but a cold sensation of failure. When the three huge main engines ignited and the solid boosters flared a brilliant white, the physical impact of the rocket blast slammed like a door in humanity's face; a massive door — nearly impossible to swing open — that she and a few others squeezed through over the years. This door, though, would never, ever, be thrown wide. She felt like screaming at that barricade built thick with compromise and latched tight with bureaucracy. She stood by the door, though, ready to pass through again and ready to slam it in the face of others, but she hated it and despised its every slow, narrow swing.

She held the scream inside her, permitting the demon roar to surround her but never to penetrate her own barriers. She would serve this beast, but would never permit it into her heart.

CHAPTER 4

I don't know the key to success, but the key to failure is trying to please everybody.

— Bill Cosby

2 February, Second Year

Gerald Cooper stared at thirteen wasted months and wondered where they had gone. In spite of President Crane's directives mandating space commercialization, funding continually failed to materialize. This, even with an odd sort of endorsement from Barry Gibbon. While never mentioning Freespace Orbital in the journals of the National Organization of Space Supporters, Gibbon nevertheless spent the last year or so taking Cooper under his wing. It was all a bit surreal.

Cooper initially met him at a symposium on space commercialization. He had known of Gibbon for years — the man, after all, had co-founded the National Rocket Society in the late 1940's and served on myriad boards and commissions dedicated to charting the nation's future in Space. Cooper, a space enthusiast from the time he could speak, joined the NRS during the Gemini missions and read in awe the prediction that there would be entire cities in orbit within thirty years. He had seen Gibbon on TV and at conventions and meetings. This time, though, Gibbon actually walked up to him and shook his hand.

"Gerry Cooper," Gibbon said, shaking the man's hand and smiling broadly. He waved a finger almost admonishingly. "I've been watching you and Freespace Orbital over the years."

Cooper felt honored, sort of, to be recognized by Barry Gibbon, but such notice mystified him. Gibbon's efforts since the end of the Skylab project — when the National Rocket Society became NOSS — focused almost entirely on the Space Shuttle, with a few glowing mentions of the Soviet space program. The organization gave little notice to non-NASA activities. He long thought that his efforts had simply been unknown to Gibbon. Now he heard otherwise.

Gibbon exhibited a jovial mood, almost like one barfly propositioning another, as if unaware of his surroundings and unmindful of the future. "Great work on that Starblazer launch system. Radical design."

Cooper smiled uncertainly. "Actually, it uses proven Apollo technology and standard aircraft manufacturing techniques—"

"That's the radical part! NASA is so conservative in the way it constantly strives for cutting-edge technology. You're far-sighted enough to dig into the past for such primitive hardware."

"Well, I..." Cooper frowned. "Thank you." It had *sounded* like a compliment.

Gibbon told him that though the second generation Space Shuttle could conceivably open the cosmos to all kinds of low-cost payloads, the need currently existed for launch systems to supplement the capabilities even of NASA's workhorse spacecraft. "The buzz around NASA is that they're offering contracts to develop a line of cheap, small boosters. Starblazer fits the bill, I'd say. Wouldn't you?"

Cooper felt very hot, as if the convention hall atmosphere had turned strangely hellish. He stared at the grey man who leaned too close to him and could only reply, "Starblazer has payload configurations, but I envisioned it more as a passenger spacecraft."

"Any crewed spaceship design can be modified into a booster." He intercepted a glass of wine from one of the circulating trays, then glanced around the room with a conspiratorial look. "I'll let you know when the bid comes up. I can't say I'll give you advance warning, but if you started thinking about designs to boost ten thousand pounds to low Earth orbit at a cost of under five hundred dollars a pound, you might have a jump on the rest when it's time to submit."

"My design already offers a payload of nearly fourteen thousand pounds for a cost of twenty dollars a pound."

Gibbon laid an arm around his shoulder. "No one's going to believe *those* figures, boy! We're talking about people who know the cost of a Shuttle payload is well over *fifteen hundred* dollars a pound! Sure, NASA subsidizes it to bring the charge down to four hundred million a flight instead of a billion, but no one's going to believe you can send up a satellite for three hundred *grand*! They're used to cost overruns, so put a little *flex* into your figures. Make it look realistic." He pointed a finger at Cooper and squeezed off a shot. "That's a hint from someone who's been watching these guys for years."

True to his word, Gibbon called Cooper the following week with the news: NASA had officially opened bids for a new generation of rocket booster to complement the Shuttle. Cooper, Brodsky, and the other partners in Freespace worked overtime for the next half-year, sometimes with no pay, to prepare a detailed bid for NASA. The design of Starblazer mutated several times during the process. To meet NASA's requirements for safety and redundancy and the Air Force's demands for other bells and whistles, the spaceship grew fatter, heavier, less powerful, more expensive. With every increase in drag-inducing size and payload-shrinking weight, Cooper had to increase chamber pressure in the engines, something that forced him to design in more exotic materials.

In an effort to anticipate what would please NASA panelists, he radically redesigned Starblazer to use a pair of solid rocket boosters similar to those on the Shuttle, but smaller. With his mind ever on safety, he designed them as hybrids: solid fuel with liquid oxygen pumped in as oxidizer. That way, if there were ever a need to shut off the engines, one needed merely to shut off the LOX flow. Such a capability might have saved the shuttle *Challenger* years back, he ruefully mused, but no one had listened to such reasoning at the time.

Unfortunately, hybrid rockets did not possess enough specific thrust to power an SSTO spacecraft, so the design now called out for hybrids to serve as boosters, with the main stage still utilizing the LOX/LH2 propellant.

Cooper spent long nights in tortured thought, watching his brainchild grow lumpy and ugly, wondering if the prize — a NASA contract to build a prototype — was worth the torment.

Seven months after the major redesign, the agony ended. Including design spec sheets, the bid weighed in at just under two thousand pages. Starblazer's payload had shrunk to ten thousand pounds and the cost increased to four hundred-fifty dollars per pound. Freespace submitted it to NASA, then waited.

During the subsequent months, Cooper carried both designs to meetings at corporations involved in the business of putting satellites into orbit. They scoffed at the design built to NASA specs, and dismissed completely the original concept. The responses were maddening:

"How can you charge so little when something as advanced as the Shuttle charges so much?"

"The Shuttle charges may be higher, but it's up and running."

"The Shuttle charges are, on a net basis, lower than the cost of the actual flight as opposed to Starblazer's charge versus cost due to NASA subsidizing a portion of the Shuttle expense. How can you compete with that, fiscally speaking?"

"How can you say your development costs would be so low? Look at the billions spent on the Shuttle!"

"Two hundred million just to build a prototype? But the Shuttle had no development costs — the government paid for it!"

"NASA wouldn't permit you just to up and launch a rocket, would they? Isn't there some law against that?"

"What if Starblazer blew up? Even NASA lost a shuttle a few

years ago with that *Challenger* thing, didn't they? And we know NASA's primary concern is safety."

"This whole launch system of yours wouldn't keep very many people employed, would it? Our managers are used to overseeing thousands of workers, not a couple hundred. It would be a step down for them, don't you see?"

Worst of all, Cooper lost several of his most faithful investors. They assumed that he lay within reach of a NASA grant and hence no longer needed their contributions. They invested in smaller companies on the farther fringes of the aerospace industry. While waiting to hear back from NASA, Cooper furloughed three draftsmen and the receptionist. He answered the phones himself, though the phones seldom rang; he cut back to one phone.

Now — thirteen months after Gibbon first approached him, Cooper stared at the letter on official NASA stationery. Actually, it was a photocopied form letter thanking him for his participation in the Medium Booster Vehicle Development Program. The bid went to General Aerospace for a scaled-down version of their Goliath III intercontinental ballistic missile. Cooper stared at the short précis of GA's bid. He showed it to Thom Brodsky.

"Liars," he muttered after glancing at the figures. "It'll cost ten times that."

"Yes," Cooper said, "but they're liars with a NASA contract and we're honest with nothing but overdue bills to show for it." He took the letter back and laid it in a file folder. "What I can't understand is how they did it. Even lying, their figures were double ours."

Brodsky shook his head. "Gerry — Ludlow Woolsey III chairs the Senate appropriations subcommittee that controls NASA's purse strings. He's from Utah. GA is based in Utah. GA will employ ten thousand people to build the Goliath III-C. We're in California. We'd employ five hundred. Didn't Barry Gibbon tell you to be realistic?"

Cooper's jaw tightened; he picked up a paper clip and worried it to pieces. "The realism is that we don't have any more money to go on. We're in a business that requires us to produce a product before anyone invests in it, but we need hundreds of millions in investment capital before we can build the product. And no one — *no one* — wants to part with that kind of money on faith. No one wants to donate surplus, no one wants to donate time. Except you and the others here." He stared at his friend for a long silent moment, then asked, "Why *are* you here, Thom?"

Brodsky smiled. "Because there's no place I'd rather be. Because I don't think this is a lost cause. And even if I did, I think lost causes may be the only ones worth fighting for, since the causes that seem to win are the worst ones possible. And you buy us doughnuts."

Cooper laughed. Thom could do that to him, even in the darkest hours. "They may have to be day-old doughnuts from now on."

The office door swung wide. Both men looked up to see Sherry Cooper burst in, her long blond hair hanging down as if she had not bothered to care for it that morning.

"Those bastards!" she cried out.

"What is it, Sherry?" Cooper asked.

"The United Nations is considering something called the Interplanetary Treaty!"

Brodsky laughed. "Sounds typically pompous and lame-brained. What is it?"

"It puts all spacecraft and satellites under UN control. It wipes out private spaceflight!"

Gerry waved a hand in dismissal. "They tried that years ago with the Moon Treaty. It didn't work. The US vetoed it."

"There's a difference this time," she said, trying to regain her breath.

"What?"

"It was written by Barry Gibbon."

Thom and Gerry stared at her with faces like poleaxed steers.

5 February

Jackson Lundy contemplated the memo on his desk. He had known for a year that it was coming, and it annoyed him to no end. As the man charged with ensuring the safety of the Space Shuttle's solid rocket boosters, the memo from upstairs was nothing more than a slap in the face. In terse bureaucratese, the waiver dismissed defects found in the current shipment of Solid Rocket Booster ignition systems and granted approval for their use on subsequent Shuttle flights.

Lundy had seen this before. He was a veteran of NASA and had lived through the nightmares of both Apollo 204 and *Challenger*. Here he saw another disaster waiting to happen: only if both SRB's ignited within microseconds of each other would the Shuttle launch safely. Unsynchronized ignition could lead to a bad trajectory. Or worse.

An overwhelming concern for safety dominated the early shuttle designs. One by one, Lundy had seen them dropped. At one time, every single piece of hardware possessed an enormous paper trail documenting its history. Over time, this procedure declined — and so did NASA. This was not the agency he had worked for in the days of the Mercury program. He continued to work, though, laboring as much as he could to maintain whatever margin of safety was permissible.

He ran a hand through his shock of silver-grey hair and re-read the memo. Another loss for him, another deadly error covered up with paper, another time-bomb set ticking with the stroke of a pen.

They learned nothing from Challenger, he thought. *Except maybe a few new ways to deflect blame.*

There already existed evidence of ignition delays bordering on dissynchrony on several flights. Yet every time a launch just barely succeeded, it proved to management the validity of their opinions. "Look, Jack," one of them once said when Lundy showed computer readouts pointing to an incipient dissynchrony, "you're telling me it's unsafe because there was almost a misfire. I'm telling you it's safe because there *wasn't*! Remember the weird power spikes we used to get at one minute, seven seconds? We didn't do anything about them and they eventually went away."

Every argument ended there. We haven't lost another Shuttle yet, therefore it's still a safe system.

He took a sip of coffee from an old stained cup emblazoned with the Apollo 11 mission emblem. The ceramic had crazed over the years, covering the eagle and the Moon with a network of small cracks and fissures. He stared at it for a moment before returning morosely to his work.

▼ ▲ ▼

Lundy lived in an older section of Cocoa Beach, in the same house he and his wife bought when they married thirty-three years before. He sat in his home office — converted from a family room after their second son, Neil Armstrong Lundy, left for college — and marveled that a third of a century had passed in this place. The palm tree seeds he had planted along the entry walk the week their first son, Alan Shepard Lundy, was born now towered forty feet high. The house, so fresh and new and... *Floridian* when they first moved in now stood in need of a good re-stuccoing. Cracks had appeared in its foundation a decade ago, but neither he nor Melissa could tolerate the upheaval in their lives that a major rebuild would cause. And neither could conceive of moving anywhere else. They, like the agency they both worked for, lay stuck in a rut, gazing on a dim goal with inexorably narrowing tunnel vision.

Lundy removed his ebony-framed reading glasses to rub the bridge of his nose. This wasn't good. Launch pressure. He had felt it so many times before. Every time it grew worse. He could not decide whether it was middle age (his own or NASA's) or simply that things were indeed growing worse for the agency.

After the demoralizing, soul-wrenching tragedy of *Challenger*, NASA recovered slowly. It took nearly three years for the agency to return to Space, thirty-two months of agonizing scrutiny and reorganization. And in the end…

Lundy slid his glasses back on.

…nothing had changed. The people responsible for the original compromises that resulted in the Shuttle Transportation System were brought back to "heal" the organization. They healed nothing, only covered up the cancer with plastic surgery; they made minor — though costly — changes to the booster design, developed an expensive escape system that would be absolutely useless in a *Challenger*-style accident — indeed, would be useless during ninety percent of the shuttle's flight regime — and spent billions to build two new orbiters: *Endeavour* a few years ago, and now *Constitution*, scheduled to fly in six months.

Nothing had changed. The STS still utilized over eight hundred Criticality One components. They had no backup components— they were, by definition, non-redundant items. If any one of them failed, at some certain point of the flight regime, it would result in catastrophic failure of the spaceship. Death and destruction as violent as *Challenger*.

Keys jangled in the front door. The office sat just off the foyer, so he heard Melissa's return clearly.

"Incoming Missile" he called out. He had greeted her with that ritual phrase since they began dating, back when a young president offered the promise of a new frontier. With her flaming hair she looked like the rocket's red glare of poem and song. Even now, over fifty, she was still a firecracker: slender, tall — in heels, taller than he — her shapely form discernible beneath the white lab coat she wore. A British racing green turtleneck sweater covered her throat — the only part of her about which she felt self-conscious. Her gorgeous mane of red hair draped down her back, only partially humbled into a ponytail. She threw her keys onto her own desk that sat on the opposite side of Jack's, facing him.

Mumbling a response to Jack's greeting, she slid her laptop computer into its home base, awakening it from its sleep mode in the process.

"Hard day?" he asked.

She shook her head. "What do you think? Now Garibaldi tells me that the success of Biosphere Three obviates the need for any more research on NASA's part. 'If we need it, we'll buy it from them' he says."

"This is the same guy who said the failure of Biosphere Two meant that research by NASA would be a similar dead end?"

Melissa smiled and nodded. "He just thinks molecular sieves are a more elegant way to scrub atmosphere." She leaned back in the chair and ran a long-nailed forefinger delicately under her left eye to wipe away a tear caused by her contact lens. She did so without disturbing the perfect edge of eyeliner that ran under the mascara-bordered lower lashes. Though more than most women wore these days, none of her eye makeup seemed excessive on her; it simply accentuated, as the best makeup should, her large, lovely green eyes.

She keyed in a password that summoned up a research file. Her days belonged to her vocation at NASA's life systems engineering department. Evenings and weekends she spent pursuing her avocation.

"Anything interesting go extinct today?" Jack asked.

She searched through the e-mail the computer had downloaded for her during the previous night. "Another frog. We're losing a lot of amphibians. Gari thinks it's because of ozone depletion."

"Yeah, well, I wish he'd stop blaming Man for the way evolution operates. Species went extinct long before we were around. What's happening now's nothing compared to the dinosaur die-off. Did you get any DNA samples?"

Melissa made a *tsk*ing sound. "No, darn it. These guys seem to vanish before anyone notices they're missing."

Jack said nothing. He had heard similar disappointing news over the years concerning The Ark Society's attempts to create genome records for endangered species. The idea — noble yet futile, Jack thought — was to decipher and store animal and plant genetic codes so that at some future date (technology willing) the lost species could be recreated in a world restored (by some fantastic and conveniently undiscussed means) to more hospitable surroundings. Melissa worked on the project with a missionary zeal, beginning a few years ago when Alan left home to join the Space Command (which title always brought a sardonic grin to Jack's lips) and Neil entered high school. So far, The Ark Society had decoded and preserved the DNA of over twelve hundred endangered species, ranging from spotted owls to sperm whales to assorted rain forest flowers, mosses, bugs, and slime molds.

The Society had its limits, though. When someone suggested that they record the genome of the smallpox virus before the Centers for Disease Control destroyed the only remaining samples, he was nixed: the CDC refused to release a sample and the Society did not want to give the future a genetic blueprint for building a biological weapon.

Jack thought it a prejudicial attitude, based more on aesthetics than morality. The biosphere of Earth overflowed with dangerous life. Why save a poisonous tree-frog? Or a man-eating tiger, for that matter?

For the most part, though, Jack admired his wife's enthusiasm in something for which she chose to work and fight. She had appeared twice before Congress to argue for the abolition of laws regulating genetic research, laws that unintentionally hampered The Ark Society's above-ground research while doing nothing to inhibit the nuts working clandestinely to engineer bizarre new life forms. Her view prevailed both times.

He wondered, gazing at his wife with adoration, if she merely seduced them into voting for the alluring redhead with the coy eyes? Knowing of the satyriasis of congressmen such as Ludlow Woolsey (both *père* in the Senate and *fils* in the House) and Zachary Taylor Peck, he was certain she had convinced them more by looks than by logic.

He had never appeared before Congress, though he considered NASA to be something for which he would work and fight. Not NASA itself, but the integrity of NASA, the purity of the space program. After more than thirty-five years, though, he felt ready to throw in the towel.

"Missile..."

"Yes, Jack?" She looked up and smiled at him, still typing rapidly.

"No one wants to talk about dissynchrony. The project manager at Hayes Poly says the SRB's are fine; any problem would be in software. The launch software has never gone through a risk-assessment procedure. The software people insist that the software is incapable of separating ignition commands; only a bad fuel bead could cause it.

"I'm afraid I see another *Challenger* coming."

Melissa kept typing. "What has Iggy done about it?"

"He doesn't care any more. It's as if he's off in some other place."

"Find out where it is. Maybe we can join him."

"I've thought about it," he said. "Thought about chucking it all. Remember when we started? It looked as if we were on the threshold of Space. You and I."

Melissa stopped typing to gaze at him. With a smile that revealed no hint of regret, only of warm nostalgia, she said, "We were going to live in orbit, maybe homestead a little crater on the Moon..."

"Occasional visits to Earth, just so our kids could appreciate what they had." He reached across the facing desk to entwine the fingers of a hand in hers. Her skin felt as smooth and soft as he remembered at their first touch.

She sighed. That was where the sound of wistfulness dwelt. "After Gemini. That's when I remember first realizing it wouldn't happen. You, you optimist, it took you until Skylab to see the handwriting."

He nodded and released her hand, suddenly more glum than when he began. "That's why it's so hard to go on. I'm just pretending at hope now."

She rose and stepped over to his side of the desk. Gentle hands massaged his shoulders, long nails stroked his neck, strong fingers ran through his greying hair. Her slender waist bent, she whispered in his ear through red, full lips.

"Don't give up the starship, my love. We've got another thirty years in us at least. It's going to happen sometime. It has to. If it's possible to do, it will be done."

"Who'll do it, though?" Jack's voice was suddenly urgent. Old, it sounded to her, and filled with a half-century of broken dreams. "Who'll do it?"

CHAPTER 5

There is no more reason for free humans to build spacecraft with twenty-three million dollar toilets than there is for a homeowner to buy a thousand dollar wrench to tighten a bolt. Yet such literal wastage is the norm for statist efforts, from road-building at millions of dollars per mile to pointless wars at thousands of dollars per bullet fired.

Are we interested in spacecraft as "instruments of national policy," or as a way to loft people into Space? Choose the former and build needlessly complicated exercises in pork-barrel construction that blow up on the launch pad from the chaotic interactions engendered by such complexity. Choose the latter and build inexpensive, simple devices in which to launch from Earth and live in Space.

Which would you choose?

That's why you're reading this book.

— **The Orbital Settlers' Guide**

10 May

The thin layer of water at the bottom of Washington Square's erstwhile fountain, punctuated here and there by islands of litter and debris, reflected its small portion of New York City skyline. The quality of the evening — warm, humid, and still young — gave free rein to the students of New York University.

Two of them, dressed in urban camouflage of black and grey, hefted an object between them that looked for all the world like an old Electrolux vacuum cleaner canister, which it in fact had once been before its current incarnation as a weapon. The students — one man, one woman — raced across Washington Square toward the university's residential area.

The nighttime city smells wafted past the pair, their footsteps lost in the city noises. Three-quarters of the way across the square, a trio of boys in leather jumped in their path.

"Evening, dudes and dudettes," the tallest one said in an amiable, musical voice. His short hair lay slicked back against his skull.

Something heavy sagged the right pocket of his shiny black jacket. "What have we here?" He pointed at the object directly before him.

The students, rather than looking terrified at being accosted after nightfall in Manhattan, appeared vaguely annoyed. The male half, a sophomore with longish hair that looked deep brown in the dim light, said nothing. The woman, short and plump and bespectacled, smiled.

"Cleanup crew," she said in a sardonic voice that could chip flint.

"Science stoonts," muttered a rare purebred Bronx accent to the gang leader's left. "They never got money."

The other raised his hand. "Perhaps we should inquire."

The third kid piped up, "I think a pat search is called for." His face looked like a topological map of Mars, red and cratered. He grinned, his anomalously well-formed teeth glinting yellow in the street lights, and looked at the woman. "Nah. *Body cavity* search."

The student's expression changed from amused to a twist of anger. She glanced over to her counterpart for approval. He nodded.

"Search this," she said, pointing the Electrolux toward the young thug and pressing a stud on the top of the device. Little grilled doors at the front snapped open. Instantly, an intense blue beam of light erupted from the depths of the machine. Leather, fabric, and flesh sizzled.

Her assailant cried out the near-universal Anglo-Saxon exclamation of surprise and pain, then jumped back to bat a leather-clad hand against his right shoulder. A thin wisp of smoke puffed from the hole in his jacket.

The other two stared at their comrade, then burst into laughter. The object of their mirth swung a savage fist at the gang leader, who took it on the shoulder with a hearty guffaw. The second punch was harder, with more injured pride driving it.

"Stop it, pus heads," the Brooklyn-throated kid said as he tore the two apart.

Having less fun now, the pair turned to look toward their intended victims.

The leader glanced around the square. They stood alone, two sets of soft footsteps vanishing swiftly into the night.

▼ ▲ ▼

The pair of physics students succeeded in penetrating security at the chem student's dorm. This was not too difficult, since their security-breech team had moments before captured and hog-tied the pair of dorm supervisors. It was just past midnight. Anyone who was not asleep was undoubtedly out committing similar mischief. It didn't matter, as long as the halls were empty.

They started at the first door on the first floor. The woman deftly slid a thin wire into the keyhole. The man pointed the laser at the doorknob and pressed the stud. The blue beam vaporized the wire with a puff and a few sparkles of intense white light. Moving quickly to the next door, they repeated the procedure. Insert magnesium wire, blast with laser, move on. The pair proceeded through the dorm, stopping at each room just long enough to melt the door lock. When they finished with all five stories, they climbed out and down the fire escape.

That was when they were spotted.

"Fizzies!" someone shouted in the darkness below.

The plump girl pointed to the left of the sound. "Fire over there, Lloyd."

Lloyd brushed the long hair out of his eyes, swung the canister around, and fired from the hip. The beam punched into the night, a bright turquoise line from fire escape to pavement. Ancient chewing gum on the sidewalk sizzled and smoked. The cement cracked noisily enough to elicit a yelp from the alarmist, who scrambled into the bushes for cover.

His shout, though, achieved its purpose. From inside the dorm rose the sounds of rattling doorknobs, followed shortly by the pounding of fists.

"Let's scram," Lloyd said to his fellow saboteur. They clattered down the fire escape in tandem, Lloyd slinging the laser over his shoulder to free his hands for the final climb down the first floor ladder.

Inside the dorm the noises abated, followed by a moment of unnerving silence.

The woman looked at her companion. "Uh oh."

The dull pressure and thump of an explosion erupted from the third floor of the dorm, followed almost instantly by similar reports. One by one, the chemistry students blew the locks off their doors with various concoctions similar to C-4 plastic explosive. Most did, anyway. Some chose the less drastic method of removing the doorknob with a screwdriver, or taking off the hinges. They were the wet blankets, though, who never went to parties and actually spent their time studying.

▼ ▲ ▼

Shortly before dawn, three chem students sneaked across the quad carrying three one-pint bottles and three narrow paint brushes. Their retaliation for the laser assault consisted merely of painting the physics dorm floors with a purple paste. Starting from the top floor and working down, they spread thin coats of the grainy compound along the linoleum floors, on doorknobs, and on the panic bars and kick plates of the hallway doors and exits. The purple paste — nitrogen tri-iodide — was a wonderful and dangerously unstable mess created by mixing ammonium nitrate with iodine crystals and then rinsing out the precipitate. As long is it stayed wet, it remained relatively stable. The three made certain, though, not to paint themselves into corners.

An hour or so later, long after the trio of painters had departed, a weary physics student dragged in through the main doors. Short, with thinning reddish hair and thick glasses, he moved, zombie-like, carrying a thick stack of library books and CD-ROM disks under one arm. He paid no attention to where his feet led him, as long as they pointed in the direction of his room. His left foot landed squarely on a smear of the nitrogen tri-iodide. The dry, unstable form of the chemical detonated with a jarring firecracker bang, startling him into dropping the books and setting off a series of mini-explosions. The noise awakened other students, who rushed out into the hallways. The resultant detonations reverberated through the physics dorm, sounding like a military attack.

Through the entrance and into the din walked one student who calmly strode across the nitrogen tri-iodide, deliberately unconcerned with the blasting beneath the soles of his shoes. He walked tall, with dark brown hair the color of an old walnut rifle stock. Tan jeans clad his legs, and over a loose-fitting beige shirt he wore an unbuttoned buckskin jacket cut in the fringed, mountain-man style. The leather briefcase he carried bore a small brass plaque that read "Property of Davy Crockett. Insured by Col. Samuel Colt." He wore a hat made out of raccoon skin, complete with its head perched on top, eyes shut, like a contented stowaway.

With unflappable determination, William David Crockett IV — graduate student of physics — walked blithely through the hallway minefield into his dorm room.

Crockett's small fifth-floor room contained a wonderworld of gadgets, books, computer equipment, charts, posters, and more gadgets. He threw the briefcase on his bed and, flopping down in an electronics-encrusted swivel chair, put his heels — soles of shoes still smoking from the chemical hotfoot — on his cluttered desk. He drew a cheroot cigar from the breast pocket of his jacket and lit it with a match struck by his thumbnail. Above his desk hung a framed antique lithograph of his ancestor: the original Davy Crockett, coonskin cap and all. He gazed at it for a moment.

After a few meditative puffs, he settled down to work on his computer. The screen displayed a schematic of the chem students' dorm, along with stress analyses. He canceled the screen and called up a file containing the fax numbers of every mail order house in the continental United States. Crockett punched the go command and the computer started dialing each number in succession, using a long-distance access code filched from the Nuclear Regulatory Commission. The faxes contained a request from the New York University Chemistry Students Association for twenty copies of each company's latest catalogue, to be sent care of Samuel Friedman's dormitory address.

Crockett switched the sound off to consider his next move. Reaching over to aim a milliwatt laser beam at a receiving lens on the chemistry students' dorm building, he flipped the switch on a small liquid-crystal TV connected to a breadboard of circuits that converted it into a picturephone. A face appeared on the screen. Curly black hair framed an intense face accented by blue eyes that normally would have been sparkling. At the moment, they gazed narrowly back at Crockett.

"Well, Sam," Crockett said. "Are you willing to concede defeat?"

"Are you kidding?" Samuel Friedman replied with a grin. *"Neither side's resorted to massive property destruction yet!"*

Crockett shrugged. "If that's what you want." Reaching over to flip an intercom switch, he said, "Let 'er rip, Bernie."

A female voice responded. *"You've got it, Davy."*

The lights throughout the dorm dimmed suddenly. Outside, a deep purple glow flickered for an instant, then steadied. A high-wattage laser beam flared across the quad, hitting the chem dorm, deftly carving away a cornice. The concrete chunk fell five stories to shatter on the pavement below.

Friedman dashed out of range of his screen long enough to assess the damage. Returning, he said, *"Good shot, Davy. How long will your capacitors hold up?"*

Outside, the purple flickering abated. From the roof of the physics dorm arose the crackling sound of electrical failure. The room lights returned to full power. Crockett glanced at his button-encrusted calculator wristwatch. "About seventeen point six seconds," he said.

Friedman smiled. *"Good work. However, this should last about four hours. Nighty-night."* He pressed a button off screen. A dozen minor, metallic detonations reverberated through the hallways.

Crockett leapt from his desk and stuck his head out the door to see that the fire extinguishers in the physics dorm had been replaced with fakes housing gas canisters. Crockett heard the telltale hiss, held his breath, and quickly stepped over to his closet.

The physics students in the dorm dropped like anesthetized flies.

On the rooftop, a lovely, raven-haired student in tight black ninja togs tried to repair the laser. She rubbed her eyebrows once and gazed blearily at her tool kit. Then she tumbled to the asphalt and gravel. Below, innocent passersby collapsed to the pavement as the cloud of knockout gas drifted out of the building.

Friedman viewed the scene approvingly from his window, watching the green images on night-vision binoculars. He turned them toward Crockett's window.

Davy Crockett sat at his desk, feet up, staring insouciantly at the computer screen through the lenses of his Israeli Army surplus gas mask. Crockett sighed, lifted the microphone to his mask and said in a muffled voice, "Nice try, Sam. And just so you'll be ready for breakfast tomorrow..."

He called up another screen on his computer, displaying a 3-D schematic of the space between Crockett's window and Friedman's, with a readout of wind speed and direction taken from the meteorological station on the roof of the physics dorm. He clicked YES on a dialogue box that asked LAUNCH?

A deep noise coughed four times from inside a device standing near Crockett's window. A quartet of farm-fresh Extra Large Grade AA eggs sailed through the air, describing a parabolic trajectory that arced high over the quad at midpoint to descend upon the alarmed face in the fifth floor window.

Friedman clambered to crank the window shut and just barely made it. The four eggs slammed against the windowpane in rapid succession, spattering their monocellular loads in impressively wide bursts. Friedman turned toward the picturephone and shook his fist, laughing maniacally.

"I shall never surrender!" he shouted. *"Nor labor under your oppressive yolk!"*

Davy Crockett's lips formed a grin beneath his mask. He switched off without a word.

11 May

Friedman walked to class in the cool morning air. Of medium height and in the habit of wearing old Army jackets and carrying his texts under his arm, he utilized the olive-drab canvas rucksack on his back to carry his laptop computer and portable chemistry set. His ebon locks strayed less wildly this morning as he strolled deep in thought.

Davy Crockett quietly strode up beside him, puffing on his cheroot, coonskin hat covering his dark brown hair completely. On his waist hung a cameraman's battery belt.

"Great fun last night," he said, slapping a hand on Friedman's neck just above his shirt collar.

Friedman jumped up two feet from the electrical shock that sparked through his nervous system, but Crockett pulled him down to ground level with both hands, maintaining his grip. The high-voltage, low-amperage current caused Friedman's hair to radiate from his head as if he were touching a Van de Graaf accelerator. It did the same to the fur and the tail on Crockett's hat. He looked like a skunk about to spray.

Friedman recovered his composure quickly enough to carry on an ordinary conversation, saying through his clenched teeth, "Feels like six hundred thousand volts this time."

Crockett grinned. "Seven-fifty."

"Good condensers."

"NASA surplus," Crockett said. "Swap them for some of your superconducting ceramic?"

"Sure." The galvanic tingle in Friedman's shoulders faded. His hair settled down, as did Crockett's raccoon tail.

They cut across Washington Square Park on their way to class when a furious voice from behind shattered the morning. "Stop or you're dead meat, Sam!"

Friedman turned to see a whirlwind of anger approaching. "Bernadette!" he cried. "Oh, temple of lust at which I worship. Oh, goddess of—"

Bernadette caught up with them. She wore an austere white lab coat over a black and extremely retro cowpunk outfit complete with atomic-symbol earrings and a pound or two of silver-and-turquoise Native American jewelry. Her black hair, though bobbed, looked straggled and unkempt, as if she had spent the night asleep on a rooftop. Between sneezes and sniffles into a scarlet handkerchief, she managed to thank Friedman *a whole lot* for gassing her. "I nearly froze to death, you worm."

Friedman shrugged. "Galahad there had a gas mask. I thought you two shared everything short of your precious bodily fluids."

"Leave my PBF's out of this." Bernadette turned her glower toward Crockett. "Well?"

Crockett mimicked Friedman's shrug. "Be grateful we do this in spring."

▼ ▲ ▼

The only class the three shared that semester was the mandatory seminar on Scientific Ethics and Social Responsibility, overseen by visiting professor Barry Gibbon, Ph.D., formerly of Yale and currently of the National Organization of Space Supporters. During the entire lecture series, he displayed a dour expression that always darkened whenever he encountered Crockett and his friends. More sour than usual today, he strode back and forth at the bottom of the auditorium, reminding everyone that he considered Science a beast only partially restrained by constant vigilance.

"But what *is* ethical science? It is best that we describe it by what it is not. It is *not* the reckless pursuit of knowledge in the absence of any societal restraint. It is *not* unbridled research without concern for social consequences..."

He climbed up the classroom steps to peer at Crockett, then at the book he held below the level of the seats. The title read *How You Can Profit From the End of Civilization As We Know It.*

"And it is most emphatically not childish rivalries such as the feud between the physics and chemistry students."

He stared at Crockett, with Bernadette and Friedman observing from the sidelines a few seats away. Crockett, without so much as looking up from his reading, replied, "Be that as it may, Professor, hasn't the research spun off many useful consumer items?"

Gibbon spoke loudly enough for the entire room to hear. "Mr. Crockett, you and your friends may fancy yourselves to be the scientific vanguard. However, your whiz-bang approach to the discipline of research is infantile and absurd to the point of being Swiftian. And I don't mean *Jonathan*, I mean *Tom*."

Some of the students — the ones seeking better grades — laughed. Crockett narrowed his gaze and muttered, "I made it a point that every prank would force me to learn something about science."

Gibbon stared impatiently at Crockett, his goat gotten. "Why couldn't you have stayed at Harvard, gotten your MBA, and become an alcoholic businessman?"

Davy closed his book, leaned back in his seat, and smiled. In a drawl that could have originated in the Blue Ridge Mountains of Tennessee, he said, "It's more fun blowing things up."

Gibbon nodded, squeezing his lips together firmly before opening them to speak.

"A fitting attitude, I suppose, for a descendant of the legendary blowhard Davy Crockett. It's a pleasure, though, to note that your opinion is no longer in the mainstream of scientific thought. Gone are the days of the lone nut researcher ready to destroy the world to test a pet theory. Today we have a grander view. In thirty years or so, *your* children or grandchildren will be living in space. Witness the planned space station *Unity*. Here we have a stunning tribute to the ability of science to transcend political differences and bring nations togeth—"

Crockett snorted loudly, then muttered, "A hundred billion down the gravity hole to build and operate something only twice the size of Skylab, which cost a fiftieth of the price." He folded his arms, rawhide fringe swinging. "I could do the same for half a billion. You're asking the same kind of minds that run the Post Office to put people in orbit. Look at what happened with the Moon. The US sent twelve guys up there, the novelty wore thin after three years, and they abandoned the project. What would the westward migration have been if the government had handled it? Build a huge, expensive land rover, send a couple of guys to Nevada and have them bring back some dirt and then never return? The government's not interested in you and I gettin' up there, they—"

"Thank you, Explorer Crockett. I suppose you'd populate the lunar surface with corncob-smoking farmers and gun-toting mountain men, in some bizarre hillbilly space program."

"It'd be better than what's up there now. A pile of overpriced metal scrap and some pretty plaques with autographs from a crooked presi—"

Gibbon slapped his palm on the dais with theatrical intensity. "Unless you and your cohorts can do better with your brand of punk science, leave the *real* achievements to the big boys and go back to your childish war games."

He turned away from Crockett to address the entire class.

"The Space Station, costing tens of billions of dollars and employing hundreds of thousands of people, will be the most complex undertaking in human history, far more complicated and certainly more life-affirming than the Invasion of Normandy... or, for that matter, Desert Storm. And — if the United Nations approves the Interplanetary Treaty — *Unity* would become a truly world-wide effort, far exceeding even the magnificent successes of Russia's late, lamented *Mir*."

"Which," Crockett interjected, "the U.S. would pay for and everyone else would leech off."

Gibbon smiled, addressing the class rather than the lone upstart. "Is it not proper that the nation that has taken the most from the world give something back?"

"This nation hasn't taken anything from the rest of the world," Crockett said. "The state that claims dominion over us may have, but Americans themselves have *given* the world electricity, airplanes, computers, medical super-science, space travel itself! As for your damned treaty, it's nothing but an attempt to put Space under the control of government bureaucrats."

Gibbon laughed. "Isn't it already? What the treaty does is make the bureaucrats of each country responsible to a higher authority — the UN."

"In other words," Crockett said, "you're just adding another layer of commissars to slow us down further. We won't get into Space that way."

"Enough, mountain-boy. No one wants *you* in space anyway. Although," he said with a smile, "perhaps some of your classmates might wish to ship you off." A large portion of the class applauded. Gibbon spoke slowly and with the cool authority that carried with it the knowledge of power. "As your instructor, I claim dominion over this classroom. I'll not have it collapse into anarchy as you would the space program." Gibbon turned his back on the student to punch up a picture on the video projector behind him. The screen lit up with an artist's rendering of *Unity*. He resumed his professorial timbre.

"What, then, in this new interplanetary order, is the role of the scientific class? First, to determine via scientific polls the needs of the electorate that pays their salaries. Second, to develop by consensus the technology necessary to meet those needs."

Crockett withdrew from his briefcase a tubular object about the size and shape of a flashlight and put it on his stack of books. Without making any overt motions, he aimed the business end of it toward the fire alarm on the wall near the stage-right exit. He casually rubbed pocket lint off of an iron pellet the shape and size of a pencil eraser and inserted it into the rear of the device. Flicking a microswitch, he folded his hands over the tube and leaned his chin on his hands as if listening to Gibbon with serious intensity. After waiting for the system to power up, he made a last adjustment to his aim and gently pressed a red button on the top of the barrel. Electromagnetic coils silently accelerated the projectile nearly to bullet velocity, sending it smack into the alarm button.

"Knowledge in service to humanity—"

The fire alarm honked into life with jarring intensity, interrupting the lecture. The class quickly flew to the exits, led by Bernadette and Friedman. Crockett pocketed his device and sauntered after them, smiling over his shoulder at Gibbon and spreading his hands in mock helplessness.

▼ ▲ ▼

On their way back to the dorms, Davy and Sam traded veiled hints at their plans for that night's battle. Bernadette walked silently beside them with her hands in the pockets of her lab coat. She seemed deep in thought and started nodding in agreement with her own interior monologue, which caused her earrings to jangle like tiny wind chimes. After a few moments, she muttered, "We could do it, you know."

"Do what?" Crockett asked.

She whispered with a childlike solemnity. "Ship off into Space."

Friedman snorted out a laugh. "Right — have you got a spare ten billion?"

She stopped walking to turn toward Crockett and grasp his arms, bracelets clanking. "You said you could do it cheap. Were you lying?"

Davy shrugged. "Do you mean build a space station or just get something into orbit? If NASA had the brains to park the Shuttle external tanks in orbit, you'd already have nearly ninety roomy space stations for the price of ten percent more fuel. I could build a simple orbital spaceship for twenty million."

"Well," she said, following him again, "what if you deduct what we could scrounge from around the campus and the city? And use volunteer labor?"

Sam smiled mildly. "No one could build a spaceship that cheaply."

Davy said, "Oh, I've seen some designs that cheap. Using aircraft aluminum and off-the-shelf equipment. Zero redundancy — pull the trigger and take your chances. There's a design I saw that uses a rotor mounted on top of the ship to give it extra lift. I've got a subscription to *The Private Space Journal*. They cover all sorts of unorthodox launch systems."

Bernadette looked at Friedman. Despite his negative assessment, he appeared to be considering the idea. Producing the laptop computer from his rucksack, he flipped up the screen, sat on the curb, and began to punch in numbers at a furious pace as he strolled.

"It would be possible," Sam said after a moment, "to build a very cheap orbital rocket, assuming volunteer labor and scrounged parts."

Bernadette slugged Crockett's arm as the trio resumed their walk. "Hear that? We've got the highest concentration of scientific minds this side of MIT and most of them don't have to work for a living. I mean, you and Sam can marshal everyone into conducting these stupid wars — why not turn it toward something that matters?"

"Why go into Space?" Davy asked. He was distracted, watching something in the distance.

"Because no one's ever gone into Space on their own, you know, without a whole lot of help. Without a whole big program. We'd be like the Wright brothers, or Lindbergh. Or your great-great-great-great grand uncle. We'd be famous. We'd be heroes. We could write our own tickets."

Crockett made a huffing noise, dismissing the whole idea with one sound. His attention focused on what he saw ahead of them.

Bernadette planted herself squarely in Crockett's path. "We'd probably get our doctorates without having to take another class."

Davy and Sam stared at each other for a moment, then said, in unison, "Sold!"

Bernadette smiled brightly at them. Friedman looked up from his computer, staring in sudden shock at the Chem students' dorm. The entryway and steps lay clogged with thousands of mail-order catalogues in stacks and slipping, teetering heaps. A Postal Service truck dumped another load on top of the huge pile.

"What the hell have you done?" Sam screamed at Crockett.

Davy held a hand against his heart. "How ungrateful! I've given you the perfect fund raiser — a paper drive!"

CHAPTER 6

Support Free Trade: SMUGGLE!

— **Bumper Sticker**

The preceding year paid off well for Marcus Grant. As a businessman, he understood and utilized the virtue of starting out small with a familiar service and a popular product. He began his enterprise with smuggling, an ancient commerce, and — profits in hand after cheerful laundering by willfully disinterested bankers — he immediately dove into less-crowded fields of endeavor. He set up several offshore corporations through which he bought an abandoned factory and warehouse on the shores of the Hudson River in Hoboken, New Jersey, a 200 foot cargo ship of Liberian registry, a vintage Boeing 707 in excellent repair, and three floors of an office building in downtown Long Beach overlooking the Port of Los Angeles.

Using these tools and his talent, Marcus Grant made his subsequent fortune. The service was still the same, only the commodities changed.

The secret of smuggling was secrecy, yet smuggling a product for sale required an end-market. A market required that customers be informed of products and services available. So no matter how secretly Marcus Grant operated, word concerning the nature of his commerce began to spread, for not even a black hole in deepest Space can hide its presence — the very fact that information about it disappears provides the means to infer its location. The stories about Grant consisted of rumors and inferences, unsubstantiated by anything that passed for evidence in a court of law.

Grant sat in his office on the twentieth floor and gazed at the screen on his computer, reviewing the day's events.

China: government officials complained that pilotless drones, apparently dispatched from an airfield in Seoul, South Korea, were parachuting shipments of contraband to dissidents on the outskirts of Beijing. One of the drones — accidentally downed over the capital city by collision with a flock of cranes — carried three separate packages. One contained inflammatory, anti-government literature. One contained Danish pornographic magazines. The third consisted entirely of Bibles. Grant did not regret the loss of the drone; the parts were untraceable, and the banned items would swiftly find their way into the counter-economy via corrupt bureaucrats. He mentally wrote off such losses as the cost of doing business, a kind of advertising that inevitably resulted in market expansion.

Nevada: High speed boats raced across the Colorado River every few minutes, carrying cartons of cigarettes from Laughlin, where the tax per pack was minimal, to California, where citizens violated the recently enacted 200% tobacco tax with impunity. Individual entrepreneurs composed much of that black market, but a plurality of ships belonged to Desert River Jet Mail Boat Sightseeing, a charter division of Grand Cayman Diversified Industries, Inc., on which Grant Enterprises held a private placement bond covering all its corporate debt.

New Jersey: The Hoboken factory lay fallow, awaiting some future use. He made a note to confer with Donahue about it.

Worldwide: Wherever a government ordered a commodity illegal, strictly controlled, or heavily taxed, Marcus Grant fed the market with quality and efficiency. Cheap American rice flowed into the agri-protectionist Japanese market; cheap Vietnamese computer chips sluiced out to electro-protectionist Canada. Video games crept into Cuba; quality cigars snuck out. Birth control devices crossed the border into Guatemala; unwanted babies escaped to clandestine adoption agencies in wealthier parts of the world. Australian beer went to the Czech Republic; refurbished Czechoslovakian AK-47 rifles made their way to African independents, Manchurian insurgents, Los Angeles shopkeepers, and dozens of other embattled groups and classes.

Grant spoke to the vox intercom. "Jo-Don!" The computer instantly connected him to Joscelyn Donahue, his second-in-command.

"Here, Marc," a crisp voice replied over the line.

"What's with the Ruthenia shipment?"

"Extra charges against the delivery division due to additional bribes of Ukrainian ministry of exports. Hasn't been entered into the spreadsheet yet. We're still in the black, but they're opening up to grey markets in electronics, so we're going to have to undercut the competition in some other ways than mere availability."

Grant mused for a moment, his fingers peaked against one another. "All right. Stop sending in the low-end computers and shift to top-of-the-line goods. Those are tariffed at one-hundred-fifty percent white market, so set the bribe maximum at five per cent of our cost and pass it through to the wholesale markup. Then start building the market for CD-ROM and VR."

"Shifting gears now." There was a pause, then the voice added, *"Marc — predictions for the coming winter are for food shortages. Take a look."*

The information appeared on his computer screen, gleaned from the CIA-KGB joint intelligence system. Grant ran a few inquiries of his own, then muttered, "Idiots. They de-collectivized farming but still maintain central control over trucking and fuel. No wonder food's rotting in warehouses while markets stand empty. All right... There must already be a link between off-time truckers and black market diesel. Strengthen it. Establish a network of freelancers and forge the appropriate paperwork so they can learn to look clean while hauling the goods. I want a return of at least twenty percent of the throughflow."

"I'll get on it." She switched off.

Marcus Aurelius Grant turned to gaze out a window that offered a sweeping view of the harbor. The sun dropped behind Palos Verdes, the fortress hill of wealthy homes that jutted into the Pacific as if wanting to break free of the rest of the Los Angeles megalopolis. Grant lived there, in a home at the top that was as much an aerie as his office. He enjoyed looking down on the world. It gave him what he considered to be a proper perspective on the human race.

He was a tall man, even seated in the oversized executive throne. In just two years his wavy black hair turned from its formerly long sandy-blond to a premature silvery-grey trimmed in short, business-like style. Dressed in an exceptionally well-tailored dark navy pin-stripe suit, pale blue shirt that matched his eyes, and navy tie sporting the tiniest and most conservative maroon dots, he now fit the classic alpha-male archetype. He looked the part he played: owner of a vast financial empire.

A few degrees above Palos Verdes hung the sliver of a new crescent Moon. It took a while for Grant to notice it in the twilight. When he did, he glanced quickly away and returned his attention to the computer.

Information was what made him strong, and information cascaded through Grant Enterprises like fish through a gill net: very little escaped his grasp. So it was that an item captured from the Combined Federal Electronic Database System was immediately routed to his attention. It was a simple list of topics for an upcoming meeting of a senate sub-committee headed by Ludlow Woolsey III, the senior senator from Utah. On that list was the name of a company only one dummy corporation away from Grant Enterprises. That was too close.

Grant Enterprises thrived on information flow. It told Grant what was illegal where, and allowed him to determine when and how to make a profit circumventing the laws. The only catch was that information never flows in just one direction. Every time the Grant octopus insinuated a tentacle into the world market, it left a trail that could — given extreme perseverance — be traced back to its source. His twin defenses against such diligence were bribery and blackmail. The elder Woolsey possessed peculiar interests in certain congressional pages working on the Hill. One of them worked for Grant, though she did not know it. He kept the photo negatives and videotapes in a vault where he stored many other sensitive items. A large vault.

Woolsey snooped where he should not. That was the trouble with politicians, Grant mused. So few were honest enough to *stay* bought.

Woolsey, now in his seventies, had reached the end of his term limit, yet was still young enough to risk losing out on private-sector positions by falling into scandal. Grant suspected counter-blackmail by a competitor. Whatever Grant had on Woolsey, someone else had something dirtier. That would require—

"Marc?" Joscelyn Donahue's voice said over the intercom.

"Yes?"

"Senator Woolsey's on line two. He says it's important."

Grant punched up the line. "Good evening, Senator. To what do I owe the pleasure?"

The voice on the other end, sonorous and dignified, spoke with equal courtliness. *"Why, Marcus, it's always a joy to hear your voice. I'm just calling as a proud parent to let you know my son Ludlow the fourth has been named head of the House Subcommittee on Space, Science, and Technology."*

"Congratulate him for me." Grant now realized the angle. Not counter-blackmail against Woolsey, but against Grant himself.

"Now, you know," Woolsey continued, *"even with such a prestigious position, he faces a tough campaign this fall..."*

"Say no more. He's got my personal contribution to the legal limit. I'll have a fifty dollar check cut immediately. On a totally unrelated subject, Ludlow..."

"Yes?" The senator knew better than to think *any* subject unrelated.

"Fidelity Security Full Faith and Credit Trust Savings Bank in Portland has quite a few non-performing loans. I think someone should question the loan officer."

"Consider it done, Marcus." The senator switched lines.

The exchange had grown a bit more blatant than he wanted, but he lacked the time to haggle. One of Senator Woolsey's bag men would soon secure a loan from Fidelity Security intended never to be repaid. The bank would simply write it off as a non-performing loan and add it to the staggering debt structure of the bank, to be repaid, perhaps, by taxes when the bank went under.

"Ah, democracy," Grant muttered, shifting his thoughts back

toward turning a profit. Marcus Grant knew the power of government and he knew the power of the market. He preferred the market. White, black, or grey, it never left as sour a taste in his mouth.

CHAPTER 7

Even as we move into Space, I fear we shall take our evils with us.

— Samuel Edward Konkin III

Barry Gibbon knew that there existed a market for the promise of power. He had promised it for over four decades and never had to deliver. He held the ears of ten presidents, thousands of congressmen, and millions of scientists, students, and common people around the world. His message never changed: someday, human beings would live and work in space, on the Moon, on Mars, and among the stars. He enjoyed filling young minds with visions of such moving immensity. The hopeful masses who saw space as a way out of their problems — as a relief valve for overpopulation perhaps, or an escape hatch for the discontented and the adventurous — flocked to Gibbon and his National Organization of Space Supporters. They needed him. And he needed them.

Gibbon had not always been interested in space. In his youth, architecture fascinated him. Though the minutiae of building design and construction failed to hold his interest, the concept of city planning imbued him with a firm sense of purpose. He studied ancient Rome and Greece for clues to the minds that devised and oversaw the construction of such huge social organisms. He pored over old maps of London and Paris, watching the cities grow. For a while, until guided away by a helpful professor, he tried to solve the mystery of the Mayan and Anasazi ruins and how such great civilizations vanished utterly, their works consumed by jungle and desert.

After a while, it became clear to him that none of the ancient cities grew out of any coherent plan. They simply appeared to spread like bacterial colonies on a Petri dish. Modern cities such as New York, Los Angeles, Hong Kong, and Tokyo were the worst. Driven by the engines of competition and commerce, they exploded haphazardly like tumors. Gibbon could not stand the sight of them. His family lived near the most planned city in his country, Washington, D.C., and it was there, in the summer at the end of the war in Europe, that he encountered his epiphany.

He held no sympathy for the defeated Nazis, yet he possessed a secret, grudging respect for Adolph Hitler's ability to inspire a nation. Gibbon understood what Hitler — another student of architecture — offered: a vision of power to the powerless masses. Gibbon, just twenty and in college during the last years of the war on a deferment courtesy of a frat brother's father in the War Department, already knew that he, too, required a vision, a vision that would unify the masses for good instead of evil.

A college chum — "Lud" Woolsey, page to a first-term senator — ran up to him with a newspaper clutched in his hand.

"We've got Von Braun!" he cried, shoving an article under Gibbon's nose.

"Von Braun?" Gibbon took the paper from his friend's plump hand and looked it over.

"The Nazi's top rocket scientist!"

"Oh yes," Gibbon muttered. "Just saw a newsreel about it."

"Right! He surrendered to the army with a slew of others and an arsenal of A-4's!"

"A-4's?"

"The rocket bomb! The V-2! Enough parts to build dozens of them."

Gibbon handed the paper back to Lud with a benign smile. "What do we need them for? To blitz Rhode Island?"

"For testing! Von Braun says that the design could be made even bigger. Longer range. Maybe even put men into space!"

Gibbon smiled wanly. He had just read a pulp story by Rex Ivarson about such a plan, though he would never admit such a failing to Lud. "You've been to too many Saturday serials. When did you first have the urge to wear silver tights?"

"This is serious, Chimp. A man in orbit with a telescope could observe troop movements, watch for storms, pinpoint sinking ships."

Despite Lud's use of his annoying nickname, Gibbon stopped walking for a moment to think. Living in outer space required food and water and shelter, everything that man originally took from the land. Yet there existed no land between planets. A city in outer space demanded a totally artificial construction, planned from the very start. Every room, every hallway, every bolt and rivet must follow a rigidly determined blueprint. A city in orbit would not grow like some fungus spreading chaotically outward but would crystallize like a snowflake suspended in the frigid night, expanding according to rigid rules.

As nature made the rules for snowflakes, so Barry Gibbon would make the rules for spacemen.

He grasped the arms of his friend. "Why, we could be living in outer space within this generation!"

"Well, I don't think it's as easy as all that, Chimp old chap. No one in government seems to know quite what to do with the huns."

"They'll know what to do with them," Gibbon said, his dark eyes alight with excitement. "They'll know because I'm going to tell them!"

▼ ▲ ▼

In the early 1950's, rocketry stumbled along through a series of hardware refinements. Flights that did not end early in a fireball lasted only a few minutes longer as even the best designs failed to lob anything into orbit. It mattered not to Gibbon. The dream was all he needed or wanted. The promise and the vision sufficiently filled his requirements.

He organized a small discussion group at Harvard, gathering around him the finest minds he could attract. Several afternoons a week, the Society for the Advancement of Rocketry met in the tearoom of an aging physics professor to discuss their plans for the newest New World. Evangeline served the tea quietly, listening intently but, Gibbon feared, totally opaque in her ability to comprehend their discussions. He allowed her to serve them more out of familial loyalty than any expectation that she might contribute intellectually to the exchange.

The group continually attracted forward-thinking young men who loved to lounge and bandy about ideas concerning how central authority could be more easily maintained in the closed environment of a space station, or how an orbiting city would be truly international, passing as it did over dozens of different countries every hour or two. They modeled their orbital government after the new United Nations, minus the concept of a Security Council in which single states held veto power over resolutions. They shared the vision of democracy triumphant, of extraordinary men working single-mindedly for the common good of ordinary persons.

Twenty years. In twenty short years, men — "and women, too, of course," he added with a languid wave of his hand — would live in outer space in huge orbiting cities overseeing the epochal march of progress.

He graduated from Harvard with a degree in political science. When asked why he chose that field instead of physics or engineering, he merely smiled and said, "There will be enough men to build and pilot rockets. Who, though, will pilot the pilots?"

Barry Gibbon never held a job; he cultivated positions: chairmanships, advisory panels, consultations. He derived an income from these and from lecture honoraria. When the Russians launched Sputnik, his career skyrocketed. Magazines and newspapers that otherwise depicted space enthusiasts as four-eyed eggheads delighted in Gibbon's urbane manner and calm assurances that the future was just two decades away. Students consulted with him about what careers to choose that would lead to a life in Space. The most promising he steered away from such ephemeral pursuits as chemistry or engineering and into psychology and the social sciences. "Why design the rockets men build," he often said, "when you can design the men who build the rockets?"

When the president announced that man would set foot on the Moon within the decade, Dr. Gibbon of the SAR declared that man would — within a generation, just thirty years or so — have a permanent foothold in space.

The Society grew, though not as fast as Gibbon's prestige.

Throughout the new Space Age, the Society published glowing predictions for the New Frontier. Copies of a booklet by Gibbon, *Your Future In Space*, were distributed free to elementary schools. Filled with gorgeous illustrations of huge orbiting space stations, the text told of a world of peace and prosperity, where teams of scientists worked together in orbiting laboratories solving the world's problems, where television communications would make the planet a single community, where — since no nation could reasonably claim outer space — all nations co-existed as one. For that reason, spacecraft and spacesuits in the illustrations always depicted the insignia of the United Nations.

None of the paintings showed a lone astronaut — they always worked in groups.

No one questioned Gibbon's optimism or his consistent idealism. He strove, after all, to make Space the new Commons.

The thirty-year prediction served Gibbon well for over thirty years. Whenever setbacks occurred, such as the Apollo disaster, the Soyuz catastrophe, or the *Challenger* tragedy, he resolutely declared such mishaps an inevitable part of the sacrifices required by such a vast and noble undertaking. Nothing, though, must stop the forward progress to establish humanity in outer space within the next three decades. Whether or not humanity ever achieved a permanent toehold in Space, Barry Gibbon possessed the pull, the clout, the power to control and guide that destiny.

11 May

Power, though, seldom resides where it seems to. Washington, DC, though it hosted the White House, Capitol, and Pentagon, actually contained little of value to the power structure of the United States. While the politicians and the news media danced in the nation's capital for all to see, the true work of Earth's final empire proceeded quietly in the surrounding states of Maryland and Virginia.

In Fort Meade, Maryland, stood the sprawling structure that housed the National Security Agency. Deep within it, in a room with no windows and only one door, sat one of the few men in the federal government who possessed a true awareness of the power he wielded.

Montgomery Barron held a small sphere suspended on the tips of his white cotton-gloved fingers. About the size of a golf ball, it was constructed of a transparent, optically perfect material. Fast inside it lay an electronic maze of sophisticated circuitry. He marveled at its intricacy, its beauty, its deadly potential.

He held in his hand the key to Space.

Barron, a smoothly handsome man of forty-eight, possessed short dark hair with a pleasing natural wave that years ago would have guaranteed him a crack at movie star status. His height, not immediately apparent while seated behind his desk, was considerable and impressive. He peered appreciatively at the sphere through dark grey eyes, then lowered it gently back into its pink anti-static nest beside two other identical globes.

Power, Barron mused, *hides in the strangest places. Not just in men or institutions, but sometimes in something as obscure as a ring laser gyroscope that exceeds all others in accuracy and reliability.*

He removed the cotton gloves and keyed his telephone.

"Stansfield," a voice on the other end answered.

"Monty here," Barron said. " 'The cook just delivered the gyros.' "

"I see. Will we be having lunch at the airport?"

Barron smiled. "I'm feeling hungry," he said, and returned the handset to its cradle.

▼ ▲ ▼

Washington Naval Air Station, compared to nearby Andrews Air Force Base, comprised a medium-sized airfield attached to a cramped military facility. One of the smaller hangers off the right runway housed an NSA project that consumed relatively little room in relation to its importance. Compared to such public secrets and well-known black projects as stealth aircraft and pulse-detonation jets, this small and comparatively inexpensive effort operated unnoticed, off the books, unknown even to the guards who stood on duty outside the hanger.

Though the ensign knew Montgomery Barron by sight, he still

performed the requisite security check every time the man arrived, as he did for the same dozen workers who arrived every morning, entered the hanger, and exited twelve hours later to be checked out by a different guard.

"Good morning, sir," he said to Barron, who strode from his limousine with the easy grace possessed by only a few men in civilian authority. The ensign had seen many important dignitaries in his time, but most of them exuded either an air of inattentiveness, as if concentrating on their performance, or an aura of nervousness, as if they constantly searched for that one betrayal that would bring them down in an instant.

Barron, though, simultaneously radiated a thorough alertness and a calm self-assurance that comforted the ensign and made him a little more proud of his country. *If only the government had more men such as he,* the ensign thought, *we'd have fewer problems.*

Barron entered the hanger through the first set of double doors, sealed them, and stroked his passcard through the checkpoint at the second set. With a sigh, he lowered his head to stare into the biometric scanner with his left eye, an action he absolutely detested.

The low-power laser fired into his eye, scanning its retinal pattern to compare with the image stored in its memory. Barron, who valued his vision immensely, had never been convinced of the safety of such security devices.

He raised his head and blinked several times. The dotted retention image floating before him alternated between red and turquoise with each blink. Amid the colors, he saw the doors part. Just beyond the threshold, in a bright blue jump suit, stood Charles W. Stansfield, a short man with unkempt greying hair and a languorous New England pattern of speech that belied a sharp intellect.

"I swear," Barron said as he stepped in, "that someday they'll be able to identify all government employees because we'll all be blind in one eye."

"Let's see 'em," Stansfield said. He held out his hand.

Barron passed the small package over. "A clutch of eggs for our bird."

Stansfield nodded. "Yeah. Let's put 'em in the nest."

The pair walked over to the object that filled the hanger. Ten workers clambered all over it, some crammed deep inside the fuselage, some standing on scaffolding around its skin, others sitting on the concrete floor to work on the landing gear.

Longer than an F-115 Eagle at sixty-five feet, its thirty-three foot wingspan narrower, the spaceplane's wings described a long, sweeping delta shape that signified hypersonic capabilities, with upturned winglets on the tips to increase the functional wing area without adding to their width. Its sleek black skeleton consisted of Beta B-120, the same titanium alloy as the late lamented SR-71. Its leading edges, though — on wings, rudder, stabilizer, and nose — bore caps of the same grey carbon-carbon material borrowed from space shuttle technology. That was all Barron wanted to use from current NASA research. The rest of the spaceplane relied on older, proven technologies. Barron took chances in many realms, but none where it mattered.

Acquisition of the ring laser gyros was an important step. Even black projects such as *Stark Fist* had difficulty procuring necessary high-tech equipment, especially when paper trails had to be disguised.

Barron walked once around the spaceplane. Nearly complete, it was the culmination of six years of secretive effort. And shortly he would face the man who sought to undo all of it.

For now, though, Barron contented himself with admiring the beauty of the bird. It looked like the killer he intended it to be.

And that made Montgomery Barron smile.

He smiled rarely, since it did not behoove a government spy to appear as if he was having too much fun.

▼▲▼

Barron's face held no trace of a smile while seated before Steven James Milton Jr., head of the National Security Agency. The two men came from different disciplines within the organization. Barron rose through the ranks of Operations, the dirty-nailed half that operated the wiretaps, devised the codebreakers, and performed the actual spying on foreigners and — as need warranted in the usual manner in which agencies flouted their charters — on American citizens. Milton ascended from NSA's Analysis division, interpreting the information supplied by operatives such as Barron and applying it under the guiding principal of national security. He viewed Barron as the trusty dog that brings in the newspaper: good at fetching, but wholly incapable of understanding the consequences of his assignments.

Barron's opinion of his superior was that analysts possessed no real-world concept of the dangers faced by the NSA. To them, the day-to-day struggle and danger were invisible, only the position of pieces on the game board held any reality to them whatsoever, and they would push the pieces around even if the walls were falling down on them.

"Monty, my boy," the director greeted him with an affable tone.

He was in his sixties, but looked younger thanks to a healthy tan from tennis games played on the courts at some of the finest country clubs in Virginia. Also, being only five feet, three inches tall, he appeared almost boyish. "I have a challenge for you." That usually meant another pointless report.

"What now?" Barron's mind buzzed with the problems of *Stark Fist*. Technical problems. Computer simulations failed to match predictions. The spaceplane design might not make it to orbit if the specific impulse of the engine on order could not be upped by three per cent or more. Weight might need to be shaved from an already minimalist structure. How much more could—

"What?" Barron thought Milton said something pertaining to him.

"I said, the House Intelligence Committee wants a more thorough accounting of all black projects."

"We're under budget on ours."

"I know. However, the Dedicated Decryption Petaflop Supercomputer is way over budget and still can't break RSA/PGP codes in less than six months of computing time. I want you to decrease your budget by seventeen per cent, retroactive to the first of this year."

The numbers cascaded through Barron's mind. "With inflation, that would be the equivalent of a twenty per cent cut!"

Milton smiled and shrugged. "Times are tight. And though there are *no* terrorist spacemen flitting about, there *are* millions of messages, financial transactions, and secrets shooting around *this* planet that we can't read."

Barron took a long, slow breath and mentally counted to ten, stopping at three to say, "As much as I would love to read every computer user's personal mail, I respectfully suggest, sir, that there is a far greater threat to national security from one single subnational in orbit than in a megabyte of encrypted messages. Just think of what it would mean. We currently have no defense against someone in even Low Earth orbit. And anyone making it all the way to geosynchronous orbit could hold a hundred million dollar satellite for ransom just by threatening to give it a kick. There'd be no need for someone to go up there with weapons and rain destruction down on us — though they could because we have no effective defense against it, thanks to the downfunding of BMDO — all anyone would have to do is go from satellite to satellite with a *screwdriver* and nearly all telecommunications *including NSA's* could be destroyed. The damage would be in the trillions. Even with the Shuttle and Deltas working full-time, it would take decades to replace what's up there!"

Milton, to his credit, listened without interruption during the tirade, though he had heard it before. "Monty," he said after a moment. "I'm not driving this. Congress is. They don't have the inside knowledge, let alone your... vision. I'm not canceling *Stark Fist*, I just need some economy."

"Then economize on that black hole of a computer!"

Milton raised his hands helplessly. "They know enough about it to support the idea of being able to examine every bank transaction, every private message, every fax transmission regardless of its encryption method. They view manned spacecraft as just some frustrated desk-pilot's wet dream. No offense, Monty."

Barron had no desire to prolong the conversation. The ship kept calling him back. "I'll see where I can cut."

"Good fellow. It'll keep your program alive and keep those fools on the Hill happy, right?"

Barron nodded, rising quickly to go. His stomach gnawed with anger even while his mind ran rudimentary cost analyses. *Meddlers,* he thought. *Short-sighted bean counters.*

16 May

The man with one arm knew the value of wealth. Wealth consisted not of the number of dollars one possessed, but of the quality of life one wrested from the universe. Larry Poubelle lived a life of extremely high quality.

Wealth allowed him the means to engineer a right arm and hand that looked real and responded to his will as would a limb of flesh and blood. Wealth paid for the artificial intelligence and fuzzy logic computer imbedded inside the device, which interpreted and acted upon the slightest electrical commands of the muscles in the three-inch stump protruding from his shoulder. Wealth bought the Beech Starship airplane that he piloted down toward the runway beside his mansion. Wealth purchased the sophisticated avionics that guided the plane to the touchdown point almost without Poubelle's assistance.

Wealth served as a tool and — in using it — Laurence Norman Poubelle was a master craftsman.

His face looked as though it had been sanded from finest teak. His tanned skin lacked the leathery quality of other sun-worshippers in their mid-forties, since he could afford the treatments to fend off damage from solar radiation. He understood radiation, perhaps better than many physicists. Radiation was his business. Larry Poubelle owned American Atomic, and owned it with a possessive passion most men reserved for a woman.

Despite its quaintly archaic name, American Atomic grew into the world's largest manufacturer of portable nuclear power under Poubelle's ownership. He built it from the economic ruins of a failing nuclear submarine facility a mere four years after returning from the war in Indochina.

Having ditched his useless A-6 Intruder in the fouled waters of the Tônle Sab, he killed his way to Pnomh Penh and down the Mekong River, and walked out of Cambodia in five days. He dragged into Chauphu with a gangrenous arm only to learn that Saigon was in the process of being abandoned to the armies of North Vietnam. He escaped — barely — onboard a fishing boat that navigated out of the Delta to deliver him to the USS *Forrestal*. He fought his way up the corporate monkey bars with equally single-minded, single-handed tenacity.

The war memory recurred while flying, especially during landings at home. His private oasis lay on the northern shore of the Salton Sea — two hundred thirty-five feet below sea level in the deserts of Southern California — sandwiched between the Kane Military Operations Area and the transition area to the airport at Thermal. On approach to his own runway, Poubelle passed over the northern quarter of the inland sea. He suppressed the sudden flash of memory about his controlled crash into Tônle Sab not because he feared his past, but only because he refused to let the past affect the present.

Poubelle touched the Starship down to the pavement with easy grace and taxied it to the hangar. Only then did he turn to the woman in the co-pilot's seat and smile.

"Cheated death again," he said.

"Don't get cocky, kid," Chemar D'Asaro said, her eyes merry, the dark, smooth flesh of her face beginning to glisten in the desert heat. Her eyes provided the most striking feature of her stunning beauty. In startling contrast to her deep mahogany skin, their irises were twin pools of gold flake stirred by hidden breezes. Men — upon first encountering her — often gazed into those eyes as if hypnotized. They stared like guileless children, ignoring all the lovely curves that in other women would be the foci of attention. Her eyes commanded notice whether they glared with anger or scintillated with joy. Larry Poubelle first met those golden eyes when Chemar served as a helicopter pilot in the Antilles. He watched the way they glowed with intense concentration as she skillfully jockeyed a rickety Sikorsky SkyCrane over a sunken shipment of plutonium pellets he sought to recover. He hired her on the spot to be his personal co-pilot and trouble shooter. She had never disappointed him.

Together, they powered down the Beech and stepped out of the hot, heavy shoreline air into the relative cool of the hangar. Inside, amid the smells of avgas, jet fuel, and oil, stood two other aircraft. One, a glistening silver DC-3, the other a cherry-red Stearman, tricked out for aerobatics. Both planes — and the Starship — displayed immaculate maintenance.

They climbed down the Starship's steps, flight satchels in hand, to face a half-dozen men in three-piece suits.

"Ah," Poubelle muttered with a grin. "My bloodsucking lawyers."

D'Asaro said nothing. Poubelle slapped on his warmest smile of greeting.

"Gentlemen!" He spread sincerity like cream cheese. "To what do I owe this charming invasion of privacy?"

A man near the middle, who looked as if the desert air had triggered a severe sinus attack, spoke through intermittent near-sneezes. "It's the press, Mr. Poubelle. They're on the warpath about the leaked report."

Poubelle locked down the Beech and walked around it slowly, giving it the careful post-flight inspection it richly merited. "It's a slow news day. They'd grill Mary about the sheep-at-school scandal if they could."

"What do we tell them?"

D'Asaro spoke up in the lush French accent of her native Martinique. "Tell them that backyard nukes are safe and feasible as a way to disconnect homes from the electrical grid, then ask them why they are serving as unpaid hatchet men for the energy oligopolies."

The man glowered and turned again toward Poubelle, who merely hooked his thumb at her and grinned. "What she said." He hefted his black saddle-leather flight satchel and strode with D'Asaro toward the hangar office.

"You can't shrug off public opinion like that, Mr. Poubelle! It only makes things worse."

Poubelle opened the office door and tossed the airplane's keys to the gorilla sitting in an easy chair enjoying a cup of coffee. The short and muscular brute wore a perpetual expression of wry mockery that curled his freckled lips into a near-permanent sneer. The freckles continued across his face up under his shock of curly red hair, stained with wheel grease and jet soot. He caught the keys easily and shifted from his chair into an erect posture. "Turnaround time, boss?" he asked.

"I'll be here a couple of days, Monk."

Monk Patterson sneered happily and left the air-conditioned confines of the office for the supreme joy of running maintenance on the Starship, his personal favorite of the three aircraft Poubelle hangared at Salton Sea.

Poubelle turned his attention back to his associates.

"Public opinion is not what the papers print. That's just their attempt to impose their agenda on the public. I'm closer to the public opinion — if there is such a thing — than they are."

"Nobody wants a nuclear power plant in their backyard," an older man with peppery hair said. "The last thirty years proves that."

"All it proves," Poubelle said, "is that nobody wants a huge tax-subsidized, zero-liability nuclear utility sucking them dry. Most people prefer independence. Why do people drive cars when they can take buses? Because they oppose transportation? No. Because they prefer to own their own vehicles. Why do people have guns in their homes when they have the police to protect them? Because they want to control the means of their immediate defense. Why do people buy washing machines when laundromats are plentiful? Why buy homes when barracks would be more economical?"

He flopped down in the same chair vacated by Monk and leaned back; Chemar snorted and leaned against the steel desk and picked up that morning's *Desert Tribune*.

"Gentlemen," Poubelle continued. "You show me anything — *anything* — that's provided now by a centralized distribution network and I'll show you something that people would prefer owning and controlling themselves. Look at how the telephone destroyed the central telegraph office, how e-mail is destroying the post office. Americans love individual action, gentlemen, because they are not of a collective mind about anything. Most Americans don't seek out a leader to tell them what to think. Sure, some continue to elect them, but look at how few actually vote. Most people conduct their affairs concentrating on the most important things in their lives: their families, business, friends. The more they can disconnect from outside control, the happier they are. The safety of my stratified-bed power cell is not the real issue with the press. The real issue is the implied rejection of central control of the electrical grid. If no central authority controls the amount of electricity a home receives, how could they ever enforce energy rationing? How could they get on anyone's case for drying clothes the wrong time of day? Or for leaving the lights on at night? How could the government penalize certain people for excessive use, in disregard of the fact that the user pays the monopoly — heavily — for electricity that ought to be considered his purchased property?"

One of the six men *harrumphed*. "Without being connected to the grid, how could a drug agency target hydroponic farms by analyzing how much power they draw?"

"Exactly!" Poubelle grinned and pulled a fat cigar from his flight jacket and rolled up the sleeve of his right arm. The lighter built into the index finger of his cyborg arm emitted blue fire to light the tobacco. He blew out the flame and after a few puffs said, "You own what you control. Control the grid, control the people."

"That's not what I meant—"

Poubelle gazed up slyly at the suits. They goggled back at him like mystified schoolboys. "I'm a betting man," he said slowly. "You seem to think that I need some favorable public relations. What would you suggest? Should I backpedal and insist that the report was old news and that we would never endanger the backyards of this nation with such dangerous devices?"

After a moment of hesitation, the man with the bad sinuses said, "Well... yes."

"How about if we just ignore it and come back with something different?" The man with one arm smiled. "Something that will deflect attention and prove my point about the American spirit?"

The men looked edgy. They hated it when their boss talked that way. It was not something they had learned to deal with at business school. The previous year's trapshooting bungee-jump wager still haunted the nightmares of the survivors.

He glanced at D'Asaro. From behind the lowering edge of the business section, her aureate eyes glowed with excitement.

"She knows what I'm talking about. On what does central authority have the greatest stranglehold these days?" He waited.

Knowing they were on the spot to come up with something, the men grasped at straws.

"War?" one asked hesitantly.

"Good guess. Except that there are about two hundred wars going on in the world today, a lot of them almost *ad hoc*." He took a deep drag on the cigar and blew a series of smoke rings. "Try again."

"Information?" another ventured.

"You're fired," Poubelle said with an icy calm. "Nobody that ignorant should be here. Information is the most decentralized commodity. Has been, ever since the microchip. Take a hike."

The others shifted nervously as the young man picked his jaw up off the deck and slowly turned to step wordlessly out of the office. No one else said anything.

"You gutless button sorters. You're just a collection of college degrees with the souls squeezed out of you. I'll give you the answer. Space. There is only one space power: NASA. Europe, Japan, China, Germany, and all the others are just lobbing up hardware. Even Russia is coasting on past glory. Only one organization has the current ability to put people in orbit and only one has the ability to seize hardware that's already up there. You own what you control, gentlemen, and right now NASA owns the rest of the Universe, as far as

Earth is concerned. That's a greater monopoly than any power utility or government service could hope to gain."

They stared at him blankly. He had never rambled so before. To them, his words made no sense whatsoever. He might as well have been discussing the Man in the Moon. Incomprehensible as it might have been to them, he was.

"Less than a decade ago, a man and a woman took off from an airport a few miles from here in a specially designed airplane and flew around the world, non-stop, on one tank of gas. They did it without any help from the government. In fact, they flew over some countries whose governments did not even know of the flight. They were small, they were high up, they were independent of any government protection or control. They were individuals, gentlemen, and do you know who paid for it?"

He knocked cigar ashes on the floor. "Other individuals. They raised the funding in the old-fashioned way: they infused thousands of people with their dream, their vision. They only wanted to set a flying record that had never been made before. Pretty frivolous. Yet in the same year that NASA was covering up the deaths of seven astronauts, these two pilots seized the imagination and hope of a nation and became the symbol of individual initiative. That's what I plan to do."

"Break their record?" a balding exec with a too-large briefcase ventured hopefully.

Chemar laughed from behind the paper, folded it away, and smiled at Larry.

"You could say that," he said. "We'll definitely be circling the world on one tankful. Only it won't take nine days. More like ninety minutes."

"You're talking crazy..." the oldest man in the group said meekly.

"Harold! You constantly surprise me with your outbursts." He turned to his co-pilot. "Chemar — increase Harold's stock options by five per cent. He's getting backbone in his dotage."

Chemar pulled a palmtop from her flight bag and entered the information.

"Crazy is American, Harold. Demanding independence from Britain was crazy. Declaring every citizen a sovereign was crazy. Recognizing the individual as the fundamental unit of society was crazy. Building trains and planes and rockets — the acts of madmen. And I'm proud to be part of that heritage. Crazy enough to build a rocketplane in this hangar and fly it into orbit. Just because it's never been done before. Just for the hell of it."

Amid the silence, only the faint throb of the air conditioner offered any evidence that time had not stopped in the room. Then the five spoke at once.

"You can't be serious!"

"The liability..."

"—can't you see the negative publicity potential?"

"You mean, go into *space*?"

"...never get permission."

Poubelle lowered his cigar and answered rapid-fire: "I *am* serious; any liability can be insured; if I succeed, the publicity's positive, if I fail, I'll most likely be dead and then it's *your* problem; yes — low Earth orbit, free-market astronauts, Horatio Alger in the sky; and I don't need anyone's permission to travel into Space any more than Leif Erickson did to travel to America. Watch and see. Now beat it. I've got a parallel team working on pre-publicity. Coordinate with them. Steinmetz is in charge there. Ask her."

The five men departed, leaving Poubelle and D'Asaro alone. He stubbed out the half-smoked cigar and shook his head. "Whenever I see those guys, you know what I wonder?"

"What?" she asked, putting her palmtop away.

"I wonder if agriculture wasn't the biggest mistake mankind ever made."

Chemar instantly made the series of logical connections and laughed with amusement. Then she shifted her long legs and said, "That was the most astounding display of extemporaneous bull-slinging I've ever seen from you."

"And what makes you think I'm slinging?"

"Because you've never discussed any of this with me. Nor with Steinmetz, I'll bet."

"You're a gambling woman," he said with an expansive grin. "That's what I like about you." His feet, shod in short-topped flying boots, clomped onto the counter into grooves worn by decades of other pilot's feet as he leaned back in the chair. "Want to cheat death for high stakes?"

"I'm game." Her face smoothed into impassive seriousness. "Can we do it?"

He flung the extinguished cigar across the room. It landed in a brass cuspidor with a hollow clunk.

"I have no idea. Let's build one and find out."

"It would cost a fortune."

"Chemar, my lovely, Americans spend a fortune on frivolous items every day. The cosmetics industry is a six billion dollar business. Candy bars another two billion. People watch TV with a phone in one hand and a credit card in another, eager to spend their meager earnings on some trinket that they think will brighten their lives. We can offer them trinkets with a purpose, overpriced collector's items that pay for something worthwhile."

The dark centers of her bright eyes deepened. "Worthwhile? A joyride for the two of us?"

"Any spaceship we build would be the prototype for a new fleet. The cargo we take with us — autographed photos, commemorative coins, patches, et cetera — will weigh as much as a small commercial satellite or a couple more passengers. This would be a short-term publicity flight that would pay off in long-term business potential."

She leaned closer to him. Close enough for him to smell the jasmine scent adorning her body. All trace of merriment faded from her face; she gazed at him with level gravity.

"Your bull was *not* impromptu, was it? You've given this long and serious thought."

"I've told you a lot about me," he said, "so you know I don't do anything halfway. Kids your age—"

"I beg your pardon!"

"—don't know what it was like to be young during the real Space Age, back when we were convinced that living in Space would be more than the privilege of a few. Back when it was just naturally thought to be the right of all. It colored everything we did, at least what I did. Why do you think I love flying so much? Why — back when we had the Learjet — did you think I kept taking it up to the flight ceiling? Remember how the Moon would look so crisp and clear and close? That's been my dream."

He raised his right arm to flick the built-in lighter. "It was a dream that the war interrupted, but never completely crushed. I built American Atomic because that's what a lunar city would need first: compact power. Power is everything. A rocket needs power to get into Space, humans need power to run an artificial environment, and the common man needs power to fend off those dull oxen with briefcases full of discouragement."

Chemar laid a hand on the cold, hard arm reinforced with magnesium struts beneath the tanned silicone rubber flesh. The sensation filled her with an odd electric thrill, as if she touched a man-machine that was more than human. "Boss," she said softly. "This visit just now didn't trigger all this. What's happened?"

"It's a small thing, really." He opened up his flight case and pulled out a manila folder. In it were two newspaper clippings: one, an article about the Interplanetary Treaty; the other, a short obituary from the back pages of the Los Angeles *Times*. This one he handed to her. "Thorald von Kleist died yesterday. I never knew him. I knew *of* him, though. He was one of the German rocket scientists who surrendered at the end of World War Two. He worked on the X-15, the rocket plane. I loved that thing. While other kids were caught up in Mercury and Gemini, I was obsessed with the X-15."

"That model on your office shelf..."

He nodded. "I built it when I was twelve." He took the news clipping back from her to return to the folder. "They're dying, Chemar. Even the test pilots. They're old dying men. Men in their sixties, seventies, and eighties who set speed and altitude records that still stand. Men who came so close to flying into orbit that only political tampering prevented them from going there. NASA was embarrassed by rocket planes. They knew that there was no way to make a big one. They took the X-15 from the Air Force and Navy, made it their own, then killed it.

"Von Kleist was just this old, poor, obscure man when he died. *I* knew his name, though, as surely as other kids knew of Ted Williams or Mickey Mantle. Even men who walked on the Moon are growing old and dying, one by one. It's as if there's some chasm between then and now. As if our fingers are loosening their grip on the past in one hand and on the future we saw in the other. We're trapped in an endless now where we mortgage our future just to stay frozen in the present." He looked up at her as if waking from a trance. "I don't want to lose that grasp." He flexed the servos on his right hand into a fist. "I'm rich now. I want to buy the deed to that future. And I want to pay off our debt to the past."

▼ ▲ ▼

The task grew more challenging than he had anticipated. He knew by heart the major facts about the X-15; he read everything he could as a boy and it stuck with him better than baseball stats had with the beer-swilling, sedentary TV addicts he was loathe to call his contemporaries.

The sleek black rocket plane, shaped like nothing so much as a mighty crossbow quarrel, consisted of a frame of titanium and stainless steel covered with a skin of Iconel chrome-nickel alloy. The Reaction Motors XLR-99 rocket engine, powered by liquid oxygen and anhydrous ammonia, produced 57,300 pounds of thrust at sea level. The sea level thrust, though, was meaningless, since the X-15 was launched from under the starboard wing of a Boeing B-52 Stratofortress.

Larry Poubelle sat in the lush and comfortable leather embrace of his office chair. Behind him, from the forty-story vantage of his panoramic office window, spread the sunlit city of San Diego. One glance encompassed the tropical greens and desert browns of the sprawling San Diego Zoo, the deep blue of the Pacific Ocean where it intruded upon the Sea World aquatic park, and the greys and purples of Cayumaca Peak, part of the mountain range that extended from Palm Springs down into Mexico to serve as the backbone of Baja California. Beneath his feet rushed the cars and trucks and messenger motorcycles that fed the business center of the city. He could see that and more if only he turned around. He rarely turned though, absorbed as he was in thought.

In the years since his youth, the spaceplane had become an antique. The people who had designed the X-15 nearly four decades ago and those who had flown it were approaching senescence. The research team he assigned to the task encountered great difficulty in procuring detailed blueprints and engineering data from the original manufacturers. He wondered whether it might be necessary to go to the Air and Space Museum in Washington, D.C., and ask to inspect the actual rocket plane hanging from the ceiling.

He doubted the necessity of such a trip. The shape was just about the only detail that would remain, and it would be upsized to accommodate a pilot, co-pilot, and cargo. He had learned enough from working closely with his power plant engineers to know that modern alloys, composites, and construction techniques could keep the upscaled version nearly the same weight as the original. And though he had not followed it closely, he knew that there had to have been improvements in rocket engine weight-to-thrust ratios in the last three or four decades.

What would a ground-up redesign of the X-15 cost? The original program cost three hundred million dollars over ten years and resulted in 199 successful flights with only one fatal crash in which test pilot Mike Adams died. Poubelle translated the 1960's dollars in the only way he knew was realistic: he took the current price of gold and divided it by the price of gold for that era, then multiplied that with the three hundred million figure to arrive at a figure just under five billion dollars. Estimating that everything the government does costs ten times as much as private industry, he brought the figure down to a cool five hundred million. He suspected that much of the avionics and the rocket engine itself could be procured off the shelf. That left the airframe and the controls. Most of the cost would therefore be in development of the prototype, so reducing the flights from nearly two hundred to just one and building a single craft instead of three would only reduce the cost to about a quarter of the total.

Over one hundred million dollars.

Not a drop in the bucket, Poubelle mused, but not exactly an outrageous amount. The used 747 he would have to buy and modify to carry it up to launch altitude would cost about a tenth of that, and ten 747's would not get him into orbit.

He could have written a check that evening to pay for the entire project. Laurence Poubelle, though, had plans that ran deeper than that.

21 May

Thom Brodsky sat in the corner of the office reading a transcript of the latest UN discussions about the Interplanetary Treaty while Gerry Cooper stared out a window at the setting sun.

"At least," Brodsky muttered loud enough for Cooper to hear, "we have the pleasure of knowing that Gibbon's little brainchild has as many nasty little hands fiddling with it as our design did at NASA. Russia demands that *Mir* be reactivated as the first UN space station, while the Chinese ambassador is arguing for Mandarin as the official language, based solely on number of speakers. She's enduring some in-fighting from the Cantonese and Manchurian candidates. The British ambassador is half-heartedly calling for 'bold experimentation in freedom,' listing fifteen proposals for social structure, at least ten of which are planks lifted from the Communist Manifesto. The Ecuadoreans and Brasilians are going at it over where the single launch site will—"

"Enough." Cooper swiveled his chair to gaze at his friend. "I can't even think about them shutting down Kennedy. It's the symbol of everything I thought was right about humanity, everything that was good about the future. Listening to them argue about how to kill it — or worse, how to encourage its suicide — it's just too much for me."

"Gerry?" The voice at the door drew his attention. He turned in his chair to see his wife framed by the flame orange of sunset. Her hair caught the last rays of daylight to shimmer the hue of gold alloyed with copper. Her athletic body, silhouetted by the fiery light and framed by the doorway, could have been the template from which to draw an idealized image of Woman. She stood there, one hand high against the jamb, the other laid along her hip and thigh.

"Are we still on for dinner?" she asked.

"That's my cue," Thom said, stuffing the newspaper into a bulging briefcase and hefting the mass as he rose. "You both have a good night." With that, he edged past Sherry as she entered. A moment later, a geriatric car engine rumbled grudgingly to life to carry Brodsky off into the sunset.

Sherry walked over to her husband and sat on his desk, legs crossed.

"Dinner," he said with a smile, "will have to consist of leftovers from the freezer. I'm tapped out."

"I know." She smiled. "I'm not in it for the food. I just want your company."

Gerry laughed. "This company? It's worth less than the leftovers."

"You know what I mean. You need a break. You've been marketing this latest version of Starblazer for almost three months straight."

"No one's interested. Not even Gibbon, who got me started on this tack. It's as if he pointed me on this direction and then forgot about me. Why did he do that? Why does he support space travel and then come up with the Interplanetary Treaty? Something that would crush all incentive to get into Space?"

"He must have a reason. Maybe he just doesn't understand how governments operate. Or how the market works. He's just a professor, you know."

Gerry shook his head. "He subscribes to Thom's journal. The articles that run about NASA interference in the bidding process for launch veh—"

"He probably subscribes to everything space-related. And probably doesn't read half of it. He *is* getting old, you know. Probably more concerned about obituaries than orbitals."

"What about the rest of them? 'The industry.' The half-dozen or so firms that *claim* they want cheap access to Space but won't invest a dime in a design that could work?"

Sherry picked up the blueprints on his desk and handed them to him. "Does this design work?" she asked in a level tone. "The one you spent a year on for the NASA bid?"

"For a price." Bitterness grew with each word. "It works, despite all the bells and whistles they demanded be part of the final design. It works even though it's loaded down with pointless redundancies, exotic components, and that ridiculous quarter-ton hatch to make it compatible with the Shuttle. It's a goddamned flying elephant, but at least it will fly. And nobody wants it because I can't subsidize the development and launch costs with tax money. Why pay two hundred million to design and fly the prototype when NASA undercuts the market?"

He slammed the sheaf of sketches into a trash can, then turned to call up the master blueprint on the computer workstation. He stared at the overall design for a long time. His wife said nothing. She simply remained seated on the desk, waiting patiently for him to come to a decision.

After long moments of silence, he said, both to Sherry and the world in general: "I'm not going to knuckle under to their way of doing things. I won't allow a committee to dictate spacecraft design to someone who knows better. A rocket, of all things anyone could build, is the purest integration of thought and matter, of will and reality. I've bent my will to theirs for too long. You can dream all you want about space travel, but if the smallest component in your spacecraft does not work perfectly in reality, you'll be dead and all your dreams with you. I know the reality of spacecraft. It's NASA that's dreaming, marching to the beat Congress pounds out on a pork barrel." He picked up the lightpen and started to alter the design. He became lost within the drawing, as if he held the pieces of metal in his hand, shaping it with fingers that handled aluminum and stainless steel like clay in the hands of the finest sculptor.

Sherry slid off the desk to drag a high stool behind her husband and sat there for the next few hours, quietly witnessing Cooper tear the guts out of his spaceship, watching in amazed silence as the man cut away every inessential part, every gram of mass that slowed it, every detail that prevented the rocket from achieving its best performance. Slowly, yet with absolute determination, the shape of the spaceship smoothed: angles that were difficult and expensive to fabricate straightened; engine plumbing that would have cost a fortune suddenly, under his eye and hand, untangled back to simple elegance and more. What he had learned in the last year he also incorporated into the blueprints: every aspect of the vehicle grew simplified, adhering only to the imperative of function. When he finished, no mere spacecraft glowed upon the screen. He gazed at the fundamentally lightest, fastest one-and-a-half-stage hybrid rocket yet designed, the essence of space travel made real by the mind and will of Gerald Cooper.

Sherry realized suddenly that she had not moved from the stool in the entire time Cooper worked at the computer. She glanced around the room. Night stole light from the office. Sherry sat quietly in the darkness, watching her husband with a satisfied warmth. Nothing pleased her more than to see him absorbed in his work. No book she could read, no movie she could watch, no vista she could observe gave her the thrill and excitement of simply watching Gerry as he made Nature conform to his demands while scrupulously obeying Nature's own stern laws.

Scrupulous. The word pleased her, for it so identified Gerry in her mind. He was the most scrupulous of men, the most honest, the most meticulous in his allegiance to reality. She loved him utterly.

16 May

SSgt. Patrick Jacobs, USAF, stood near the corporal who held a finger over the red switch.

"Five," the commanding officer intoned over the loudspeakers. "Four."

Jacobs watched the corporal's finger rest lightly on the glowing crimson circle.

"Three... Two... One... Fire!"

The corporal pressed the button firmly. Two miles away there bloomed a mighty explosion. The white fireball rose upward, shooting out miniature glowing white meteors that left smoking streamers in their wake.

The sound reached the group, a thundering boom followed by the rush of wind from the blast. Jacobs turned his eyes from the rising cloud to gaze at the Russians. They smiled heartily, as did the Americans and the newspeople rushing about to photograph this historic occasion. Today marked the beginning of the end for nuclear weaponry. Everyone looked happy. Everyone except SSgt. Patrick Jacobs.

The explosion was not nuclear, it was chemical. The object destroyed was not a nuclear warhead — that would be dismantled elsewhere and the plutonium stored for future contingencies, such as a return to bomb-building if the treaty failed to achieve its goal. What had gone up in an instant of flame and smoke was the missile to which the warhead had been attached. To glory in blowing up a missile made about as much sense to Jacobs as cheering the demolition of a murder weapon while letting the murderer escape scot-free. A missile is only a tool, he thought, and Jacobs watched those who had been ready to use the tool for destruction cheer the destruction of the tool, as if it contained the evil.

Jacobs turned away from the scene and returned to his squad's jeep. In the driver's seat, Sgt. Deborah Gunn stared at the cloud slowly dissipating in the Utah sky.

"Damn shame," the short woman said, tapping her fingers wavelike along the steering wheel. Blond hair cropped far shorter than required by military standards framed an intense expression that conveyed seriousness without looking hard or worn. Sometimes she broke into a smile that reminded Jacobs of Peter Pan. This was not one of those times.

Jacobs slid into the passenger seat. "Yep." He nodded slowly, gazing at the cloud of vaporized solid fuel, then at the crowd of backslapping, gladhanding politicos. "You could take a Titan, yank out the warhead, and lob a little orbiting platform into space. Or use it to send hardware up for the space station."

"Even strap a couple together for more payload."

Jacobs shook his head in wonderment. "I came from a dirt poor family. Pappy always said 'Use it up, wear it out, make it do, or do without.' " He started the Jeep's engine. "How he hated it when the revenuers would come in and smash up his stills. Always said that showed how wasteful the government was. At least a regular crook would make off with the goods and use 'em or sell 'em. He considered revenuers to be nothing more than vandals."

Gunn nodded in agreement. "Yeah, well, what can anyone do about it? Can't fight city hall."

Jacobs hit the gas and spun dirt as they raced away from the officials' photo opportunity. "I just wish," he said over the engine noise, "that someone would try!"

▼ ▲ ▼

A world away in Kazakhstan, a colonel of the Russian Military Space Force watched in silence as the barbarian hordes advanced. That was how Vladimir Tuchapski thought of them, the Kazakhs who had never quite abandoned their nomadic impulses. He watched from the gravely berm as they descended upon Tyuratam, not on horseback, but in military vehicles emblazoned with the Kazakhstani flag.

The barbarians had won. Russia fought hard to retain control of the Tyuratam launch site. In the end, though, as with so many empires in the past, world public opinion forced the Russian bear to let the jewel in its crown slip through enfeebled paws. The task of militarizing the base had failed; his superiors finally surrendered to the United Nations General Assembly vote ordering the closure of the deceptively labeled "Baikonur Cosmodrome" and its cession to the Kazakhstani government.

"Cossacks," he muttered, watching the jubilant troops race through the cosmodrome. Col. Tuchapski ensured, though, that nothing of value remained for them. The spacecraft and launch vehicles were long gone, used in the retrieval of the last cosmonauts from the *Mir* space station. With Baikonur gone, the only functioning cosmodrome would be the military's own facility in Plesetsk, at a much higher latitude. Manned spaceflight would be difficult from there.

Rifle fire cracked across the barren and rocky desert flatland. Victory shots. The death of Russian manned spaceflight. Though he'd had his run-ins with the Space Agency, Tuchapski firmly supported *Mir*. The thought of it circling the Earth empty and cold foreshadowed Russia's own fate. As a child, the glowing vision of a Soviet Moon enchanted him with its vast possibilities. Over the decades, as he matured, the promises of Soviet space grew smaller and quieter, until only the tiny sardine can *Mir* comprised the Soviet cosmonauts' paradise.

Now even that no longer remained.

The trucks disgorged their cheering cargo. The troops trotted through the gutted remains of Tyuratam. After a while, it dawned on the horde that of the cherry they seized only the pit remained. Col. Tuchapski smiled. Seeing their disappointment spread imparted some small satisfaction. They could take back their land, but Russia had smuggled its heart and soul to the mother country.

The colonel, a lean man in his fifties who still possessed the Nordic qualities of the Viking Rus from whom his country derived its name, turned his back on the overrun cosmodrome and walked slowly toward the helicopter. His work there was done. Now he moved on to an even more onerous task: overseeing the destruction of the last five hundred SS-18 intercontinental ballistic missiles. The end of the ICBM's would signal the end of any possibility that Russia could regain the empire it once had.

He did not cringe from the word *empire*. He had long ago seen through the fiction of world communism to the core truth: his nation had been the *second*-mightiest empire in history. Now there remained only the undisputed master. *America*.

As he calmly witnessed the betrayed Kazakhs run riot through Tyuratam, smashing windows and setting fires, he saw a vision of the same fate for Moscow, Ekaterinaburg, St. Petersburg. There, though, the invading hordes consisted of blue jeans and stereos, vacuous sports and television comedies, hamburgers and soda drinks. The flames that consumed Russia would be those that had already reduced to ashes the American soul: hedonism; the sacrifice of long-term goals to short-term pleasures; the elevation of infantile athletic disputes into national concerns. These weapons destroyed far more thoroughly than any atomic bomb. As a child, he once believed that a dedicated Soviet could be killed but never stopped. Now he realized that a soul can be slaughtered just as easily as a body. Perhaps, he mused, more easily.

Colonel Tuchapski considered himself an atheist. He did not join the rush back to the Church during the temporary weakening of communist power. He did, however, believe in a particular kind of spirit: a national spirit in the heart of every Russian. That spirit started to die by suicide long before the empire ended.

A rifle bullet cracked through the air a dozen yards from where he stood on the berm. A few instants later, he heard the rifle's report. It was time to go, the colonel mused, when Kazakhs pulled close enough to identify as a target a man standing on a hill, let alone to aim in his general direction.

As the helicopter lifted off, the colonel took a last look at the abandoned spaceport and saw every dream and hope he possessed evaporate from him like the black smoke of the fires below. He sought a way to grasp that fleeting ghost of his spirit, some way to hold on to one tiny hope, one small chance.

He only saw the coming fire, the explosions and flames that would mark the destruction of the SS-18s. It would be his responsibility to oversee the demolition of Russia's only remaining instrumentality of defense against conquest and decline.

His head swam. Something stirred within his ravaged soul, something that refused to allow the dream to die.

The missiles!

He felt drunk, light-headed, giddy, terrified, all at once. An insane thought, a mad idea. Reckless ultra-left adventurism. Something only a desperate man would consider. Something only a man with no future would try.

Vlad realized that he had become such a man. The Russia he knew and loved no longer existed. It had fallen years ago, and crows now circled the corpse to pick it clean. One spark of vitality remained, though. One microbe of life still stirred within the dead shell. From it could grow *Novii Rossiya* — New Russia.

The tides of history flowed around him. He suddenly grinned like a crazed Viking warrior, no longer feeling any pain at the loss of Tyuratam. It lay behind in the old world. Vladimir Tuchapski suddenly saw brightly spread before him a vision of the new world. Above it all flew a red flag of golden stars in the shape of the constellation *Ursa Major*, the Great Bear in the sky.

He would need help. After they crossed the border and switched aircraft, the long flight home would give him time to build a list of men and equipment.

His soul returned to him in that moment of decision, he thought with a mad glee, and with it the spirit of Mother Russia itself.

21 May

Everyone has a true work, whether one pursues it or not. Chad Haley pursued his true work with a secretive zeal no one ever saw. He pursued his true work without uttering a word to others. That was simple enough — he had no friends. No friends, at least, that he ever met or spoke to. Haley possessed acquaintances. Shortly after five o'clock, he would rejoin them.

Right now, he stood on an island dotted with palm trees and brightly colored towers. From the shore of Long Beach, the island looked for all the world like a fancy resort or condo or aquatic amusement park. In fact, Chad Haley worked on Island White, an oil pumping station in the Long Beach Outer Harbor, one of four inside the harbor and the center island of the three named after the Apollo 204 space martyrs, the other two being Island Grissom and Island Chaffee.

Haley's job was that of a flow control supervisor, ensuring that the spaghetti tangle of pipes and valves flowed smoothly, delivering oil to the mainland like blood through arteries. When all went well, Haley took the time to stand on the earthworks that concealed the pipeworks from the eyes of touchy natives and tourists, who demanded that the gleaming steel and honest grime that fed their cars and lit their homes hide from view as if work were a sin and the façade of mere decoration a virtue.

Behind him, a waterfall cascaded down a gracefully sloped tower enshrouding a tall rig. The tower and rippling water looked lovely, but Haley saw no difference between its beauty and that of the intricate steel skeleton beneath. Others did. As a young man, this mystified him. Past his mid-twenties now, he had encountered enough people with a mania to make useful things look like anything-but to understand it as a symptom of arrested intellectual development, a child's desire to be surrounded by toys. How else to explain Nouveau Kitsch, the latest fad of making everything in the home look like something else? Clocks that looked like quilts, chairs that looked like open mouths, skillets that looked like tennis racquets.

He gazed at what he had just entered into his wristwatch computer. The device, he noted with comfort, looked exactly like what it was.

> Chaos theory proves central economic planning fundamentally impossible. As with weather forecasting, predictions tend to break down beyond a fairly short time horizon. Too many variables. Billions of human minds making trillions of choices every day. How else to explain the unanticipated nature of fads, stock swings, and irreversible monetary collapses?

Not bad, he thought. Could be a new broadside. He ran a hand through his short crop of red hair and squinted out toward the white bubble of the dome that once housed the largest airplane in the world and now served a the first all-weather, all-hours drive-in movie complex.

He could have passed for a local surfer with his lightly freckled tan face and slim, muscular arms; Chad Haley, though, dedicated his life to catching a newer wave.

A horn barked twice. Five o'clock Friday. For the next two days, his life was his own. He pulled the sleeve of his oil-stained orange coveralls over his watch and walked down the berm to a small spit of concrete that served as a harbor for the island. As the other workers filed up the gangplank of a weatherbeaten 24 foot motorboat, Haley jumped into a tiny inflatable raft and cast off, switching on the minuscule electric motor.

The warm May afternoon kept the harbor waters steady. Chad maneuvered the black and red raft around the spit and toward the mainland, steering north by northwest toward the section of bluff above the beach that marked the eastern end of a line of buildings stretching from the regally towering Villa Riviera at Alamitos and Ocean to the small and humble Queen Motel at the end of Cherry Avenue. That gap beyond Cherry marked Bixby Park, where he would make landfall in ten minutes.

The watery commute soothed him. Though it would take as much time for him to use this shortcut, he enjoyed the slap of the waves against the rubber hull, the firm ripple of the living sea a fraction of an inch away from the soles of his feet. He rode atop a gigantic living thing, gliding across the soft skin of Gaia (after spending the day, he admitted, sucking out her vital essence); yet this did not make him feel in any way small. He felt a part of the larger being. Every atom and molecule within him came from the Earth, would return to it, would become part of others who came after him.

He sang a loud pirate chantey as the boat caught a wave that propelled it to the shore. The afternoon beach crowd stared at the man with the matching hair and overalls as he dragged the boat ashore, deflated it, then carried the bundle of rubber and motor up the stairs and into the gaily painted mouth of the pedestrian tunnel running under Ocean Boulevard.

He emerged at the south end of Bixby Park and walked alongside it up Cherry. The Viking had returned from the sea.

▼ ▲ ▼

Haley earned about as much as any mid-level worker in the oil industry. It proved enough to suit his purposes. He spent the minimum necessary on living, which practice led him to live in a less-than-modest apartment building in East Long Beach. The eleven unit brown-stucco building — one of the survivors of the 1936 earthquake — stood unobtrusively on Seventh Street like so many other unimpressive old apartment buildings and homes from the 1920's. Here and there modern three-story apartments and condos replaced some of the homes and older apartments. The differences imparted a glaring disparity to the street, as did the constant rush of old Chevies, new Mercedes, and freight trucks of all sizes and ages along the four-lane street — technically a section of California Highway 22.

Haley toted his boat up the steps to the second floor. Excitement filled him as he approached the door. He'd spend the whole weekend with Sophia. Two days and three nights in which she would be all his. Sixty hours to use her in any way he pleased.

His key slid into the lock and turned.

"Honey, I'm home!"

At the sound of his voice uttering that particular phrase, Sophia came to life.

"Good afternoon, Chad," a sultry voice whispered. "I missed you. It's been hours."

Haley smiled, stashing his boat beside the well-worn sofa bed. He reached over to the back of the door, took the ash-grey fedora from the coat hook, and set it rakishly on his head.

He smiled. "Let's play."

At those words, Sophia booted her optical disc drives, loading programs to prepare herself for Haley's pleasure. She automatically connected up via the apartment's optical fiber cable to The Net, the world's largest VR computer information service.

Haley plucked a pipe from the rack beside Sophia, loaded it with his favored variety of smoking herb — Long Beach Rooftop — and sat in Sophia's chair. The chair was the only piece of furniture in the apartment of post-space age production. Designed for comfort, it was more cocoon than seat. Haley nestled into the soft leather padding that conformed to every angle of his shape. With a gentle buzz the chair rotated so that he lay nearly supine. Soft music — more accurately, rock and roll played back softly — surrounded him via the chair's speakers. He slipped on his Sky Pilot brand goggles, a pair of motion-sensing HyperGloves and entered the world of online virtual reality.

The goggles' twin liquid crystal color screens displayed three-dimensional images transmitted by light-wire from a super-computer in Omaha, Nebraska. Connected to that computer were Haley and thousands of other users whom The Net comprised. Each of their computers, when connected to The Net, added to its power. The more people online, the more rich and varied the experience. Some of the images he saw changed daily on the whim of either the programmers or of the members. Some he could change himself.

He floated before a towering citadel of multi-hued, jewel-like facets. In the base of the glittering fortress stood a huge door closed and bolted with massive timbers. He raised his right hand. The sensors built into the HyperGlove detected the motion and sent the information to Sophia, who interpreted the delivered information into an image on the goggles. In the VR world, Haley watched a metal-clad hand rise into view. The armor gleamed like polished stainless steel. He rotated the hand in a precise manner that told Sophia to create a mirror in which he could see his virtual body. This actually ran a systems check. Haley gazed at the face before him in the oval mirror framed by entwined snakes. If Sophia's software detected any error in the programming, it would appear as a wart on his face. Any known computer virus entering Sophia via The Net would appear as a squirming maggot.

The face, which he modeled after that of an idealized version of another redhead — young Thomas Jefferson — displayed no mark of imperfection. A small video camera attached to the chair scanned Haley's face and converted any expression he might make into a similar expression on Tom. He ran his hand through his hair and the mirror cracked apart to reveal once again the gate. He pointed in the direction of the tower and suddenly surged toward it at a dizzying velocity. He clenched his hand into a fist. An instant before he hit the door, Sophia transmitted his password to The Net and the barrier vanished in a shower of glitter.

That was a good one, he thought.

Chad lay almost completely at rest, yet glowed with an energy and excitement that would have amazed his coworkers at the pumping station.

He stood inside the Virtual Mall, the nexus of The Net. Wandering through on a programmed "walk," Haley gazed at the other people around him. As usual at this hour on a Friday, crowds clogged the promenade. Every avatar he saw represented a user online at that very moment. If they walked in the mall proper, they were either entering, leaving, or browsing the system. If they stood inside a particular store or office, they were shopping or participating in virtual discussion groups. In The Net, "face to face" meant avatar to avatar. Tom Jefferson might speak to Emily Brontë or John Wayne and neither could be sure to whom he or she spoke in real life. One's avatar in The Net projected whatever persona one desired.

He recognized some avatars. Some waved at him. He waved back. If he pointed at anyone (a body language not considered impolite on The Net), he could enter into direct dialog with that person, no matter that he might be ten thousand miles away. He avoided doing so and pointed instead to an office with a sign overhead that read "The War Room."

He flew toward it and entered, looking for familiar faces. Seeing none with whom he cared to converse, he lifted his left hand in a manner that caused a briefcase to appear. Opening it, he scanned the available messages in Sophia and plucked out Broadside Forty-Six. He slapped it on the bulletin board where it unfurled like a piece of parchment. The action loaded the text of his message into the war discussion group's reading file. Some of the members clustered around, indicating that the users were reading the message on their own VR goggles. Several dogs and cats scampered up to the message, too. They indicated users who set their software to download messages automatically while they were away from their computers.

He lit his pipe. Since he did so whenever he was on The Net, he had programmed in the movements so that he saw onscreen an intricately carved virtual meerschaum in his right hand being lit by a cartoon blowtorch in his left.

He took a long puff and said aloud to Sophia, "We'll see how they respond to this idea. Right, babe?"

"Yes, lover," she replied whenever she heard the triggering question. Haley had digitally pored over hundreds of female voices in films, television programs, and commercials to gather all the necessary phonemes to synthesize just the right sound for Sophia. The result was a voice that purred feminine approval with every utterance.

He blew a ring of smoke across the room, though he could not see it and had not programmed in a hand movement that would signal a virtual smoke ring to appear onscreen. Sophia's main components resided safely in the smoke-free environment of the bedroom closet. He smiled. This was what he lived for.

Words appeared on the parchment.

> Civilian-based sabotage is an important component of civilian-based defense, and one that has received short-shrift among pacifists. Is it violent to destroy the machinery of an oppressor — either foreign invader or domestic tyrant — as long as no living thing suffers?
>
> Slashing the tires of a troop carrier is something any schoolchild can do. It harms no one, yet immobilizes many more troops than the child could hope to by any other non-violent means.
>
> What we need is a definition of non-violence. Is it the utterly passive assembly of large groups of people as practiced by Gandhi (untenable here in an America that still retains a vestige of individualism, and unnecessary among an armed populace, as Gandhi respond-ed in the only way he could, noting

that "among the many misdeeds of the British rule in India, history will look upon the Act depriving a whole nation of Arms as the blackest"), or can it include acts of sabotage that simply wreck "property" of the State (property which, by the way, had to have been stolen or paid for with stolen money, since States do not create wealth, only plunder it)? Is the sudden rearrangement of non-living matter a violent act? Or does violence only involve harm to living things?

Civilian-based sabotage is far more accurate than any sort of bombardment that a State offers as "defense." The civilian-saboteur *knows* who is the oppressor, *knows* what equipment belongs to the invader, *knows* the difference between "liberator" and "new master."

The civilian-saboteur is the hero of any war or revolution.

Instead of re-entering the Mall, he took a shortcut to the Economics Room by pointing to a sign on the bulletin board. Once in the nearly deserted grey-upon-grey room, he reached for a virtual microphone to dictate a message, which Sophia's digivox translator converted to a text message for storage.

It is with the discovery of the Chaos theory that economic planning finally receives its fatal blow. The fundamental observation of Chaos is that small, individual changes in the initial state of a complex system can multiply until their effect becomes vast and impossible to predict. This is true of weather, where a small patch of snow suddenly sliding off a branch can alter the albedo of that small area, which changes the thermal output of the surrounding area, which modifies the airflow around the forest, which pushes the jet stream in a way no one can ultimately predict, because there are millions of snow patches and tree branches, billions of insect wings flapping and animals moving and breathing, quadrillions of air molecules bouncing randomly about.

Is it any wonder that no one can predict exactly what the weather will be like next Thursday?

And so it is with the economy. Billions of people, each making economic decisions every day. To buy or not to buy this or that item. To save or sell or invest or squander. How can any central authority predict the economy for more than a few moments, when one person suddenly, capriciously buying a diamond ring for a loved one can make the day profitable for a jeweler, who in turn decides she finally has enough to buy a car from a car dealer who takes the profit but needs just a little more to improve his building so he sells a block of stock, which triggers someone's programmed sell order on the stock exchange, which... Well, you get the idea.

Macroeconomics is a fraud. We greet Chaos as the great liberator of individual choice and the final vindicator of spontaneous order.

"There," Haley said. "Sophia — mark it as broadside fifty-five."

"Yes, lover," the purring voice replied. "Done, big boy," it said an instant later.

He wandered over to another room, this time a futuristic rocket cockpit that contained the Outer Space Round Table.

The joint was packed. When Haley entered, the hatch slammed shut and alarms wailed to indicate that the discussion group was full. The Net needed to allocate more memory space to this extremely popular area, but had not done so yet.

This time, one of the virtual members — a beefy, bearded rouge of a spacefarer over six feet tall and almost as many wide — strode right up to Haley. He knew the creator of this avatar, a mean-spirited little woman in her fifties who considered the group her own personal bully pulpit.

"Haley!" She pointed at him, putting them in private mode.

"Mathilda," Haley said with a Jeffersonian grin. "You look so... burly today."

"Can it, Chad. Topic Seventeen is supposed to be concerned with drug manufacture in zero-gravity or microgravity environments. By that we mean medicine drugs, not *drug* drugs. I've deleted everything you posted about how to grow crystalline cocaine hydrochloride. The Net will not permit any discussion of illegal activities—"

"*Talking* about theoretical chemistry," he said, "is not an illegal activity. Look it up in your Constitution." Haley smiled. *Got her adrenaline pumping, at least.*

"My room," she said through the stout brute's fat lips. "My rules."

Haley shrugged. That motion did not transfer to his avatar because Chad still could not afford the full-body VR sensor suit (with optional GenitoMatic to enhance virtual sex) that some members of The Net possessed. So he winked at her instead and switched back to public mode.

"Censorious minx," he muttered, knowing full well that a mutter could be heard by everyone in the room.

"Free-speech fetishist!" she retorted, storming into a sub-category.

Haley took an instant liking to the appellation.

That was when he felt it, the sudden and distinct impression of someone standing behind him, watching. He turned his head. Sensors in his goggles detected the movement and rotated the scene accordingly. People crowded behind and all around him. Some even looked in his direction.

That was not what he detected, though. He felt as if spied upon, a ridiculous feeling in a computer network whose inhabitants existed as mere images — digital masks — and everything lay out in the open. His Sky Pilot goggles and HyperGloves contained no circuit to channel emotional feedback. This was entirely an internal, psychological reaction.

To what, though?

No software allowed him to feel evil gazes boring into his back, no *frisson* interface sent a chill up his spine. Yet he felt watched, observed by someone lurking at the edges of The Net. He called up the mirror again. No warts. No bugs. Hence, no infectious software. The Lurker was something — or someone — else.

He clenched his right fist and stuck his thumb back toward his shoulder as if throwing someone out, his signal to disconnect from The Net, which Sophia did quickly. He removed his VR goggles without even watching his virtual self fly out of the castle as the gates swung shut and the huge bolts slammed home.

An hour had passed. He could usually spend four or five at a stretch. He took a deep breath to calm down, gazing at the pipe in his left hand. *Too much of this, maybe,* he thought.

"Sophia," he said.

"Yes, master?"

"Run the Grand Tour."

"I tremble with delight at the prospect, lover."

Haley snorted. He had programmed in all sorts of responses by which Sophia could indicate affirmative or negative, then put them on random choice. That one came up rarely, but he enjoyed the sarcasm now and then.

Slipping on the goggles, he watched as computer animation launched him from Earth into Space. He raced through starry darkness past the Moon, swinging low to pick up speed. Then he accelerated toward Mars, made a few orbits, explored the asteroid belt, flew a crazy, gravity-defying series of loops around Jupiter and a dozen of its moons, then sped toward Saturn. False-color rings of crimson, emerald, and peacock-blue encircled the jaundiced gas ball.

Music accompanied the tour. Music that soared triumphantly and murmured worshipfully. Regal horns, lush violins, imperious drums.

His eyes grew moist, blurring the view. He put the tour on hold long enough to wipe them dry, then ordered Sophia to resume.

Uranus and Neptune slid by, cold and icily colorful. Pluto, frigid and tiny, sailed past view. The music faded. The eyescreens dimmed to black.

The tour of the planets always boosted Haley's spirits. This time, though, he felt an odd longing. He lit the pipe again, took a deep drag, and held it.

Time for introspection, he mused. *A mental systems check.*

"Sophia. Run Brainstormer."

"Okay, sugar."

The goggles lit up with pulsating colors. A rhythmic sound throbbed from the speakers in the chair. The sensory stimulation relaxed his mind by directly altering his brain waves into an alpha pattern.

Calm, yet alert, Chad tried to pinpoint his disquiet. *Was it work?* No, all was well there. Pay was acceptable, stress was moderate, coworkers were easygoing. *Friends?* Not many offline. No need for them.

Lady friends? Lovers? Sophia gave good speaker, he knew, but without a penile interface, she provided no sexual outlet. Haley knew no women offline. This realization troubled him little. He knew plenty of women on The Net and had even exchanged some pretty hot e-mail with a few. All talk, no action, though.

The thought reverberated. He relit the pipe by feel and took another deep mouthful. *All talk, no action.* This meant something and not just in regard to women. Women he could do without. Ideas alone excited him. Recently, though, ideas on their own had lost their edge.

I'm twenty-six, he thought. *Does that have something to do with it? Is this some form of middle-age panic?*

All thought, no action.

All theory, no practice!

All his life, the importance of ideas fascinated Chad Haley. The obsession turned him into an electronic pamphleteer, an online proselytizer for all manner of causes he thought vital to the future of humanity: freedom of thought and speech (to the point of fetishism, apparently), the right to control one's own body (he took another toke and watched the flashing lights) and one's own property, and the freedom to travel (even though he had never left his native Southern California), most especially to travel into Space.

He had written and written and talked and talked online and sometimes offline about these things.

Have I ever put them into action?

He thought and wrote and spoke as he pleased. He certainly put whatever he wanted into or on his body. He ignored every law and social convention he disliked.

What am I doing about Space, though?

The lights and sounds enveloped him, locking him in a tiny room with his perfectly rational mind, cut off from the rest of the world. There he lay, thinking.

What can anyone do about Space? One man alone can't just build a rocket and take off. And the Shuttle is a joke...

A memory hit him. The Shuttle launch scheduled for next week. That triggered all this. Some astronaut going up, about his age. Tammy Reis. That explained it. He fast approached the age that other people were astronauts and he was not.

All talk, no action.

For years he had believed that one day he would live in Space and, as far as actually achieving that goal, all his talk about it had added up to a big fat zero.

Deeds, not words, shall speak me.

Chad Haley laid down his pipe. It was time for action.

▼ ▲ ▼

The search program would be a snap to run, though it would take time. Haley mused about time while coming down from the high. Meditation consumed time, as did action. Action, however, achieved goals whereas contemplation could only recognize and set them. He spent too much time visualizing his desires, and too little reaching for them.

The time he spent in his advocacy, though, gave him one powerful tool: contacts. Via The Net, he knew thousands of people. More important, in The Net he possessed access to information, the most important possession possible.

The Net allowed him to search billions of words of news stories and magazine articles, millions of financial reports and public documents. Just a few years before, he would have done this through an exhaustive list of key words. Now, though, in his goggles and gloves, he stood before a towering golden Buddha on whose serene face lay the burden of wisdom and the barest hint of an understanding smile.

Chad adjusted the boom mike attached to his headset.

"Oh, master of all knowledge," he said, "before whom I am a mere flyspeck on the light bulb of inspiration, who knoweth all that passeth before thee in thine—"

"Get stuffed, you runny-nosed, gob-faced, pestilent twit," the Buddha replied in a high-pitched British accent gone awry, "and get to the bleedin' point. I haven't got all day."

Chad grinned. "I need to find someone with a lot of money who in his personal or business life has shown an intense interest in space travel *or* who has the capability to engage in space travel *and* who is not currently involved in any way in government-sponsored space travel."

The Buddha immediately said, "Define 'space travel' more precisely."

"Manned venture beyond Earth with the goal of inhabiting outer space and other planets. In the short term, either living in Earth orbit or on the Moon."

"Define 'government-sponsored' more precisely."

"Receiving tax subsidies for space projects. Voluntarily subjecting oneself to government control, regulation, or oversight. Involvement with the National Aeronautics and Space Administration *or* the Department of Defense *or* Space Command to any degree whatsoever."

"Define 'capability to engage in space travel' more precisely."

"Someone wealthy enough in his personal holdings to finance construction of a spaceship costing hundreds of millions of dollars."

The Buddha closed his eyes. His voice was suddenly low and commanding. "This search will take time. Return to me in one hour, thirty-seven minutes and twenty seconds, not counting timeouts. That is all."

▼ ▲ ▼

Haley spent the time at his virtual keyboard, composing another broadside. The elaborately carved hourglass next to it marked the time. When the last grain of polished black sand fell through, trumpets sounded. He saved his work and rushed over to Buddha.

"I find but two names engraved upon this book," the all-knowing one intoned. "Laurence Poubelle is one. The other is Marcus Grant."

Haley frowned. *That's all?* "Tell me of them," he said, "while downloading."

The Buddha spoke while Sophia copied in-depth information to her optical disc.

"Laurence Poubelle is a billionaire who recently issued public queries on the whereabouts of former X-15 engineers, conducted a patent search on X-15 components, and filed a Freedom of Information Act request for all X-15 design data."

"And the other? How could you have possibly picked Grant?"

"Grant Enterprises has never received any money from the government, such as federal subsidies or guaranteed loans. Marcus Grant personally holds all company assets. He has no investment in any space-related field."

"And no one else made the list?"

"Nearly all companies I examined have taken advantage of some federal program or another. Grant is scrupulously clean in this regard."

"He ought to be," Haley muttered. "He makes enough in the black market. How can a nuclear plant owner not consume taxes, though?"

"Upon purchasing American Atomic, Poubelle sought to abolish the Price-Anderson liability limitation act. He was defeated. He has been involved in numerous clashes with the Nuclear Regulatory Commission in his efforts to remove his plants from the category of public utility. Most are still pending in the courts. He has lost the rest."

"Why does he keep trying?"

"I have no information to answer questions of motive."

Haley signed off of The Net and removed his gear. What a meager choice. Just two billionaires. One a flake in the nuclear power industry and the other a notorious underworld figure. Poubelle, at least, was making a stab at building a spaceship. Haley considered that aspect for a moment. Would it be better to hitch his wagon to that star? Or to try to convince someone who appeared to have no interest whatsoever?

Posing the question answered it.

"Sophia. Fax resume code-named Bootstrap to Grant Enterprises. Circumvent Personnel, address to chief executive officer."

"Sure, sugar. Searching fax number database."

▼ ▲ ▼

He received an answer to his query via an unusual route.

Three days had passed. He was willing to give them a week before calling, and spent the interim time on The Net, uploading broadsides, quarreling with the other denizens, and experiencing the virtual world through pot-tinged eyes and fingertips.

All talk, no action. The thought once again resonated in the large red cavern of his mind as he ran through various rooms in The Net, hammering up text and listening to other people's postings. Suddenly, a pigeon landed on his wrist. This signaled a personal message to him. He plucked the paper tube from around its leg and unrolled it. A woman appeared before him, a gorgeous redhead in a skin-tight crimson spymistress action outfit. That got his attention.

Haley turned down the music to listen as she spoke in a voice as low and sultry as Sophia's.

"I find all your postings here very interesting. You faxed me a job resume and did not mention that your hobby is electronic rabble-rousing. My true name is Joscelyn Donahue, Chief Executive Officer of Grant Enterprises, and I don't normally answer job inquiries this way. Come to my office at eight-thirty Wednesday morning. Bring a disc of your best ideas."

Haley unconsciously gulped back a feeling of unease. *Talk's over. Now here's some action.*

What sort of corporate VP — outside of the computer industry — perused the round tables of a computer network? Sure, he knew that business types had personal computers and a lot of them linked into The Net, but such things were considered perquisites, and perqs of value often languished unused, the point being simply to receive them. Just his luck that a busy and apparently driven executive such as Donahue signed on to The Net and actually *used* it. *Whatever happened,* he mused, *to high-tech pursuits being the exclusive domain of tinkerers and fanatics? Maybe she* is *a fanatic. That's why she works for a counter-economist such as Grant.*

▼ ▲ ▼

"Mr. Haley."

Joscelyn Donahue spoke his name with a firm, crisp voice. She remained seated in the black leather chair, looking down at something on her desk. Her auburn hair cascaded over her shoulders, almost brushing the desktop with its ends. She looked just as alluring as her spymistress disguise. Her hands moved constantly, now tapping at her in-desk terminal keyboard, now manipulating the ten-key, now lifting a black-and-gold stylus to jot a note on the screen.

An unfamiliar tremble forced its way through Haley's gut, like a minor tremor in the earth around a volcano. He faced the necessity of action, rather than just talk. And person-to-person, at that.

"Have a seat," she said, waving a hand toward the pair of Zimbabwe chairs in front of the black-lacquered desk.

He pulled out the one on the left and sat. Air whooshed out from the thick cushions. Though the chair supported him comfortably, it did nothing to ease his disquiet. All the calm he sought to muster vanished in the quiet room. His left leg began to bounce lightly at the heel.

She tapped out a few more lines, typing with the pads of her fingertips in such a way that her long, blood-red fingernails avoided tangling in the keys. This close to her, Haley inhaled the perfume draping her. The sweet floral fragrance reminded him of fresh air in a meadow. It was the only thing about her that put him at ease.

Donahue looked up at him with deep green eyes.

"You wrote all these?" She raised the terminal screen toward him. In sharp black letters on a glare-free white background glowed the title

Black Market Morality
by Chad Haley

It had to be that one, he thought, gazing at the words as if they were the edge of a guillotine racing toward his upturned throat. Decapitation, though, seemed almost preferable to a job interview run more like an inquisition. He nodded guiltily.

"It's an interesting discourse," she said, watching him for his reaction. "I read your others, too." She leaned back in her chair.

"It's really just a hob — "

She interrupted him with a raised hand. "Why don't you apply as much ingenuity to your day job as you do to this after-hours effort?"

Haley said nothing; he only stared. *Think. Say something.*

"We're interested in employees who can contribute something of value," she said, "not those who simply punch a clock." She reached over to swivel the screen back and down into the desk. Her nails clacked softly against the scarlet monitor case.

"I..."

She waited patiently. Haley knew that the selling moment had come.

"I reserve my talents for companies that merit them. That's why I sought out Grant Enterprises. I've reached the point where I can apply my abilities to any problem you have."

"Grant Enterprises has no problems," she said with a smile.

"Every diversified company has problems." Haley desperately searched his memory, wishing he possessed Sophia's random-access capability. "His — I mean its — problem with the Interstate Commerce Commission over unlicensed truckers..."

"How did you know about that?"

Haley took his turn smiling. "I'm on The Net. I asked Buddha to do some information-base searches. I didn't get far, which in itself indicates a company that exerts a great deal of effort to keep its affairs private."

"Thank you for coming by, Mr. Haley," she said crisply, turning her attention back to the realm of her desktop.

For a moment, Haley sat and stared. Then, slowly, he rose, turned, and walked out of the office.

Only after the doors closed did he permit himself the luxury of breathing.

▼ ▲ ▼

Donahue reread the electronic pamphlet, modifying it with the addition of underlining and bolding for emphasis. She typed in a few notes at the top of the file and closed it out. Smiling, she addressed the file to GRANT.1. In an instant, the file moved to where Marcus Grant would read it.

In that instant, she sealed Chad Haley's fate.

▼ ▲ ▼

"Very impressive," The rich baritone voice spoke from behind the plush leather chair. "But can he be used?"

Two hours had passed since Donahue sent Grant the document. Now she sat on the edge of her boss's expansive desk and said, "He's all right. A little wimpy, but his ideas aren't. That disc has some bell-ringers. Check them out."

The chair rotated. Grant's eyes met hers. "I don't want another Morgan Brennen."

"He's no maverick, boss. Classic risk-averter."

Joscelyn gazed at Marcus Aurelius Grant. "Risk-averter? Then why does he publish this stuff?" Grant flipped his fingers toward the computer screen inlaid to his desk surface. " 'Chaos Theory and Macroeconomics,' 'God and Man as Fractal Progressions,' 'The Technological Resolution of the Abortion Dilemma,' 'Space Programs Versus Space Travel,' 'The Soul as an Electro-Chemical Ordering' "

"He's totally caught up in theory, Marc. He didn't inherit a *goforit* gene the way you did."

Grant shook his head in wonderment. "A guy with ideas such as these ought to be rich. What's wrong with him?" He leaned back in the chair and hooked his thumbs in his vest pockets. "I'm no rocket scientist and I've done all right. Doesn't the kid have any initiative?"

"He pumped up the nerve to approach us."

"Well, snare him in."

"Right." She slid off his desk, lowering her long legs to the carpet. Walking to the carved-wood double doors, she added, "I'll have the smelling salts ready if he faints in your presence."

Grant smiled. In a creaky voice, he cackled, "Excellent, child, excellent."

▼ ▲ ▼

Haley stared at the approaching woman with a sense of dread. *Not twice in two days!* he thought.

Joscelyn Donahue neared him, dressed in a dark grey business jacket and skirt that did little to hide the stunning curves of her body. Her eyes, though, terrified him. They stared so deeply when they gazed at him, as if laying all his life bare before her.

"Mr. Haley," she said.

"Ms. Donahue! What a pleasure to meet you here." He continued to nail up a broadside. She glanced at it, pulled off a copy, and slid it in her jacket pocket.

"Take a walk with me," she said, glancing to her left and right. "I'd like a private talk."

The statement became a command and a door appeared beside them that read **PRIVATE**. He followed her into a forest through which golden sunlight filtered. Birds chirped and squirrels scampered.

"You've got the knack for VR, I must say."

She waved her hand dismissively. "I pay someone to program this stuff. I've no time for details. Here's the offer. We turn your ideas into usable products and services. You earn one percent of gross cash inflow or ten percent of net return on investment. Take your pick."

"What's your overhead?" he asked.

"None of your business unless you're working for us."

"One percent of gross, then."

She smiled. "Always the better choice. Here's another. You can work through The Net, but I'd prefer for security purposes to set up our own local area network at the office and have you physically present. Mr. Grant travels quite a bit and you'll undoubtedly be accompanying us."

Haley's head swam. It was all going too fast. "Why... are you putting me on such a fast track?"

Her gaze narrowed. "Don't you *want* to be on the fast track?"

"Sure. It's just that... how do you know I can do the job?"

She pulled the broadside from her pocket. "This is how I know. Any personal boldness you lack can be learned. I'm a damned good teacher. See you tomorrow at six AM. We like to get a jump on Wall Street." She turned toward the exit, then pivoted about, her hair sparkling in the shafts of sunlight like crimson flame. She held the broadside toward him.

"Incidentally," she added, "You're working for us now. Stop giving it away."

Haley stared at the departing Donahue and said nothing. His mind raced to grasp the implications of the last few moments. He'd unconsciously sought this sort of influence for years. To reach with his ideas someone who could actually change things. Someone who could act upon his ideas. However...

"Ms. Donahue?"

"Yes?"

"I'm pleased that you — and Mr. Grant — appreciate my articles. But the ideas haven't been tested in the real world. If I take this position and something we try fails, what then?"

She raised one sardonic eyebrow. "Aren't you the one," she said, "who claims it's possible to calculate the exact cost of trading risk for profit?"

CHAPTER 8

There is no such thing as a professional pioneer. The men, women, and children who settled the New World were not ex-navy test-sailors, even though the science of intercontinental sea travel was still in its infancy. These people poured their life savings into a venture that cost many of them their lives. None had ever settled a savage new continent before. And while none of them may have been fully aware of all the risks, most of them knew that their decisions were total, irrevocable, and permanent.

How does space migration differ in any fundamental way?

— **The Orbital Settlers' Guide**

19 May

It rained a hot, muggy rain that evening, when the three held a brainstorming session in Bernadette's dorm room. Bernadette sat on a reversed chair, her arms dangling over the chair back to prop her chin. She wore an embroidered crimson Chinese robe and smoked a joint from a foot-long black-and-gold cloisonne cigarette holder. Davy's cheroot imparted its own aroma to the room, rising in a Morse code of streaks and swirls as he puffed slowly. Sam paced hyperactively about when not rushing to his laptop to run a few more calculations.

"There are ways to make it cheap," Friedman said. "We can scrimp on payload, since we won't be taking much more than ourselves up."

Davy blew a smoke ring. "We pass the savings on to you!"

"We won't need much life support, if we're only going up for a day or two."

Bernadette chimed in with Davy. "We pass the savings on to you!"

Friedman began to chuckle. "And forget all that systems redundancy and safety equipment!"

"We pass the savings on to you!"

"Tracking devices? Out the airlock with 'em!"

Bernadette and Davy collapsed to the floor in laughter, not all of it induced by the verbal exchange. "We pass the savings on to you!"

Sam couldn't contain himself. "Landing gear? Cabin pressure? Who needs it!"

"We pass the savings on to you!"

"All right, all right," Davy said after a moment. Climbing out from under a dragon lady that seemed obsessed with tickling him mercilessly, he regained the bed to say, "Payload requirements for us *will* be different: computers are a million times more powerful per cubic foot than they were in the Apollonian era."

A snicker escaped from Bernadette. "The *what*?"

"The Apollonian era," Sam explained. "The golden age of space travel. The—"

"The golden age of space travel," Crockett said, "begins when we launch this puppy."

Sam nodded, tapping at his laptop. "We could have the equivalent of NASA mission control onboard the spacecraft itself. We wouldn't need any ground support."

"Aren't you forgetting a minor technicality, Earthwise?" Crockett stared up at the ceiling. "Aside from paying for all this, where are we going to build and launch it?"

Bernadette and Friedman exchanged puzzled glances.

Crockett took a long drag on his cheroot, then said through the cloud of smoke, "We need to operate in secret — NASA abhors competition. We'll require a large, enclosed area so the spaceship won't be seen from the air or on satellite photos. We need a construction site where nobody will notice loads of material coming in. And, most important, we need an area with those factors that is also uninhabited so that when we launch, we don't toast everyone beneath us."

Bernadette took an equally long drag on her long holder, held the smoke deep in her lungs, and thought about the problem. Then she grinned.

"I've got just the place!"

20 May

"You read about it all the time," she said, walking with Crockett and Friedman through the South Bronx in the grey light of dawn. She wore a black leather biker jacket with matching shorts, her pale white legs a sharp contrast to the second skin. The spike heels of her boots clacked on the brick sidewalk. Sam wore his army jacket and fatigue pants, Davy his rawhide.

"This area fits the bill perfectly — it's been a wasteland for years. Look!" She pointed at the buildings down the empty, clutter-strewn avenue. The windows of abandoned factories were boarded up from the third to top floors — the windows on the first two floors were *bricked* in to keep out transients and gangs.

"Some of these buildings — unbeknownst to their absentee owners, if they even have owners — house operations of dubious legal nature." She turned a corner and waved at one of the larger buildings — a sealed-up factory of red-brown brick and rusted iron. "That's a likely prospect."

Crockett gazed at the sprawling, rickety relic with disdain. From one of the pockets inside his fringed jacket, he pulled a slab of beef jerky and bit off a piece. "It's a dump. Think we can afford the rent?"

Bernadette smiled with glee. "What rent? That's the joy of being a squatter!"

"Yeah," Sam said. "Well, let's squat through that hole in the wall and check it out."

Others had entirely trashed the place. Garbage, ruined machinery, and collapsed girders littered the dim interior landscape like the aftermath of war. Water dripped ceaselessly somewhere. Rats scurried about on their own errands, oblivious to the invaders. It exuded all the warmth and welcome of a vampire's crypt.

"We won't have much problem bringing the roof down when we're ready to launch," Friedman said, looking up at the sagging skylights.

"The trick," Crockett added, "will be keeping it up till then." He kicked at a pile of rags. Cockroaches raced away toward safer hideouts. "Gee, gang, I'm *very* enthusiastic about such a glamorous project. Let's do it."

"Low Earth Orbit or Bust!" Bernadette shouted. Her words echoed through the cavernous factory for long seconds before it faded away.

Friedman's voice grew quieter. "Now how do we pay for it?"

Crockett's replied in a matter-of-fact tone. "The same way anything's paid for these days: with other people's money. Other people's effort. We couldn't afford this if we had to pay for anyone or anything. There's a fortune, though, in idle hands and idle goods all throughout New York City. We're going to con them into the future."

Thus began the South Bronx Space Project.

26 May

It did not look like an ordinary kegger to Penny Giannini. When her friend Bernadette had told her to grab ten other friends and venture into the South Bronx for a party, she was suspicious. When Bernie told her to take along her acetylene torch, it only served to confirm her suspicion of work in the offing. Not that she objected to work — her youth in Brooklyn had included a lot of that. She only objected to work inadequately disguised as fun.

One look at the building let her know that fun was not the reason for this excursion.

"A clean up party?" one of the guys shouted. "What a gyp!"

Another one poked Penny in the ribs with his elbow and whispered, "Who's the cowboy?"

"Davy Crockett."

"Yeah, right. Hope *I* don't flip out after four years here."

Penny tilted upright the oxy-acetylene tanks she had wheeled in. She smoothed out the wrinkles in her scarlet jumpsuit and straightened up. Though shorter than Bernadette, who was a bit of a sprite herself, every inch of Penny's frame consisted of hardbodied muscle. Her black hair, short and straight, clung to her scalp like a helmet. Her chestnut eyes surveyed the rotting factory behind the ludicrous figure of the man in rawhide and coonskin hat.

"You made it!" Bernadette, equally incongruous in a pink lab coat with black pockets and belt, jangled over to the new arrivals. Her hair today bore streaks of pink and orange, the silver hardware hanging from her earlobes depicted a planet orbited by a sleek, old-fashioned rocket with winglets. On closer inspection, her lab coat was smeared with dust and rust and other varieties of filth.

Giannini nodded and leaned an arm across the tank-cart handle. "What's the deal, Bernie?"

"Isn't it great? All we have to do is spruce it up and we've got a searing place to hang out."

"If you don't mind getting shot at on the way over. We just about—"

"Are you the welder?" Crockett's voice boomed across the floor. "There's a beam that needs to be cut in two so we can drag it out of the way."

Bernadette smiled that sort of smile reserved for introducing embarrassing friends. "Penny, Davy Crockett. Davy, Penny Giannini."

Not everyone got off to as bad a start. Most of the undergrads and postgrads viewed the opportunity to do something — anything — other than study as a godsend. Davy directed the cleanup crew; Sam, as chemist, ran the bar; Bernadette oversaw the influx of tools and equipment. They started Friday night by the light of borrowed lanterns connected to NASA surplus fuel cells. By Sunday morning they had dragged all the trash out to vacant lots or into other abandoned buildings in the surrounding area. The hung-over masses returned to their dorms, there to remain comatose through Monday.

Only the Unholy Trinity, as Penny branded Sam, Davy, and Bernadette, knew the truth about their efforts. Now that they had their construction site, that had to change.

The three conspirators sat within the cleared factory by the fading light of an ultra-bright luciferin/luciferase compound Sam had concocted. The last remaining party-ball of beer squatted between Davy's legs like a bad case of elephantiasis. Even so, he drank his own beer from a can, dispensing the draft to the other two.

"The spacecraft's frame gotta be light but strong," he muttered, peering blearily at the can. "Aircraft-grade aluminum. Nothing fancy. Not like those Titan rockets where they spend a fortune reaming out little triangles on the inside of the skin."

Friedman shook his head. "Composites. Lighter than metals. Better protection from meteoroids, too."

Bernadette, flat on her back staring at the skylights six stories up, voted for aluminum. "It's cheap, plentiful, and doesn't need a genius to assemble. I'm not going to spend my time *knitting* a spaceship!"

Sam yawned and nodded. "Fine, fine. We're only dealing with one atmosphere of negative pressure. Not 'zif we're building a sub or anything."

"I died." Bernadette rolled over to lay her head on Davy's lap.

"Can't slow down now," Crockett said, adding to the yawn quotient. "We have to come up with a money-pump scheme. There are some things that just can't be begged, borrowed, or restored to the private sector. We need some serious mazuma."

Bernadette's face gazed up at his in bleary despair. "We'll never pull it off. Where're we going to get *money*?"

Crockett tossed his empty beer can into a bag of recyclables. "New York is the richest city in the world. All you need is an angle." He stared at Friedman with glazed eyes. "You're a chemist. We're physicists. Where's the money being made?"

The three answered as one.

"*Programming!*"

27 May

That morning — still awake and tipsy — Crockett and Friedman descended on the Computer Science department. At a terminal, almost hypnotically staring at the screen of a Cray III supercomputer, sat an intense computer addict. Thickly spectacled of eye, obsidian black of skin, colorfully penned of pocket-protector, and heedlessly surrounded by a days-old accumulation of empty White Castle hamburger containers, soda cans, and Twinkie wrappers, "Hacker" Sewell barely acknowledged their existence.

"Where's the robot, Hacker?" Crockett waited for an answer. He asked once more. Receiving no answer from the possessed figure at the keyboard, Crockett and Friedman nodded to each other and — in unison — lifted Sewell from his seat, scattering burger wrappers to the floor. Hijacking him to a storage room, Crockett presented Hacker with a proposition.

"We need your robot prepped for work in wet environments and equipped with a simple pattern-recognition program that I'm sure you'll have no problem writing."

Hacker roused from his spell. "Unhand me," he said with authority. He had, in his junior year, forsaken the accent of his Harlem birth for something vaguely British. He found that it helped in dealing with upperclassmen.

Crockett unhanded him and Friedman assured him, "You just program it, set it free, and forget about it. We'll handle the rest."

Hacker frowned. "What's in it *por moi*?"

"In exchange," Friedman said, "I'll give you the security code to Dr. Welch's computer files so that little uranium hexafluoride incident can disappear from your permanent record."

Sewell nodded. "I can see the utility in that. Deal."

28 May

The next day on the streets of Manhattan, a man reached into his pocket to pay a cabbie. A quarter and a pair of nickels fell to the pavement and rolled down a storm drain. Inside the sewer, an electric whirring grew louder and louder. A robot — about the size of a suitcase — equipped with treads, twin stereoscopic cameras, and manipulative hands, rolled on balloon tires over the soggy bottom of the drain, pausing every few seconds to reach out and pick up this or that. It lifted a thick metal washer up to its eyes to scan, its onboard computer employing a fuzzy-logic pattern-recognition program to identify the piece of metal as such. It tossed the disc behind it and proceeded onward.

The lost coins clattered through the drain grating and into the sewer, splopping directly in front of the robot. Stopping to examine them, it recognized that they were coins, picked them up, and dropped them into a storage box attached to its back. The area under the grate turned out to be a rich vein, and the robot continued to discover other coins. It identified a wedding band as a ring, kept it, and then found another washer, which had a hole wide enough that the robot could not decide whether it was a washer or a ring. It spent a few nanoseconds deliberating the problem before its programming defaulted to saving the object for humans to decide. In it went with the other booty.

Back at the chem students' dorm, the Postal Service still dumped catalogues on the front steps. As soon as they landed, though, a troop of students carted them over to a blue trailer-sized trash container on the side of which hung a banner proclaiming the "Chem Dept. Paper Drive."

Friedman looked away from his fifth floor window to gaze at Crockett. The physics grad stoked the emptied front third of his cheroot with leafy material taken from a baggy.

"We won't get into Space on paper drives and spare change, Davy."

"We'll hit the big time," Crockett said with a cheerful grin. He sealed the baggy, twisted the end of the cheroot, and snapped his Zippo open to light it. After a deep drag, he said, "We're going to tap the people that have just enough brains to make money and not enough to use it properly."

"How?" Friedman gazed at his friend. "Sell them dope?"

"We're going to sell them something worse." Davy grinned even wider. "Something far worse."

At that moment, the sewer robot clattered in. Crockett lowered his cheroot to gaze at the crud-dripping machine. Friedman nearly gagged before he could pinch his nose in reaction to the scent carried back from the depths. It stopped, scanned the area to confirm its whereabouts, then dumped its wet, slimy load of corroded coins, tarnished jewelry, soggy currency, and rusty washers at their feet. It may have been what he smoked, but Crockett began to laugh, starting with an uncharacteristic chuckle that grew to a guffaw when Friedman donned bright blue chemical gloves to handle the mess and increased to an uncontrollable horselaugh as he watched his friend try to sort the valuables from the junk.

The robot sat impassively, observing the scene without comprehension, dripping green-black storm drain scum on the beige dormroom tiles.

"*Eeeyiuu!* What's that smell?" Bernadette walked in holding a stack of newspapers. She saw the robot and Sam beside it, sorting corroded coins and rusty washers. Her smiled collapsed into a pout. "Do we really want to get into Space that badly?"

Crockett jumped from his seat and seized the papers. "Is this it? Did they run it?"

"Page seventeen," she said, pulling a green and gold cowboy-style kerchief from her emerald green sequined knapsack, dousing the cloth with perfume, and covering her mouth and nose with it. The color went well with what she wore that day: a severely straight, waist-length red wig, a Lincoln-green mini-skirt, and rust-hued boots that rode up to her knees. She sniffed and said, "Could you open a window?"

Crockett opened the top copy of the paper and turned it toward Sam. Friedman looked at the full page ad in *The Village Voice* and groaned.

"I can't believe I'm doing this."

Bernadette, her own copy of the *Voice* opened to the same page, said, "Just think of it as the price you have to pay to leave Earth."

"Every shred of my dignity. Every ounce of my self worth."

"I think it's inspired," Crockett said, tearing the page out to pin it to his bulletin board. "And it beats sorting sewer finds."

"Does it?" Friedman asked. "Or am I jumping into a bigger sewer?"

The ad proclaimed, in ninety-six point type:

YOUNG URBAN PROFESSIONALS —
SWAMI RAMA BEN SAMESH
WILL TEACH YOU HOW TO HAVE
EVERYTHING YOU WANT
WITHOUT *GUILT* OR *STRESS!*

Below the blurb lay a huge photograph of Friedman in a turban and Fu Manchu moustache. His expression was that of a man forced at gunpoint to appear mystical.

"I tell you, Sam — I mean Rama — this'll drag them in off the streets. You could be the new spiritual guide for this generation."

"But what do I tell them?"

Davy shrugged. "The usual mystical crap mixed with self-help truisms dating back to Norman Vincent Peale and Napoleon Hill. Add a dash of crackerbarrel wisdom and you're set."

Bernadette pulled a thick file out of her knapsack and handed it to Davy.

"I got this from Ken Potter. His dad worked on the Apollo program back in the Sixties. It's all about aerospike engines."

Davy took the manual and added it to a pile under his bunk. "Great. I've received a lot of material about the Starblazer from those guys in California. It's amazing what people will send you just to brag about their work." He kicked at the pile. "We'd better start asking for stuff on microfiche, though. It's getting crowded in here."

Friedman removed his gloves and smiled, reaching into his army jacket. "I've done you one better." He produced a plastic jewel case. "An entire set of blueprints for a liquid-fueled single-stage-to-orbit spacecraft on CD-ROM."

Crockett's eyes widened. "CAD-CAM?"

Sam handed the CD to Davy and spread his fingers wide. "Hook a laptop to a computerized mill and away we go."

"How'd you get it?"

"Okay — Mike Dreesen knows this math major named Bill Einstein. And Bill's brother-in-law works for the drafting company that transferred the blueprints to disc. He made a copy of the archival disc for Bill, Bill gave it to Mike, and Mike gave it to me. Be warned, though — the design's a tad unconventional."

"Our going into Space is a tad unconventional," Bernadette muttered, her head buried in a *Voice* article.

"No," Sam insisted. "This is *really* out in left field. It's an orbital *helicopter*."

That made the others sit up and listen.

"A *helicopter*?"

Sam nodded, running a hand through his black curls of hair. "It's not as weird as you think. The numbers look impressive." He slid the rainbow-hued disc into his laptop and called up a schematic of the spacecraft, which looked for all the world like a beer can with a conical top. From the base of the cone, four rotor blades sprouted, each displaying at its tip a slender rocket nozzle.

"Are you sure," Davy asked, "that you didn't get plans for one of those portable hand-held fans?"

"Not unless the fan is sixty feet tall with a forty-foot wingspan."

The physicist in Crockett immediately took control as questions erupted from him at machine-gun pace. "How come the rotor blades don't break off or burn off during the ascent phase?"

"It doesn't rise as fast as a normal rocket," Friedman replied, in an equally staccato manner.

"What about cavitation? When the rotor tips go transonic?"

"That's a control, stability, and noise problem for true helicopters, not this. The rotor acts more like a vertical propeller in the lower atmosphere, then the whole thing goes supersonic as it transitions to pure rocket propulsion, but only in the upper atmosphere and doesn't stay that way for long. The reduction in maximum dynamic pressure more than compensates for the increased drag from the rotor. Even though it's inefficient compared to helicopters or propellers, that's not what we're comparing it to; the lift is superior to conventional rockets, meaning more payload or smaller vehicle."

"What about the tip rockets? How do you feed the fuel?"

Sam smiled. "That's the neatest feature. They're high pressure rocket nozzles fed by centrifugal pumping. The rockets burn, the rotor spins, and the suction draws up the fuel resulting in turbopump efficiency coupled with pressure-fed simplicity!"

Bernadette *harrumphed* and put down the newspaper. "I'd like to see someone design a rotating seal for cryogenic fuel."

Friedman called up a wire-frame diagram of the seal. "It's all here. The rotational velocity at the tips may be high, but at the hub it's just a few dozen feet per second. The pressure at the hub runs between five and fifteen p.s.i., and lots of rotating machinery have seals that exceed the requirements. According to the designer, there are some good ones as stock items in aviation catalogues."

"And the rotor blades burning off on reentry?" Bernadette's voice dripped with sarcasm.

"High altitude deceleration. You come in horizontally, or nearly so. The rotor blades provide drag to decelerate you while providing lift so that the re-entry is slow and smooth. It sounds weird, but the numbers seem to support it. The tip rockets can provide further descent rate reduction. You can hover this thing for a landing practically anywhere that's flat!"

"Wow." Davy nodded in admiration. "I'd like to meet this guy someday."

"Copy this design," Sam said, removing the CD from the laptop, "and you *will* meet him... in court."

Crockett laughed and pocketed the disc. "I think if we got one of his babies off the ground he'd be our biggest supporter."

"Rehearse that line. The jury will want to hear it."

Crockett's grin grew wider, his eyes sparkling with glee. "Sam! You still haven't gotten it through your head, have you? We're leaving this planet. Not only does that put us out of reach of the law, that makes us heroes. And heroes don't sweat the small stuff."

"Gee, remind me to rob a bank and kill a few people before we blast off." Sam gazed at Davy with a sudden intensity. "We can't leave Earth with dirty hands. Heroes don't do that."

Bernadette leaned forward on the bed, the hair of her long red wig spread out over the covers. "What do you suggest we do?"

"Build it, I guess," Friedman said. "And be ready to offer some sort of *post facto* restitution to the designer in case he objects."

"Good. Agreed." Davy glanced at the wall clock. "Hey, Sam. Don't you have a dead spirit to channel or something?"

29 May

At class the next day, Professor Gibbon noted — more by the silence than by any direct indication — that several students were missing and, now that he recalled, had not been there for at least a week or two. That Crockett hillbilly and his clique. And a few others. He pondered why he should have noticed their absence, especially with Laurence Poubelle, the Interplanetary Treaty, and other matters on his mind. Then it came to him.

Prompted by one of his young friends in the class, he once gave an impromptu discourse on NOSS and its achievements over the years, including a complete pedigree on its evolution from the Society for the Advancement of Rocketry, through its absorption of a score of other space interest groups, to its current status as the largest and most effective pro-space lobby in the country. He asked for a show of hands to indicate who were members or intended to join.

Crockett and the others did not raise theirs.

Their response — their lack of one, rather — troubled him. NOSS had something to offer anyone interested in Space. He even developed a Space Freedom Special Interest Group devoted to continual debates on the role individual liberty played in contributing to the common good. Crockett was a young idealist. Why did NOSS hold no interest for him? More important, Gibbon thought, why was he unable to persuade Crockett with his logic?

They started skipping class, he realized, shortly after Crockett's outburst regarding the Treaty. About the same time those infantile student wars stopped.

For a moment, Gibbon lost track of what he had been saying to the class and looked again at the empty seats. He feared putting his finger on something he dared not consider.

CHAPTER 9

Work is of two kinds: first, altering the position of matter at or near the Earth's surface relative to other matter; second, telling other people to do so.

— **Bertrand Russell**

7 July

Larry Poubelle faced Chemar D'Asaro across a conference room table and smiled. Between them sat less-than-appreciative members of the board of directors of American Atomic. He scanned their visages carefully, though equally careful not to reveal that he was doing so. It would be a hard sell, harder than to the American people at large. He stood.

"Ladies and gentlemen," he began in an upbeat tone. "American Atomic has always cultivated the virtue of forward-thinking community service. Not only are we the single largest provider of nuclear-generated electricity to the Pacific Northwest, we are also involved in scores of charities and community programs that benefit not only the needy, but also our own corporate image."

Smile benevolently, you bastards. Probably never donate a cent of your own money.

"The opportunity is at hand to open a new era for humanity, and American Atomic must be at the forefront — in a leadership position — to marshal the talents, resources, and dreams of a new generation toward the greatest adventure of all: the economic exploitation of Space."

He paused, staring at the group with a forceful, positive expression, one hand on a thick report, the other fisted on his hip.

One of the younger board members made a sour face. "Space? *Outer* space?"

"Yes! The final frontier! That distant realm that's held our fascination for millennia, that we who are alive today are at last able to reach, to claim, to sett—"

"Space is boring," the man said. "Bunch of guys dressed up like Frosty the Snowman pushing dead satellites around, playing stupid games with water blobs, women dressed like gas station attendants. What's your point? Flying an experiment on the Shuttle's no claim to fame. It's strictly a dead loss. Might as well send the money up and let them throw it overboard. That, at least, would get some press."

"Forget the Shuttle," Poubelle said. "Space doesn't belong to NASA. It belongs to anyone with the courage and wherewithal to get up there. Here's our angle: American Atomic will sponsor the first *private* astronauts in the first *private* manned spacecraft. And as for gas station attendants..." He extended his robotic hand toward Chemar.

She stood to remove her grey business jacket. Underneath, she wore a tight-fitting silver-lame jumpsuit with a plunging neckline that reached down beyond her solar plexus to reveal more than corporate discretion should have permitted. The fabric clung so tightly to her flesh that if the temperature were to drop, everyone in the room would know it just by looking at her.

One of the older men cleared his throat. "With all due respect, Ms. D'Asaro, you look like something out of an old science-fiction movie."

"Exactly, Mr. Trevor." She poured on the sultry tone. "Sex appeal is what Space is all about. Climbing into a long, round rocket ship to thrust into the unknown blackness of eternal night; floating free of all earthly bonds where every possible position is neither up nor down; the law of gravity broken and all other laws put into question..."

"NASA," Poubelle waved a hand at D'Asaro, who smiled sardonically and resumed her seat. "NASA has sucked all the sex appeal out of space travel, exactly as you pointed out, Frank. They made the astronauts virtually faceless, devoid of personality. They developed an argot wiped clean of excitement. The only word they seem to permit is 'fantastic,' which we hear with such relentless repetition that the word itself becomes meaningless because it denotes anything and thereby nothing.

"Gentlemen, ladies, I propose that American Atomic seize the high ground in more ways than one. Without using a cent of AmAtom funds, we could construct"— he punched a button that dimmed the lights and powered up the projection video to display computer animation of a souped-up X-15 rocketing into orbit from the back of a 747 — "an aircraft-launched rocketplane that would safely put two people into orbit and return them to Earth. All funding would come from private donations to a non-profit organization. Our only input would be to include mention of the effort in our image advertising. Other publicity would be donated or paid for by the NPO."

"What if it fails?" asked one woman who had endured too many face lifts.

"It won't fail. The technology was proven in nearly two hundred successful flights over thirty years ago. And if it does, you can blame it all on me because I'll be the dead heroic pilot."

"You?" a man in an ill-fitting toupee muttered. "How could you with your..." He gestured toward Poubelle's prosthesis.

"This?" Poubelle reached into his pocket with it, drew out a quarter, flipped it, and smacked the coin down on the back of his living hand. "Heads or tails?"

"What?"

"It's heads, the cyborg with the inhumanly sensitive palm said." He withdrew the robot hand to show the coin around the room. "I paid good money for this arm and I could put enough computer power into it to fly the ship without me. Besides"— he grinned with a wicked, feral gleam in his teeth —"Think of the publicity we'd generate using a wounded Vietnam vet!"

There followed an uncomfortable pause from which Trevor was the first to recover. "See here, Larry, you can't expect that consumers will just throw money at such a project. Even our own charitable contributions have been cut back. Money's tight—"

"Tight? Americans spend six billion dollars on makeup every single year. They spend twenty billion on soft drinks, fifteen billion on beer, ten billion on cigarettes, twenty billion on sports and another twenty billion to go to the movies. Get smokers to send us the cost of one carton of Old Nic, or drinkers one six pack, or girls a lipstick, or anyone movie ticket and we could pay for this ten times over. In fact, we'll offer them value for their contributions, ranging from cloisonne pins with the mission logo, through embroidered baseball caps and autographed photos, up to VIP passes to the launch site and breakfast with the pilots. We're setting up an eight hundred number to take MasterCard and Visa and a nine hundred number for straight cash donations where callers hear daily mission updates. And don't forget collateral advertising support for everything from the engine we use to the underwear I'll have on."

A younger board member — a pleasant-looking woman in her forties — spoke up. "You want to be the man who sold the Moon, is that it?"

Poubelle smiled and pulled a cigar from his jacket. "Right now I'd be satisfied merchandising Low Earth Orbit." A flame danced at the end of his fingertip. He took a few puffs and said in a conspiratorial voice, "If this cigar could get out of Havana, my friends, simply because it has value to people, then we can get into orbit. All we have to do is demonstrate a value. We've seen how promises of long-term manufacturing potential and thirty-year plans for colonization bring about a big yawn from short-term thinkers. Offer them a quick thrill, though, the equivalent of a car race with loud noise and the chance to witness flaming death, and the dollars will roll in.

"I'm doing this, members of the Board. On my own if I have to. Will American Atomic be a sponsor? That's what I want to know." The one-armed man waited for a reply.

Whispers and mutters followed, then Trevor asked, "This project, Larry, that everyone is so worked up about. Does it have a name?"

Oops, Poubelle thought. *Better think of something.* He waved his cigar about as he spoke. "Well, the name of the rocket will be *Nomad*. As of this moment, though, the project—"

—"is called Daedalus," Chemar interjected. "The Daedalus Project. Named for the Greek inventor who stuck feathers on his arms with wax and flew out of the Labyrinth he had constructed for the Minotaur."

"Didn't he fly too close to the Sun?" one of the asked.

"That was his son, Icarus." She turned her eyes toward Poubelle, pinning him with their golden gaze. "He got cocky. Flew too high. The Sun melted his wings off and he died in the Aegean Sea." She turned her attention back to the Board and smiled. "The Daedalus Project will just graze the edge of Space. It will make history — *safely*."

Her words and tone mollified the board members. They talked among themselves for a few moments, then Trevor spoke for the group to say, "Larry, Ms. D'Asaro, we'd all like a while to discuss this in greater depth. Thank you for an intriguing proposal."

The pair smiled and made a quiet exit. Outside in the dark, wood-paneled, green-and-burgundy carpeted hallway, Poubelle let go a pent-up breath.

"Hooya. Thanks for the quick save in there. I hadn't thought to give the whole deal a name. Fast thinking."

"Actually," D'Asaro said, "that name was what first came to me when you mentioned the idea. I want you to take care. You're too valuable to scatter across the stratosphere."

"Well, I guess I'll have to find a good co-pilot. Maybe I can get an Air Force jet pilot. Or a former MiG pilot. It would have to be someone competent, trustworthy... a fast thinker..."

"Laurence Norman Poubelle, you know damned well who it ought to be and I'm going to strangle you for keeping me hanging these last three months!"

He grinned. "Someone with an outrageous French accent."

She swung a mock blow that he deflected with his metal arm.

"Mr. Poubelle?" One of the younger board members stuck his head out the conference room door. He looked as if he too expected to be slugged. "The Board has come to a decision."

Once inside, the president of American Atomic realized immediately that the board had come to a negative conclusion. He and D'Asaro declined the offer to be seated.

"Mr. Poubelle, Ms. D'Asaro," Trevor said, his voice wavering just a bit. "The Board has concluded that the interests of American Atomic and its stockholders would not be served by—"

"All right." Poubelle kept a smile on his face as he stubbed out his cigar in the only ashtray on the table. He had smoked less than a quarter of the expensive import. "I'll use my own money and hog all the glory. Don't say I didn't give you the chance."

"It's not that we don't—"

"Save it."

▼ ▲ ▼

Fax machines across the nation and around the world hummed that night, spitting out thousands of copies of the first press release from The Daedalus Project. One lay on the desk of Joseph Lester the following morning.

He took a few moments to read down through other faxes, memos, and wire service stories before reaching the single page of information.

"Whoa!" he cried, leaning forward in his seat. He re-read the entire page several times.

FOR IMMEDIATE RELEASE

Billionaire businessman Laurence Poubelle today announced his intention to create aviation history by building and flying the first privately funded manned spacecraft. The Daedalus Project — named for the mythical inventor of human flight — would be supported entirely by contributions and the sale of collectible merchandise, similar to the 1986 Voyager around-the-world flight.

Poubelle — president of American Atomic, which is not involved in the project — announced that volunteers were invited to work on the design and construction of the spacecraft, dubbed *Nomad.* Based upon an up-scaled version of the historic X-15 rocketplane, the black, arrow-shaped *Nomad* will be carried aloft by a jet aircraft and released. From there, powerful rockets will thrust the spacecraft into orbit, something never achieved by the original X-15 in 199 flights.

The Daedalus Project plans to keep the spacecraft in orbit around the Earth for 24 hours, then bring it safely to a landing in the Mojave Desert in California.

Poubelle, a Vietnam veteran and accomplished aviator, will pilot the spacecraft. Asked why he devised such a project, Mr. Poubelle said, "The American people — and people all around the world — need something hopeful to hold on to. They need a frontier to look toward and NASA is letting them down. Travel to other planets seems at once both boring and unattainable to them. I intend to put some excitement back into what should be the greatest adventure of all. I designed the Daedalus Project so that anyone and everyone who wants to participate can have a hand in lifting us to the stars."

The time schedule for design, construction, and launch is a short two years. Project manager Chemar D'Asaro stated that advanced super-computer design and testing, coupled with VR flight simulation training, makes the accelerated timetable realistic. "Besides," she pointed out, "we're not NASA. We don't have career bureaucrats building little baronies at Daedalus. We're seeking sponsors and volunteers who are involved because they want to put a spaceplane in orbit, not because they want to draw a fat paycheck."

Both Poubelle and D'Asaro have taken leaves of absence from American Atomic in order to work on the Daedalus Project.

-30-

For a complete press kit, please call or fax the numbers at the top of this release. The third number listed is for the 24-hour, touchtone-controlled *Nomad* Update Hotline.

nomad@daedalus.org

There's a gauntlet thrown down at NASA's feet, Lester thought while dialing the vox number.

"Hello," a voice at the other end said. *"You have reached the offices of The Daedalus Project. If you are calling to volunteer your services, press One. If you are calling to make a non-deductible donation, press Two. If you would like a copy of our souvenir catalogue when it becomes available, press Three. If you are a media representative, press Four. If you have any—"*

Lester pressed 4 and waited. When a woman answered the line, he immediately requested an interview with Poubelle.

"Mr. Poubelle will grant interviews," she said, "but only in person at Mojave."

"I'll be there," he said, and gave her the address to which to Federal Express his press packet.

He rose from his desk to seek out Hillary Kaye. A flash of feathery blond curls marked her location. Lumbering over to her, he tapped a big hand upon her shoulder.

"Big news out of the Wild West, Kaye. Maverick rocket jockey plans to beat NASA at its own game. I'm going. I'll need a lensman. Want to join me?"

A throat cleared behind him. He turned to see his editor, Brent Marley, glowering from a foot below.

"Hey, Brent!" Lester said. "I'm following the big news out in Mojave. I figure I can do an interview and get a lead article in three days. Save me column one on the front page."

"Forget it." Marley's voice projected all the friendliness of a spitwad. "I ain't springin' for no joyride to the coast."

"Brent, this is big. Bigger than it looks. I've been following the underground space movement. Something's happening, and when it breaks, it's going to be the last scoop of the millennium!"

"Underground space?" Kaye said. "Doesn't that have something to do with the Hollow Earth theory?"

Lester waved his hand dismissively. "I don't know what else to call it. Look, Brent, I've got a stack full of clippings and a megabyte of newswire downloads about all these guys trying to compete with the Shuttle. NASA's been stomping them for thirty years. The boot's growing weaker, though, or maybe the hobnails are wearing thin, because now we've got someone who's not just a dreamer with a nifty artist's painting. Poubelle's one of the ten richest men in America. He could write a personal check tomorrow and buy a complete Shuttle. But he's taking this weird route of collecting donations as if he's running a charity telethon for space travel. I've got to cover this."

"We can get the story from the wires. It's not a Fort Collins story."

"Oh, no?" Lester peered down at his boss. "Fort Collins has the largest chapter of the National Organisation of Space Supporters in Colorado. Bigger than Denver, Boulder, and Colorado Springs combined! I tell you, Brent, something's in the air, something's gonna pop soon. You know about IT, right?"

Kaye piped up. "I know IT conquered the world!"

"IT just might. The Interplanetary Treaty's up before the UN. It's another stab at exporting socialist ideals. It's worded as if it supports access to Space for everyone, but the text establishes strict UN control of every spacecraft and satellite. The crazy thing is, it was written by the head of NOSS—"

"Look," Marley said with an exasperated sigh. "You're not going.

I can't afford to pay for it and I can't afford to give anyone time off. We're understaffed as it is."

To Lester's surprise, fury overcame good sense. A catalogue of what he saw as petty injustices and career delays suddenly scrolled through his thoughts, totaling up to a big, fat zero. He poked at Marley's chest with two fingers, emphasizing every sentence.

"God damn it, Marley, I've had it with covering gang murders and cop beatings. You can read that in any town, big or small. The paper's become nothing but a police blotter! Here's someone crazy enough to offer this country hope and rich enough to follow through and you don't think it's worth covering! Well, rot in your own sludgepot, because I'm covering this one. I quit!"

Hillary gawked for just an instant, then said, "Was that Joe the misanthrope speaking? Or are you channeling Pollyanna?"

"And I'll take my own damn' pictures!" He strode over to his desk, turning to wedge himself between tight obstacles as he went. He looked for all the world like an infuriated Winnie the Pooh marching out of the Three Acre Wood, but instead of a honey pot, he carried with him his laptop computer and a tray of floppie disks.

Marley did nothing to stop him. In fact, he allowed the faint suggestion of a smile cross his purplish lips. Kaye simply stared in surprise.

When Lester pushed past the pair to make his escape, she said, "Joe. You're not really leaving, are you?"

He shouldered by her. "Hey — I'm freelance now. I'm going to follow this story to the Moon if I have to. I'm going to be the Horace Greely of the third millennium. Go Up, young woman, and tame the new wilderness."

The double doors swung wide to pass his bulk, then shut with a *thupp*ing sound, as if blowing a watermelon seed out of a mass of chewed pulp onto unplowed ground. After years of dormancy, Joseph Lester sought a more fertile field.

▼ ▲ ▼

Home in his apartment, he surveyed his belongings. Books, mostly, and back issues of the *Sentinel* containing his articles. He had all of them on disc, so those and the books could be put into storage. The furniture was worthless, bought for low cost and comfort more than heirloom value. No music — that came free from the alarm clock radio. That left his computer equipment: optical storage disk with data cartridges, laser printer, and the portable setup he had dubbed Lex Looter: his laptop, a handheld scanner, and an optical character reader program that allowed him to walk into any library and copy the text of any book or magazine into the laptop's capacious memory.

He gazed at the wall of bookshelves holding hundreds of books, then at the foot-high stack of optical discs holding thousands. He knew which he would take along with him.

His only camera was a low-end 24-bit Kodak Digital Stereocam, more suited for 3-D snapshots than serious photography, but it would have to do in lieu of Hillary Kaye's 64-bit Hasselblad with its ten interchangeable lens pairs and auto-parallax. He put it in the center of the living room along with the computer equipment.

That left his guns, a matched pair of sequentially serial-numbered Wildey Survivors, chambered for the .45 Winchester Magnum; the stainless steel, gas-operated autopistols were the foremost component of his only recreation: steel profile shooting. Nearly every weekend, he and a few friends trekked out to a target range to blast away at thick steel plating cut in the shapes of various animals and placed at precise distances. He had to use low-power hand-loaded cartridges; his first attempts to use the pistols with factory ammo resulted in his shelling out a week's pay to replace the profiles through which he had unwittingly punched finger-sized holes. With the proper loads, he was a fairly good shot.

No more of that. Southern California had become a no-man's land where most citizens carried guns for self-defense despite multifarious laws, but no one had any opportunity to practice with them since the ban on shooting ranges had been enacted. Concealed weapons were the megalopolis's everyday reality that dared not speak its name.

He could not legally ship them to California; no gun store owner could receive high-powered pistols anymore. He'd have to stash them in the car. That made him smile. He would become a renegade the instant he crossed the state line.

He opened up the walnut pistol case to look at the Wildeys. The deep blue velvet inside snugly held the pistols and two each of the six interchangeable barrels, plus magazines and a box of ammunition. It weighed in at over thirty pounds. He added a custom-made double shoulder holster to the pile of goods on the living room floor.

He lived lightly — shooting was his one indulgence — so he could get by on his savings for a few months, especially if he stayed in a cheap motel in the desert. Decisions made, he used his laptop to reserve a room at the Mojave Motel Sixty-Six, e-mail his shooting buddies, send a formal resignation to Marley, print a note to his landlord announcing his move, close out his utilities and phone, pay a few bills, check his bank account for available cash, and receive a paperless fax of road conditions from the National Auto Club. Then he stripped, showered, brushed, climbed into bed, and slept fourteen hours.

By noon the next day, he had crossed the Continental Divide in his geriatric Aerostar, which was more rust than finish, following the Sun on his way to what he hoped would be a journalistic Mecca.

10 July

Two days later, exhausted, Lester arrived in the desert town of Mojave in the middle of a typical July day. The cloudless night sky permitted the previous day's heat to radiate away from the desert, the temperature stood at a comfortable seventy degrees just before sunrise. He turned off the two lanes of Highway 14 that cut through the business district like a main street and followed the signs toward the airport. A pair of zigs and zags brought him to the Mojave Airport. Pulling into the parking lot composed of crumbling asphalt and brown desert earth, he stepped out to watch the advent of a desert dawn.

The stars still shone as the sky lightened, turning from black to an eerie purple to a frigid deep blue. Dust in the air, still suspended from the previous day's winds, tinged the blue with hints of an almost tropical green. The air was still as Lester walked quietly out toward a tiedown area. The runway and taxi lights shimmered like stars on the ground. Beyond them rose mountains turning ruddy as the eastern sky reddened. The air smelled fresh, with just a hint of desert dust and plant aromas.

Suddenly that air shook with the sound of an explosion. Windows in hangar offices rattled. Lester turned about to scan the sky. Behind and to his left he saw an F-16 climbing straight up, cracking the sound barrier in a vertical ascent as it caught the first rays of sunlight.

Edwards Air Force Base was only a few miles southeast, Lester realized; morning flights must have begun.

The glow of dawn reached the airport and Lester saw a blood-red phalanx of jet airplanes lined up along the northern side of the runways. Hundreds of commercial airliners sat wing-to-wing, preserved in the dry desert air. Lester had never seen anything like it before. The colors of major and minor airlines graced the fuselages and tails of the mothball fleet. Names of companies that had not flown for years peppered the landscape. Engines cocooned to keep out dust, windshields covered with reflective Mylar to block the relentless desert sun, the aircraft stood silent and still; most of them, perhaps, forever.

Sunlight teased the mountain tops, creating bright red deltas that grew and spread downward. The east glowed bloody crimson with rays of pink. Then it broke over the horizon, a ruddy orange crest of light that dazzled and warmed the instant it appeared. All around, desert insects roused from silence to click and buzz in the warming rays of the Sun. Lizards began to dart from cover to cover, from scrub brush to rock. Lester turned to gaze at his long shadow stretching across the tarmac. An electric-blue vintage Corvette Stingray pulled into the parking lot a few dozen yards away from his van and a dark-haired man jumped out, opened a hangar door, and jumped back into the car to guide it into the hangar.

What Lester saw in the hangar compelled him to stroll over just as the man sought to slide the doors shut.

"'Morning!" he called out to the man, who looked a few years older than he.

The man acknowledged the greeting with a nod. He wore a grey business suit that seemed so out of place in the desert that Lester could have used that alone as a starting point to conversation. Instead, he asked, "Is that a rocket you've got in there?"

The man nodded and said, "Spaceship, actually. One-fifth scale mockup of a single-stage-to-orbit hydrogen-lox aerospike reusable spacecraft. This one's configured to carry two crew members and a two thousand pound payload."

Lester knew that the man must have had to repeat that description hundreds of times. He pointed at the twelve-foot-high gumdrop shape and said, "This isn't *Nomad*, is it?"

The man in the suit shook his head with a bitter smile. "No. You want the Larry-come-lately in Hangar One-Fifty. My name's Cooper. I'm not a billionaire."

"You dress like one."

"Thanks, but I've met Poubelle. He dresses like a tripwire vet. Or as if he's going on safari."

The other smiled, his instincts shifting from those of a tourist back to those of a reporter. "My name's Joe Lester," he said, extending his hand. "I'm a reporter." They shook. "Freelance," he added, as if it explained and forgave all past and future sins, gaffes, and errors.

Somewhere nearby a piston engine chugged and roared into life, followed by another and another.

"Dawn patrol," Cooper said, nodding toward the runway. "They love desert flying, even with the restrictions of being under the Military Operations Area. Want to go inside?"

Lester hesitated.

"He won't show for a couple more hours," Cooper said quietly. "I'm worth at least a sidebar."

Lester nodded and followed the man into his hangar. Inside, clustered around the mockup like mission control, stood a circle of drafting tables, CAD-CAM computers, workbenches, and desks, all facing inward as if surrounding an altar to some high-tech goddess. No one else occupied the hangar at the moment, though some of the computer screens glowed from being left on all night, their screen-saver utilities painting bizarre images of snakes, flying burritos, and even one of the spaceship blasting off and circling Earth.

"I call this class of spacecraft the Starblazer line," Cooper said, checking the coffee maker to affirm that the timer had started everything brewing.

"Looks kind of stubby. What does it sit on top of?"

"A launch pad." Cooper poured two cups of java. "I know it looks like a bloated Apollo Command and Service Module, but believe me, that's all there is to the spacecraft. The fuel tanks are inside and twenty small engines surround them in an annular ring inside the ablation shield on the bottom. We use aerospike techniques... Say, are you an aerospace writer?"

"Science writer," Lester said with pride, accepting the brew.

Cooper's smile crooked a bit off center. "Close enough. Aerospike engines adjust to the two different requirements of the flight regime. In the olden days, the exhaust bell on a rocket worked well only half the time. A narrow bell gave great thrust in the atmosphere, but was inefficient in a vacuum. A wide bell worked wonderfully in Space, but created too much drag at liftoff. Some designers tried to develop expanding exhaust chambers, but then some bright boy decided that the rocket plume itself could act as a variable bell. On a Starblazer, the sixteen engine nozzles can gimbal inward during atmospheric flight, then gimbal outward after Max-Q for exo-atmospheric... Are you really interested in this?"

"Actually, I am. Don't you get much interest?"

Cooper sipped at his coffee for a while before answering. When he did, his voice possessed a mystified tone. "All my life I've wanted to build spaceships. My earliest memory is from when I was about three years old. I woke up on a Saturday and snuck into the rumpus room and sat down at my mother's desk, a curving wedge of a thing that looked like a rocket command center constructed of blond wood. I made a crayon drawing on a piece of cardboard and tried to make a tube out of it, but I didn't know how to roll it up and staple it, so I just folded it and made a flat rocket. I stuck a little plastic Easter bunny charm in it and pretended I'd built my first animal-launching rocket.

"From there, I moved on to the usual kid's toys. But unlike my friends, I never put away those childish things. I built model rockets and messed around with chemistry sets. And I noticed something about people around me: the longer I adhered to my dream, the more distant I grew from others. It was as if *I* were the one standing still. Do you see what I mean?"

Lester shook his head.

"Okay. You know how popular science-fiction is, right? Blockbuster movies about galaxy-spanning civilizations, best-selling novels, million-dollar VR environments. Billions of people are fascinated about the future, millions fantasize about living in Space, but what are they doing to get from here to there? From now to the future? They spend all their time dreaming and no time working or even saving toward the day when I can offer them airline-style service to orbit. Why is that?" Cooper looked his companion in the eye with sincere bafflement.

It was apparent to Lester that the man had grappled with the question for years, perhaps to the point that it was rhetorical. "Don't you get any support?"

"Some. Mostly from a very few people at the fringes of the aerospace community. The huge number of people who show an interest in futurism, though, are indifferent or unbelieving. I used to go to science-fiction conventions. It seemed as if there were always a handful of people there ready to pick my ideas to shreds. People who should have been supporting me. 'How do you know it will work?' they'd ask. I'd tell them nothing's certain until we build the prototype, but the figures indicate success. 'Nobody's proved that the aerospike will have enough specific impulse.' Well, exactly. That's what I'm out to prove. The place was full of guys dedicated to being naysayers. I don't understand such belligerence; it's not their money, after all. I'm not asking for tax dollars. Actually," he finished off the cup, "I did ask for tax money once. I never will again. NASA is a naysayer with a velvet glove over a mailed fist. First they string you along, then they deliver the knockout blow..." He gazed out the hangar door at a Beech Starship taxiing past. He nodded toward it. "That's Poubelle's plane. He's got the money and the panache to pull off a one-time stunt. I've got the design to make space travel available to everyone. Want to take a bet on who succeeds? Why don't people put their money where their dreams are?"

"Leaving Earth is a scary idea," Lester said, setting his cup down half-consumed. "I had second, third, and fourth thoughts about leaving Colorado to come here. It meant quitting my job, leaving most of my belongings behind. How do you think most people would feel about doing that *and* moving to a hostile wilderness?"

"The West in the nineteenth century was more hostile than Space. Within decades, millions of people migrated here." Cooper turned to gaze at the spacecraft model. "I think we've lost our pioneers."

Lester glanced furtively at the Beech, then back at the speaker. He wanted to catch the billionaire, but he did not want to alienate Cooper, sensing important stories on both sides.

"I think the pioneers are out there, Mr. Cooper. What they don't have are their Conestogas. And what Space lacks, at least what low Earth orbit lacks, is resources. No trees to fell for log cabins, no animals to hunt for food, no land to farm for a living. Pioneering types know that they won't find freedom out there for a while. Some very expensive apron strings would be dangling down to Earth. No one wants to go until they can go and be free."

"And no one," Cooper said with a weary tone, "will be free until they make the effort to go." He rose from his chair with a faint attempt at a smile. "Thank you, Mr. Lester. My day's started off with a great rallying cry—"

"Don't be discouraged," the newsman said. "Poubelle's project can only help you. Interest in *Nomad* can just as easily become interest in your Starblazers. All you need is publicity. You'll get some from me." He pointed at the mockup. "And roll that out when the press shows up to cover Poubelle, and I guarantee you even more coverage."

Cooper mulled over the idea, then brightened. "Thanks. I'll do that."

Lester shook the rocketman's hand and lumbered out onto the tarmac. The Beech stood silently a few hundred yards away. Two figures moved about in the cockpit performing shutdown procedures. Lester considered climbing into his van, then changed his mind. Out of shape as he was, something about the cool morning desert air impelled him to stroll the distance. He did so, watching the airport activity increase. Hangar doors rattled open to spill trapezoids of light onto the airfield. Tools clattered. Voices laughed or cursed depending on the condition of the aircraft they discussed. Engines huffed, buzzed, or thundered into life. Planes taxied out onto the runway and lifted off, first a Cessna, then a Piper, then a 737 with fading paint. The Boeing circled the airport and returned for what appeared to be an urgent landing.

Lester smelled kerosene, avgas, and hot exhaust mixed with the morning air. Yellow sunlight glinted off of painted airplane fabric, polished metal skin, and bright white composite. To the north, bright red gyroplanes flew close to the mountains. In the east, squadrons of military jets performed dogfight maneuvers from nearly ground level to tens of thousands of feet high. Lester had never seen so much aerial activity crammed into one place.

A man climbed out of the Beech clad in a black flight suit. He extended his hand upward to take that of a woman similarly dressed.

"Mr. Poubelle!" Lester called out. "Joe Lester. What can you tell my readers about the Daedalus Project?"

"What paper are you with?" the woman asked. She gazed at him with startlingly golden eyes framed by the rich, dark hue of her beautiful face.

He smiled. "I'm freelance."

"Aren't we all," she said coolly, lifting the flight satchels from the hatchway and handing them to the pilot.

Poubelle took them — the lighter one in his right hand — looked at Lester, then glanced up at D'Asaro. "I told you we'd get at least one."

Lester, his voice incredulous, said, "No one's interviewed you yet? I've been on the road three days to get here!"

"Oh, we've had interviews," Poubelle said. "By phone and VR. Nobody's made the pilgrimage to the desert yet, that's all." He walked inside, leaving Chemar to lock up the aircraft. "*Aviation Week* will be here on Wednesday to follow up the PR and short phone interview with some preliminary photos. But you're first as far as people who'd come here in July." He glanced at a dollar-sized LCD display imbedded in his right arm. "Seven AM and already eighty-five degrees. If you like heat, you're in for it today."

"I'm from Colorado."

"Then come on in and sample our highly conditioned air."

Poubelle turned out to be a gracious host, both to Lester and to D'Asaro. The reporter spent much of his time simply observing their interplay. Whether they were lovers or not he could not tell from their demeanor — they never touched. Their relationship was definitely not that of an employer and employee. The most apt label he could slap on them was *partners*, either business partners operating as equals or an old married couple who knew each other so deeply that they thought and spoke as one. *Mature*, he thought. *These two people know what they want from life and work toward it with secure determination*.

Feet up on the new mahogany desk within the teak-paneled office that imputed the luxury of a downtown Manhattan address, Poubelle toyed with an unlit billy club of a cigar and summed up his spiel: "So I plan to have a team working to upsize the supersonic drop tanks used on the X-15 A-2, which got up to Mach six point seven and one hundred-two thousand feet 'way back in sixty-seven. Thirty years of successive research should allow us to triple the velocity and quadruple the altitude. I have people crunching the numbers now."

"Paid people? Or has anyone volunteered?"

"Volunteers?" He looked at his watch, then said, "It's seven-fifteen. Take a look at this."

He rose and crossed the room to an inner door. Opening it, he waved Lester through to a hangar filled with scores of people, but only a few desks and terminals. Sleeping bags littered the concrete floor. Backpacks and suitcases stood lined up along one entire wall. People sat on the floor hacking away on laptops, palmtops, any computer they may have brought with them or that Poubelle provided. People peered over shoulders of people peering over shoulders.

"Sixty-five at last count. Some of them are laid-off aerospace workers, some are retired engineers from the Apollo era, some are kids still wet behind the ears. And they've been here for two days now. We've got the phone bank coming in today and then we'll be in business."

A chirping sound emanated from Poubelle's right arm. He gazed at the readout, touched the screen in two places, and said, "I've got an appointment with a promotional supply company at eight. Chemar and I have to go over some ideas now. Did you get a press kit?"

Lester nodded. "I'd like to wander around and do some interviews with the volunteers," he said. "And shoot some photos."

"Anything you want."

They said their good-days and Lester strolled through the hangar, snapping shots with the Kodak. He introduced himself to several of the volunteers who were more than eager to give him their life stories while simultaneously working away on computers or flipping through research files. He soon cut his questions down to one: "Why are you here?" elicited detailed and lengthy responses.

"Because," a young man sorting microfiches said, "Larry Poubelle's the only one in the country who has the guts to put his money where his mouth is."

"I'm here because nobody else needs hypersonic flow-separation studies," a soft-spoken woman with short brown hair said.

A man in his fifties agreed. "NASA laid me off. At least here I can be of some use."

A man with a Texas accent drawled, "Hey, *somebody's* got to pilot the jet that takes *Nomad* up. Might as well be me."

"I've worked for three different launch vehicle companies," a young, long-haired man in t-shirt and torn jeans said. "None of them ever had enough money to do anything. I think Poubelle's hit on the only way to fund this: the people, not the corporations or the State."

Half of those he spoke to not only volunteered their time but had already donated sizable amounts of their own savings to the project. When asked why, nearly all of them replied that they were investing in their future, in the future of humanity.

Something's definitely brewing, Lester mused.

▼ ▲ ▼

Barry Gibbon, meanwhile, publicly greeted Poubelle's press release with indifference. He went so far as to solicit air time on talk shows and morning news programs in order to announce his indifference and that of the National Organisation of Space Supporters.

"Amateur wish-fulfillment by a dilettante, at best," he told one morning anchorman. "At worst, a dangerous threat to anyone under their flight path." He spoke with nearly regal authority, lacing his argument with a few comments on payload masses, specific impulse, and reentry heat, but mostly discussing liability.

"What a wealthy dabbler such as Mr. Poubelle does not understand is that treaties exist giving the government of each nation full liability — and thus total responsibility — for any spacecraft launched from their domestic airspace. I've seen no request from Mr. Poubelle for NASA oversight on his alleged project. How serious can he be? I fear we may be seeing the birth of yet another money-raising scheme with lovely brochures and pretty trinkets and absolutely no intention of building a working spacecraft."

"So NOSS does not endorse Poubelle's project?" the anchor asked.

Gibbon sighed and gazed at the newsman with weary indulgence. "If you only knew how many crackpots we hear from each week with plans to build a giant Space Ark, you wouldn't greet this new proposal with any less skepticism than I. Besides," he said, shifting in the chair and suddenly warming to the subject, "all this sort of independent pipe-dreaming will be a thing of the past within a year or two. You see, the United Nations will be voting this fall on the Interplanetary Treaty. Very soon we'll see an end to the useless duplication of effort we've endured in the last four decades of the Space Age. Combined together under one flag, the United Nations Interplanetary Treaty Organization will coordinate all space programs and launch facilities for the benefit of *all* mankind, rather than the enrichment of a select few. With the finest minds in the world controlling the resources and directing the efforts of all the national space programs, we shall at last have a coordinated and rational program that will see human beings living and working routinely in low Earth orbit within the next thirty years."

On the ride back to the Central Park East penthouse lent to him by a wealthy alumni whenever he lectured at NYU, Gibbon fielded two radio and three newspaper interviews on his cellphone. Each time he inquired whether the caller had plans to contact Poubelle. Each time he received the deferential answer that his interview appeared to sum things up and confirm that this new project was just an inchoate publicity bid.

Gibbon, on the other hand, privately held a grave concern about the Daedalus Project. All previous attempts at building spacecraft without government assistance were indeed pipe dreams, lone nuts such as that Roberts fellow in California, pouring every cent they owned into hardware and never having quite enough, or discussion groups that endlessly debated spacecraft design, hoping to come up with something that was perfect on paper before daring to lift a screwdriver. The former were doomed by their poverty, the latter by their timidity.

Gibbon did not like Laurence Poubelle. The man was, after all, ex-military and the head of a nuclear power conglomerate. He was too rich to join NOSS for its financial clout, too successful to join it for any feeling of political empowerment. He represented the man Gibbon had for decades feared would someday arise: a man of wealth *and* vision.

He opened his cellphone and autodialed a number.

"Barry Gibbon for the senator," he said.

After just a few seconds, Ludlow Woolsey III said, *"Hello, Chimp you old chump. I hear you're popular again."*

Gibbon had long ago ceased to chafe at the annoying nickname, having learned the value of accepting humiliation with good humor. He prided himself in possessing no ego to wound.

"Only in the reflection of another's efforts, Lud. Tell me, what do you think of this Poubelle fellow?"

"You're the expert. Is he full of hot air?"

"I think he's opening a regulatory nightmare for himself. His stated plans appear to overlook entirely the congressional oversight involved in any space activity."

The sonorous voice on the other end said, *"My committee's always up for a challenge. I'll have my staff look into it."*

"Wonderful, Lud. And put that nice young staffer of yours, Bradley on it. He's a NOSS member and can round up all the information your committee needs."

After the requisite exchange of goodbyes, Gibbon switched off and called home only to receive a busy signal. Though it proved that Evangeline was home, it annoyed him that she spent so much time gabbing on the phone to friends whose names he did not know and about whom he could not have cared less. What possible topics could someone as quiet, bland, and dim as his sister blather about? Spinsterhood?

Gibbon sighed. Ever since their parents passed away, she had been his burden. At least she kept the house tidy and performed most domestic chores with a simple-minded graciousness.

He allowed the barest trace of a snicker to escape. *Imagine someone such as she,* he mused, *being born on the Moon.*

He shut the cellphone off to watch the scenery of New York City drift past the car windows. The graffiti, the garbage, the wandering homeless, the bustling crowds filled his view. It amused him to think of such people transplanted to the Moon or Mars, running back and forth in their spacesuits with pressurized briefcases carrying stale sandwiches. Bums begging for spare oxygen. Gangsters tagging crater walls with their slogans.

So few men proved worthy of the honor of space travel, his observations reaffirmed. And with the Treaty so near to approval, he would soon be able to pass judgment on anyone who presumed to represent humanity to the Universe.

It was all he wanted from life.

2 August

The catalogue arrived, as fate would have it, on a day when the old man was unable to concentrate. Rex Ivarson's wife sorted the morning mail, holding on to the fan letters to answer on her own, retaining the bills to pay, and passing on only the items that she thought might awaken his interest for even a brief moment.

He had carried the catalogue with him to the clinic and now gazed at the thin, colorful booklet, attempting to look at the illustration of a sleek, black rocket plane with stubby wings blasting into Space off the back of a Boeing 747. Shaking hands flipped to the next page to reveal arm patches, coffee mugs, belt buckles, posters, key chains, and a dozen other goodies emblazoned with the image of the modified X-15. He put the catalogue down to stare at the rhythmic motions of his left hand.

Rex Ivarson could not force the trembling to go away. A companion even more constant than his wife, Grace, the shakes were the legacy of Parkinson's disease. Rex Ivarson, now eighty-eight, had given up trying to write at eighty-two. His last novel had been published seven years ago to gentle, respectful, sadly negative reviews. His golden years, wrote one critic regretfully, were not Rex Ivarson's Golden Age.

Now the man once called the Beethoven of science fiction sat with his wife in a doctor's waiting room, his hands shaking listlessly, his body racked with unstoppable spasms that possessed a rhythm not of his making. Once a literary giant, he was now just a small, old man trapped in a body that refused to obey him.

Grace, as white-haired as Rex was bald, sat beside him, taking one quivering hand in two of hers, stroking it gently as if doing so could soothe her husband into quiescence. She wore pleated beige slacks with a white blouse and matching beige military-style tank jacket. Her husband wore blue jeans and a red-and-blue Pendleton shirt. He looked like an old cowboy, still able to maintain a stern dignity despite his condition.

"If I could just beat this," he muttered to Grace. "If I could just get writing again. If I could just *think* straight again. Concentrate."

Grace nodded and patted his hand. Nothing would please her more than to see him at his typewriter, hunched over in thought, the keys clattering at furious speed. In her deepest inner soul she feared that she would never see that again, that his decline would continue unto death, and that death was near, if not for his body, then certainly for his mind, for his soul.

"Mr. Ivarson?" The nurse spoke his name from the doorway. Grace stood to help her husband rise. He attempted to walk without her aid and accomplished a slow shuffle across the waiting room toward the inner door. His left hand never stopped shaking.

The examination room was stark and white. On the counter hung a model of a human spine. At least Grace thought it was a model, though she knew Rex would be fascinated if it were real. The world had always fascinated him. When he was able and they could afford it, they had traveled extensively. Since the rewards of a lifetime of writing had come only after most of that lifetime passed in building generations of readers, their window of opportunity to enjoy their wealth had been narrow. Comfortably well-off in their mid-sixties, they enjoyed their journeys like newlyweds for over a decade. Then his hand began to shake. Then the money went to doctors instead of cruise ships.

Rex Ivarson — award-winning author, inspiration to thousands of boys and girls who gazed up at the nighttime stars — sat as straight as he could in his chair and tried to ignore the hand that shook and shook and shook...

"Good morning, Grace, Rex." Dr. Kerberos entered with Ivarson's file. A lean man, he looked taller than his actual height of five-eleven. His fingers embodied his most striking feature. Long and graceful, they exhibited the strength and control of a concert pianist's. He performed his concertos, though, on that most delicate of instruments — the human brain.

Kerberos sat on the examination table with one leg on the floor and one hanging. He glanced for a final time at a magazine tucked in Ivarson's folder, then said, "I'll be straight with you. L-Dopa isn't working in your case. Parkinson's is a disease that destroys the cells responsible for creating the neurotransmitter dopamine. L-Dopa is a precursor to dopamine, and by raising its concentration, sometimes the remaining cells can be coaxed into making a little more. Understand?"

"Doc." Rex Ivarson's voice was shaky, but still strong. "I'm not losing my mind. I'm losing my body. If you're telling me it's over, say it and let me go so that you can spend your time on someone who has hope."

"There is hope," the doctor said quietly. "And it may sound bizarre..." He smiled at the old man. "Then again, you've written some pretty bizarre things yourself."

Ivarson said nothing, but gazed at Kerberos with a level intensity.

"The problem with L-Dopa," the doctor said, "is that not enough crosses the blood-brain barrier to get where it is needed. If something inside the brain could generate dopamine—"

"A dopamine pump," Rex said quickly, his mind already racing with the possibilities. "Like an insulin pump for diabetics. But how much could it hold? How often would it have to be replaced?"

"Not a pump," Kerberos said.

Grace interjected with: "A factory?"

Kerberos nodded, pulling out the journal in Ivarson's file. "It's fascinating. The researchers spliced the gene for human dopamine into rat brain cells, cultured them, then put the cells into a membrane that allows nutrients in to nourish the cells and lets dopamine out. Since the rat cells are never in contact with your immune system, there's no opportunity for rejection. And I think this also overcomes your aversion to using human fetal brain cells?"

"First question," Ivarson said. "Will I be able to write?"

"It's not impossible."

"Second question: when do we do it?"

Dr. Kerberos slipped the journal back into the folder. "I think we can get you into the program within a few weeks."

Grace spoke up. "The side effects from the L-Dopa were unpleasant. What are the side effects from this rat-cell implant?"

"As far as I can tell — beyond that of the operation itself — none." Dr. Kerberos smiled. "Though he may develop a fondness for cheese."

16 August

Brain surgery is surgery of the most intimate kind. An outsider drills a hole to enter the most sacred vault one owns. Once inside, the intruder moves as carefully as possible, knowing full well that the slightest misstep through this holy place may destroy the greatest treasure in the universe — a human mind. And as a counterpoint to that danger, the operation occurs while the patient is awake and aware. Horribly enough, if the trespasser destroys anything of value during his foray, neither will ever know. The intruder cannot know what memory he has sundered, and the owner would be unable to remember.

Rex Ivarson knew he would be awake. That was why he courteously but firmly requested that a video monitor be positioned so that he could see his own brain for the first time in his life.

Hello, old friend, he thought, gazing at the pinkish-grey mass on the monitor.

CHAPTER 10

The function of a State Space Programme is to police space. The State's programme will pick up spectacularly the moment a lot of marketeers start appearing up there making untaxed money and capital.

— Samuel Edward Konkin III

3 September

"Just how far can I take this?" Chad Haley asked.

"To its logical extreme," his boss answered.

Joscelyn Donahue gazed around her at the seedy little office in the light of a fly-specked bulb overhead. Dented, ancient wooden filing cabinets overflowed with dog-eared files. Yellowed newspaper clippings cluttered the desk, along with an ashtray holding a ziggurat of butts and a bottle of whiskey only partially full, the tumbler next to it holding a liver-killing amount of liquor. She craned her head about to take in every detail. She was impressed. Glancing over to a dusty mirror, she observed that she wore a tight-fitting red dress and a broad-brimmed fedora. Haley's clothing consisted of brown chinos, a dingy white shirt with the sleeves rolled up way past the elbows, brown suspenders, and a narrow-brimmed hat that looked as if it had been slept upon.

"Then here's the plan." Haley pulled the sheet of paper from the black Remington Standard typewriter and handed it to her. Another sheet appeared under the paper bail with the identical words on it. He referred to the organizational chart on that one.

"The only way to make a leveraged buyout profitable these days is to purchase the company and — before the first interest payment comes due — sell off all assets *except* its core money-maker — in this case, the handgun manufacturer — then move the capital equipment to that empty factory you've got sitting in Hoboken, then begin operating the core business on all three shifts. The day shift manufactures completed guns and spare parts in the traditional, BATF-approved fashion. Swing and graveyard shifts manufacture pistols and receivers lacking serial numbers or manufacturer's marks in order to sell at higher prices in the counter-economy."

Donahue thought for a moment, then said, "How do we maintain security?"

"Swing and graveyard crews consist of one systems analyst and two gunsmiths. Pay them well so they don't rock the boat."

"Too risky. People get drunk. People blabber."

Haley stared up at the screen. "You... could make the number stamping an automated final phase overseen by just the analyst. It would be computer controlled, switched on and off automatically at the appropriate times. And..." He stared at the chart for a moment, then typed in an extra level. "There. Use robotics when at all possible."

Donahue nodded. "Distribution channels?" she asked.

"Since they're off the record and lack any tracking numbers, the production runs can just vanish from the loading docks. I have a multi-level marketing plan that involves a trio of national distributors who recruit regional marketers in the high-crime areas. They make contact with the more radical elements of Neighborhood Watch. You know — the people who realize that the cops aren't going to be there when they need them. Or who view police as just a gang of thugs in blue."

"And if the operation is busted anyway?"

Haley smiled and shrugged. "You sold the company to a paperchase corporation and parked the stock with another dummy, didn't you?"

She patted him on the back. "This is a good one. Save me a copy."

"Save changes," Haley said.

"Yes, boss," a sultry voice responded from the front part of the office. Donahue turned to see a buxom blond in a tight turquoise sweater dress slip a folder in a desk tray marked "JD."

"Where did you get her?" Donahue asked Haley with a puzzled expression on her face.

"Built the voice up byte by byte. Movie stars, radio deejays, commercial actresses. Totally synthetic."

Donahue lowered her voice. "I see," she said in a susurrous breath.

Haley frowned. "How did you do that?"

She laughed and tossed her hair over her shoulders. "Any woman in heat can speak that way."

Haley sat there composing a reply, but Donahue beat him to the punch when she picked a newspaper clipping and scrolled through the text. "What the hell is *this*?"

Haley shrugged. "It's just a think-piece. The concepts certainly don't have to be applied in the way I suggest." He hoped that she would take the bait. The headline she gazed at read

Low-Altitude Cruise Missiles as a Transport Method of Consumer Goods from Colombia to New Mexico

"Colombia? We are not a company of drug smugglers, Mr. Haley!"

"Of course not, but you gave me wide latitude in what — "

"That will be all," she said sternly, removing her Sky Pilot HG II goggles. She blinked a few times, readjusting her focus to take in the dimensions of Haley's actual office in the Advanced Systems Division. It was not spacious, but neither was it as small as the 1940's detective's office Haley created in his VR computer workspace. The real office lacked no amenity. The lighting — soft, low, and golden — came from a pair of antique Tiffany peacock lamps on the ends of an equally venerable desk at which Chad very rarely sat. He spent most of his days in his electronic cocoon — a copy of one in his apartment, he told her, except for the more powerful supercomputer it accessed — spinning threads of thought into maps of action.

"Joscelyn..."

"Yes, Chad?" Donahue glanced at her wristwatch and adjusted the jade comb in her hair.

"I figured out the source of the New Mexico missile some time ago. That's why I ran this idea past you."

Her dark crimson lips formed a wicked smile. "I know."

"Should I be worried about all this?"

"All what? All the money we're making?"

"All the laws we're breaking."

Her smile faded just slightly. With a weary shake of her head, she said, "I do the worrying for Grant Enterprises. And I do it weekends and holidays."

Concerned at her tone of voice, he exited the VR program and removed his goggles to look around the office. Donahue had already departed, her own headset and gloves lying on the polished walnut desk, still emitting the scent of her perfume.

▼ ▲ ▼

"I need to know what you think of him." Grant stared at Donahue from the vantage of his leather Recaro executive chair. His penthouse office occupied the entire top floor of the skyscraper. "What sort of a risk is he? Would his fully informed assistance be an even greater asset?"

Donahue stared quietly out at the Long Beach Naval Shipyard, a jumble of grey ships and rusting steel cranes. The sea breeze had cleared the shoreline of smog, and a sapphire sky stretched out toward Catalina.

"I think you should ask him yourself. Up front. He's a radical thinker."

Grant snorted. "I'll admit that." He leaned back in the chair, his right hand grasping the handle of a simple black coffee mug that looked almost quaintly austere amidst the wealthy trappings of his workplace. The fingers of his left hand beat out an idle march: one-two-three, one-two-three, one-two-three-four-five. "He's got wild ideas."

"Ideas that work," she persisted. "Ideas that have brought us money. Substantial money."

"So why not keep it at that? Why pull him in further?"

"Because," she said, sitting on his desk to perch one leg against his chair and swivel it toward her, "I think that, somewhere in the convolutions of the three pound universe that serves as his brain, sits an idea that will shake this planet and bring us more wealth than we can handle. I just have to find that idea."

Grant took a sip of the coffee. "I had ideas once," he said in a rueful tone. "Real ideas. Big plans. Now my ideas are simply... *mechanistic*. I can look at something and make it run better, more efficiently. I have the ability and the power to take the well-worn path and pave it, raise the speed limit, throw up the billboards." He gazed out at the sea. "That power is nothing compared to the simple ability to blaze the next trail."

▼ ▲ ▼

Haley detected the eerie presence of another. The Lurker had returned to the Virtual Mall. He turned swiftly about, so fast that the computer could not generate the illusion of motion. Instead, the image flickered and the new point of view appeared. There, darting out of view, ran a figure in black cloaked in a voluminous cape that reflected no light.

Pointing his finger toward the exit, Haley flew past the crowds and returned to his own virtual office, this time designed like a Louise XIV palace boudoir. He turned toward the virtual keyboard — now the ornate organ from *Phantom of the Opera* — and typed madly.

> Don't know what Lurker wants. Perhaps trying to drive me crazy just by hiding nearby. Doesn't anyone else sense him? If not, how can he appear on private face-to-face if I didn't give him my public key access? Is it someone I know? Or did he hack my number?

A hacker would be fairly benign, he thought. Someone is making a concerted effort to follow him, to unnerve him. Perhaps even to spy on his work stored in the Grant supercomputer.

Something scratched at his door. He turned, his point of view shifting to the door. The headphones shrieked with the grating sound of nails against slate.

How can he do that? Any attempt to get his attention would cause Sophia's voice to say "Someone at the door, lover." Screeching fingernails were simply not in the sound files. Unless...

Unless someone has *hacked into my own system!*

The nails screeched again. He reached toward the ghostly door and yanked it open.

And saw no one.

He saw, in fact, nothing at all. His LCD spectacles registered blackness where there should have been his message room and bulletin board. Shuddering, he pulled the unit from his head, severing the connection.

"Sophia," he said. "Return from Erehwon. Run check for virus, Trojan Horse, tapeworm, logic bomb... *anything*."

In the minutes that followed, Haley collected his thoughts and tried to calm down. He gazed at the goggles and feedback gloves, suddenly aware that wandering the Virtual Mall might not be any safer than cruising any realm that welcomed the masked and the anonymous.

"Chad?"

"Yes, Sophia," Haley answered.

"I can find no evidence of corruption in my system."

"Thank you, Sophia. Take a message." Hesitantly, he slipped on the spectacles to see Sophia's busty form sashay into his office, notebook in hand, and sit cross-legged on his desk.

"Ready, Chad," she murmured.

Haley took just a moment to point his glove at the office door. It opened to reveal the message room and bulletin board exactly where they should be. He closed the door and locked it; this put the system into an encrypted mode.

"Message to Joscelyn Donahue, carbon to Marcus Grant. Subject — Safe operating environments." He smiled. Sophia gazed at him, hanging on his every word. He purposely had not programmed in the action of her writing down what he said. He thought it was more amusing this way.

He took a deep breath and began what he considered to be the ultimate test of his position at Grant Enterprises. For a long moment he said nothing. He had spent several months at Grant, building his reputation. Everything he suggested, he and Donahue implemented to the benefit of the company. The time had come to make his case for the most daring black market investment of all time.

"Industry in the modern world is once again coming under fire from the Luddite forces of anti-technology, this time flying the banner of environmental concern. Already free trade, except in the counter-economy, is non-existent. Though the risk of government interference in counter-economic market activity is low and can be lowered even further by the intelligent application of ounces of gold or grains of lead, I suggest that the twin concerns of environmental safety and lowered operating risk can be met by the relocation of manufacturing to a neutral zone.

"This neutral zone would have to be so isolated as to be out of the reach of any government that might try to claim it, and so barren that any environmental pollution could not affect any living part of the planet."

Haley grinned. *This will do it*, he thought. *This will probe how far I can go and how much they'll spend*. "Since all deserts are claimed by one State or another and the high seas, though nominally free, are the soup-bowl of life on Earth, there would seem to be no place in the world that can satisfy both conditions. Therefore, Grant Enterprises must leave Earth."

Sophia did not raise an eyebrow.

"Whereas environmental laws and restrictive trade practices make white market business unprofitable and black market business risky, orbital manufacturing with re-entry delivery of goods allows for operations free of government interference. Such an orbital platform could become a base for manufacturing *anything* without environmental risk. It would be of great interest to the genetic-engineering and fusion power professions, both of which are being legislated against on Earth. And though certain governments may *claim* to extend their authority into space, and the UN will soon attempt to claim the entire Universe, such laughable pronouncements fail for lack of any realistic means of enforcement. The High Ground is completely defensible.

"That means that — in addition to legitimate manufacturing and services — *anything goes*. Uncensored — and uncensorable — TV and radio broadcasts. Drug and weapon manufacturing. Zero-g brothels. Unmanned reentry vehicles delivering any type of good to any point on the globe — for a price. If Grant Enterprises can be the first to get a toehold in space, it will become the richest, most powerful company on Earth or off of it.

"Details upon request."

▼▲▼

This time, Marcus A. Grant called Haley to his office. Less than two hours had passed since Chad transmitted the message to Donahue and Grant. Haley was working on a list of illegal activities that an orbital facility might house when a great globed head like that of the Mighty Oz appeared before him and — in a voice that thundered in his earphones — demanded that he come to Grant's office in five minutes.

Haley entered the large, bright penthouse office to see Donahue sitting in one of the Zimbabwe chairs in front of Grant's spacious, vehemently neat desk. The afternoon sun was a deep purple dot on the tinted picture window behind him.

Marcus Grant, Haley noted, was tall, yet not a large man. He was so well-proportioned that he could actually look shorter than his true height. Silver-grey hair lay combed back over his head in the style of a symphony conductor. The grey appeared to be premature; the quality of his facial skin denoted an age of no later than early forties, possibly just mid-thirties. The man's age held vital importance to Haley: knowing it, he could judge what part of the Space Age influenced Grant's childhood. This just might help.

Grant made no effort at introduction. His first sentence hit Haley like a hammer blow: "No spaceships, Mr. Haley."

That was not the greeting he expected. "Mr. Grant, there's no reason why the company can't expand into Spa—"

"No spaceships, no rockets, no Moon-bases, no astronauts, no crazy Rex Ivarson crap."

Haley's gaze narrowed. "You've read Rex Ivarson?"

Grant's jaw tightened. "Who hasn't — as a child? We grow up and put away childish things, though. I'm willing to discuss secure sites with you. Siberia, Antarctica, even the ocean floor. But no rockets. Understood?"

Haley frowned. Something was not right. Everything he had studied about the company indicated that Grant ought to embrace the concept. "Mr. Grant — with all due respect, the attitude of businessmen toward Space — which you seem to share — leaves the cosmos wide open for the first company with enough courage and ingenuity to—"

"I said no rockets!"

Donahue nearly jumped from her seat. Grant never raised his voice. If anything, she considered him very nearly emotionless when it came to the cool calculation of business and market position. His rejection of Haley's idea bordered on the hysterical.

"Perhaps," Haley ventured, "we should speak candidly. About ballistic missiles to New Mexico, for instance."

"That was a long time ago, Haley, when I needed to generate operating capital. They were unmanned missiles. You're proposing a black market manned-space program. It's an insane risk with so much profit to be made right here on Earth."

"We trade risk for profit. The opportunity for immense profit exists in Space. Yet no one is willing to risk tapping into it. That's a sure sign of a market niche begging to be exploited."

A palpable pressure welled up in Grant, an inner conflict made manifest by a ruddiness in his face that brought with it small beads of perspiration.

"No spacecraft. You may think I'm some heartless profiteer, but there's no way I'm going to build something that can blow up the way *Challenger* did. There's no way I'll build something that could roast people the way Grissom, Chaffee, and White got roasted in Apollo 204!"

My God, Haley thought with a shock of insight. *This man isn't anti-Space at all.* Not one in a thousand people remembered the crew of the Apollo fire. Not one in a hundred thousand knew the correct designation of the Saturn 1-B rocket on which the crew sat. Most who had any memory at all of the event called it Apollo One.

There's got to be some way to get to him. Something needs to be awakened.

"Those were government attempts," Haley ventured.

"If the government can't do it, nobody can." His voice dripped with acid irony.

"You don't believe that, or you would never have built those drug missiles."

Grant let out a laugh that released his ill-disguised tension. "Who told you they carried drugs?"

"Logic. The payload had to have a high value-to-mass ratio, it had to be relatively sturdy to withstand launch and landing, and it had to be something illegal to smuggle from south of the border."

"And you don't think that something else — let's say, supercomputer chips with high import tariffs — might not be even more profitable?"

Haley turned the conversation back to the direction he wanted. "It doesn't matter what the rockets carried. They carried the merchandise *safely* and *profitably*. They could carry people the same way."

The billionaire asked, with deadly seriousness, "If you're so smart, Haley, why ain't you rich?"

Haley mulled over the question. After a short pause, he said, "Because I've never — until now — put my theories into action."

"*Right!*" Despite the assertive reply, Haley's boss radiated a troubled unease. "I've made a lot of money because I take the initiative. I've also lost a lot of money because there seemed to be factors operating in the world that defied my analysis." He pulled an optical disc from the inside pocket his navy pinstriped jacket and waved it lightly at Haley. "You propose concepts and reach conclusions that are utterly at odds with everything *I* grew up believing. And yet they fit right in with everything I know *works*. Do you have a theory to explain *that*?"

"Perhaps because, while I've never put my theories into action, *you've* never put your actions into a theory."

Grant placed the disc gently on his desk and leaned backward in his chair, his eyes glazing. "What do you mean?"

Haley leaned forward, weighing every word he was about to say. "I mean that you have allowed the market to make your choices. You have gone where the money already is—"

"What's wrong with that?"

"—rather than where it will be. You are simply reacting to existing markets rather than creating new markets. Reactionary investing rakes in existing money, no doubt about it, but *visionary* investing can create new wealth."

"There's nothing visionary about space stations, Haley. They've been promised to us for half a century."

"On what basis, though? As government outposts, as military bases, as scientific playgrounds. All those ideas received the tax subsidies and all have collapsed under government's lack of vision. Space is not a desert fort or exotic laboratory. Space is the only frontier left for humanity. And I think we're all going a little bit insane because we're not reaching out to it."

Grant shifted in his chair as if roused from a troubled slumber. "Insane?" he asked.

"Look at the world around you. A hundred minor wars going on continuously. Murder-suicides of entire families. Rape and brutality, poverty and despair, starvation and slaughter. And nowhere to escape. Nowhere to find freedom, to be left alone to build a new life. People need that. Frustrate that need and insanity — mass, cultural insanity — is the result."

"So Grant Enterprises should build spaceships to relieve all this worldwide suffering? What a load of horse—"

"Marc." Joscelyn stopped Grant without even speaking loudly. "Chad isn't talking about charity. What Chad means is that things are so bad on Earth because there is no place to escape. What he is implying, I suspect, is that some people will pay any price to leave

Earth. And if Grant Enterprises can provide either transit or destination services, they'll pay that price to us."

"No!" Grant pounded a fist on his desk and rose to stare into the purple sun. "Don't you understand that the future of man is not my concern? We have no future! They stole that future and smashed it! They crushed it in their mailed fist and threw it in the gutter. It's from there that we gaze longingly upward at the sky." He turned to face them. In his eyes smoldered an anger Donahue had never seen before. "I swore I'd never again gaze at the stars. The gutter is where all the loose change falls."

"Where does the change fall *from*?" Haley demanded. "And how much *doesn't* fall and so stays out of your reach?"

"That doesn't concern me. Earth is a gutter unbelievably wide, deep, and rich."

"You could—"

"Think of something else, Mr. Haley. Something... practical."

Haley nodded. "Something more down to Earth."

The grey man turned back toward the setting sun. The window tint colored the sky like a vast, ugly bruise. "Yes," he said quietly. "Something down to Earth."

▼ ▲ ▼

Donahue joined Haley in the corridor, genuine concern on her face.

"He's never reacted that way," she said. "You hit some sort of nerve. I've brought up aerospace investing before and he's just dismissed it lightly. He looked ready to tear your throat out just to shut you up."

Haley punched at the elevator call button. "So Space is out. We concentrate on other schemes."

Donahue laid a hand on his. "No," she whispered. "Your proposal is important. It could make us a fortune. Marcus knows that, but he's built up some sort of barrier, something I know nothing about. Keep working on it. Develop a step-by-step program. Accumulate the facts. Run a cost analysis. Generate a database of people in aerospace who might be available for hire. I'll help you on this one."

Haley looked at her with a puzzled expression. "You're up to your eyebrows in alligators already. Why take on a speculative project."

"You don't understand people," she said. "There was hatred and despair in that room. Where there's that much emotion, there's even more passion. I've never known Marcus Grant to be passionate about anything. When he's with you, though, it's as if you challenge his world-view. He thinks he's smarter than anyone; cagier, more aware of how the world really works. You come along and he's suddenly hungry for your opinion, eager to act on your ideas. Then you offer up your best idea and he just as suddenly clams up."

"So you want me to keep at it? In spite of his objection?"

"No — *because* of his objection." Donahue stepped into the elevator with him and stood even closer to him. The scent of her excitement touched his nostrils. "I want you," she whispered, "to hit him with a plan so overwhelming that it will shatter his defenses."

25 September

The effort required all the research of a full-scale business plan. Haley and Donahue spent the following weeks analyzing the market for a space-based counter-economy. Haley discovered that The Net stored a daunting amount of information on the subject in the form of old surveys conducted by space groups. None of it was very helpful except as a guideline. No legitimate group, for instance, asked how much what percentage of those polled would pay for a night with a zero-gravity hooker. Nor did any of the cost-benefit analyses include estimates of the return on investment of designer drugs manufactured in an orbital facility versus the expense of defending against space narcs. Even the concept of orbiting pirate TV satellites barely received a nod from researchers.

The pair worked in *spatia incognita*, where every idea implied a dozen preceding points requiring investigation and confirmation. After three weeks, they possessed a report long on speculation and short on hard numbers.

Over those weeks, Haley noticed a warming on Donahue's part, a genuine joy in the study of orbital mechanics and spacecraft design as applied to market analysis. Her calls to him occurred more often as the days went by, the time the spent together after hours grew longer and involved late dinners. Sometimes, she even drifted off to sleep in exhaustion on Chad's couch. Most significantly, her image on their VR system dressed in more alluring clothing and carried itself with an ever more seductive energy. He wondered how long he could resist the attraction he felt toward her.

One evening at his apartment the two lay side-by-side on the couch bed, VR goggles and gloves connected to Sophia. In VR, they stood on a vast desert plain near a huge white balloon that glinted brightly in the morning sun. Below the balloon hung a white cylinder surrounded by six smaller cylinders. Chad — looking more like an idealized version of himself rather than Tom Jefferson — wore a khaki safari jacket and pants. Joscelyn wore tan shorts cut about as high on her long legs as they could be and still have a one-inch cuff. Her blouse was white and split open past her navel to disappear at the belt line. An inch or two had been edited from her waistline, Chad noted, and the little diamond plane just below the bridge of her nose that he found so sexy on her actual self had been deleted from her virtual features. He wondered whether she did that intentionally or simply forgot to include it when designing the walking, talking icon.

A flash of sunlight caught his attention, reminding him of the presentation underway.

"Here's an idea that's rarely mentioned in the literature," he said, pointing to the balloon, "even though the technique was used for unmanned rockets decades ago." At the urging of his finger, the huge gas bag rose into the deep blue sky. "The Piccard-style helium balloon is constructed of ICI Melinex polyester bonded to ultra-thin DTEX rip-stop nylon. I'd considered metalizing it for a hot-air balloon, but that would add the weight of the metal and the unacceptable weight of the propane tanks. Also, the metalized surface would be a radar reflector."

She watched it rise. "How long would it take to lift the rocket to the balloon's service ceiling?"

Chad smiled and stretched out his arms to fly into the air after the glittering object. Joscelyn joined him. They shot up after the balloon, which rose upward at very nearly a rocket's pace. Behind it — writ across the sky in towering numerals — the altitude, rate of ascent, and speed of simulation rolled past. They watched the lighter-than-air craft rise at one hundred times its real-world rate.

She found the impression of speed and altitude delightfully dizzying. The sky turned to a deep purple hue. The balloon envelope expanded to nearly double its volume, making the spacecraft suspended below it look like an earring. When the readout displayed 115,000 feet, the simulation suddenly slowed to one-half real time. All seven rocket engines ignited in unison, propelling the spacecraft into and through the balloon canopy. Erupting from the topside, the vehicle roared upward, the flaccid remains of the balloon instantly incinerated in its fiery wake.

Arms outstretched like super heroes, Chad and Joscelyn followed the simulation up into Space, watching as — two by two — the boosters extinguished and separated until there was only the payload orbiting amid star-spangled blackness above a blue Earth.

"That's one possibility," Chad said, gazing at Joscelyn floating two hundred miles above Earth without benefit of space suit. He made a motion with his hand and suddenly they hovered above a placid blue sea. For her information, huge turquoise letters floated on the surface spelling the name "Caribbean."

"Here's a second method. Whereas the first design saved fuel and increased payload by launching above ninety-five per cent of the atmosphere, this design takes advantage of economies of scale and simplicity by launching at sea."

They flew over a cylinder the size of a very small supertanker. On the water floated a legend indicating a length of five hundred feet. For comparison, two 747's perched nose-to-tail on the huge rocket then evaporated.

Two barges accompanied the leviathan. The forward ship towed it into position. Off the deck of the aftward ship slid a massive concrete block attached to the rear of the spacecraft. The block sank, slowed by buoyancy bags, until it dragged the exhaust bell underwater. Slowly the nose cone of the rocket arose. Within moments the vehicle pointed perpendicular to the surface of the sea, half submerged, half above water.

"The beauty of this design," Chad commented, "is that you can use standard drydock construction methods, standard barge-handling techniques, and the ocean becomes your launch platform. The water acts both to quiet engine noise and confine the exhaust. No expensive gantries or flame-suppression systems. More important" — a 3-D rotating image of the engine and fuel tanks appeared amid the azure sky — "the size of the rocket provides such a gravity pressure gradient that no turbopumps are necessary. Chamber pressures can be much lower than those of the Shuttle — three hundred p.s.i for the first stage and sixty p.s.i. for the second — because the fuel is gravity-fed. It's amazing how much weight a four-hundred-foot column of cryogenic fuel—"

"Why don't the sides burst under all that pressure?" she asked.

He halted the playback; the gentle waves froze, the wispy clouds ceased motion. "We'd use heavy-gauge, high-strength steel rather than lighter high-tech stuff."

"Wouldn't that make it too heavy and reduce the payload?"

Chad shook his head. "Remember your solid geometry. A rocket is mostly propellant tanks. The weight of the propellant versus the weight of the structure correspond more or less to volume versus surface area. If this thing were a sphere, it would be the classic cube-square ratio: as the size goes up, the volume increases by the third power while the surface area increases only by the second power. The larger the vehicle, the greater the ratio of propellant to structure. Do you know the basic rocket equation?"

"Vaguely."

"All other things being equal — *caeteris paribus* is the term you MBA's use, right? — the total weight injected into orbit increases at the same rate as the propellant weight. Since the structural weight increases less rapidly than the propellant weight, the bigger the rocket, the greater the percentage of its GLOW — its gross liftoff weight — it can devote to propellant instead of to structure."

"Well, that settles that." Even in VR, she smiled wryly.

"Just for comparison," he said, and a chart spread across the sky.

	Saturn V	**Leviathan**
GLOW	6.4 million pounds	40 million pounds
1st stage thrust	7.7 million pounds	80 million pounds
LEO Payload	240,000 pounds	1.5 million pounds

The simulation continued and the chart vanished. They dove beneath the waves to see the single house-sized engine ignite, generating a cloud of steaming bubbles. Explosive bolts released the concrete ballast and the lumbering ship rose upward.

"Slo-mo?" she asked softly, though Chad heard every word over his headset.

"Nope. Real time. It's slow on lift off, if only from the skewed visual cues you receive from something so big."

The spaceship rose nearly three hundred feet in the air before its exhaust bell cleared the surface. When it did, the water erupted like an undersea volcano. The flame — a bright orange-white — reached down to lap at the deep crater its pressure made in the water. Clouds of steam billowed outward in all directions like a bomb blast.

"Let's follow it!" Chad's excitement was not the least bit simulated.

Into the sky they dogged the burning giant. At the region of maximum dynamic pressure, where the ship received the most buffeting from the atmosphere just before going supersonic, Chad pointed out the structural strength of the solidly-constructed rocket by switching to a false-color image that demonstrated aerodynamic forces at Max-Q. Few points on the structure showed any signs — in the simulation, at least — of undue stress.

At staging, the huge first stage separated spectacularly, drifting along behind the second stage, which sprouted an expanding exhaust bell like an unfolding corrugated sheet-metal umbrella. The engine ignited and pulled swiftly away from the first stage, which sprouted a drogue chute to reduce its tendency to tumble and to prepare it for splashdown and recovery.

They followed the second stage into orbit, Chad commenting: "The wider exhaust nozzle is more efficient in a vacuum. And since the chamber pressures are so low, radiation keeps the bell cool. No need for fancy plumbing. Internal gas pressure is all you need to keep it open."

The engine shut down. They were in orbit.

"Here's where you get a true idea of the scale."

Tiny figures trooped out of a cargo hatch. They looked like ants swarming over a length of sugar cane. Out of nowhere, an entire Space Shuttle appeared, external tanks, SRB's, and orbiter. The complete spacecraft could have fit inside the payload bay with just the tips of the orbiter's stubby wings sticking out.

"This is amazing," Donahue said, almost breathless. "This is as good as going into space for real."

Suddenly, the spacecraft, Earth and stars vanished into a murky grey.

"No," Chad said in a level tone. "We can't fool ourselves into thinking VR is as good as real." He removed his goggles and gloves. "True, I can take a tour of the planets on this thing that blows my mind every time, but we can't become so obsessed with the simulation that we neglect going there for real."

Joscelyn removed her own feedback devices. "Well, those two plans are both magnificent steps along the way. Especially the big one."

"Leviathan. Yes, I'm partial to that one myself."

"How did you ever come up with that?"

Haley smiled. "I didn't. It was once called Sea Witch and proposed by a guy named Ace Roberts."

"And no one's built it yet? It's such a brilliant, cutting-edge concept, why hasn't anyone jumped on it?"

"Ask NASA. They rejected the proposal in the nineteen-sixties."

Donahue's jaw dropped. *"What?"*

"Too simple a concept. Practically no funding needed for research. NASA hates mature technologies. They never wanted to be in the *business* of space travel."

"We've got to show this to Marc."

▼▲▼

Montgomery Barron crashed *Huntress* five times that morning. True, he practiced in a simulator, and even more true, he would not be the pilot of the hunter-killer. Still, Barron wanted to know all he could about the spacecraft. In that, he was an unusual operative in the NSA. He possessed no interest in codes and ciphers, no desire to decrypt and listen in on the terabytes of information flowing around the planet on phone lines, data fibers, and satellite beams. He knew what he had to know: that *something* happening right now on Earth could soon affect the cosmos.

His inferiors performed the drudge work of snooping and spying. The reports they handed him sufficed to tantalize and worry him. Most blatant, of course, was Laurence Poubelle and his X-15 knockoff. A success there might encourage a dozen other crackpots. Then what?

Next down stood startup launch-vehicle companies such as Freespace Orbital, Singapore Spaceways, Ltd., and Deutsche Raumschiff GMBH. NASA and DOT controlled the American ones easily enough, but other governments lacked such efficient chokeholds on access to Space.

Their failures defined Barron's mission. He unstrapped from the simulator and took the data discs with him, performance information on *Huntress* being his own personal responsibility to keep secret, which he did with ferocious care.

Another cloudy, humid, windy day clobbered Bethesda, where the simulator occupied a small warehouse on a back street. The hurricane season, in full swing, lashed South Carolina and made the local weather about as lousy as it gets in late September.

Barron slid his substantial body into the confines of a nondescript federal four-door sedan and headed back toward the Capitol to do what he dreaded: perform emergency osculation on the *gluteus maximi* of seven senators in order to keep Project *Stark Fist* going. This peculiar feat had to be performed without informing the subcommittee exactly why he needed the money.

The atmosphere in the committee room hung as stifling as the air outside, even though conditioned and de-humidified. Barron broke into a sweat born more of anger than trepidation as he gazed one-by-one at the members of the oversight group. Dean, McWhirter, Juliano, Phan, and Woolsey.

Sounds like a law firm, Barron mused, then realized that it could have been, every one of them being attorneys.

Ludlow Woolsey III picked up a sheet of paper to peruse through the reading glasses perched low on his bulbous nose. Silver-grey wisps of hair, still curly decades after losing their color, lay combed back in dignified — if archaic — argent waves.

Hides his alcoholism well, Barron thought, *but his body reveals it nonetheless*. Barron's respect for the legislative branch had evaporated years before and he chafed at every command performance.

Woolsey, as chairman of the oversight committee, led off the inquiry.

"Mr. Barron, I hold in my hand a photocopy from you of yet another budget requisition with the entries concerning your project blacked out with what I can only assume is a very broad and very messy marking pen. Or was it a crayon?" He passed the copy around to the other members.

"Senator Woolsey, gentlemen," Barron said. "As I have stated previously, this is a black project concerned exclusively with national security matters of high-reaching importance. This committee receives enough annual paperwork to orbit the Earth, and I would not want to take up a disproportionate amount of your time if it were not so vital to maintaining the high ground for the United States." *There. You'd have to be an idiot not to get the drift.*

"Mr. Barron, it has been the tradition in such proceedings for the general outlines of such black projects to be presented to the committee in closed session so that we may ascertain a sort of... *outline* of what you intend to do with the taxpayers' money."

As if the taxpayers had a choice. Barron's heartbeat rose. His right foot began to tap imperceptibly against the lush carpeting beneath the table. "With all due respect to the committee — and most of all to its distinguished chairman — may I remind the members that it is within NSA prerogatives to limit access to sensitive material and information even to members of the oversight committee."

Woolsey puffed up like an owl splaying its feathers, bringing to Barron's mind the observation from another senator that some men grew in public service — others simply swelled. He knew that the senator was about to become extremely polite in response to Barron's own forced politesse, a sure sign of contempt on the Hill.

"No one is as quick to acknowledge the honorable and meritorious service of the NSA and its worthy and competent public servants." *Here comes the slam-dunk.* "Nonetheless, the committee finds that without something more to consider than a series of parallel black lines with your name at the top, we must put the matter of your funding into abeyance until such time as we receive something approaching a general idea of what you are up to with seventeen million dollars of the taxpayers' money."

Funny how it's only the taxpayers' money when they don't want to give it out.

Barron nodded in their direction and rose to leave.

"Has this committee dismissed you?" Woolsey asked with a raise of his feathery eyebrows.

Barron bit the inside of his cheek, then forced a smile. "No, your honor."

Woolsey smiled with amused satisfaction and said, "You may go, Mr. Barron. And remember whose money it is you have been spending."

Barron picked his briefcase off the floor and rose to leave, thinking: *As if you thought about it when you spent it on your mistresses, you bloated, boozy tick of a plutocrat.*

That evening he flew the simulator a dozen times, scoring devastating hits on every sortie.

CHAPTER 11

When all else fails, steal the documentation.
— J. Neil Schulman

1 October

Davy Crockett welcomed the return of fall classes with a joy he had not experienced in years. The population of NYU nearly tripled with the start of the new school year, which was good news for the South Bronx Space Project, since it relied on one notorious law of nature: that college students tended to have few compunctions about spending their parents' money.

Over at the warehouse, the skeletal form of their SSTO space chopper took shape. They paid for very little of it with cash. The students donated their labor. The aircraft-quality aluminum-lithium struts came from Penny Giannini, the metal-shop student, who had sweet-talked them out of a surplus-aircraft dealer in Arizona. The propellant tanks were, quite literally, woven in a class on composite materials used for cryogenic storage. The students received top scores for the quality of their work. Ditto for the graphite-fiber rotor blade wrapped in an outer skin of Iconel-X alloy. Off campus — in Passaic — another team constructed the tip rockets using CAD-CAM machinery.

Bernadette spent most mornings and every evening at her computer, stacks of technical journals around her, studying the digital blueprints onscreen, constructing a virtual prototype to put through simulated flight tests, stress analyses, and emergencies. She spent the summer accumulating several megabytes of notes on subjects ancillary to spacecraft design: life support, waste management, celestial and inertial navigation, radiation, and physiological effects of spaceflight.

"Sometimes" she told Davy on their way to the chemistry department, "I think my brain's going to explode from data overload."

She wore an enticing retropunk outfit that day: black t-shirt razored in strategically alluring places, black jeans peppered by shotgun pellets, and more of her silver bracelets and necklaces. She put it all to good use keeping a chemistry prof distracted while Crockett and Friedman — in lab coats — spirited away a cart of elaborate laboratory glassware, chemicals, and solvents.

Sam ferried the equipment to the warehouse while Bernadette and Davy retreated to a wing of the physics dorm that they had gradually appropriated for the South Bronx Project. In a room marked "For Post-Grad Study Only," a dozen technofreaks labored away over computers and microfilm readers.

Bernadette clapped her hands in glee. "This is ten times the computing power I've got!"

Crockett grinned. The doors opened to admit six more undergrads maneuvering a machine the size of a phone booth. Crockett immediately joined in and helped position the machine lengthwise by a section of bare wall.

"Image digitizer for microfilm," he announced to the room at large. The students glued to their consoles did not even hear him, but Bernadette's eyes widened. "Anything those guys find of value, we can now convert to e-text or CAD blueprints!"

"Where'd you find it?"

Davy smiled. "Let's just say it was checked out from the drafting library."

"Library!" Bernadette whipped her wrist up to look at her atom-shaped watch. "I'm supposed to be helping Natasha design spacesuits from our NASA library downloads!" She impetuously gave Davy an impulsive kiss on the lips and raced out of the room.

She had mastered the art of running in spike-heeled boots. For years she walked and ran in the normal human manner of heel-toe, heel-toe. Not only did she wear out her narrow heels, she was also prone to stumbling and turning her ankle. Then it dawned on her that high heels were an inherently unhuman — very nearly *in*human — fashion item. It required a totally different method of ambulation. She learned the fine art of walking and running exclusively on the balls of her feet so that the heels of her shoes and boots barely touched ground at all.

It was one of the myriad reasons she had accumulated for leaving Earth. In free fall, heels were not a problem.

▼ ▲ ▼

Natasha chuckled. Her long black fingers raced across the keyboard, entering data from over two hundred measurements Bernadette had taken from Crockett. The sewing CAD program, which Natasha had specially modified, mulled over the inputs for a few moments, then piece by piece created cutting templates for a customized pressure suit. She ran both hands across her short-cropped hair and locked her fingers behind her head, saying with a note of triumph, "There it is, girl. No muss, no fuss. Are you sure it'll work, though?"

Bernadette looked up from the sewing machine. "Space suits for NASA cost a million bucks a shot and are about as comfortable as wearing pork barrels. I found this research report from the nineteen-sixties by a team that ought to have won the contract bid, except that their suits only cost a thousand dollars each and could be done by any seamstress. NASA probably figured that would have looked cheap, so for three decades astronauts have been lugging around thirty layers of cloth and a refrigerator when they could have been dressed in Spandex tights."

She unfurled the test piece on which she worked. A glistening ebony, it looked like a sheer, form-fitting top from a dominatrix fantasy. "I'm gonna try it." Bernadette removed her blouse and bra.

"I still can't believe those videos were real," Natasha said, helping her slip into the precisely cut and fitted garment.

Bernadette's hair — a luxurious strawberry blond this week — blossomed out of the neck hole. She Velcroed shut the opening and pulled her hands through the sleeves into the cat-burglar gloves. "It was real, all right. Think of it this way..." she slid the tight fabric around her breasts, which gratefully popped into their custom-fit cups. "The difference between down here and up there is only one measly atmosphere of pressure. Our skin is strong enough to withstand that gradient. It has quite a bit of tensile strength. The only problem is that it stretches *too* well. That means we swell up, which drops the pressure in our bloodstream, so our blood outgasses and vapor-locks our hearts. With just this second skin to keep our body volume constant, we don't expand. So we don't boil."

She looked at her figure in the full-length mirror on the inside of the door to Natasha's room. The glove-sleeves revealed every soft curve of her arms. She moved her fingers and wrist to observe the supple ease with which she could move. A deep breath proved that the Spandex stretched enough to allow for easy breathing. A side view, a frontal gaze, and an over-the-shoulder peek evoked a smile of satisfaction. The skin tight fabric described the twin circles of her nipples and areolae.

"Girl, that's a fine form," Natasha said with a smile.

"Sure beats dressing like a polar bear." She struck a fists-on-hip pose, chest thrust proudly outward, and turned toward Natasha. "South Bronx Space Project recruitment poster."

"Take it to Wall Street, hon, and get us some venture capitalists." Natasha saved her screen work and called up a different program. This one displayed a skeleton view of the spaceship with the ventilation system highlighted in 3-D graphics. "Because I just priced our life-support system and molecular sieves are not the cheapest way to filter out impurities."

"Sam can probably order them through the chemistry department."

"I'd just go with lithium hydroxide to scrub the CO_2. I mean, how long do you plan to stay up there?"

"Davy thinks a week would be sufficient time to garner enough positive publicity so that we're not arrested the moment we land."

Natasha rubbed the bridge of her nose and turned her attention toward the computer display. "Don't count on the Man having such a short attention span."

▼ ▲ ▼

Barry Gibbon, even though his busy schedule kept him off-campus most of the time, found that his guest lecturer status allowed him time to lobby the UN members on behalf of the Interplanetary Treaty while still having contact with his most valuable investment — tomorrow's leaders. He began to smell a rat at NYU, though; a space rat in the form of Davy Crockett.

His first hint of something in the air was the wholesale boycott of his class by the Crockett clique. At first, he chalked it up to politics: the boy obviously possessed an antipathy toward the space program. Crockett's father, after all, was a notorious conservative businessman with investments in military hardware. Such nationalist fools, Gibbon mused, never possessed the imagination to view the sublime importance of a humanity united behind a single goal. Some of it must have rubbed off on the son.

An indication that something more ominous might be in process arrived in the form of an off-hand comment by one of his other students. This one — Johnson, Jones, something like that — walked past him one day while talking to a student with whom the professor was unfamiliar. The only phrase he heard distinctly was "I bought the line about it being the set for a student film until they brought in four very real rocket engines." Then the boy saw him and shut up, turning three shades of crimson. Gibbon knew better than to let on that he had overheard the conversation. Time would bring the truth out.

He suspected Crockett, though. The post-grad's silly little wars had ceased abruptly at the same time that he had stopped attending class. He and his cronies were not signed up for the subsequent class this fall, but out of sight rarely meant out of mind to the professor.

He picked up his office phone and punched in a number. The

greatest benefit to being a guru was that one acquired a limitless number of chelas, each one willing to play spy or mere rat-fink.

▼ ▲ ▼

Everett Stevens, NYU administrator of finance, received a troubling report from one of his subordinates. His deep ebony eyes glanced over the report, which chronicled rather complicated attempts to cover up equipment missing from the Physics and Chemistry departments. He smiled coolly.

"Are you going to speak to Professor Gibbon about this?" his assistant asked.

"No," Stevens said. "I'm going straight to the top on this one."

▼ ▲ ▼

"*Crockett!*" Stevens's shout caught Davy's ear from across the fountain in Washington Square Park.

The tall Stevens, immaculately attired in a three-piece suit that contrasted sharply with Crockett's tan fringed jacket and jeans, sat on one of the concrete benches and patted the empty space beside him. His sinister smile intrigued Crockett, who sauntered over to the man, a mask of curiosity on his face.

Stevens calmly mentioned the existence of the report to Crockett, concluding with, "May I point out that it has the Davy Crockett *modus operandi* scrawled all over it."

The post grad slipped into his Tennessee drawl. "Now, what would *I* want with seventy rolls of Kevlar and a ton of graphite fiber?"

"It had better not be for that bulletproof lingerie scheme you had last year."

"I think you're pointin' the stick at the wrong man, Mr. Stevens. I've given up on kid stuff. I'm totally devotin' myself to pursuin' my doctorate."

"In what?"

Crockett gazed at the sky. A gibbous Moon rose between two buildings. "Shucks, Mr. Stevens, I ain't rightly commenced to figure that out yet. But I'm devotin' to it."

"Oh, for God's sake, man." Stevens grasped the student's shoulder with firm brown fingers. "I have seen years of wasted potential in students such as you. School is not a con or a hustle. You should be here to take what knowledge you can get from us, not to grab whatever's not nailed down. I'll be watching you. One hint that you're ripping off this university and it's not just going to be a bill sent to daddy, it's going to be cops and courts. Understand?"

Crockett stared at him with genuine hurt. The accent disappeared from his speech. "Mr. Stevens, I am doing nothing that would injure the reputation or standing of NYU in any way."

"Keep it that way," Stevens said, rising to head back toward the university.

Crockett stayed on the bench, gazing heavenward. Posters for Rama Ben Samesh were stuck on bench backs, on poles, or blew lazily in the breeze. He watched the Moon, faint in the afternoon's hazy air. Bernadette's shadow fell across his face, interrupting his daydream. He turned his eyes to see that her lab coat only partially concealed an unbelievably revealing black catsuit. The electric-blue gym bag at her side bulged spherically with the helmet he knew must be hidden inside.

She frowned. "We tested the skintight pressure suits in the city pound's decompression chamber," she said. "They work. But now we have trouble with the fuel supplier. Dynamic Cryonics wants cash up front and we don't have enough."

Crockett nodded. "Y'all are doing your part. It's time I got off my backside and pulled some strings I hadn't wanted to."

"You don't mean — "

Crockett nodded with weary sadness.

▼ ▲ ▼

In the hotel hall where Sam Friedman conducted his seminar, the crowd numbered over two hundred, mostly composed of wealthier twenty- to thirty-year-old professionals from downtown brokerages and banks. They stood, dressed in a variety of clothing; most evident were karate *ghis* and aerobics outfits. Friedman wore a simple white *ghi* with a red headband and belt. He walked on stage in a lithe, catlike (for him) fashion. Taking a deep breath, he rubbed at his Fu Manchu moustache and spoke in a tone he hoped conveyed a commanding presence.

"Amra the Hunter brings you greetings from the souls in your past. From this humble channel to infinite truths, learn the discipline of Sam Chi to open up your *chakras* and release your *ek*."

He began a clumsy, freestyle attempt at Tai Chi that the entire group faithfully followed as best they could. Bernadette stepped out of the wings to whisper in his ear.

"Davy's going to ask his father for money!"

His right leg in the air, Sam craned his neck back to stare at Bernadette in shock. "But they haven't spoken since he dropped out of Harvard Business College to come here!" He tried to regain his balance with a wild propellering of his arms but stumbled to the floorboards.

The entire seminar — as one — craned their necks back, whirled their arms, contorted their faces, and collapsed.

Bernadette bent to pat Sam's shoulder. "Keep it up, Amra."

▼ ▲ ▼

William David Crockett IV faced William David Crockett III. The elder Crockett's office, richly appointed in expensive, ultramodern chrome and glass contained no hint of a past stretching beyond 1975 in either design or decor. Significantly, no Davy Crockett memorabilia were anywhere in sight. On the smooth, green glass desktop lay a stack of military specification books. Some visible to the younger Crockett displayed titles such as "F-15 ASAT MISSILE BID," "HARDENED ORBITAL DEFENSE INSTALLATIONS — PLANETOID PHASE," "BMDO CONTRACTORS DIRECTORY."

Davy had barged into his father's home — dressed in his finest Brooks Brothers suit — with a simple request. "I'd like to establish a line of credit with the family's investment banker."

In a polished Boston accent that made the Kennedys sound like yokels, the elder Crockett asked, "Now William, what could you possibly want with something so crass as a million dollars?"

Davy, his accent unconsciously reverting to a virtual mimic of his father's, said, "It's for a little... real estate speculation."

His father *harrumphed* and strode to the window overlooking the conservatory. Outside the office, the remainder of the estate revealed the more traditional look of colonial design.

His father possessed strong shoulders and a middle-aged girth that made him look like a college quarterback gone on to comfortable wealth. His hair, still deep brown with just a peppering of grey at the temples, did not have a follicle out of place. Even at home, he wore a three-piece suit. He stood gazing out the window awhile, then asked, "What sort of real estate? Where?"

"I'd rather not say at the moment. It's highly speculative. And I would want to grab it before anyone else has the notion to."

The older man shook his head. "I don't think you have the head for real estate."

Don't get riled, Davy thought, *you're asking a favor, not demanding a right*. "I have to start somewhere, father. Even *the* Davy Crockett dabbled in longshot land investment."

"And in the process lost his buckskin shirt," the other added with quiet contempt. "When he regained what little sanity he had, he entered politics. Had he built upon his heroic image, he might have become President. He didn't learn the art of compromise, though. Instead, he foolishly *believed* his legend, refused to support President Jackson, and went off like a damned sulking fool to the Alamo." The elder Crockett stared at his wayward son. "Now what have you *really* got up your sleeve?"

Davy realized that his father was a dead-end for financing. "Nothin'," he said, his accent reverting to Tennessee. "Just a pie-in-the sky idea."

Father gazed at son. Though they stood roughly the same height, to Davy it seemed as if his elder stared down on him from a considerable vantage. "William, this maudlin fixation on a long-dead ancestor has been the undoing of scores of Crocketts over eight generations. I rejected that ridiculous hero-worship and struck out on my own—"

Davy's hackles raised up. "Davy Crockett wouldn't have had anything to do with lobbying the military."

His father made a disparaging sound. "You really do believe his inflated legend. That's exactly *why*, however, I pursued the career I have — because *he* wouldn't have. And it's brought us everything we own. I now have the influence to put you in the White House within fifteen years. I could still do it if you'd channel your ambition along reasonable lines. This mad scientist route you're pursuing..." He shook his head. "I deal with scientists and engineers all day long. Bean counters and button sorters, all of them. They spend their time writing up grant requests and where do they go with them? To *me*, hat in hand. The days of the pioneering men of science are over. They're all employees now. They work for the MBA's. If I want a bomb, I tell them to design a bomb and they go off and do it. If you choose to become one of them, you're just selling yourself and your family short."

Davy answered with a bitter anger. "If you'd ever instilled in me any real values, something worth selling short, I'd — " His eyes widened. A grin of inspiration and hope spread across his face. "Thanks, Paw!" he cried in his loudest ring-tailed roarer voice. Calculated to annoy his status-conscious father, it achieved that effect grandly. The young Crockett triumphantly drew a cheroot from his inside jacket pocket, lit it up with a match struck on his thumbnail, and took a puff. With an artful snap of his fingertips, he flicked the match across the room. Trailing smoke, it landed squarely in the smoked-glass ashtray an inch from his father's hand. The older man instinctively flinched.

"Paw," he said in his most Southern drawl. "You're going to be proud of me. I'll make my own fame and fortune on my own terms. Y'all wait and see."

His father turned his contemplation back toward the outside view. "I trust," he muttered, "the wait will be a tedious one."

CHAPTER 12

More than 30 years ago, the Air Force was routinely dropping the X-15 spaceplane from a B-52 bomber, flying it to the lower reaches of orbit, and bringing it back for standard landings on runways. The X-15 program was put together quickly, didn't cost much...

The spaceplane does have one drawback that drives NASA crazy: It would be impossible to build a huge spaceplane.... It is for this reason that NASA hates, hates, hates any mention of the word spaceplane.

— **Gregg Easterbrook**

25 October

The design stage for the Daedalus Project ended when Larry Poubelle sat in a VR simulator and flew a successful hypersonic flight to the edge of Space. The specs fed into the computer created a virtual *Nomad* 70 feet long, eighteen feet longer than the X-15 A-2, which it more or less accurately copied. Forty of those feet consisted of the propellant tanks, ten feet of two-seat, tandem cockpit and avionics, and twenty feet of rocket engine. Dry weight tipped the scales at 20,000 pounds; GLOW, the gross liftoff weight with fuel and including the hypersonic drop tanks, maxxed out at 85,000 pounds. The engine, a surplus Rocketdyne J-2 with 68 tonnes of thrust, provided a specific impulse of 390 — just enough to tweak out orbital velocity.

Chemar, sitting behind him in the simulator, backhanded sweat from her forehead. "Deadstick landings," she cursed.

"Nothing to fear," Poubelle said, climbing out of the cockpit and extending his hand to her. "Energy management is a snap using the onboard computers."

The difference between the old X-15 and *Nomad* had less to do with any size or shape changes and more to do with nearly four decades of materials development. Iconel steel remained Poubelle's choice for the main skeletal structure of the spaceplane, but nearly everything else benefited from lighter construction. The drop tanks and inner fuel and oxidizer tanks utilized a spun graphite-fiber composite material. The dorsal and ventral fins used a similar composite. The onboard navigation and flight-control computers possessed as much power as a building-full in 1962 and weighed only ten pounds. The fly-by-light system likewise weighed much less than the original pioneering fly-by-wire system, and responded with nanosecond speed.

Much of what Poubelle used came off-the-shelf from aerospace suppliers hungry for the business — and the publicity. The official logo of the Daedalus Project, the spaceplane rampant surmounted by a disembodied arm-and-wing, appeared in advertisements in industrial magazines, encircled by the phrase "Official Parts Supplier for the Daedalus Project."

Since the X-15 had flown 199 flights, twenty-one in Phase IX, the X-15 A-2 design phase, there existed a mountain of flight data that Poubelle's bright boys pounded into the simulator, then adapted for the upsizing and up-powering of the spaceplane. The simulator utilized a massively parallel supercomputer more powerful than anything used in flight research outside the military, which had long ago abandoned the hypersonic flight regime almost entirely, except for the persistent rumors of pulse-detonation jets flying out of Edwards and Groom Lake, Nevada, to rattle windows in Los Angeles at Mach 7.

All the groundbreaking, trailblazing work done by NASA in its vigorous infancy convinced Poubelle that they would not need many test flights. In fact, he had only planned one. One flight that would earn him the last remaining aviation cherry: the all-time, absolute aircraft altitude record.

Outside the simulator, he addressed the assembled crew of volunteers and salaried genii, Chemar at his side. They had been working for months, most of the volunteers on a come-and-go basis, most of the paid workers on 14 hour days with overtime enthusiastically provided.

"I don't know how many of you have had time to learn the history of the X-15," Poubelle said, standing before a screen that replayed his simulator flight, "but there's a fascinating fact that the Daedalus Project is going to exploit, both for publicity and as a personal salute to the original builders.

"The X-15 achieved the enviable velocity for an aircraft of Mach six point seven and a still-unbeaten aircraft altitude record of three hundred fourteen thousand feet, though never simultaneously. The X-15 actually flew higher, to three hundred fifty-four thousand, two hundred feet with pilot Joe Walker at the stick. Here's the weird part, though: *it didn't count as an altitude record!* Since the official organization that bestows such records — the Federation

Aeronautique Internationale — defines space as beginning at one hundred thousand meters, which is three hundred twenty-eight thousand feet, and since an aircraft would have to beat pilot Bob White's altitude by 3 per cent or about ten thousand feet, there's only one final, slim opportunity to exceed White's altitude and not be disqualified by entering Space at three hundred twenty-eight thousand feet. Only the narrow zone between three hundred twenty-four thousand and three hundred twenty-seven thousand, nine hundred ninety-nine feet will be acceptable to the FAI. It's that altitude range that the simulator's training me to achieve. We're going to shoot our arrow there and hope we hit the mark."

Smiles and applause arose from the group. To set two different and enduring records with *Nomad* was more than they had expected.

An assistant burst into the room carrying a cellphone. "Better take this, sir," he said. "It's Senator Woolsey's office."

Poubelle cracked a smile and held up the phone in his robot arm. "Getting a call from someone's office is like getting a letter from someone's desk. Good afternoon, Senator..." He listened for several moments, the sardonic smile fading then relighting wickedly. "Well, Mr. Barkley, tell the senator that I'd be more than pleased to accept his gracious subpœna." He shut the phone, placed it back in the young volunteer's hand, and said, "Friends, nomads, countrymen! It appears that the Senate subcommittee on Space requests my presence. Consider it more free publicity. I'll do my best to make you proud."

With that, he and D'Asaro retired to his office to plot strategy.

"Woolsey's out to nail us," she said once the door closed.

"Now, why do you think that?" Poubelle said, lighting a cigar with a flourish of his arm. "Perhaps the servants merely want to be informed as to what one of their bosses has planned."

"Naif republican," she muttered.

"Cynical anarchist," he retorted.

"Get on the desk."

"Tempting," he said. "However, I want a disc copy of that simulator flight, a screen large enough for the audience, separate SkyPilot goggles for each committee member, and patch cords so that the networks can download the video portion for added impact on the news. Contact Bill Braverman personally."

He clapped the errant arm around her shoulder. "Let's take some press kits... what, five hundred or so? Bring a thousand. Plus buttons and patches to hand out. Find out which senators have kids and bring them model kits, and the premium mahogany models for the senators themselves. I want a cheering section of about a dozen scattered throughout the room, and have publicity dispatch a mass-media fax about this. Oh, and wear something sexy."

"You've got your nerve, monsieur."

"We'll need all the nerve we've got to turn this to our favor."

28 October

Ludlow Woolsey III displayed nerve in spades. His stout frame no longer possessed the rugged attractiveness that had won him so many votes in the Eisenhower era. His nose, as ripe as a rotting tomato, revealed a network of alcohol-ruptured capillaries and leaned slightly to the left where it had been broken in a literal floor fight during the Watergate hearings. His eyes, somber and very nearly dead, hid darkly beneath folds of flaccid skin and bushy, wayward eyebrows that not even his wife had the temerity to suggest he trim.

His hair, what little was left, sparsely covered a liver-spotted scalp with grey-white strands. His age-enlarged ears earned him the cruel cloakroom nickname Toby, from the mug handles they mimicked.

He could have coasted through the last few years of his final term. Instead, the impending end instilled in him a furious activism, as if many scores remained to be settled before he departed the federal zone.

"Mr. Poubelle," he said in a low rumble. "How can you sit there and tell this committee that your rocket plane is safe when it hasn't even been built yet, let alone tested?"

Poubelle sat next to D'Asaro at the green table facing the elevated panel of committee members. He smiled in wry amusement at the attempted optical illusion. He knew his own stature, and no trick of architecture could rob him of that. He realized, though, that the illusion was for the benefit of the other members of the audience, as well as for the committee members themselves.

D'Asaro sat beside him with regal aplomb, dressed in a light-rust jumpsuit with emerald piping. The front of the suit, zipped modestly up, revealed as much to the imagination as it pretended to hide. The panel addressed questions to Poubelle, but their attention constantly wandered back to her.

"May I remind the committee," Poubelle said, "that the original X-15 flew nearly two hundred flights with only one fatal crash, pilot Mike Adams, twenty-five November, Nineteen sixty-seven, and few enough survivable crash landings to count on one hand? The design proved far safer than the design of the Space Shuttle, which has already killed seven and stands poised — by NASA's own estimate of the odds — to kill again."

"Neither NASA nor the Shuttle are in question here, sir." Energy slowly returned to Woolsey's face as he warmed up for confrontation. "What I want to know is how you think you can plan this without any coordination with NASA, the Department of Transportation, or the Department of Defense, all of who have jurisdiction over outer space."

Poubelle smiled. "The first flight of *Nomad* is not intended to enter the realm of Space, senator. And as with any experimental aircraft, we are keeping a meticulous log of the construction procedure, including photographs and video, for final inspection by an FAA official. As far as the law is concerned, sir, that is all we need to do. We mailed our application for an N-number on September seventh."

"But you do plan to make an orbital flight, am I correct?"

"If *Nomad* checks out on the test flight, yes."

"At that point, then, you will submit to NASA oversight?"

Poubelle shook his head. "No."

"And why not, sir, since it is the law?"

The subpoenaed man leaned on his artificial elbow and eyed the senators one by one, then said, "Because, ladies and gentlemen, it is not the law. There are *statutes* on the books, and *regulations*, yes; but these are not the *law*. If there is any law in America, it is the Constitution, and that law is not a restraint upon *me* as a citizen, it is a restraint upon *you* as members of the government. I do not have to apply for a permit to pursue life, liberty, or property. I do not need your approval to build, to travel, or to explore a new frontier. May I remind this committee that with the American Revolution, the sovereignty devolved to the people, and that as government employees, all of you act not as our masters but simply as our agents?"

"Well, Mister Poubelle, this 'agent' works for many more of the people than just you. I have a sacred duty to protect—"

Chemar spoke up. "How many people *do* you work for, senator? According to published figures, you received three hundred-eighty four thousand, two hundred ninety-one votes in your last election. We have received votes of confidence in the form of purchases and contributions in excess of five-hundred sixty-seven thousand people."

"Mr. Poubelle, Miss D'Asaro. I am afraid I cannot allow — this country cannot allow — such historically blind and obstinately reckless attitudes to prevail. Understand that one of the purposes of these hearings is to establish guidelines for the transfer of spacecraft and facilities to UN control in light of the expected passage of the Interplanetary Treaty. And if you are such a Constitutional scholar, you will know that international treaties supersede even the Constitution."

"As a constraint of government, not as an infringement upon—"

Woolsey's voice rose to near-filibuster strength. "I do not need to be lectured on the document I have sworn an oath to protect. These proceedings are about outer space and about preventing its exploitation by publicity-hungry peddlers of cheap knick-knacks who would risk the safety of millions of persons just to satisfy his own monomaniacal desire to play space cadet with the wealth he's plundered by exposing Americans to the risk of nuclear power pla—"

"*And I say*," Poubelle clenched his fist in a manner deploying several utilities from his robotic arm so that it looked like a Swiss army knife on steroids, "that it's an honor to be labeled a space cadet by one committed to keeping us in the trees eating grubs. This show trial is over." He and Chemar rose as one.

"You have not been dismissed, sir." Woolsey's voice dripped with the polite viciousness.

"No," Poubelle slammed his fist on the table, denting the surface and crazing the finish. Cameras strobed with mad abandon. He raised and pointed a titanium finger toward Woolsey. "Public servant, *you* are dismissed!"

The pair turned and strode out of the chamber, past clots of reporters and onlookers. Some visitors cheered. No senator or senate employee smiled. An attack of such a nature against one constituted an attack against all.

Woolsey shook his head almost imperceptibly when the sergeant-at-arms looked in his direction. *No need to bring him back*, the senator thought. *It's war, now*.

▼ ▲ ▼

Montgomery Barron watched the proceedings on his office TV with an ominous foreboding. *This is just one. One audacious enough to flaunt his plans. There have to be others*.

With both a sense of dread and an overpowering elation, Barron realized that *Stark Fist* may very well see a clear and imminent mission. And Laurence Poubelle's *Nomad* might be its first taste of blood.

▼ ▲ ▼

"*Hooyeh!*" someone shouted over the general din at the South Bronx spaceship factory. "That's a gauntlet thrown if ever there was one!"

"All right already!" Crockett hit the remote to turn off the screen. "This guy's a zillionaire and could have something in orbit within a few months. We've got the jump on him and we've got to maintain it!"

"So we're in a race, Davy?" Penny Giannini lowered the TIG torch she sought to repair rather than replace. Her olive skin dripped with sweat from the welding work, unrelieved by the pervasive humidity this time of year or by the break she took to watch the interrogation. Her short, buzz-cut hair made her look like a butch Marine cleaning a weapon.

Crockett shook his head. "No race. I just intend us to be first." He gazed over at the skeleton of the spacecraft. Beside it stood sixteen wooden crates, each of which held a man-sized rocket engine. "We've got a lot of plumbing to do. Let's get back to work."

▼ ▲ ▼

Instead of watching Laurence Poubelle, "Ace" Roberts took a break from adjusting the gimbals on the forty-foot long cylinder in his driveway to watch something more significant to him. Over his satellite dish, he received live, unedited footage of the rollout of the sixth Space Shuttle orbiter, *Constitution*.

An anonymous NASA announcer spoke as the orbiter, mated to the external tank and solid rocket boosters, moved slowly on its massive conveyor toward pad 39B. "It's a stately pace befitting the sixth and undoubtedly last of the first generation orbiters. *Constitution* — built as a bailout for aerospace companies hurt by cutbacks in military spending — was designed for fast turnaround and long-range missions. Its first flight — scheduled for November fifteenth — will be the much-anticipated month-long Enduro flight. Several firsts will be established on this ninety-third flight of the STS: first flight of *Constitution*, first use of the South American Laboratory for Space Agriculture, first test of the Advanced Crew Cleanliness System, and — most significantly — the first flight with a female shuttle commander, astronaut Tammy Reis."

Ace perked up his ears and put down the grease can. He had followed Tammy's astronaut career with the pride of a surrogate uncle, taking the time to watch her two previous flights. This, though, was news to him. She never wrote him anymore.

11 April, 1981

The first time he met her, she was just this runt of a teenager tagging along behind an older boy in a Saratoga surplus yard where Roberts loaded up his truck with sheet aluminum and — found purely by luck — the tip tank off an old Beechcraft. He looked at it and knew immediately that the front third would make an ideal nose cone for his rocket. Nearby, he heard two adolescents arguing.

"I told you it wouldn't go up." The boy's face held no trace of self-satisfaction. If anything, he looked angry that he had won their bet.

"Launch delays," the girl said, "are inevitable. Especially on the first *manned* flight of a spacecraft that's never even been test-launched before! Admit it, you never expected the STS to be built and there it is, ready to go!"

The duo rummaged through some bins. The boy looked to be about seventeen or eighteen, though his serious, steady gaze revealed a mind operating with a much older, almost anachronistic maturity. Ace's grandfather, who long ago regaled him with stories of travelling the Oregon Trail in a prairie schooner, had that look in his eyes. Roberts even had that look once, before it became a narrow peer from too many nights spent preparing reports, rewriting permit applications, and returning the stare of bemused visitors watching him build a rocket in his driveway.

The intense young man peaked out at six feet tall. He wore navy blue cargo pants with multiple pockets and a surplus Swiss Army leather cartridge belt on which every pouch was stuffed to overflowing with necessities. He kept his sandy hair trimmed short and functional and wore an olive drab baseball cap with military-style scrambled eggs on the brim and the appellation *Space Cadet* embroidered on the front. The young woman, only just beginning to achieve her teenage figure, stood a full foot shorter. Her long black hair lay braided and pinned into a tight bun a few degrees to the rear of her head's centerline. She wore a blue jumpsuit of her own making, a copy of what the shuttle pilots would wear on the upcoming flight of *Columbia*. She, too, sported a cartridge belt, draped bandolier-style across her chest. They could have been visiting spacefarers in some science-fiction adventure film, and both appeared to like the feeling.

"Look at this." The boy held up a canister of crackers. "Civil Defense, vintage Nineteen Sixty-Two. Bet they taste great." He put it down. "Anyway, I didn't say it would never fly, just that it would never meet the ridiculous promises they made. Two-week turnaround, launch-on-demand — we saw what a joke that was, yesterday — and especially the hundred-fifty-dollars-per-pound-to-orbit costs. They may *charge* customers that much, but the rest of the cost is subsidized by you-know-whom."

"They have to attract customers—"

"Hey, if they built something cheap and easy to mass-produce, you and I and a million others would be customers. They just wanted something that would look nifty and sluice tax doll—"

"You two kids talking about the Shuttle?"

They both turned toward Roberts to see a leathery man in his mid-fifties, dusty fedora perched way back on his head, gazing at them with intense interest. Draped over one arm was his last (he promised himself) purchase of the day: a surplus Air Force high altitude pressure suit, complete with a helmet, which he grasped under his other arm.

"Yes," the girl said brightly. "He thinks it's a flying pork barrel and I think it's the *Mayflower* of Space."

Ace smiled. "Could be both, you know."

"Could be the *Titanic*," the boy muttered. "It's irrelevant, anyway, since humanity will find other ways to get there."

She shrugged in agreement. "In fact, we're working on our ow—" An elbow to the ribs from her friend cut off her sentence, but not before the listener caught the gist.

"Is that so? We seem to be birds of a feather. My name's Roberts. My friends call me 'Ace.' So can you."

"Truman Roberts?"

Roberts grinned, threw the pressure suit and helmet into the cab of the truck, then turned to say, "Call me 'Ace.' I haven't used 'Truman' since Truman was president."

"I'm Paul Volnos. This is Tammy Reis" — he hooked a thumb toward the runt, who could not have hit fifteen years, at least not very hard — "and we'd love to see your rocketship."

Ace laughed out loud, tanned skin wrinkling around his eyes. "Didn't your folks teach you not to talk to strangers?"

The boy smiled. "You're no stranger to me. You invented the ocean-launched solid-rocket missile for the Navy and worked with Von Braun and Kraft Ehrike on the XSL-01 Moonship with aircraft re-entry concept back in the late Fifties. Then you went to work for—"

"That's okay, son, I know my own resume."

Tammy's eyes widened. "What sort of rocket is it?"

Ace smiled. "One-man orbital intended to use three Aerobee Three-Fifties, two for the first stage, one for the second."

Paul performed swift mental calculations and said, "You won't make it. It wouldn't even lift the re-entry capsule."

"Who said anything about re-entry? It's intended to be a one-way trip to the Space Station, when it gets built. Two hundred-fifty pound payload, max."

Paul snorted. "They wouldn't let any of *us* onboard. We're just mere citizens. We just pay for it."

"I don't think they'd turn me away. They might send me home on the next shuttle, though."

"I'd like to see it!" Tammy said.

"No free peeks. If you come, you've got to do some work."

Tammy looked up at Paul with imploring eyes.

"You don't need *my* permission," he said.

She frowned. "I don't *want* your permission. I want you to come, too!"

He gazed at her with a big-brother glower. "I wouldn't let you run off alone. You're not big enough to cross the street by yourself." That earned him a quick jab in the solar plexus.

Ace smiled and clapped a grizzled hand on the boy's shoulder. "You're okay, kid. All right. Hop in your car and follow me up Bear Creek Road."

▼ ▲ ▼

Paul maneuvered his AMC Pacer — bought in extremely used condition more for price than because it looked like a futuristic bubble-car — up the long driveway to Roberts's ten acre property. Tammy jumped out and ran to the garage as Roberts disappeared inside it, gazing with her eager eyes at a pack-rat paradise: two long work benches on either side of a central trailer rig supporting Ace's Space Age version of the Model T.

Two-thirds of the spacecraft extended beyond the confines of the garage, but was covered by a canopy consisting of geodesic triangles of aluminum framework and rainbow-colored sheets of parachute nylon. The central cylinder measured sixty feet long and three feet in diameter, flanked by two forty-foot tubes of the same diameter. Two of the Aerobee 350 engines lay in place in the boosters, their exhaust bells cocooned in blue shrink wrap. The third engine lay in parts on one bench and what was presumably the guidance system lay on the other bench in even smaller pieces. Beneath the benches were stacked frayed cardboard boxes and wooden liquor crates filled to overflowing with dusty, rusty, or grime-coated remnants of a fading technology that once had been the promise of every kid's future.

Paul still saw that future and brightened instantly upon entering the sacred temple. The engine captured his attention and he hovered over it, examining every bend of the plumbing that wrapped around the exhaust bell, serving the dual purpose of both cooling the bell and pre-heating the fuel and oxidizer.

"Wow!" Tammy said, her eyes wide. "It looks like a miniature Delta!" She ran a hand over the sleek aluminum cylinders.

Ace smiled at the two of them in perfect understanding. There was something about aluminum that fascinated him even more than cold steel. Aluminum was light, both in weight and in its silvery color. Soft and ductile, it could bend in his hands; yet it was also strong enough to stand the flaming violence of a launch into Space. It all depended on how it was created, how pure and consistent it was, how one handled it while shaping and forming it, how well one knew its properties and could predict its behavior.

Paul ran his fingers along the engine tubing, feeling the cool, smooth texture. Roberts saw that and said, "Whoa there, son. White gloves only on the engine. One greasy fingerprint could ruin it!"

"Sorry." The young man joined Ace in unloading the truck. "What can we do to help you?"

The old man lowered the tip tank to the driveway, then jumped down to assist Paul in placing it on a dolly. "You're doing it, boy. Things seem to be getting heavier every year."

▼ ▲ ▼

That spring and summer, Paul and Tammy spent long days working with Ace on his rocket, scrounging at junkyards for bits and pieces required from steering controls, fuel piping, fins. Tammy hollered with joy when she discovered a scratch-free acrylic submarine porthole at a marine surplus store: it became the viewing port for the pilot, who would fly the rocket standing up. Some days they would return home dog-tired to the sound of worried and irritated parents. More than once, Ace had to placate the adults with a phone call or three.

Over the next few years Tammy earned her private pilot's certificate at the youngest age possible; Paul, at Ace's urging, entered his model rocket designs in state-wide contests and routinely won. He became bored with the accolades and impatient with the small stuff — seven-foot tall rockets that regularly hit 50,000 foot altitude — and threw his efforts into Ace's project. He learned first hand about liquid-fuel rockets, about phenomena of large spacecraft such as pogoing, wherein the thrust of a poorly designed rocket creates a devastating vibration that can tear the vehicle apart. Most important of all, though, were the values tacitly imparted to him by working with Ace. The old man never let any setback deter him. If a part would not fit or if something broke, he simply set about to fix the problem with a dogged, purposeful effort.

While Tammy began to spend more and more time at the airport, Paul learned more about the truth of backyard rocketry. He watched as Ace accumulated stack upon stack of forms, correspondence, and notices concerning his efforts.

"There's an old saying," he told Paul more than once. "When the weight of the paperwork equals the weight of the spacecraft, it's ready to launch."

"Why do they make it so hard to go into Space?"

Ace snorted out a good-humored laugh. "I could be generous and say it's that they want to ensure that everyone below us is absolutely safe from falling debris, but they don't slap the sort of regulations on aircraft that they do on spacecraft, and falling airplanes kill hundreds every year. With the exception of a few Russki cosmonauts, no one's ever been killed by spacecraft. Missiles, yes — governments intend for people to be killed by missiles, and somehow that's all right — but rocket flight's pretty damned safe. No..." he put the greasy rag down and leaned against the work bench. "I'd say — and this comes from personal experience, mind you — that NASA simply doesn't want to be shown up by anyone. The Shuttle's pretty impressive, but I could build a water-launched rocket using standard supertanker construction techniques and facilities that would carry thirty times what the shuttle carries to orbit at one seventieth the cost per pound. NASA looked at my design in the 'Sixties. They rejected it. Couldn't spread the work around to employ enough congressional districts to ensure funding, though they wouldn't admit that was the reason. It could be built in one dry dock by one shipbuilding company." For a moment, his gaze turned far from where they were, then he shook his head and concentrated once again on the matter at hand.

28 October, Year Two

Ace watched with immense pride *Constitution*'s crawl toward Pad 39B, almost as if his own daughter were about to punch through the sky in that contraption. Then he thought of Paul, since Tammy and he were inseparable in the older man's mind, and was overcome by regret at the lost talent, the vision Paul had abandoned. He gazed at the shuttle and wondered why the boy could not have settled for half a dream instead of none.

CHAPTER 13

How tragic. Is that the one the schoolteacher was on?
— President Ronald W. Reagan
Immediate reaction to news of *Challenger* disaster

What NASA did was illegal. Against the law. I don't know how to make it any plainer or what good it will do. The whole thing stinks.
— Dr. Ronald Wright
Broward County medical examiner,
on NASA's refusal to allow legally-required
autopsies on astronaut's remains

The sacrifice of your loved ones has stirred the soul of our nation, and, through the pain, our hearts have been opened to a profound truth.
— President Ronald W. Reagan
Eulogy for the Challenger *Seven*

30 December

"Get them in the cans," a voice boomed.

"What if they fall off the truck?" another voice asked with nervous hesitation.

She feared that just such a disaster might happen. That somehow one of the garbage cans would roll off the truck and dump its contents onto Highway A1A. Dump a black body bag containing the water-soaked, shark-eaten remains of a *Challenger* astronaut.

An ominous presence watched her in the night as she lifted one of the limp, heavy bags and lowered it into the trash can. It slid in like a sack of wet kitchen scraps. The body within was no longer whole; impact with the sea had torn it apart, sliced into pieces by its restraining straps.

Safety belts, she thought with bitter irony, putting a lid on the first can and moving on to the second. She read the name tag on the bag and started to weep.

"Keep going," the distant voice demanded. "We've got to bury the evidence."

She stood now above the mouth of an open missile silo. An impossibly huge flatbed truck dumped the shattered remains of *Challenger* down into the black depths of the hole. Suddenly, her truck tilted, too, and the three garbage cans rolled off the back and into oblivion, followed by four more black, limp bags, then the volumes of the Rogers Commission report.

"There," the voice said. "Out of sight, out of mind." Concrete poured into the hole, sloshing back and forth in a watery grey stream to drown the shattered orbiter and the seven bodies until nothing was visible but a flat circle of cement. Workmen troweled it flat. Children knelt at the edge to press their handprints into the fresh surface.

She turned to face the voice. Behind her stood seven dark figures: five men, two women. They reached out to push her into a yawning chasm a hundred times larger than the burial shaft. Cold, clammy hands shoved her, sent her spiraling over the edge. Falling, falling into endless black.

Tammy awakened overcome by a wave of nausea. Then she realized where she lay and what day it was.

Today she would be the first commander of Orbiter *Constitution*.

▼ ▲ ▼

She could not shake the dreams. They always centered around *Challenger*. They always ended in falling; falling out of the sky or falling into darkness. She knew other astronauts sometimes experienced such nightmares, though how often was a question best left unasked. These images came to her on the average of once a week or more. She dared not mention it to anyone out of fear that she might be grounded.

Far greater than blowing up was an astronaut's fear of being grounded. With so few Shuttle flights — averaging five a year — one could train for half a decade just to spend one week in Space. To be grounded was tantamount to professional death; any intentional act that resulted in a grounding the equivalent of professional suicide. More than any other factor, this fear of being yanked from the crew roster engendered the tight-lipped, frosty exterior many in the astronaut corps exhibited. Their stoic silence masked the quiet dread of losing their chance to ride that towering pile of high explosives into the unknown.

Tammy remembered a time before the nightmares. A time when the world seemed fresh and open and beckoning to her. The feeling never lasted long.

She celebrated her nineteenth birthday the day before *Challenger* flight 51-L, and took her car down to Cape Canaveral to watch the twenty-fifth Shuttle launch as her own private birthday gift. The nation's youngest astronaut trainee — as the press billed her upon her acceptance the month before — still found it necessary to use her good looks to finesse an automobile pass for the NASA Causeway from someone in order to park her car within view of Launch Complex 39. The chillingly cold day provided sharp and clear air. Everything stood out in crystalline relief like a snapshot of Heaven.

For some, it was Heaven frozen over. Orchard owners struggled to save their orange groves, setting out heaters and smudge pots to fend off the ice. School children bundled up as they seldom had before. Waiting for their busses, they played breath-frost games under the deep blue, cloudless Florida sky. Commuters cursed their cars, some of which refused to start, some whose freeze plugs had pushed out, saving their engine blocks but disabling the machines for the day.

At Kennedy Space Center, a larger piece of machinery stood immobile.

Video cameras planted around Pad 39B channeled images back to the Launch Control Center. Everywhere they looked, long, clear icicles hung like crystal daggers from cables, tubing, hand rails and stairways.

To Tammy, far from Pad 39B and away from her TV set, it was the most beautiful day imaginable. As she sat bundled up in her convertible with the top down and a thermos of hot chocolate, she pondered her bright future as part of NASA and its glorious mission. She felt a kinship with one of the crew members, and it wasn't the one with whom most of the nation identified. The press made a big deal about Christa McAuliffe, the teacher, the first common citizen-astronaut, as if all Americans *must* cheer her on. Tamara Reis, however, admired the other woman on the flight, Judy Resnik, a trained and experienced astronaut.

Tammy ran a hand through her dark hair, cut and curled to resemble Resnik's trademark shag style. She often fantasized how it would feel for her hair to drift around her as Judy's had in videos from her previous flight.

The countdown proceeded on the car radio. At T-minus six seconds, the three shuttle engines flashed into life. At her distance, there was no sound at first, just an eerie silence. Then came the solid rocket ignition. Instantly, in a white-hot cloud of smoke and flame, *Challenger* leapt upward. The low roar of the engines washed over her, followed shortly by the stunning thunder of the SRB's. It struck her solidly, like humanity's fist pounding on the heavens. She gloried in the sound that enveloped her like the hand of a titan, watching the ascending column lengthen and thicken with every second as if it were that giant's arm reaching up into the sky.

Within a minute, *Challenger* receded to near-invisibility. Only by the condensation trail it left could Tammy tell where it was. She hefted a pair of binoculars to track the vehicle. A dot of white at the top of the smoky pillar, just above an orange glow, marked the spaceship's location.

"Go, Judy," she whispered, though she could have shouted and still barely have heard it above the receding thunder. "Go, space rats!" Paul had called her a space rat once, a term she immediately embraced with perverse joy. It was just about all she had left of him, now.

After half a minute, she turned on the car radio to listen to the coverage. They should be throttling back the three main engines to sixty-five per cent power as they passed through Max-Q, the region of maximum dynamic pressure where the force of the supersonic spacecraft hitting the thin atmosphere nine miles up generated pressure of thousands of pounds per square foot on every forward part of the shuttle. Safely past that region, pilot Mike Smith would throttle up the SRB's to one hundred four per cent of their rated power.

"Challenger, *go with throttleup,"* the voice of Mission Control said.

"Roger," Commander Dick Scobee confirmed. *"Go with throttleup."*

Watching through the binoculars, Tammy saw something wrong. Something horribly wrong.

Red-orange flames exploded around the spacecraft. Her breath froze in her chest as a cloud of vapor and smoke blasted outward from the shuttle, expanding to fill the view through her binoculars. Letting them drop, she stared at the sky in terror. There, at the top of the perfect arc of the exhaust trail hung a growing, billowing rust-hued cloud from which two horns of white emerged, corkscrewing wildly about. Below it, like a devil's beard, thin streamers of debris trailed smoke downward along ballistic trajectories.

"One minute, fifteen seconds," Mission Control calmly reported, as if the explosion had not happened. *"Velocity twenty-nine hundred feet per second, altitude nine nautical miles. Downrange distance seven nautical miles."*

No! her heart cried out as she watched transfixed. The cloud continued to expand, the SRB's flew uncontrolled on divergent paths, smoking pieces rained from the fireball. Then, its incomprehensible energy expended, the cloud ceased to billow, appearing to freeze in the icy air.

Tammy searched the sky in vain for some sign that the shuttle still climbed. She tilted the binoculars in desperate hope of finding an exhaust plume, or the flash of sunlight on the orbiter's wings. Her mind screamed *RTLS! RTLS!* Deep inside, though, she knew there would be no return to launch site. The all-consuming blast erased *Challenger* from the sky, from her life, from their families, from the world.

As if in a delirium, the voice of Mission Control spoke with a stunned incomprehension: *"Flight controllers are looking very carefully at the situation."* Then he added, with terrifying understatement, *"Obviously a major malfunction. We have no downlink."*

A whirling emptiness grew inside the pit of her stomach. The high-altitude winds slowly dispersed the aborted trail that led halfway to heaven. *No!* was all she could think. *No!* As if the invocation could drive the flaming fuel back into its tank, as if the prayer of denial might pluck the pieces of *Challenger* from the sky and reassemble them, as if the force of her will could breath life back into the astronauts.

It took her a moment to realize that the astronauts were dead. The orbiter contained no ejection seats, the crew wore no parachutes. If the blast consumed the orbiter, then all seven doubtless burned to death an instant before shattering at hypersonic speed against the wall of air from which *Challenger* no longer protected them.

Around her, cars started up and moved down the causeway at a slow, somber pace. She once attended an air show where an old P-51-D flew into the runway after an inside loop. First came the shock of impact and the horrified cries from the onlookers, then the unforgettable sight of the fireball sliding down the concrete trailing oily black smoke, then a stunned silence as the audience wandered back to their cars in a daze. The show went on, though, for the other pilots always knew that death flew alongside them on every flight.

Tammy Reis knew that the remaining astronauts would want to continue, but she also knew that NASA's show would not go on. And for two and a half years, it did not.

CHAPTER 14

We absolutely cannot get anything done anymore. We've stopped thinking and stopped innovating. All NASA energy now goes to endlessly rejustifying the budgets for bad ideas from the past....

The way you get ahead inside NASA is by denying there are problems and being the loudest one to attach the blame for anything that goes wrong to critics.

— Former NASA official

29 January, 1986

Astronaut trainee Reis reported for work the next morning to witness a space program as fragmented as the remains of *Challenger* on the ocean floor. Though the level of activity was high — workers and managers rushed to and fro carrying enormous stacks of documents, reels of data- and videotape, and trays of printout — everyone moved as if in a horrible nightmare.

Upon reaching the classroom, she learned that a lecture concerning the shuttle's robotic arm had been canceled. Instead, the dozen astronauts in her group gathered to mourn, in their muted way, their fallen compatriots. A television set broadcast the latest news, which consisted mostly of speculation, since NASA management had uncharacteristically clamped down a total news blackout to the point of seizing all film and video from cameras at the Cape and official viewing sites up and down the coast. The mourning turned quickly to angry speculation.

The first to broach the subject was Jon Franck, a former naval aviator and test pilot now astronaut specializing in solar research. He was tall for an astronaut, with a blond and lanky mountain-boy look to him. A three-time shuttle commander with a midwest twang part Hoosier and part Jayhawker — Jayhoosier, Tammy labeled it — Franck turned to glower darkly at the rest of the astronauts.

"I heard all sorts of things last night," he said, running the back of his hand along the tip of his chin. "The self-destruct charges going off on the ET, premature SRB separation, O-ring burnthrough, Libyan terrorists, Soviet particle beam weapons and Tesla scalar devices. Even rumors that the CIA did it to *blame* on Libya or that NASA did it to create a new generation of space martyrs now that nearly no one remembers Grissom, Chaffee, and White."

"You mean," a weary man's voice said, "you didn't hear the one about Voyager passing by Uranus last week and setting off a Sentinel to fire a warning shot at us? Or Comet Halley bringing its curse back to Earth?"

The attempt at gallows humor fell flat. "I vote for something going wrong with the SRB. We've had O-ring charring on half the flights."

"And the ET didn't explode," Scott Boyd offered. Boyd was a compact man, short, muscular, intelligent and driven; astronaut material of the old school. He'd make shuttle commander someday, Reis was sure of that. "At nine miles up, there's practically no atmosphere. An explosion would have created a rapidly expanding fireball spreading over the sky. What we saw was the ET rupturing and voiding its contents, which subsequently caught fire and burned. That was a cloud of water vapor. I'd estimate that we saw less than a sixth of the energy that would have been released by an actual explosion."

"So *Challenger* broke apart under aerodynamic stress?" Tammy asked. It was odd to participate in such a discussion, as if it were just another in the long string of classes that she had to attend as part of ground school.

Boyd nodded slowly. Most of the others knew what that meant. Franck voiced it. "That means they weren't incinerated."

Boyd nodded again. "I think they're going to find the crew compartment."

Tammy shuddered.

"Gentlemen," a voice behind them said. "Ladies."

The twelve turned around to see J. E. B. Manners — "Bad" Manners, as other NASA personnel called him — standing in the doorway. Manners was once an astronaut and now served as an instructor. His curly hair had long since turned grey and receded. His usual wry smile was missing, replaced by a set jaw and bloodless lips.

"I've been directed," he said in a level tone, "to speak to you about the importance of maintaining an even strain while the investigation into Fifty-One El progresses. You all have families. You all must know what the families of the seven are going through right now. The astronaut corps does not want to do or say anything that would increase their grief. Do I make myself clear?"

Silent assent. The astronauts all served on the same team; all knew the pain their own families would feel. Franck asked, "Any news?"

Manners nodded. "Over a score of aircraft and vessels searching six thousand square miles. Some floating debris. Maybe the top of the ET off of Savannah. Not much."

"What about the crew cabin?" Tammy asked hesitantly.

Manners pinioned her with his gaze. "Won't be found," he said. "Disintegrated in the explosion. End of story." He continued to stare at her for a few seconds longer, as if sizing her up or silently reproving her. Then he looked grimly at the whole group.

"During the investigation, NASA wants no one talking to the press. Any speculation or leaks about our progress could bring unwarranted grief to the families of the crew. Now let's all get back to work."

"For what?" Franck asked coolly. "The program's not going anywhere now. There's not going to be another flight for months, maybe years. I was scheduled for one sixteen months from now. I may not see it until the 'nineties."

Manners glared at the man. "I think it's high time we stopped thinking about our own selfish concerns and pull together on this. The crew would have wanted us to go on."

8 March, 1986

NASA moved on — in the fashion of an automobile lurching as it ran out of gas — for more than a month as revelation after revelation stunned the tight-knit astronaut corps.

The investigation teams concluded from video footage and telemetry that the cause of the disaster was most likely an O-ring burnthrough on the right-hand SRB. The president used his powers of rhetoric to comfort the nation, which only polarized the astronauts even more. Some resigned. Others transferred to non-flight positions. Some, such as Tammy Reis, stuck to the corps despite everything, and wondered why they did.

"Target Sixty-Seven," Jon Franck whispered to Tammy Reis, "is the crew cabin."

Reis stared at her fellow astronaut. They sat in the rear annex of a night club called The Heat Shield, a bar catering to the spacefarers. The owner of The Heat Shield, Ed Laird, an ex-astronaut, understood the need for a place of refuge from reporters, gawkers, and astro-groupies. The black-tiled Ablation Room in the rear served the astronauts privately, exclusively, and discreetly. A pair of surly, burly bouncers kept reporters and other groundhogs out. Ed protected his special customers well.

Jon Franck was never one given to whispers, especially in the privacy of the Ablation Room. Now, though, he spoke like a spy in a den of spies.

"Divers from *Preserver* found the Five-Seven-Six bulkhead. Intact."

Reis shook her head. "I figured they might." Her whisper was just as low. "They weren't blown up, then. Just blown out."

Franck nodded his head with its shorter-than-regulation hair, recently trimmed now that he was part of the presidential commission investigating the *Challenger* disaster. Reis noticed that it had changed him.

"They found the crew," was all he added. He took a sip of his bourbon and branch water, leaned back in the soft vinyl chair, and gazed around the room.

Other tables supported the glasses, ashtrays, and elbows of nearly half the astronaut corps. Back in the heyday of Ed Laird, a bar on Highway A1A always hosted at least a trio of astronauts at some point every night. And they all looked nearly the same. White men in their thirties and forties, crewcut, short, friendly but quiet (until a few drinks lit their engines).

Now, the Ablation Room hosted nearly two dozen men and women. White, black, yellow, brown, red, and startling pink. From astronaut trainees fresh out of college — of which Tammy was the youngest — to a mission specialist in her sixties. Not all of them had been into Space yet. Little more than a month after the fall of *Challenger*, many wondered whether they would get there at all.

Reis took a deep breath, let it out slowly. Her hand shook lifting the Kahlúa and cream to her lips. "Dead from impact, then," she said softly.

"I doubt that they drowned." Franck finished off his drink and upended the glass, which was swiftly replaced by Laird, who personally tended his flock and frankly overlooked the fact that Tammy was underage. Old enough to fly spacecraft, he figured, old enough to drink.

"You heard, right?" Ed Laird looked nothing like a former astronaut. His leonine grey hair hung down to the collar of a black turtleneck sweater beneath the navy blue seaman's coat. His beard — still jet black — formed a sharp spade on his chin. He looked for all the world like a ship's captain from an old pulp adventure story. Only the small silver astronaut wings on his lapel revealed that he had once left Earth's surface to sail upon the New Sea.

Reis and Franck nodded.

Laird shook his head and wiped his hands on a bar towel. He was not the sort to waste his breath on "if only," and "might-have-been." He strode back to the bar with just a mutter to himself about "suit-and-tie scum."

Reis's mind dwelt on the might-have-beens, though. If only they hadn't launched on that cold January morning. If only NASA management hadn't been so eager to have the shuttle up in time for the president's State of the Union speech. Sure, there'd been no actual presidential order to do so, but everyone *knew* that's what was wanted. No one asked about the coincidence of the two events being planned for the same day. Everyone knew why — it was in the blood to know instantly what higher-ups wanted. Anyone without that knack did not rise in the organization. It was natural selection for bureaucracies. And Tammy Reis was as prone to act unquestioningly as any other government employee.

"Impact," Reis whispered. "From nine miles up." Unbidden, her mind calculated the time it took to fall that far. Two, maybe three minutes. Terminal velocity of something shaped like the crew cabin would be in the 180 to 250 mile-per-hour range, depending on how much junk trailed behind it.

Her mind would not leave the image alone. She had to know more.

"They found the crew?" She could not utter the word *bodies*.

Franck nodded. He gazed at her levelly, unblinking. "Six weeks under ninety-five feet of warm water. Not much left."

Reis sipped slowly at her drink. The shock of *Challenger* had long since passed. Even though the point had very rarely been driven home, they knew the risks inherent in space travel as much as everyone else knew the risks of highway travel, or every pilot understood the dangers of flying. Once in a while, reality taught the lesson in painful, personal ways. That did not scare many people out of cars or planes, and would never stop an astronaut, at least not one with the right stuff.

Once, she had witnessed the recovery of a body from the Florida waters while on a team in search of a missing T-38A trainer jet. The pilot had been down for a week when civilian skin divers located the wreck. The remains gingerly hauled up looked like whitish-grey gelatin out of which sea life had snapped greedy chunks. Much of the skeleton lay exposed to the sea, serving as anchor points for small crustaceans.

She dully took another sip. The astronaut corps comprised an unusual group — tight-knit in that everyone knew and worked with everyone else at some point in their professional lives, yet tight-lipped, reticent, and aloof among one another in so many ways. She, being a newcomer, knew even less about her fellow astronauts. It was not until she read the memorials that she discovered Ellison Onizuka was a Buddhist, or that Judy Resnik — they called her "J.R." — could play the piano.

The thought of them on the floor of the Atlantic seemed ignoble. Somehow, back when everyone thought they had burned up in what looked like a fireball, their deaths seemed purer, more appropriate for astronauts. To be cremated in the flames of your own spacecraft, to be scattered into Space or up into the atmosphere of your home world seemed hauntingly poetic.

The poetry turned into abomination as the truth revealed itself. *Challenger* had not risen from Earth and exploded into space.

Challenger fell.

And so fell Tamara Reis's heart.

CHAPTER 15

Immediately upon your arrival to Space, your body begins to make accommodations to free fall. Some are not so pleasant. The liquids in your body redistribute themselves. No longer pulled by gravity (which your body has learned to compensate for over a billion years of evolution), your legs force the fluids to the "upper" part of your body. Your face puffs up and turns ruddy. The pressure on your sinuses makes you feel as if a cold is coming on. Your eyes get a little bloodshot. You may sneeze a lot, or sound nasal when you speak. Your legs will get skinny, almost looking as if they are atrophying.

Blood pooling in your chest cuts down on your lung capacity. You'll begin growing a few inches. This is due not just to the fact that you are weightless. The fluid redistribution flows to your spine, too. The discs between your vertebrae absorb this fluid and swell, pushing the bones farther apart. So you're getting taller.

At the same time, this redistribution of fluids sends jumbled signals to your body. You no longer feel thirsty, since your brain is getting a "full" signal from your thoracic zones. You have to remind yourself to drink regularly or you'll get dehydrated. Even so, you'll lose five pounds or more (in terms of mass) over the next few weeks. None of these changes are permanent: if you return to Earth, you'll get shorter and regain your water-weight.

But you don't intend to return to Earth, do you?

— The Orbital Settlers' Guide

30 December, Year Two

Distracted by all the preparations, Tammy did not notice the relative silence of the crew cabin until the whine of the *Constitution*'s turbopumps set it in sharp relief. Then came the roar of the main engines, then the terrible six-second wait. As *Constitution* strained at its massive clamps, computers verified all three engines firing and operating properly. Only then did the command go out to ignite the SRB's. The pair of solid rocket boosters had to fire simultaneously and with identical thrust. If one engine failed to ignite, or ignited too late, or delivered sub-critical thrust, the STS would tumble over sideways like some giant pinwheel firework and demolish launch pad 39A . With no way to shut down the solid rockets — as they could the liquid-fueled main engines — once the SRB's roared, the Shuttle crew irrevocably committed their bodies to Space — or to Eternity.

The SRB's ignited flawlessly. Tammy felt only a slight pressure from the liftoff. Within seconds, however, the pressure grew greater and greater. The dizzying sensation of being shoved forward, as if from a catapult on an aircraft carrier, excited her more than could a kiss from any lover. Unlike the catapult though, the sensation lingered, increasing. She knew that her childhood decision to train for an astronaut career by riding roller coasters had been the correct one. She lay strapped onto an infinite elevator with the UP button punched good and hard.

They hit Max-Q at eight miles up, over the Atlantic, and *Constitution* trembled like a stallion galloping at heart-stopping speed. Within seconds, the worst Earth's atmosphere could do lay behind them, and the engines throttled up to one hundred four percent of their rated power.

The renewed force of acceleration pressed her into the hard, narrow seat at four times her earthly weight. She sought this her entire life, this overwhelming rush of power directed by human will, unbelievable energy pointed like a finger of fire at the heavens, the triumph of the human mind over that most ancient of masters: gravity. She was free, now, finally free...

An overwhelming cry of unbridled joy escaped, startling her pilot, Lt. Cdr. Scott Boyd. He understood instantly, though, for he also let loose with a cowboy whoop that sounded archaic in the spaceship, yet struck Tammy as completely appropriate. *Constitution* was the ultimate bronco and Space the ultimate wide-open range.

Then the engines cut off, and the feeling of freedom struck her even harder, like a doubled fist. On the KC-135 jets that dropped through parabolic dives to tease her with a half of a minute weightlessness, she never had time to feel and consider all that her body was going through. Onboard *Constitution*, she felt suspended at the center of the Universe. She felt light and free.

Not all the sensations were pleasant. Her head felt stuffed with mud. In free fall, no longer working against gravity, her body redistributed fluids, concentrating them in the upper torso and head. Her eyes grew bloodshot, with puffy patches appearing under them; her high cheekbones rode even higher, giving her an exotic, exaggeratedly Oriental appearance; her head throbbed and swam with every movement; her breasts floated high beneath her blue flight suit; her hair drifted around her head like a dark nebula; her internal organs shifted upward, narrowing her slender waist even more.

She ignored the unpleasant sensations, even the bout of nausea that NASA euphemistically labeled "early flight malaise." She chose to focus on the fulfillment of her dream.

Everything she had dreamed about since childhood had come true. With this, her third flight, she became a fully fledged space shuttle *commander*. She felt an uncompromised freedom in her flight above Earth. She closed her eyes to savor the emotion.

▼ ▲ ▼

Tammy maneuvered from the flight deck to the mid-deck. Entering head first, she glanced around and a familiar feeling of disorientation overwhelmed her. The enclosure hung upside down from her point of view, and even though she was a veteran of two previous flights, her mind still refused to interpret the altered angles. They called it *jamais vu*, the feeling of never having been in a familiar place. And it could set off sudden and violent nausea.

She fought it, thinking back to her youth, of the hours she spent at amusement parks on roller coasters, tilt-a-whirls, scramblers, and hammers in her own private effort to desensitize her to space sickness. It worked; the rising tide of malaise subsided and she positioned herself before the camera. Rotating about, the image of the mid-deck suddenly matched her mental map and her stomach quieted. She resolved that she would not embarrass herself or the mission with any unscheduled demonstration of zero-g fluid dynamics. She was not too sure about the congressman, though.

"I think I'm going to throw up!"

The congressman stared sickly at Tammy, his skin pallid, his eyes jerking about as they sought to process information that conflicted with what his inner ear relayed. The only part of him that looked as it did on Earth was his wavy brown hair, held firmly in shape by whatever epoxy politicians used for photo opportunities.

"You can't throw up in Space," Reis told him as she floated around his shuttle seat. "You can only throw *out*." She smiled, trying to calm his obvious panic with the lame old joke.

Ludlow Woolsey IV tried to hold back, but the sensations created by free fall relentlessly assaulted his guts.

Tammy kept her right hand near the pocket on the right thigh of her dark blue shuttle overalls. With her left hand, she skillfully undid Woolsey's straps.

Woolsey — on Earth, at least — had become a handsome man in his late forties, quite unlike the awkward rocket club supervisor Tammy had observed with disdain back in Los Gatos. His wavy salt-and-pepper hair had probably won the carpetbagger as many votes in his Oregon district as sharing the name of the powerful and respected Utah senator Ludlow Woolsey III, his father. In orbit around the Earth onboard *Constitution*, though, he looked like a sick and miserable child. Free fall caused fluids to accumulate in his face, puffing it out. That happened to everyone, though on Woolsey it looked worse. Even the extra blood circulating in his face did not give him the ruddy look the others possessed. In fact, space-sickness paled him and covered his flesh with beads of clammy sweat that refused to run off, simply clinging in place like the heads of rivets.

"Oh, nuts," Reis said, reaching quickly into her pocket for the sick bag.

An instant too late. The Honorable Ludlow Woolsey IV blew his cookies.

"Jon! Get the vac!" she cried out.

"Busy!" Jon Franck's voice shouted from beyond the fllight deck.

Vomit rocketed forth from the politician's mouth like campaign promises, spreading outward in a noxious, churning swirl of pulsating globules of red, green, and brown chunks suspended in viscous yellow bile and stomach acids. Woolsey gazed at the meteor of puke for only an instant before the sight of it made him retch again. This time, Tammy got the bag in place.

Nausea was nothing unusual to an astronaut. Reis knew that every stray droplet had to be removed from the air before it reached the ventilator ducts. A billion-dollar spaceship could ill afford circulating as powerful an agent of corrosion as stomach acid. She withdrew a tightly bound piece of cloth from what she called her puke pocket and unfurled it. The green mosquito netting, while not an official piece of NASA equipment, passed all the strict requirements for inclusion onboard the Shuttle: its fireproof fibers would neither break off nor create lint, and the material would not outgas any chemical vapors.

The net made a very efficient air strainer.

While the congressman continued to heave into the sack, Reis bounced toward the main cloud of debris and pinched the edges of the mosquito netting to create a small parachute. Waving it back and forth, she strained the mess out of the air. It took a good ten minutes.

The average Space Shuttle flight cost about one billion dollars and lasted about a week, though this one cost two billion and would last a month. The crew this flight consisted of four astronauts, not counting the slightly green representative. Reis's ten minutes of cleanup, by such a scale of measure, cost the taxpayers about one hundred sixteen thousand dollars.

On the other hand, had she not cleaned it up, the damage could have run into the millions.

Tammy Reis maintained a painful awareness of the true costs of spaceflight and resented providing an orbital junket for Ludlow Woolsey IV, not to mention mopping up the messes of the useless tagalong. As chairman of the House Subcommittee on Space, Science and Technology, his official purpose was to confirm the flightworthiness of the newest Shuttle and to inaugurate once again the Civilians in Space program.

She cursed mentally and — glad that free fall also disabled her sense of smell — used an absorbent towel to wipe off the locker door where the first salvo made impact. Finished, she wadded the towel and netting into a wet ball and propelled gently toward Woolsey's seat.

Lud, as he insisted on being called, acted affably, broad and friendly in his gestures, politely solicitous of his old acquaintance Tammy, respectful of the astronauts' knowledge and skill, and quietly awed by the power of the shuttle. Right now, though, he looked as if he had been hit with the worst case of flu on earth. His stomach ceased convulsing for the time being, and he wordlessly gave her the bag when she extended her hand to him. She replaced it with an empty one, just in case.

She stuffed the towel and net into the bag, sealed it, and used her gold Fisher Space Pen to mark the date and time of the incident on the label, along with the name of the source. That done, she kicked over to one of the many lockers that lined the bulkheads of the middeck and opened it. A piece of tape written in black marker designated the refrigerated unit as the VOMIT VAULT. Below it, a note in another hand commanded: SECURE ALL BARF BEFORE REENTRY! She tossed the plump bag inside and shut the hatch.

"Thank you, nurse," Woolsey managed to say with a sickly, weak grin.

Reis flashed a crooked smile. "Just one of the many and varied services we offer our honored guests."

Woolsey laughed, some of the color returning to his puffed-up face. "It's not exactly the Ritz, is it?"

"No," she said as she unstrapped him. "On the other hand, you can't beat the view."

The straps retracted and he floated free.

"This is amazing," he said, his sickness all but forgotten. His arms, relaxed, drifted into a loose sit-up-and-beg attitude. His waist and knees bent a third of the way chestward. "Did you ever believe when you and Volnos were kids that you'd actually make it up here?"

"Yes," Reis answered seriously. "All the time. And a lot sooner than it turned out." She put an arm around his waist. "We're not going to do any acrobatics. You'll need at least a couple of days to get used to free fall. Let me take you to the flight deck and we'll give you the best window." She glanced at her wristwatch, an unpretentious black Casio Data Bank calculator watch in which she also stored a digital crib sheet of emergency commands for the ship's computers. "We should be over Madagascar right now."

▼ ▲ ▼

Once he hovered in front of the viewing port, Woolsey's stomach calmed and he floated in wonder. Outside, two hundred-ten miles below, crawled a stunning panorama of color and texture. The greens and browns of Madagascar drifted past, the cities of Majunga, Tananarive, and Tamatave smudged by visible brown hazes of smog. Nothing to compare to New York or London, perhaps, but a visible mark of human existence. There followed a stretch of twinkling sapphire-blue Indian Ocean. Suddenly, the twin Mascarene Islands appeared off the bow, moving slowly aftward.

After observing the congressman's adhesion to the window for a few moments, Reis silently drifted back and away from him, softly making contact with the far bulkhead to work her way hand-over-hand through the shaft to the mid-deck.

Jon Franck hung in front of the controls for the remote manipulating arm, running a test on the system and reviewing procedures with Mission Specialist Federico Kayanja, in charge of deploying the experimental solar panels for Space Station *Unity* stored in the rear of the cargo bay. They would share duties, too, in the South American Laboratory for Space Agriculture.

"If only they allowed us to send down a video of *that*," Franck said, turning toward Reis. "What a reelection bid that would be! 'Vote for Woozy Woolsey, the—' "

"Can it, Jon."

"Don't take such good care of him," he continued. "He might start following you around like a puppy."

"Tammy? Are you down there?" Woolsey's voice sounded distant even though he was only a few feet away in the shaft.

"See what I told you?" Franck said.

Reis saw the direction in which Woolsey's feet popped through the hatch.

"Don't come in that way!" she shouted.

"What?" Woolsey entered the mid-deck feet first and looked around him. From his point of view, Reis and Franck levitated on their heads below him; the mid-deck seats hung from one wall, instruments and lockers lined other walls at a crazy angle. He really did turn green this time.

Reis hollered, "Your local vertical's wrong—*No! Use the sick bag!*"

▼ ▲ ▼

"Commander Reis!" The voice awakening her sounded muffled by the persistent stuffiness in her head. The shout erupted from shuttle pilot Boyd. He maneuvered into the mid-deck area and hung there upside down — at least to her point of view. "Franck, Kayanja," he said. "Time's up. Start earning your keep."

Reis emerged from her sleep restraint — a sleeping bag attached to the mid-deck bulkhead to prevent crew members from drifting around like so much flotsam — ahead of the others. Gently kicking off a bulkhead, she rammed a shoulder against Boyd's soft space boots. Franck, the astronaut with all the seniority, had pulled a mere flight crew position on this maiden flight of *Constitution*. Reis suspected that the ill treatment resulted from the conclusions he had espoused about NASA years ago while serving on the *Challenger* investigatory commission, conclusions that were not greeted with warmth by NASA management. Franck denied it, stating that he had pulled what duty he could to be part of the historic first flight on *Constitution* and the first STS flight with a woman commander.

"First assignment this morning is an interview with GSN." She glanced at her wristwatch. "Seven minutes from now."

Boyd nodded, then went on his way. Boyd established a down-link to Houston and the Global Satellite Network. Tammy gave her head a shake, setting in motion waves of jet-black hair. The other astronauts flanked her.

"Good morning, Constitution,*"* Tom McDermott, the GSN news anchor said, *"and good morning Commander Scott Boyd. How's the view from up there?"*

"The view is fantastic, sir, utterly fantastic."

Reis fought to keep from rolling her eyes. *Leave it to an astronaut to come up with a lifeless description.*

"That's great, Commander. And I see Mission Commander Tammy Reis there. Good morning, Tammy."

"Good morning, Tom." Two, she thought, could play the first-name condescension game.

"How does it feel to be the first woman to command the Shuttle?"

She smiled to hide her annoyance at the question. "Being in command of the Shuttle Transportation System is the most thrilling adventure anyone could ever experience. Just to be a part of the space program is an honor and a—"

"So it's pretty fantastic for you, too," the reporter stated.

Reis stopped. "Yes," she concluded, adding in an acidic tone, "It is utterly fantastic."

▼ ▲ ▼

Joscelyn Donahue's forehead wrinkled imperceptibly as she frowned at her boss. Marcus Grant never followed the shuttle, yet there he sat in his office watching one of those banal orbital interviews on the wall screen, feet up on the desk, hands behind his head, fingers interlaced. He was not smiling, and did not seem to be enjoying the experience.

She observed him quietly for a while, then said, "Pretty insipid, huh?"

"Shh." Grant waved a hand to silence her, then slipped it back behind his silver-grey head.

The newsman asked the commander of *Constitution* about the cost of flights. "Aren't you concerned that America can't afford the Shuttle?"

Reis set her jaw and took a deep breath. It was time to defend NASA. "That would be a legitimate concern if there were some alternative to the Shuttle. There isn't any. Russia built the *Buran* Shuttle and only flew it once because of the cost. They abandoned it because they had a working alternative in the form of their heavy-lifting Proton series of disposable launchers. America doesn't have the equivalent. We did, once: we had the Saturn Five. That's gone, now, and private enterprise has dropped the ball despite active scientific and financial encouragement from NASA. We may be exploring Space in a luxury sports car, but that's only because there aren't any Model T's around."

Lt. Cdr. Boyd opened his mouth and raised a hand to interrupt her when she added, "And I know you've been seeking the 'woman's viewpoint' this time around because it's another 'first woman' flight, so here it is: speaking in my political capacity as a woman, I'll state emphatically that I want my children to be born and grow up on other planets and I will do anything I can to ensure that it happens in my lifetime. Not thirty years from now, but ten years, five years. The US space program is the only program that will allow us even the hint of a chance at that dream, at making that dream a firm reality."

There was a long silence after she finished, the newsman requiring a moment to gather his thoughts after the gentle tirade. "Um, thank you, Dr. Reis." He searched for a segue, finally saying, "Well, here's hoping that your next first will be the first baby born in orbit. Now — Colonel Kayanja, as the first Kenyan to ride the Shuttle, does *your* wife want to raise children on the Moon?"

Visible only on Grant's huge hi-def wall screen, Tammy's eyes rolled toward her eyebrows.

During the exchange with Reis, Joscelyn watched Grant instead of the TV. His knuckles were white, his laid-back posture tense — almost forced. His narrow, intense gaze hid something she had never seen before. She was certain that it was hatred, but a hatred that transcended the mere subject of space travel, a topic he usually avoided. A darkness dwelled behind his eyes, an anger and a contempt as deep as the foul sediment beneath the dark waters of a poisoned well.

"Fetch Haley," Grant said in a low voice that chilled Joscelyn with its belying calm. "Tell him to finalize his affairs as if he had only one year to live."

▼ ▲ ▼

Haley clasped the SkyPilot goggles lightly in his left hand while tapping his gloved right hand against the chair arm. The urge to jump over to Grant and help him was nearly overpowering. His boss fiddled with something in VR, wiggling his fingers, nodding his head this way and that, reaching, twisting, pointing as if conducting some invisible symphony or molding a phantasmal sculpture. Beside Haley sat Donahue, also patiently awaiting her boss's demonstration.

"All right," Grant said, waggling a finger in their direction. "Suit up and come in."

They donned their goggles and adjusted the headphones.

"I liked your ideas for the sea rocket and the balloon launch, but I can't use them for security reasons. First off, the big booster is great, but towing it out to sea is like dragging a five hundred foot banner that says 'Hey! Track me by satellite! I'm a gigantic rocket!' And keeping the crew building it quiet is a challenge in itself."

They floated above a virtual airfield at about two thousand feet, the horizon obscured by clouds and haze.

"Second," he continued, "the balloon launch, while elegant, is also slow and leaves us vulnerable for hours to aircraft and radar sightings."

"I've considered that," Haley said. "The balloon would be constructed of radar absorbent—"

"The key is secrecy." Their view of the airfield changed as if they were diving toward it. "What do you see down there?"

"Airport," Joscelyn said. "Hangars, aircraft, three runways."

"Good. Let's drop into the landing pattern." The view shifted with vertiginous speed to four hundred feet on final approach. Instead of lining up with the runway, though, they buzzed the tiedown area. "What did you see there?" Grant asked as they pulled out of the pass.

"Airliners." Haley's voice sounded impatient. "Six of them. Boeing Seven-Forty-Sevens."

"Let's watch." At Grant's command, the aircraft taxiied swiftly onto the runway and one by one lifted off at fast-forward speed, tearing past clouds and into the sky. Their point of view paced the airplanes at a dizzying velocity.

Haley spoke dumbfoundedly. "You're not suggesting what I think you're—"

"Watch."

The half-dozen 747's flew a loose delta formation. In the lower left of the image appeared airspeed and altitude indicators. At 45,000 feet and 600 miles per hour indicated air speed, flames erupted from the rear of all six aircraft. Off they flew at a breathtaking pace, angling higher and higher into the purpling sky. When the sky turned black and stars appeared, the engines shut off and the airplanes began to behave unstably, pitching, yawing, and rolling this way and that. Tiny flashes of light on the wing, nose, and tail countermanded the motions, keeping the airplanes-cum-spacecraft in a synchronized attitude.

Grant, with a gesture, moved the three of them to a point of view that placed the aircraft between them and the Earth. The view of the aircraft high above the clouds, moving across the planet at nearly five miles a second, stunned the two new viewers.

The aircraft shifted about in a decidedly non-aerobatic maneuver. Using the tiny impulses of the attitude rockets, five of the planes rolled over on their backs at precise sixty-degree angles, their wingtips almost touching. They formed a belly-out hexagon, wingtip to wingtip.

"You can't be serious," Haley said as they zoomed in to see space-suited workers welding the wingtips together. Steel cables were strung from attach points on the dorsal centerline of the planes to every other plane. Zooming back out to a thousand feet distance, they watched as the reaction motors slowly imparted a spin to the tethered 747's until the unit became a bizarre rotating space station wheeling through Low Earth Orbit. A blazing red and orange logo flamed into the black sky reading SPACE STATION GRANT-ONE.

"I'm quite serious," Grant replied. "Jet aircraft are cheap, plentiful, and made to withstand nearly an atmosphere of negative pressure. With just a few modifications and the addition of either internal or conformal external boosters, we could have a functioning space station in operation within a week of launch. Moreover, nobody in the spy satellite biz will notice anything on the ground, since we can work in existing hangars at remote airports worldwide. We don't even have to launch them together, but could launch from different parts of the globe and rendezvous for maximum secur—"

"You didn't just come up with this, Marc," Donahue said, removing her goggles. "This isn't some sudden inspiration." Her voice possessed an angry edge that mystified Haley.

"It's an idea," Grant said, slipping his goggles off to gaze at her, "that's been percolating in my head for —"

"Ever since I've known you, you've never given a thought to Space. You even seemed to hate it, or fear it or something. Yet you've been thinking about *this*!"

Grant spoke in a calm, quiet tone, as if explaining to a child. "I'm a planner, Jo-Don. I've always kept my mind on possible profit centers. Space is just one of the places I've entertained over the years, holding back because I could not see a short-term profit. Now — with Haley's and your input — I'm beginning to see the light. So I'm dusting off an old idea and seeing if it flies."

Donahue slung the goggles on her chair arm and peevishly removed her glove. "I could have told you it was a brilliant idea," she said. "Years ago, if only you'd confided in me." She rose from the chair. "I move that we implement this plan immediately. If you have nothing more for me, I'd like to start working on it. We'll need to study the market for used aircraft and pick the best six—"

"Jo-Don." Grant's voice sought to soothe.

It failed to remove the bite from her tone. "Yes, boss?" she said.

Grant glanced at Haley, then back at her. "We'll discuss this later. Thanks for your... positive response."

She strode out of the office without a word of reply.

CHAPTER 16

...if your career involves space science or engineering, you cannot be on record criticizing NASA. It is a monopoly, the only game in town.

— Gregg Easterbrook

31 December

The party wasn't going well. With *Constitution* launched just the day before, the technicians refused to stop talking shop.

Jackson Lundy had seen it constantly in his thirty years at NASA; after all, he too possessed that mixture of intelligence and monomania mandatory for spacecraft engineers. Sending people into Space was no ordinary job.

Here he stood, though, throwing the archetypical New Year's Eve party. Balloons, streamers, loud music, animated conversation. And as with all parties filled with coworkers, the conversation inevitably turned toward work. Here a pair of balding, spectacled men punctuated their dialogue with fingertaps at each other's chests. There an attractive chemical engineer entranced a coterie of younger men and women with tales of the Good Old Days. And across Lundy's living room, Igor Svoboda sat in the apex of the cigarette-smoke-tan corner group, holding court with other malcontents.

Though the banter coruscated loudly over the music, and hands swung cigarettes and drinks in grand arcs and imperative thrusts, no one seemed to be having a good time in the here and now.

And only ten minutes to midnight.

Lundy gazed around the room. "Missile!" he called out.

A rocket's plume of red hair swirled about; an emerald lame strapless evening gown glittered like pirate treasure; Melissa Lundy turned toward her husband at the sound of her nickname.

His wife was a beautiful woman, still in possession of the charms he had seen over a third of a century ago, before men rode in rockets. She glided toward him, a slight flush on her tawny skin highlighting her feline green eyes. She smiled.

"It's almost time, sweetheart." She slid a lightly-tanned arm around his waist, her long nails gently tickling at his midriff. She held a wine glass in her other hand and gazed at him from a height almost equal to his by virtue of her four-inch high heels.

Jack nodded, slipping an arm around her. "And no one's going to notice or care, the way things are going. Look at Iggy."

"The sourpuss." Melissa smiled. "Don't let it get to you."

"It does. It does because he's so right." He gave her a hug and pulled away, drifting toward the knot of gloom.

Igor Svoboda, almost ten years younger than Lundy, exuded a Slavic grimness that made him seem a century older. Hunched over, forearms on knees, he sat in the corner group staring at the others around him from tobacco-hued eyes buried under dark, thick eyebrows. His words grumbled out from lips framed by a black beard that refused to maintain any degree of orderliness.

"*Constitution* is a case-in-point," his deep voice growled. "Take this flight—"

"Please!" someone interjected.

Svoboda continued, oblivious to humor. "Two delays before launch. There is no way we can turn it around for the next liftoff in February! SSME's must be swapped, no time to refurbish the ones on the orbiter, HPU's need upgrading, SRB's are late coming out of Utah. What gives with these people?"

Lundy listened and nodded. They lived in a world of acronyms, where jumbles of letters — meaningless to outsiders — denoted items or systems as instantly recognizable to them as chemical symbols to a chemist, or magical phrases to a wizard.

"If *Constitution* can't launch," Svoboda said, "then *Atlantis* is delayed. Delays multiply right down the line. And *blam*, our launch schedule is blown to pieces."

"Whatever happened to our commitment to Space, damn it!"

The young man who made the outburst was unfamiliar to Lundy. Probably someone's date.

"It seems," the stranger continued, "that the only thing we do is make proposals to get funding and then make up excuses why things aren't happening so we can get more funding to correct the problems. Then when we get a chance to go into Space, we delay, delay, delay. It's as if we'd rather draw our pay tinkering with the damned spacecraft than launching them. When did we stop looking at the sky?"

"At about the time we started working here." Svoboda stared gloomily at the young man, then up at Lundy. "Jack! Come join the mutineers, *tovarisch*."

"Maybe it's best," Lundy said with a wry smile at the young guest near Svoboda, "that we delay and delay. After all, that would make sure that the UN won't get off the ground."

"Don't start me on that Interplanetary Treaty." Svoboda hefted his glass of whiskey toward Lundy while addressing the young man. "Jack here's got a twisted sense of humor. Has ever since they began conducting experiments on week-long flights to see how humans adapt to 'prolonged exposure to weightlessness.' As if they had no data from Skylab. Funny, eh? Right, Jack?"

Lundy smiled only slightly, looking down at his wristwatch. The second hand ticked toward the new year.

"Almost midnight, Iggy. It's almost the year of the fifteen-launch schedule."

The short, bearish man on the couch ran a hand through his black, straight hair, making a point of straightening up and taking a deep, shuddering breath. He held both arms aloft to stretch.

"Damn the administrators," he cried, "full speed ahead!"

"Hey!" someone said. "Fifteen seconds!"

The countdown began.

"Ten!" everyone shouted, even Iggy Svoboda. "Nine! Eight! Seven!"

"Ignition sequence start!" someone called out.

"Six!"

"SSME's functioning!" another voice hollered.

"Five! Four! Three! Two! One!"

All together, everyone shouted: *"Torch the SRB's!"*

Lundy shuddered. Outside, the rolling thunder of explosions reverberated.

The new year had arrived.

▼ ▲ ▼

Barry Gibbon paid scant attention to Tammy's flight. Though responsible for her career direction and her values, he invested no time in enjoying the fruits of his patronage. He preferred to labor on the Treaty. Unlike the logical intricacies of writing subjective law, of drafting a treaty that seems to support space travel while actually seizing control of it, the emotional nature of human beings complicated matters and created challenges that kept Gibbon in a constant state of nervous anticipation, as if the wrong word here or the too-strong push there might cause his entire life's work to collapse about him.

He sat in his home in Langley staring at the dim glow of a computer screen, putting final touches on the draft of the Interplanetary Treaty that he hoped the General Assembly would approve. As close to his lifelong goal now as he would ever be, he felt the warmth of it like the glow of a candle toward which a moth is drawn.

In his youth, Barry Gibbon once made a concerted effort to help the poor and the suffering. Fresh out of high school, he spent the first two weeks of summer in a shanty town in Mississippi, helping to construct cheap shacks that were at least dry and windproof compared to the tents and corrugated steel lean-to's thrown together by black veterans who had come home from the war to a jobless future. Some rejected his assistance, rudely suggesting that they didn't need any guilt-labor from a rich white boy to get out of their predicament, all they needed was to be left alone to work it out for themselves. Such rudely ingenuous behavior bruised his youthful enthusiasm and sent him back to Maryland with the sour impression that the collective good could not be served by operating at the individual level.

Then Gibbon discovered something incontestably immune to error, something incapable of protesting his attempts to preserve it, something unable to foil his defense of it. Barry Gibbon discovered the vast emptiness of Space.

The chance concurrence of two events captured his attention and redirected his goals. One autumn afternoon in 1945, he emerged from a Boston movie theater running a newsreel of captured German film of V-2 tests at Peenemuende. He knew all about their rain of death on London, but the images he saw of the sleek, cigar-shaped missiles shooting into the grey Teutonic sky aroused an unfamiliar excitement within him.

Then, on his way back to the dormitory, he passed a newsstand and saw — in garish reds and yellows — a pulp magazine with a cover illustration of six V-2's linked in a circle rocketing high above the Earth. The artist painted little cockpit bubbles on two of the rockets, totally out of proportion with what Gibbon knew to be the actual size of the missiles. It depicted a scene from a story by Rex Ivarson entitled "The Man Who Bought the Night."

A little embarrassed, Gibbon purchased the raggedy-edged magazine and snuck it back to the university to read the story with some distaste. Ivarson painted a broad picture of the near future in which a millionaire simply bought V-2's from the US government as surplus, souped them up with expanded tanks, bolted them together into a two-stage affair, twelve on the bottom and six on the top, and succeeded in orbiting a two-man spaceship. The story ended on what Gibbon interpreted as a melancholy note, since the two men had no way of returning to Earth.

The story was patent trash to Gibbon, since he knew from firsthand experience that millionaires could not see beyond the end of their wallets. All his father thought about, for example, was tires, tires, tires, as if the entire fate of America rested on how many tires his company could produce and how fast they could overcome the slump caused by wartime tire rationing. The man possessed no vision, certainly no more than this Ivarson chap who naifly assumed that the government would surrender such awesome power to the private marketplace.

The story, though, stuck in his mind. What *could* the future of rocketry bring? Might it not bring an opportunity for humanity to start anew? To begin from scratch on other worlds with a single purpose and a modern political structure?

He brought these questions the next day to his mentor, Ian Mansfield-Rayne, professor of economics. It was he who convinced young Gibbon to abandon his plans for a major in architecture and enter Harvard with the new goal of a degree in political economy.

"Don't trust your own feelings on this," the leonine don told him. "Listen to others. Keep an ear open to the masses. When you detect a collective glance heavenward, then you will know it is time to act. When that time comes, give every ounce of your effort to involving as many ordinary people as possible. Only they have the mass strength to condition the intellectual class to move in a new direction."

That afternoon, Gibbon ran into Lud Woolsey, all flush with excitement over Operation Paperclip and the surrender of Wernher Von Braun.

Barry Gibbon found the pulse of the body politic.

Nearly half a century later, his thin, aged fingers raced with surprising speed over the keyboard, deleting a word here, adding a phrase there, creating an ever more subtle proposal to establish absolute hegemony over the Universe. He did not permit himself to think in such terms, however. He often laughed out loud at the idea of mere humans controlling anything so vast. A megalomaniac might envision such an ultimate outcome, but Gibbon sought a much more modest goal: to control access to Space so that only a hand-picked few would lead humanity to the stars with a single, unified, and immutable social structure. Peace and harmony, rationally guided and centrally administered. And Robertson Barrett Gibbon intended to be the architect of this new Eternal City.

CHAPTER 17

There's not a hollow cave or lurking-place,
No vast obscurity or misty vale,
Where bloody murder or detested rape
Can couch for fear but I will find them out;
And in their ears tell them my dreadful name—
Revenge, which makes the foul offender quake.

— **William Shakespeare**
The Rape of Lucrece

1 January, Year Three

Falling again.

A brief instant of light and thunder, a dreadful tumbling, and then the meteoric drop from the sky. A disembodied voice calmly reported the descent.

"All systems nominal," the man's voice said. "We are Go at breakup."

Falling, falling. Toward Kennedy this time. Toward the Space Center. Toward the marshy tidelands. Toward Pad 39A.

"We are Go for death," the voice said as levelly as any CapCom would report altitude, downrange distance, and velocity. "You are dead, Judy. You are dead, Mike. You are dead, Christa. You are dead, Ellison. . ."

She struggled against her chest restraints as the voice droned through the crew list. A voice behind her shouted with brave finality: "Give me your hand!"

She kicked and flailed but could not break free. The straps tore through her clothes, cut into her skin, grated against her ribs. She hung there, pressed against the restraints by the hideous deceleration.

Pad 39A grew visible in terrifying detail: the gantry, the water cannon, the dark exhaust shaft that seemed to disappear deep into the earth. She fell straight toward the darkness. It consumed her.

"You're dead, Tammy."

Her entire body spasmed into waking. The restraints still held her tightly, all but her arms. Her eyes jerked open. She struggled for breath, only to see a pair of dark eyes gazing at her a few inches away.

She flailed her arms about, but two strong hands quickly seized them to prevent her from hitting her sleeping crewmates.

"Tammy," the voice of Ludlow Woolsey whispered calmly. "You had a nightmare. Everything's all right. You're safe."

"Oh God," was all she could say for a moment. She took a deep breath and looked around. She floated inside her sleep restraint. The others still slept, suspended in their bags, arms floating halfway out from their bodies like zombies in cocoons. The sight in the semi-darkness always teased some primordial fear in her. After the dream she just had, the image did nothing to soothe her.

She gazed back at the man holding her arms. "Sorry," she whispered.

"I can't sleep either," Woolsey said, gently releasing his hold. "Is there a way to get coffee around here?"

"Sure." She undid the Velcro seals as quietly as she could and pulled herself out. Floating over to the galley, she produced two bags of coffee from a compartment and filled them with hot water from a gun-shaped injector.

"Let's drink in the flight deck," she said, "so we don't wake anyone."

Woolsey nodded and carefully followed her through the shaftway. He watched as she floated upward — or was it sideways? or down? — into the white plastic and metal passage. Her black hair floated around her head like a corona of lovely dark waves. Her shoulders, athletically broad and strong, accentuated the fascinating way her breasts behaved in free fall. Beneath the utilitarian blue flight suit, they moved in a manner that was not a jiggle, but more accurately a demonstration of the laws of inertia: when she kicked off a bulkhead to move forward, they shifted ever so slightly lower on her chest; when she stopped suddenly, they continued to drift, attaining a youthful high-breasted appearance. Woolsey — despite his earlier bout of space sickness — noted the effect from the first moment he saw her move. She was not merely the only woman for at least two hundred miles around, she was someone with whom he felt a connection going back years, back to a time that he possessed dreams of his own, dreams long abandoned to practicality.

She had followed her dreams with firm consistency and had achieved them. He longed to taste such joy, such energy, such drive.

Her slim, athletic waist disappeared into the passage, followed by her narrow hips and a pair of glutes, Woolsey noted with growing interest, that made the smooth muscular transition to thighs that only skaters and certain other physical types possessed. Even the thoracic blood-pooling that weightlessness induced could not suck the firm beauty from her legs.

"How's the stomach?" she asked when they reached the flight deck, making certain that the congressman aligned himself with the local vertical of the cockpit. Through the overhead window hung a bright blue-and-white beauty of the Pacific. Soon they would approach the terminator and pass over the night side of the world.

"I'm pretty much over the nausea," he said, floating near the pilot's seat. He eyed her with the keen gaze of a man trained to size up others. He squeezed the coffee bag and sucked on the spigot. "Lukewarm," he muttered.

Tammy shrugged. "Best we can do. Sorry."

"No problem." He let the bag float in front of him, watched it with a smile for a moment, then looked at Tammy and asked, "What sort of a nightmare were you having?"

She said nothing.

"Come on," Woolsey said. "It's just you and me, your old supervisor."

She inclined her head toward a corner of the flight deck. "You and me and Houston." A red light glowed beneath a lens. "Video monitors. I'm not sure whether they keep the mics open all the time, but I don't discuss personal matters."

"They're watching us everywhere?" he asked, looking around at several other minicams that covered every angle of view.

She nodded. "Everywhere except the toilet and shower. We insisted on that. Anyway, there may not be anyone staring at a screen every minute, but it's all being taped. The psychologists love it. And you should see the tape someone made once called *Space Bloopers*. They—"

"I think I saw it once. Funny stuff." Woolsey suddenly looked embarrassed. "You reminded me — I've... had a problem with the toilet. I haven't... gone... since we got into orbit."

"You trained on the simulator, right?"

The congressman nodded.

"You don't get thirsty in space — are you drinking enough water?"

He nodded again. "I feel somewhat self-conscious about this. Do you think you could sort of talk me through it?"

His discomfiture seemed genuine and not a little urgent to her. "Well," she said, "I *am* the mission commander, and one of my duties, if necessary, is to assist crew members in the jettison of cargo. So let's go. Quietly."

▼▲▼

The Space Shuttle Waste Management System cost a cool 23 million to produce and still could not overcome the problem inherent in defecation: that it is a gravity-dependent bodily function. Negative air pressure in the bowl and aftward-directed jets of air attempted to duplicate the method of separation that — on Earth — was easily accomplished by the 32 ft/sec^2 acceleration of gravity.

Space Shuttle Mission Commander Tammy Reis floated outside the drawn curtain of the toilet imparting to The Honorable Ludlow Woolsey IV the benefit of her extensive spaceflight experience.

"Now bounce a couple of times against the seat. That helps the air jets."

From inside the cramped booth came a thumping sound.

"That's got it," he said. "Thanks."

There was a long period of silence. Tammy allowed him long enough to clean up, but when several minutes had passed, she whispered, "Lud?"

There was no answer.

She asked again and heard nothing. Hurriedly, she threw the curtain aside, which caused her legs to fly backward and her head forward into the enclosure.

She stared in shock at the congressman — flight suit doffed and floating beside him — holding onto the toilet seat grip with one hand and nursing an erection with the other.

"Oh, shit," she said, pulling back and reaching toward the curtain.

"No — wait!" he whispered urgently. "Let's do it here. Out of camera range!" His hand shot out to seize Tammy's wrist. "I've always wondered what it was like in free fall. Show me everything."

"Go fuck yourself," she snarled. Bracing one leg and her free hand against the side of the toilet, she had the leverage she needed to break free of his grip. He shot to the top of the chamber and hit his head. The surprise and pain resulted in a rapid detumescence that, because his crotch drifted to Reis's eye level, was plainly obvious to her.

"I'd rather fuck you," he said, pushing toward her face. "You know I wanted to back when you were thirteen?" He grinned conspiratorially, whispering, "Actually, even when you were *ten.*" His congressional member again swelled halfway toward full.

Until it met Tammy's backhand.

The force of her blow propelled her backward, out of the way of his crumpling body.

"Two things you learn in Space," she said, loudly enough to rouse the others. "One: Never assault the commander of your vessel. Two: Never assault anyone whose favorite sport is squash."

"Tammy?" Jon Franck was the first to awaken and fly to her aid.

She nodded toward the congressman balled up in the overhead of toilet clutching his groin. "Lud there has misconceptions about Shuttle etiquette."

▼ ▲ ▼

"Houston — we've got a problem."

Pilot Boyd floated before the flight deck communicator. In front of him and slightly below him hung Commander Reis. Flanking her were Kayanja and Franck. They all stared with cold anger toward the videocam built into the instrument panel.

"Copy, Constitution*,"* crackled the voice of Dan Cunningham, CapCom at the Johnson Manned Spacecraft Center in Texas. *"What's wrong?"*

"This is a private conversation," Boyd said. "Please take the transmission off public feed and encrypt it."

"Roger, Constitution. *One moment."*

Reis glanced at Boyd. He nodded agreement.

"Ready to copy, Constitution.*"*

Reis cleared her throat. "Get Bryan on the line please, Dan. Over."

"I'm here, Tammy." The deep voice of NASA Administrator Bryan Kirk at KSC cut through the static. *"What's up?"*

Jon muttered to Federico, "Nothing of Woolsey's, that's for sure."

"It's the congressman, Bryan. He's acting in a manner that jeopardizes the safety of the crew."

There was a silence of several seconds before Kirk spoke. *"Can you elaborate?"*

"Not at this time," Reis answered.

Federico cut in, his dark eyes glowering, his voice no less harsh despite his gentle Kenyan accent. "He tried to rape her, Bryan, all right? What sort of pig did you send up with us?"

Reis tried to interrupt. "Fred—"

Kayanja shook his head and continued to speak. "He came on to her in the toilet. She whacked him in the balls and that was the end of it. Need more detail, man?"

Another period of silence. Kirk's voice, when he responded, carried a tone of cautious dread.

"And where is the congressman now?"

"Check your monitors," Boyd said. "He's in the mid-deck. I ordered him to stay there."

"*You ord—?"* They heard Kirk take a deep breath and release it.

"I *am* shuttle pilot, Bryan."

"I know, Scott, I know. And you know that he's chairman of the Subcommittee on Space, Science and Technology."

Reis's tone grew chilly. "He wanted free fall sex, Bryan."

Another gap of silence. After several moments, Kirk said in a weary tone, *"I'm going to talk to him on the mid-deck. Privately. Out."*

"Roger, Bryan," Reis said, switching off the radio link. She glanced around at the other three. They all wondered about the final outcome. Whatever it would be, they knew that politicians could hold long grudges.

▼ ▲ ▼

The next several days moved at the usual hectic pace. Kayanja and Franck deployed and tested the Space Station *Unity* solar cells, encountering several glitches along the way. When the panel finally extended fully from the rear of the cargo bay, though, it glittered like the great black wing of some mythical giant bird.

Boyd and Reis worked in the South American Laboratory for Space Agriculture, a hydroponic module that occupied the forward three-fourths of the shuttle cargo bay. More spacious than the flight deck and mid-deck combined, Reis found it a perfect refuge from the insanity of the previous day.

The Honorable Ludlow Woolsey IV sequestered himself on the flight deck, watching the view out the window and even participating in interviews with C-SPAN and the networks. His demeanor gave no hint of the turmoil he had created onboard *Constitution*.

Night was signaled by a message from Houston after dinner. Weary from the day's effort, the crew sealed themselves up in their sky blue sleeping bags.

"Where's the ballast?" Franck asked the commander. Reis shrugged.

Boyd looked toward her. "He's strapped into your seat. I think he's going to sleep there tonight."

Tammy ran a hand through her drifting nebula of jet hair. "Remind me to scrub it down in the morning."

CHAPTER 18

...the idea of citizens being fully informed about what the government is doing is merely another nonsensical notion.
— **Ferdinand Lundberg**
The Myth of Democracy

5 January

Within NASA there dwelt a number of spies. However, as with many other federal agencies, these spies worked for no foreign power. NASA's brace of spies reported to competing federal agencies such as the Department of Defense, the Central Intelligence Agency, the National Security Agency, the Sandia National Laboratory, and even — for arcane reasons related to the federal budget— the Department of Housing and Urban Development. They routinely monitored encrypted communications between the Shuttle and the Johnson Space Center in Houston, the Kennedy Space Center at Cape Canaveral, or the Marshall Space Flight Center in Huntsville and devoted a good deal of supercomputer time in redundant efforts to decode one another's transmissions. Many considered this task a vital part of the checks and balances that keep a republic alive, or at the very least lively.

Montgomery Barron wasted no time with interagency intrigue. With a diligence that bordered on monomania, he spent his days and evenings and sometimes nights in the hangar at Washington Naval Air Station, overseeing Project *Stark Fist*, watching the nearly organic growth of the spaceplane from simple titanium frame to where it stood now: an impressive black skeleton housing the high-tech entrails of propellant tanks, plumbing, turbopump, and high-pressure engine that awaited the connection of weapons, fly-by-fiber controls, and heat-inhibiting skin to make her complete.

Barron, no lady's man, liked to think of the spaceplane in traditional feminine terms. He picked the name *Huntress* and even ordered low-resolution decals with that name, surmounted by nose art of a woman in a black trench coat and slouch hat gazing mysteriously at the observer. Since hypersonic flight and reentry would sear the artwork off every flight, he ordered scores of copies.

The fuselage and wing tanks gave her lines a solidity lacking in the basic skeleton. Her graceful wings swept back more sharply than those of the shuttle orbiter, which made for a smoother transition to hypersonic speeds, and their tips bent upward into winglets, which served to extend the wing area without adding to wingspan. Her fuselage bore some of the traits of a lifting body, though nowhere nearly as fat as the Lockheed X-33 or as round in the belly as the old Dyna-Soar. If anything, *Huntress* shared kinship more with a delta-winged version of the X-15 once proposed but never built. She also shared lineage with an aircraft that would never fly, the National Aerospace Plane.

Huntress would fly, though, for she was small and sleek and not designed to please Congress or the aerospace business community. He ran a hand over her frame as he approached the cockpit.

A pair of engineers hung heads-down in the cockpit, legs up in the air like celery stalks in a cocktail glass. They worked quietly without argument or agitation. They paced themselves even though the pace was swift.

"How's it going in there?" Barron called up to them.

Without disengaging, one of them said, "The specs on the light fiber were off by a fraction of an inch each, so the bundle won't fit the holes. Tim's going to enlarge the holes, but we'll stay within the stress limits. Barely within."

"Keep at it." Barron saw no need to double check their work. He trusted the men as far as any NSA operative could trust anyone. When finished, *Huntress* would fly.

Charles Stansfield stepped up to him, tightly holding a fat file folder conspicuously marred by purple classification stamps. "General Dardanelle is waiting at the hotel."

Barron nodded. Dardanelle was not his real name. And though it irked Barron to purchase weapons for Project *Stark Fist* from the Israelis rather than buying American, he had shopped the entire war market and the lightest, simplest, and most reliable weapons to serve his purpose were those coming out of an industrial park in Hadera.

There was no way he would let the general see the spaceplane, though. NSA files contained reports of a Hassidic sect attempting to reconcile space migration with Talmudic law and openly promoting a new Exodus to construct an orbiting City of the Chosen. He might have dismissed the report, except that several of the Hassidim were former Soviet rocket scientists who had made *aileyah* to Israel just a few years before.

Barron sighed. Leaving the hangar meant staring into that damned retina scanner again.

▼ ▲ ▼

Haley delivered the bad news to Grant in an almost apologetic tone. Beside him in Grant's office stood Donahue, looking grim in a grey business suit and clutching a thick sheaf of corroborating data in her left hand, pressed against her thigh for support.

"I've crunched the numbers and run the simulations, Mr. Grant, and there is just no way the 747's can do it."

Grant sounded irritated, if not downright peevish. "I ran my own numbers, Chad. That's where I came up with the VR simulation."

Garbage in, garbage out, Chad thought, judiciously choosing not to say it aloud. He picked the more diplomatic route. "Let me say that the case for orbiting a 747 is good, but hardly practical. To lift something that heavy into orbit requires going supersonic—"

"They took one supersonic once," Grant cut in, looking for weakness in Haley's argument. "The airframe can take it."

"Only barely," Joscelyn said. Her red hair hung down past her shoulders, unkempt and bespeaking the days of relentless work on the problem. "You get tremendous transonic drag because the shock wave forms over the wing while the rest of the plane is subsonic. Look, Marc, I know you thought that flying up to the service ceiling puts it above most of the atmosphere, but it turns out that the energy required to take it up to forty or fifty thousand feet and six hundred knots plus is..." She plopped the stack of printout and notes on his vast desk. "Marc, it's just *infinitesimal* compared to what you need to get from that speed and altitude to seventeen *thousand* miles per hour and a hundred twenty miles altitude!"

"But I ran the numbers myself!"

Still the diplomat, Haley said, "It's marginal. Very marginal. And in the real world, we have to have firmer numbers than that."

"What if we jettison excess weight?" The others watched Grant's mind at work, wheels turning. "Jettison the landing gear just after liftoff, then have the wings and empennage rigged with explosive bolts to blow at altitude, just before firing off the boost—"

"Mr. Grant... Marcus." Haley pulled up a chair and sat, leaning his arms against the edge of the desk and spreading both hands. "The wings of a Boeing are the main structure to which the fuselage is attached, not vice versa. And blowing the empennage means coming up with a new bulkhead to maintain the cabin pressure. The cost of retrofitting six planes to do all that and do it *safely* and then go supersonic and orbital, well..." He glanced at Donahue for support. She nodded. Haley gazed at Grant with eyes that implored and commanded simultaneously. "Well, it would cost just as much to build an entirely new system from scratch. That's all. And Joscelyn and I think we've found one."

Grant leaned back in his chair, still digesting the fact that his space station concept had just gone down in flames. "Found one?"

Haley deferred to Donahue, whose power of persuasion over Grant undoubtedly exceeded his own.

"It's nearly forty years old," she said, "but don't let its age fool you. When it comes to space travel, a lot of good ideas came out in the 'fifties and 'sixties, only to be ignored or suppressed by NASA. This one's called a Neuffer Ring." She slipped a CD-ROM into Grant's computer and the wallscreen displayed a digital slide show to accompany her pitch. The first image looked like a sketch of a woman's bracelet, round and composed of sixteen spheres intersecting together so that their points of contact were actually circles, much as bubbles share a broad area when squashed together.

The bracelet imaged was belied by a width mark from edge to edge that denoted a diameter of two hundred feet.

Grant let out a low whistle and leaned forward, elbows on desk.

Donahue knew better than to let a smile overtake her. "The design is optimized to permit a single-stage-to-orbit launch of a fully assembled space station consisting of sixteen pods, each forty feet in diameter. The pods"—the image changed to a cutaway diagram of one of the spheres — "serve as fuel tanks on the way up and — once in orbit — are voided of hydrogen and filled with what remains of the oxygen from the LOX tank for atmosphere. Neuffer's design did not allow for very much payload other than the station itself, but modern structural materials such as composites and aluminum-lithium can bring the mass down so that a crew of twenty and a minimal amount of life support and machinery can be added."

Grant peered at the diagram until it changed to a close up of the engine itself. "What is that?" he asked. "An aerospike?"

Donahue nodded. "Classic design. Four concentric rings of one-hundred-eighty combustion chambers each, arranged around a central plug. The plug contains a tube bundle heat exchanger sec—"

"Save the details for later," Grant said. "Will this thing work?"

Haley laid a hand on the stack of printout. "It stands a better chance of working than the 747's and you don't have to assemble it in orbit. All the work is done of nice, safe terra firma."

Grant mused on it for long moments before asking, "What would it cost to build?"

"Less than a modern skyscraper," Donahue said with a smile, "but more than a supertanker."

"Less," Haley added, "than buying the planes and retrofitting them and buying the boosters to lob them into orbit. We're not a government space agency. We don't have to waste money the way they do. We can be cheap *and* safe. This" — he pointed at animation of the space station climbing into orbit — "is Grant One."

After a moment considering the idea, Grant had only one question: "While we're building it, where do we hide it?"

CHAPTER 19

What is the point in vilifying all politicians or bashing bureaucrats? After all, waste, fraud, and abuse can never be totally eliminated from human commerce, nor can vanity, ambition, and hatred be wiped out of human nature.

— Allen Thornton
Laws of the Jungle

15 January

Gibbon moved in for the kill.

He had done it before and was master of the art. The Space Migration Society dangled out there in the midwest like a ripe apple ready to be plucked. Now he saw a sign of decay on the stem and jumped to exploit it.

"Theodore, Theodore, Theodore," he murmured into the telephone, his voice as deep and understanding and filled with empathy as it could be. "I know we've had our differences in the past, but I'm quite honored that you would turn to me in your time of need."

"It's so hard to ask for help," the voice at the other end of the line said in a halting tone. *"I've run SMS for fifteen years and I've watched it grow to ten thousand members and then I watched it just sit there."*

"I understand. It's difficult for anyone to work with such devotion and not see his dreams pan out. I'll bet you expected to be living in orbit by now." Gibbon permitted a wan smile to cross his face. He was alone in the darkness of his library.

"Then I met Genevieve. I don't know. She messed my mind up. And with the membership starting to decline..."

Gibbon listened without comment to Theodore's lament, mutely pleased that his strategy had succeeded. The National Organisation of Space Supporters, with its four hundred thousand members, held its annual convention in Cleveland last Labor Day. Gibbon steered the con committee toward a space migration theme, and NOSS offered new members a number of snazzy gifts for joining, including an 8 X 10 color print (suitable for framing) of a proposed space habitat cribbed from a design by an Arizona architect, a ten-color embroidered arm patch, and a photo ID card made and laminated right there at the convention.

SMS members joined in droves, many not bothering to renew their memberships in the rival organization. It offered no arm patches. In fact, its only draw was an opportunity to place money into a growth fund earmarked for construction of a spaceship. Gibbon, after leaching off SMS members, aimed for the weak spot of the fund: Theodore Straite.

"Oh, yes," Gibbon softly interjected in the middle of a recitation of Theodore's woes. "I remember Genevieve. You know, I think she made a pass at me at that convention. Imagine! A man of my age."

"She was so beautiful, but she had these... appetites. I couldn't concentrate on my job, on the newsletter, on the club. I got fired. Pretty soon, I started dipping into the mutual fund—"

"Theodore!" Gibbon sounded horrified. "That fund was a sacred trust, the future of humanity."

The voice half a continent away sobbed in anguish. *"We went through it in weeks. She just... It went."*

The older man heard inarticulate noises over the line. He waited until he adjudged the man's suffering to be at its peak, then said, "Theodore, you know I don't own or operate NOSS, but I *am* on their advisory panel. They've helped out troubled clubs in the past, usually by offering to take on members at no charge for a full year, then asking if they would like to renew. How many members do you have?"

"Now? Less than six thousand. Plus another two thousand who just subscribe to the newsletter."

Gibbon already knew the numbers — Genevieve had kept him apprised every step of the way.

"I'm certain I can convince the board to relieve you of that burden and of any... personal liability you may have incurred as far as membership is concerned. I'm afraid they won't be able to do anything about that depleted mutual fund, though. I know a fine attorney in Kansas City who handles embezzlement cases. I'll include his number when I express a package to you with the papers for membership conversion."

"Thank you," Theodore said almost imperceptibly. *"God bless you. You've kept the torch burning all these years when so many weaker... people would have let it go out."*

"That's very poetic, my dear friend, very poetic. The movement needs more poets. Write you feelings down in a letter of apology and I'll see that they run it in the next issue of our journal."

Thanking him again, Theodore rung off. Gibbon placed the telephone handpiece back in its elegant cradle and smiled. The Space Migration Society clung on as the last holdout. Now every major space group will have been absorbed into the structure of NOSS. That accomplished, his attention returned to his lead article for the next NOSS journal, an analysis of the Interplanetary Treaty by its author. Since the article would come out after the UN vote, he wrote of it as if it had passed already. It pleased him, this pretense, because he possessed the confidence that it would be so, and he did not believe in jinxes.

He punched in the command to save his work and received a curious message:

Low on memory

Evangeline entered with a tray of *hors d'oeuvres*-sized sandwiches and sought to leave it beside his desk.

"Go away, Angie!" he snapped.

"Why, what's wrong, Barrett?"

"Nothing you'd understand." He tapped at the keys. "According to this, I have only three hundred seventy megabytes used up on this disc and yet I'm getting an 'out of memory' message." He looked up at her. "You don't let anyone use this while I'm out, do you?"

Baffled, she said, "Why, no."

"And you haven't used it?"

She looked flattered. "Barrett, you know machines and I don't get along."

"Well, it's damn' curious, that's all. I should have nearly two hundred megs left." He popped one of the tiny triangular sandwiches in his mouth and almost immediately spat it out. "What in God's name is this?"

"Pate, Barrett."

"It is not!" He sniffed at it. "It's *cat food*!"

Evangeline blushed frightfully and stammered, "I must have gotten the cans mixed..."

"Oh, just get out! You can see why no one ever married a scatter-brain like—"

He paused, took a deep breath, and said, "Angie, I'm going to go rinse my mouth out, and then I require uninterrupted silence for the rest of the day. Can you remember that?"

"Yes, Barrett," she whispered, head down.

▼ ▲ ▼

Tammy, a pilot since age fourteen, believed in gremlins. At least, she harbored a deep-seated uneasiness about the complexity of the Orbiter and the competence of the thousands of employees and contractors involved in maintaining and refurbishing the five craft space fleet. The last three weeks onboard *Constitution* were clouded not only by her run-in with Woolsey, but by persistent nightmares. Less of *Challenger* as often as of a multitude of other disasters.

In one, she stood on the back porch of her parent's rural home in the hills overlooking Los Gatos. Overhead flew a huge flying-wing aircraft with hundreds of windows delineating three or four levels of seats. Incredibly detailed and colored with the alternatively subtle and intense colors of her dreams, the airplane slowly, ponderously drifted toward the town below, trailing a thick black cloud of smoke from an engine pod. She could do nothing to stop it. She could only watch as the magnificent flying machine crumpled into the center of town and burst into flames. Even at that distance, the heat seared the flesh of her dream body.

In another, she stood on an unfamiliar desert plain to watch a long, fluted cylinder lined with portholes — an Art Deco spaceship out of an old comic book — slowly crash in flames like the Hindenberg. The crashes were always in agonizing slow motion, as if the machines were so huge that relationship between size and the acceleration of gravity and resistance of the atmosphere imparted a dreamlike languor to the disaster.

She assured her troubled mind on waking that they *were*, after all, just dreams. She could handle dreams after awakening, but the feeling of helpless dread while she slept took its toll on her attitude and outlook.

Woolsey, for his part, behaved as if nothing had happened. He was courteous and quick with a smile at first. The other four crew members shunned him, relegating the lawmaker to the rear of the SALSA where he performed his makework assignment of administering nutrients to the zero-g hydroponic system. The South American Laboratory for Space Agriculture — after more than three weeks in orbit — possessed a primordial, jungle-like serenity that the astronauts, even Woolsey, enjoyed. Rain forest plants grew willy-nilly in every direction, unbound from the twin pulls of earthly gravity and sunlight. Dense greens, vibrant reds, and lush yellows lined the bulkheads.

Reis could not muster the self-control required to treat her attacker with civility, so she avoided him whenever possible. As the days turned to weeks on the Enduro flight, a persistent cabin fever slowly took hold of her.

"Tammy?" Franck asked, approaching her work station at the forward end of the SALSA.

"What?" she said in a startled, angry tone.

Franck did not cringe. He was used to this by now. "Fuel cell number three is on the blink. The hydroxide's overheating."

"So what else is new?" She pounded a fist against the bulkhead, sending a reverberating thud throughout the lab. At the far end, nearly hidden amid the foliage, Woolsey glanced toward them, then back to his work.

"Tammy," Jon said softly. "We've got just a few days left. He's kept away from you. When we get back to KSC, we'll figure out what to do. Just keep cool."

She nodded agreement, though rather than cool, Tammy smoldered like an incipient prairie fire.

▼ ▲ ▼

The time had come.

Barry Gibbon mounted the dais in the arching cavern that housed the United Nations General Assembly. Nearly two hundred countries were represented by the tide of faces of all colors and types. Hundreds more spectators lined the far reaches of the chamber. He revealed no trace of disappointment at the meager number of news cameras. The masses did not need to know what was about to transpire. They would learn soon enough, though a deep and true awareness would only come years hence.

Gibbon walked at a deliberate pace, not from any infirmity of age, but from a somber sense of history and a desire to savor his destiny. He held in his hand a copy of the treaty, noting that the desks of the ambassadors all bore the white rectangles of their own copies.

He spoke slowly, both for the sake of drama and the convenience of the interpreters.

"Ladies and gentlemen, representatives of all the free and democratic nations of Planet Earth." He knew the ambassadors believed that, even though practically none of them represented nations that were either. "Today we stand on the threshold of a new age, a new frontier, a new challenge to the collective wisdom of the human race. Within the next three decades — well within your lives and the lives of your children, though probably not within mine — humanity will grow past its infancy in the cradle of Earth to reach out to other planets.

"We shall inhabit the regions above the Earth and return to the Moon not as jubilant, flag-planting winners of some infantile contest but as united workers following a rationally directed common goal of human expansion and exploration. The great masses of humanity will gaze up into the night sky and know that you, their leaders, have chosen the wisest, freest path for mankind to follow: free of competition, free of duplicated effort, free of strife, free of greed, free of exploitation. In the quest to sail this new sea, the nations of the world have a chance to unite for a purpose that transcends all boundaries of nation, race, and creed."

Gibbon cleared his throat, regretting the necessity and hoping it did not mess up his tempo. Gazing out at the plain of faces, he noted smugly that he held their rapt attention. They rarely heard much more than jingoistic bluster, so his message of hope carried its impact throughout the chamber.

"The Security Council has approved UN Resolution Thirteen Ninety-Three, introduced by twenty-two nations, that is known as the Interplanetary Treaty, from which I now read:

" 'We, the Nations of the world, United, do hereby resolve that one year from the signing of this Treaty, all programs of space exploration, colonization, and development by signatory nations shall fall under the exclusive control of the United Nations. Further, that all spacecraft, launch systems and facilities, and personnel shall operate within the purview and coordination of the Security Council and that the Council shall form an United Nations Interplanetary Treaty Organization to administer the quotidian functions of the united space program.' "

Gibbon read the entire eight page resolution, which covered such minutiae as the existing launch sites that would immediately fall under UN jurisdiction and what compensation current satellite cartels would receive for the internationalization of their spacecraft.

He finished with the closing paragraph: " 'Resolved, therefore, that the United Nations shall be truly and perfectly united in their quest to create an United Solar System wherein all share the benefits of space exploration and none shall profit by its exploitation. In the name of, and for the sake of, all humanity and its posterity, so mote it be.' "

There was a momentary silence while the interpreters finished reading their own copies of the text. Then the ambassadors began to applaud. It was polite, at first, but then built with the assistance of some vociferous members of the visitor's balcony.

Looking pleased, humbly honored, and suddenly venerably frail, Barry Gibbon acknowledged the applause and stepped down from the dais.

The Secretary General of the UN took her position at the podium and called for discussion of the resolution. Hearing no requests, she called for a vote.

Leaving the center stage, Gibbon at last allowed himself a smile of triumph. This was the pinnacle of his success, this was all he strove to achieve. Now, the nations of the world would speak to the stars with one voice, and that voice would be his.

Goodness, he thought with amusement, *could that be a touch of hubris?*

▼ ▲ ▼

He made certain that he was in place in a news room for the signing of the Treaty. His organization had set up an interview on *A.M. United States*, the morning talk show for the Global Satellite Network. The hostess, Marilyn Jordan, adored Gibbon and his elderly grace and wit, and hung on his every word.

"We are so honored to have you with us, Dr. Gibbon," she said, brushing a strand of her honey-blond hair over her ear and leaning toward him on an elbow. Her turquoise eyes gazed at him with wide admiration. "How does it feel to be part of such a momentous occasion?"

Gibbon smiled. "I'm honored to give whatever small assistance I can to the brave men and women who will go forth into the unknown. Now, they will go forward with a common purpose, united under a single banner."

"That's been important to you, hasn't it? You've fought waste in the space program for years with your opposition to quick-fix efforts at space colonization."

"Oh, yes," he said, crossing his legs and settling comfortably into the seat. "It is no great accomplishment to send a multitude of bodies into orbit using half-century-old technology. NASA's privilege and gift to humankind was its boundless ability to push ever forward the limits of technology. We may call it a virtue that NASA has never put more than eight people into space for more than two weeks at a time, and now only five for the month-long Enduro flight; the pointless and excessive cost of pampering so-called "colonists" is money that might as well be shoveled into a rocket and fired into the sun for all the good it does in promoting humanity's future.

"When the time comes for humanity to venture into space colonization — as it will within the next thirty years — NASA's role shall be to develop the most advanced, technologically superb living accommodations for those few brave souls, not some cheap tin can rattling around the Earth like the first shack of an orbital shantytown."

"Will NASA exist under your treaty?"

Gibbon let an embarrassed chuckle escape. "Good heavens, Marilyn, it isn't *my* treaty! It's the legacy of an entire civilization! I just gave the treaty the input of the hundreds of thousands who are members of the National Organisation of Space Supporters. And as far as NASA goes, it will be stronger than ever as the American branch of UNITO. No longer will it waste resources in pointless 'firsts' or lose lives in the dangerously ludicrous attempt to be space truckers. Now they will have a single purpose which they may pursue with singular dedication."

"Inspiring, Dr. Gibbon. And now we have a surprise for you." She touched her ear, listening to instructions from the sound booth. "Yes, we have contact with some people you know who will be witness to the historic vote."

Gibbon raised an eyebrow. He disliked anything that smacked of a plan other than that of his own devising.

"Hello *Constitution*!" she said, raising her voice as if to compensate for their distance.

"Hello Marilyn," crackled the voice of Scott Boyd. *"And hello Dr. Gibbon and everyone on the blue planet."*

Gibbon hid his annoyance at the intrusion. Glancing at the monitor, he saw that the camera was now on Jordan with the crew of *Constitution* inset at the lower right.

"Tammy Reis," Jordan said. "I understand that today is an important day for you. Not only is the UN set to sign the Interplanetary Treaty, but it's also your birthday, isn't it?"

The astronaut gazed at the camera with a grim expression. *"I was born the day three astronauts died in a burning space capsule. Now on this same date, another traged—"*

Too-convenient static broke up her last few words. She appeared unaware. Off-camera, Gibbon smiled. Fate, or someone controlling the NASA feed, had silenced her dissent. He knew she opposed the Treaty. He considered her his only partial failure. That led him to think about the Crockett boy. He banished the concern from his mind when he heard Jordan say, "I understand, Dr. Gibbon, that shuttle commander Reis is one of your proteges, and that Oregon congressman Woolsey is the son of a very good friend of yours, Senator Woolsey of Utah."

"Indeed yes, he is," Gibbon said. "Good morning, Lud. How are they treating you up there?"

"Just fine, Barry!" His voice came through full of cheer and enthusiasm. *"They have me doing everything around here, including donating about a gallon of blood to the cause of science. Not to mention that*

Commander Reis has promoted me to Permanent Latrine Orderly."

"Well, I'm glad you made it into orbit, Lud."

"I am, too, but I'm only here as a representative of the American people and I feel their hopes and dreams riding with me. And now all the people of the Earth can share in this dream. The Interplanetary Treaty, thanks to you, poises us on the brink of a great leap forward for the human race. I think it is appropriate that the word 'humanity' has imbedded in it the word 'unity,' don't you?"

The camera switched to Gibbon, who smiled with a gracious inclination of his balding head. "You know I do, Lud, my boy. Unity and peace and harmony among the planets."

"What a lovely sentiment," Jordan said, turning toward the camera as it zoomed slowly in on her face. "Next up on our show, a look at spring fashions with"— she touched her ear again — "Ladies and gentlemen, Dr. Gibbon, Commander Reis. I've just been told that the vote of the General Assembly is one-hundred thirty-eight to forty-one with seven abstentions... The Interplanetary Treaty is now interplanetary law!"

The studio audience applauded after a bewildered pause. Most of them had no idea what had just occurred.

Two hundred miles above the Earth, Tammy Reis knew. She turned and kicked away from the mid-deck to retreat to the flight deck and spent a long moment staring at the Gobi desert passing over her head. It looked as bleak and barren as the emptiness in what was once her soul.

Part Two

The Mailed Fist

CHAPTER 20

...the ultimate order of a Western-type 'democratic' government is just as severe in its effect as the order of a Stalinist or Hitlerite government.

— **Ferdinand Lundberg**
The Myth of Democracy

27 January, Year Three

"The god-damned sons of bitches have killed us!"

"Gerry?" Sherry stood to see him shove his way through the door. Sweat covered his face like a thin plastic mask. He was a furious caricature of the Gerald Cooper she knew as he thrust the crumpled newspaper at his wife.

"They've killed us. They voted on humanity's death sentence and passed it!"

She stared at the front page and only saw news of an ax murder in Waukegan, a school bus crash in Seattle, food riots in Sri Lanka, and a preview of the Super Bowl.

"Page twenty-seven," he muttered, looking out of the living room window into their back yard. The scrubby zoysia grass lawn was in need of a thorough trim — they had canceled the gardener weeks ago as a cost-cutting measure. "Buried with the fur coat ads."

"The treaty?" She read the five column inches swiftly. "The US abstained."

"Abstained!" His hand sought his forehead, found it, pressed tightly against it. "What a noble show. A no vote in the Security Council would have vetoed it. They abstained there, they abstained in the General Assembly. They let it go through without dirtying their hands. The UN is now the sole master of the Universe. For the sake of all the people, which means for the sake of the UN, for the sake of a world state."

"It can't be as grim as that," she said, putting her arm around his shoulder. "You remember how worried *I* was at first, and how *you* dismissed it. It really is just a piece of paper."

"So's a death warrant. This is the law, now. Treaties supersede the Constitution. The UN now owns every spaceship on the planet. Even ours."

"No they don't." She shoved the paper in front of him. "Not for a year."

Cooper huffed. "A year. We couldn't put Starblazer up in a year."

Sherry stood and gazed down at her husband. "And why not, Gerald Cooper?"

"Material flow, development time, testing. It's all—"

"Details, Gerry, details!"

"That's what makes rockets fly, Sher—details."

She slapped him with the paper. "Details are what keep rockets on the ground. *Vision* is what makes them fly. You've let those weevils at NASA eat at you and eat at you until they devoured your dream. Well, I'm not going to stand for it! I want my husband back. I want that dream." The paper crinkled in her grasp. "We have one year and I want us in orbit by then!"

▼ ▲ ▼

"*Zhopu kozina*," Colonel Vladimir Tuchapski muttered. The goat's hindquarter in question was the lieutenant who delivered the latest issue of *Novii Pravda* to the damp blockhouse that served as his office in Novosibirsk. The demilitarization of the former Soviet Union was progressing at its usual turtle's pace: after three months in this frozen wasteland, Tuchapski had succeeded in demolishing only five SS-18 intercontinental ballistic missiles. They were far from meeting the goals of INERT, and the colonel could hardly have cared less.

Flipping through the magazine, printed on rough, grey paper, he paused to read a short piece about an upcoming UN treaty. His feet slid from the desktop as he sat up in surprise. The Interplanetary Treaty, he quickly surmised, would take control of the entire Russian space program — what there was left of it — finishing, in his mind at least, the ravishment that the breakup of the USSR had begun.

Nothing more than internationalist Kazakhs, he thought, throwing the magazine across the small room. He ran a cold hand over his close-cropped blond hair and fulminated. News was slow to reach this frozen part of the planet, and he suspected that the treaty had no doubt been approved. In an effort to shake the constriction in his soul, he pulled a stack of missile reports toward him and turned to the specifications section.

He knew the specs for the SS-18 by heart, but seeing the facts in bold Cyrillic type reassured him that his mother country indeed possessed a mightiness that was once unquestioned.

Designed to deliver atomic death to America and elsewhere, the SS-18 was a powerful liquid-fueled missile capable of reaching targets on the other side of the world. The specifications began to play in his mind. He decreased the payload and attempted to calculate what altitude and final velocity he could achieve. The calculations quickly became too complex for mental consideration, so he withdrew a calculator — a cheap Chinese knockoff of a Japanese model — and began working with it and a sheet of yellowed stationery from the desk. The paper bore the insignia of the old Soviet Space Force. The old Russian proverb still rang true for the military: use it till gone, use it till broken, live with it, or live without it.

After reducing the payload to ridiculously small masses, he took the different tack of clustering the rockets together. Even without factoring in the added mass of explosive bolts connecting the boosters, it was marginal at best. And the reliability of the SS-18...

Still, INERT mandated the destruction of the missiles. To him, it was insane to destroy the rocket when it was only the warhead that was the evil.

Tuchapski stroked at his smooth, cold chin. *We are here surrounded by tundra. Who is to know what we blow up? Treaty inspector is bundled up in his office blue with cold. Some kerosene barrels, extra explosive...*

The pride that once dwelt within Colonel Vladimir Tuchapski began again to grow. Could he do it? he wondered. Could an individual stand up against the collective will of the world?

He would need help for such ultra-left adventurism. He would pick them from his troops. He had one year.

One year to reach, reactivate, and snatch away from the UN Russia's abandoned outpost in the Cosmos: *Mir!*

▼ ▲ ▼

Ace Roberts heard the news from the UN over the little transistor radio perched on his workbench. He shook his head in amusement. Thirty years ago, he might have flown into a rage. Now, he simply continued to polish the surfaces on the third Aerobee engine that lay in pieces on the table. After more than two decades working on his dream, he felt no sense of urgency, simply the calm pleasure of slow, methodical effort aimed at a distant goal.

Not too distant, he thought. By his estimate, the rocket required another eight hundred man hours or so before static testing could begin. Even though he was in no hurry to thumb his nose at the United Nations, he could be ready to within the next year or so.

▼ ▲ ▼

Hacker shoved the printout under Crockett's nose. "What does this mean to us, Davy?"

Crockett shoved back his coonskin cap to read the article captured from the computer news network. Behind him, the framework of the rocket stood nearly thirty feet tall. Three narrow metal seats surrounded the central support column, heads in and feet out. The rotor blades, each twenty feet long, sprouted from the base of the command module like four popsicle sticks glued to the wide part of an inverted, cone-shaped paper cup. The cup rested atop the fifteen-foot-tall cylindrical framework comprising the fuel and oxidizer tanks.

Crockett shook his head. "Doesn't mean jack to us." He handed the paper back to Hacker. "The same way no one expects gangsters to obey gun laws or squatters to obey zoning statutes or illegal aliens to obey immigration codes. We're space squatters, Hacker, vacuum-backs. Besides" — he hefted a nitrogen tank to carry over to Penny — "we'll be up, around, and back before that thing even becomes law. At least, we will if you can calculate that flight program."

"It's not as easy as that, Davy."

"Why not? The basic rocket equation I could do on a pocket calculator. And the rotor gives us greater than ten-to-one thrust augmentation. That's an effective specific impulse of nearly three thousand seconds."

Hacker walked alongside him, adjusting his glasses. "Yes, but the answer you get is worthless unless you can plug that in to higher order equations to yield a trajectory. And even if you can figure out the integration for a specific trajectory, you won't be able to guess what the *optimum* traject—"

Crockett put the nitrogen canister down with a clang and patted Hacker on the back. "You're right," he said with a grin. "*I* won't be able to. That's why *you're* helping us."

"But even I—"

He stabbed a finger into Hacker's chest. "I'm entrusting you with our lives. I have complete confidence in you."

Hacker took a deep breath and let it out, shaking his head. "I've never been responsible for anyone's life before."

"Yeah," Crockett said casually. "Well, college has a way of deferring adulthood for 'way too long. It's about time we grew up, huh?"

▼ ▲ ▼

Joseph Lester heard two pieces of news that day. The first concerned the Interplanetary Treaty. The second concerned his career. The series of articles he wrote about Laurence Poubelle and Gerald Cooper, picked up by a wire service, had apparently piqued the interest of somebody in the news bureau of GSN. He played back the message on the answering machine in his motel room. Outside, one of the desert's winter storms turned the streets to mud.

"This is Belinda Helman calling from GSN New Orleans. We'd like to talk to you about turning your articles into a series of reports for GSN News. We think there's been enough nationwide coverage that we'd like to discuss your being the on-screen talent, if that's feasible. Call me at—"

Lester jotted down the number and keyed it in. While waiting for the connection, he glanced down at his girth. Six months in the desert, mostly in summer and autumn heat, had inspired him to shed about sixty pounds. Though he considered himself much more trim at two thirty-five, he possessed the objectivity to know that he was still not telegenic enough for GSN. All his professional life had been spent behind a keyboard. He regularly refused to provide his photograph to head up columns in papers that encouraged such a barbaric practice. Yet the allure of television reporting drew him to the full-length mirror on the motel door.

His face appeared lean enough, at worst athletically stout; his shoulders sloped off a bit, though his arms were not as heavy as they once were. Most of his weight concentrated around in his midriff, the classic pear shape — the most difficult weight to lose.

Part of him rebelled. *Why do I have to conform to some idiotic mass-media notion of good looks?* Another part of him pondered the health question. Before dropping the sixty, his breath grew labored after mere moments of mild exertion.

He decided that he would try to lose some weight, but to do so, he based his program on a piece of trivia he encountered in talking to Gerry Cooper about spacecraft design. Every extra pound of payload, Cooper told him, added over three extra pounds to the gross lift-off weight of a rocket, due to the added structure and propellants require to loft it into orbit. If he were an astronaut, every pound he lost would shave three times that from the GLOW of his spaceship. His goal, he decided, would be to reduce the GLOW of an imaginary rocket by one hundred-eighty pounds. At the safe rate of a pound a week of payload equaling three pounds a week of GLOW, that gave him fourteen months. He could do that; he had a reason to.

He glanced back at the article about the Interplanetary Treaty. By the time he lost that weight, Space would belong to the UN. His stomach growled with a gnawing sense of despair.

▼▲▼

"I say we need *Stark Fist* more than ever now, Steve." Barron stared directly at Milton in the NSA director's office. He stood with his hands in his suit pockets while Stansfield sat next to him, hands resting primly on his grey leather attache case.

Milton gazed back at the pair from the deep recesses of his large executive chair in which he looked like a limp doll propped up in a normal adult seat. He was a small man who commanded a massive and powerful agency.

"I don't see how we can justify it, Monty." Barron's superior nearly squirmed in his chair. "Frankly, the thought of UN control and oversight of *Stark Fist* gives me the willies. I think we should just terminate the project and destroy all the records. Otherwise, it's strictly can of worms time."

"I say we don't tell them," Stansfield muttered, gazing down at his attache.

Milton shook his head. "The President backs IT. He's been informed about your project. He'd turn it over to the Security Council for their uses. It would still operate to suppress subnationals."

"Look," Barron said, pulling his hands from his pockets to lean on Milton's desk. "This treaty is a pile of crap from that one-worlder Gibbon. We've got files on him going back to Harvard. I can unravel this whole mess with eighty grains of lead. He's the impetus behind it all. Get rid of—"

"May I remind you that he has the full support of President Crane?"

Barron muttered something about an extra two hundred grains, then said, "If I can arrange a demonstration of what *Huntress* can do, if I can come up with something before the implementation date, will you kill it on paper and keep it operating in deep black?"

Milton simply sat there, breath and pulse rate suddenly racing. He hated this part of the job, circumventing and even subverting the desires of the chief executive.

"Don't embarrass us," was all he replied. He knew that Barron would interpret it the appropriate way, but the NSA chief could always insist he meant the opposite.

Barron nodded. "I won't."

Deniability established to the satisfaction of both parties, Barron turned to leave, followed by Stansfield.

"All we need now is a suitable target," he said *sotto voce* to his assistant.
"We may have one," Stansfield replied. "Out in California."
Barron snorted. "We've got at least a dozen out there."

▼ ▲ ▼

One of that dozen lowered the newspaper and grinned at the woman at the other computer. "First congress and now this," Poubelle said. "I think someone's egging me on."

Chemar glanced up from the screen upon which ran a simulation of a drop-tank jettison at Mach 3. "It's going to have a chilling effect on people such as our neighbor, Cooper."

"You think so?" Poubelle folded the paper and set it down. "I'm feeling inspired."

"You think folk hero status will save you?"

"I've got half a million on the mailing list. The project's yielding world-wide coverage. Whether or not we can get it up within the year, what do you think the reaction would be if I called a press conference the day IT takes effect and blew *Nomad* to bits?"

She gaped at him. "You're joking!"

Poubelle's teeth glinted white in the center of his grin. "*Nomad*'s a tool, milady. It's a tool to get me into Space, it's also a tool to inspire others. If I have to destroy it to make a point, it'll be the best hundred million I've ever spent."

D'Asaro smiled back at him with mock wariness. "I don't think psychiatrists have a name for your pathology."

"Give that Lester fellow a call. I want to give him another story."

"About what?"

Poubelle eyed his prosthetic arm, rotating it this way and that. "Just something I've had up my sleeve for a while."

▼ ▲ ▼

Onboard *Constitution*, the conversation turned on the UN treaty. Only Scott Boyd gave it anything approaching support, and that was more in the form of resigned acquiescence.

"If we have to fly for the UN, we'll fly for the UN," he said, floating amid the SALSA's dense foliage. "After all, we just swap this patch" — he patted the American flag on his left shoulder — "for a UN one."

"You don't see anything wrong with that?" Reis glared at him suspiciously; she looked that way most of the time now.

Boyd shrugged. "It's not as if we've been conquered. When Congress ratifies it, that makes it legal enough for me."

Kayanja spoke up. "I didn't ratify it. None of us was asked. Yet we'll have to fly them. You people have little experience with the UN. I do. We had peacekeepers in Ethiopia and Somalia, right next door to Kenya. We considered them nothing more than colonial troops. To them, peacekeeping means defending a status quo that retards any attempt at change for the better. That's what they'll do to NASA. They'll freeze us."

"NASA's been frozen since *Challenger*," Franck said, plucking an unripe bell pepper from its stem and spinning it around in the air between his fingers. "Since way before, even. I'm dropping out when we get back. I've got an offer from a VR firm to develop and market a spaceflight game. I'd be a veep. Have lots of perqs."

"You sound really ecstatic," Tammy said.

"NASA," an acid voice behind them said, "is performing the function for which it was devised." Ludlow Woolsey drifted through the foliage. His face looked puffier and ruddier than ever on the flight — on Earth, it might have been a flush of triumph; in Space, it merely made him look like a petulant child holding his breath.

He smirked at the other four, most pointedly at Reis. "NASA was created to monopolize space exploration within the United States. Except for one or two rigidly NASA-controlled unmanned launches, it has succeeded magnificently. Now UNITO will monopolize Space on a global scale, with you, the Japs, the Europeans, the Russians, and everyone else jumping through one single, solitary hoop."

"Has the smell in here gotten worse?" Kayanja asked.

Boyd inclined his head and the other three followed him out of the SALSA. "Let's get back to work," he said when they gathered in the mid-deck. "He'll be out of our face within twenty-eight hours and then we can go on with our lives. All right?"

The other two men nodded. Reis, however, frowned and said, "As long as he's on the Space committee, he'll be in our face."

Boyd laughed. "You showed us how to handle him, Tammy. He responded well to a slap in the gyros."

Tammy laughed in spite of herself. "Well, who hasn't had to deal with horny politicians while orbiting Earth in a billion-dollar rust bucket? Happens every day, right?"

Even the usually glum Jon added a smile. "Something for your memoirs, right? Every astronaut writes a book sooner or later."

"More's the pity, my friend," Federico added.

"All right!" The commander grinned. "We're back up to speed. Let's go through our work list and get this pooch ready for home!"

They went their separate ways, each with a task to perform that had been determined by NASA months before.

28 January

Night is an arbitrary thing in space. Orbiting the Earth at 17,590 miles per hour, a spacecraft passes through the planet's shadow every ninety minutes.

Shortly after midnight, orbiter time, Tammy Reis again dreamt of falling, of being onboard *Challenger*, of hearing the voices she had only heard on the garbled final radio transmissions that NASA had kept secret for so long.

Uh oh.

Houston...

Give me your hand!

She could not breathe. Or shout. Or move. The restraints cut into her flesh like knives. The air screamed. The ocean grew closer, sunlight shimmering on its placid surface.

It had never happened before in the dream: this time she hit.

The awesome force of the nine mile fall shattered the crew cabin as if it were a glass bauble. On impact, the seven astronauts' bodies flew forward through their restraints, the straps cutting them to pieces.

Judith tried to scream, but realized she was dead. She could not breath. Only a deathly, watery silence covered the broken remains of *Challenger*. Through a red haze of blood and torn flesh swam a school of fish, intrigued by the scent. They began to feed.

She could not scream. She could not breathe.

An eel tore into her with vicious greed.

"Oh God!"

Tammy Reis awoke with sudden terror to a ripping sound.

She could not breathe. She could not scream.

Duct tape covered her mouth, bound her hands, hobbled her ankles.

She could breathe through her nose, though, and saw the angry face of Ludlow Woolsey as he dragged her from the sleeping bag. He pulled close to whisper in her ear.

"You like it rough, kitten? That's how it'll be. I've waited a month for this. No. I've waited *years*. Free fall and rough trade."

He wrapped his arms around her and gently kicked off the bulkhead. Tammy struggled against him and tried to form a scream in her throat and nose. It was not loud enough to pass through the thin air and reach the fluid-clogged ears of her crewmates. Together they sailed toward the hatchway to the SALSA.

With all its lush vegetation, SALSA could have been an idyllic Eden in the dead of Space.

For Tammy Reis, it had become Hell.

Woolsey huffed and puffed, pushing feet-first through the hatch.

One tennis-strengthened arm pulled his captive by her sable hair. She hissed furiously, the sound erupting through her nose.

On Earth, Ludlow Woolsey IV was a handsome man, winning elections with the aid of men and women who voted as if they were picking beer-buddies or boyfriends. After a month in space, however, his wavy hair — impossible to coif in free fall — radiated from his scalp in a madman's frazzle. The exertion, added to the normal fluid buildup, puffed his face into a caricature of an alcoholic.

He sealed the hatch shut and locked it.

The lab itself was a quiet place. Only the steady hiss and click of the nutrient cycler competed with the nearly subliminal whir of air conditioning. In this soothing orbital forest, Woolsey's grunts of effort sounded wild and animal-like.

Another length of duct tape zipped off the roll to bind her wrists to the bulkhead hidden by the broad, thick leaves of an immature plantain banana tree. He produced a Swiss army knife — the commemorative one with a silver space shuttle inlaid on its crimson side — and used the blade to split the tape binding her ankles. Legs free, she delivered a kick toward his face that he blocked easily, squeezing her ankle with numbing force.

Her left leg he taped to a grip near the control panel. Her right, far to the other side against a strut. She hung there, wrists together overhead and legs spread, her blue flight suit stretched taut at her crotch.

Woolsey closed the blade of the knife and unfolded the scissors. He rotated about so that his thighs hovered before Reis's face, his head positioned in front of her groin. He held the scissors level with her eyes.

"I know you have a change of clothes," he said. "Don't worry, though. I don't need to shred these. Just a short, inconspicuous little—"

Reis heard but could not see the operation. All she saw was the congressman's body suspended a few inches away, his swollen presence outlined under the fabric of his flight suit.

She glanced desperately around the lab. They *had* to be in view of one of the video cameras. She located it a few feet beyond his left leg. Its lens pointed directly at them.

Can't they see? she thought. *Why don't they wake up the crew?*

Then she saw it. She saw and realized at just the instant she felt cold, trembling fingers begin to explore her.

The diode that should have been glowing red was dark. The camera had been switched off.

No one was watching.

No one on Earth knew what was happening.

Then a thought shuddered through her as the congressman

flipped about and the sound of tearing Velcro filled the lab like the snarl of some terrifying jungle monster, a thought that robbed her of all hope, all resistance.

What if they did *know?*

Then she saw the camcorder — *his* camcorder — nearby, taped to a strut with a length of the same silver-grey material with which her captor bound and gagged her.

Tears of terror, rage, and helplessness welled up in her eyes, clouding her vision. In free fall, they did not run down her cheeks, but spread across her eyelids and face like a viscous gel. Though she could have wiped them away on her upstretched arms, she let the tears remain, let her sensations blur. All she sought now was to disappear, to pull away from herself, from the inevitability of her attack.

She closed her eyes.

She was falling.

▼▲▼

Lud completely forgot his stomach awareness. His awareness concentrated about a foot lower. Wild sensations coursed through him, electrifying the thrill of her violation. All his senses, dulled by free fall, grew sharp once again. Every snip of the tiny scissors sounded like the slash of a saber through a harem tent. The scent of the woman, suddenly released, filled his nostrils with its musky aroma of hot, energized fear.

The congressman pondered the historic nature of his act as he reached teasingly inside her, past the harsh, fire-resistant fabric, past the silky undergarments the color of which he could only imagine.

"You've done this before," he murmured. "Gangbanged whole crews, I bet."

Tammy said nothing beneath the silver-grey tape that covered her mouth, did not even make a grunting attempt. Her face glowed a furious red, the skin so taut with blood and hatred she could have burst.

"Don't bother trying to excuse it." He withdrew his fingers and marveled at the way droplets of her sweat and juices behaved in zero-gravity. "It's better than having an all-male crew and their suck fests." He wiped off his hand on her thigh. "Oh, I've heard the stories. They have to be more than rumors. I mean, how could anyone resist trying?" Grasping her slender waist, he hung just a few inches away from her captive form. "Not exactly something you tell the grandchildren, but how many astronauts know for sure if they'll ever get into space again? So they at least go for the Onan Orbit, right? And some are more bold." He tugged at the seal on his flight suit, pulling his arms from the sleeves to let the top half trail behind him. It floated like some bloodless Siamese twin joined below his waist. "You train with your crew for months before a launch. Friendships will form. Grow, perhaps, a bit more intimate on the ground."

His hands grasped the seal on her flight suit, one near her name-plate, the other near her NASA patch. They pulled sharply apart. The Velcro separated with an angry rip that fueled his excitement. He felt a wave of heat escape from inside, as if he had just cut open a doe felled by his arrow. Beneath the blue of the suit, bordered by the twin black stripes of the Velcro, she wore a light tan t-shirt. Body heat had stained it with sweat. "Then you make plans," he whispered, "to consummate that intimacy among the stars."

The tiny scissors snipped at the bottom of the shirt. With a single motion, he slid the blades upward to rend the cloth.

"I knew it," he said, gazing with a sly smile at the blue Jogbra binding her chest. "I knew you were hiding them." He held the Swiss army knife up before her eyes and snicked the scissors twice.

She swung her head rapidly forward in an attempt to hit his. He floated just beyond her reach. Instead, her dark black hair whipped forward like a thousand tiny whips to lash his face. Rather than fall as they would on Earth, they snapped back and forth for a few sways, then floated again around her head like turbulent storm clouds.

He laughed at the flogging. "I might ask for more of that."

The scissors did their work again, unleashing her breasts from their bonds. He casually extended his hand and released the knife. It floated, scissors open, a foot away from them.

He observed the way her struggles made her breasts move. With no gravity to drag them down, they drifted with her motions in a way that excited him madly. They rode high and firm on her, as if they belonged to a teenage girl, the kind who were so plentiful back in California to the first-born son of a powerful senator. Except one. The one who worshipped Space first, then Paul Volnos, and nothing and no one else. The one for whom he no longer had to control his desires.

He gazed at her face, then quickly looked away. It spoiled the moment. Apart from the duct tape across her mouth — which excited him — weightlessness caused fluids to amass in her face and permitted flesh to rearrange. Her cheekbones, already high on Earth, looked even higher. Almost Oriental, he thought; that was no good — he secretly loathed Japs and Chinks and Gooks, the epithets running through his mind like a perverse mantra. Veins in her forehead and neck were swollen, dark semi-circles bulged under her eyes. Her throes of rage only made things worse.

He turned his attention back to other parts of her body. Though he vaguely understood that free fall also shifted her internal organs upward into her thorax, he could plainly see that her waist was as slender as a that of a fashion doll. He wrapped his hands around it and pulled closer to her, rubbing his naked flesh against her exposed chest and flat, muscular belly. Twist as she might, she could not turn away from him.

He surrendered to the importunate urge within. Whispering every obscenity he knew in a single stream of unconscious hatred masquerading as lust, he sought out the hole in her clothing with trembling fingers, spread her lips, and thrust inside her.

She was dry, which caused him some pain. His body responded with rougher, deeper attempts. She did not groan. She did not scream. No sound emerged from beneath the tape. She did not even breath heavily through her nose. She seemed to be on some distant world now, separated from him, from this event.

She possessed, he decided, no sense of history or their place in it.

He shoved harder, deeper, as if he could find some source of moisture farther in. He glanced at his camcorder, flashed his best re-election grin, and turned back to his pleasure.

Every inward thrust caused his upper body to pull away from her, rotating at his loins. He solved this by grasping her upstretched arms and wrapping his own arms tightly around them. Every outward pull threatened to throw his legs back and away. He slammed his outer thighs up to press hard against her inner thighs, tight and spread wide by her captive posture.

Sweat beaded all over his face, held to the skin by surface tension. A quick shake into her flowing hair wicked it away. He inhaled deeply her musky scent and pulled back for a moment to observe how her breasts moved in so unearthly a manner with every violent motion he made.

He grew closer now. Closer to his particular goal for the space mission. "I'm bringing you down, you haughty bitch," he muttered between grunts. "I brought your little boyfriend down to earth and I can drag you down, too. That's power, whore. The power to change lives."

▼ ▲ ▼

Tammy drifted, disconnected from the world around her. She closed her soaking eyes and sought solace in the only place she could — the future. This would be over soon, she tried to assure the terrified child inside, though that part of her feared that it would go on forever.

The thrusts grew faster. Suddenly a cold sensation filled her, as shocking as ice water, and the motions within grew slick and less painful, though they sped up and rammed deeper. The cool spurts continued; she refused to count them.

He was done.

He released his grasp and floated apart from her, connected now only by his one piece of invasive flesh. This he slowly withdrew, fascinated by the long pearlescent strand that stretched between them until it snapped apart into several spheres that drifted away like wandering planetoids.

"Star whore," he muttered. "Space tramp. Shuttle slut." His face twisted into a mask of hate. "Just because you made me come, don't think you have any power over me. Whores don't have power, that's why they're whores. But I'll do you a favor. *I* have the power to get more flights for you, treaty or no treaty. Maybe I'll even be on one. And maybe I'll share you. With UN astronauts. Whores have no rights, but they receive privileges. Would you like that, you tramp slut? You'd better. No fucks, no Buck Rogers."

He reached out where he had left the Swiss Army knife and encountered emptiness. Glancing about, he saw that the lab's air circulation caused the tool to drift toward the filter vents. He nabbed the slow mover, folded away the scissors, and opened the large blade. This he slid under the tape around her right wrist. His voice changed timbre, softening to a murmur of feigned concern intended as comfort.

"It's time to go back to bed now, little sweetie. Daddy'll put you back to bed for sweet dreams."

The knife sliced through the duct tape, perilously close to veins and tendons. All it cut, though, was her silver-grey bonds. She made no motion. Her arm hung upward where it had been. The same for her other arm. Both freed now, they floated rigidly above her like the arms of a catatonic.

He drifted down to free her ankles. Before he could, she locked her fingers quietly together in a double fist. Using her strapped legs as bracing and her hips as a pivot point, Reis contracted every muscle in her arms and stomach to swing her stiffened limbs downward with swift, crushing force. The fist caught Woolsey in the back of his head with a sickening crack.

Pain seared through her hands and wrists. A scream sought to escape from beneath the tape across her mouth. Bones burned as if broken. A flex or two assured her that they were throbbing but intact.

Lud rotated about from the force of the blow. He vomited, sending a bilious stream of ejecta around the lab. Floating away from his hand, the knife threatened to drift out of Tammy's reach. Once more she contorted, her fingers shooting forward through a quivering, foul mass to seize the tool tumbling just beyond it.

The congressman moaned and grasped the back of his head. She had only seconds. Bending down, she slit the tape around her ankles. Using the blunt side of the knife, she pommeled her attacker twice on the side of his head. The blows rendered him unconscious, but he twitched and jerked in a horrific dance unlike anything she had expected.

No sympathy for his plight welled inside her. She tore the tape from her mouth, taking some skin with it. Then she cradled his head in her arm, steadied the both of them by locking a leg around a stanchion, and poised the knife above his face.

"Kiss the future goodbye, fucker."

CHAPTER 21

By wire and wireless, in a score of bad translations,
They give their simple message to the world of man:
'Man can have Unity if Man will give up Freedom.
The State is real, the Individual is wicked;
Violence shall synchronize your movements like a tune,
And Terror like a frost shall halt the flood of thinking.'
— W. H. Auden

29 January

"You mean you've both been building spaceships at the same airport and you've never met before?" Lester stared in disbelief at Poubelle.

The billionaire puffed on the cigar and shook his head. He wore all white, from polo shirt and cargo-pocketed bush pants to running shoes only lightly laced with desert dust. "Haven't said word one. Know all about him, though, from your articles. Now that you're about to hit the TV screens, I think an historic encounter is called for."

They walked along the tarmac from Poubelle's hangar toward Gerry Cooper's. "This treaty," Poubelle said. "Gibbon's been an enigma to me for years. Now I know what he's up to. He's been offered NASA posts and has turned them down in order to 'maintain his independence.' What he really aimed for all these decades was to become the top space bureaucrat for the entire planet."

"And that's a problem for you?" Lester swung the wrist weights at the ends of his arms as they walked, his ankle weights rustling with the sound of small sandbags at every step.

"When a man achieves a global ambition, he becomes a global problem."

"And your solution?"

Poubelle stubbed out the cigar and tossed the butt into an ashcan. With a wide smile as white as his clothing, he said, "Where's your cameraman?"

Lester backhanded sweat from his forehead. "I just found out about this job yesterday. I recommended someone I've worked with before. If they approve, she can be out in a few days."

Poubelle stopped and shook his head. "No good." Pulling a

celphone out of his pocket, he switched it on and said "Braverman." Within seconds, the autodialer connected him with the office of the head of GSN. "Jane. Larry Poubelle. Let me speak to Billy. Thanks." He smiled at Lester's gape and flexed his robot arm. "Same country clubs. I beat his butt at golf and he beats me at squash. One time on Maui it started to rain and I took my arm off when it shorted. You don't forget a golfer who does tha — Hey, Billy! I hear your news department's hiring competent reporters for a change..."

After a minute or less of banter, Poubelle got to the point. "Bill, there's a young man here who's just started working for you and he needs a video crew pronto... For what? To cover *me*, you sandtrap miner. He's got someone in mind..." He looked toward Lester.

"Hillary Kaye. Fort Collins *Sentinel*"

"Her name's Hillary Kaye. In Fort Collins. Tell your Putzpuller Prize winner to fly her out to Mojave pronto... I tell you, Billy, it's news... Hey, all I do is flash my Erector Set arm and I *make* it news! Yeah? Sorry, I don't like the taste of implant... Yeah, you too. Twice on Sunday." He switched off the phone and grinned. "Braverman's a guttermouth. I have to reply in kind. Better call and warn her." He handed the phone to Lester and turned back toward his own hangar.

▼▲▼

The Cessna Citation landed at Mojave in the frigid chill of a desert winter morning. Though it would be pleasantly warm within hours, Hillary Kaye wore a thick down jacket of forest green and dark brown slacks. An ambivalence about the entire affair permeated her thoughts. She specialized in still-camera work — traditional and 3-D; she considered video a hobby, though she had amassed professional quality equipment over the years. Lester's phone call had come out of the blue, but the salary offer had come straight out of New Orleans: double what she made in Fort Collins. Times being as they ever were and always would be, she accepted the offer without hesitation.

She scanned the flight line for a glimpse of Joe but saw no one. The plane taxiied to a stop and the co-pilot opened the hatch. She stepped out into the cold to see a man trot up to the steps. "Jesus, Mary, and Joseph Lester," she said in shock. "Is that you?"

Lester nodded.

Kaye nodded right back. "You look as if you lost the equivalent of an English schoolboy. And I like the hair style."

"Thanks," he said, running a hand through the short waves that had once been longer curls. "We don't have much time if we want to make the satellite feed for the morning news in New York, so grab your stuff and we'll set up in the hangar."

"What's the deal? Someone declaring war?"

"Could be. It may not sound like it right now, but I think what'll happen today is going to set the future of the human race for the next millennium."

Kaye pulled her equipment cases from the luggage compartment. "So they'll have hot coffee and fresh donuts?"

▼▲▼

The donuts were fresh, procured from the airport coffee shop whose cook prepared them in the time-honored manner. Kaye noticed that Lester, who once consumed a baker's half-dozen every morning, abstained, drinking a black coffee and glancing nervously in a small mirror.

The Freespace Orbital hangar hosted three other news crews from local Los Angeles area stations with network affiliations. Lester, however, was the only reporter promised an exclusive interview after the press conference.

Kaye fired up the Canon DigiVid II and verified that the optical disc pack was receiving the data. Then she mounted the hardware on her shoulders, lowered the monocle, and moved into position. The digital steadier compensated for her motion, so she closed her left eye and simply watched through her right.

Lester, finger against earphone, received instructions from GSN and awaited his introduction. He nodded toward Hillary and looked into the camera lens.

"Good morning, Bruce," he said to the distant anchorman. "The Mojave Desert is a wasteland of dry lakes and bristling Joshua trees. Today, though, the airport at Mojave is a beehive of Space-related activity as nuclear industry billionaire Laurence Poubelle — the man behind the Daedalus Project — calls a press conference at rival rocket designer Gerald Cooper's spacecraft hangar."

Hillary panned the camera past Cooper's mockup of Starblazer and zoomed in on Poubelle, who stood with Cooper and D'Asaro on a platform in front of the model. Cooper wore his trademark dark suit, white shirt, and skinny tie, while Poubelle and D'Asaro were decked out in matching black and gold flight suits with Project Daedalus patches sewn prominently over their hearts.

"Good morning," Poubelle said in the same voice he used to address soldiers in Vietnam and workers at American Atomic. "Two days ago, the United Nations approved a treaty that will signal the end of the American space program. Some may mourn its loss, but the truth is that NASA has done nothing to achieve a permanent home in Space for humanity since it let Skylab crash in flames in the Australian desert twenty years ago. The Moon, once promised as a new home for us, has been abandoned for nearly three decades. Our children have no memory of what it was like in those days, thinking that the future was within our grasp.

"There is something more ominous, though, in the Interplanetary Treaty. It does not just abolish NASA and seize the Shuttle and Cape Canaveral. It also authorizes the UN to control or seize *any private spacecraft or launch company*. The creator of the treaty, Barry Gibbon, holds up the example of the Antarctic as a paradigm of how the UN should control Space. Antarctica, however, is a small continent full of life. Space is infinite and — mostly — sterile and dead. No world body has the authority to restrict anyone's migration into Space.

"I'm here with my co-pilot on the Daedalus Project, Chemar D'Asaro, and my neighbor and fellow Space Cadet, Gerry Cooper, to announce the formation of an organization directly aimed at building a private, non-governmental presence in Space. It's called the Experimental Spacecraft Association, modeled after the venerable Experimental Aircraft Association, and as its inspiration does, it will serve to give experimental spacecraft builders a network of information, volunteer assistance, and moral support."

Poubelle put his hands on his hips and gazed at the cameras with a smile that promised the world. "In order to inspire ESA members in this goal, whoever constructs a reusable, single-stage spacecraft that *within the year* puts a human being into orbit around Earth will receive, from me, the sum of five hundred million dollars."

His words made Hillary's camera teeter for an instant, then recover.

Thom Brodsky, there both as Cooper's friend and partner and as reporter for his *Private Space Journal*, shot his hand up to ask, "Why only one year?"

"The treaty," Cooper interjected. "IT becomes effective next January twenty-seventh. We feel that if we have spacecraft in orbit by then, the UN will have no way to enforce the treaty. They may be able to pin us down next year, but they have no way to bring us down once we're up there. These are peaceful, private efforts to inhabit Space, and the world would view any attempt to down such spacecraft as an unwarranted act of genocide against a minority group."

"Minority group?" someone from a local TV station said.

"Under the terms of the UN's own Genocide Treaty," Poubelle answered, "any government that acts to eliminate a political movement is guilty of genocide. We believe in the unrestricted right to travel into Space and create a free and prosperous culture there. As such, the ESA represents a politic—"

"What about NASA?" Lester asked. "They've kept Starblazer on the ground for years. And Congress seems to have it in for you, Mr. Poubelle."

Poubelle's smile twisted to an amused angle. "We won't let personal vendettas get in our way. And we urge the American people to write and call their representatives. You know"—he raised a finger, his voice shifting to a conversational tone—"Americans spend six billion dollars a year on makeup products, twenty billion on sports. If everyone who wanted to be out there in Space themselves within their lifetimes, instead of watching a handful of high-cost astronauts play with water globs, if they just sent in the cost of one lipstick or one football ticket or one movie or one cable channel, we'd be sending up rockets like the Fourth of July."

He nodded toward the reporters. "I know I've used more than a sound bite or twenty, so I'll just leave you all with that half-billion dollar prize floating out there. I've got that in escrow. That's my personal fortune, it doesn't come from American Atomic or anything like that. And, by the way"—he winked at the cameras—"I intend to keep it by being the first up with Project Daedalus!"

"There you have it," Lester said as Kaye turned the camera toward him. "A five hundred million dollar prize in the Great Space Race. How many contestants there will be and whether the governments of the world will permit such unbridled competition remains to be seen. Back to you, Bruce."

"And… we're clear," Kaye said, lowering the camera.

"Geez, I used the most clichéd opener and closer in the book!"

"Joe, it's your first time. Take it easy. You were fine. Hey! They're still doing questions!" She switched the camera on and refocused on the trio.

"No," D'Asaro said in answer to a question. "The Shuttle does not count. It is directly subsidized by the government."

"But satellite owners pay to use it!" a reporter countered.

"Paying a few hundred million when the actual cost of a flight is nearly a billion sticks the taxpayer with the deficit."

"What if the government forbids the contest for safety reasons?"

"*Some* governments may forbid it," Poubelle said, "but one can launch from anywhere to qualify. And if someone wanted to share part of the winnings with an impoverished equatorial country…"

"Yet you plan to launch from right here in the USA."

Poubelle nodded. "Damn' right. I'm an American. I fought and lost an arm for America. And I think anyone in government who tries to stop an American from settling this wild new frontier is just a grub-eating tinpot tyrant more concerned about limos and mistresses and obsequious lickspittles than about the future of the human race. I say, eat my exhaust plume!"

"Fighting words," one reporter said into her camera, "in Round One of a new Space Race."

"Hey!" Lester muttered to Kaye with a grin. "I ripped off that name first!"

"Trite minds think alike, Joe."

▼ ▲ ▼

Reporters gone, Cooper took Poubelle on a tour of the hangar, including a close-up look at the Starblazer model.

"Even if I had the money," he told the billionaire, "I don't think I could have a prototype built within a year."

"Why not?" Poubelle asked. "*Nomad*'s only a few months away from completion. I figure a September launch—"

"Look, it's not as easy as you seem to think. There is component testing—"

"We're both using off-the-shelf. What's your problem?"

"Safety is an important issue here, it... Look, what happens if your spaceplane crashes and takes a city block with it?"

Poubelle narrowed his gaze. "What happens when an airliner with two hundred people does the same? A few headlines, a ton of lawsuits... Gerry boy, I think you've internalized all of NASA's propaganda over the years. The only difference between a rocket crash and an airline crash is that a rocket crash kills fewer people! If Chemar and I went down in flames and hit an orphanage run by nuns we'd get plenty of coverage. Not that I'd care, because I'd be dead. The death toll, though, would be less than an average holiday weekend on the highways." He grasped Cooper's shoulder in his robot grip. "Good God, man, if we worried about death all the time, we wouldn't go anywhere. And that's just what NASA and Gibbon want. Do you think the men setting out on the Oregon Trail worried whether they were leading their wives and children to death?"

"Yes, I do."

"But that didn't stop them, did it? A lot of them died. Hell, I can guarantee you there'll be people dead because of this race." He tightened his grip. "We all die, Gerry. *We all die*." His titanium fingers released the man. "Do you want to die later, gazing up at the stars from some rest home bed on Earth? Or do you want to die up there? And if you want to die among the stars, does it make any difference *when*?"

Cooper stared at the man in black, speechless. His words were those Cooper might have used on doubters, years ago. He suddenly felt much older than Poubelle, weary of the world and the battle he had fought for so long.

"Look," Poubelle said. "I think your problem is that even your simple Starblazer concept is made complex by all that plumbing for so many engines. If you want to win that prize, why on Earth are you using solid rocket boosters?"

"When I redesigned the ship for a NASA contract, I wanted to use something derived from Shuttle research that was also throttlable."

"Did the original design need hybrid boosters?"

Cooper frowned. "No."

Poubelle walked toward a CAD station. "It was reusable, though, right?" An arm of flesh and an arm of metal shoved Cooper down into the seat. Poubelle switched on the draft mode and called up the design of the blunt cone Starblazer, deleted the boosters hanging off the side, and began rearranging internal components with the mouse. "I've seen your original designs. They're based on Max Hunter's designs for SSTO's, so you know it's feasible. Hell, the Delta Clipper proved that before NASA pulled the plug. Just dump that NASA-pleasing mindset —"

"I've never wanted to please NASA!" Cooper took the mouse from Poubelle's mechanical arm and raced through the changes, improving the LOX/LH_2 design beyond even its original parameters.

Poubelle smiled and stood back, content to observe the rebirth of Starblazer under Cooper's frenetic CAD input and spoken notes digitally recorded and converted to text by a simultaneously running utility. He turned to leave only to encounter Sherry Cooper, who had been standing silently behind him during the entire exchange.

"Thank you," she whispered. "I just witnessed my husband's return to life."

Poubelle shrugged. "Business motivation seminar jabber coupled with a layman's interest in rockets. Preaching to the choir is important. It keeps them singing." He pulled a black cap with a Daedalus patch on it from one of his cargo pockets and put it on in order to tip it in a gentlemanly way toward the woman. "Now, if you'll excuse me, Mrs. Cooper, I've got to go to my own hangar to ensure that your husband does not denude me of my fortune." He winked. "Although I wouldn't object strenuously to a dead-heat tie."

▼ ▲ ▼

Onboard *Constitution*, barely controlled chaos reigned.

"All I can tell you," Boyd said frantically into the microphone, *"is that we must deorbit* now *for a medical emergency involving Congressman Woolsey!"*

"You're scheduled to de-orbit tomorrow. Is the emergency life-threatening?" Bryan Kirk's hand pressed against his earphone as if it could push the words deeper into his head so that no on else could hear. He stood in his office out of earshot of anyone else at Mission Control. No one else, as far as he knew, could intercept or decode the encrypted channel he used to communicate with *Constitution*.

Several seconds passed. Boyd's voice was cautious. *"I doubt it. Believe me, though, this mission is over."*

"What's with him, Scott? Spit it out!"

"He's received multiple lacerations to his face. It's stopped bleeding, but he's going to need plastic surgery right away."

Kirk's voice exploded into orbit. "Tammy! It was Tammy, wasn't it?"

"Sir, she was—"

He gripped the boom mic until it bent. "I want her restrained and put under guard. Pump her up with Thorazine if you have to. I don't want her endangering the orbiter. Keep this quiet until we can develop a contingency plan to explain why she went berserk."

Boyd spoke in slow, precise words. *"I don't think you'll want any of this to get out, sir."*

"We've got to handle her somehow."

Jon Franck interrupted. *"The government's handled her quite enough,"* the astronaut said coldly. *"Woolsey tied her up and raped her."*

An icy sensation like the terror of free-fall seized Kirk's stomach. His voice lay trapped inside lungs that refused to breathe. After a long moment, he quietly said, "Initiate procedures for emergency deorbit."

▼ ▲ ▼

Constitution landed safely at Kennedy, with Boyd and Franck at the controls. The usual half-hour wait for explosive fumes to disperse from around the orbiter passed at an irritatingly slow pace. When the ground crew opened the hatch, Woolsey disembarked first, his forehead bandaged. NASA issued a cover story that he hit a bulkhead while flying around in free fall and suffered a concussion. He angrily shoved aside any assistance walking down the stairway and stomped into the ambulance under his own power.

Lights flashing, the van sped down the runway to a waiting congressional jet, destination not divulged to anyone at KSC.

Reis stepped out of the orbiter to see the jet take off. Jon Franck could not tell whether she was merely squinting in the sunlight, or whether the smallest trace of a vicious smile momentarily crossed her face.

A separate ambulance waited to receive her.

▼ ▲ ▼

Doctor Culver was the best plastic surgeon at Bethesda, and in his time he had worked on a number of badly carved sailors as well as a politician or two. No facial laceration, though, had ever impressed him with the degree of creativity shown on the honorable Ludlow Woolsey's brow. Though Astronaut Reis had confined her damage to the congressman's forehead, each stroke sliced deep enough to touch his skull.

"She can't spell, can she?" Dr. Culver muttered as he examined Woolsey.

The raw crimson wounds combined to spell the epithet

RAPEST

"Fix it!" Woolsey said through the clouding effect of painkillers. "I can't have a trace of it visible. I've got to maintain my integrity. I'm a congressman, for God's sake!"

"I'll bet she started to spell either 'rape' or 'raper,' then changed her mind and decided on 'rapist,' but it was too late to make corrections," the doctor mused. "Now it's spelled like a superlative. Rape, raper, rapest."

Woolsey looked up at the doctor with searing hatred. "Shut up and fix it! Flawlessly. Or by God I'll personally legislate you into bankruptcy and suicide."

The surgeon's firm hand on Woolsey's shoulder pushed him back onto the examination table. "I have no sympathy for you, sir. No woman would do this to another human being without cause, so I can only assume the worst." He sighed and signaled his anesthetist. "Still, I'm a military man and have to follow orders." He aimed one more light on his fleshy canvas. "If you hadn't taken thirty hours to get to me, though, this might have been easier. As it is…" He shrugged and waited while the anesthesiologist injected her customized cocktail into Woolsey's IV.

After a moment, she said, "He's out," and turned to monitor his chemical slumber.

Dr. Culver took a deep breath as his assisting surgeons flanked him. "All right, boys. The horizontal cuts we can hide in the creases of his brow, but these verticals and that runic 'S' are going to be problems..."

▼ ▲ ▼

Tammy sat in the examination room feeling nothing like the heroic first female shuttle commander. Bryan Kirk, who before had treated her and the other astronauts like his own brood, had escorted her almost wordlessly to the medical center and left her there, alone. A nurse took an unusually large blood sample — six tubes — and departed. For a quarter of an hour, Tammy stared at the light green walls and the speckled tile floor and pondered her situation. Only confused and distorted thoughts tumbled through her mind, inchoate and at times incoherent.

Should have killed the bastard. Then at least they couldn't cover it up as easily.

Why are they keeping me waiting?

Bastard.

A woman in a white lab coat entered carrying a folder. "I'm Dr. Thomas. We're still waiting on the blood test. It takes awhile."

"Blood test for what?"

"EPF. Early pregnancy factor only shows up in trace amounts, but it can tell us just twenty-four hours after the fact if you're pre—"

Reis raised her hand. "Wait. You're giving me a pregnancy test? Aren't you supposed to do some sort of exam to prove that he raped me?"

Dr. Thomas looked uncomfortable. "We're assuming that... sex took place. What we want to establish is whether a pregnancy termination is—"

"You go to hell!" she screamed. "Where's Kirk?"

The doctor nodded toward the hallway. Reis stormed out and searched for him.

"Bryan!" she shouted when she saw him.

Kirk made gestures for quiet with his hands. She lowered her voice to an angry hiss.

"What the hell is going on?"

His silencing motions transformed into placating ones. "Tammy, things have gone crazy here. Upper management hasn't got a clue what to do about it. In here."

He stepped inside an empty room, pulled a black box the size of a pager out of his pocket, and switched it on. The LED glowed green. "Okay, look," he said, satisfied that the room hid no bugging devices. "There's more here than right and wrong. I'd kill the guy myself, but the Shuttle's a tool of national policy and that means that what happens onboard affects national security."

Reis glared at him. "The last refuge of a coverup."

"The NSA's involved. I can't stop them."

"Who's got the tape?"

Kirk's face drooped into stunned confusion. "Tape?"

"The son of a bitch videotaped the whole thing. While *your* damn' camera was *off!*"

Kirk shook his head. "I don't know. I… Didn't you look for it?"

"Boyd wouldn't let me anywhere near Woolsey. He said he looked for it, but I don't think he looked hard enough."

"I'm sorry, Tammy, but it doesn't affect what's happening. I've got a meeting with Steve Milton slated for this afternoon. I'm telling you a black eye like this could… Woolsey's a vengeful man—"

"I'm a vengeful woman."

"We can't have it!" Kirk's voice verged on sheer panic. "We can't have anything other than the image of business as usual. Now, you'll be in on this meeting with Milton—"

"*What?*"

His voice leveled out to a dreadful tone. He gazed at her with eyes that displayed the management-level equivalent of raw animal fear. "If you want to save your career, you'll be there."

▼ ▲ ▼

The mundane world intruded. Tammy returned to her Cocoa Beach apartment to find her mail box jammed with bills and junk circulars, her potted plants in various stages of droop, decay, and death, and the smell of something like rotting broccoli tainting the air.

Now she felt truly down to Earth.

She had left the hospital without learning the result of her EPF pregnancy test. As far as she was concerned, the incident was over, or so she tried to convince her turbulent mind. She locked the door, threw the deadbolt, and slid home the chain, yet the actions imparted no feeling of safety. She stood to gaze at herself in the mirror at the end of the hallway.

Her shag of jet curls hung limply, a month of post-perm growth revealing over an inch of straight black hair at the roots. Around her eyes lay the crinkles denoting too much time spent in the sun, none of it recreational: desert survival maneuvers, tropical splashdown rehearsal, even orbital exposure to naked solar radiation unleavened by earthly atmosphere.

Her rational mind knew the cause of this feeling of ugliness and tried to discount it. The feeling would not depart, though, and another more insidious emotion crept in: the thought that she somehow deserved this, that Woolsey had been the divine sword of retribution for some pervasive evil that had stained her life.

She shook her head. *Original sin. Unearned guilt. Can't believe how ancient nonsense survives.* She could not shake the impression, however, that there was somewhere in her life a guilt that she had rightfully earned.

▼▲▼

She showed up at Kirk's office the next day. The small, cramped office belied the importance of his position. She sat across from his desk waiting for the arrival of NSA chief Steven James Milton Jr. Kirk said nothing about their previous meeting, said nothing at all, in fact, merely sitting with his head bent over a stack of papers, reading and signing, reading and signing.

Tammy suddenly felt an odd sympathy for the man; he spent his life sending other people into Space but would likely never follow them there. Most everyone at NASA was like that — they burned with the dream of space flight yet were condemned to live that dream vicariously. Meanwhile, monsters who possessed not the least iota of interest in Space parlayed their power into junkets as if Space were their plantation and astronauts their slaves...

"Tammy?"

"Huh?" She looked up at Kirk.

"Director Milton's in the building."

Milton strode in a moment later, followed by two men who performed a physical and electronic security sweep. Kirk's office was clean despite the piled clutter of manuals and reports.

"Bryan. Ms. Reis." Milton nodded at them perfunctorily and sat in the chair alongside Tammy. "To say we have a problem here is a gross understatement. The congressman has taken a two-week leave of absence, which we are attributing to the effects of a month in orbit. To say that he is not pleased with your actions is another understatement. He not only wants you out of the astronaut corps, Ms. Reis, he is ready to savage NASA's budget. This flight was supposed to convince him of the value of a manned presence in outer space."

"Bribe him, you mean." Tammy's voice dripped loathing. "Ply him with fulfillment of his fantas—"

"*Tammy.*" Kirk's voice, level but deadly earnest, silenced her.

"Meanwhile, we at NSA have encountered another threat to NASA's program. Our intelligence operatives have determined that something is afoot in the realm of subnational launch efforts."

Tammy frowned, but refused to acknowledge her ignorance by asking what Milton meant.

"Clues abound, all of them tantalizing but inconclusive: a shipment of imported solid-rocket fuel intercepted off the coast of Florida; forged interstate shipping papers for large amounts of lithium hydroxide that have apparently left the country; dummy corporation purchases of accelerometers, laser gyros, inertial navigation and guidance software, all of this during a downturn in aerospace business. All of it done with cash, not even ninety-day-net payments."

Milton looked more often toward Reis than he did toward Kirk. "On the face of it, no single episode appears incriminating, but putting them all together one is faced with the ominous possibility that someone, somewhere is secretly building a missile, perhaps more than one group. We've already got that nut out in California trying to build a spaceplane. We're pretty sure he's just fleecing people, but we're keeping an eye on him. And of course there are those companies trying to build private launch systems that we're keeping in check via the regulatory route."

The man shifted in his chair as if uncomfortable with the topic, as if something he was about to discuss deeply disturbed him.

"I don't know if you've ever thought about it, but what if someone could secretly construct a manned spacecraft and put it in orbit?"

Kirk, puzzled by the topic, said, "I suppose the military would shoot it down."

Milton snorted. "The military. They're still trying to win the Cold War. The Ballistic Missile Defense Organization — if it ever gets anywhere — is set up to defend against missiles coming *in* toward the country. What if a missile launched from, say, Nebraska? Arizona? It would catch everyone by surprise. Even if the military could launch something in an attempt to intercept it, the clandestine launch would have precious minutes of lead time. To say nothing of operations outside the forty-eight. A launch from Hawaii? How about Ecuador?"

"I don't understand," Kirk said. "What does this have to do with Tammy?"

Milton leaned forward, as earnest as a child in a high chair. "Simply this. With the congressman in the mood he's in, NASA would be unable to withstand the humiliation of an unauthorized — and cheap — private launch. I don't mean Larry Poubelle's egotistical self-promotion, we can defuse that. Something more sinister — a plot to turn space into a kind of orbital Bangkok. I'm talking about drug runners dropping their filth wherever they choose, insurrectionists broadcasting unrest from an invulnerable high ground, outright thieves holding satellites hostage, demanding ransom so they won't... I don't know, won't kick the Hubble telescope out of orbit. Ms. Reis, your country has a mission for you."

"I already have a mission. On the Shuttle."

Kirk cleared his throat so that she would turn to see him shake his head. "You've already been grounded. That was what I thought we were going to discuss."

Milton splayed his hands placatingly. "That need not be permanent," he said. "Temporarily, though — if you agree — you'll be quitting NASA."

Reis stared blankly. "No, I'm not."

"You are for the record." Milton produced a file folder from his attaché case. The bright red folder bore the seal not of the NSA but of NASA. "You are quitting the space program in disgust with the way in which it is being handled."

Reis's stomach tightened — *who finked?*

"You'll make it known to all your acquaintances," Milton said, "that your piloting skills are available — for a price."

"Why?" How could he have known it was what she had been contemplating in her moments of desperate frustration?

"Your past is not invisible to us, Ms. Reis. When you were a teenager, you assisted a man named Roberts in the construction of a rocket, so we know you are familiar with some of the so-called 'civilian' space efforts. A few years ago, there were over a dozen transportation companies attempting to offer alternatives to the Shuttle. You more than most should appreciate how that might have bled business away from your agency. The Department of Transportation helped NASA quite a bit when they set up the licensing bureau. And international agreements to set limits on launch contracts have slowed attempts to privatize the Russians and Chinese agencies. There are only a couple of spacecraft manufacturers left in the US, and they're both contracted to the Air Force for stuff the Shuttle can't handle."

"Unmanned missiles never threatened the Shuttle in the first place."

"Don't play dumb with me, Ms. Reis. I know that you were concerned enough about one possible competitor to go as far as to direct interference his way."

She gritted her teeth beneath her calm expression.

"Everyone in your bloated agency—"

"Hey!" Kirk protested.

Milton continued without comment, "—knows the shuttle's overpriced even with heavy subsidies. The only reason you've survived this long is that you've got friends in Congress and DOT, not to mention the NSA. We're just as worried as you about space technology falling into the wrong hands."

Reis frowned. "You just said the Russians and Chinese have been—"

"Not the damn' Russians, girl — *civilians*." The word sounded like a curse.

"But *we're* civ-"

"I don't mean NASA. I mean *private people*. Subnationals like your old pal Roberts. The yahoo on the street."

Kirk lit up a cigarette — he had taken to chain-smoking again — and leaned in toward Milton's lecture. "You're worried about Tom Swift offering cut-rate service?"

Milton turned away from the man's smoke to gaze out the narrow window at a sliver of the Atlantic Ocean. "The analysis sector of Puzzle Palace is worried. They want to determine the extent of the threat. Operations, however, wants a credible mole. An infiltrator to be invited in to filtrate." Milton smiled at his attempted witticism, then frowned when it was obvious Reis was unimpressed. "What they want is a double agent in the counter-economy."

"The *what?*"

"The underground. The black market. We have a fairly extensive think-tank report indicating how easy it would be for someone with a few million dollars to build a small, functioning spacecraft and put it in orbit."

Reis glowered at the administrator. "The *toilet* in the Shuttle cost twenty million dollars — no one could build a whole ship for — "

"According to this report, the counter-economy doesn't tolerate cost overruns. Things are done in the cheapest way possible, as you well know. We're not talking about people on the technological cutting edge, here. We're talking about Robert Goddard minds tinkering with Air Force surplus goods."

"You're just talking about bad PR."

Kirk stubbed out his cigarette to say, "Right. After the embarrassment of *Challenger*, a stunt like a civilian space launch could ruin the shuttle program. Why use a Cadillac when a Model T can get you where you want?"

Is that all it is to you after a few years pass? she thought. *An embarrassment?* "You don't seriously believe that, do you?"

Milton glanced at her, a genuine concern clouding his expression. "NSA does. That's why we want an experienced shuttle pilot out on the streets, waiting to be approached."

Reis stood up. "I don't do cloak-and-dagger crap."

"Then you don't do flying crap," Milton said.

Kirk made a placating gesture with his cigarette hand. "Tammy — how would you like to be the mission commander for the first construction flight of Space Station *Unity*?"

"That's been five years away for the past fifteen years. With the UN treaty, it may never happen." She could not believe what she uttered. It sounded like bargaining. "Anyway, why should I have anything to do with NSA or NASA or..." She could not bear to utter Woolsey's name.

"Because," Milton said, "your deepest desire is to be an astronaut. It's not simply a career goal with you, it's not just the 'top of the pyramid.' You *need* the space program and you know it's the only avenue for you. It's in grave danger, now, because Woolsey is going to take vengeance on the agency. You took a knife to a powerful and vindictive man, Ms. Reis, and an entire organization is going to suffer for it. Tens of thousands of employees may lose their jobs. Earth's only space fleet may be grounded forever. All because of one... amorous encounter in—"

"I don't have to take this," she said, rising to stare down at the little man.

"No," Kirk said. "You don't." He pointed toward Milton. "You told me you were going to make Tammy an offer she could live with, one she'd be eager to take. Now you're acting as if she's to blame in all this. Well, she *isn't*. Make that offer or get out."

The edges of Milton's mouth inched upward to a near-smile. "In brief, pretend to quit NASA in disgust—"

"That'll be easy," she muttered, still standing.

"—and wait to be contacted by subnationals. Someone out there will want your knowledge and skills. If you hook a good prospect, we'll have Operations neutralize them. Quietly. Then I guarantee that Bryan and I will coordinate our efforts to secure your flight status in spite of any objections from certain legislative quarters."

"How secure will that flight status be?" she asked.

Milton smiled. "That depends upon what fish you net for us."

▼ ▲ ▼

Reis spent the evening getting drunk with a couple of her crewmates in The Ablation Room.

"Putting me on furlough," Reis muttered to her Jack Daniel's. "What does that bastard Kirk want?"

"Funding!" two of her friends said simultaneously. "No bucks," Mission Specialist Samantha Madison said, "no Buck Rod—"

"Spare us," Jon Franck drawled. His lanky, mountain-boy looks seemed perfectly at home with a bourbon in one hand and a tumbler of branch water in the other. "Anyway, if Kirk is going to be that vindictive, we should call him on it." He muttered a low curse, taking a sip of the Wild Turkey. "Wouldn't *that* perk up the news for a week or two."

"Yeah," Madison said, running her fingers through her light brown hair, her face a mask of confusion. "Just happened with Woolsey up there, anyway?"

"Shuttle's the only way to go," Reis mumbled, staring into her drink. "We've got the space bug. Want to be up there. Who else is going to let us go? The Russians?"

The others laughed. "Can you speak Japanese?" Franck asked.

"If I thought they'd take me," Madison interjected, "I'd learn to be a samurai."

Franck snorted. "If you knew the feudal history of the samurai, you'd know that's what we are right now."

Reis had enough for the night. She rose to leave without finishing her drink. Outside, the night air from the Atlantic blew across her face and arms, cool and bracing. She maneuvered her car homeward, weaving only occasionally.

Her night in bed passed without nightmares or dreams; the long hours drifted by in a sleepless and troubled jumble of confused thought.

CHAPTER 22

It is inconceivable that a secret intelligence arm of the government has to comply with all the overt orders of the government.

— **James Jesus Angleton**
CIA counter-intelligence chief

3 February

"Half a billion bucks is nothing to sneeze at."

Marcus Grant smiled wanly at Donahue. "I intend us to beat everyone else," he said, "but I don't think we'll need the prize. First, we won't be returning to Earth to claim it, and, second, our immediate action upon achieving orbit will be to broadcast a declaration of independence."

"Politics?" Chad Haley leaned in the doorway of Grant's office. "You?"

Grant swiveled in his chair to glance at the newcomer. Haley wore a light tropical outfit that contrasted sharply with the rainfall hammering the Long Beach harbor area. Strapped to his overnight bag, though, was a telltale dripping umbrella.

"It just so happens," Grant said, "that I was quite political in my youth. Anti-political, you might say. I think I can get it up for a blistering attack on UNITO. How was Uganda?"

"I spent a few weeks there yesterday." Haley flopped down in an empty chair, his face a mask of exhaustion. "Speaking of politics, I think the situation is too unstable even for us. There were two gun battles near the airport the one day I was there. Six Ruwenzori protesters dead. Constant announcements from the government that there was no cause for alarm. I couldn't even sign onto The Net over there. However..." He pulled a handful of flyers from his overnight bag and tossed them on Grant's desk. "There aren't a lot of choices when it comes to equatorial launch sites, especially with uninhabited land or ocean to the east. In the Celebes Sea, you've got Malaysia, Indonesia and such. Borneo would be a good location, as would Celebes or New Guinea; over seven thousand of the smaller islands are uninhabited. Biggest problem is that it's under fairly constant satellite observation, due to intense shipping."

"Heck, the whole planet's under surveillance," Grant said. "That shouldn't stop us."

"It rains a lot there, too, which limits launch opportunities. In South America, you just have Brazil. Lots and lots of Brazil. Macapa's a coastal city at the mouth of the Amazon. Good political stability, but maybe too close and cozy with the U.S. That leaves the east coast of Africa. Somalia, to be precise. Kismayu."

"Kiss your what?"

Haley shook his head. The long hours were getting to all of them. "It's a port town smack dab on the equator, give or take a quarter degree. Climate is desert-like, with occasional monsoons."

"Political stability?" Grant asked.

Donahue sighed. "Rotten. Tribal warfare disguised as civil unrest. Somalis versus Bantus. You remember the U.S. was involved a few years back. Dead soldiers dragged around. It's quieter now, but not what I'd call placid."

"Those are our choices?"

"If you want an equatorial orbit. If you decide otherwise, there's—"

"No," Grant said with an emphatic finger jab at the desk. "This station, this *first* station, has to be in an equatorial orbit. I intend to use it as a way station for geosynchronous rendezvous." He let go a disgusted snort. "Let me think about it. Have you finalized the station blueprints yet?"

Haley shook his head. "Still checking out contractors to do the combustion chambers. We need over eleven thousand of them. And we were going to go to Mojave and check out a composite fabricator for the propellant tanks."

Grant's voice brightened. "Mojave Airport?"

Donahue nodded, smiling. "Across the field from Laurence Poubelle and the Daedalus Project."

A wide grin spread across Grant's face. "When's their gift shop open?"

▼ ▲ ▼

The rainstorm drenched the desert, too. Grant maneuvered the luxurious Jeep El Capitan through and around sheets of water spilling across Highway 14.

Haley kept his gaze glued to the Jeep's navigation terminal, reading weather information and simultaneously watching a real-time map of the storm enshrouding them. "Flood watch for the area," he muttered, "but no flood warnings yet.

"We're almost there," Grant said, pointing to a faded sign.

Donahue peered out at the sign. On it was painted a bizarre-looking white aircraft with long, thin wings, an engine pod with both pusher and tractor propellers, and twin fuel pods parallel to the cockpit. "Hey! Did you know that this is where Voyager flew out of?"

Grant nodded. "And a few miles down Highway Fifty-Eight is Edwards Air Force Base, where the shuttle lands sometimes."

"There!" Donahue pointed at a small sign indicating the way to the airport. Grant executed a skidding turn that sent a sheet of water splashing against the side of a small diner. A few lefts and rights later, the Jeep slid to a halt behind a series of hangars.

After a few moments struggling into rain gear, the trio popped open umbrellas outside the doors and galoshed into muddy puddles, splashing their way toward the Daedalus Project building. Haley and Donahue headed for the office and Grant for the hangar.

The office was a wonderworld of merchandising: hats, shirts, mugs, keychains, model kits, pamphlets, pens, lunch boxes, postcards, and much more lined the walls and the point-of-purchase displays. The two visitors stood in the entrance shaking off the water and collapsing their umbrellas before venturing forth into the souvenir Mecca.

"Not too crowded today, is it?" Donahue fingered the black corduroy cap with the Daedalus patch.

The lady behind the counter smiled. She was plump and matronly, though her face bespoke too many days in the searing desert sun. "Some people just don't like weather."

Joscelyn slipped the cap over her auburn hair. "How do I look?"

Haley laughed. "Like a wet gas station attendant."

She turned to the woman. "I'll take it."

"Poubelle's really paying for the rocket with all this?" Chad picked up a photo book of the progress so far on the project, along with artists' conceptions of the flight itself.

"Souvenirs and donations." The cashier pointed to a mayonnaise jar by the cash register, stuffed with coins and currency.

Haley and Donahue glanced at each other, then broke out into laughter, both imagining what souvenirs from their own scheme would look like.

In the hangar, meanwhile, Grant observed the dozen or so workers laboring tirelessly on *Nomad*. His gaze darted everywhere, absorbing details, analyzing strengths, searching for deficiencies. *This is the market at work*, he thought. *Competition fueled by cooperation, driven by a vision. No need to pay them hush money, either*.

"Beautiful sight," a voice behind him said.

He turned to face Larry Poubelle, dressed in a glistening wet black leather trenchcoat and carrying a thin Zero-Halliburton aluminum case. A worker ran up to him; he handed the case to him and said, "Gyros and accelerometers. Give them to Pierce."

"Mr. Poubelle." The visitor extended his hand. "Marcus Grant."

Poubelle reached out merrily, then hesitated upon hearing the name. "*The* Marcus Grant?"

Grant smiled. "I've heard that often enough that I'm going to make it my first name."

Poubelle shook his hand anyway, saying, "I don't believe everything I read in the papers. Considering how they treat me."

"Believe half of it." He reacted only slightly to the grip of the mechanical hand. Upon release, he pointed toward the skeletal aircraft. "You know, the X-15 A-2's drop tanks added a lot of weight and drag for only two more Mach numbers. And the proposal to make it orbital by hitching it to a Navaho booster included the pilot ditching the aircraft to parachute back to Earth."

It was Poubelle's turn to smile at the man. "For a billionaire, you seem to have done your homework."

Grant ran a hand though his grey hair. "We're more or less contemporaries. The original program held my interest as… a teenager."

"What brings you out here?" Poubelle asked. "Rotten weather for limos."

"Business," he said in the politesse of the wealthy that implied it was none of Poubelle's damned business and he was better off inquiring no further. "This part of it is the pleasure I try to mix in whenever possible."

"Would you like the four-bit tour?"

"No, thanks." Grant looked about. "I know you've got a deadline to meet." He paused, then looked Poubelle straight in the eye. "Do you think they'll just let you fly off out of their reach?"

"What?" Poubelle stared at the man with a baffled look.

"You were a military man. How would they—"

"Oh, *them*. I don't worry about *them*. The three C's, you know: Cost, Competence, and Conspiracy. Right now, they can't afford it, they probably can't hit an accelerating target over the continent, and there are undoubtedly conflicting factions of the power elite whose divergent interests would probably paralyze any response. Hell, you must have encountered such ruling class intrigue, right?"

A thin smile distorted Grant's lips for a moment. "Spake as one billionaire to another."

Poubelle laughed like a banker in a melodrama. "Don't you hate inherited wealth?"

Grant nodded. "If you don't earn it yourself, you can't appre—"

"Gun!" someone cried.

Poubelle whipped about to see a woman in the hangar door pointing a revolver at him. He cut to the side, covering his face with one arm, his heart with the other. She followed his motion and commenced firing. The shots reverberated in the sheet-steel building as workers jumped from *Nomad* and dove under desks and behind equipment.

Grant raced toward her and launched into a flying tackle just as her last round fired. They slammed against the concrete together, her head hitting with a sickening crack. A brunette wig flew from her scalp exposing matted, henna-orange hair beneath. Her face was lined like a map of homelessness and misfortune. Blood trickled from her nostrils and ears.

The .38 caliber Colt Cobra skidded from her grip to lay a foot away from her. Grant elbowed it farther away. "Don't touch it!" he shouted to a worker running toward him. "It's got her prints on it."

A strange whirring sound approached him from behind. Pinning the assailant's unconscious shoulders to the ground, Grant turned to see Poubelle approach, his right arm twitching in spasmodic jerks. He fumbled with a pocket on the shirt sleeve; it tore away with the ripping sound of Velcro to reveal an access hatch that he opened to press a finger inside. The arm suddenly froze as if it had been placed in a cast.

"Took a slug in the servos," he muttered, then hollered over his other shoulder, "Antonio! Bring my other arm! It's behind my desk!" He bent over Grant and the woman.

"Who is she?" Grant asked.

"You tell me," he said, looking curiously at his rescuer.

▼ ▲ ▼

The local constabulary and paramedics eventually arrived to cart the groggy woman away. The rain, at least, had let up. None of the cops lifted an eyebrow of recognition when Grant reluctantly identified himself for their reports. He was mostly known to a higher level of law enforcement than small-town flatfeet.

When the assailant's identity had been sufficiently established, along with it came her disoriented attempt to explain a motive. Joseph Lester and Hillary Kaye were there to tape his response.

"Have you ever heard of Lana Lane before?" Lester asked, turning the microphone toward Poubelle, who sat at his desk on which lay his ruined arm, two bullet holes punched in it, a golden puddle of hydraulic fluid staining the newspaper beneath it.

"Never. And her claim that she had lost some big investment in American Atomic is equally untenable. My people are checking into her claims, but if she has any beef, it ought to be with her stockbroker, not with me." He pulled a cigar from his pocket humidor and rolled it in his living fingers.

"Do you find it suspicious that such an assault would take place in the middle of a winter storm out in the Mojave desert just days after you announce a half-billion-dollar Great Space Race?"

Poubelle glowered at Lester as if he had been asked what color underwear he was wearing. "I don't want to speculate on anything that's even more far out than my offer." He suddenly grinned as if a switch were thrown. "Why don't you ask me if I had it done as a publicity stunt?"

While Lester wrapped up the interview, Poubelle noticed that Chemar had returned from her daily rain-or-shine run to stare in alarm at the crime scene tape blocking the entrance. When she saw Larry, a look of overwhelming relief enveloped her. She rushed over to embrace him, staining his clothes with rainwater. Then she smiled up at him and said, "I'm gone an hour and this is how you treat the crew?"

Poubelle nodded. "No one's hurt," he said, "though I think we may have to address the security question."

"What did I tell you?" she said in a somber tone.

Gerry Cooper sloshed by to say that he had heard about the attack.

"Bad weather brings 'em out," Poubelle replied.

"It must do something," Cooper agreed. "I took a call this morning from General Davis of the Air Force. They've agreed to let us conduct launch tests from Vandenberg."

Poubelle raised a wary eyebrow. "I'll pencil your name on the check," he said wryly, then added, "Watch your back."

Cooper frowned, perplexed. "Thom Brodsky said the same thing. Don't you guys see that they're finally coming around? That our arguments and examples are convincing them to loosen up?"

"I see them trying to cover all bases." Poubelle flexed his spare arm.

"I know for a fact that there are people in the military and civilian space programs who don't like the Interplanetary Treaty any more than we do."

The robotic arm whirred and slapped Cooper across the back to give him a comradely squeeze. "Then maybe they'll all quit their jobs and join us, eh, Coop?"

5 February

Jon Franck and Samantha Madison, while commiserating with Reis yet another night in The Heat Shield, both regretted the pilot's decision. As far as they knew, she quit the corps without even consulting them. A chill permeated the Ablation Room as they discussed the future, an icy atmosphere that distanced her from her closest friends.

Madison coolly suggested that Reis go to an airline. "You're attractive, you could always get a good PR job."

Reis eyed the younger woman with sullen pain. "You could say my looks got me where I am today," she agreed. "Listen, I want to fly *spacecraft*." She felt miserable and wondered whether she had made a truly idiotic decision. What did *she* know about spying, anyway?

"Not too late to learn Japanese," Franck said.

"Very funny."

"I'm serious. NipponAero is just a few years away from their first crewed launch. Forget the PR potential, they might just offer you a chance to pilot the ship because of your expertise."

"Maybe," she said. "But I'd prefer something that'll knock Kirk's ass onto concrete. Something right under his nose." Her voice rose enough for other tables to hear. "I'd like to blast off right out of the middle of Omaha or someplace on a pile of nuts and bolts that cost ten bucks to build and show those bloated little empire-builders in management how a space program ought to work!" *There*, she thought. *That wasn't too hard. Just keep talking that way. Subtle and indirect.* She took another sip of her Jack Daniel's.

Franck entertained the idea seriously. "Well, there are private launch systems struggling for a market. That media hog Poubelle is one of the least credible. It's all the regulations, though, that keep them from making any headway. Who can afford to post a hundred million dollar bond before each flight? Governments can — they print the money, so it's just a bookkeeping entry. Private companies, though, you're talking real money."

"And convincing the satellite industry," Samantha added. "They see the STS and EuroSpace and won't invest in a new system until they see a prototype and no one can afford to build a prototype without investment from industry."

Tammy slugged back her drink as if it were water cooling a fire and slammed the shot glass down. "It's pointless." Her voice was slurred from the third drink. "There're too many little petty *cowards* in NASA who'll sabotage anything that might threaten their damned funding!" She looked around her and loudly said, "Any one of you think you've got a future in Space? I mean for more than a few days out of your entire lives?"

Samantha touched her arm. "Come on, Tammy. Sit down."

"Everyone talks about how we're like Christopher Columbus," Reis said, nearly in tears. "Columbus didn't matter. Sooner or later someone else would have hit the coastline. The one's who mattered were the Indians who showed up three hundred centuries before and actually *settled* here! And Virginia Dare, first baby born here from English settlers."

Jon pulled her down into her seat. She stared mournfully at the tabletop. "We're just *tourists* pretending we'll move there someday, but the boss won't let us transfer. He won't open a branch office. 'Too expensive,' he says. 'No one out there.' Well, I say 'Build it and they will come!' "

Jon shook his head and stood to raise her up. "Let's take her home. When she starts quoting inspirational sports stories, she's had it."

▼ ▲ ▼

Milton read the flash report carefully. It described the pistol attack on Laurence Poubelle in general terms, closing with the observation "investigators conclude that the assailant was a disgruntled former investor in American Atomic with a history of mental illness. Suspect was under the care of a psychiatrist and was being treated with fluoxytine hydrochloride. Police view suspect as LNA."

LNA was agency shorthand for Lone Nut Assassin.

Milton smiled. The mark of a successful hierarchy was how well a particular task could be accomplished without its goal being mentioned at all. Strategy, discussed at the highest levels, translated into tactics at middle levels — without the specifics ever being communicated — and from there trickled downward to operatives as individual actions with no apparent trail of actual orders leading back to the top. This had been the technique of leadership long before Henry II had established plausible deniability in the assassination of Thomas à Becket by uttering no more than the rhetorical question, "Will no one rid me of this meddlesome priest?"

Milton knew that merely by asking if Poubelle might be in danger because of his public battle with NASA, he had communicated to his aides the need for Poubelle's removal. The assistant quickest to intuit his wishes would be the one who would most quickly find an underling to whom another vague implication would be made. From there, the chain of imply and infer continued until someone contacted the psychiatrist and — perhaps — suggested an increase in the dosage of fluoxytine or an in-depth discussion with the patient about her feelings toward Poubelle, or maybe a session on "acting-out" or whatever was the *shibboleth du jour.*

Milton slipped the report into the shredder, which sliced it in six different directions and ejected it from the underside as a minor snow flurry of small paper flakes.

To rule by decree was pleasing enough, he thought, but to be surrounded by minions skilled at interpreting unspoken wishes was far more sublime.

Milton worked late nearly every night. It was not that he needed to, but that he chose to. Something about the NSA offices — constantly abuzz with intrigue, incessantly flowing with information plucked from a conniving humanity — filled him with a sensation of standing on a firm rock in the middle of a vast, turbulent river watching the political and historical waters flow around him. More than anything, he gloried in the giddy realization that he could alter that flow with less than the point of a finger; with an ambiguous wave, a casual word.

When he first achieved the high water mark of the bureaucracy, he discovered that agents would make mistakes in interpreting his wishes. It soon grew apparent, though, that it was an organic, evolving process that winnowed away the ineffective to leave only those who could most consistently execute his unstated desires. To his surprise, he also saw that the mistakes seldom mattered, since undesired results could be explained away as random chance or even turned once again toward his own ends. The only danger in a mistake, he realized early on, was if it caused damage to the secret wishes of those even more powerful than he.

Such an irredeemable foulup had never happened. The only proof that he was consistently pleasing his superiors was empirical: he was still alive and still NSA chief.

"Mr. Milton," the voice on the intercom said. *"Call from Mr. Kirk."*

Milton realized that he was about to make another part of the river suddenly splash up and shift course. "Put him on," he said, "and secure the line."

CHAPTER 23

Anyone who puts his own conscience above the state is an anarchist.

— **Allen Thornton**
Laws of the Jungle

6 February

The Lurker still followed him.

Haley raced through The Net as fast as he could issue commands. He understood now that the impression of being watched was not a mysterious, impossible case of telepathy. Running through the Moroccan bazaar that functioned as this week's central meeting zone, he saw the cause of his apprehension: the meticulous programmers of The Net had created such a scrupulously lifelike virtual world that polished objects reflected light and images. Haley had never paid much attention to the finer aspects of the illusion until this morning — when he saw in a green glass fishing float the reflection of a figure standing behind him: the shadow of the Lurker.

In an instant Chad was off, flying out of the bazaar at eight megabytes per second, the fastest his equipment could cycle the image over the fiber lines. The shadow followed him. All bets were off now. No more subterfuge. Whoever tracked his whereabouts on The Net no longer cared about stealth. He glanced backward to see that *only* a shadow followed him; that was a sure sign that the Lurker's presence was encrypted. He had seen shadows before in the moreadvanced experimental realms, but they always stayed on the sidelines.

Now one pursued him, presumably to frighten him, for there was no way Chad would do any work while being chased. He fumbled with one-way trapdoor functions to enter private sections of the system: the Pornorium, this month featuring an *hareem* out of a triple X-rated version of Burton; the Mad Scientist's Lounge wherein — for educational and curio purposes only — lab-coated, shock-haired researchers and their hunch-backed assistants worked this week on revivifying a virtual corpse; and the Wilderness Retreat, set up for one viewer, one vista. Chad emerged from the tent and zipped the flap shut, locking out all other users.

The shadow of the Lurker penetrated the tent like smoke through a veil.

Haley stood his ground. Pressing a stud on his outfit, he assumed the form of Horus, the mighty hawk-headed Egyptian sun god.

The shadow merely stood amid the desolate splendor of Destruction Bay, on the northern base of the Klondike's Saint Elias Mountains. Behind him lay Kluane Lake, deep blue beneath a sky scrubbed digitally free of any trace of worldwide pollution.

"Okay," Haley said through his flesh-rending beak. "I know you've been following me around for months. You may have gotten something interesting in the first few weeks before I realized what was going on, but I've isolated my system from The Net since then, and Sophia's endured no penetration, so you're just chasing shadows as immaterial as you. You're just trying to unnerve me and it won't work."

The shadow hung there amid the vegetation and the rocks. It flickered now and then, nearly imperceptibly. Haley suspected that whoever was behind the shadow was not connected via fiber line but by way of a satellite linkage. That could place them anywhere in the world.

He switched off his mic and spoke to Sophia's microphone mounted on the computer itself. "Sophia. Correlate those flickers on the shadow with satellite hand-offs. Try to intuit an origin for the signal."

"Sure, honey," the seductive voice responded.

Switching back on, he said, "Maybe you're just trying to waste my time. Or maybe I'm wasting yours."

The shadow remained unmoved. "You could be on automatic pilot, I suppose." Haley drifted toward it. "A genuine shadow, intended just to follow me around." He switched his glove to handshake mode, a way to identify another Net member with a touch. With a swift motion, he plunged his fingers toward the wraith.

Pain shot through his hand as the feedback servos in his glove suddenly constricted. They could not break his hand, but the pinch served as a potent warning that no data would be forthcoming by normal channels.

He shook his hand out, which sent all manner of conflicted commands to The Net. His point of view shot up Mount Kennedy, across to Mount Vancouver, and stomach-lurchingly downward into Yakutat Bay. After a brief ascent to the summit of Mount Seattle, he gave the finger signal for return to origin and stood once again before the tent.

The Lurker was gone.

Fingernails scratched at the inside of his tent. "Who is it?" he demanded.

"Joscelyn," came the muffled reply. She was the only one he had given an unlimited exemption to his Do Not Disturb default for such areas of The Net.

"Come on in."

The tent unzipped and the digital Joscelyn entered the great outdoors, dressed in an unnervingly sexy *lederhosen* getup with a blouse cut low in a manner the Swiss never intended.

"You just missed the Lurker," Haley muttered, losing Horus and restoring Tom Jefferson, this time in an 18th century hunting outfit.

She strode up to touch his shoulder, putting them in encrypted one-to-one communication. "How's the purchase going?"

"We have a single source for the thrust chambers as well as the fuel tubing," Haley said. "And an alloy fabricator in South Af…" He paused to gape at her. Her image flickered for an instant.

"Where are you?" he asked in what he hoped was a casual manner.

She gazed around her, then looked at the compass on her wrist. "Pretty far from here, actually. I'm in Florida, waiting for a pilot. A good one, too. How about you?"

"I'm assembling an excellent team. I'll tell you more in person. Gotta go now." He strode past her through the tent to make an orderly exit from The Net rather than just switching off.

Doffing his SkyPilot goggles, he gazed at his office and let out a slow, unsteady breath. His pulse raced and sweat dampened his brow.

"Sophia? Were the Lurker and Joscelyn ported through the same satellite links?"

"No. The first set of hand-overs indicate somewhere on the eastern seaboard. The second visitor was definitely from Florida or Georgia, though with only one hand-over to—"

"Thank you, Sophia. Could a single source access The Net through two different satellite paths to hide its origin?"

"Possibly."

Haley grunted. Whoever the Lurker was, it attempted to make him doubt even his allies. An east coast source certainly pointed toward the alphabet soup of snoopers concentrated about the District of Columbia. CIA, FBI, NSA, DIA, and a dozen and more. Instilling paranoia was a standard destabilization technique in their portfolios.

He shut down the computer and headed to Grant's penthouse office.

▼▲▼

Colonel Tuchapski worried about his own single brand of alphabet soup: GRU. Though the destruction of the Soviet Union liquidated much that was unsavory about the military security organization, its remaining members found a new endless enemy against which they could continue their employment. *Nalevo*, the left hand of Russian economics, the black market. Nalevo was a worthy enemy, for was it not the underground economy that brought the Kremlin to its knees, providing food when the government markets were bare, selling vodka in the midst of Gorbachev's anti-alcohol crusade, and importing Western clothing, music, and electronics right under the noses of corrupt officials?

Now, here on the outskirts of Novosibirsk, Col. Tuchapski was one of those corrupt officials, moving products out of the right hand of government control into a shadowland of left-hand use. Corruption for him, however, took the form of his adherence to an abandoned Russian goal: the conquest of the Cosmos.

Thirty SS-18's had so far been destroyed in this phase of INERT. Five of them were fakes comprising spare casings and loose parts. The genuine articles lay hidden in warehouses around the southern part of Siberia. Today he would acquire the sixth and final missile.

"Colonel Tuchapski?" The man entered the office bringing with him a flurry of snow and blowing ice. He wore a heavy wool overcoat of modern Western design topped off with a traditional hat of expensive beaver fur. It was an odd mixture of styles that managed to betray the integrity of both fashions.

"Yes?"

"Aleksander Baumhoff, *Geh Er Uoh*."

Tuchapski frowned. The man was one of the East German bastards that stayed with the Soviet Union after German reunification, then somehow remained in the GRU after Soviet dissolution. Tuchapski usually admired loyalty, but this man obviously possessed no concept of motherland. Or fatherland, or whatever gender he used to anthropomorphize his nation, if he did at all.

"Good morning," the colonel said cheerlessly. "Would you like a glass of tea?"

"Coffee, if you have it."

"The coffee is mud."

Baumhoff smiled. He was a man of medium height, with the rounded, fleshy contours of well-fed Teutonic physique. More unnerving to Tuchapski, though, was his impression that the GRU man's smile was a happy one. He detested that, especially in a German.

"At least not frozen mud, yes?"

The colonel shrugged and poured the coffee into a cracked red mug, one of several still in active use around the base that bore the golden star of Soviet supremacy, tarnished though it was with age and neglect.

"Ho!" Baumhoff said, receiving the cup. "Collector's item!"

Vladimir inwardly fumed at the comment. He considered the mania seizing the West, in which any trinket from the former Union became a fashion accessory, to be nothing more than the tasteless humiliation of a conquered foe, vultures picking at the corpse of a fallen titan.

"What brings you to this cold place, *Herr* Baumhoff?" The foreign honorific was about as much insult as he dared allow.

The GRU man sipped at the acrid beverage, then smiled over the edge of the cup. "The UN inspectors contacted us concerning... *irregularities* in the demilitarization process here."

Tuchapski maintained his placid military composure. "Such as?"

Baumhoff sighed and wrapped his hands around the warm cup. "These people have been through several verification processes. SALT, START, INF, START II. Several of the more experienced have a certain *intuitive* feel for how a proper missile explosion should look. In at least three instances, they were... *dissatisfied* with the... *quality* of the detonations."

The other man shrugged. "It is cold here. Sub-zero temperatures play havoc with the explosives. Additionally, some of the plastique we use is over a quarter of a century old. Very unstable. Very unpredictable. Sometimes we have no explosion at all. Sometimes..." He flung his fingers lightly outward and mouthed a silent *poof*. "We lost a nearby truck last month when a burning piece of explosive hit the fuel tank *then* exploded from the shock of impact."

Baumhoff smiled and nodded his head. "You hear? Another mystery. No one saw that explosion, but the truck is reported destroyed. A large truck, also, as I understand it. The Kremlin is thinking perhaps enforcing INERT could be a little less expensive."

"So you are here as an accountant?"

Baumhoff lowered the cup. He no longer smiled. "I am here to take account."

▼ ▲ ▼

For the first time since his military career began in Afghanistan, Vladimir Tuchapski considered that career at risk. Sudden disappearance was no longer a threat as it was in the past, but losing one's rank in the current economic climate was nearly as bad as death, there being no pensions or guaranteed employment. He knew the only place he would be able to work under such conditions: *nalevo*.

Boots crunched across the ice as the small cluster of personnel and inspectors trudged to the missile destruction site. It was three in the afternoon and not yet dark, though the heavy, low clouds washed all color from the landscape. The frigid air burned Tuchapski's nostrils. He enjoyed the harsh assault, as he enjoyed the vast grey expanse of the slate skies touching the snow-ash tundra all around him.

The UN team consisted of eight observers from Security Council nations, four of them missile scientists, four of them demolition experts. While Russian troops prepared the missile for destruction, the UN team observed every step of the process.

Tuchapski and his accomplices worked with great caution in stealing the missiles. They could not salvage an entire SS-18 at once, but instead picked components from each of the two dozen rockets destroyed since hatching their scheme. This time, under the noses of UN observers, they were after the rocket motor.

Tuchapski's men made certain that the mounting bolts had been cut away from the inside, leaving the engine in position, though precariously so, and the outside untouched. Timing would be crucial.

In the stinging cold, the UN representatives gave the most cursory of inspections to the missile. They had seen so many demolitions so many times before that the repetitive task numbed their minds as thoroughly as the Siberian winter chilled their bones. The SS-18 lay in sections on a cheap iron support frame that would be sacrificed along with the rocket. Surrounding its perimeter, a long, thick snake of grey putty formed an oblong loop along the bottom, almost as if the weapon had been mounted on a wad of modeling clay. Four wires extended from the plastique, running five hundred meters to the blockhouse.

A few degrees colder, Tuchapski mused, *and wires could become superconductors.*

The UN inspectors each raised a hand to indicate assent to the procedure. Baumhoff watched with interest as everyone trudged away from the blast zone without a word.

The demolition area lay in a shallow depression about one hundred meters in diameter. Their boots sought traction in the snow as they climbed out, and Tuchapski gave a quick final glance backward before ushering the group toward the blockhouse.

His men worked swiftly. As soon as the UN team passed the point where they could no longer see the missile, six men rushed in, heads down, maneuvering a low, wide dolly toward the rear of the SS-18. On the dolly lay pieces of an old rocket motor, which they dumped beside the demolition stand. Muscles tearing with the effort, they rapidly slid the good engine out of its housing and onto the transport. A steel cable ran up the eastern side of the depression to a hidden winch.

Heading toward the blockhouse, Vladimir calmly watched the inspectors — and most of all Baumhoff — with his peripheral vision. None of them looked back, though Baumhoff glanced at the colonel now and then.

The blockhouse was just that: a square bunker with walls of meter thick reinforced concrete and a roof about half that thickness. It housed the simple-but-effective controls for the detonator, a vented outhouse, mercifully indoors, a radio, and a dented old samovar in which water stood hot and ready for the crowd of frozen men and women.

Tuchapski kept a mental count of the time. At the moment they reached the door of the blockhouse, his men were winching the engine up the side of the pit. When he walked over to the samovar and began to draw glasses of water for their tea, they ought to have been over the edge, struggling to guide the slippery burden down the shallow incline toward the waiting truck.

"To peace and disarmament!" he said, raising the tall glass. The others muttered the oft-repeated toast in limpid tones and sipped at the hot drinks. At that moment, the truck would be slowly clattering away from the site with its precious burden. He smiled toward the head demolition expert. She nodded back, rubbing her hands together for warmth.

Reaching toward the simple detonator, she threw the first switch to arm the system. It warmed up slowly. As soon as the green light on the black, crinkle-finish box glowed, she could depress the detonation button, an impressive, overly large red protuberance surmounted with the word DETONATOR in Cyrillic.

By the time the explosion would take place, the colonel's men and their precious cargo would be out of the danger zone and on their way to a warehouse.

The light glowed green. The demolitionist pressed the button while gazing through the bunker periscope to observe her handiwork.

At that moment, however, the six men and the rocket motor were not motoring toward safety as planned; they stood at the edge of the depression pulling at the steel cable in an effort to raise the engine without the aid of the winch, which lay on its side in the snow, motor smoking, victim of a corroded central shaft that shattered on startup in the sub-zero temperature.

One of the men took a precious instant to glance at his wristwatch timer.

"Too long!" he shouted. "Run!"

A dozen boots clambered up the icy embankment while the pristine engine slid back toward the blast zone.

The grey twilight flared to a dazzling orange-white. The six men felt only the pressure of the blast at their backs, then nothing, as shrapnel from the explosion riddled their bodies, punching through layer after layer of coat, sweaters, and shirts to penetrate flesh, muscle, organs, and bone. The shock wave tore apart the two men closest to the missile. Another was crushed by a large, smoking chunk of debris. The rest merely fell forward into their own entrails and lifeblood where they steamed for a moment before freezing solid.

Tuchapski knew none of this as he sipped his tea with the others, secretly relishing the knowledge that he would soon have enough equipment for a cosmic endeavor that would stun the world and awaken the sleepy oafs that peopled the Kremlin.

"Shall we inspect the damage?" the GRU agent said.

The colonel stared at Baumhoff. "We must let the noxious cloud dissipate first."

Baumhoff edged the UN woman aside to peer through the periscope. "I see only some smoke from fire. There is a brisk wind blow—"

"Very well," Tuchapski said curtly. "We go."

Within a hundred meters of the site, Tuchapski realized that something had gone horribly wrong. Dark forms littered the left edge of the snowy depression. Even in the growing darkness the crimson stain of blood leapt out with stomach-churning vividness. He realized what had happened long before the others could comprehend. They raced toward the smoking pit to gape at the carnage. All except Tuchapski.

Baumhoff was the first to turn his head from the horrific sight. He saw the smashed dolly and the twisted remains of the rocket engine. Fumbling inside his overcoat, he reached for his concealed Makarov 9mm pistol while simultaneously struggling to work his index finger out of the slot cut into the glove for the purpose of trigger-work.

Auto-pistol out, he completed his turn to stare at the barrels of Col. Tuchapski's decidedly non-regulation pair of Ithaca M1911A1 .45's gripped in white, gloveless hands.

The twin pistols spoke out of turn, one shot penetrating Baumhoff's throat with explosive force, the other disappearing into his overcoat and pushing outward the heavy fabric on the other side. The GRU agent stared sightlessly at Tuchapski with the dying expression of a man who could not comprehend how all his dreams and plans could end in a single instant. It was a visage of such uncomprehending disappointment that the colonel endured a momentary twinge of compassion before suppressing it beneath an icy contempt and an equally cold dedication to his task.

The UN observers stared in horror only a moment before making a break in all directions. They could not run fast enough.

The Colt .45 clones in Vladimir's hands held sixteen rounds fully loaded. Down to fourteen, he knew that he would have to be deliberate in his targets in order to slaughter the remaining dozen lives. He fired at the two women first, in an effort to spare them the pain of seeing their compatriots die. Both fell from single shots to their chests.

He spun toward one brave fool who attempted to rush him and blew his skull apart with a left-handed shot. Something burned inside him now, a battle-fever he had not encountered since a firefight against the *moujeheddin* on the outskirts of Kabul. His forehead pounded, his hands glowed pink with supple warmth in defiance of frigid nightfall.

He lunged forward, racing after his shrieking prey, laughing with every shot that downed a victim. Three with his right pistol, two with his left. Two at once from left and right combined. One of his targets, the slender Pakistani running in a random, evasive manner, required an annoying three shots to dispatch. The shots rang out hollowly, incapable of echoing anywhere on the tundra. Dark puddles of blood smeared across the snow, sinking into it and freezing solid like the fossilized record of an ancient conflict.

Two more still lived. He gazed about. One man — the British member of the team — cowered behind the cooling wreckage. A shot from the right pistol dispatched him with a hammer blow to the upper spine. The slide on the .45 locked back, the magazine completely empty. He pocketed the heavy automatic and transferred the other to his right hand.

Footsteps crunched across the snow. A truck door slammed. Vladimir scrambled out of the pit to see the other American inspector furiously monkeying with the ignition on the truck the colonel's men would have used to haul away the engine.

Tuchapski pounded toward the truck, his lungs searing with each intake of super-cooled air. The furious heat departed his body and soul almost as fast as it had come upon him. With time to ponder his deed, he almost regretted this final killing if for no other reason than it was indeed the last.

His bare left hand gripped the truck door handle, where the sweat of his exertion promptly froze, firmly adhering his skin to the painted metal. He paid no attention to the burning pain, but leveled his pistol at the American.

The engine caught and the truck lurched forward. The pistol shot punched up through the truck roof and the slide locked open.

He swore and reached through the side window to pistol whip the driver. The American blocked his blow and floored the accelerator.

The Russian's frozen grip held tightly to the handle and he swung his arm again, this time hitting the driver's laryngeal cartilage.

With a curse directed toward both god and devil, Tuchapski tore his fingers from the door handle, leaving behind a good deal of grey, frozen skin, and jumped from the uncontrolled truck. He rolled in the snow, coming to a stop when he slammed against a concealed rock. The truck, bouncing wildly onward, also hit a rock and tipped lazily over, still in gear with tires spinning.

Tuchapski rose, searched for his other pistol, and pocketed it. Then he sat down in the snow to take a deep breath while slipping his gloves back over his cold, stiff, bloodied hands.

He knew that he would have to rig a second explosion after gathering all the bodies to the center of the demolition pit. It would take several hours in the dark and cold. He would do it, though. It would buy him some time.

Time enough to escape.

CHAPTER 24

Big institutions, if unwatched and unchallenged, make big mistakes.

— **Ralph Nader**

8 February

Too many variables, Jack Lundy thought. *Too many different things being changed all at once.* It was almost like the old days before *Challenger*. President Crane wanted to make a big deal of the quick turnaround time on *Constitution*, seeing it launched next month, less than six weeks after the end of its Enduro flight. Whatever happened on that previous flight remained a mystery to Lundy, who only knew that Congressman Woolsey maintained his seclusion after ten days and the shuttle commander, Tammy Reis, quit the program to become a drunken fixture at The Heat Shield. Rumors spread like a plague, and he knew of at least seven different theories concerning her plight, all of them fraught with sexual implications. Though the gossip threatened to distract many technicians from their duties, Lundy kept his attention planted squarely on his work.

With changes to the firing-sequence programming *and* the delivery of the latest solid rocket engines *and* the dizzying turnaround for *Constitution*, Lundy feared that safety was once again taking a back seat to political necessity. Crane had a point to make about the Shuttle and the Interplanetary Treaty. NASA management apparently concluded that UNITO might choose one launcher to be the sole transportation system for the entire planet, and they hoped to influence the choice — among the STS, Europe's Ariane 2000, Japan's N-2, and Russia's venerable Proton — with a good showing in the next few months. President Crane concurred, hence the sudden acceleration in launch schedules and the attempt to reinstate the "can-do" enthusiasm of the 1960's.

Lundy knew better. He gazed out his office door at the people walking to and fro. Career bureaucrats, half of them, who boasted of management skills while almost proudly professing their ignorance of engineering. The rest... burnout cases such as he, dinosaurs from the growingly distant Space Age, hanging in there for the pension or trying to rescue a scrap or two of the dream. There may have been a handful of young people who possessed some vision of humanity living in Space, but they burned out even faster, leaving within a few years to pursue positions at foreign launch efforts for lower pay, or using what skills they may have picked up at NASA as résumé filler in search of higher-paying work in the domestic private sector. Some simply vanished completely, apparently leaving aerospace altogether.

He looked once again at the thick printout of programming for the launch sequence. The recently redesigned rocket motors required new sequencing commands. New commands required new programming. New programming demanded meticulous debugging. Debugging consumed time. And President Crane let it be known in his State of the Union message that time was something NASA would not be allowed. The UN vote could not have come at a more inconvenient time.

The SRB ignition sequence alone consisted of over ten thousand lines of code. Jack realized that he would have some evening and weekend reading ahead of him.

The phone buzzed. "Hello?" he muttered to the speaker grill.

"Dad!" The voice over the speaker was deep and strong.

"Alan!" Immediately, Lundy's face and voice brightened. "How are you, son?" He unconsciously sat up straighter, his shoulders squaring with pride.

"Fine, Dad. Guess what — the promotion came through! You're talking to Lieutenant Colonel Alan Shepard Lundy, United States Space Command." Even with his masculine baritone voice, he sounded like a kid to Jack, as if his son had come running home with news of a home run that won the game.

"Alan, I'm very proud of you. And I know your mother will be, too."

"Where is she? I tried calling her over there, but they said she was on vacation."

Lundy laughed. "She's in California. At the San Diego Wild Animal Park for the Ark Society. Up to her elbows in white rhino semen, no doubt—"

"Dad!"

"—she and crazy friends. Did you hear that they found a female passenger pigeon in some old guy's freezer in Vermont? They're all agog about finding a viable strand of DNA to clone. I told her 'as if we need more pigeons,' and she—"

"Father."

Jack paused. Alan only used the term to get his attention. "What?"

"I've been transferred to Vandenberg. I'll give you my number when I'm settled in."

"Are they taking the Shuttle launching facility out of mothballs?"

"I can't tell you that, Dad. It's a big step up for me, though."

"That's great son. I'll tell your mother."

They chatted some more, then said their goodbyes and disconnected. Jack pondered the meaning of his son's transfer. The Vandenberg launch site had never been used for Shuttle flights. It was one of the most expensive boondoggles in history: the military cared nothing for the STS but demanded a piece of the action in an effort to control the spacecraft's design and use. The Air Force insisted on all sorts of modifications, such as the capability to land practically anywhere on the planet despite a notable lack of suitably long runways; such changes raised the cost and delayed launches from the mid-Seventies until the early Eighties. The west coast launch site cost way over a billion dollars, back when that was a huge sum of money. Never used, it was summarily mothballed after the destruction of *Challenger* when the military abandoned any publicly professed interest in manned space travel.

Now it jumped suddenly to the front burner again. Lundy could see no other reason for his son to be promoted and moved to Vandenberg. As far as the world knew, Space Command was nothing more than a debris-tracking service for NASA and the military, keeping tabs on the thousands of satellites, living and dead, and the boosters, fragments, nuts, bolts, and paint chips circling the planet in the Sargasso that was Low Earth Orbit.

Lundy frowned. *Little more than a week after* IT *passed the* UN, *this happens.* He tried to make sense of it, but his mind simply had no capacity to generate conspiracy theories. That was more Igor Svoboda's hobby. He turned back to the printout. It would be a long six weeks.

▼ ▲ ▼

The six weeks passed for Tammy Reis in a fog of alcoholic incoherence. Far from being flooded with calls from clandestine space colonization cabals, she had not even received a single call back on the résumés she had faxed to aerospace companies in the first week of her unemployment. After that, her visits to The Heat Shield became more frequent. It was her attempt to drown out the incessant dreams. Doused with liquor, the dreams either never surfaced or were forgotten upon waking, she was never quite sure which. She did not want to be sure of anything ever again.

Had it all been an act — former astronaut Tamara Reis hits bottom — it would have been superb in its realism. Tammy, though, was in a tailspin out of which even her friends could not pull her.

"Shuttle's actually going to go up next week," Jon told her as she sat on a bar stool among the bar's non-spacefaring clientele, well outside The Ablation Room.

"Who cares," she muttered. " 'Nother Sputnik!" she yelled at the bartender.

Ed Laird slid the drink, a vodka highball, to her, a sour expression crossing his Captain Nemo face. "Listen, Reis, you're downing these things as if you've taken out a contract on your liver. Ease up or I'll jettison you on your retro."

"Ed, shut up with that stupid space lingo. God, ten years I've been coming here and you still talk like someone from a stupid comic. It was stupid when I first heard it and it's stupid now and it'll be stupid when I'm..." She lowered her head and started to cry.

"Jon?" she said. "Is Sam around?"

He shook his head. "She's in training, Tammy. She's mission specialist on the flight next week. You're not remembering anything anymore. You're not aware of anything."

"Aware." Her crying turned to a disdainful snort. "I'm aware of one thing." She downed the Sputnik in three pained gulps. "Samantha's not here?"

Franck shook his head.

"Damn. This is girl stuff."

"What girl stuff?" he asked in a cautious tone.

"You know," she said, her speech slurring as the alcohol fraction of her blood continued to increase. "Like, whether getting blasted every night makes you miss your period or is it just a body fat thing?"

Something akin to vertigo seized Jon. The edge of the bar became a precipice from which he clung in fear. "You missed your... ?"

She could see enough of him to tell that he was counting backward.

"No," she said weakly. "No, that's not it. It's gotta be body fat. I read it somewhere. I haven't been keeping food down, so I must've lost weight."

"Tammy, you've got to see a doctor. This could be—"

"*No!*" she screamed, sliding off the bar stool and pushing away from Franck. "I've gotta be *here*! NASA needs me! I'm part of the *team*, don'cha unnerstand?"

Franck looked at Laird. The barkeep nodded and came around to help the astronaut strongarm Tammy back home.

The interlude did not go unnoticed by the patrons of the establishment, including one who had more than a tabloid reader's interest in the fallen angel.

CHAPTER 25

Every decent man is ashamed of the government he lives under.

— H. L. Mencken

10 March

Though Larry Poubelle generally loathed lawyers, he acknowledged their necessity by doubling the number working on his problems with the government. In the first three months of the year, the team faced down a cease-and-desist order from the Interstate Commerce Commission regarding sales of Daedalus memorabilia, performed an end-run around both NASA and the Federal Aviation Administration regarding certification of *Nomad* as an experimental aircraft, brought suit against the Department of Transportation for technical violations of the Paperwork Reduction Act, and successfully quashed a suit by the Center for Space Exploration in the Public Interest seeking a restraining order against a launch from any federal facility.

The core of his team had honed their claws at American Atomic, battling all manner of lawsuits relating to nuclear energy litigation. For them, the whole question of space travel constituted a finger exercise. Enough vagueness and contradiction existed in US and international space law for them to storm about the courts like rampaging bulls or slither through loopholes like pencil-thin snakes.

Poubelle had no affection for people whose entire lives revolved around finding exceptions to everything, but he appreciated their dedication to the specialized trait and rewarded it.

He knew the other side was desperate when they sicced the Bureau of Alcohol, Tobacco, and Firearms on his hangar with an eye toward charging the Daedalus Project with "construction and possession of an explosive device," specifically, the explosive bolts that would detach *Nomad* from its mother aircraft. One of his lawyers, permanently stationed at the hangar, discovered seven errors in the warrant, including an incorrect address for the airport and the lack of the approving judge's signature. With Joseph Lester and Hillary Kaye on the scene delivering a live feed to GSN, the BAFT retreated, blaming the mistake on flawed information from an investigator in the Justice Department who had a drinking problem. The Justice Department declined comment later that day.

Poubelle let the lawyers perform their arcane incantations and cast their Latinate runes. He was more intrigued by the interest generated by the Experimental Spacecraft Association. Already over two hundred people had joined, half of them submitting designs for the contest with about half of *that* group indicating that they intended to construct working models. Most were obvious nonsense or distant dreams, but at least a dozen consisted of detailed specifications, parts lists, and price sheets.

If we get a dozen members with realistic plans, he wondered, *how many more are out there around the world, quietly constructing their ships rather than trying to deal with the crap I've had to handle?* A sudden grin spread across his face. *Maybe I really* do *have a contest on my hands.*

▼ ▲ ▼

Poubelle's nearest contender sat in his office reading the latest issue of *The Private Space Journal*. Thom Brodsky's lead story concerned the threat of the Interplanetary Treaty and the responses of Laurence Poubelle and Freespace Orbital. There followed updates on such obscure efforts as "Ace" Roberts in Northern California and a few others that were more talk than action. He glanced up from the screen to ask, "Thom, you're more hip to politics than I am. I just design these things. Do you think there's a concerted effort to keep us grounded?"

Brodsky guffawed. "Comes the dawn after twenty years!"

"It's just that this thing with the AFT. It's so... vicious. They showed up armed."

Brodsky twirled his Project Daedalus cap on a finger. "Remember that Rex Ivarson novel back in the Seventies? *Pindown*? I don't doubt his contention that the military will never allow a civilian spacecraft to launch. I don't care how much money Poubelle has, he's in danger of an 'accident' at any point."

Cooper turned his attention back to the page layout on the computer screen. He ran a hand through his hair. "What about us?"

Brodsky sighed and let the cap spin across the office to hit with a thunk against the water cooler. "I don't think we have anything to worry about at the rate we're progressing." He glanced in the direction of Poubelle's hangar. "I wish he'd share the wealth. A guy such as he ought to be more willing to—"

"We can do it on our own," Cooper said sharply. After a pause, his voice dropped to a calmer tone. "If we just keep working at our grand plans, someday someone will walk through that door with a smile on his face and an offer to invest in—"

The office door swung wide to slam against the wall. Both men looked up to see a woman standing there, framed by desert sunshine. She was short, chestnut-haired, and feisty, dressed in green and black.

"Those bastards!" she cried out.

"May we help you?" Brodsky asked.

"If you have nothing to do with those bastards at NASA, you might."

Cooper started at her. "Nothing whatever."

She flopped down in the chair before Cooper's desk and picked up a copy of a recent *Private Space Journal* to fan herself. "That rat at the top of NASA, that Jack Craver, said — officially, mind you — that the Shuttle could not be made available for tourist flights. Safety concerns, he said. Liability. Lack of available payload space. UN treaties. Geez. And me with zillionaires that wouldn't think twice about popping a mil per seat."

Cooper looked at Brodsky. Brodsky raised his eyebrows, then shrugged.

"Excuse us," Cooper said. "May we ask… who *are* you?"

She stopped fanning herself and stared back at them in shock. "Leora Thane. Society Orbital Tours." She tossed the *Journal* back on the desk. "Geez, you mentioned me in your rag a year ago!"

Thom recovered first. "I'm so sorry, Ms. Thane. I've never seen a photograph of you. Please have a seat — you already do. Of course. Coffee? Doughnut? Ice water?"

Cooper watched as Brodsky spent the next few moments soothing the woman's ruffled feathers. She wasted no time after that.

"Those NASA pinheads have jerked me around once too often. I came to them six months ago with an offer to send up eighty-five tourists on *Constitution* for a one-day flight. One measly day! And I'd pay them eighty-three million dollars. What sort of profit does that leave me? Who gets by on less than two percent these days? That's what they charge anyone else for a stinking satellite. So what, so people can get more TV channels? Geez, just what we need, more reruns of *Lucy*. I was talking cultural enrichment! I was even going to give a seat *free* to some kid with polio or something. What more could I offer? Blood?" She collapsed back in the chair, then pulled a green-and-black leather cigarette case from her matching handbag.

"Damn' bastards. I had twenty-three people lined up. Twenty-three! At ten percent deposit! So I came here."

"Excuse me?" Cooper watched her light the long, black cigarette.

"Here," she said, using both hands for emphasis. "To this — you should pardon the expression — *egg crate.*"

"Egg...?"

"Look, I've got people who want to take a spin around the planet. They've got the bucks, but the suits at NASA tell me — officially, mind you — to take a flying one. So here I am. Let's talk."

Cooper stared at her with as much incredulity as her behavior warranted. "About building a tourist spacecraft?"

"No, about getting an even tan. Of course about spacecraft. I'm a busy lady. Did I tell you NASA kept me waiting four months?"

Cooper jumped from his seat. "Let me show you our prototype. It could carry twenty as is, not counting a crew of two pilots and two flight attendants."

"That means I could only get twenty million a flight!"

Cooper smiled. "But if you pay us eighteen million, that's a *ten* percent profit to you."

Thane nodded, smiling. "I like you. You know how to set priorities. Now how do *you* make any money on this?"

He held out his arm to her, which she politely took, and spoke as he led her into the warehouse. "For less than the recurring cost of a single Shuttle flight — for a mere three hundred million — we could perform *all* of the development necessary to build a fleet of single-stage-to-orbit spacecraft within one to two years. With an average spacecraft lifespan of one thousand flights, the cost can be amortized per vehicle per flight to five grand for development and twenty-five grand for the vehicle itself. Oh, did I mention that if we can orbit one by next January, we could split half a billion dollars between us?"

Brodsky watched the pair disappear into the hangar. He shook his head and muttered, "Not hip to politics, huh?" Turning to the computer, he rearranged the layout of his newsletter to insert an announcement of a pact between Freespace Orbital and Society Orbital Tours.

He reached for a doughnut. Things were looking up.

CHAPTER 26

The biggest mistake we have ever made was putting SRB's on the shuttle.

— Dr. Max Faget (ca. 1978)

16 March

The morning dawned clear and cool. Any day less than balmy reminded Lundy of the frozen morning when *Challenger* died. This morning, though, he paid scant attention to outside temperature. Inwardly, he had hit his own boiling point.

"Don't reroute me!" he yelled into the telephone. "I want launch director Geddis and I want him now. We've got to hold the launch until we can recycle the ignition sequen—" The distinct click of the call transfer caused him to curse. A new voice spoke on the other end.

"Marshall Space Flight Center," it said. *"How may I direct—"*

"Damn!" Lundy slammed the phone down. His stomach churned. *It's happening again. As if nothing's changed from before.* He gazed at the computer simulation on his workstation. Something in the new programming was causing a dissynchrony in the two boosters and he had no idea what it was. The only answer was to stop the launch.

He faced a battle as uphill as a launch into orbit. With nearly seventy successful launches since *Challenger*, the agency was more complacent than ever. All the changes instituted by the Rogers Commission had gradually unraveled over time, all in the name of increased efficiency and cost-cutting. A line engineer such as Lundy — for a few years able to access launch directors without interference — once again saw layers of bureaucracy and chain of command laid between him and fire control.

He seized his windbreaker and rushed out of the building. Perhaps if he barged in on Launch Control physically…

Igor Svoboda saw him outside and shouted.

"Jack! Meet my mother, Tanya!" The woman beside him looked like a recent arrival to Ellis Island, all wrapped up in a dark wool coat with a wine-hued, moth-eaten wool scarf wrapped numerous times around her throat. Her grey hair hid beneath a black and white polka-dotted babushka, the gayest item of clothing she wore. Her hands lay deep within the recesses of an aged muff that may once have been mink or fox. It looked stiff and old, yet regal and warm — very much like its owner.

"No time," Lundy replied. "I've got to get to Launch Control. Bastards won't let me get through on the phone."

"What's wrong?"

Lundy looked physically ill. "It's *Challenger* all over again, Iggy. I've found a glitch and I can't convince anyone of it. The whole damn' chain of command is committed to the launch."

"That's because of the UNITO guys they're taking up. A big show of solidarity."

"Solidarity!" Tanya muttered in a thick Slavic accent, embellishing the word with a dry spit at the end.

"We can still hold at T-minus thirty minutes if I can convince someone that there's a problem." Lundy disappeared into the crowd of workers and gawkers milling about between the buildings.

His worst fear was realized when he reached the launch control center: his security badge would not admit him during countdown. Out of breath and weak-legged, he nonetheless ran to a telephone booth on the far side of the structure. He punched in the number for Hayes Polysulphide in Utah. Arguing his way up from operator to management, he made a quick introduction and explained *Constitution*'s problem.

"So it's not a problem with our boosters?" the voice on the other end asked.

"No," Lundy said with clipped speed. "But a dissynchronous ignition will destroy them just as thoroughly."

There was a silence on the other end, followed by, *"Then I think you ought to take this up with your division head."*

"They're ignoring me here! I need someone higher up to reach the Launch Dir—" A click ended the conversation.

"Oh, Jesus," he whispered. "Christ, you bastards." The choking inside grew more profound.

T-minus thirty-five minutes. Still time. They could stop it at T-minus ten seconds if he could just break through. His legs pumped like a sprinter's as he raced back to his office. Out of breath, he collapsed in his chair and grasped the phone. It was his only hope. He called the off-site company that wrote the program. The team leader there insisted that there was no problem, that Lundy's simulation hung up because of system incompatibilities between his workstation and the actual launch computers. For a moment, she almost convinced him. He wanted to believe that, but could not allow such a comforting thought. The lives of eight astronauts were at stake.

The beauty of the morning was lost on Lundy, but not on the thousands of VIP's who crowded the viewing stands. For many of them, members of the National Organisation of Space Supporters, this was the culmination of years of effort. Finally, NASA and the United States put aside all nationalistic interests in the space program and instead aimed at a higher, more worthy goal: the unification of humanity under a single banner, to be taken to the stars by *Constitution*. Though some may have balked at the choice of shuttles — the Constitution, after all, was considered (in not so many words) an archaic nationalistic document of capitalist white male domination arrogating to themselves the all-inclusive phrase "We the People," — the irony of it pleased others. After all, now the United Nations Charter would be the fundamental foundation of humanity's future on other worlds.

One personage was notably absent: Barry Gibbon, founder of NOSS and author of the Interplanetary Treaty watched the launch from his seminar at New York University, a superb photo op for the attending news media.

The highest ranking US government official present — Vice President Schield — spoke of the importance of a shared tomorrow in Space.

"For the future," he said over the loudspeakers and television cameras, "belongs not to nations and to governments, but to the people of all the Earth. It is in their name that we humbly, and with reverent resolve, take this small jump into space, that a far greater leap to our home in the stars may someday be possible. And it is with a unified, single purpose that we move forward — slowly, cautiously — to test the new waters of this infinite ocean in the hope that our children and grandchildren will touch the dream that we can only distantly envision. Thank you."

The applause was light and respectful and rang as hollowly as his amplified words did over the tinny loudspeakers. The audience preferred to save their awe for the launch itself.

Also in the bleachers sat dignitaries from the United Nations. Ambassadors, mostly, with a handful of heads of smaller states who still gloried in whatever recognition they might receive from the globe's last remaining fully certified superpower. Beside them lounged several astronaut-hosts and invited guests such as congressmen, senators, governors, and large contributors to President Crane's upcoming campaign.

Most dressed lightly against the cool mid-March morning. Spring was just around the corner, but a cold front descending through the Midwest threatened the launch with high-altitude winds.

Jack Lundy prayed for a weather hold. In that, he was disappointed.

His phone calls to Launch Control went unrouted. He tried circumventing the chain of command by calling over to Johnson Space Center. No good. Johnson took over *after* launch. He called an old friend at Dryden. He was on vacation. In desperation, he called Vandenberg.

"Hello," he said. "My name is Jackson Lundy. Please connect me to my son, Lieutenant Colonel Alan Lundy, U.S. Space Command. This is an emergency."

"One moment please." It took a hell of a lot longer than a moment.

"Dad?" the deep voice at the other end asked in a querulous tone.

"Alan! I'm at my wit's end down here. We're at T-minus eighteen and I can't get through to anyone that there's a glitch somewhere in the ignition sequence for the SRB's. I keep coming up with a dissynchrony that doesn't show up when they run it on the mainframe."

"Have you checked your PC for—"

"Christ, son, I need your help! You're in charge of making sure the trajectory is clear—"

"Not any more."

"Well, you've got to have some sort of hotline to the launch directors. Maybe if we both go at it from two directions one of us—"

"I'll do what I can."

"Thank you." Lundy pressed his thumb against the cradle switch and lifted it. He knew his son would do everything in his power. He looked at the computer screen. T-minus seventeen. There was still time.

▼▲▼

Igor Svoboda and his mother were not VIP's. Except for the astronauts, no NASA employee was allowed to take up space on the hard metal benches that accommodated the posteriors of the world's élite. Instead, they took Iggy's car several miles in another direction to park on the NASA Causeway that runs between the Cape and Merritt Island.

"Will we see it from here?" Tanya asked.

"Can't miss it."

"What about your friend's worry?"

Her son shrugged. "I gave up long ago any concern about NASA. I do what I'm told and I do the best job I can. The astronauts know that they're sitting on the largest non-atomic bomb in the world. They all remember *Challenger*. I can't butt my head up against Fate."

"Fate!" She made that spitting sound again. "Fate is the cry of a *svolotch*. You know what is a *svolotch*?"

Iggy smiled. "I helped grandfather fix cars. Diddi never minced words."
She nodded firmly. "A *svolotch* gives up and blames Fate."
He glanced at his wristwatch. T-minus twelve.

▼ ▲ ▼

Lundy's phone rang on the second line. He switched over from being on hold to take the incoming call.

"Dad. I got through to Washington."

"Great, Alan."

"Not great. They told me to route it or they can't consider it a legitimate request to hold."

Sweat stung Jack's forehead. "We've only got ten minutes!" He made an instantaneous decision. "I love you, Alan. Tell your mother I love her too."

"Dad? Dad!"

Lundy put the phone back and ran from his office. In his haste, he knocked over his coffee cup, which shattered on the black and white linoleum. He paid no heed.

Outside the office, he glanced at the huge countdown display in the distance. With less than nine minutes, his only hope to put a hold on the launch was to violate launch site security.

Lundy's knowledge of the spaceport, gained over decades of working at KSC, served him well. He knew where to find holes in the fences, ill-maintained areas of high brush. He had to remain out of sight in order to penetrate deeply enough. Then he had to become visible, so unrelentingly visible that a security-breech hold would be placed on the countdown.

At his age, though, he wondered if he could make it. He was two miles away from pad 39-A. He only needed to be within a mile of the pad to be seen on the surveillance cameras. It put him well within the danger zone from the blast of liftoff, so they would hold the countdown while conducting his arrest.

His legs pounded across the pavement and into the brush. Cranes squawked as he burst through their dominion, stumbling now and then over the uneven, marshy soil.

He discovered that one hole in the cyclone fence had recently been repaired. There was another one, though, a few hundred yards away.

Under the gap between the hole and the dirt below, he pulled and wiggled. T-minus four minutes. The wide service road that led toward the shuttle launch pads lay five hundred feet away. He scrambled toward it, grass and gravel sliding around under his shoes.

A terrible pounding thundered in his head with every wheezing breath. *Not too old,* he thought, *I can make it.*

Racing up the crushed limestone that composed the wide shuttle roadway, he saw the surveillance camera mounted on a tall, slender pole a hundred feet away. T-minus two. Still enough time.

He sprinted toward the launch pad with renewed energy, though his lungs and legs threatened to give out. His heart pounded like a turbopump and his vision tunneled until all he could focus on was the camera. He drew near and began to shout, waving his arms.

"I'm out here. Security! Hold the launch!"

What Lundy had no way of knowing was that the surveillance camera in front of which he gestured had been disconnected three weeks before in anticipation of a new replacement that would have been installed on a post thirty feet farther down the road. The replacement had been held up at the Port of Los Angeles along with ten thousand metric tons of electronic equipment from Singapore in a dispute over recently re-imposed tariffs.

T-minus sixty seconds.

"Come on, come on!" Lundy continued to wave. Then he heard the klaxon. Turning around, he gazed toward *Constitution*.

"Son of a bitch," he said, wheezing as he sat wearily on the white, sun-warmed limestone gravel. "First goddamn' launch in twenty without any holds."

At T-minus thirty seconds, he began to laugh uncontrollably.

"They must be proud," he whispered. "They must be so goddamned proud."

He could not hear the countdown from Launch Control, but he could tell from the sudden cascade of water roaring into the depression at the base of the pad that — at T-minus eight seconds — he had no time left. He took a deep breath and thought of Melissa. *She'll think I was the biggest fool who ever lived.* Then he smiled. *Maybe her friends'll have me cloned.*

At T-minus six seconds, Lundy watched in awe as the liquid-fueled SSME's ignited. He counted, just the way he did with Florida lightning. By the time the gut-rumbling roar hit him, the twin SRB's ignited, apparently in unison.

Constitution edged a few yards upward from the launch pad amid a white cloud of solid-fuel smoke and steam. Lundy watched in wordless amazement as it tilted sharply over to point straight toward him.

Dissynchrony!

He marveled as the colossal beast turned on its side and roared toward him, nosing into the marshland, the ET crumpling like tinfoil. It was his last living thought. Cryogenic liquids erupted from the mass that cartwheeled across the roadway toward him. In a heartbeat, the hydrogen and oxygen mixed; rocket exhaust ignited the half-million gallons of fuel in one single, devastating explosion.

▼ ▲ ▼

Staring at computer readouts, oblivious to the roiling disaster, the woman at Launch Control performing the countup said, “We have liftoff. Liftoff at twenty-six minutes after the hour. *Constitution* is clearing the tow—” Then the information on her screen turned to

SSSSSSSSSSSSSSSSSSSSSSSSSSSSSSSSSSSSSSSSSS
SSSSSSSSSSSSSSSSSSSSSSSSSSSSSSSSSSSSSSSSSS
SSSSSSSSSSSSSSSSSSSSSSSSSSSSSSSSSSSSS

indicating static. In utter shock, she looked up at the main video screen.

The viewers in the VIP bleachers knew within an instant of ignition that something had gone catastrophically wrong. Only the astronaut-hosts, though, knew the impending totality of the disaster. The right SRB fired first by only a fraction of a second. By the time the left engine ignited, the shuttle had begun to yaw over. The eight explosive bolts holding the entire spacecraft to the pad separated on schedule, but by then the left engine nozzle, bent and crushed against the launch pad, pinched shut, building up enormous pressure instantaneously, adding no compensating thrust and only increasing the sideways rotation of the spacecraft.

Constitution turned over with an agonizing shriek of metal lost in the volcanic howl of the tortured boosters. It twisted about and thrusted west toward the Vehicle Assembly Building. A mile away from it, the shuttle nosed over into the marsh. At that instant, the external tank spilled liquid hydrogen and liquid oxygen across the pavement. An instant later a fireball exploded like an atom bomb. The rising orange-white sun seared the flesh of everyone jumping from the stands and running madly about nearby. Then the shock wave hit them, blasting skin and muscle, shattering ears and bursting lungs, throwing bodies against buildings like bugs against windshields.

No one there lived to see the final horror, as the crushed, unrecognizable debris that was once *Constitution* reeled out of the fireball, propelled by its own monstrous momentum, trailing a toxic cloud of hydrazine from it auxiliary power units, which ignited hypergolically in a blinding streak. The SRB’s broke apart at their four joints, each segment under its own power as the fire inside the cores burned uncontrolled. The bottom three segments of each SRB, lacking caps, vented their thrust in both directions. The top segments of either booster took off like skyrockets, one corkscrewing upward into the blue, the other screaming southward to burn out over Lake Okeechobee and crash into the Everglades. The others pinwheeled around the marsh like so many colossal fireworks, sending thick streamers of orange flame and white smoke across Merritt Island.

Blown free from the boosters by the explosion of the ET, *Constitution* turned over and over, tumbling across the marsh like a rampaging beast, leaving scratch marks and deep furrows in the soil and limestone. Guided by its powerful initial thrust, it tore through fences and barriers to smash with irresistible force against the press and VIP bleachers, scattering aluminum tubing and human bodies like straws in a hurricane. Without slowing, the smoking ruins of the orbiter slammed into the Launch Control Center, penetrating it like a battering ram to expend the last of its kinetic energy against concrete walls and steel beams, shoving all aside until finally it came to rest amid the rubble and carnage, a flaming, charred mass of metal, plastic, and silicone tile.

▼ ▲ ▼

"Oh God!" someone cried in The Heat Shield as the morning drinkers watched the Shuttle's vain attempt to lift off.

"It's tilting!"

The small clot of people viewing Ed Laird's big screen TV fell silent. Behind them rose a drunken snort that became weak, bitter, half-sane laughter.

"Your *Constitution*'s burning, America. Hope you're watching." Tammy raised her glass toward the infernal scene and downed the drink in a single chug. The laugh transformed into weeping and she lowered her head, matted sable hair splaying around the arm she wetted with sobbing tears. " 'Bye, Samantha. That damn' pooch screwed you worse than it screwed me."

The doors to The Ablation Room burst open. A handful of astronauts — who had up to a moment ago been too jaded to watch the liftoff outdoors — burst through to race back to KSC. None of them noticed Tammy Reis raise her head blearily to watch the swirling flames engulf the spaceport. None of them knew the secret comfort she drew from seeing the instrument of her violation reduced to cinders. Not one of them, in their shock and alarm, could have known or even imagined the emotions that warred within her knotted soul and rotted mind.

Some of them, though, saw — from the corners of their eyes on their way out the door — a twisted smile on her pale, dry lips and the glint of vicious triumph in her dead eyes.

▼ ▲ ▼

"Turn on the TV!" Haley screamed, slamming through the doors into Grant's office.

Grant stared at him in surprise as Donahue instantly reached to switch on the wall screen. The lights automatically dimmed and the blazing images flared into view.

"What is thi—" Grant began, then saw the silhouette of a rocket gantry amid the flames.

"*Constitution*!" Haley cried, taking deep gasps for air. "It tipped over. I saw it hit a building. Look — they're replaying it."

The trio watched as the flames vanished, to be replaced by an intact Shuttle on the launch pad. The SSME's ignited and the entire spacecraft seemed to lighten, rising a perceptible few inches. Then the solid boosters lit and the ungainly assemblage leaned sideways and rammed into the earth, turning end over end. They watched from the safe, objective vantage of a distant camera as the ET fireball exploded, solarizing the video with incomprehensible candlepower.

"My God," was all Joscelyn could say. It was just about all anyone watching could think of to say. She had seen the black and white film of the destruction of the Hindenberg, had experienced the shock as a teen of watching the billowing breakup of *Challenger* on TV while in class at school. Neither matched the heart-gripping nightmare of what she saw on the screen.

When they saw the fiery remains of the orbiter emerge from the fireball to skid across the space center and smash into Launch Control, they fell into an inarticulate silence.

The news network, as shocked and unprepared for this as anyone, wordlessly replayed the footage. They stared once more at a healthy Shuttle, only to see it collapse and explode yet again.

Marcus Grant was the first to say anything, and he spoke in a tone that Joscelyn had never heard before. "The beast is dead," he said with an almost reverent whisper. "This changes everything. Chad — go full speed ahead with the office complex in Kismayu. We're relocating ASAP. Jo-Don — how is the crew coming along?"

She only stammered, staring at the screen in fascination and dread at the awesome power of a rocket releasing its stored energy all at once.

"Snap to it, Joscelyn!"

Her entire body jerked as the command broke the hypnotic grip of the endlessly repeated image. "Um, we have twelve of the crew of twenty lined up for sure, I'm still scouting the rest. I've got my eye on a damned good pilot and co-pilot. We've assembled an American construction crew — mostly ex-aerospace — willing to relocate at the wages we're offering. Semi-skilled labor will be local Somalis. Management will be completely from Grant personnel. Slots are about sixty percent filled."

Grant ran a hand through his grey hair. "Not good enough. Begin immediate move of all personnel to Somalia through the diverse routes we discussed. Establish a six-level paper chase of companies and dummy corporations. Make the company that interfaces with Somali bureaucrats appear to be a naïve bunch of humane Americans with a lot of foundation money to be sucked up by savvy officials."

"How," Haley asked, "do you plan to hide construction of the station?"

"Right out in the open," Grant said absently, gaze riveted on the screen. "The individual pods will be fabricated in Germany at an amusement park ride manufacturer — they look like mini-theaters or some sort of enclosure. Then we'll ship them to Africa, switch the manifests, and they'll arrive as pre-fab housing. We'll even landscape the center of the ring structure. They'll believe dumb, good-hearted Americans would build a huge, expensive housing project in the middle of a starving desert nation. Happens all the time. Remember to ship them some grain for the army to steal off the docks. That'll keep them occupied. Begin an aggressive recruitment campaign for crew." He looked once more at the screen. *Constitution* cartwheeled once again through the grandstands and into the Launch Control complex. "Go ahead and query NASA personnel. The space program is dead and gone now. Any survivors will be ripe for whatever straw of hope they can grasp in their grief. Be careful, though. I don't trust any NASA stooge to be more loyal to Space than to the State. And that goes double for astronauts." He nearly spat the last word.

"I'll... get on it." Donahue rose to leave. His last words threw her thinking off-track, and she required a moment or two to return to normal.

"One more thing," Grant said.

"Yes, boss?" Her voice held an odd, nervous edge that might have been expected under the circumstances, but that caused Haley to observe the tension between the two with an uncomfortable wariness.

"Feed me a list of the dead as it comes out of KSC or Washington. Also compile a list of surviving NASA personnel from interviews, posted reassignment lists, et cetera. You'll be working that up in the course of your recruitment anyway."

"Surely," was all she said on her way out.

"What are you gawking at?" Grant snapped Haley. "Isn't this what you predicted? Another catastrophe for NASA? They couldn't have suffered a more thorough destruction than this!" He pointed at the screen. "Pad 39A — gone. Launch Control — gone. Hundreds of top-level people — gone. It's as if God's fist came down upon Cape Canaveral and crushed the infidels in holy fury."

"Infidels?" Haley peered at Grant. The older man seemed suddenly to have grown young with an energy and fervor he had never seen before.

Grant splayed his fingers across the desktop, gazing not at Haley but at the relentless video of the incineration of the space program. "You and I, Chad," he said, mesmerized. "We're puritans. We see the necessity of a stoic dedication to our chosen goddess. We are the zealots, the fundamentalists, the fanatics. They... *they* were the unfaithful, the usurpers, the infidels who desecrated Space with spy satellites and war machines. *They* were the Pharisees who barred the true believers from the infinite temple, only to see the wrath of the righteous smite them with its terrible swift sword."

He paused as if awakened in the midst of sleepwalking. Turning his gaze toward Haley, he drew his fingers up, tapped the desktop lightly, and said, "We have a precious few months now. The US government will be in total disarray over this, and UNITO has lost its only manned space fleet, and I don't expect the Russians to revivify their program in any reasonable time span. We can do this. Let's go." He once more exuded the impression of a man fully in charge. Haley nodded in agreement, despite the red alert that sounded in his pounding heart.

▼▲▼

Davy Crockett and the others actually attended class that day — Crockett had a perverse interest in sitting in the front row of Dr. Gibbon's Advanced Space Ethics guest lecture as the countdown progressed. Beside him sat Bernadette, wearing a black, fringed buckskin vest-top and matching Daisy Mae shorts and boots. Against the mid-March cold outside, she had with her a powder-blue one-piece ski outfit in a dripping heap in front of her feet. Sam Friedman flanked her on the other side, dressed in a heavy *ghi* and snow boots.

The projection TV image of the Shuttle glowed on the overhead screen while Gibbon spoke of the mission's import.

"Never before has the US space program carried so visionary a crew, nor so vital a cargo. Only three Americans on this flight: Mission Commander Vance Rader, Co-Pilot Jarrod Heinz, and Mission Specialist Samantha Madison. The other five represent an astonishing cross-section of world's space programs: Yohiro Tagawa from NipponSpace; Colonel Alain St. Jaques for CNES, the French space program; Dr. Marie Klausner representing the European Space Agency; Dr. Nikolai Gagarin — no relation to Yuri, I understand — from Russia; and as an indication of the new interplanetary order, Mr. Nguyen Trahn Phu, the new UNITO undersecretary and only the third civilian to fly aboard the Shuttle since *Challenger* over a decade ago. The new age heralded by such universal cooperation can only — ah, here we go."

The class quieted down as the launch entered its final seconds. *Constitution* crept upward, yawed over, and exploded into blazing debris.

"Oh my God!" several voices cried out almost in unison.

"This isn't happening," a girl in the back whispered.

Friedman, unable to tear his gaze away from the screen, hoarsely said, "Davy!"

"I see it." Crockett said in a calm voice.

Bernadette clutched his arm with a terrified grip. "Davy. That could be us up th—"

"No," he whispered, his voice harsh, his tone firm. "Don't be discouraged by the failure of that... elephant."

Gibbon, staring upward at a severe angle from the podium, saw the screen flare with orange and white. "Oh my," was all he could say. "Oh my." Thin fingers touched thinner lips. He walked on unsteady legs toward one of the seats in the front row, only a few students away from Crockett and friends.

Crockett turned to gaze at the professor. Gibbon's face had become an inscrutable mask after a moment of incomprehension, displaying neither shock nor agony nor any other emotion. He simply watched, quietly, eyelids partially narrowed as if they sought to block a truth from escaping — or entering.

▼ ▲ ▼

"Oh God, Gerry, look!" Sherry Cooper turned the small color portable toward her husband, at the moment deep within thought and gazing at his computer screen refining yet again the aerodynamics of Starblazer. Nearly every other aspect of the spaceship design was frozen, since work had begun at the subcontractors. The outer skin, though, he could still tinker with.

He glanced up at the tumbling wreckage crashing against the building and instinctively tapped the keys that would save his work up to that point. He knew he would get nothing more done that day.

"What happened?" he said.

"It just tipped over."

"Dissynchrony," he muttered. "Nothing could be worse than this." He shouted without turning his head. "Everyone! *Constitution* just blew up on the launch pad!"

Gasps of shock were followed almost immediately by moans and sobbing. Many of his workers had been involved with space program or at least retained some residual fondness for it.

For the next hour or so, they clustered around the TV set, watching the horror endlessly repeated, listening to the frantic voice-overs, the announcements of the names of the suspected dead, including the Vice President of the United States and his family, the wide-ranging speculation as to what went wrong, the dire predictions concerning the future of spaceflight.

Cooper shook his head bitterly after an hour of it. Sherry put an arm around his shoulders. He pulled her closer and said, "I thought they would help us, and instead they used every trick in the book to freeze us out and scuttle our plans. I ought to cheer, but this..." He raised a hand and let it fall to his lap.

"It's not good for anyone," Sherry said. "No one's going to put a cent into Space now. Not for years."

"I will."

The Coopers turned at the sound of the Brooklyn accent to see Leora Thane standing behind them, fists on hips. Her thick mascara was missing, wiped from her red, wet eyes.

"You know why I started my travel agency? Because I like to travel. Why? Because when I was a kid there was a TV show with this couple who traveled all over the world with their kid. I wanted to be that kid and get the hell out of New York and see the world. I've seen the world now, every part of it. I've seen the night sky draped by the Arctic lights in Alaska, I've seen the Southern Cross from New Zealand. I watched the Moon blot out the Sun in Baja and saw the planets align from Mauna Kea. I squinted at Halley's Comet in the Australian Outback and hunted meteors in the California desert. The Earth has been my backyard and now I want to jump the fence! Humans are nomads. We have been for a million years. Ask anyone what they would want to do if they didn't have to worry about money and they'll tell you — *travel*. It's in our blood, in our genes. We can't fight it now that we've made the planet a sardine can. If we resist the urge, we'll go insane. We *are* going insane. As a race, as a people."

She clutched her silver lamé handbag against her shimmering grey silk dress. "I'm a millionairess and while that impresses my family and old schoolmates, I know it's small potatoes when it comes to aerospace. I have connections, though. Billionaires. Real money. They may not have the courage to take a spin in orbit, but I guarantee you that their good-for-nothing offspring will badger them for a ticket if we just *build the goddamned rocket*."

She took a deep breath, then sighed and gazed at Gerry Cooper with an uncharacteristic humility. She nodded toward the TV set. "You'll probably get bids from satellite companies, maybe even the military now, if you can get a working prototype built. All I'm asking is, if I invest in your company, that you make manned spaceflight one of your priorities. Pioneers are nothing more than uncomfortable tourists."

Cooper smiled with genuine appreciation. "Thank you. I would do it anyway, but thank you."

"Don't thank me," she said, regaining her composure. "Build the damned thing so we can gouge the bastards!"

▼ ▲ ▼

A few hundred yards away, Larry Poubelle and Chemar D'Asaro hung upside-down with the sound of rending metal thundering in their ears.

"Well, *that's* not it," Poubelle muttered, slapping the reset switch. The VR simulator rotated to place their fake cockpit upright. On their helmet goggles, the image of the Mojave Airport runway reappeared.

Chemar reached out with her sensor-gloved hand to punch the appropriate buttons. The image quickly changed to what it would look like to sit in *Nomad* atop a 747 cruising at its operational ceiling. The sky above was a dark blue, the color of the deepest ocean at high noon.

"Okay," Poubelle said. "Let's give it one more try before breaking for lunch. Launch to orbit, then jump forward to de-orbit and let's try not to skip out of the atmosphere this time."

"Better than augering into Santa Barbara the way you—"

"Larry?" a voice said in his headphones.

"Yes?"

"I'm porting a satellite feed to the simulator."

The two saw the world suddenly explode around them, the flames and spacecraft fragments menacingly close.

"*Sacre merde!*" Chemar cried.

Poubelle watched the entire sequence play over once, then removed his goggles and gloves. "Robert Hutchings Goddard," he whispered, "thou art avenged."

▼ ▲ ▼

Montgomery Barron stared blankly at the computer screen before him. A moment ago, he was patched in to an encrypted downlink from one of the Tracking and Data Relay Satellites and now all he saw was a line consisting of nothing but the capital letter S marching across his screen until it was full. He checked the downlink. TDRS still responded, but the Shuttle did not.

His interest in *Constitution* was more than just academic. The orbiter carried in its cargo bay a small experimental package — one of many making the voyage — that was part of an NSA black project; so black, in fact, that NASA was unaware of what it carried. For one second during the spacecraft's fourteenth orbit, the experimental device was to have sent out a pulse that would jam all transmission frequencies of every satellite within line of sight. The jam would be short enough, NSA hoped, to be interpreted as only a glitch by anyone monitoring, and would not result in any significant disruption of communication or uncorrectable interruption of data flow. The ability to destroy communication was as important as the ability to intercept and read it. NSA wanted absolute mastery of both abilities.

Barron switched his monitor over to visual and saw an inferno sweep across the Florida marshland.

He felt no horror, no loss. The emotion that filled Barron was one of cold anger.

They've blown it, he thought. *They've blown their only chance for hegemony.* Without hesitation, he seized his phone and punched up Milton's office. "Are you watching it?"

"Watching what?" Milton asked.

"The Shuttle! It's gone! The U.S. has no space fleet. UNITO has no space fleet. Earth has no space fleet! I want top priority on *Stark Fist* and that means unrestricted funding."

"You and every little corner of the agency."

"The difference is that *Stark Fist* is the only project that can bring down the subnationals who'll take advantage of this tragedy."

He heard a sigh on the other end of the line. *"Run it through proper channels, Monty. Please."*

"Steve, this explosion"—he watched the numbing repetition of the disaster—"looks intentional. If I wanted to destroy NASA, I'd blow up a Shuttle on the pad in just that way. It took out the VIP seats and a whole building. NASA will never recover from this. They must have lost all their supporters in Congress and the UN as well as their top management! NASA's dead, Steve, and it won't be what it was. Ever. Meanwhile"—he flipped open a folder—"we're finding liquid hydrogen shipments moving from Ukraine to Libya and then vanishing, laser gyros from Israel intercepted on their way to South Africa, a plant under surveillance in Pakistan that's manufacturing chlorine pentafluoride and hydrazine — that's what we're using! It's got the highest specific impulse of any storable fuel at three hundred-fifty sec—"

"Monty, all those can simply be weapons manufacturing, and the CIA has means to deal with that."

"Anything a missile uses, a spacecraft can use and vice versa."

Milton's voice grew impatient. *"You're interpreting information to suit your argument, which is an admirable trait under most circumstances. However, there are meetings where we can hash this out. Now, if you don't mind, I have two calls backed up and I'll bet they have to do with* Constitution *or something even more important. Goodbye!"* He made a point of ramming the phone down with audible force.

Barron did the same, but an instant too late for it to be heard on the other end. He leaned back in his chair and fumed.

Without NASA to serve as the main instrument of spaceflight suppression and — more important — the main organization drawing enthusiastic spacefarers into a dead-end bureaucracy, those energetic dreamers will drift elsewhere. To places, perhaps, where they could not be monitored and influenced... or neutralized, if necessary. Then what?

Then *Stark Fist* would be the government's only hope. The thought failed to fill Barron with a sense of pride, only with a feeling of urgent inevitability. He glanced at his watch. Today would be a good day to make a few calls to check on the status of the LEAP's, the Light Exo-Atmospheric Projectiles that would serve as *Huntress*'s talons.

CHAPTER 27

It [NASA's Challenger *story] just unraveled like Watergate. We felt betrayed. It was one thing to understand the technical reasons for the solid rocket explosion. But NASA had always put its people above everything. To hear how they put off and covered up the needed repairs and how it killed your friends is a little hard to take.*

— ex-astronaut John Fabian

21 March

One week after the *Constitution* tragedy, NASA finally released the body count: 2,105 dead, 658 hospitalized, another thousand or more treated and released. Among the dead were Vice President Schield and family; five senators, sixteen representatives, and dozens of legislators from space-industry states; Britain's Prime Minister and his wife; the Secretary General of the United Nations; two-time Academy Award-winning actor Randolph Trent; several heads of small foreign states; the governor of Florida and her husband; three venerable network news anchors; the CEO of Hayes Polysulphide; Japan's foreign trade minister; the Russian Space Agency representative; the top man at CNES in France; Karl Ganzel, the top scientist-advisor to the National Organisation of Space Supporters; a high school marching band from Ames, Iowa; family members of the *Constitution* crew; and eighty-five percent of Launch Control personnel including the Director. Astronaut manager Bryan Kirk was among the names listed under MISCELLANEOUS PERSONNEL.

Among the survivors — amazingly, though lost in the general climate of shock and mourning — were two members of the *Constitution*: Samantha Madison and Nikolai Gagarin. Both had been seated in the mid-deck. When the shuttle cartwheeled, the crew cabin broke loose and slammed into Launch Control as a nearly intact piece. The flight deck crumpled, killing four, and the other two on the mid-deck died of internal injuries while awaiting rescue. The remaining two, though, had survived because their intact PEAP's, the breathing apparatus, provided them with oxygen amid the smoking ruins until a member of a body-removal team reached the crew cabin four hours after the crash. Both were comatose, in critical condition, and not expected to live.

The world mourned, at least that was what the press insisted. Flocks of child psychologists descended upon schools in an effort to locate and soothe any traumatized ids. Finding only a few, they worked diligently at opening up repressed emotions with video replays of the disaster, followed by art and writing projects designed to elicit the hidden pain. After a while, they discovered all the anguish they knew had to have been there. Grants to study the effects of the tragedy were swiftly filed.

Congress, mourning the deaths of its members and of the Vice-President, launched an inquiry into the cause of the disaster, headed in the House by Ludlow Woolsey IV, chairman of the Space Science and Applications Subcommittee, which lost two members in the holocaust. President Nolan Crane, still stinging from the leak of his first words upon hearing of the disaster — "Was that the one with the UN guys on it?" — called for an independent blue ribbon committee to be chaired by the one man all the world could trust to be impartial and insightful, Barry Gibbon, Ph.D.

Damage assessment continued. Pad 39A was a total loss. Pad 39B could be operational once the road connecting it to the Vehicle Assembly Building was repaired.

Most of the bodies still could not be identified. The names in the death roll were assembled by implication: most of the survivors had been identified, so — once crossed off the lists of those present at the VIP stands and those personnel clocking in to Launch Control — the remaining list yielded the names of the likely dead.

▼ ▲ ▼

For the families of the dead, the tragedy assumed unspeakable proportions. For those intimately involved in the space program, the pain was heartfelt and personal. For most Americans, the sense of defeat and sadness varied from individual to individual. Among a small minority, the disaster evoked either a raging feeling of betrayal or a secret *frisson* of smug glee.

Shocked into sobriety, Tammy Reis felt none of these emotions. Inside she was simply cold, her sensibilities as dead as the bodies of the two thousand-plus at KSC. She had been denied visitation to the ICU at Walter Reed, where Samantha had been delivered by military helicopter after stabilizing into her coma. Ex-astronaut non-relatives counted for little, even if Samantha was her closest female friend. So she sat in Jon Franck's living room with Jon and two others, awaiting the afternoon call from Samantha's brother. Afterward, they would call the homes of other astronauts and spread the word through the telephone tree. Then Jon would post an update on The Net.

This had gone on for the latter half of the week. Most of the astronauts — indeed, all of NASA — had been cut adrift by the disaster. Their managers, superior officers, and many of their compatriots were nearly all dead or hospitalized. No one existed to give them orders, so they waited at home, some mourning, some awaiting progress reports, most simply on hold.

The phone rang. Jon punched up the speaker.

"Franck here."

"Hi," Samantha's brother said in a weary but brightened tone. *"The doctor says she's showing some intermittent signs of awareness."*

"Fantastic!" Franck said, adding "Pipe down!" to the astronauts around him who broke into cheers and applause. "What's it mean?"

"It's a good sign, but she's still in ICU and will be until her internal injuries have healed more. Her mom and I... We brought her headset and powerglove and hooked her into some of her favorite music VR videos. The nurses all say that talking to her and playing the verves help. I've hooked up a recorder so if she opens her eyes to track the video or uses her glove to interact, we'll know the time and extent and whether it was conscious or reflexive."

Reis cut in. "That's great, Garrick. Has she spoken?"

"No, Tammy. And I asked again; they say no visitors except Mom and me. This place is crawling with Russians, though. I guess Gagarin's people have pull."

Madison ended the call with a hasty goodbye. Tammy gazed at the others and broke the silence. "It's good news."

"She'll wake up," one of the others said. "She's got what it takes to pull through."

"What sort of world will she wake up to, though?" Franck said. "The new darkness after the false dawn?"

An older astronaut, her black hair streaked with grey, said, "We've been through groundings before. After Apollo One, after Apollo Seventeen, after Skylab, after *Challenger*. None of them was the end of space flight."

"This is," Tammy said, even though she agreed with the woman. She still clung to the faint hope that there was some way to set all of this right. That hope ebbed and receded on an almost daily basis. She thought back two years to the way she stalled Freespace Orbital's threat of competition. What if she had not interceded? What if she had simply warned Cooper the way Paul Volnos had warned her?

Might Starblazer have been an operational launch system today, ready to take on at least part of the Shuttle's manifest?

Could she have become a Freespace pilot?

Something burned at the base of her throat like battery acid. Here she sat, setting the stage to foil another rival. "NASA will never recover," she said, not knowing whether she believed it or not. "Congress will never rebuild KSC. They'll turn it into a museum, wait and see."

"There's always Vandenberg," the other woman said. "I hear it's being reactivated."

Nods of agreement. "Polar inclinations and expensive doglegs to equatorial," one dissenter muttered. "No one's going to allow an eastern trajectory over the continent."

"We'll rebuild!" the older astronaut insisted. "We've got to. America is our only hope for real space travel."

"America maybe," Tammy said with a bitterness made all the more veritable because it was genuine, "but the United States, never. NASA never existed to get people into Space. It existed solely to monopolize Space. And now we have UNITO to do that! They'll just take NASA funding and ship it to Europe or Japan or Russia."

Franck put a hand on her shoulder. "Tammy—"

"What happened on *Constitution* was just a symptom," she said to no one in particular. And not even Jon was sure whether she meant the crash or her own incident. "The dream is dead, the dreamers are dead, and what you see is just opportunists feeding on the corpse!"

She knew she had gone too far. She was supposed to develop an image of dissatisfaction and something within drove her beyond what was necessary.

"I give up," she said quietly to Jon. "May I puke in your toilet and go home?"

Franck gazed at her steadily. "I *thought* you were starting to show."

She almost hissed at him. "It's a beer gut."

"What are you going to do about it?" he whispered.

"Poison it with whiskey," she muttered, elbowing past him toward the door.

"No, Tammy! Don't start agai—"

The door slammed shut.

31 March

"It's desperation, don't you see?" Brodsky waved a hand toward the spacecraft's framework. "The DOD's just throwing some bucks at you to keep their options open. They have their Goliaths from regular stock and from the INERT transfer."

Cooper shook his head. "Forget the Defense Department. That's just pocket change. Leora's the main source."

"Tourism is a very volatile market. Don't count on—"

"When did you become the naysayer, Thom? Look around you!" Cooper spun once, his arms outstretched.

Nearly a hundred workers scurried about, laying lithium-aluminum frames into place. Heli-arc welders sparked and glowed with pure white light. The aroma of ozone and aluminum oxide filled the hangar air with the scent of progress. Computers encircling the work area each sported an operator surrounded by at least two kibbitzers flipping through stacks of spec sheets generated by the not-quite-paperless office.

"We're doing it, Thom! Twenty years of dreaming, dreaming since we were kids and now it's going to happen! We've got brand new surplus engines coming in from Stratodyne, we've got a contract with Kelvin Kryogenic for fuel, ablative coating from DuPont... It's all coming together."

Brodsky raised and lowered his shoulders in something more hopeful than a shrug. "I guess that I've spent so many years chronicling your setbacks and those of others that I just can't believe it."

"Evolution," Cooper said. "It doesn't happen in a smooth continuum. It moves in fits and starts. Nothing happens for a long time, then in eight years you go from dogs in space to a man on the Moon. Then the doldrums set in for over a quarter of a century. I think we're ready to see a blossoming, a new dawn. And we'll be right there with Aurora... Hey! Starblazer is just the name for our class of spacecraft. Each ship needs its own name." He turned toward the conical framework and shouted. "She's going to be called *Aurora*!" A few workers heard and gave him a thumbs up.

Thom smiled. "That's better than the name I'd thought of." At Cooper's smile of query, Thom said, "Back when it was a hybrid rocket — solid fuel, liquid oxidizer — I thought *Chimaera* might be appropriate."

"A she-beast *and* an impossible fantasy, eh?" He watched the sparks for a few moments, then, clapped an arm around his friend's shoulder. "Fantasy no more, Thom. The dream is real."

1 April

The FAA inspector grinned with pure joy at the sight of Poubelle's spaceplane. Parts of it had the black alloy skin in place, held on with aluminum clecoes that looked like stubby pencils sticking out of the rivet holes. In the open spaces, the big composite-material fuel tanks took up most of the fuselage. In the forward end, technicians wove smooth tresses of optical fibers from the cockpit to all parts of the frame. The system handled not only flight controls, but all sensors and data-gathering nodes.

The inspector was a middle-aged man with a slight paunch and a perpetual glower; his pleasure upon viewing the work seemed so inappropriate. He circled the stubby-winged vehicle with a mixture of glee and respect.

"Mr. Poubelle," he said to his host, "I have rarely seen such meticulous workmanship. Not even on airliners. The welds on the frame, the way your prepregs and composites cured, the thoroughness of your static load tests... Will she really take plus fifteen gees and minus nine?"

Poubelle grinned. "She'll take it. I don't think I could, though. That's why I have the most advanced compact supercomputer linked to the fly-by-fiber."

"That's my only problem. Just one computer. No backup. What if it fails?"

"It's a massively parallel neural net computer. It's like the human brain: knock out every tenth neuron and it can still think well enough to maintain control. If the whole thing goes, well, Chemar and I will break up into little pieces over Arizona. Or over the Pacific, on the return home."

"I just want to thank you for inviting me out to look at this," the inspector said. "It's a real pleasure."

Poubelle nodded warmly and reached for a cigar. "I wanted to keep the FAA fully informed during the certification process."

The inspector maintained his appreciative smile. "Well, of course, the FAA has nothing to do with certification."

"Mmm?"

"This is a space ship. Only NASA can certify it as spaceworthy."

Poubelle nearly bit an inch off the cigar. "Whoa. Wait. It has wings. It flies through the atmosphere. It lands on a runway. It's first flight is being certified for an aircraft altitude record. It's an aircraft."

The inspector spread his hands helplessly, the smile never fading. "It's rocket-powered. It goes into orbit. It's a spaceship."

Poubelle's gaze narrowed. "NASA is in shambles. Nearly all upper management is dead. Having them certify this might take years. It might never happen!"

The older man shrugged. "It's not my jurisdiction. We defer to NASA on anything designed to fly above fifty miles altitude."

Poubelle yanked the cigar out of his mouth and pointed it at the inspector as if about to say something, then he paused. After a moment of thought, he calmly said, "So no jurisdiction means no oversight or interference?"

"I'd have to approve the modifications made to your 747, but that's as far as I'd go."

"Then let's have Hector take you to the other end of the airport and show you what's going on there. Cigar?"

"Don't smoke. Can't accept gifts."

After seeing the inspector off with a smile and a wave of his prosthetic, Poubelle frowned. He always thought he possessed enough wealth that he could push through whatever he needed to be aboveboard and legitimate. Yet there was no way to buy NASA approval in time to beat the deadline; they would stall, if only through the confusion created by a shattered chain of command.

He wandered over to the flight simulator. Chemar was inside, practicing what she called "the pilot-out contingency." Poubelle preferred to call it "the Dead Larry scenario."

"Chemar."

"*Oui*?"

"Brainstorm time."

▼ ▲ ▼

Joseph Lester scratched his head. "A TV show?"

Poubelle and D'Asaro nodded simultaneously. They sat opposite the reporter in their office. The sound of the air conditioner drowned out the construction noise from within the hangar.

"We've got to stir up greater public support for this project," Poubelle said.

"You've got support. Don't you get a thousand letters a day? Fifty thousand dollars or more a week?"

"That's a small fraction of the population, Joe." Chemar gazed at him with her stunning golden eyes. She knew it never failed to grab his attention. "We need to influence a major bloc of viewers. Cable or network, it doesn't matter."

"How would you like to produce a ninety minute special on space disasters?" Poubelle asked. "Point the finger right at NASA? Lay out all the screwups, all the coverups, all the lies and betrayals?"

Lester took a sip of soda and said, "Sounds depressing."

Chemar raised her hands as if offering him a platter of steak. "End it with an upbeat tone. Fifteen minutes on Daedalus and Freespace. And anyone else who's working on alternatives."

"I like that. Will anyone air it, though? NASA can come down hard on any—"

Poubelle dismissed the comment with an imperious wave of his cigar. "Forget NASA. They're still reeling. The old boys' network is six feet under. You want to know who'll air it?" He spoke to his wrist. "Phone. Braverman." After a few moments, the call connected to the speaker phone.

"Mr. Braverman's office."

Lester raised an eyebrow.

"Yolanda my girl! This is Larry Poubelle. Let me talk to Billy Boy, *s'il vous plaît*." He winked at Chemar, who shot back a patient smile.

"One moment."

"Larry?" William Braverman's voice was gruff but dignified, like that of an old lion content in his den. *"Are you still in that California sand trap?"*

"I like zero humidity. I never sweat anymore. It sizzles off like spit on a skillet. Listen — I've got a producer here who has the plumb line on a great concept for a news special. Squares off with NASA over *Constitution* and *Challenger* and so forth. No libel, just facts in the public record. Ought to enrage every widow's son. Can I count on your help?"

"You've always leveled with me, Larry. Send it to me and I'll air it."

The billionaires said their goodbyes and rung off.

"See?" Poubelle said, pointing a finger at Lester. "Bang — you're a producer for the Global Satellite Network." The lighter in his finger sprouted a flame. He blew it out with the flair of a gunslinger and grinned. "Your move, pilgrim."

▼ ▲ ▼

Lester used The Net to make their task simpler. Flying with Hillary through a vast landscape of film clips, he progressively narrowed their search until he located the high-def digital versions of what they needed. As for textual research, he already knew — in the best tradition of reporting — what he wanted to prove; the search consisted of finding material to bolster his argument. In the case of NASA and space disaster coverups, he encountered no paucity of data. The hardest task was actually to read it all.

Ducks in an orderly row, Lester blazed through writing the narrative with an arcade-marksman's thoroughness. The toughest part turned out to be the segment dealing with *Constitution*. Though he knew the remnants of NASA management struggled madly, almost ludicrously, to turn the disaster from an indictment of the agency into an example of the tragedy that results from inadequate funding, not enough of the truth was yet known to reveal the enormity of their statements and actions.

He would have to wing it with the old journalistic standby: "it remains to be seen..."

At the end of a week, he called Poubelle to make a totally insane request: "I want Truman Collings to narrate this."

The billionaire laughed. *"The most pro-NASA reporter in the known Universe? The man who's covered every flight since Friendship Seven? And I thought* I *had lofty fantasies!"*

"He's been retired for years. I think he's seen what has become of the space program and has simply kept a gentleman's silence. This will give him a chance to say what he's probably wanted to for years."

"We don't have time to sweet-talk an old curmudgeon such as Collings. I think we should go with that right wing motormouth Haste Purgatory. He's popu—"

"Who's the producer here? Look, Larry, if you want this program to convince America to support you and come down on NASA, you've got the classic hard-case test in Collings. Convince him to narrate it and we can convince anyone."

"Hand me the program and I'll hand you Collings."

Using The Net's digital editing room, Lester and Hillary produced the test print of a 72-minute documentary with all the appropriate commercial breaks in eleven grueling days — without resorting to anything higher on the speed spectrum than caffeine.

12 April

He handed the optical disc pack to Poubelle in his office, saying, "Hail Caesar! We are victorious."

"Good God, Joe, you look as if *Constitution* rolled over *you*!"

"Not funny, Larry. I've included some of the less disgusting photos of the crash site. It's been an unrelenting descent into death and duplicity to produce this."

"I hope you gave it the cheerful ending we agreed upon."

"Yeah," Lester said listlessly. "Really upbeat."

"You'll be pleased to know that Truman Collings has agreed to view the work print. No guarantees."

"When can he see it?"

Poubelle slipped the disc pack into his office unit and summoned up the telecommunications utility. "Now. Chemar is in Waterbury charming him and setting up the modem. If he likes it, he says he can narrate it this week."

"Great! All I'll need to bring is Hillary, the HD camera, a sound board and DAT, blue screen, three spots, and a mic. We can build the set on a virtual sound stage and—"

"Here goes." Poubelle made the phone connection and started the playback of the documentary. As sure as Lester was of the persuasive quality of his work, he nonetheless endured the onset of a full-fledged anxiety attack.

An hour and a quarter later, Lester was on another phone, booking his flight to Connecticut.

CHAPTER 28

Ideas are the factors that lift civilization. They create revolutions. There is more dynamite in an idea than in many bombs.

— John H. Vincent

14 April

Rex Ivarson stared blankly at the equally blank screen before him. His hands hovered over the keyboard for a moment, then dropped back into his lap. He ran a thin-fingered hand over his nearly completely bald scalp. Then he took a long slug of coffee and savored the cocoa Grace had added to the mocha.

"Got to try," he muttered to the empty room. "Come on, rat-brain."

Aged eyes experienced some difficulty focusing on the dark screen, despite the glasses he wore — his "cheaters," he called them. Fingers positioned over the keyboard, he slowly typed

`MURDER IN THE SKY`

He stared at the green glowing letters for a long time before taking another sip of chocolate coffee. Then he killed the line. He typed again.

`ICARUS DESCENDING`

Rex Ivarson — at eighty-nine — looked his age and more. The scar left behind by the implant operation covered a quarter of his skull. He sat at his cluttered desk in comfortable old chinos and a crisp, clean Hawaiian shirt. Outside, the chirping around Grace's birdbath filled the air with hope. Right now, though, Ivarson felt a little hopeless.

Staring again at the screen, he leaned forward to type

MASTERS

Masters, he thought angrily. *Masters sitting in Washington and New York on executive leather thrones plotting to seize the high frontier and then screwing it up, killing good men and women who thought they were helping to build a future in Space.*

He shook his head, slugged down another gulp of coffee and felt woozy. He typed three more words.

OF THE SKY

Now that *is a proper use of the word 'Masters,'* he mused with a snort.

"Not the masters of people," he muttered, "but the masters of nature. Of science. Of Fate itself." He peered at the screen again.

MASTERS OF THE SKY

Okay, he thought. *Okay. I won't write about how they screwed up. I'll do something else. About how it would have been if they* hadn't *betrayed the dream. If they* hadn't *screwed up.*

He took another sip. *What if Goddard hadn't let the war interfere with his plans? What if Von Braun, Oberth, and Ley had escaped from Hitler's clutches? What if Tsiolkovsky had lived long enough to meet them in a Parisian exile? Korolev... What if he had escaped the GULag?*

He began to type:

MASTERS OF THE SKY

by

Rex Ivarson

The sun rose over Peenemuende with a crimson glare that bathed the land in blood. Wernher Von Braun felt no warmth from the new dawn. Instead, a cold feeling like liquid oxygen ran through his veins — burning him without warmth, searing without comfort.

He had come to build rockets. That was all. He suppressed the odd sensation in his stomach, forcing down the queasiness that came whenever he thought about what the rockets would carry, where they would fly.

He had come to build rockets. To prove his theories. To show the world the machines of a new age. Nothing more. He was a scientist. Global politics were not his expertise — the war confused him and filled him with terror as much as it did anyone else.

It would be after the war that his vision would see its triumph. For now, he had to cooperate. Who else, after all, could pay for such a mighty effort?

An icy wind blasted at him, cutting through to his bones.

He paused to stare at what he had written. *Not bad.*

Five thousand miles away, in Roswell, New Mexico, Robert Hutchings Goddard spoke animatedly to the Army Air Force colonel. The colonel shook his head with an air of tolerance hardly concealing his contempt.

"Mr. Goddard," he said with only minor condescension, "Your rocket is quite impressive, but a rocket with a two mile altitude can hardly hope to match a B-17. I really can't see what you're getting at."

Goddard explained one more time. "These are just models I am working with. There is no upper limit on the power or range of rockets. They could become an irresistible force that might turn the tide in the war. The nation that masters rockets could—"

"Rule the world?" the colonel asked with a smirk. "Every inventor I talk to has a touch of the mad scientist in him."

"Free the world, Colonel. Liberate it. Isn't that what the war is all about?"

The colonel made a dismissing motion with his hand. "I hear you've been offered contract work from the Navy."

Goddard felt as if he were arguing with a tar baby. There was no way to put any pressure on this man.

“It has little to do with rockets.” Goddard folded his arms. “You’re saying, then, that the Army also has no interest in my work?”

“I’m instructed to tell you to keep it up, Mr. Goddard. After all, you’ve got that Guggenheim grant.” The colonel rose to leave. “Maybe Lucky Lindy will fly one of your rockets to liberate Paris, eh?”

“They would not only be weapons,” Goddard said. “Rockets would be an entirely new form of transportation.”

The military man stood in the doorway of Goddard’s home. “You really believe that moon man stuff, huh?”

Goddard bristled at the use of a nickname he found irritating in the extreme. “I believe I’ve had enough. Good day, Colonel. Good day.”

As he watched the back of the man’s uniform, Goddard marveled at the stupidity of the world. The wastefulness of war. The shortsightedness of the military mind, always planning to re-fight the most recent war.

And I stood here offering to contribute to that waste. He shook his head. *Never again. I have a different path to follow*

He turned to face the woman who had walked in from the living room. “Esther,” he said, “We’re leaving Roswell.”

“For Annapolis, dear?”

“No...” He paused, deep in thought. “For Pike’s Peak, in Colorado.”

▼ ▲ ▼

Rex Ivarson grinned a grin that made him look decades younger.

“Dear?”

Ivarson turned. Grace rarely entered while he was working. “What is it, darling?”

“There’s something on TV I think you’ll want to watch.”

“Can’t you tape it?”

“I am,” she said. “But I think you’ll want to see it as soon as possible.”

▼ ▲ ▼

Thousands of miles away from Ivarson another pair of aged hands hovered above a keyboard. Swiftly, deliberately, passionately they struck the keys in a creative scherzo.

The Orbital Settlers' Guide
by Luna Celeste

Just as Christopher Columbus, supported by the Spanish State, made four relatively meaningless trips to America, so the Apollo project, supported by the taxes of the American State, made six relatively meaningless trips to the Moon. Both series may have scored historic firsts, but neither made any lasting contribution to settling their respective frontiers. Columbus left syphilis and brought back not much more than a few Indians for the amusement of his financiers. The astronauts left millions of dollars worth of litter and brought back a few pounds of rock.

Who truly settled America? The malcontents. The misfits. The ones who rejected the States that claimed power over them and sought a new world, free commerce, and private property. Some may have had baser motives — we can never be rid of them all. And many may not have understood or respected the property and rights-to-life of the Indians. The vast number of people, though, who flooded into early America were those who made it there under their own power, with not a cent of money expropriated through taxation.

So shall it be with Space.

Various governments have visited Space, have timidly trod upon Luna. It will be the people, though — free men and women — who break the bonds of Earth and State to sail *en masse* across the sea of stars.

And this time, we shall not carry the myth of the State with us.

▼ ▲ ▼

"Ace" Roberts fiddled with the old television set until the picture improved. The makeshift connection to his small satellite dish made the image jump every now and then. He stepped back to his cluttered workbench and alternated glances at the screen with his work on the instrument panel for his rocket. The newspaper accounts of the preemption of regular GSN broadcasting to bring a special report on the *Constitution* disaster caught his interest. For weeks now, the networks and cable stations had been fumbling for some sort of a handle on the tragedy. Most had lost their finest science reporters in the explosion. For once, the news people had been as stunned and speechless as the ordinary people in whose faces they stuck microphones and camera lenses.

▼ ▲ ▼

Poubelle flew out with D'Asaro, Lester, and Kaye to William Braverman's GSN office to watch the program air. Braverman's office took up half of the top floor of the GSN building in downtown New Orleans. Entirely decorated in exotic woods and fine antiques, it could have been an Edwardian drawing room but for the presence of the most sophisticated HDTV viewing room between the two coasts.

They sat in plush, wide theater seats from another era, along with Braverman's family and staff. To the side of the movie-screen-sized HD panel stood the InstaRate Incremental Viewership Monitor, which delivered the minute-by-minute ratings for the show.

▼ ▲ ▼

The first seventy-eight seconds of the program consisted of *Challenger*'s fiery flight: the magnificent liftoff, the seemingly flawless ascent, the sudden sputtering of flame between the orbiter and the fuel tanks, the squawk of static accompanying the flash, then the horrifying long shot of the explosion, the orange-pink cloud of flame and vaporized fuel, the twin solid rocket boosters flying crazily onward, their payload obliterated, their fuel still burning unquenched.

The familiar image faded, replaced by another familiar one — the publicity pose of the seven *Challenger* astronauts. The announcer's voice intoned their names gravely.

"Mission Commander Francis R. Scobee; Mission Pilot United States Navy Commander Michael J. Smith; Mission Specialists Judith A. Resnik, United States Air Force Lieutenant Colonel Ellison S. Onizuka, Ronald E. McNair; Hughes Payload Specialist Gregory B. Jarvis; Teacher-in-Space Christa McAuliffe." He paused for a short moment.

"Seven men and women from all walks of life, many races, many creeds, all Americans. Seven adventurers on their way to the unknown. Seven lives destroyed in a fiery instant. Seven heroes in America's space effort."

The image was replaced by that of *Constitution* cartwheeling across the Florida marshes.

"As if every generation requires a spaceflight tragedy, last month saw the fiery immolation of thousands in the destruction of the sixth Space Shuttle, *Constitution*. A nation, a world watched with horror as the fury of Hell consumed America's Space City. To name the victims would take this entire show, and we have much more to tell you."

An image of the multi-national *Constitution* astronauts faded, replaced by the image of the announcer. He was an old man, with dignified grey hair; an aging news anchor with a deep, theatrically mellifluous voice. He walked a few steps toward the camera amid a set (created within the depths of The Net's supercomputers) decorated with backlit photographs of scenes from the U.S. space program. Here Alan Shepard waved at the crowd. There Neil Armstrong stepped on the Moon. To his left, Sally Ride floated through a hatchway. John Glenn gave a thumbs up, Gus Grissom gazed forward with a hang-dog face, Ed White walked in space above a blue and gorgeous Earth.

"Good evening," the host said. "I'm Truman Collings. For most of the nearly four decades of NASA's existence, I have covered the American space program with pride and enthusiasm. Tonight, though, I want to take you on a voyage of a different kind. A journey behind the veil of lies created by NASA's efficient public relations machine to the facts about America's spaceflight disasters. Tonight, we will discover whether such heroes as the Apollo trio or *Challenger* seven or the *Constitution* thousands were victims of unavoidable catastrophes or pawns sacrificed in the deadly gambits of bureaucratic and political intrigue."

▼▲▼

William Braverman watched the program from the front row of the three row theater. He was a small, round man with a fringe of white hair around a bald melon of a head. His soft, unlined pink skin gave one the impression of an old elf from Santa's workshop. This elf, though, could have bought and sold Santa a dozen times over. "More brandy?" he asked his guests.

Poubelle waved away the offer. Lester nodded, holding out his snifter, as did Hillary. Chemar sipped at her Coke. Braverman reached to refill the glasses, then gazed at the InstaRate.

"Viewership's acceptable," he said, gazing at the screen, "but not thrilling. As I suspected, not many people are interested in this stuff."

Poubelle lit up a thick cigar. "Just wait," he said.

▼ ▲ ▼

Truman Collings continued as the camera slowly dollied in. "Tonight we'll ask the tough questions. The questions no other reporters dared to ask. And you'll get the answers."

The scene dissolved to photographs of a gutted, blackened space capsule.

"*Constitution* was not NASA's first space-related disaster. On January 27th, 1967, Virgil I. Grissom, Edward H. White II, and Roger B. Chaffee died in a fire that consumed Apollo One during a rehearsal for the first flight in the race for the Moon. Gus Grissom was the second American to travel into Space. Ed White was the first American to walk in Space."

▼ ▲ ▼

No one said a word inside The Ablation Room at Ed Laird's Heat Shield. Tammy Reis — allowed in for the somber affair — leaned forward to stare at the big screen. Jon Franck leaned back, taking a long drag on his cigarette, alternating exhalations of smoke with sips at his glass of bourbon.

"I can't believe they're showing this," Reis muttered.

"It's about time somebody kicked the suits in the ass," Franck said.

Someone in the back muttered, "Don't trust it. I hear Larry Poubelle's paying for the whole show."

▼ ▲ ▼

"While ground testing, the Command and Service Module was filled with one hundred percent oxygen at sea level air pressure," Collings explained. "And nearly every available surface inside the Apollo capsule was covered with Velcro, which had proven so useful for securing small items during the Gemini flights. It proved to be a deadly mixture, though. Some wiring, placed where its insulation could be abraded by a storage-compartment door, generated a spark. In the pure, high pressure oxygen atmosphere, nylon webbing under the crew's seats caught fire, igniting the Velcro and everything else in a flash, killing the astronauts with heat and choking, toxic smoke."

Ancient newsreel footage of NASA management rolled.

"The official word from NASA mimicked the official reports that initially followed the *Challenger* explosion and now are flowing forth in the wake of *Constitution*. They said that the Apollo astronauts died instantly, painlessly, burned beyond recognition in a raging fire that they could not have escaped under any circumstances."

Collings stood before a matted-in image of the Apollo capsule. It looked as if the capsule was right there on the set. "NASA lied. The astronauts died of asphyxiation, not burns. NASA kept lying until the *New York Times* revealed that tape recordings existed of their final moments. Gus Grissom's widow Betty filed a lawsuit to force the truth out of them. Then it was revealed — safely, quietly, long after any national grief might have turned to outrage — that Grissom, Chaffee, and White suffered for over a minute and a half, screaming and pounding on the spacecraft hatch, before they died. Those screams were heard by hundreds of NASA employees over an open microphone. They had been forbidden to reveal publicly what they all privately knew."

Collings reached behind the image of the capsule to withdraw a fancy wrench. "The three-layered hatch, once sealed, could only be opened by using this ratchet. It would normally take ninety seconds or more to undo the hatch from the inside. In the smoke and panic, it is easy to see how that might not have been possible. Opening the hatch from the outside took over five minutes. By then, the astronauts were dead."

Collings walked slowly over to an image of *Challenger*'s flight deck. For a geriatric newsman, he possessed an actor's understanding of how to play to an empty set so that it looked as if he wandered among actual artifacts.

"NASA officials lied outright, then defended the lie by implying that the truth would have been too devastating for the astronauts' families and for a nation mourning the loss of its heroes."

The camera slowly zoomed in on Collings. "Too devastating? For a nation already mourning tens of thousands of heroes dead in Viet Nam? Or, perhaps, too damaging to NASA's image of competence, to its tradition of placing the safety of its astronauts first and foremost? Might there have been — instead of concern for the astronaut's families — an atmosphere of panic and bureaucratic coverup and blame-shifting?"

▼ ▲ ▼

Braverman glanced at the computer. "Ratings are climbing."

Poubelle smiled. "People are calling other people, telling them to watch. Everybody loves to see scandals exposed."

Lester said nothing, simply smiling and watching the television with a producer's pride in his creation.

Braverman grunted. "I just wish we could have gotten some advertisers other than our own internal spots and your ads for Daedalus."

Poubelle shook his head, still smiling. "You think anyone would want his company sponsoring this duck shoot? You might as well have commercials during an impeachment."

"I would," Braverman muttered.

▼ ▲ ▼

The images around Collings changed suddenly from the familiar NASA photographs to those of crude-looking rockets standing on barren plains.

"As tightly as NASA hoped to keep lids on the facts about its various failures, all of them took place under the watchful eye of public scrutiny. However, the United States was not the only government involved in space-disaster coverups. Even more adept, due to the military nature of its space program, was the former Soviet Union. In October of 1960, in a distant place called Tyuratam in the Soviet republic that is now the independent state of Kazakhstan, more than three hundred rocket scientists and technicians died in a launch pad explosion of a Mars-bound spacecraft.

"The engine failed to ignite. Because of political pressure to launch the rocket during Premier Nikita Krushchev's visit to the United Nations, the program's top military official, Field Marshal Mitrofan Nedelin, violated a major safety precaution by ordering an inspection of the failed rocket before the fuel had been unloaded. While surrounded by the cream of Soviet space experts, a worker mistakenly plugged a second-stage umbilical cord into the wrong connector, opening a fuel valve on the second stage. The engine ignited, setting off fuel trucks, killing nearly everyone in an explosion as devastating to the Soviet program as *Constitution* is to ours."

Collings stared directly into the camera lens to say, "How often has political pressure — or merely the *perception* of pressure — caused government space bureaucrats to order unsafe launches? Apparently *every single time*. This happens regardless of nation or form of government, as we shall see when we return after this."

▼ ▲ ▼

"Turn that thing off!"

It was well after dawn on the outskirts of Rubcovsk, just a few miles from the Russian/Kazakhstan border. At 51° 33' latitude, it was as far south as the renegade Colonel Tuchapski was going to get after his hasty departure from Novosibirsk. He was in no mood to hear the small television with its jury-rigged parabolic antenna picking up a signal from some European satellite.

His fellow thief, Capt. Sergei Brajnikoff, responded to his superior's request by saying, "This show, it mentions Tyuratam and Nedelin!"

"Good for them. We have work to do." Vlad lit a cigarette. "The grain silo is topping off today. Once it is done, we can move the missiles in and assemble them."

Brajnikoff turned away from the commercials to face his leader. "We know when to avoid most Russian satellite surveillance, but we know nothing of current American intelligence."

"That is why God made cloudy nights."

▼ ▲ ▼

"In the aftermath of both shuttle explosions," Collings said, "NASA repeated its Apollo history to the letter. The *Challenger* crew, the *Constitution* crew, and all the victims on the ground, they flatly stated, died instantly. The astronauts never knew what hit them. It was an almost ethereal death, a sudden blaze of light and fire, an instantaneous, painless end. That was the way heroes — if they must — should die.

"America and the world grieve, but are comforted."

The scene shifted to footage of recovery ships. Collings voice was low and filled with scorn.

"What would not have comforted them was to discover that the *Challenger* astronauts had survived the explosion, that they lived to experience a horrifying plunge downward into the Atlantic. That they were fully aware of their fate and that, rather than dying instantly in a blaze of fiery glory, the *Challenger* Seven died when impact with the water shattered the crew cabin, when the harness straps across their laps, legs, and over their shoulder dismembered their bodies and scattered the pieces across the ocean floor."

▼ ▲ ▼

Tammy stared at the screen. During Collings's last few words, her heartbeat began to race, her breathing grew short and rapid. Her incessant nightmare had reached into the waking world to envelope her in fear. Blood pounded against her ears. A swirling prism of multi-faceted colors pulsated in her field of vision. Falling, falling.

She felt the impact, but at first did not realize that her head lay against the table. Nervous macho laughter jackassed somewhere far away. Jon lifted her up and back into her chair.

"Tammy?"

"A-OK," she said softly. "I just had a bit too much to drink." She marveled at how pervasive lying had become.

▼ ▲ ▼

"*Challenger* had no emergency locating transmitter," Collings said, "something that costs a few hundred dollars and is required equipment on every aircraft that flies over American soil. While this would not have saved the astronauts, it would have sped recovery of the bodies. An ELT weighs ten pounds. NASA, ever concerned about excess weight on the shuttles, did not include one, nor have they included any on subsequent shuttle flights.

"What did they include on *Challenger*?"

A series of photographs kept pace with Collings' list.

"A deflated soccer ball; 700 embroidered mission patches; sixteen hundred flags of various sizes from various states and foreign countries; medallions, patches, pins, and ornaments. And a frog. But no emergency locating transmitter."

Collings looked grim. "For an organization that paints itself as being overwhelmingly concerned about safety, the absence of an ELT belies such concern. And it is worse than that."

He stood now beside a model of the shuttle.

"Something that actually *could* have saved the astronauts' lives was proposed but never added to the shuttle, for reasons of budget. However, at a cost of two hundred-seventy million dollars over the entire life of the shuttle program, a small kick motor here"— he pointed to an area just below the three main shuttle engines —"could have served two purposes. First, even at a two percent weight penalty, it would not have been dead weight, for it could have been used in every flight to give the shuttle a final push into slightly higher orbits. Second, in an emergency, it could have been used to throw the shuttle clear of the boosters and external tank, a capability that could have saved seven lives and the half-billion dollar *Challenger*. Yet this simple device was not on *Challenger*, nor was it installed on any of the other orbiters, including *Constitution,* despite the fact that it might have saved the orbiter and crew in this disaster, too. Why? Where is NASA's concern for safety when it comes to such a simple solution?"

▼ ▲ ▼

Gerry Cooper stared at the TV screen set up in the Freespace warehouse, transfixed. Finally, after all these years, he was seeing the lid blown off NASA, exposing the worms that crawled inside. If any remaining humor had lurked in his soul, he would have laughed with glee. Instead, he simply shook his head and watched, feeling the wasted years spent believing in the space program slip through his fingers and away from his life.

Sherry put an arm around his shoulder. She knew what pain this was for him. Even though he sought to compete with NASA — and NASA sought to neutralize him — his sincere fondness (nostalgia, perhaps, she thought) for the space program died a slow and painful death over the years. This show merely hammered the final stake through its heart.

▼ ▲ ▼

Collings turned his attention toward the shuttle boosters. "NASA officials knew since the first flights of the Shuttle that the booster O-rings had a tendency to burn through. Simple burn-through wire sensors wrapped around each segment joint in the booster — *had they been installed* — could have alerted computers to abort the flight. A pyrotechnic charge that blows open a vent in the top of the boosters — *had it been installed* — would have neutralized the thrust, allowing the shuttle to break free with the abort motor — had *it* been installed. And those same thrust-negation devices might have saved thousands of lives last month, rendering the Solid Rocket Boosters incapable of propelling *Constitution* toward the viewing stands."

Collings looked scornfully toward the camera. "Monday morning quarterbacking, you ask? Easy to find solutions to problems *after* they become apparent? Well, McDonnell-Douglas's proposal for a booster back in 1972 took O-ring burn-through into consideration and suggested exactly the sort of sensor and thrust-negation devices mentioned here. In 1973, Aerojet Solid Propulsion Company suggested building a booster in one solid piece, rather than in segments, totally avoiding the problem of gaskets, O-rings, and burn-through. Since the resulting booster would have been too big to transport by train, Aerojet proposed building the rockets in Florida and shipping them to Cape Canaveral by barge. Yet Aerojet lost the bid to Hayes Polysulphide, far off in Utah. Why?"

Collings shook his head as if all the evils in the world could be summed up into his next revelation.

"NASA claimed that the Hayes bid was the lowest of four bids. Well, maybe that's the reason that it was picked even though it also ranked as the least desirable of the four. NASA denies that Senator Ludlow Woolsey of Utah — chair of the Senate committee controlling NASA's budget — unduly influenced the decision. Nor did NASA administrator Joe Feather, an ex-president of the University of Utah whose wife hailed from Hayes Polysulphide's home town of Young City. In one case, though, seven lives were snuffed out in a horrifying plunge into the ocean. In the other, hundreds of innocents died because of a chain of anticipated and avoidable decisions. Decisions that would never have been made in any organization with any degree of accountability."

▼▲▼

Braverman turned toward Lester. "You have all these facts on file? My lawyers are probably sweating missiles."

Lester nodded. "It's all there and only you had the guts to help me point at the emperor's wardrobe."

Chemar pointed at the InstaRate. "More people are tuning in. The more Collings goes into the coverup, the higher the ratings go."

Braverman nodded. "Good. Good. Look! We're even pulling them away from pay-per-view!"

▼▲▼

Collings stood beside footage of the *Constitution* disaster, followed by news video of a subsequent press release. "Even now, NASA repeats the same mistakes and identical contempt for the truth. Within hours of the destruction of *Constitution*, the surviving members of the agency's press relations team issued assurances that the crew died instantly, painlessly, unaware of their fate. Anyone who watched the slow, inexorable fall of the spacecraft knew otherwise. Even as the press liaison spoke, crash crews struggled to extinguish the fires and release surviving crew members Samantha Madison and Nikolai Gagarin from their partially intact crew cabin.

"Both crew members are still alive, though barely so, and hospitals along the eastern seaboard strain under the burden of hundreds of the severely injured. How could it have happened, in light of the managerial changes wrought by the *Challenger* investigation years before?"

The camera closed in on Collings's face. "*Challenger* Flight 51-L was the twenty-fifth shuttle flight. Since then, there had been more than twice as many successful flights. NASA management believed that its reputation for safety had once more been recaptured. So when a mid-level engineer named Jackson Lundy questioned the safety of the new SRB ignition sequence program, he was directed into a maze of overlapping and contradictory jurisdictions.

"And what did Lundy discover that extinguished the lives of over two thousand innocents?" The camera zoomed in until Collings's face filled the screen. "A left parenthesis in one line of code was missing. One solitary character out of hundreds of thousands. Yet its absence threw the entire ignition sequence off by a fraction of a second, and in that blink of an eye, America's space program ended in flaming tragedy."

▼ ▲ ▼

Melissa Lundy sat alone in the darkness of her home, staring at nothing. When the telephone rang, she answered it with a deadened voice. One of her friends spoke softly on the other end to tell her that a TV program just mentioned her husband's name. She quietly thanked the woman and returned the phone to its cradle.

It had only been a week earlier that the mystery of her husband's death had been solved. She watched the destruction of *Constitution* from the causeway. She hoped against hope that he had somehow survived. When her son called her on the car phone, though, she knew that Jack must have done something desperate. She knew he was dead.

A crash investigator visited her a month later, with the news that Jack's scorched ID badge had been found beneath a body on the road to Launch Complex 39. Pride and anger overcame her: Jack had died trying to save his beloved shuttle, and it made not an iota of difference.

She refused to watch the news reports, working instead on her DNA project with The Ark Society. Her only concession to grief was to add a digital record of Jack's DNA to the Ark's database. In some dimly distant future day, her husband would live again.

▼ ▲ ▼

Collings continued after a station break. "Space Command Lieutenant Colonel Alan Lundy — Jack Lundy's son — has verified that he received a frantic call from his father moments before the disaster. No one in Washington or at Kennedy would interrupt the countdown. Why? Some survivors blame President Crane, who, they allege, desired to have the shuttle orbiting Earth to coincide with a speech he planned to give the following day to representatives of the United Nations Interplanetary Treaty Organization. The President, however, cannot order a launch against the wishes of Launch Control.

The highest levels of NASA management are to blame, as they were in the *Challenger* disaster. The major difference between then and now is that after *Challenger*, no one in upper management was fired. The destruction of *Constitution* resulted in the death of nearly every high-ranking NASA official, except for a handful who were in Washington, DC, at the time.

"What changes this portends for NASA — indeed, for the entire American agenda in Space — is impossible to predict. It remains to be seen what further truths can be recovered from the ashes of Kennedy Space Center, and what those truths will mean to a nation mourning the shattered ruins of the final days of the Space Age."

Collings's funereal voice lightened just a bit to say, "When we return, a look at an alternate future in Space for America. A future far removed from NASA's way of doing business."

▼ ▲ ▼

"Here comes the payoff for sitting through all the scandal," Davy Crockett said, passing a bowl of popcorn to Bernadette. She ferried it over to Swami Sam, who seized a hefty handful to cascade into his mouth. They sat in their South Bronx warehouse, surrounded by other members of the NYU conspiracy, plus a few minions of SBX-13: Crush 69 ran the popcorn popper; Maus, a diminutive crony who happened to be heir to a weapons-company fortune, doled out the product.

"God," Penny Giannini said, "I had no idea they dragged the astronaut's bodies around in garbage cans. That's gross beyond belief!"

"Think they'll mention us?" Sam asked through a mouthful of corn.

Crockett laughed, then turned to look toward their creation. The pencil-stub shape of the rocket stood twenty-five feet tall at the far end of the warehouse. Though the rotor and blades had yet to be attached, most of the interior work on the upper section had been done, and the lower two thirds — where the fuel tanks were — was still an open framework skeleton.

Crockett wondered what Dr. Gibbon would think of it. The old man looked as if he had been cut adrift when *Constitution* consumed his blessed UNITO crew. Gibbon had spoken of the flight's symbolism. Davy wondered what he thought of symbolism now. Gibbon had rushed from NYU to DC moments after witnessing the devastation and had not been seen or heard from since. The university subsequently canceled the seminar series.

"Ooh," Bernadette said, leaning forward. "Here comes the neat stuff!"

▼ ▲ ▼

"Does the end of NASA mean the end of the dream? Or have we awakened from a nightmare to the cool, hard light of day?" Collings walked over to the images of *Nomad*, *Aurora*, and nearly a dozen other bizarre and beautiful spacecraft models.

"There may in fact be a new dawn for space travel, if any one of these dreamers can put their creations into orbit. What you see here are designs from members of the Experimental Spacecraft Association, founded by billionaire space enthusiast Laurence Poubelle in reaction to the tremendous response to his announced half-billion dollar prize for the first person to orbit the Earth in a spaceship built entirely with private funds. Some of these spaceships exist only on paper, or in a computer. Others, however, are in the construction phase and should be ready to fly by the end of the year, if not earlier."

He described each design quickly and simply, sometimes with the studio shot giving way to footage of the actual spacecraft under construction. That done, he painted a broader picture of people living and working in Space, "not, as suggested by some, thirty years from now, but within the next two or three years. Living in orbit is not difficult, as the makeshift Skylab and the clunky Mir space stations proved. And if the simple space habitats are supported by people who *want* to live there, instead of temporary residents with a home on Earth, genuine progress will be astonishingly swift."

Collings faced the camera and looked as sincere as he ever had. "I've been reading a script for the past ninety minutes, but what I'm about to say are my own words. When I agreed to preview this program, it was with great hesitation. I have supported the space program for over half my life, and as a boy in the midwest used to gaze in wonder at the night sky and dream of someday living there. Even though I have a photograph of me dressed in a Shuttle uniform, I knew back then that I had no real chance of getting into Space on a NASA vessel. One of these spirited adventurers, though"—he waved a hand at the spacecraft models—"might have room onboard for an old workhorse willing to sign any waiver necessary. So if you see me broadcasting once more someday soon, don't be surprised if I've managed to beg, buy, or barter a ticket to the New Frontier."

He raised his left hand in his traditional signoff, which made this more than just another narrating stint for him and his viewers. "And that's the way I see it. This is Truman Collings — Good Night."

▼ ▲ ▼

Marcus Grant turned toward Chad Haley to say, "Are you thinking what I'm thinking?"

"Not seriously."

Grant pointed to the HDTV screen. "Bring along whoever produced that documentary, a cameraman, and Truman Collings. Hell, we could make the biggest box office hit in history: 'Filmed entirely on location in Outer Space!' "

"I really think," Joscelyn said, "that we need every bit of available space for supplies and crew. The design was not intended to carry much — if any — payload. The original idea was to orbit the station, then supply it via the Saturn Five. We've been able to improve the performance and reduce the dry weight of the station enough to permit a crew, life support, and some machinery. You put me in charge of the personnel requirements and I've come up with—"

"Is this going to turn into a meeting?" Grant asked, shutting down the entertainment center with a single squeeze of the remote.

"You saw all those projects the ESA has going." Donahue tossed her long hair over a shoulder and continued. "I don't want to overinflate the time factor here, but if any one of those small-scale efforts gets up before we do, we can kiss the element of surprise goodbye."

Grant shook his head. "It may not matter. The feds actively look for smuggling and only catch a small percentage. The counter-economy is more resourceful and quick to adapt than the government is to react and respond."

"Still, it's nothing to spit at. Half the pods are finished and are arriving in Kismayu. With Chad's assistance, I've created manifests for each pod. We'll split the personnel up among the sixteen pods, one each, except for the cockpit pod that will contain the pilot and co-pilot. The opposite pod will hold extra machinery as ballast."

"No navigator?" Grant asked.

"Navigators," Chad interjected, "are obsolete. We'll be hooked in to the same Navstar, Glonass, Inmarsat, and other GPS systems everybody else uses. The launch itself is all up to the computers anyway."

Donahue continued. "So we'll have twenty people up there, who each ought to have multiple skills we can exploit. I presume the three of us will be going, so that reduces the remaining crew to seventeen. The two pilots bring it down to fifteen. We absolutely require a doctor/paramedic pair. Of the remaining, I've decided we need some space-agriculture people, since we're going to have to grow our own in the absence of any restocking flights; an electrical engineer to hook up the solar panels and keep everything else working; a metallurgist, preferably one who can also do welding; a vet to tend the rabbit warren, our only source of fresh meat; an expert in zero-g manufacturing for both the crystal bath and the high-temperature furnace; a chemist for the peptide unit and other mini-factories; and I think we should also have at least one expert on military communications and weaponry, just in case we have to face that threat."

Grant nodded.

"Systems engineer, nutritionist, city planner, radiation experts—"

"Whoa! City planner?"

Haley smiled. "You intend there to be a Grant Two, Grant Three, and so on, don't you?"

"Yes," Grant said. "But a city planner?"

Donahue nodded emphatically. "There are a few who don't spend their days plotting land scams and taking bribes. Some actually understand how cities evolve and have the brains to channel that evolution rationally. Most of them don't work for city planning commissions, though. Think of them as macro-architects."

Grant raised a hand. "Fine, fine. Who else?"

"Computer programmer, maintenance, general handyman. Oh, and one space law specialist."

"We're going to despoil outer space with lawyers?" Grant sounded full of disgust.

"No, Marc. I said a specialist. That could be anyone with the knowledge."

Grant mentally reviewed the count and said, "That's more than twenty."

"I'm looking for people with dual skills. A doctor who's a chemist, or an electrical engineer who can program."

"No astrophysicists or spaceflight experts?"

Donahue nodded. "I was hoping that one or both of the pilots would be former astronauts."

Grant's face suddenly pinked. "No. That's out. No NASA pilots. Ex-ground personnel, maybe, but no astronauts."

Haley frowned. "Why not? No one else is more familiar with—"

"No one else," Grant said, reddening, "has been as hypocritical in their support for an agency that kills their own kind. Anyone who stayed or became an astronaut after *Challenger* is either monumentally stupid, irrationally suicidal, or in it just to climb the ladders of power. Forget them. We don't need their poison." He emphasized his position with a slap of his hand against the chair arm. "Just forget they exist."

Joscelyn pondered this facet of Grant's personality. She had never known him to grow furious over anything, and though his interest in Space was apparently long-suppressed and now given vent, his antipathy to NASA bordered on the pathological. She had been to the astronaut watering hole, and the level of discontent there was high. Especially in one ex-astronaut named Tamara Reis. If she could reach that bitter wretch and revive her with a new vision and goal, she would be, Joscelyn suspected, a most enthusiastic member of the crew.

She would have to work behind Grant's back, though, until the deal was done. She gazed at the man sitting silently at his desk, fuming, and feared what his reaction might be. *I hope I'll be able to make my case for astronauts before he strangles me. And them.*

CHAPTER 29

Blood alone moves the wheels of history.
— **Benito Mussolini**

15 April

Tammy lay strapped in Samantha's seat on *Constitution*, her belly swollen enormously. In the midst of the countdown, Lud Woolsey appeared from nowhere, naked and swollen in his own vile way. He was on her in an instant, tearing her clothes away and thrusting into her with animalistic force. She turned her head to the left and cried to the next astronaut, "Please..."

The helmeted head rotated toward her and its visor slid upward of its own volition. From within glistened the water-bloated, unrecognizable face of a *Challenger* crew member. "At least you survived," it gurgled.

"At least you survived," echoed three charred skulls atop the flame-tattered remains of three ancient Apollo-era space suits.

"Go at cartwheel," Launch Control announced over the loudspeakers.

Woolsey's jerks and spasms caused *Constitution* to rock back and forth on the launch pad. At the point of his climax, the spaceship teetered on its left SRB and seemed to hold that position for an eternity. Tammy saw just beyond the other astronaut that President Crane stood at the port bulkhead. "Get this thing *moving*!" he shouted, and slammed a fist against the lockers.

Constitution's solid boosters ignited, first one, then the other, and the spaceship fell slowly, slowly to one side even as it accelerated toward the grandstands.

She saw them all applauding, nodding appreciatively as the flames rushed toward them. Her point of view shifted to an omniscient, godlike overhead vantage as if looking down upon an aerial photo or a map. The flames roiled across the three miles separating Launch Control from Pad 39-A, spreading like a wave. Then the crew cabin shot out from the flames like a bullet and tore into the bleachers and building.

Suddenly, a chorus of thousands chanted, "You survived. You'll even have a family. You'll move on. We're gone. Cry for us, not for you."

Tammy lay in place of Samantha in ICU, tubes of all sizes penetrating her nose, mouth, and veins. She could not move, she could not feel. Lud Woolsey sat in the room with her, the word **RAPEST** bleeding on his forehead.

"She doesn't matter," he said to a dark figure behind her. "She is only an instrument of national policy. I just want my son, Lud the Fifth!"

He plunged his hands into her abdomen, each of his fingers an engorged male member piercing through flesh and blood—

"God!"

Tammy awoke in a sweat that smelled of whiskey and worse. She was in her own apartment, of that much she made certain with a flick of a light switch. Wiping the soaking perspiration from her face, she began to weep and add more wetness.

She reached for the bag on her night stand and pulled out the passport and airline ticket to assure herself that she had made a firm decision.

18 April

The office, Reis noted, was clean and modern, even by Brazilian standards. Clad in her white, open-backed gown, she settled onto the cushioned table and put her feet into the stirrups.

The doctor entered. She was tallish, middle-aged, greying at the temples, and possessed a firm self-assurance moderated by just a touch of world-weariness. She smiled.

"Good morning, Tammy. I'm Dr. Fletcher." She strode over to the examination table and raised the metal stirrups a few inches. "You've come quite a long way to have your pregnancy terminated."

Tammy nodded. "I came to you because you're out of the country. Nobody can know about this."

Dr. Fletcher's smile never wavered. She wheeled a cart over to her patient and picked up a speculum. "You've come to the right place for that," she muttered. "Let's take a look."

Reis stared at the ceiling and tried to think of the beauty of Space as the cold, impersonal device entered her. All she could see were the eyes of the man who had stolen her life.

"You're pretty far along here."

"Two and a half months. The rape occurred January Twenty-Eighth."

Dr. Fletcher raised an eyebrow. "And you came to me?"

Reis nodded. "I want this done right. I don't want any lingering doubts."

"I can terminate it today, then, if you want. Do you have any preferences regarding the... disposition of the fetus?"

Tammy's jaw tightened. "Yes," she said with grim determination. "Very specific preferences."

CHAPTER 30

It takes two to speak the truth — one to speak and another to hear.

— Henry David Thoreau

15 April

"Yes," Barry Gibbon said gravely, "I understand that the show pulled in excellent ratings, Billy. However, that was just a single ninety-minute program. And in those ninety minutes, you poured incredible suffering on the families of the dead. A world mourns and you allowed these insensitive boors to dredge up old pain, open old wounds. Frankly, I expected a higher level of discourse on GSN than what I saw last night."

On the other end of the line, William Braverman's embarrassed voice tried to make apologies. *"Well, yes, the ratings were quite good, but I see what you mean about old wounds. It did go farther back in history than I thought warranted, but Larry Poubelle was the sponsor and generally called the shots..."*

"Joseph Lester — the producer? Is he not a GSN reporter?"

"I believe so. Yes. I'm pretty sure."

Gibbon's voice sounded sympathetic, but the words cut through with his message. "Don't you see how that makes the show's viewpoint ineluctably tied to GSN's editorial position? Surely your corporate headquarters has received negative phone calls as a result."

"Yes. Yes, we did. Quite a few, in fact. Many, many members of NOSS."

Gibbon smiled. He sat in his drawing room, dressed only in a long, quilted robe with a dark paisley pattern. "NOSS members look to GSN for its thorough coverage of space news. They do not want to dwell on failures and setbacks and finger-pointing. They want to see the future unfold before them. They are already mounting a letter campaign to Congress urging increased funding for NASA. It's NASA's critics who condemned those people to death, you know. Naysayers and nitpickers who stifled the agency's cash flow so that safety concerns could not be affordably met."

"Why, yes, I know they were once highly concerned about—"

"Most Americans support NASA. They enjoy watching their heroes shoot upward, and don't want to see or hear any defeatist accusations."

"It was a one-shot, as you said. We won't rerun it."

"I think a disclaimer would be in order, too, don't you?"

"It would make sense, I suppose."

Gibbon smiled. "And that producer that works for you. Joe Lester? His perspective might be broadened by taking him off the science reporting beat. He needs to take a look at the real suffering in the world that Space Station *Unity* would alleviate. Africa. Asia. Europe. Anyplace where there is starvation and disease. You would do him a favor to humble his arrogance."

"I would, wouldn't I?"

"Yes, Billy, you would. I won't take up any more of your valuable time, except to say that you still haven't taken me up on my offer of a round of golf at the club when you're next in town."

"Oh, I'll be there, you can count on that."

Gibbon smiled and replaced the handset in its cradle, thinking, *I can count on a great many things.*

23 April

A week after the success of his program, Joseph Lester stood in Mogadishu's crowded airport with the stunned expression of a steer hit by a pneumatic maul. During the entire flight, he pondered his reassignment to Africa. The documentary had been a qualified success, with a good rating and an impressive share and even leading to calls in Congress for a special prosecutor to investigate possible criminal misconduct contributing to the *Constitution* disaster, as well as a demand to reopen the *Challenger* case. And yet here he stood, passport in hand, with only Hillary Kaye and two cases of camera equipment to accompany him to Africa for a story about UNICEF's mission to Somalia.

The air hung hot and dank in the months between the northeast and southwest monsoons, a time the natives called *tangambili*, and — despite his continuing weight loss — Lester's breath grew labored as they walked the entire length of the terminal after leaving Customs.

He was never much of a fighter, and his only real choice when facing Bill Braverman's second-in-command had been to quit GSN or acquiesce. So here he was, trying to make the best of it.

Kaye threw her equipment in the back of the cab, insisted that the driver prove to her that the trunk actually locked, then collapsed onto the cracked vinyl cushions of the back seat.

"Another fine adventure you've gotten me into," she said.

"If we can avoid liver flukes and Ebola virus," he said without a smile, "I'm certain we'll have a great time."

▼ ▲ ▼

The grave had been neglected. A man wearing an Air Force uniform with the insignia of a Colonel stood at the foot of the plot. In his mid-thirties, with wavy dark hair and clear, quiet eyes, he silently read the headstone.

JACKSON LEE LUNDY
HUSBAND, FATHER, SPACE PIONEER
"THE EARTH IS THE CRADLE OF THE MIND.
BUT ONE CANNOT LIVE FOREVER IN A CRADLE."

The cemetery, one of the largest yet least ostentatious in Orlando, received few visitors this cool February morning. One of them — Alan Shepard Lundy — bent down on his knees to scrub aside the mud that had accumulated in one corner of the headstone, set too deep so that every morning the sprinklers watered the lawn and caused mud to flow over the stone where it would dry and efface his father's memory. He would inform the management to correct the problem.

He rose up again, feeling distant from the emotion of seeing his father's resting place for the first time. He was unable to attend the funeral, since the destruction at KSC resulted in highly classified operations at the Vandenberg shuttle complex. Due to the loss of several Space Command brass, it also brought about Lundy's hasty promotion to Colonel.

Now, though, reading the inscription on the black granite, Lundy allowed the sadness to envelop him. *He tried to interest me in his rockets,* he thought. *Tried to turn me into a little astronaut. Named me after one, took me to all the right movies, bought me all the right books. Didn't expect me to turn toward mil-space, couldn't understand my fascination with Space Command.*

"Dad..." he whispered. "I'm sorry I wasn't the space nut you wanted. I'm sorry if it hurt you." It sounded insincere. He was not sorry he led his own life. He was only sorry his father could not understand a Space Age youngster's disinterest in civilian space. Now he would never have a chance to explain it.

He wondered with a sharp pang of guilt whether his father and all the others would be alive today if he could only have broken through the layers of Washington's bureaucracy to halt the countdown. He knew it was pointless to dwell on what might have been, but he swore that a similar disaster would not occur on his watch.

Ten minutes had passed since Lundy arrived at the cemetery. He crisply saluted his father and turned to walk back to his pool car, casually reading other headstones as he walked past, oblivious to whether or not he stepped directly on any of the other graves.

His mother declined the invitation to visit her husband's grave. "I went there once," she said, "to say goodbye. That's all he would have asked of me." She told her son that she was quitting NASA to devote more time to The Ark Society. In fact, she was leaving for Africa that week on a safari to harvest some DNA from endangered species in Kenya. Her guide was to be an astronaut who hailed from there and who was on leave during what would probably be a years-long hiatus.

"The heart's been torn from the space program," she told him. "You at Vandenberg should know that you are the country's only hope now."

"I do, Mother. We do."

"Your father gave everything for NASA," she said, "and in the end they let him down. Betrayed him and everything they stood for. Don't let it happen with Space Command."

"I won't."

CHAPTER 31

He is richest who is content with the least, for content is the wealth of nature.

— **Socrates**

11 May

Chad Haley — a theorist now in charge of producing the actual system for putting the station into space — realized early on the difficulty of keeping secret something that needed so much technical know-how and sheer man-hours to design, manufacture, assemble, and launch.

"May I hire, umm, *experts*?" he asked in Grant's Long Beach penthouse office. "After all, I'm not an engineer."

"Sure you can, Chad — as long as you organize things along your 'modular agorist' lines." The man smiled like a grey-maned lion. "See, I've been reading your stuff. I *like* the idea of not having anything remotely resembling regular employees. Work with Jo-Don on hiring the engineers and independent contractors for all phases of the project — as long as each group doesn't know what the others are doing. The overall plan must be known only to a select few."

"That's no problem," Haley said, "until the point of recruiting the flight crew. Joscelyn must tell *them* what's going on. If we're going to keep this as counter-economic as possible, though"—he grinned—"I'm going to have to know what types of companies you actually control. So we can keep supply purchases and services all in the family."

Grant smiled back. "Pal, *I'm* not even sure what I've got."

"And I do want to approach Truman Collings and that producer," Haley said. "When we launch, we had better be ready with publicity and rhetoric to counter the cover story the US and others are going to use as an excuse to shoot us down."

"Shoot us down?" Grant's smile looked forced and almost quirky.

"You don't expect them to allow anyone into Space whom they don't control, do you? We may be well-protected in orbit by virtue of our high-ground position, but that won't stop them from trying to down us because of a perceived threat to national security. The space station will be in a stable, predictable, low-Earth orbit. Easy pickings if they ever decide to down us. Short of that, they'll denounce us as reckless or criminal or highly suspect. We've got to seize the *moral* high ground and hold onto it, and high visibility is the only way to stay their hand. Keeping a news pipeline open is just as important as getting up there."

Grant thought about this for a moment. "All right. You and Jo-Don handle the research and recruitment. *I'll* handle the delicate political maneuvering."

"Okay, but I—"

"Have you ever bribed anyone?"

Haley frowned. "Not rea—"

"I do it daily. Leave it to me."

▼ ▲ ▼

Haley spent weeks learning all he could about plug-nozzle rocket engines, aluminum-lithium parts fabrication, hydrogen-oxygen catalysis as a way to convert unused fuel into water for the space station crew.

Using 3-D design software, Haley slipped on his VR equipment and gazed at a model of the space station. No engineer, he would leave the actual stress, weight-and-balance, center-of-gravity, and other calculations to the software, with input from experts Joscelyn would soon hire. For now, he hefted the virtual spacecraft in his hands, feedback devices allowing him to feel the shape of the knobby toroid. Like a string of raindrops joined together, the sixteen pods were rounded on the fore end, tapering at the midriff where they connected, and sharpening to points aftward.

With a flick of his fingers, he separated out a single pod and expanded it to look inside. The upper two-thirds of the teardrop contained the hydrogen tank, the lower third the oxygen tank, fitted into the tapering cone of the aerospike. Inside the hydrogen tank were three decks made of aluminum-lithium latticework. While allowing for free flow of the fuel during launch, once they had achieved orbit and catalyzed the excess hydrogen into water the empty tanks would immediately have three levels of work and living space available to the crew.

The crew and cargo occupied relatively cramped quarters during launch, packed into the topmost portion of the pod riding above the fuel tank, separated by a few inches of insulation. Chad designed in a small polycarbonate window for each crew member, then added an interior shutter for those too nervous to watch.

The most important part of the project would be in deciding what to take into orbit with them. Though he had no doubt that Grant could resupply the station once it was successfully operating, it might be some time before such a second launch was possible. That indicated the need for more than prepared food, hence the hydroponic tanks and seeds. The necessary water would come from combining the residual hydrogen and oxygen in fuel cells to provide electricity, heat, and water for the space station until solar panels could be deployed.

That thought caused a momentary digression. What, he wondered, would be the weight and drag penalty if amorphous or crystalline silicon solar cells were glued to the skin of the spacecraft before launch? Since they intended to spin the toroid artificial gravity, most of the station would receive sunlight for at least a portion of each rotation. If each pod had its own rechargeable batteries, as well as an electrolysis unit to break down waste water into hydrogen and oxygen for the fuel cells, how would that alter the payload requirements? And the cost? And the fire danger of more electrical equipment...

Haley began to sweat. Designing a space station was no simple exercise. It required knowledge of science, engineering, aerodynamics, chemistry, horticulture, human physiology, plumbing, biology, architecture, pyrotechnics, metallurgy, cryogenics, recycling, cybernetics, air conditioning, nutrition, ecology, radiology, and higher mathematics of a head-numbing depth and variety.

A stunning amount of work over the last fifty years provided a wealth of data to utilize for the project, but Haley still needed experts to marshal all their knowledge into a final product. He telephoned Donahue to remind her of the need for speed.

"I'm on top of it," she said cheerfully. *"My plan is that some of the people who will design and oversee construction of the station will be the ones who go up in them. That ought to ensure quality control, right?"*

Haley agreed. "How do we keep this from mushrooming into a long-range, NASA-style never-ending project?"

"We have the classic skunk works setup in Kismayu," she said. *"Isolate a small group of genius-types with a fascinating challenge, pay them practically nothing, and give them a firm finish date. It's worked so often in so many fields, from aircraft to computers to movies, that it may be the natural adjunct to your concept of the extremely horizontal modular agorist organizational chart."*

"How many people do you have under contract?"

"A few. I'll be going for more this weekend." She became serious. *"Including a few ex-astronauts and cosmonauts."*

"Grant won't like that."

Joscelyn's voice grew even more emphatic. *"We need input from people who have actually been in Space. An astronaut-doctor would be ideal. Anyone who may have done space construction would be invaluable. Pilots — I think that's the most important of all. None of this will be worth it if we can't reach LEO."*

God, he thought, *she's beginning to use acronyms.* "Any prospects?"

"I'm working on a few right now."

19 May

Donald MacIntyre watched as the woman from the mailroom wheeled in this morning's mail.

"Congressman Woolsey's very popular with the ladies," she said, nodding her head toward the colorful pile of card-sized envelopes addressed in feminine script.

"Thanks, Carol." He gazed at the cartload.

"Does he ever see any of these?" Carol asked.

MacIntyre winked at her. "Only the ones with photos." *That meet my approval*, he secretly added.

Carol laughed and moved on to her next stop. MacIntyre ignored the obvious love letters to pluck a red, white, and blue airmail envelope from middle of the pile. It was thick, but he was certain nothing dangerous lay inside since the mailroom always X-rayed and neutron-scanned anything that might harbor explosives.

The envelope had been very neatly typed, the high-denomination foreign stamps applied crisply and squarely. No return address, though the postmark indicated its origin to be Sao Paulo, Brazil. He slit the envelope open to withdraw the contents: a sheaf of pink papers stapled at the top corner. Despite the Brazilian origin, the copies of the airfare and medical bills were written in English, along with the note hand-written in tense script that read, *I FELT IT UNREASONABLE THAT EITHER I OR NASA SHOULD PAY THESE.*

What he read made his eyes narrow.

So he did *bop the astronaut,* MacIntyre mused with a mixture of cynical pleasure and mild disdain. *And she's got the balls to send him the bill for the abortion.* He smiled. *Maybe we should bill* her *for Woolsey's plastic surgery.*

He laughed quietly, but knew it was not a matter to be taken lightly. The congressman's reputation as a womanizer had more than once threatened him politically, and something as crass as knocking up a national heroine might be the last straw if it became common knowledge.

MacIntyre slipped the envelope and its contents into a manila envelope stamped **TOP SECRET** at top and bottom and added it to the stack he would personally discuss with Woolsey. He picked up the next mail item, thinking, *Brother, if I ever write that book...*

CHAPTER 32

The gratification of wealth is not found in the mere possession or in lavish expenditure, but in its wise application.
— Miguel de Cervantes

30 May

"Gaze at the power of money, Ger." Leora Thane watched with smug satisfaction as *Aurora* rolled out of the warehouse upright on its landing gear, which had been equipped with a caster-like arrangement of ballooning aircraft tires. Leora wore her finest evening gown of gold and bronze and copper lame, despite the intense desert heat. She looked like a millionairess — which she was no longer, after investing so heavily in Freespace — witnessing the delivery of her newest limousine.

"All my life," she said, "I've wanted to be part of something big. I didn't know how to create anything, but I knew how to give people a good time. I started out delivering balloon bouquets, did you know that? I must have racked up a hundred thousand miles schlepping all over Manhattan with those helium-filled monstrosities, wedging into elevators, getting stuck in revolving doors. Then I organized parties. Murder-mystery weekends, Regency High Teas, romantic retreats. That gave me the bug, you know? So many rich people who for whatever reason wanted to forget their own lives and be somewhere else for a while. So much money itching to be spent. I became a travel agent. Spent years booking flights, arranging cruises, and couriering tickets out to businessmen running late."

Cooper looked at *Aurora* in the light of its namesake, dawn, and nodded. The framework above the sliding hangar doors had been removed to allow *Aurora* a dignified rollout. The spacecraft consisted of a blunt cone thirty feet in diameter at its widest point — the ablative reentry shield — and fifty feet high, that looked like an old Apollo command module with a thyroid condition atop a longish cylinder with a flared and curved base. Instead of ordinary bell-shaped exhaust nozzles that would have required actuators for pivoting and cover doors during reentry, *Aurora* contained twenty liquid-fueled combustors arranged in an annular ring-nozzle configuration around its base. Mounted flush with the ablative stern, it resisted reentry heating and used differential throttling for attiude compensation.

Painted an extremely pale blue that looked white in the desert sunshine, *Aurora* trundled past the constantly critical eyes of Cooper and his team to the outside world and a small group of reporters and onlookers.

Cooper noted the absence of Joseph Lester, who might have given him the most comprehensive coverage. The GSN reporter present gazed at the rollout with a faint disdain, as if Cooper were a modern sculptor displaying a pile of junk shamelessly palmed off as art. Others in the crowd expressed a greater enthusiasm, oohing and aahing. Scattered applause greeted the spacecraft when it stopped, and cameras clicked and hummed to capture the moment.

His attention clearly lay focused on the slow movement of the spacecraft. A single large dent in its aluminum-lithium alloy skin could conceivably deform the thrust structure — the main internal weight-bearing frame — since it was integral to the hull. Such damage could lead to destruction of the spacecraft during liftoff or re-entry.

So many ways to fail, he thought, but only for a fleeting instant. The simplicity of the Starblazer design served as its greatest protection against failure. Where the Space Shuttle employed hundreds of Criticality One components, *Aurora* utilized only a few — none of them in the engines. Even the failure of several motors did not guarantee loss of the spacecraft: low thrust on one side could be compensated for — much in the manner of an engine-out procedure on a multi-engine aircraft — by throttling individual combustors to compensate for differnetial thrust. The onboard computer, monitoring the engines' performance thousands of times each second, could make the appropriate alterations before anything could go wrong.

Leora Thane continued to rhapsodize. Cooper did not blame her. He would have whooped in triumph if it were in his personality. Dressed in a somber navy-blue suit, though, he could have been a quiet accountant come by to watch the spectacle.

"I've never seen such quick results from just taking a pile of other people's money and throwing it at a challenge," she said, this time to Sherry Cooper.

Sherry, attired in a light beige safari shirt and matching shorts, nodded from behind her dark glasses and smiled. "Gerry spent ten years fiddling with the original design on CAD and lining up suppliers. So when you appeared with the investment, it was just a matter of modeming the specs to the sub-contractors' computers. He didn't design *Aurora* to consume a million man-hours and billions in taxes."

Leora nodded her head merrily. "It should say on the ingredient label 'No Pork,' which — for more than one reason — is OK with me."

Sherry walked with her husband around the base of the elongated gumdrop of the Starblazer prototype. From its gently curving base extended three sturdy landing gear through hatches in the ablative shield. Encircling the gear was the annular ring within which hid the twenty rocket nozzles. She admired the nearly seamless way in which the sprayed-on composite ablative material had been applied. Far cheaper than individually unique and hand-made thermal tiles, the coating could be reapplied within the seventy-two hour turnaround time allotted for the production version of the spacecraft.

Small attitude rocket nozzles that controlled pitch, yaw, and roll formed little trefoils of two oval exhaust ports on a transverse line with a single oval above them on the vertical. These were placed above where the center-of-gravity would be once the ship was in orbit with much of its fuel consumed.

The only other visible openings were the twenty trapezoidal viewing ports just above amidships (for the tourists) and the three clustered together higher up on one side of the flight deck (for the pilots). Here and there, streamlined bumps protruded from the fuselage to enclose the various antennae for navigation and communication. Unseen beneath the blunt nose cone lay the universal docking adapter for which — currently — there was nothing in orbit to mate. Unless one counted the dead husk of *Mir*.

Sherry hazarded a glance at her husband. He beamed as any other father would at a son hitting a home run or a daughter performing a perfect gymnastic floor exercise. Or vice versa, she thought, and wondered whether they would consider starting a family, now that Gerry had given birth to his dreamchild.

Larry Poubelle wandered over from his hangar to watch the event. He left behind him a nearly complete *Nomad*, awaiting only the delivery and installation of its single powerful rocket engine.

"Hey!" he shouted in a jovial way. "Coop! You trying to beat me out of my own half-billion?"

"Better cut the check!" Cooper hollered back. "We static-fired the engines at Skull Valley last week, slapped them in, and now we move on to Vandenberg!"

Close enough now that he did not have to yell, and not wanting his voice to carry, Poubelle said, "Are you sure you want the Air Force involved in this?"

Cooper shrugged. "Someone at KSC convinced someone at Space Command to let me use the facilities, so even what's left of NASA knows that the game's changed. I think they want a reliable spacecraft as much as we do."

Poubelle made a *tsk*ing sound. "My design allows me to lift off from any long runway and launch in the air."

"Well," Cooper said, "I don't need *much* in the way of a spaceport to take off and land. Besides, *you're* receiving Air Force largesse, too!"

"It's not like either of us is accepting money from them, just using public property for as long as we're standing on it, reluctantly surrendering it back to an ownerless condition once we move on. I'll only be using Edwards for the landing strip on Rogers Dry Lake, if I can wrest permission from them."

"And if not?"

Poubelle smiled and drew a cigar from his safari jacket. "Then I'll just land at Cuddeback Lake and have the damned thing trucked out."

"You're not going to light that, are you?" Cooper asked.

Poubelle looked at the oversized cigar and handed it to Cooper. "Congratulations, new dad."

Cooper slipped it into an inner pocket. "Thanks. I'll smoke this after we orbit."

A man in a beige suit with a pale blue shirt and a paisley tie — annoyingly tied in a Windsor knot — stepped up to them. He was young, probably mid-twenties, with brashly expensive shoes and a meticulously fashionable hair style. "Gerald Cooper?"

"Yes?" Gerry flashed a proud smile, then saw the other man's odd smirk.

"Thiel. Department of State. I'm here to inform you that you have not obtained an export permit for that shipment of munitions."

"I beg your pardon?"

Poubelle listened in, one eyebrow raised in interest.

"The State Department classifies rockets as 'munitions,' and — in order to satisfy the mandates of the 1967 Treaty on the Peaceful Uses of Outer Space — requires an export permit for any munitions that leave U.S. territorial limits." Thiel smiled, reached into his jacket, and withdrew a thick, folded sheaf of paper to hand to Cooper, then turned to Poubelle and pointed a finger at him, pistol-like. "I'll be seeing *you* next week."

Cooper flipped through the papers incredulously. "I'm not exporting anything. I'll be sending it up from Vandenberg, orbiting, and bringing it down again. It's not going to any foreign country!"

Poubelle cut in. "Yeah. In fact, since he doesn't touch down anywhere else and returns to his point of origin, the FAA would classify it as a local flight!"

"A permit," the man in beige said, "is required to allow the vehicle to leave the country regardless of where the vehicle goes or whether or not the vehicle actually changes ownership." His smirk widened. "Have a good one." He turned and departed.

Poubelle laughed. "You know, if he came here with agents to seize the ship, he'd have made sure the cameras were on him. He preferred to do this quietly. That ought to tell you something."

"What?"

Poubelle slid the papers out of Cooper's hands. "That he doesn't have a leg to stand on and would look like an idiotic spoilsport on TV. Let my lawyers handle this and just do what you need to."

"What I need is to borrow your Boeing to fly this baby to Vandenberg."

"If you've got the attach points, we've got the struts. I won't need the plane for months."

13 June

It took two weeks for State to back down from the export permit demand. Thiel did not even bother to attempt to serve papers on Poubelle. In that time, crews lifted *Aurora* by crane and gently lowered it on its side atop the Daedalus Project's 747. It had been Poubelle's idea to offer to design strut attach points on the airplane and suggested that Cooper design in matching points on the Starblazers. Though the points differed for *Aurora* and for *Nomad*, due to different centers of gravity, Poubelle magnanimously offered to set the Boeing up for Cooper's ship first, knowing full well that a launch from an Air Force facility would take far longer than an air launch from the back of his plane. He had no doubts that he would precede Cooper into orbit, retain his prize money, and open the door for widespread repudiation of UNITO.

At Vandenberg, the Coopers stood side-by-side in the chill, damp pre-dawn ocean air and watched *Aurora* move slowly into position on the launch pad. Very little pre-launch preparation would need to be done to the spacecraft, in keeping with its short turnaround-time design. Loading the cryogenic fuel and oxidizer was the only time-consuming process, and it would take only an hour or so. A compressed helium-hydrogen mix, used to pressurize the LOX, was already onboard in smaller tanks. The helium worked better if preheated, so the hydrogen was mixed in to provide the heat, flowing through a catalyst chamber where it reacted with precisely metered oxygen to form water and release sufficient heat to warm the helium and increase its pressure. This obviated the need for a more complex heat exchangers in the engines.

The toughest part of the whole pre-launch process, Cooper mused, had been convincing the Air Force range safety officer of the safety of the Starblazer design. The twenty rockets, each sixteen feet long, provided seventy thousand pounds of thrust during their eight minute burns, leaving enough unconsumed fuel for re-entry braking and a landing back at a wide, clear area of Vandenberg. The ship was diminutive and light — any high-altitude disaster would result in the ship breaking up and falling to Earth in small, relatively harmless pieces. A lower-altitude disaster would be not much more destructive than the crash of a corporate jet — and would kill far fewer people. Even so, Space Command insisted on strapping self-destruct explosives to the fuel and oxidizer tanks. If activated by range safety, they would rip open the tanks, allowing the two components to mix and ignite. The explosive power of the propellants would perform the actual demolition of *Aurora*.

This time, when the light of dawn came over the mountains to bathe *Aurora* in its golden light, Gerald Cooper felt a mixture of pride and exhilaration compete for supremacy within him. He slipped an arm around Sherry's waist.

"It's so beautiful," she said. "As simple and perfect as a robin's egg."

He nodded, then said seriously, "Let's hope it doesn't crack."

They headed back to Launch Control, where Freespace personnel mingled with Air Force and NASA people. NASA insisted on handling the launch, the Air Force overseeing range safety and flight control, which left Freespace to do the actual work. This was to be a crewless flight to fifty miles altitude. Straight up, straight down. No frills. It would verify the ability of the SSTO design to launch *Aurora*, shut down in mid-flight allowing the spaceship to decelerate and then plummet ass-backward toward the ground, and re-ignite at the proper instant to lower the spacecraft safely to the surface a few dozen yards from the launch pad.

If all went well, Cooper hoped to prove the ship's fast turnaround time by launching a crewed flight into orbit one week later.

The presence of three different groups in Launch Control provided no end of confusion, exacerbated, Cooper suspected, by a reluctance on the part of either NASA or the Air Force to cooperate with a private launch so soon after the *Constitution* disaster. Very few of the NASA people were experienced launch personnel — half of Cooper's people, in fact, comprised retired NASA personnel whom he had hired to fill in the gaps. And the Air Force people seemed more than rigorous in their efforts to root out problems with the vehicle. Cooper had no objection to that *per se*, but the range safety officer — Lieutenant Chet Rollins — spent much of his time checking and rechecking the arming mechanism for the Flight Termination System — the euphemism for the spacecraft-destruction explosives

— and very little time reviewing the abort-and-return-to-launch-site sequence.

The relatively short two-hour countdown proceeded without incident. Cooper — absorbed in the process — felt as if he and *Aurora* became one, straining toward the moment of ignition like a thoroughbred horse at the starting gate. Only a successful launch would release the pent-up energy within him. Thom Brodsky, who would be monitoring telemetry, felt just as much pre-launch *angst*.

Conversations flowed on four different audio channels simultaneously. Monitors glowed with a dozen different camera angles, some on the entire ship and launch pad, one on the lines feeding the fuel and oxidizer tanks, one on the engines, several on security checkpoints around the complex.

"All systems nominal," the calm voice of the launch director said. *"T-minus one minute. APU's functioning."*

Sherry stood near her husband, who bent over a display near the range safety officer. The intense concentration he radiated was a palpable thing to her; it made her stomach knot with tension. Soon, though. Soon it would be over.

"T-minus thirty. Internal power. Pressure. Telemetry coming in."

"Roger on TM," Brodsky replied.

"Downrange clear," Lt. Rollins said. Since the flight was nearly vertical, the only "downrange" consisted of a small footprint where debris might land. Range safety, however, consisted of several hundred square miles of surrounding land and sea area.

"T-minus ten, nine, eight..."

Adrenaline sluiced through Cooper's body, creating an otherworldly sense of heightened reality. Turning his gaze away from telemetry and toward the monitor, he watched as seagulls flew past the spacecraft standing in the misty morning.

"Three seconds. Ignition sequence start."

"Valves open," a voice on Channel One said. *"Release clamps."*

"Abort!" cried a voice on Channel Two. *"Subnormal thrust!"*

Half of the engines on *Aurora* flared briefly into life and burned with a languid flickering. Instead of blasting out the exhaust nozzles with lifting power, the flames licked upward, blackening the composite structure.

"Abort! Abort! Stuck valve! Keep clamps locked!"

Lt. Rollins held his palm over the large red abort button, prepared to destroy the bird if necessary. Others stood frozen in place, expecting anything, including the prospect of their own deaths in another ignition dissynchrony.

Cooper immediately shouted, "Vent the helium tanks! Vent through the engines!" The commotion was pointless, since the computer had already reacted to the problem and done just that. The helium, with the hydrogen already removed in the catalyst chamber, vented downward under pressure to act as a fire extinguisher, forcing the oxygen out of the combustion chambers.

"Fire out!" someone said.

"LOX still flowing!" a voice said on Channel Four.

"Close the valve!" Cooper yelled, running over to the launch control panel.

"It's stuck," the director said in a level voice. "Won't move."

"Confirm flameout," another voice on Channel One intoned. *"Vent oxidizer tank."*

On the monitor, a cloud of white vapor erupted from the midriff of the spacecraft. In a moment, the cloud dissipated to reveal *Aurora* encased in a thin crust of ice crystals everywhere but around its scorched stern.

Lt. Rollins reluctantly removed his hand from the destruct button.

"Damn!" Thom Brodsky said from the telemetry console. "I show the main oxidizer valve stuck one-third open. Thrust was only twenty percent. Give a medal to whomever kept the clamps on. If they'd released, it would have tipped over."

"It's safe," Sherry was the first to observe. "Damage looks minimal. We can fix it and try again."

"After we find out what happened," Gerry said.

"Valve froze," Colonel Alan Shepard Lundy said as he strode into the blockhouse. The military men sprung to attention but he waved them down.

"That didn't happen during the static firings," Cooper shot back. The alarm of the previous few moments faded into a weary, sullen anger. It was an anger Cooper directed at himself for missing a detail, but the words came out clipped and irritated.

"The ocean air out here does that unless you keep the chambers flushed with dry nitrogen." Lundy turned to the launch director. "Captain Fortney?"

Fortney pursed his lips, then said tersely, "It was not in our purview to determine if the customer had knowledge of what the dew point is, sir." The word "customer" came out with an unusually ironic edge.

Lundy narrowed his gaze. "My father and a couple of thousand people died at Kennedy, Captain Fortney. That won't happen anywhere at Space Command, not even with private contract work. Is that understood, *Captain*?"

"Yes, Colonel."

Lundy turned toward Cooper. "After all systems are safely shut down, I'd like to invite you and Mrs. Cooper to the officer's dining room for lunch."

Cooper nodded distractedly. Sherry smiled and inclined her head slightly with gracious appreciation.

▼ ▲ ▼

"There are a lot of people in the US government who don't like what you're doing, Mr. Cooper." Col. Lundy sat with the Coopers in a private dining room separated from the rest of the officers by luxurious wood paneling.

"And my wife," Cooper replied. "We're a team."

Lundy turned to her and said, sincerely, "Of course. I apologize. My father and mother both worked for NASA. I didn't mean to imply—"

"Your mother — did she also..." Sherry let her question simply hang.

"No. She saw it all, though, from a causeway. My father died on the crawler path. He had no business being there. He was trying to stop the launch. He knew what was going to happen." Lundy spoke the short, simple sentences as if he had recited them hundreds of times to hundreds of listeners. Sherry knew that his pain must be deeper than anything she could imagine.

"That's pretty much what we learned from that documentary." Gerry observed Lundy with no small degree of admiration and empathy.

"Range Safety is very important to monitor," the colonel said.

"We're addressing every aspect of safety issues," Gerry said. "As we saw, the design has several feature—"

"Range safety," Lundy said again, this time with disturbing emphasis, "is *very* important to monitor."

Sherry could tell that he wanted to say more. It showed in the pain knotted into his eyebrows and creased along his forehead. "Thank you," she said. "We'll monitor it. Closely." She glanced at her husband. His eyes gazed into space, his mind lost in contemplation of repairs and retrofits to *Aurora*. She knew that was where he had drifted to, and knew that Col. Lundy's veiled warning had utterly eluded him.

She returned to her meal, formulating a plan that she dared not reveal even to her own husband.

CHAPTER 33

The universal regard for money is the one hopeful fact in our civilization, the one sound spot in our social conscience. Money is the most important thing in the world. It represents health, strength, honour, generosity, and beauty...

— **George Bernard Shaw**
Major Barbara

14 June

The failure of *Aurora* passed with little notice except in the commercial space newsletters. *Aviation Week* ran a paragraph about it that week, and the following week included a letter from Barry Gibbon in which he wrote: "The failure of this minor-league attempt to capitalize on the heart-rending tragedy of *Constitution* is sufficient proof that space travel is a dangerous undertaking, and that the UN is correct in its decision to assert international control over this new wilderness. Because of these dangers, it is only proper that the environment of outer space be preserved and that access be permitted only for the good of humanity, not for private gain. And most certainly not for rubbernecking tourists from the millionaire elite."

The Private Space Journal, in contrast, ran a twelve page special supplement with photos and an exhaustive analysis of the failure. Thom Brodsky managed to paint the upset in the best possible light, beginning with the headline "Inherent Safety of Starblazer Design Proven."

It was big news in Mojave, too. The local paper ran a front page headline, which Larry Poubelle was reading when Chemar shoved open their office door.

"You're not going to believe this!" she said.

"I might," he said, lowering the paper to eye her. She was dressed in aquamarine shorts with a matching floral print Hawaiian shirt knotted at the waist and unbuttoned halfway to her navel. The colors accentuated her dark skin and made her golden eyes seem even brighter and more piercing. "I'm a fairly credulous fellow. I believe it when you say you love me for my money and not my mind."

"Take it from me." She signaled to somebody outside in the shimmering noontime heat. "Your mind is about to bring in a truckload of money." She pulled a folded envelope from the back pocket of her shorts as one of their workers dragged in a sack of mail as big as a St. Bernard.

"It started to build right after *Constitution*. Then I found out why." She unfolded the letter to read aloud. "This is from a kid whose letterhead reads 'From Wapakoneta, Ohio, the Birthplace of the First Man on the Moon.' It starts out, 'Dear Mr. and Mrs. Poubelle" — she lowered the page to peer at Larry and raise a shapely eyebrow — "I already like the kid. 'I saw you on the news when you announced that you would be building an X-15 to fly into Space.' It's cute how it's capitalized. 'I sent in five dollars and got all sorts of neat stuff from you. I am eleven years old and I wanted to be an astronaut since I can remember. Then the Space Shuttle exploded and killed everyone and I felt really really sad like we would never be able to go into Space again. The people who died were my heroes. I know it will cost a lot of money to rebuild the Space Center, but my Dad says they'll do it by turning the screws a little tighter on everybody's kahonies. He said kahonies were how they collected taxes, so I guess the Shuttle will be paid for.'

"Isn't this priceless?" she asked.

"Sweetheart, we get those every day." He half-smiled. "Except for the kahonies, maybe."

"Not like this one, you don't. 'But then I thought, what about you? Your newsletter said you were supported by donations and sales and I wanted to help. So I figured I'd tell all my friends that buying a *Nomad* souvenir was cooler than motorskates or a six-pack of soda. I booted up my almanac disc and checked. Makeup and stuff is a forty-billion dollar business. Toys are fifty billion. Soft drinks are sixty billion! So I figured if I could get a whole lot of kids to buy your stuff instead of other stuff, they'd still get neat things, but *Nomad* would get the money."

Poubelle put his feet up on the desk and leaned back in the chair, absent-mindedly flicking the lighter in his finger.

"Here's the part," she said, pointing a long-nailed finger toward the mail sack, "responsible for *that*. 'My Dad's computer has a fax modem, and my whole family is on The Net, so I started posting messages wherever I could and I faxed letters to newspapers and magazines. My Mom says we're a nation of spenders, not savers, so I said that if everyone's going to spend, they might as well spend their money on something really important. They'll still get neat stuff for their money, but they'd also get to see *Nomad* do what the Space Shuttle can't right now. I think the Astronauts and the Vice President and our Governor would have wanted it that way."

Chemar lowered the letter. "This kid"— she glanced at the bottom of the second page — "Darla Jean Corbett, is the one responsible for the quadrupling of our donations."

He gave her a look. "*Constitution* had something to do with it."

She shook her head. "That shook people up. This girl directed whatever they felt — grief, anger, betrayal, hopelessness — into helping us. This sack is just a tenth of today's mail. Well over half of the letters mention this kid or that they read or heard her reasoning. I've had to hire three more people to process the checks, and the manufacturers are having trouble keeping up our inventory." She gazed at him with renewed vigor, as if she had just climbed a mountain to see an incredible vista.

"We're going to do it, *mon homme*. We're going to light that candle."

"I never doubted that. I'd have paid for it myself."

"It's not the money," she said, waving a lithe arm toward the sack. "It's the support. The people are on our side. Every one of those envelopes contains a vote in our favor. Every passing day makes it tougher for the government to denounce us."

Poubelle jerked a thumb toward the bullet-pierced robot arm mounted on a wall-plaque. "It's not denunciation I'm concerned about."

CHAPTER 34

Many ideas grow better when transplanted into another mind than in the one where they sprung up.
— Oliver Wendell Holmes

16 June

The shadow followed Haley through every nook and cranny of The Net. Afraid that the Lurker might trace his data stream back to Grant Enterprises, he tried every evasive tactic he knew.

Finally, he gave up and stopped. In the middle of the Mall, the shadow caught him. For a moment it simply stood before him. Then, pixel-by-pixel, the shadow metamorphosed into the female robot from *Metropolis*. She held out her hand to offer a scroll to Haley.

Hesitantly, he reached out to accept it.

In an instant, she vanished. He read the scroll.

The Orbital Settlers' Guide
by Luna Celeste

THIS IS A POLEMIC. A practical polemic, meant to refute the notion that only governments are capable of conquering Space. We, as free, thinking human beings, do not seek *conquest*, we seek the expansion of humanity into the stars. Can it be done without the State? It can and must, for the State is the enemy of space travel.

Why is the State our enemy? One need only gaze around to find the answer. The State murders. The State plunders. The State crushes beneath its jackbooted heel all those who presume to disagree with it. The State is the greatest and most powerful criminal organization in history.

We, the free humans, see its strangling tentacles reach toward the stars and oppose with all our might this incursion of War and Theft into the peaceful quiet of Space.

What is the State? The State is people. People who believe they have a right to rule others. These people are the thieving, murdering brutes responsible for war, conscription, taxation, massacres, slave camps, gas chambers, killing fields, nuclear missiles, and endless death stretching back ten thousand years. The State arose through conquest and shall not confine its ambitions to Earth alone.

Luckily for all, the State is *only* people. And, generally, the least competent of people. They are the ones who cannot innovate, only steal. They cannot reason, only kill. They are brutes who see the greatest efforts of mankind as loot to seize and control. Yet when they seize the creations of greater minds, the works crumble in their hands, for they cannot control what they are incapable of understanding. They tried to seize space. The fall of *Challenger* and *Constitution* proved their folly. UNITO and its effort to monopolize all the planet's space activity is likewise doomed to failure.

Space travel requires free, thinking human beings willing to innovate and experiment. It cannot be accomplished by centralized authority issuing orders at interplanetary distances, paying for everything with stolen money. Nature will judge the State, and punish it mercilessly, automatically.

We, the free humans, declare that we can and will out-compete the moribund State. History is on our side. The government expeditions of Columbus did not settle the New World; Pilgrims and Puritans did by pouring their own fortunes into escape from the Old World. The highly funded government bureaucrat Stephen Langley did not make human flight possible; the struggling Wright Brothers did. A statist airplane did not fly around the Earth without refueling; the private venture of *Voyager* did. It will not be a bloated bureaucracy that sends multitudes of humans into Space, it will be we, the People.

By the indomitable spirit of mankind, we dedicate our every breathing moment and all we possess to humanity's future in Space. This book will tell you how we can do it...

▼ ▲ ▼

It read as well, he thought, as anything he had written. Better, in fact. And the only aspect of the piece that amazed him was the fact that he had *not* written it.

Joscelyn appeared, wearing an all-too-alluring leopard pattern on her virtual skin. "What's up?" she asked.

"Read this," he said, nodding toward the parchment. She leaned over his shoulder. "Where are you right now?" he asked.

"Florida again. You know."

He nodded. He read further, the text on the parchment scrolling at his command.

▼ ▲ ▼

Look up in the night sky. Gaze at those bright points of light. Seek out Luna, Venus, Mars, Jupiter, Saturn. Squint at the Sun just before morning to see Mercury. Sit in the desert on a moonless night to find Neptune and Uranus. Consider the darkness between us and them. This darkness, this empty black expanse, is the new sea on which we must sail. For we cannot stay bound to the land forever.

We are the new pioneers, the nomads, the wanderers. We are the ones who will advance our species. If the fact of evolution and the theories of natural selection and punctuated equilibrium are correct, our leaving Earth will result in a rapid evolution of our species. We shall change while the earthbound shall stagnate. We shall become the new, vigorous race. *Homo Sapiens* will languish while *Homo asteralis* flourishes.

Space travel is the stuff of destiny.

▼ ▲ ▼

"Pretty stiff drink you're serving," she said.

"I didn't write it."

She stared at him for a moment. "You mean these ideas are percolating around the *zeitgeist* on their own?"

Haley nodded.

"Who wrote it — Rex Ivarson?"

Haley shook his head. "The Lurker."

▼ ▲ ▼

Chapter 1
BREAKING THE SPELL

The idea that *only* the State can engage in space travel is as much a myth as any other. The State builds dams, but does that mean that *only* the State can build dams? Let's ask the nearest beaver. Only the State can build roads, or so the story goes. Tell it to the owners of thousands of miles of private highways.

What the State is good at, it turns out, is *seizing* from private hands the land for roads and dams. It excels at *confiscating* at gunpoint the funds for construction. When deemed necessary, the State *enslaves* the manpower needed for construction.

Beavers don't have to be drafted to build dams. Neither do humans need to be conscripted, taxed, or forced aside to make way for progress. They will either join gladly, be open to bargaining, or hold out heroically to what is theirs. All the State does in the name of progress is trample human rights and dignity.

So it is with Space.

The self-aggrandizing statists in the space program have assured us that space travel is incredibly dangerous, unbelievably complex, and overwhelmingly expensive.

And for them, it is.

▼ ▲ ▼

Donahue whistled lowly, impressed. "I think she deserves an e-mail fan letter."

17 June

Montgomery Barron wondered whether to share the information his subordinates had gathered with Milton. The slaughter at Novosibirsk had been confirmed, explaining why the CIA's mole in GRU, Baumhoff, had not reported back about subnational space efforts in Russia. For Barron, that was all the confirmation he needed. He shredded the report. The tiny diamond slices of paper fell like snowflakes into the waiting bucket of water and bleach beneath, where they dissolved into unreconstitutible mush within moments.

He turned his attention toward *Huntress*. The spaceplane stood in its hangar like a bird of prey eager to do battle, surrounded by scaffolding as if caged to hold its fury in check. Long, sleek, and white as death it was, its delta wings forming a sharp, narrow-based isosceles triangle. Along the center line lay the wasp-waisted fuselage. At every inch of its winged length, the cross-sectional area equaled that of every other inch. This allowed acceleration to hypersonic speeds with minimal control problems at transition to higher Mach numbers.

The cockpit hatch formed a mere blister on the forward dorsal area; the flush-mounted cameras, forward-looking infra-red sensors, and phased-array radar that would provide data for the pilot's VR headset were nearly unnoticeable.

The engine, tucked away in the stern, was the spacecraft's crown jewel. Rescued from MacArthur-Truitt when NASA funding ended for the National Aerospace Plane, the turbojet/ramjet/scramjet/rocket engine — a successfully fired 1/3 scale test bed model — fit *Huntress* superbly. NASA never publicly admitted that NASP constituted an impossible boondoggle, that there existed no way to build a huge spaceplane. Yet NASA and the trough-feeders wanted a massive project. They obfuscated a fact that Barron discovered in his research, though: *small* spaceplanes were feasible.

The proof — he hoped and believed — lay in the fruits of Project *Stark Fist*.

There could be no test flights of this secret project, however. That was why he spent so much time in the simulator, even muscling out the actual pilot now and then. Barron wanted to know — pre-need — that when the time came to unleash *Huntress*, nothing would go wrong.

With the exception of the engine itself and the actual weapons, Barron's crew thoroughly tested and impeccably maintained all systems. Storable rocket fuel and oxidation-inhibited jet fuel guaranteed that the spaceplane could be operational within moments of need, once they removed the scaffolding.

That would happen within a week, when the ablative material cured completely. Meanwhile, Barron again heeded the urge to bump the pilot from the simulator.

18 June

A number of pallets marked

LOCKHEED SR-71 SURPLUS TITANIUM
FOR AUTHORIZED SALE ONLY

stood outside a South Bronx warehouse. Davy Crockett shook his head in annoyance, which caused the tail of his coonskin hat to wag back and forth like an impatient animal.

Next to the pallets of titanium struts lay a few more crates with such stenciled information as

JR. PROSPECTOR FIELD ANALYSIS KIT

FARM-IN-A-TUB HYDROPONICS

ALGAE, BLUE, WATER-ACTIVATED, 100 KILOS

"Bernie!" he shouted through the doorway.

Bernadette emerged wearing a white Tyvek painter's overall. The bright sunshine turned her into pure glare. Crockett shielded his eyes.

"How'd your final go?" she asked.

"Aces, I'm sure," he said. "What's all this stuff doing here?"

"Provisions," she answered.

"We're going up there for a day or two, not forever."

"So I'm thinking ahead. It was free."

"Well, can we get someone to move it inside?"

She shook her head. "Two-thirds of the crew are taking finals, and some of the rest have already gone home for summer."

"What about Crush and the gang?" He stepped inside and raised the warehouse door just enough to bring out the pallet jack.

"They're off on their own business. Gang business. I don't *wanna* know."

"Where's Sam?"

"Where do you think?" she said with a crooked grin. "Proselytizing like the proselytute he was born to be."

▼ ▲ ▼

Friedman stared at the audience before him in the hotel meeting hall. *Boy, I wish we had some other scam going instead of this.*

He stroked at his Fu Manchu moustache — the real one, finally grown long enough to replace the lip wig he had started with — and adjusted his white *ghi* so that it would look just baggy enough for him to appear at ease but not so loose as to make him look geekoid.

He strode out on stage after a brief introduction by Natasha, who had a way with New York crowds. No one applauded, but some members of the audience began to hum *Om*.

"Half a millennium before our souls incarnated in their present vessels," he began, weaving as lithely as he could on the hotel stage, "in the ancient Orient, the Chinese invented gunpowder. They used it to power skyrockets, fireworks to send messages to the gods. The human soul has always sought the divine in the night sky, among the stars. Gods and goddesses live up there, or so we believe. Why do we believe?"

He stopped moving, threw his head and arms back in an adoration worthy of any evangelist.

"We were children of the stars!" he cried. "The stuff of our bodies was formed in the heart of exploding suns! We weren't meant to live on Earth, but in the depths of Space. Gravity drags us down, crushes our bones, sags our flesh, collapses our arches, and gives us *stretch marks*!" Many in the audience nodded. It all made sense now.

"We belong in Space! Our ancestral home! Our dreams of flying saucers are memories of our homeland! We must return to the stars!"

For over half an hour, he channeled an impassioned, mystical speech, urging everyone to contribute to the building of a great Space Ark in which the faithful may return to Space.

It brought in sixteen grand. Less the hotel fees, they cleared fourteen and a quarter.

We still need more, Sam thought at the end of the evening. *Space is a drug and we need to score.* That brought a smile. *We need to mainline is what we need.*

21 June

"Hey!" Poubelle said, pointing his cigar at Marcus Grant. "The last time *you* showed up, I got shot." He hooked the thumb of his cigar-holding hand and pointed it back toward the trophy mounted on his wall. It looked like a damaged prop from a science-fiction film.

Grant strode into the office with a wide grin. His grey hair sparkled in the morning sun angling in through a window. He gave every impression of a man on top of the world.

"You don't associate me with that bit of excitement, do you?"

The other man shook his head. "Nah. My detectives traced her psychiatrist back to a CIA shop in the Eighties."

Grant's smile straightened out to something more worried. "You mean you suspect it was an agency wet job?"

Poubelle mocked a look of horrified surprise. "I'm so shocked! Would my own government attack one of the citizens it is sworn to protect?" He took a puff or two on the cigar and said, "You're talking to a graduate of 'Nam University during the Great Disillusionment. I have the highest regard for my government — it is capable of anything." He eyed his fellow billionaire. "So what *are* you doing here?"

Grant turned to gaze at a 747 sitting on the taxiway, awaiting clearance for proceed. Purchased by Grant for the purpose of ferrying equipment and people from all points of the planet to the eastern shores of Africa, the used aircraft bore no paint job, looking bright and polished and smart and new, despite its age.

"Oh," he said casually to Poubelle, "a little desert business." He fixed his attention on the one-armed billionaire. "So I thought I'd sneak a peek at *Nomad*."

"She's ready for her test flight." He rose from his desk. "Let me show you around."

The warehouse bulged with people. Separated from the crowd of tourists and enthusiasts by a red velvet cord and armed security guards, the ground crew tinkered with the black bolt of a spaceplane. With the exception of a few close-out panels, through which workers made endless adjustments and corrections, *Nomad* appeared complete.

It's family relationship with the X-15 was inescapable. Though larger by almost thirty percent, the proportioning nearly matched the original design. The only visible difference was that the cockpit enclosed a two-seat tandem configuration and seemed roomier nonetheless.

All the gorgeous curves and angles of the four-decade-old original had been reborn with the Daedalus Project: the twin bulges that ran alongside the fuselage to contain the rocket fuel; the Q-ball nose widening along the line of a prolate parabola, slightly flattened; the stubby, wedge-like wings and tail surfaces, designed for the rigors of hypersonic flight; the streamlined holes for the reaction control system that provided attitude control outside the atmosphere. It also possessed several features the original did not, including extremely powerful guidance and navigation computers, a complete energy-management system, and a pilot/co-pilot ejection pod that could serve as a reentry vehicle on its own.

Grant walked once around the spaceplane with its creator, asking a few questions now and then. He wanted to ask a million questions, but thought that such boyish excitement might tip his hand. He maintained the appearance of a rich man visiting another rich man's aircraft collection.

"And you'll launch this from the back of a Seven-Four-Seven?"

"Yep. Just like the old Space Van concept from the early Eighties."

"No heat shield tiles?"

Poubelle lightly stroked the black skin of the spaceplane. "Nope. The reentry temperatures will be far lower than those of the shuttle orbiter, since the planform loading is less than half. She's a light bird and we're carrying almost no cargo except for a few collector's items. A combination of high-temperature metal and heat-sink methods — more heat-sink mass than the original, in fact, since the internal-volume-to-surface-area ratio is greater — ought to give us what we need."

"Ought to?"

Poubelle threw his mechanical arm around Grant's shoulder. "Hey, we can run computer simulations up the kazoo, but you never *really* know until you try."

Grant thought about that as he glanced out the hangar doors to see his 747 lift off into the summer sky.

▼ ▲ ▼

Leave-taking occupied Chad's thoughts as the aircraft in which he sat as a passenger performed its slow and stately takeoff roll, climbing into the cloudless June sky to leave behind the brownish haze drifting into the Mojave desert from neighboring Los Angeles. Haley glanced south toward the metropolitan area and made his mental goodbyes.

It was a strange thing to leave his native land. Born in California and raised there, he grew up immersed in America's odd combination of melting-pot and pressure-cooker that turned most people into non-cosmopolitan eclectics. He appreciated all cultures but never felt the urge to travel to and immerse himself in them. Now he embarked upon a non-stop trip to Somalia, a place the location of which he had not even been certain a few months before. And after a few months there, he would relocate to an even stranger place.

In the rush of events, the hustle and bustle of designing the revolutionary spaceship, Haley found little time to think about the enormous change he and a handful of other people would soon undergo. He had not even visited all of the western states surrounding California, yet here he stood on the verge of bidding farewell to Earth forever. While enough of an optimist to expect that in a few years travel to and from Grant One would be commonplace (if it weren't, they would all quite probably be dead), he also entertained the possibility of the unpredictable. The engines could blow up in flight; the airflow through the center of the toroid could choke off at transonic speed, causing the flat-plate area to rise sharply, increasing drag beyond any ability of the engines to overcome; unknown factors in the supersonic flight regime might lead to catastrophic destruction of the vessel...

He wondered if he had made his goodbyes properly or sufficiently. He kept few friends, except on The Net, and he could maintain *those* friendships via satellite links. With no family to speak of, that left the Earth itself. Astronauts, cosmonauts — they all departed on their trips knowing that they might die, but fully expecting to return to Earth after a mission of determinate length. They were truly *residents* of Space: there for a specific time and purpose, intending to leave when their goals were accomplished. This trip would be no mere residency for Haley and fifty-nine others; Grant One would be their *domicile*, their permanent home, their settlement in Space. They would no longer be citizens of their respective states or nations, they would be settlers in a new land — if one could call the void of Space a land — as immune from retaliation *or* assistance as the inhabitants of Plymouth Rock, and with fewer resources than they carried on *Mayflower*.

Even the most rag-tag and shoddy expedition to the New World, Haley mused, *had air, water, and food waiting for them at their destination. We'll have nothing but what we bring.*

And what *would* they bring? Grant remained peculiarly mute on the subject. He took in advice from Haley, Donahue, and a small cadre of experts hired to research the subject, mostly poring over the manifests of Skylab and *Mir*, and released nothing. He claimed to have the matter well in hand. Haley suspected that Grant had been pondering the subject for some time and already possessed his own list.

The browns of the desert and the ochre of LA smog gave way to the crisp blue of the Pacific. The silvery aircraft carried a great deal of cargo intended for the work crew in Kismayu. Stripped of seats in its lower passenger section, the jet contained sealant and pressure-test devices to ensure complete integrity of the hulls; welding units and every conceivable tool that the construction crew would need to assemble the sixteen individual spheres into humanity's first real space habitat; sewing and serging machines and Kevlar III stretchable ballistic fabric with which to tailor the custom-made pressure suits (and ten full-body sewing dummies piled against one bulkhead like crash victims); test brands of packaged food to determine the best menus for the spacefarers; and — at Haley's insistence — scores of water bottles filled with fresh, pure mineral water as an alternative to the local supply.

He tapped at his breast pocket to ensure that his passport still rested there. He pulled it out to admire the forgery. Grant's counter-economic connections could provide anything at a price. They had provided him with the bogus — yet fully documented — identity of Murray Rothbart, VP of International Operations at World Habitat Missions. There was something about possessing a passport, even if not in his real name, that filled Chad with all the excitement of a boy playing spy-counterspy. Just a little booklet with his photograph, it identified him as a world traveler. Within half a year, though — weight restrictions forbidding such useless mass — it would be left behind on the planet's surface and Haley would become a citizen of the Galaxy.

It would be a long flight to Somalia. Haley settled back in the wide leather seat, shifted it to recliner, and gazed upward at the sky-blue overhead, thinking about the future. This was his first work break in months, and his first opportunity to consider the emotional impact of space travel. Not just space travel, though: space *migration*. This would be no visit, no week-long Shuttle cruise, no months-long tour of duty onboard an American or Russian space station. That might come later for visitors to Grant One. For the original station inhabitants, though, this was as permanent a destination and as complete a break with America and Earth as the Massachusetts Bay Colony had been for Europeans. He was comforted by the fact that Grant Enterprises apparently would not impose on the occupants of Grant One the sort of communalism imposed on the Massachusetts Bay Colony by John Winthrop. Grant seemed more like William Bradford, who helped establish private property in the colony, leading to its survival and growth.

Haley had no doubt that the space station could prosper. What he doubted was whether outside forces would permit it to.

It was the leaving, though, that troubled him the most. He had never considered himself a pioneer. Though he may have dreamt about space migration and fancied himself one of the vanguard, he never dwelt upon the actuality of departure. This was *it*. The moment those nearly 12,000 mini-engines ignited, he would be thrown into an adventure as great as anything ever experienced. He tried to envision exactly what it meant. Death, of course, denoted the extreme negative outcome. What about success, though? What if everything went absolutely right?

He would spend every subsequent day of his remaining life inside the curving confines of the rotating metal toroid. No backyard in which to roam. Or, looking at it another way, a backyard bigger than anyone ever dreamed.

Haley gazed out at the shimmering azure Pacific as the plane turned inland for its flight to Orlando, Florida. Above him hung the sapphire sky with the Sun converted by the crazed acrylic window to a pointed star surrounded by concentric golden arcs. The biggest difference in Space, he thought, would be that he would see much more of the Earth below him in one glance and the sky around him would be black, the atmosphere they struggled so hard to penetrate nothing more than a thin veil on the horizon.

He sat up, unstrapped, and ran down the spiral staircase into the depths of the aircraft.

Despite the cargo it held, it looked positively cavernous, stripped of all its seats and class partitions. He tried to envision it as being curved sharply, part of a corridor five hundred feet long that looped back on itself. That would be about the length of the middle level of the space station, with the outer level a bit longer and the inner level a bit shorter. It seemed roomy enough for twenty people to live and work in. Lots of space for private cabins, materials to be sent up on subsequent flights for such niceties as partitioning and beds.

Twenty people in an expansive space station with a magnificent view. It need not be like an Antarctic base, where isolation sometimes drove people mad. Grant One would not be a remotely ruled government outpost performing subsidized activities with no profit allowed or freedom permitted. With a hydroponics farm and rabbit warren providing food they could live without outside assistance; the free-flying microgravity manufacturing plant they intended to take up with them contained equipment and raw materials to make a number of pricey products, which the crew would package and ship back to Earth in simple, unmanned aerobraking reentry capsules.

He had no idea what other cards Grant played close to his vest, but he knew that not one of them would lose money. That is, if the governments of Earth — and Grant's industrial competitors — declined to interfere.

The notion of defending an orbital platorm kept him awake nights. He touched the fuselage wall. Made of aircraft-grade aluminum, it was similar to the wall of the hydrogen fuel tank that would serve as their home in Space. The tank wall — four-tenths of an inch of aluminum-lithium alloy and strong enough to contain the 75,000 p.s.i. internal pressure of the fuel — would easily maintain the pressure differential between the hard vacuum of Low Earth Orbit and the interior 10-15 p.s.i. atmosphere the inhabitants required. The outer wall would also be proof against solar radiation and cosmic rays, but would it withstand the occasional meteoroid or chunk of orbiting space junk? Could a light exo-atmospheric projectile such as those devised by the Ballistic Missile Defense Organization devastate and destroy the entire space station?

He returned to his seat and gazed once more through the thin Lexan pane separating him from the frigid, nearly airless realm of the upper troposphere. Chad Haley did not fear the prospect of leaving Earth, he discovered, so much as he feared not leaving it far enough behind.

CHAPTER 35

Destiny is no matter of chance. It is a matter of choice:
it is not a thing to be waited for, it is a thing to be achieved.

— William Jennings Bryan

19 June

In the world of high-tech counter-economics, goods and services flowed in certain directions while the paperwork — or digital information — moved in other, far different ones.

The 11,520 individual thrust chambers — each one a rectangular block 25 inches long by five square with an hourglass-shaped interior combustion chamber tapering down to three inches at its narrowest — came from a manufacturer in Wichita, Kansas, based on a CAD-CAM design delivered by Joscelyn Donahue via computer. All the Wichita firm knew was that the finished pieces were to be shipped to New Orleans by rail. There, Donahue faxed paperwork showing them shipped to an oil field in Belize when they in fact they were barged to Fort Lauderdale, trucked to Orlando, and placed onboard the airplane carrying Haley to Somalia. There, the containers were marked as plumbing parts to be delivered to World Habitat Missions. Plug nozzles, cryogenic liquids, composite structures, and miscellaneous tools and cargo all arrived by even more complicated routes, while the digital bits indicating their bogus official descriptions for tariff and permit purposes moved along entirely fictional paths. Any errors or discoveries by vigilant bureaucrats were dealt with in two traditional ways: bribery and/or blackmail. Murder — an option so far unused — remained the last resort for only the most recalcitrant of government employees.

Luckily, Donahue's search for crew members involved less chicanery. The fiery end of NASA trickled down through the aerospace industry as, one-by-one, contracts collapsed, funding evaporated, and projects died. Many a skilled technician and able scientist discovered that their talents were useless to an earthbound society. Donahue had her pick of them.

She had her pick of pilots, too. Despite Grant's objections, she wanted astronauts. Due to *Constitution*, all sat on the sidelines on semi-permanent furloughs. Many quit, unable to envision hanging around a moribund NASA waiting out the years that may pass before the remaining shuttles made a comeback. Rumor that the slowly reconstituting agency — filling up with newcomers more familiar with paper-shuffling than with spacecraft — would once more "redirect its priorities" and abandon the STS created a hemorrhage of workers at all levels except management.

When Joscelyn hacked into NASA's personnel computers to search their employee lists, she found that the finest people, as rated by their periodic reviews, were long gone. These she tracked and located all around the world. One, whom she had seen passed out in a bar in Cocoa Beach some time back during her preliminary investigation, particularly came to mind.

22 June

Tammy's phone warbled like an insolent bird. She rolled over in her sweaty sheets to reach out blindly toward the offending intruder.

"What?" Her voice growled with the mellifluousness of library paste. Abdominal cramps — aftermath of the pregnancy termination — seized her with sudden, numbing pain. Gritting her teeth, she listened as a computer-distorted voice of indeterminate gender greeted her. *"Good morning, Dr. Reis. I understand that you're fed up with NASA."*

"Who is this?"

"You'll find out eventually. I understand that you have recently resigned and you're seeking new challenges."

"I'm not exactly receiving a pension," Tammy said, suddenly wide awake, heart racing, pain forgotten.

"Are you interested in a piloting job?"

"I'm not interested in airline work, cargo transport, smuggling, flight instruction, foreign military, or barnstorming. Does that still leave you in the running?"

"Yes," the eerily inhuman voice replied. *"Are you prepared to 'disappear' from family and friends?"*

A chill ran through her. After a moment, she quietly replied, "Yes."

"Do you have a current passport?"

She laughed with an inadvertent amusement that made her hungover head throb. "Hey, I've been around the world nine hundred eighteen times!"

The altered voice on the other end of the line betrayed no humor.

"Do you have a current passport?"

"Yes," she replied soberly. "As an astronaut, I traveled worldwide, for training, research, and publicity trips."

"Fine. A limo will arrive at six tomorrow morning to take you to Orlando. Bring only carry-on luggage."

"Wait a sec. How do I know—"

The caller hung up. Tammy immediately punched in her call return code. A telephone rang somewhere in the world. Once. Twice.

"Heat Shield," the familiar voice of Ed Laird said.

"Ed?" she said in utter shock. "Ed, this is Tammy! Who was just on the phone?"

She could hear Ed's shoulder-shrug in the sound of his voice. *"Tammy, I'm setting up bar. How should I know?"*

"This is important, Ed!"

After a pause, the baritone voice said, *"Sure, kid,"* and grew faint as he asked someone nearby. In a moment, he came back to say, *"Nobody, Tammy. Ricardo said he's been trying to get a dial tone for the last fifteen minutes."*

She muttered thanks and goodbye, then pressed a finger against the hangup button. She next called Steven Milton, the only man she knew to contact now that Bryan Kirk was dead.

"What do I do?" she asked after telling him of the offer.

"You accepted. That's all you have to do. I'll be over in half an hour with... someone I'd like you to meet."

▼ ▲ ▼

Tammy examined the gift she held between her fingers, a gold Shuttle Astronaut pin identical to hers. This one, though, contained a microchip and power supply that emitted an encrypted signal detectable by satellite. The signal — to anyone not in possession of the decryption key — would be indistinguishable from background radiation. Red noise.

"We won't desert you," the nameless visitor who arrived with Milton told her. He was a fat and smiling man with a beard and long, thin red-brown hair and a T-shirt that read THE ONLY THING CONSTANT IN MY LIFE IS PLANCK'S. "In the event of a life-threatening emergency or an imminent launch," he explained, "gently bend both wings of the shuttle upward— that alters the signal from tracking to distress. We'll be on your tail within minutes."

"What will happen to the group I infiltrate?" she asked.

Milton spoke with pleasant coolness. "Leave that to us."

For the second time that night, Tammy Reis felt a chill in her soul.

▼ ▲ ▼

"Tammy?"

Reis turned at the sound of the voice. She stood in the room to which the limo chauffeur had led her. The face she turned to see was just as familiar as the voice — Jon Franck entered, led by another chauffeur. Dressed for travel in light loose clothing, the same as Reis, the astronaut gazed at his former crew mate and grinned in bafflement.

"What in the hell are you doing here?" she demanded in a tone more terrified hiss than angry whisper.

"I got a phone call," he said. He looked tanned and relaxed. "I thought I'd finally take some vacation time and view the world from a new perspective. You too, I see."

Tammy clasped her hand over her throat in a gesture of concern — and an unconscious attempt to cover the tracking pin. "You don't even know what you're getting into."

Franck shrugged and hefted a stuffed carry-on bag onto his shoulder as if it were a deer carcass. "Neither do you. Isn't that the essence of adventure? Isn't that what we joined NASA for?"

This may be a bit more adventurous than you suspect or I want, she mused as he sat in the lounge chair next to hers.

The room wasn't much, one of many empty offices converted for use as a passenger holding-pen. A few chairs, a self-service bar, some packaged snack food. An overhead speaker played light instrumental music. Outside the tinted window rumbled jets coming and going to one of the biggest tourist destinations in the world.

Nobody had noticed them coming in, a couple of travelers amid hundreds of others. Astronauts no longer held celebrity status. There was an irony in that. The Mercury Astronauts — most famous because they flew the first missions — served little more function than human ride-alongs, performing far fewer flight-related duties than the average shuttle astronaut. Yet their names and faces burned on in the memory of an entire generation. Gus Grissom's perpetual hangdog expression, John Glenn's clear and steadfast gaze, Gordo Cooper's brash and youthful look of derring-do. They were all old men now, some of them dead, and except for the one who turned his fame into political currency all could now pass unrecognized on any American street.

Even though they had been dead or comatose only six months and were mourned as heroes, the *Constitution* Eight probably could not have been identified in a lineup by more than a small percentage of Americans, most of them schoolchildren.

"So how did you get involved in this?" Franck finally asked.

Reis avoided his inquisitive gaze. "Phone call, same as you."

"Meet with anyone?"

Her pulse suddenly quickened and she felt a flush warm her face. "Nope. You?"

"Nope. This is like some spy game I used to imagine as a kid. Globetrotting, man-in-a-suitcase kind of intrigue."

Totally unexpectedly, she said, "It's not too late. We can bail out now."

Franck smiled and ran a hand through his wavy blond hair. "Why would I want to do that?"

"This could be dangerous. We could get killed!"

Franck's laughter broke through the perpetual buzz of airport chatter. Completely free of sarcasm or fear, it was the laugh of a man who — because he loved life — viewed death as an unimportant consequence.

"And we're safer with NASA?" was all he said.

▼▲▼

She stared out the window at the sunshine and blue skies above. The 747 flew straight and steady above an endless expanse of Atlantic waters. She stayed awake for the entire flight, gazing out the window. A pilot by inclination and profession, she rarely encountered the opportunity merely to sit and appreciate the scenery.

Franck sat beside her, not talking much for the entire flight. The only other passenger, a man who introduced himself as Chad Haley and said nothing more, sat in a seat on the opposite side of the sky lounge, working away at a permanently installed computer workstation. He stayed there for the entire flight, erasing his screen whenever curiosity got the better of Reis and she wandered over to attempt conversation.

She detected the change in altitude before she heard the engines alter their whine.

"Ladies and gentlemen," the captain said over the speakers and headphones, *"We're descending into Madrid and will be landing at Aeropuerto Barajas within twenty minutes."*

Tammy touched the shuttle pin on the lapel of her aquamarine floral print blouse. Her heart raced with anticipation. With only one piece of luggage, she was about to embark on a journey that could lead anywhere, even to her death. What sort of gamble was that? Violated by Woolsey, savage in her revenge, she saw little chance of NASA actually delivering on its promise to reinstate her to the flight schedule. Certainly not before the STS became chattel of UNITO.

Why was she doing it? she wondered. Was her devotion to NASA so strong that she still clung to the belief that it was her only road to

Space? So much so that she would infiltrate and betray a rival enterprise? Or — the very thought of it made her feel edgy — was she searching for kindred spirits? Someone on the planet who looked up into the night sky and saw the possibilities she envisioned?

She fought back the urge to remember the past. Too much joy and pain lurked there for her to visit it yet again. Instead she looked forward, out of the window.

I wonder what happens next?

She did not have to wait long to find out.

▼▲▼

Somewhere in Fort Meade, Maryland, a tiny orange dot slowly moved across a computer-generated map of the world. Steven James Milton Jr. watched the computer project the path toward possible destinations for a moment, then placed a call to an agent in Spain.

▼▲▼

After an overnight in Madrid — their mysterious benefactor had arranged rooms for them at one of the more expensive hotels plus ten thousand dollars in walking-around money — they boarded yet another flight, this one to the Mediterranean and south across Africa. Tammy took three hours out of the short stay in Spain to change her hair style at a renowned boutique. When she joined Jon in the limo to the airport, her raven hair sported a straight pageboy, oriental style, that curled gracefully inward at the neckline. Her bangs, straight and severe, cut across her forehead just a fraction of an inch above her eyebrows. She wore an outfit — also purchased at the boutique — that perfectly matched her new look: a shiny black patent leather jumpsuit designed more to show off her figure than with any thought of function. Unless its function was to follow her form.

"Whoa!" Jon cried out at first sight. "You win the spy costume contest!"

She flinched at his use of the word. Either he knew something — perhaps Milton had enlisted him, too — or his joke simply hit too close to home.

Franck wore clothing more suited to their suspected destination: light white woven shirt and matching cotton cargo-pocketed pants cinched at the waist with a military web belt. He held in his hand a white Panama hat with a light grey band. His own gold Shuttle pin glittered on his lapel. Tammy wondered whether it, too, sent out a signal.

They said little on the flight from Madrid to Mogadishu. When they arrived, the mysterious Haley gave them directions to their next flight, bade them farewell, and set out to oversee unloading of the pallets and crates of cargo.

As the pair of astronauts acquired their next set of tickets from a small, recently erected ticket counter for an obviously new and tiny company called Velocet Airways, Franck merrily said, "Have you wondered who has the money to do this?"

"Not the Russians, that's for sure."

"I figure it's some up-and-coming Asian government. One that may still be an international pariah."

"That narrows it down," she said in a biting tone.

"Tammy—" His voice grew suddenly serious as he put an arm around her shoulder. "I want you to know that I've been watching you..."

She tensed up, this time consciously fighting to keep her hand away from her shuttle pin.

"And I'm very proud of you for not having a drink during the entire flight."

Her eyes widened a bit, then — despite her conflicting emotions in the crowded terminal of the densely populated little city-state — she smiled. It was as warm and honest a smile as had escaped her in years.

"Thank you, Jon. I don't seem to feel the need anymore."

He nodded. "We're wild dolphins."

"What?"

"Dolphins. In the wide open sea, they lead pretty normal lives. In captivity, though, where they have to jump through hoops to please the crowd, they behave neurotically: nervousness, aggression, sexual dysfunction, depression. Human beings are the same as dolphins or rats or just about any other animal: crowd us together"—he wedged past a cluster of Somalis gazing at the strangers with inquisitive, vaguely suspicious glares—"and we go nuts. Give us our elbow room and we grow civil again."

"Elbow room?" she said, using that part of her own body as a wedge and a defense through a sudden crowd surging toward a gate. "The old *lebensraum* argument?" She handed her boarding pass to a Bantu woman in a maroon flight suit with grey trim. They boarded a small eight-seat Cessna Citation.

"Not exactly. *Lebensraum* with no one else *leben*ing in it. Space changes all our notions of what constitutes Land. Land was always something nearly mystical to some people, since there was only so much of it on Earth. It was a form of property different from others. It had to be — you couldn't manufacture more, you could either stack more people on what you had or go out and settle what little unclaimed Land remained. In Space, though, the concept becomes irrelevant. You could plop down onto a planet and have a whopping huge increase in the amount of Land available, or you could stay up there in the void and have something even greater: a vast volume in which to build structures with all the attributes of Land, such as dirt to farm, air to breath, water to drink, yet different from Land: you can move it anywhere you want and you can make more of it."

He took a seat and stuffed his bulging flight bag in the overhead compartment, then flopped down into the comfortable first class accommodations. She sat next to him, sliding her case under her seat.

He continued. "A new frontier to settle, without the accompanying necessity — or opportunity — to seize Land from others. If you can build your own Land, you're more likely to do that than try to take someone else's, especially when someone else can pick up and move. Imagine if the Jews could have taken their pieces of Israel with them during the Exodus. Not just goods and livestock, but the Land itself, leaving a void, leaving nothing for the Pharaoh to grab? What if Caesar rolled into Gaul and found nothing but a gaping chasm? What if the Poles could have moved Poland out of Hitler's grasp? Or out of Stalin's?"

"Sounds like a lot of moving."

"Maybe 'Luna Celeste' should change the name of her book."

"What book?"

Franck pulled a diskette out of his shirt pocket. The label read: *The Orbital Settlers' Guide*. "Maybe she should have called it *The Orbital Nomads' Guide*."

"Who's 'Luna Celeste'?"

"I have no idea, but she's written the longest anti-NASA screed I've ever read. Must have bottled it up for years."

She turned the disk over as if expecting to find jacket copy written on the other side. "May I read it?"

Jon smiled. "If you have time. I suspect our mysterious benefactors will want to get their money's worth out of us."

Her voice dropped to a whisper close to his ear. "What do you think we'll be flying?"

He shrugged. "Something that requires our unique skills. Say"— he gazed around the small aircraft at the sound of the hatch sealing shut — "we're the only ones onboard!"

24 June

The desert-beige Range Rover that met them at the small airstrip in Kismayu was driven by a Bantu named Ali. Tall and lean, he maneuvered the truck over the dusty road, all the while asking questions."

"You speak Italian?" he asked. "My Italian be much, much better than English. Whole family live in Moqdisho — in Italian Somaliland — before independence. You hot in that outfit?"

Reis had to admit that she sweltered, but she had not found time to change and just wanted to get to wherever they were headed so that she could shower and rest. "Where are you taking us?"

"Lovely place. Lovely. Just outside town. New housing development. Very modern. You both Americans, right?" The Rover hit a pothole in the dirt road and flew into the air, landing with jarring impact. Ali seemed not to notice. "Yes. America help us big. Very big." His words bespoke gratitude, his tone, caution. "End starvation. End civil war. Very happy to have America here."

"There are still US troops here?" Tammy asked.

"Just a few. Just with UN. Just up north. Nothing bad happens down here."

Jon frowned. "Then why do you have that gun beside you?"

With a wide grin, Ali patted the 9mm automatic. "Because we learn from Americans: better to have a gun and no need than need a gun and no have, yes?"

Tammy snorted, her gaze scanning the horizon. As they cleared a hill, something completely anomalous came into view.

The twisting road lead down to a small vale. In the center at the road's end, bright yellow Caterpillar and dark green John Deere equipment dug at the brown earth, digging a precise circular scar twenty feet deep, about the same wide, and half a football field in diameter. In the center of the circle stood ten single-width mobile homes that served as temporary facilities, around which grew small patches and swaths of grass. The ubiquitous small herds of cattle that roamed the land tended by nomadic Somalis gazed across the dry moat with miserable desire. The land outside the circle sported the usual scrubby brush and dry grasses on which they eeked out their existence. The one bridge to the center consisted of a railroad flatbed car sunk level with the edges of the channel. A cyclone fence extended several yards in either direction to support the gate guarded by a lone Somali sitting under a bright yellow beach umbrella.

Most striking, though, was what straddled the ditch. Six bulbous structures — hemispherical on top, tapering, truncated half-cones from midline down — sat atop rusty steel girders placed across the circular chasm. Two more sat on massive truck beds awaiting placement by a titanic crane nearby.

"What the hell is that?" Franck said.

Ali steered the Rover toward the bridge. "That's going to be big new hotel. Bring lots of guests to visit." He waved at the guard, who opened the gate.

"A hotel without windows?" Tammy muttered to Jon as the Rover rumbled across the big ditch.

▼ ▲ ▼

"Looks more like a tank farm." Franck lowered his flight bag to the patio deck of one of the mobiles to gaze around at the activity. Workers swarmed around the six identical pods. An airy framework of scaffolding encased the two pods on the ends. Sparks flew here and there from the blue-white centers of heli-arc and TIG welders joining the edges of the spheres together. Something clanged with the jarring sound of metal against metal. Drills whirred, riveters pounded away, and air-driven wrenches whined like a hundred tire-changers gone mad. The muggy air hung thick with smells: engine oil, scorched aluminum, perspiration, exhaust fumes, and the pervasive odor of cattle.

"Dr. Franck! Dr. Reis!" an unfamiliar voice cried out. They both turned to see a slender, auburn-haired woman run up to them. "I'm Joscelyn Donahue," she said. "Your official welcoming committee."

Tammy took her proffered hand and shook politely. "Then you're the one we get to interrogate about all this."

"Certainly! Step inside the office and we'll get started."

▼ ▲ ▼

The half-hour briefing, complete with VR presentation of the construction and launch of the SSTO space station left Jon and Tammy limp. They stared at each other, then at Donahue. Jon's left eye developed a tic. Tammy, filled with terror and awe, attempted to convert her emotions into an aire of ebullience.

"That was great! What do you call it?"

"It's technically called a Neuffer Ring, in honor of its designer. Mr. Grant calls this particular structure Grant One."

"It's an astounding concept," she said. "In one step you'll — *we'll* — accomplish something that's eluded NASA for decades! Can we meet Neuffer?"

Donahue bit her lip. "I don't think so. He designed it in the early Nineteen-Sixties. NASA, of course, rejected it totally as part of their tacit Not Invented Here policy. We..." her finger traced a circle on the monitor screen, then tapped it twice lightly, "sort of... *lifted* it from some microfilmed proposals Mr. Grant discovered."

"About this Grant guy," Franck said, caution in his tone. "Who is he?"

"Just a shrewd businessman."

"I've heard otherwise," Reis said. "About the business part, not the shrewd part. The news media call him a smuggler and money launderer. And worse."

Joscelyn smiled. "Bring it up when you meet him. He convinced me of his intentions."

Tammy's fingers unconsciously gripped the chair arms.

▼ ▲ ▼

"She did *what?*" Grant stood and rammed both fists onto the desktop. This gesture — made in Long Beach, California — converted into electronic bits and became a similar movement on The Net, which Haley saw from his vantage point in Kismayu, Somalia.

"Two astronauts. Ex-NASA. Both with extensive piloting exp—"

"Put her on. *Now!*"

Haley — in goggles and glove inside the office mobile — reached over to punch the intercom.

"Speak," her voice erupted tinnily from the speaker.

Haley said, "I'm on The Net. Get on it. Grant wants to ask you something."

"Uh-oh."

"You've got that right."

She found Grant had summoned up his own avatar — Orson Welles as Harry Lime, the black marketeer from *The Third Man* — and was waiting for her in an encrypted room designed in Early Foreign Intrigue: dense wicker furniture, bands of light and shadow striping through the bamboo blinds, and a slowly rotating fan overhead. Joscelyn entered as Honey West, tied up her ocelots, and faced the music.

"I specifically ordered you not to hire astronauts," he said in a tone made all the more icy by the computer reprocessing.

"*Constitution* made them all *ex*-astronauts," she said in terse reply. Long, perfect nails tapped impatiently against the table top. Behind her, one of the digital cats yawned and stretched. They served as security program icons, constantly checking the room for attempts to decrypt their message thread.

"The only ex-astronaut is a dead astronaut," Grant shot back. "Their loyalty to NASA is as fanatical as the *schutzstaffel*'s was to Hitler. They're a threat and I want them out."

Joscelyn stood her ground. "The two I hired are nothing like that. Jon Franck was passed over for advancement and then furloughed with everyone else. Tammy Reis quit in disgust after that medical incident on—"

"Tammy Reis?" he nearly shrieked. "She's the worst of them all! She's their little press darling, their poster girl for NASA recruiters!" Harry Lime's mesmerizing eyes knifed at the woman. "I want her out of there before she compromises the entire project."

"Marc," Joscelyn said with a firm intransigence, "I located her in a bar where she'd been drunk for a month. She quit NASA within days of her return from orbit. Something happened up there, something neither she nor her crewmate Franck will talk about. I've seen the tabloid stories, though. Rumors that Congressman Woolsey was stabbed onboard *Constitution* and that's why he was in the hospital for weeks afterward. Even a man can figure out what must have—"

"We don't need someone prone to violence, either. Get rid of her."

"No, Marcus. She and Franck already know too much for us to let them leave. They've been into *Space*, Marc. They can tell us what to expect. We need experts now, and astronauts are experts."

Grant paused, deep in troubled thought. The fan turned quietly, blade shadows crossing his face. "Keep them out of my way when I get there. I don't want to meet them, I don't want to see them. And I don't want them to see me. Not even a photo, understand?"

"No, I don't."

"Just do it, Joscelyn. I leave them to you and I pray it doesn't jeopardize the project. If one of them betrays us, we'll all be dead."

"I'll watch them, Mr. Grant."

Moving to another room on The Net, Grant questioned Haley. "Did you check them for tracking devices?"

"No," he answered slowly.

"All right" — Grant rubbed at his chin — "I want everything moved up. A December launch leaves too much time for more leaks. Let's all crack the whip and aim for a September launch. Early September. Daedalus hasn't even started test flights and Freespace just had a fire on the pad. We'll beat them both by weeks or months if we do that. How are you on the rest of the crew?"

"Eight people already here, four on their way. Donahue's contacting the last few this week."

"Get them. I want intensive seminars for everyone, especially for their input on the cargo manifest. I've made my estimates and everything's on order, delivery dates over the next three weeks."

Haley frowned. "Early September just gives us ten weeks. I don't know if I can have the whole thing ready for launch by—"

"Nothing is impossible when price is no object. I'm putting everything I have into this. I'm closing down or cashing out all operations."

"Putting your eggs all in one basket?"

"No — I'm taking them *out* of Earth's basket. Now let's *move!*"

CHAPTER 36

Passion is in all great searches and is necessary to all creative endeavors.

— W. Eugene Smith

24 June

Joseph Lester felt more than conspicuous. Not only was he a white man wandering an African city, he was a big man among a nation of the starving.

The ongoing sub-Saharan drought contributed to the starvation, but the major cause was the eternal one of power. Disguised as tribal warfare between the Bantu-speaking minority and the Somali majority, or as religious conflict among Muslim sects, or as political struggle between ideological splinter-groups, the real battle murdering Somalia and nearly every other nation in Africa and the world was between those who would rule the lives of others and those who wanted simply to be left to tend to their own lives. The former, minority group currently held the upper hand — the one with irrigation water and relief food in its grasp.

Lester waded through the emaciated victims of the perpetual struggle in an effort to locate Hillary. She had wandered off again to some damned slum for more video of hungry street urchins. How many more of them did she need? Lester considered the subject of hunger thoroughly covered. Yes, people starve in this world. People have always starved, there will always be marginal living — human nature pushed systems to their limits, filled in every niche, survived at the extremes. Human nature also accepted such conditions and usually ignored them, and the news bureau chiefs to whom they sold their stories were extremely human in that aspect.

His celphone warbled for his attention. He pulled it out, flipped it open, and said, "Yeah?"

"Joe — are you anywhere near the airport?"

He snorted. "The whole city is near the airport!"

"Then get over here. I have something to show you."

"God, I hate that sort of teaser. Just tell me what's up."

"I just saw Drs. Edvard Dobroshevsky and Laura Tutihasi. He's a Russian rocket expert and she's a Japanese scientist specializing in orbital struc—"

"I've heard of them both. Why're they here?"

"I don't know. Just get over here. I — my God, they're being followed. A couple of locals. I'm going to video. Hurry!"

The connection broke.

The airport lay northeast of where he roamed. Lester debated looking for a cab or making a run for it at least part of the way. He looked down at where his stomach had been. In the year since he had made his decision to lose weight, he had dropped an average of two pounds a week — about double what a safe weight-loss program ought to accomplish. He still felt overweight. Now down to one hundred eighty, he was within ten pounds of his target liftoff weight (as he liked to think of it) and much of that remaining weight he had turned into muscle through daily exercise.

He chose to run.

▼ ▲ ▼

Twenty minutes of running brought him to the airport. On his arrival, he saw Kaye standing outside a blue-black line of airport police. She nodded toward him surreptitiously; he caught on instantly and walked in another direction. She followed and intercepted him around a corner.

"I'm glad you got your cardiac workout," Hillary said with tight-jawed severity. "Take a look at what you missed."

She hit the playback button and held the camera up for Lester to watch through the eyepiece. The tiny speaker mounted on the side replayed the audio with low fidelity. She had kept the camera supremely steady while rushing through the crowds to follow the hit men. The lens caught the panic of the onlookers as the two mysterious men withdrew silenced pistols and aimed at Tutihasi. The scientists turned at the sound of the commotion to see both men drop from shots to the head; shots that appeared to come from nowhere. The camera panned and tilted. No source for the protective fire was apparent.

Drs. Tutihasi and Dobroshevsky were ushered out of the video frame by a red-haired woman.

"Did you follow them?" Lester asked in an annoyingly demanding tone.

"Not in that stampede."

Lester huffed. "I want us to stake out the airport after the excitement's worn down. If we recognize any more scientists or anyone important, I'll want to see where they're going."

He did not have long to wait.

Six hours later — after the bodies were removed, the police investigation finished, and some semblance of normality restored — a flight from New Zealand arrived. Two women and a man among the arrivals hastily strode to the Velocet Airways counter to pick up connecting tickets. They were the only ones in line.

"Recognize them?" he asked Hillary.

"One of the women," she whispered, "is Dr. Joan McLaughlin, an expert in space medicine from Brisbane. The others, I don't know."

"I've seen the other woman. She blew the whistle on some government contractor or something a couple of years back. Really bitter exchange of accusations, including attempted murder. She claimed they tried to run her off the road. Something to do with the company faking test data on inertial navigation systems for missiles."

"And the man?"

Lester peered at the skinny, nervous man in the drab brown, ill-fitting suit. "Could be anyone. Pretty expensive laptop he's carrying, though."

After the three left the ticket counter, Lester strode up to it and asked the woman when the next flight was departing.

"Where to?" she asked.

He pointed at the three walking out to the Cessna. "Same place they're going."

The woman's smile grew. "And where would that be?"

Lester paused. "I don't know," he said slowly. "All I know is I'm supposed to be with them."

"Regrettably," she said, returning to her fixed smile, "the flight is booked. Very small airplane."

"I'm really in a hurry. What about the flight after?"

She made a show of looking down at a computer screen, tapped a few keys that Lester could see did nothing, then said, "All flights booked. Small planes. Sorry." Her English grew worse the more he pressed her. When she shifted into rapid-fire Bantu with a decidedly harsh tone, Lester gave up and walked over to rejoin Kaye.

"I think we have a bogus airline here," he whispered.

"What next?"

He nodded toward another cubicle. "Let's charter a scenic flight."

▼ ▲ ▼

Lester — only a semi-skilled haggler — let the local dollar speak for him. Hillary — videocam awhir — sat in the rear seat of the dust-coated green Beech Bonanza while Lester, from the right-hand co-pilot's seat, gripped at his frayed seat harness and observed the ground fall away from them.

"Velocet a new airline," the pilot — a middle-aged Ethiopian woman clad in deep blue, oil-stained overalls — said in broken English. Her dark brown eyes gazed intently at the horizon, rotating downward every few seconds to scan the instruments in a precise pattern. "They come and go so fast here now. Not enough dollars in capital equipment." She banked hard to the right, leaving the take-off pattern at eight hundred feet. "I fly here sixteen year. Always pay heavy for good maintenance. Little dust okay, as long as engine purrs good, yeah?" She grinned at Lester with a mixture of pride and impishness that belied her matronly visage.

"Do you own this plane?" Hillary asked, turning the camera toward the pilot.

"Oh, yes," she merrily replied, pushing the throttle in to gain altitude and lowering the nose a tad to increase airspeed. "I flew route between Adis Ababa and Goba in sixties and seventies. Then come Mengistu and his Dergue party"— she made a spitting sound and touched a Coptic cross hanging from a necklace — "so one day I just keep flying from Goba across the border into Somalia. I own outright property from then. No bank loans. Banks same as the Dergue — think they own *you*. See that patch there?" She pointed at a palm-sized piece of aluminum riveted to the left wing's leading edge. "I fought against invasion of Somalia in seventy-seven. When Mengistu finally go, I stayed here. Like living on the coast."

She made a smooth turn without so much as a slip or skid and dropped down toward Kismayu. She pointed. "There is your target."

The Cessna — cruising at a stately speed yet still ahead of the Bonanza with its throttle rammed all the way in — was a grey-and-maroon spot above the horizon.

"They're heading toward airstrip at Kismayu," the pilot said.

"Take us there, then." Lester eased his grip on the shoulder harness and gazed out of the crazed acrylic side window at the browns and greens of the coast thousands of feet below. What would they find in this far-off place? he wondered.

▼▲▼

What they found, an hour later, was an armed escort presenting them to Chad Haley, who cordially introduced himself and asked what they were doing taping the exterior of the World Habitat Missions' latest housing project.

"Joseph Lester, GSN," the reporter replied. "And this is Hillary Kaye, my crew. We'd like you to comment on why a charitable organization would be host to experts in space medicine and spacecraft guidance. And, for that matter, why you need armed guards."

"Somalia's not exactly the most... pacific place in world. Still a lot of what you in the press call warlords running around. Put that thing down," Haley calmly said to Kaye. "Global Satellite Network, eh? You produced that documentary about *Constitution*, didn't you?"

Lester nodded. He would have smiled at the recognition if it were not for the gunmen flanking him.

"We tried to find you, and here you show up on our doorstep." Haley rubbed at his sharp chin. "Can you two keep your mouths shut for a few months in exchange for the scoop of the millennium?"

"Define keeping our mouths shut," Hillary said.

"Not leaving this development unescorted. Not communicating with the outside world. Not snooping where you shouldn't."

Lester said, "Define scoop of the millennium."

Haley smiled like the Cheshire cat. "Deal first, then secrets."

Lester and Kaye glanced at each other and shrugged.

"Deal," they said in unison.

Haley beamed. "Ms. Kaye, you may switch on."

▼ ▲ ▼

Haley spoke candidly about the project and its far-reaching goals. Both Lester and Kaye barraged him with questions. The technical ones he answered easily. The ones about motive, though, gave him pause.

"Why did you offer to let us cover this?" Lester asked. "I should think secrecy would be of paramount importance."

"Secrecy before the fact, yes. Afterward, though, we can provide mutual aid to one another. You two get an exclusive on the biggest story of the century, and — in exchange — Grant Enterprises presents its position as clearly as possible, so that no government would risk the bad publicity of trying to sabotage our efforts."

"We're not going to do a puff piece on you," Lester said. "We'll call it the way we see it."

"Fine," Haley said. "What you see will amaze you."

CHAPTER 37

Any system of entrusting the government to judge and correct its own abuses is the same as appointing the accused criminal as his own judge and jury: Don't expect many convictions.

— **Allen Thornton**
Laws of the Jungle

3 July

Milton mentally debated about informing Barron of Reis's contact with the subnationals. *Stark Fist*, though, was Barron's baby and would undoubtedly be employed if more standard procedures failed.

He shook his head. The National Security Agency began in much the same way as had the Central Intelligence Agency. Chartered only to intercept and decrypt foreign messages, it quickly evolved — as had the CIA — from an intelligence gathering and analysis agency into an activist agency, performing sabotage and wet jobs abroad and at home. Downing subnational spacecraft and destroying all traces of their existence constituted just one task of many.

Barron sat across the desk from him, a smug expression plastered across his beefy brow. "Tammy Reis, eh?"

"The signal's been stuck in Kisdmayu, Somalia, for over a week now. Our section agent says the location is some sort of construction site inland. Some futuristic-looking hotel."

"Futuristic?" Barron tapped a finger to his smiling lips. "Close to equatorial. Pacific to the east. A good launch site. Less fuel, safe trajectory."

"It could just be a hotel."

Barron shook his head. "You drafted her to find spaceships. She's not going into the resort business. She's in training over there. Do we have any satellite images?"

"Probably. But Photo Interpretation is backed up so much that rush jobs take a week. Forget trying to push them about something so low priority. I'm going to contact Stahl, the new NASA administrator, about this and we can—"

"No!"

Milton leaned forward, miffed at Barron's commanding tone. "What did you say?"

"NASA is irrelevant at this point. Space Command has already laid claim to *Atlantis* and nothing's going to fly out of Kennedy for years. Leave them out of this. There's more at stake than their useless shuttle and any overpriced joyrides they may *someday* get around to. We're dealing with an event that would do more to undermine the security of the United States than anything a foreign power could hope to do. It would open up Space to anyone who had the guts to go. The British Empire suffered and ultimately collapsed because of migration to the New World. I don't want the same to happen to us. Any subnationals that leave Earth will be forever beyond our reach. The destabilizing effect on world affairs would be catastrophic. *We* must be the only ones to hold the high ground."

"There is evidence that the people contacting Reis *are* Americans."

"When I say 'we,' Steve, I don't mean *Americans*. I mean the *United States*. An American subnational in orbit is a far greater threat than anyone else. We can denounce foreign citizens as tools of their own governments. Denouncing an American is much more complex."

"I've seen the figures from NASA. I know how difficult and expensive it is to get into orbit. *That's* our protection. And if it were dirt cheap, do you think you could *stop* anyone from getting up there?"

"All I want," Barron said in a level tone, "is to slow them down until *we've* established a firm foothold. If that costs a few lives, well, a nation is glued together by the blood of its enemies."

When Barron left the office, Milton sunk back into the soft confines of his swivel chair. The wetboys retained by the agency always gave him the willies with their snake-eyed willingness to kill not so much for abstract ideals, but for the sheer joy of homicide. Barron left him with a far more ominous feeling — the stomach-churning sensation of being in the same room with an ideologue whose capacity for killing was driven and controlled by his far-reaching vision of a world transformed.

▼ ▲ ▼

The 747 arched over. An instant later, the three support pylons released their grip upon *Nomad* and the spaceplane — lacking the hypersonic drop tanks, but with interior fuel tanks fully loaded — lifted swiftly up and over the modified twin-tailed empennage.

"We have a clean release," Chemar D'Asaro said breathlessly into her helmet microphone.

Larry Poubelle, in the forward pilot's seat, said nothing as he worked the controls.

High over the Mojave desert, a deep blue sky hung above them like a second sea, while below lay the chocolatey mist overlying the Los Angeles metropolis. An icy wind whistled past them at seven miles altitude, almost overpowering the shine of the auxiliary power units. They both wore pressure suits consisting of precisely fitted Spandex covered with outer layers of puncture-proof Kevlar III and fire-resistant Nomex. Locked on to the neck rings were their dual-purpose helmets. Not only did they provide the standard head protection, they also contained sophisticated electronics.

"All right," Poubelle said. "She handles like a drive shaft with wings. Let's put the spurs to her."

Poubelle flicked the ignition switch. For an instant, nothing happened. Then the APU's whined louder, powering the turbines that pumped the liquid oxygen and liquid hydrogen into the J-2 engine. Within a second, the rocket throttled up to full power, crushing them in their seats with three gravities of acceleration.

Neither of them spoke. The simulator failed to prepare them for the pressure. Huffing to the point of hyperventilation, Poubelle monitored the programmed flight plan.

The engine burned for an unbelievably long two minutes, during which the rocket plane climbed two hundred thousand feet at speeds up to Mach six.

The engine throttled down and the pressure lifted from them. Now came the hard part. Momentum carried *Nomad* upward along a ballistic trajectory. To beat Bob White's altitude record by 3 per cent, the upgraded X-15 had to achieve an altitude of 324,000 feet without straying any higher. If the black thunderbolt climbed a mere 4,000 feet higher, it would enter Space and lose FAI certification of an aeronautical record.

Achieving such accuracy, given the nature of aerodynamics involved, depended more on luck than on science. Flights of the original X-15 routinely deviated from their projected altitude by as much as five per cent. Poubelle could not afford to miss by a mile. Not even four-fifths of a mile. He watched the plane's altimeter numbers closely. The FAI altimeter sealed in the cargo compartment recorded the official altitude. He prayed that they would match up.

The plane continued to soar upward through 300,000 feet. At 318,000, he used the reaction motors to ease *Nomad* level. This created some small degree of drag in the thin atmosphere, but did not significantly alter the rocket plane's trajectory. It still ascended, now passing through 325,000 feet.

"Come on, baby," he muttered. "Slow down." He rotated the plane further, now into a nose-down position.

"Dorsal skin temp's climbing," Chemar noted.

At 326,500 feet, Poubelle realized that they would overshoot their mark. "Diving!" he called out, igniting the engine to 10% power.

Nomad creaked and popped like a cast-iron stove, then shuddered with a frightening vibration.

"Pushover!" Poubelle radioed. "Over the top at three hundred twenty-seven thousand one hundred feet! We're coming in!"

In a mild power dive, *Nomad* picked up speed, punching through Mach numbers as if through paper. Poubelle cut off the engine and activated the energy management system for landing.

"Switching to VR," he said.

He touched a button and suddenly the spaceplane around them disappeared. Merging the video images from a dozen cameras — each no larger than a roll of dimes — placed strategically around the fuselage, the main computer displayed on the mini-HUD inside their helmets a 360° view of the outside world as if they flew in an aircraft made entirely of glass. Poubelle looked down between his feet to see the golden-brown, rumpled Tehachapi mountains far ahead and way down, their ridges dotted with the remains of bankrupt wind-farm turbines. He turned his head up toward the control panel — visible as if suspended by a magician's illusion — and checked some instruments that did not appear on his helmet screen. The programmers had offered him a completely virtual instrument panel, but he had no desire to be elegant to the point of self-endangerment. If he lost the entire VR system, he could still pilot *Nomad* to a safe landing using standard seat-of-the-pants techniques learned flying taildraggers in his teens.

"Okay, babe," he said. "You take it for a while. Give us a thirty degree right banking turn."

"Larry," a man's voice said in his helmet. *"Advise that* Nomad *not land at Rogers Lake, over."*

"Why in hell not, Jeff, over?"

"Advise you not land anywhere in Charlie MOA. Return to Mojave, over."

"Jeff, you're playing hell with my energy management. And the runway will play hell with the skids. What's up, over?"

"Nothing but a military greeting committee ready to seize your little black arrow. Over."

"Mojave is inside Alpha Military Operations Area, Jeff. Over."

"Not under twelve hundred feet AGL, Larr. You'll be landing on non-military pavement. Over."

Poubelle said, "Chemar, we'll come out of the turn at heading three hundred. Set the Loran for Mojave and establish a glide slope. And Jeff?"

"Roger."

"Get the bloodsucking lawyers on the horn. Find out why—"

"They're here. It seems your friend in the Senate's been putting pressure on the Air Force in addition to a nicely typed subpoena inviting you to appear before a Select Committee investigating space commercialization companies."

Poubelle sighed. "Bastards."

"Roger that, over."

The hypersonic glide back to Mojave passed with nominal performance on the part of the EMS. The oval-shaped footprint it displayed on the screen always included the airport inside — a sure indication that they would reach it without relighting the rocket.

At two thousand feet over Mojave Airport, Poubelle jettisoned the lower half of the ventral fin, then attempted to cycle the landing gear. Where he thought he reached with his robotic arm, however, was not where it went.

"Chemar!" he shouted. "Drop the gear!"

Without asking why or hesitating an instant, Chemar's hand darted to the redundant control and activated the blow-down devices. Immediately, skids and nose wheel bit air, the drag causing a notable decrease in airspeed and an increase in rate-of-descent.

"RF interference with the arm," he said tersely to inform both his co-pilot and the flight recorder. The disturbing glitch in Poubelle's arm subsided and he established the best glide ratio while gazing down at the runway below. The VR system proved its worth in the landing sequence. In *Nomad*, as in the original X-15, the runway lay below the field of view from the cockpit. Without the VR, he would have had to perform a series of left and right rolls in order to catch glimpses of the approach. With the HUD operating correctly, he simply gazed at the horizon over the instrument panel as if possessed of X-ray eyes and kept the centerline of the runway pinned in his peripheral vision.

Chemar said nothing during the final approach. Poubelle handled the fly-by-light instruments with the skill of a pilot with nearly 8,000 hours flight experience. Even for him, though, the sensation of flying *Nomad* was new, thrilling, and intensely demanding. The breathable Spandex pressure garment allowed his perspiration to be wicked off by the outer layers of fabric into the cool, nitrogen-filled atmosphere of the pressurized cabin.

At eighty feet off the runway and an airspeed of 170, he prepared for touchdown. He did not perform the landing flare normal for most aircraft. He held it steady until the skids touched, then forced the nose wheel down to avoid the aircraft's characteristic rebound into the air. The flight simulator he practiced in benefited both from one hundred ninety-nine X-15 flights and from the speed of modern parallel processing computers. He had learned well; the nose wheel touched the centerline of the runway and stayed there. He opened the air brake on the rudder to little effect. Nothing was left to do but skid to a stop — *Nomad* had no other brakes.

"Welcome back, Nomad*!" the tower controller said. "Do you plan on stopping at any point?"*

"Roger, tower. What's your overrun? Over."

"Two hundred feet. Why?"

"I'm going to need it!"

The crew in the tower — and dozens of people on the ground who had come out when they heard what was landing — watched as the sleek black arrow darted down the airport's longest runway, twin roostertails of dusty smoke erupting behind the skids. Down and down the runway it slid like a skater with blades locked forward. Hearts caught and breaths seized as the spaceplane approached the broad yellow lines marking the end of the usable runway, crossed them — leaving twin scrape marks — and headed toward the abrupt end of the pavement. Beyond lay desert dirt, scrub brush, and Joshua trees.

Poubelle gritted his teeth and said, "Hang on, sweetheart!"

Chemar shook her head in cynical amusement. "Does a drag chute seem like such a luxury n—"

They rolled off the runway at thirty miles per hour. The nose wheel caught dirt, dug in, and snapped off, permitting the nose to slam down firmly and bury itself in the desert. The sudden stop threw both of them against their harnesses, knocking their breath out.

Poubelle labored to inhale deeply when he was finally able and reached over to cycle the hatch. The electrical system still operated, so he had no need to blow it manually. Pulling off his helmet, he watched as the virtual image faded, replaced by the confining reality of the cockpit.

"Chemar?"

"I'm fine. How's the plane?"

He unstrapped and climbed out, sliding down the side of the aircraft into the soft, hot earth. It was silent but for the whir of a cicada off in the bushes and the distant, hollow wail of the crash truck siren.

"Nose is dented up pretty well," he shouted up to her. "Skids are bent. Ventral fin's lying about ten feet behind the rear. Nothing that can't be fixed. Cheated death again."

"I wish you'd stop saying that," she said, sliding down to join him. "What do we do now?"

He waved to the people in the crash truck as it pulled up beside them.

"Now we make it go higher."

CHAPTER 38

The heights by great men reached and kept
Were not attained by sudden flight,
But they, while their companions slept,
Were toiling upward in the night.
— Henry Wadsworth Longfellow

4 July

Haley worked nearly twenty-four hours a day, deep under technical problems that exceeded his capacity to handle. From all around the world, though, experts recruited by Joscelyn Donahue arrived. Nearly every one of them went through three phases: a sort of angered disbelief, as if they had been conned into an illegal activity; then nervous worry, as they contemplated the enormity of what they had been hired to do; then the final stage — a nearly giddy enthusiasm — which appeared anywhere from a few minutes to a few days after arrival. How long it took any one member of the team to pass through these phases depended on how tangible each individual's results seemed. For the design people and modification crews, the results sprouted over the circular ditch right before their eyes. For the emigrating specialists, merely drawing up their equipment manifests and seeing the items delivered and stored in the upper reaches of the pods served to generate unbridled optimism.

For the pilots, though, who had to rehearse constantly in a simulator, the only impression was one of claustrophobic tedium unrelieved by the freedom of actual flight. And the more troubled of the two astronauts was definitely Tammy Reis.

"She's only had two weeks to dry out," Donahue said, watching test results scroll up the screen in her office.

"Oh, she's sober," Haley agreed. "As sober — and sour — as a judge. She performs well on the simulator, but there's no... *interest* there. It's as if she's waiting for something to happen."

"They're both itching to get out and fly the damned thing."

"She's not. She's listless. I think you picked a clunker."

Donahue spoke with a firm, level tone. "She's no clunker. Don't you get it? Something happened on her last Shuttle flight. Something that made her quit and sink into despair. It'll take a while for her to recover—"

"It'd better not take more than eight weeks."

"Trust me," Donahue said. "Trust her."

▼ ▲ ▼

Trust her, Haley thought, watching Reis in the simulator. She performed superbly, handling the bizarre flying doughnut with consummate skill. Reis always nailed it right into orbit. So did Franck when they traded places. In Reis, though, he saw no joy at successful maneuvers, no disappointment at minor flaws. Even stranger, no alarm at any of the failure scenarios the computer threw at her. She handled everything in a machinelike manner. No emotion, just stimulus and response. *Maybe that's good,* he mused. *Maybe she's exactly what we need: a machine with a human mind.*

11-12 July

Marcus Grant — dressed in a tropical khakis — stepped off the Cessna to face Chad and Joscelyn. Both of them wore safari outfits and looked a bit like novices in the Great White Hunter Club. It was the first time in weeks all three had been together. Two men and one women disembarked with him, the last of the flight crew.

Grant inspected the construction site with the meticulous attention of a race-horse owner inspecting a thoroughbred. All sixteen pods now stood connected into a single unit, and the construction crew labored in the hot confines of the circular trench to install the thirty-foot-diameter tapering cones that were the plug nozzles. The nozzles were built in Germany and flown in pairs to Libya, where they sat on the runway for a few hours without inspection before heading directly to Mogadishu while paperwork indicated that they had been inspected and shipped to the Sudan as desalinating irrigation pumps. They looked the part, their interiors crammed with plumbing, the actual purpose of which was to cool the aerospike and preheat the cryogenic fuel via a heat-exchanger.

Grant was impressed. The spaceship dwarfed the cluster of mobile homes now located outside the circle, behind a protective berm.

"I sure wish we could test-fly this baby for real," Grant said. "We can't know if our simulation is one hundred percent accurate."

Donahue and Haley shook their heads almost in unison. "A test flight," she said, "would blow our cover as surely as an actual flight. We have one shot and one only. The crew understand this — either I or Chad've explained it to every one of them. They're willing to trade the risk for whatever personal reasons they have for going up."

"And what," Grant muttered in an irritated way, "is Reis's personal reason?"

"What is your problem with Tammy? She's performed superbly."

"She's right, boss."

Grant eyed Chad, then turned his attention back to Donahue. "She's spying on us. I know it. I had a detective check out the bar she practically lived in the last few months. The owner ran a bar tab for her. A big one. It got settled the day *after* she left for here."

"Marc, we need her. We need Jon Franck. They have both contributed their knowledge, skill, and wisdom without any hint of... of *duplicity*. If she *is* a spy, I think she's on the cusp. I think she can be turned."

Chad cut in. "Reis and I got into a sort of argument a few days ago. She was miffed that nothing we were doing was by the book, at least not the way NASA wrote it. First, she criticized the pressure suits. I explained to her that the concept was nearly forty years old and actually developed by NASA and then dropped for political reasons: a thousand-dollar space suit couldn't win the congressional support that a million-dollar one could. Then she protested that the tools we'll be using in orbit were bought on sale at Sears. Then she objected that there was only one onboard guidance computer! I asked her how many times one of her five redundant shuttle computers had broken down. When she said nearly once every other flight, I said 'This station's only going on one flight, so we have a fifty-fifty chance that we'll make it. You can take a parachute if you're worried about not possessing the Right Stuff.' You know what she did?"

Grant said nothing. He merely stared more darkly at the younger man.

"She thought about it for a moment, nodded, and then went back into the simulator."

Grant sighed and headed toward the four-story structure. "Biting her tongue all the way, I'll bet. Didn't want to blow her cover."

"I don't think so," Haley said, following. "If that was the case, why did she bring it up in the first place? If she was going to turn us in and run, why any concern about whether we make it or not?"

Grant hesitated, unable to come up with an answer.

"Look, Marc"—Donahue laid a slender hand on his arm—"I'll try to draw her out some more. I really think she's on our side."

"Then you don't know her." Grant looked at their curious gazes, then added, "Read any interview she's ever given, damn it! Watch tapes of her on TV! I did, after you told me you'd hired her. She's as big a NASA stooge as Barry Gibbon!"

Joscelyn climbed down into the trench. Heli-arc welders illuminated the curving pit with a bright white glow. "All right, Marc. I'll feel her out."

"Wish you'd leave that to me," Chad said with a wicked grin.

"Shut the hell up," Grant muttered, turning away from them to gaze up into the shadowy depths of one of the pods. Its oxygen tank in place, engine plumbing hanging downward awaiting connection to the plug nozzle, it looked like the underside of some tentacled sea creature floating overhead. Or perhaps the inside. The oppressive equatorial summer heat, exacerbated by the welders, transformed the trench into a hellish bowel of torment.

Grant noted that the workers held up well under the brutal conditions, though several sat against the relatively cool earth, downing gulps of water from bota bags provided by youngsters, children of some of the native work force.

Short of sabotage by NASA spies, Grant thought, *this will work.*

▼ ▲ ▼

Reis possessed no interest in sabotage, but she spied as much as she could, conducting her own investigation of the Grant Enterprises operation. Under the guise of agreeing to an interview with Joseph Lester, she intended to sneak in an interrogation of her own.

Hillary recorded the two in the cramped interior of the space station cockpit. Lester scrunched behind the chairs, asking questions. The pilot sat — back horizontal, head level with feet — in one of the two wide, padded seats, fingering a softly burnished metal buckle connected to the five-point harness she would wear during liftoff. The photographer knelt on the other seat, leaning as far back as she could to achieve a decent wide-angle shot encompassing Reis and the control panel. Light from the overhead window had been blocked out with a reflective cover in order to keep the cabin cool and protect the delicate electronics The only source of light was a pair of dollar-bill-size fluorescent panels set into the low overhead.

"On the shuttle," Tammy said as if conducting a tour, "our seats were narrow and hard, based more on the design of a John Deere tractor seat than on that of a plush airliner. They worked just fine, since you only needed them for about fifteen minutes going up and half an hour coming down. After we go orbital, though, we'll spin this baby to impart artificial gravity. Since it's small, we can't spin it at six RPM to mimic a full Earth gravity — Coriolis forces and the gravity gradient would make us sicker than we'd ever be in free fall. At three RPM and a quarter gee — the maximum we can safely give it — these seats will feel pretty comfy at the end of a hard day." She looked up at the camera, inadvertently, then at Lester. "Every day is going to be a hard day up there, as far as I can tell."

"Do you miss the shuttle?" Lester asked.

"I miss what NASA was. I miss its promise."

"And UNITO?"

"If I believed UNITO could do what NASA had done, I wouldn't be here. If I believed NASA had a future, I wouldn't be here." The answer was more true than Lester knew. If NASA had a future, it would only be because she had penetrated a rival program that could show up the space agency.

"I'm fascinated about the man behind this," she said.

"Yes," Lester said, "but this interview is about you."

She sighed and leaned back in the chair. "Can we take a break?"

Kaye turned off the camera. "Good idea. I've got to switch discs anyway."

"You've both met him, right?"

They shook their heads. "We've met Haley. Grant hasn't shown his face to us."

Hillary added, "I think he's been around, though."

"Where do you think the money came from for all this?" Tammy turned onto her stomach and planted her chin on a fist. Dressed in a grey and maroon flight suit, she looked like a visitor from the future, curious about the local inhabitants.

"Black market. Grey market." Lester tried to get comfortable in a space behind the seats smaller than a refrigerator. He liked nothing more, though, than a good talk about classy crooks. "He's great at staying out of the limelight, just as a lot of billionaires do."

"So there aren't any pictures of him?"

Kaye shook her head. "None that we've seen. And Haley won't let us interview him."

"Grant is here?" Reis said slowly.

"The crew said he's been here." Lester frowned. "Wait a minute. You remember last February when we were at Mojave and Larry Poubelle got shot at? The police report mentioned that Grant was there."

Hillary's forehead wrinkled in a frown of thought. "We might have caught him on video." She reached into the equipment case by her feet. Inside were dozens of discs from the last few months.

"Any idea how old he is?" Tammy felt suddenly close to answering the riddle of the entire conspiracy. Perhaps knowing the mastermind behind the project would give her an edge, a chink in the armor that she could exploit without resorting to calling in Milton's NSA cavalry.

"Neither of us saw him," Lester said, watching Kaye riffle through the disc cases. "He must have just come and gone."

Kaye pulled a disc out and said, "Here it is." She loaded it into the videocam and set it on scan, looking into the viewfinder to watch the playback. After a few moments of searching, she muttered, "I'll be damned — look who's there!" She handed the camera to Tammy.

"Watch as the view pans right, past *Nomad*. You can see Haley and Donahue, and the one in the middle with his back to us is most probably Grant."

Tammy held the viewfinder up to her eye and stared at the image within. A crisply focused, professionally smooth pan right lingered on the graceful lines of the sleek obsidian-hued spaceplane. The black fuselage provided a background against which three people stood, silently surveying their rival's work.

She recognized the other two immediately. Haley like a mountaineer in his rain-soaked down parka, Donahue a blaze of red hair in an emerald green slicker.

Even more familiar, she realized with a shock that froze her heart, was the man in the middle. He turned to glance behind him, then frowned at the camera. Despite his prematurely grey hair and lines added by more than a dozen added years of age, she had no difficulty recognizing the face of Paul Volnos.

Part Three

The Open Hand

CHAPTER 39

Actually, everything is a countdown.
— **Alan B. Shepard, Jr.**

11-12 July

Reis handed the camera back to Kaye, saying nothing, speechless with the sudden knowledge that more was at stake than her seat on an upcoming shuttle flight, more than thwarting an upstart rival to NASA hegemony.

Paul Volnos — Marcus Grant — constituted a different, far greater class of enemy.

She knew Paul, knew his past, and knew that in the last decade *something* must have driven him to this point, and — having come this far — nothing would stop him, not even she.

▼ ▲ ▼

Security cameras discreetly placed around the inner, outer, and underground periphery of the toroid allowed Grant to view every part of the operation on his office computer screen. At the moment, he scanned the entire area, admiring the sleek, orderly operation. The scaffolding had been removed from the last pod and all work proceeded below ground level.

Each pod's upper section contained seating for either one or two crew members, along with as much cargo as they could safely carry. The design tolerances were few: the design optimized the trade-off between number of spheres and engine nozzle geometry. He might have added or subtracted a few pods, but the requirements of weight and wall thickness (even using modern materials), volume and engine nozzle area all converged on the dimension of the flying ring he saw before him. And it would carry into Space what Grant told everyone would be the mainstay of the orbital city: a free-flying microgravity manufacturing platform. He envisioned it floating unattached smack in the center of the rotating space station, visited only when necessary by the crew, but always within easy reach and safe from attack.

Marcus Grant worried about attack, especially from the US, though he rarely allowed all his fears to surface. He rubbed his eyebrows and gazed at the screen. Coming out of the boarding hatch of pod number one — the cockpit — Tammy Reis gazed around her at the magnificent machine entrusted to her. She stepped into the cherry-picker lift at the end of a crane that served as their elevator. Behind her followed the reporter and photographer Haley had taken on to chronicle the project.

Grant zoomed the security camera's view in on Reis.

She was just as beautiful as the day they turned their back on each other. Up until that day, Space — and Tammy Reis — had been his life.

11 November, 1966

The morning called to Paul, urging the five year old to come out and play. Great thick rays of yellow gold beamed into his bedroom, touching his pillow, piercing his dreams. Dust motes in the air sparkled like stars and his eyes opened to the sight. For a moment, his dreams traveled with him into waking and he watched the stars flow around him as he floated freely in Space.

It was Friday. A school day for his older sister, Patty, but not for him yet. He heard her stirring in the other bed. Then the door burst open.

"Who wants to stay home," their father bellowed like a boisterous Russian bear, "and watch Gemini blast off?"

Then the realization hit him. Today was the day. Everything in his short few years of life, it seemed, had led up to this moment, and he was here — awake and alive — to see it, feel it, live through it.

Paul could not remember a time when he did not love Space. Nor could he remember just when or how he fell in love with it. Ever since he was small, the heavens struck him with a wonder the same way other people were stricken upon entering cathedrals or museums. The stars and planets were shimmering gems he desired to touch, the Moon, a gleaming white pearl he sought to hold in his hand.

Paul's parents told him that his first spoken word, aside from the obligatory "mama" and "dada," consisted of the Russian word for satellite: *sputnik*. His mother and father, who spoke Russian at home, found nothing unusual in his choice of the language, but drew great amusement from his choice of that particular word. Aside from meaning "companion" and "satellite," it also meant "fellow traveler," something the Volnoses — White Russians to the marrow — most certainly were not.

He bounded out of bed, throwing the covers aside in a heap and slipped into his scratchy, deep plum robe with the white piping — a smaller version of the one Daddy wore. Carefully lifting his Col. McCauley Space Helmet from its red, white, and blue box beside his dresser, he bounded from the bedroom into the hallway. This was it! It had been two months — *two months!* — since the last Gemini rocket launch. This one — Gemini 12 — ended the program. At his age, two months spanned an eternity, and the concept of something being the last of its kind was too enormous to grasp. He only knew that his father loved to watch the rockets go up and so did he.

Paul's father, mother, and sister (until she lost interest) watched every rocket launch since Alan Shepard went up half a decade before. He bounced his toddler son on his knee when Wally Schirra's Mercury-Atlas 8 flight occurred on October 3, 1962.

Television. What a wondrous invention. It had been with Paul all his short life, like a window on the world. It took him inside Mickey Mouse's own clubhouse, it showed him exotic realms on *Passport to Adventure*, and it plunged him into the most exciting universe of all in his local channel's reruns of *Men into Space.*

And once more he watched *real* men shoot into Space. Paul knew that his TV hero — Col. Ed McCauley, USAF — was just an actor named William Lundigan. And though he thrilled to the tales of the conquest of Space and wished he could be there himself, he knew that Col. McCauley was nothing more than a character in a story. These men, though — the Gemini crew — were *astronauts*. A new breed of man. The future of mankind.

Paul would be an astronaut, too. He would be riding his own column of fire someday. He would be a part of the American space program, part of the incomparable National Aeronautics and Space Administration and its noble mission. He believed this with every fiber of his young being.

▼ ▲ ▼

The television image of the Titan rocket looked like a blowtorch burning furiously. The sound of the engines came over the speaker as a flaming crackle.

Paul Volnos watched the greyish ghost on the screen. His heart pounded. This was the greatest adventure that could ever be! Man was actually taking another step toward the Moon.

"*Gospodi polimoi!*" his mother cried when a billow of smoke punctuated the rocket's slender exhaust trail. She sat behind him with his father. His sister, Patty, had walked to school that morning rather than play hooky to watch something as passe as a rocket launch.

"Don't worry, Mommy," Paul said. "It hasn't blown up. That's just staging."

"Well," she said, "I don't see why they have to scare us like that."

"That's just the way it works," her husband said. Even though Lev Igorovich Volnos had emigrated from Russia at the same time as Pavlovna Alexandrovna Abakonovich, his accent was virtually absent. He sounded like any other liquor store clerk at Ernie's Cork 'n' Keg, which suited him, Ernie, and the customers just fine.

They called him the Mad Russian, though, to get his goat.

That morning, Leo and Paula Volnos and their son Paul sat before the TV screen in the living room, as did so many other American families, and watched two fellow Americans plunge into space.

"*Ochen krassnaya*," Paul's father muttered. Like Paul, he was fascinated by the beauty of space travel. Paul suspected, though, that if Daddy were offered the chance to jump aboard a spaceship, he would hesitate. Paul had no doubts. He would go up in an instant.

27 January, 1967

Another Friday, less than three months later.

The end of Gemini brought close on its heels the promise of Apollo and a manned mission to the Moon by the time Paul would be seven. That's what President Kennedy once said, before his birth, and Paul knew that presidents never lied. Paul raced around the house, awaiting his sister's arrival from school and then — several hours later — his father's weary return from the liquor store.

The television filled the living room with its glow. His mother ironed while watching a late afternoon soap opera. On his next lap through, Paul realized something had changed. His mother sat before the television set, her eyes intent. For a moment, he was not sure what was happening. A network newsman spoke onscreen, his voice somber. His mother turned to gaze at him with a look of concern.

"Paul," she said, "come sit here."

He sat and stared at the screen as she draped an arm around him to pull him close, to protect him as best she could from the brutal intrusion of the real world into her little boy's dreams.

The reporter continued in a stunned monotone. "The crew testing the Apollo capsule — Virgil I. Grissom, Edward White, and Roger B. Chaffee — died instantly in the fire on launch pad 34."

Son and mother listened and watched as the horrifying news trickled in.

"At least," his mother murmured quietly, "they died instantly." Her Russian accent made everything about the moment surreal and bizarre. His Russian parents despised everything Soviet. They gave birth to the archetypical American son, who now watched in horror as America stumbled in its space race with Russia, immolating its effort in a towering pyre.

Paul Volnos began to weep along with his mother. Too young to associate names with their histories, he only understood that they were astronauts and they were dead.

"Will they be coming back, Mommy?"

"No, Paul. I'm sorry." She knew for whom she was crying. For Gus Grissom, who had suffered more grief as an astronaut than anyone else. For Ed White, who had been the first to walk in space (she was sure the Soviets had lied about Leonov). And for Roger Chaffee, a rookie who had died without ever reaching space. To die was terrible. To be an astronaut, though, in the glorious Space Age and to die without ever having a chance to touch the heavens was an unfathomably cruel jest. It was evil.

"Why did it happen?" Paul asked. "Why did it burn up?"

"Accidents happen," she said quietly. "Even to astronauts." She hugged her son tightly. "At least they didn't suffer."

▼▲▼

It was only months later — long after other events in a young boy's life had supplanted conscious thought of what was now called Apollo One — that investigative reporters and the widow Betty Grissom finally forced NASA to release tape transcripts revealing that the trio died hideously, screaming and banging on the cockpit for nearly a minute and a half.

Unknown to Paul, a man named "Ace" Roberts grew disgusted with NASA over the revelations and resigned from his position at Kennedy Space Center to move to Saratoga, California — far from Cape Kennedy but still in the aerospace environment near Moffett Field.

11 October, 1968

The Saturn 1B roared into life. A flaming spear of destiny, it broke free from its earthly bonds to blast upward into the sky.

Paul lay on his stomach in front of the TV set, pounding the blue-grey carpet with his fists.

"Go! *Go!*" he shouted. He had waited an eternity for this. Nearly two years had passed since Apollo 204. Twenty months brought such milestones as the beginning of school, and a growing consciousness of the world around him, of how truly vast and wonderful it was.

As usual, his mother and father watched with him. His sister, Patty, left for school. Five years older than he and very pretty, other items filled her personal agenda.

He sipped at a glass of fresh orange juice through a straw. The glass rested on a blue paper napkin that rested on a china saucer that in turn rested on a larger plate. His mother intuitively understood the need for multiple redundancy in unstable systems.

The juice tingled his throat. He had tried to acquire the taste for the artificial orange juice Tang, since the astronauts drank it, and wondered whether liking it was a prerequisite for spaceflight. He hoped not.

The spear of crackling fire wavered on the TV screen as the camera struggled to keep the distant, moving image centered. Paul wondered with whom he would travel into space.

It wouldn't be anyone he knew, that was for sure. He had friends, but they seemed now to express only a cursory interest in space. When Paul talked or thought about it, though, it was always *Space*, spoken with either wild enthusiasm or reverent awe. His friends — schoolmates, neighborhood kids, contemporaries encountered at stores and the beach — viewed Space as one more fantasy adventure from their childhood, discarded and picked up periodically like the Old West or Sherwood Forest or the world of spying. They once had played at being Buck Rogers or Flash Gordon or Colonel McCauley or Captain Kirk with as much true belief as they had when they had played Davy Crockett or Robin Hood. Now, though, they no more thought about someday living in Space than they seriously considered moving to the middle ages or the wild, wild West.

Paul was seven years old, watching the fiery pinpoint on the screen and dreaming of being a thirty-year-old astronaut, confidently riding that column of terrifying power to burst free of earthly bonds and float above the clouds among the stars.

On TV, the image of the rocket brightened suddenly, accompanied by a billowing plume of smoke.

"*Bojemoi!*" his mother cried out. "What's happening?"

He turned to look at her sourly. Won't she ever figure it out? "That's the first stage separating. Everything's nominal."

She sat back in the easy chair. "Why do they have to do it like that? I thought they'd blown up."

Paul laughed and sipped some more juice. *Imagine being startled by staging*, he thought. *Doesn't she listen to the voice of the capsule communicator?*

"It'll happen again when they drop the second stage," he said aloud, "but by then they'll be out of camera range."

"Well," she said, folding her arms grumpily, "I don't think they should scare people like that. What if they had really blown up? How would we know?"

Dad snickered. "Your mother," he said. "Always the optimist."

Paul watched the screen, sucked his orange juice, and tried to imagine the thunder of the engines.

▼ ▲ ▼

Within the span of his seventh year of life, Paul witnessed a breathtaking blur of activity in Space. The Apollo program sped — in a matter of months — from a brief orbital flight to the first circumnavigation of the Moon. It was the greatest Christmas present anyone could have received, and he knew he was a member of the luckiest, most blessed generation in the history of humanity.

The next year brought an even greater triumph. The greatest triumph of all time. Just days before Paul's birthday, Neil Armstrong became the first man to set foot upon another planet. Paul made a solemn vow that day that he would be the first man to set foot on Mars.

"That's one small step for... man," the static-distorted voice said from the lunar surface, *"one giant leap for mankind."*

Paul's father frowned. "Man and mankind are synonymous. What did he mean by that?"

Paul's mother shrugged. "Maybe he said '*a* man' and we just didn't hear it."

"Maybe he blew his lines," Patty said, running a brush through her long golden hair. She was home for this one. Everyone on Earth was home for this one.

Paul thrilled at the moment, his gaze glued to the blurred, black-and-white image beamed from a quarter of a million miles away. He knew all about Neil Armstrong, how he had once flown that most beautiful of airplanes, the X-15; how he and Dave Scott survived a wild spin during the flight of Gemini 8; how he escaped from a nearly fatal malfunction of the "flying bedstead" lunar-landing trainer. This man was a hero of classic proportion.

Paul only wished his hero could describe what he saw without continually resorting to the word "fantastic."

The perfect end to his seventh year on Earth — and the perfect beginning of his eighth — arrived in the form of a birthday gift two weeks after the triumphant return of Apollo Eleven. The gift was a model rocket kit. Not just a plastic model kit such as the ones that littered the house, but an actual working rocket complete with a series C motor!

In less than a week, he had it built and took it out to Oak Meadow Park with his father for a Saturday flight. The morning — bright, clear, and hot — echoed with his shout of *"Fire in the hole!"* He pressed the ignition switch, and watched as a part of him, a creation of his own hands and mind, flew into the sky.

He launched rockets all the time, but most fervently during lunar missions. With the first lunar landing came a slowing of the frenetic space race to a more stately progression, with five more landings over the subsequent three years.

Paul remembered Apollo 204. When Apollo Thirteen made its unlucky flight around the Moon and back to a tense return to Earth, Paul once again encountered a crisis of faith. How could NASA fail to keep its astronauts — the most important people in the world — safe from harm? His parents patiently explained that space travel was a difficult and complex undertaking. He accepted that, and the fact that it was better to fly into Space in something unsafe than not to go at all. Yet instead of admitting the obvious, NASA always seemed to blame their critics and declare that if Congress gave them more money, all would be well.

And then — like a clock unwinding — all motion and momentum ceased. Apollo Seventeen climaxed the Apollo program, even though at least three more flights had been planned. NASA pulled the plug in a series of political maneuvers of which Paul Volnos — and the rest of the nation — remained completely unaware.

Man abandoned the Moon, with only the dimmest promise of return. Someday.

Paul, disappointed in NASA's behavior — which he likened to that of a dog that constantly chased cars until, having finally caught one, suddenly realized it had no idea what to do next — continued to refine and build larger model rockets.

It was a year after the Skylab era that Paul, a lanky thirteen year old, met little Tammy Reis, someone who shared his intense interest in Space. More important, she gloried in the novelty of it all. He became her mentor, forging between them a bond that they both thought impossible to rend. With young Tammy in tow, he moved up from series C to series D rocket motors, multiple stages, multiple motors, then onward to the mainline for rocket junkies: series G and H motors as a member of the High Thrust Rocket Society.

The Skylab project once again had exposed Paul to the dark side of the space agency. With the three Saturn rockets left over from Apollo, NASA decided to establish a space station. Paul thought it a magnificent effort, to put into orbit a habitat the size of a three-bedroom house and staff it with astronauts. After more than three years of nothing but robot probes shot into Space, here arose another grand effort to establish a foothold in orbit. Perhaps from there would grow a larger space station, then perhaps a return to the Moon. Paul thought that perhaps he *could* become an astronaut and make it to the Moon, Mars, and beyond. At one time he had feared that he was too young, that someone would make it to the red planet before he was old enough to qualify. Then, with the end of Apollo, it seemed as if he might grow old and die before anyone ventured out into the void again. Now — with Skylab — a new hope filled him that perhaps the timing would be just right. That a renewed space program might have the pacing to put him on Mars by the time he was thirty.

Then the news from Space turned sour. The first two Skylab crews complained of long hours, endless pushing from the scientists Earthside to perform scores of pet experiments. The third crew, though, showed Paul something he had never imagined before: open rebellion against NASA. The reports coming from Space astounded him. The Skylab Three astronauts went on strike when faced with overwhelming workloads. This might have occurred in one of his cherished science-fiction books, but nothing prepared him for the video image of bearded, wild-looking astronauts peevishly denouncing their managers and the scientists they were ordered to serve.

NASA tried to keep a lid on things, but even popular comic strips mocked the fiasco.

Paul, who at thirteen could look at NASA with an eye jaundiced by years of disappointment, saw the episode as something akin to the American Revolution, with the space colonists in revolt against their distant oppressors. Tammy — five years his junior and with less awareness of past incidents — thought the astronauts behaved with extreme ingratitude toward those who labored mightily to loft them to their exalted orbit.

Neither had any idea how their childhood disagreement would carry over into their adult lives.

16 June, 1983

Tammy sped up Ace's driveway in a rattletrap racing-green 1954 MG and screeched to a halt. Sixteen now, she had matured into a young woman who regularly turned heads at every airport she visited. She still dressed in shuttle-blue jumpsuits, though now her nubile body curved lusciously above and below the slender belt line.

"I did it!" she cried with glee, jumping over the car door and running up to Ace, Paul, and four other volunteers.

Paul pointed a wrench at her, grinning. "And on the first date, too, I'll bet."

"Gutterbrain," she said gaily.

"You passed you're exams," Ace said. "Right?"

Her dark eyes twinkled with excitement. "Yes! I'm graduating high school two years early—"

"Say!" someone said. "Today's the twentieth anniversary of the first woman in Space. Twice the reason to celebrate!"

"And that's not all!" Tammy pulled an envelope from her thigh cargo pocket and withdrew the letter. "With the help of my career advisor, Mr. Woolsey, I'm going to college courtesy of the Robertson Barrett Gibbon Space Scholarship!" She practically squealed with joy.

Paul's expression darkened. "Gibbon? And his NASA fan club?"

"Paul!" She sounded genuinely wounded. "NOSS is the biggest group of space fanatics in the world. And Dr. Gibbon is the most dedicated man. He's been at this for nearly forty years—"

"Yeah. Promising every generation that the *next* generation will be living in Space. NOSS is just a money pump for Gibbon. Have they built one single rocket with all their millions in club dues? Have any of their members pooled their life savings into trying what Ace is trying? Or do they pay their dues, buy their stupid pins and thumb through their monthly magazines looking at pretty color pictures content that Barry Gibbon has everything planned out for them? Woolsey's dad and Gibbon are old buddies. I wouldn't put it past Lud the Pud to have pushed you for the scholarship so he can get his pothead hands on you and—"

She stuffed the letter back in her pocket. "Paul Volnos, that is the meanest, most paranoid lunacy I've ever heard you spout!" An angry finger pointed toward the summer sky. "The Shuttle is flying. Right now! There are people in orbit around the Earth as we speak, and I am not going to stand around here tinkering with a... a... ground-bound bottle rocket when there's a functioning space program on the verge of building the first real space station—"

"Don't forget Skylab," someone interjected.

"Or *Salyut* or *Mir*," another said.

Ace quietly ignored Tammy's assessment of his effort, and calmly continued to tinker with a small attitude jet.

"You people," she said slowly, "are the most self-absorbed, negative-thinking wet blankets I've ever known, and—"

"You say that about *us*?" Paul threw his wrench down at the driveway so hard that it chipped the concrete. There flared in his gaze a furious anger, a volatile mixture of dread and revulsion at her decision. "What about you? You've bought into the whole NASA fraud. How can you ignore the figures? With what it costs just to *launch* one shuttle flight, Ace could have put a whole space station into orbit on a Leviathan! The shuttle's a fraud — an *expensive* fraud — and Gibbon's role in all this proves that he is *not* dedicated to space migration."

The others watched the pair go at each other, not knowing if they should or *could* choose sides. Most of them objected to NASA, but not with the vehemence expressed by Paul. And if any one of them had been offered the chance to join the astronaut corps, they most likely would have jumped at it.

"You're a loser, Paul. All your ideas about bootstrapping into Space, they've been shot down. The Shuttle is the only key to Space. NASA's won. They're doing what you only dream about, and that's what blows your mind. You can't admit that they're back on track while you're stuck in the mud!"

"You are not going to get into Space working for NASA," Paul said with the grave certainty of prophecy. "You will either disappear into bureaucratic nothingness or be incinerated by statist incompetence. Don't forget Grissom, Chaffee, and White!"

Tammy stared at Paul with her mouth partway open in shock at his death sentence. In a voice low with dispirited pain, she said, "I would never wish that on you," and strode to her car. Without a look at Paul or Ace, she gunned the engine, backed out, and turned at the base of the driveway.

▼ ▲ ▼

He never saw her again, at least not face-to-face, until Donahue brought her to Somalia. Now he watched her walk purposefully away from the toroid toward the office mobiles, a grim expression on her face. She disappeared inside Haley's office. A moment later, the phone outside Grant's office warbled for attention. He punched up the line with a smile and — switching on the voice-alteration unit — said, "Marcus Grant."

The woman on the other end said, in a clear, steady voice, *"Paul."*

His heart pounded. For a long moment, hung out in time like meat on a hook, he said nothing. Then, clicking off the voice distorter, he said, softly, "Come over."

He did not move from his chair as he heard her footsteps ascend the uncarpeted steps to his double-wide mobile. She knocked on the door with a single firm tap.

"Come in, Tammy."

She entered to see a man sitting in an expensive black leather executive swivel chair, palms down on the rich, dark walnut desktop. The place looked like an executive suite in downtown Manhattan, not like the inside of a poorly air-conditioned mobile home in the middle of an African coastal desert. His grey hair was even more startling to see in person, the judgmental gaze of his blue eyes piercing through her as they had nearly half her life ago. He rose, apparently without conscious thought, as she approached him.

"If anyone could have done this," she said, "I knew it would have been you."

"Why are you here?" he asked.

She shook her head. "No. My life is public. You know why I'm here. Why are *you* here?"

He gestured toward a chair and spoke after she gracefully sat. "I'm out to make my fortune."

"You'll hardly break even given what I've seen here."

"Overhead is low in the counter-economy. No taxes, no regulatory costs, minimum wages, or mandated benefits."

Not even a hint of amusement crossed her face. "Isn't that canceled out by the cost of bribes?"

"I'll ask you again, Tammy, why did you come here?"

She stood suddenly to lean over his desk, fists planted vehemently on its surface. "I came here to see if there really was such a thing as an underground space movement. I didn't think it was possible to marshal the money, the expertise, the material, and the secrecy to do so. I wanted to find out if it was true. And maybe I thought I'd find an answer to a mystery."

Grant merely raised an eyebrow in inquiry.

"Why you stayed with Ace instead of coming with me."

"We've been through this before. I—"

"We could have both been up there, Paul. I've been into Space *three times*—"

"And *came back* every time!" He rose to meet her eye-to-eye. In his expression was something inscrutable: not rage, not pain, not anger, not hatred, but a firm conviction that had endured years of struggle. "Don't you see? You followed a course that took you to the place of your dreams, then yanked you away again and again. And now, you'll probably never see Space again. NASA's in ruins and there's no way UNITO's going to revive it. I stuck with Ace because he was building a spaceship without one cent of government money. He didn't force anyone to support him. He didn't have to beg for funding from drooling cretins whose definition of public service is screwing their constituents!" He frowned at seeing a shudder come over her, then said, "I stopped working with Ace the day he received notice from the Department of State denying him an export permit on his rocket components. He wasn't exporting it anywhere but to orbit, so the ruling was a bald-faced attempt to frustrate his plans or bankrupt him if he tried to fight it in court. I learned the nature of the beast that day. I realized — finally — that all the talk about the pioneer spirit and free enterprise was just a smoke screen. The people in power didn't want any of that. They wanted us to believe it just enough to work hard for their corporations, keep our savings in their banks, invest in their stocks, and pay taxes to their treasury. But the moment anyone tried to create his own success, strike out into a frontier they don't — they *can't* — control, down came the mailed fist."

Tammy's heart raced and her palms sweated. She had brought that fist down at least once — on Gerald Cooper. She unknotted her hands and sat again, releasing a pent breath and gazing at Grant levelly. "What did you do? Where did you go?"

He sat, laughed bitterly, and turned to look at the wall to his right. On it were hung photographs of the Moon and the planets. "What did I do? I gave up. Of the only two people I'd called my friends, one was hitting his head against a bureaucratic stone wall and the other had leapt the battlements to join the other side. So I surrendered to superior force." He turned to stare at her. "Guess where I went. Forget it, you won't. I went to Lud Woolsey and bought some LSD from him. I liked the irony of that. I hated Lud, so I rushed to him first thing for the means to escape the world his father and friends had made. He was more than happy, even a bit smug, selling me the finest stuff he had. I chose to retreat to inner space rather than face a planet of cowards who could not accept the enormous possibilities of outer space."

Tammy said nothing, simultaneously shocked and mesmerized by his confession.

"I surrounded myself with beautiful things: my model rockets, those photos there, music that evoked in me the same emotions that Space did. I put a square of blotter acid on my tongue, tasted its sting, and swallowed it. Immediately, I felt the way you must have felt on your first shuttle flight, when the SRB's ignite and there's no turning back. I knew that nothing could stop what was to happen to me.

"It took nearly an hour. I'd gone through Beethoven's Ninth and was listening to the *Blue Danube* when the photographs seemed to become more than pictures. They moved, they radiated some incredible emotion that cut me in half. I obsessively examined every step of my life. I roamed around the room playing with every space toy I still owned from childhood. I cried with joy at the memories. I huddled in fear that I'd be discovered, locked up and never allowed off this world."

"It was a bad trip, I take it." Her voice was cold and distant.

"No," he said with frank simplicity. "It was a very good trip. It had all the elements of beauty and thrill and adventure. That was when I realized that I didn't need Space to be free. I could be free anywhere I wanted to be. So I became a pioneer — of the inner frontier. And I became a free enterpriser — in the underground economy. I never looked at the stars again."

Her fingers tapped against the chair arm. "Until?"

"Until I met Chad Haley. He reminded me of me, of my true dreams and highest aspirations. He forced me to realize that as long as I stayed on Earth evading the laws of the power elite while still within their grasp, I simply played their game in their sandbox. I had fooled myself into thinking that the cop-outlaw game is somehow superior to the master-slave game. It isn't. They merely set the rules I would break instead of the rules I would obey. Soon"—he glanced down at the image of the space station on his desk monitor—"the only law I'll be breaking is the law of gravity." He gazed across at her. "Let me show you something no one has seen yet. Not even Chad or Joscelyn know all my plans."

▼▲▼

They walked past the space station's base. In the trench swarmed scores of furiously busy workers. Tammy nodded toward the pit. "What sort of air-movers will you be using during fueling?"

Volnos looked puzzled.

"For the pit," Tammy added. "To evacuate the hydrogen."

"Hydrogen is lighter than air," Paul said. "It'll just float away."

Tammy sighed and shook her head. "This is why you need astronauts, Paul. Why you need *me*." She waved broadly at the trench and said, "Cryogenic hydrogen is *denser* than air. It will fill the trench and suffocate any workers down there, or mix with the oxygen vapors and explode at the smallest spark. You've got to bring in some positive-displacement blowers with sealed motors designed for use in Class B explosive atmospheres."

He stared at her, wondering how to receive the benefit of her experience. "Duly noted," was all he said.

▼▲▼

The pair stood in a mobile adjacent to the construction site, gazing into pitch blackness. Paul threw a panel of switches to illuminate the area. Tammy saw two large objects on aluminum support racks. One looked like a small version of the Centaur booster the shuttle once carried aloft to kick satellites to synchronous orbit or to send robot craft on planetary missions. The other, which looked as if it could mate with the booster, was an ungainly hodge-podge of tool cases, parts boxes, and tethers sprouting from behind a cylindrical balloon less than eight feet wide and ten feet long.

"The crew cabin's an inflatable Kevlar-web supported balloon. Just a big space suit you can live inside. It's a two-seater," he said matter-of-factly. "Low mass, small payload volume. Once we're in equatorial orbit, we deploy and inflate it. The booster can take a crew up to geosynchronous orbit where they can repair satellites or recharge them, using fuel salvaged from the maneuvering units of other satellites too far gone to be fixed. The computer has a database on every geosynchronous satellite and its needed repairs. We know to the ounce how much and what kind of fuel is out there, what work needs to be done. We'll repair the first satellite on spec — to advertise our service — and then broadcast our rates. These communication and data satellites cost hundreds of millions. What their Earthbound owners will pay for repairs will cover subsequent flights, plus a hefty profit. That ought to make Space Station *Volnos* a successful venture from the first week."

"*Volnos*, huh? I thought it was called Grant One. Going public with your true identity?" Tammy reached out to run a hand along the side of the space taxi. An emotion stirred within her that she refused to acknowledge.

"In good time," he said.

"You could also hold satellites for ransom with this thing, threatening to kick each one out of alignment or saw off an antenna."

He gazed at her in amusement. "I could, but I won't. I'm a businessman, not a terrorist."

"There are some who think the two equivalent."

"There are some," he replied, "who confuse politics with progress. I'm not one of them, which is why I'm here."

"Did your hair turn grey from all that philosophizing? Or was it the drugs?"

For a moment, he said nothing. Then he laughed lightly. "It's colored this way. I thought looking more like an old alpha-male would help me in the business world. I think it has. The lines you see, though, *they're* real and I earned every one, courtesy of the joys of high finance."

"What makes you think," she slowly asked, "that any government would allow you to keep money paid to you on Earth for your work in Space?"

Grant said nothing. Sliding his hands in his pockets, he gazed at the two pieces of space hardware as if reviewing the entire process that brought him to this point. Then he smiled a deliberate, forced smile. "I plan to make *them* customers, too. I'm certain they'll accept. They have their own satellites that desperately need repair or placement in proper orbits, and NASA can't do anything for them, now. I can."

"And you don't consider that to be dealing with the enemy?"

His smile grew more relaxed. "No. I consider it selling to all sides without prejudice. That is the open-handed nature of the market. My dealing with those who try to destroy me can only strengthen me and weaken them, for the corrupting influence of free trade is more powerful than the destructive impulses of power and monopoly."

"Is that what you are? An agent of corruption?"

"Only to those in power. To corrupt evil is to twist it toward good."

Something within Tammy — deep within her soul, beneath a decade of patience and compromise — stirred. She felt it, fought it, blurted out another question.

"So NASA is the evil and Paul Volnos is the good?"

"Functionally, yes. NASA's funding comes from taxes, money taken at gunpoint. My funding comes from my profits. I don't force anyone to pay for my efforts. What better definition of evil and good can there be?"

For his part, Grant waged his own internal battle. Part of him — the conscious, thinking part — answered her questions, offered ripostes, met logic with logic. Another part of him — the realm from which grew his passion for Space and from which flowed the strength to persevere — burned like a rocket's blazing flame.

She turned away from him to examine a detail on the small spacecraft. "I think you've made a valiant effort, but the hubris you display may well be your undoing."

She turned back. He stood close to her. Heart-stoppingly close.

Without a word, he grasped her arms to pull her closer still. For an instant, a chill seared through her, a rapid-fire replay of all that had happened onboard *Constitution*. Then, as if breaking the sound barrier, all the pain and degradation fell from her in one shuddering instant and she threw her arms around Paul to press close, burying her face into him, inhaling his scent, feeling the heat of his body, the passionate pressure against her.

He whispered her name with an urgency she longed to hear so many years ago. She heard the same sound, she suddenly realized, whenever one of his model rockets sizzled up into the sky. It was he, calling her name in love and desire. She knew now that she had felt it even then.

And here he stood, holding her, kneeling with her to the floor, hands tearing at clothing, swiftly releasing all restraints. Outside, the sound of evening wind beat against the building. Inside, a cyclone of desire threw her to the ground and pinned her there.

Time ceased to have meaning. He gazed at her and simultaneously saw her and the young woman she had been. There existed no gap, no separation in time or space between then and now. Every struggle, every setback, every betrayal and failure along the way no longer existed; such petty obstacles faded into unimportance. The universe consisted only of their union's loving fury, and the world they forged together in their crucible of desire.

She whispered his name into his ear, then kissed him deeply as they united. Every movement became exhilarating acceleration. She surrendered utterly to emotions she once thought slain and dead within her. Now they resurrected, erupting again like the flames of an engine that could move the world.

She succumbed to the fire.

▼ ▲ ▼

At the blazing instant of shuddering release and shattering awareness, he knew why he had turned away from the night: she had not been in it. Now that she lay there in the night with him, the universe exploded with possibility. Arms wrapped around each other, ecstatic captives of passionate yearning and boundless love, they bridged their years of separation and grew closer than they had ever been.

She whispered something in his ear.

"What?" he whispered back.

"I said I've been sent to destroy you."

"You can't," he softly murmured. "Not now. Not ever again."

"Yes, I can," she insisted, pushing away from him to grasp at her clothing. "I was sent by the NSA. I'm a spy."

He smiled at her with genuine warmth. "I know. I've always known. I had Joscelyn scan your belongings. Your shuttle pin's a homer."

His equanimity suddenly frightened her. "You knew? And you still—?"

"Forget the NSA." He pulled the clothes away from her and drew her close once more. "Forget NASA. Forget your masters. Here you're free. Once we're orbital, you need never fear anyone again."

She searched his face for any sign of self-deception, any hint of his own fear. She saw none. She saw in Paul Volnos, in this man now called Marcus Aurelius Grant, an incomprehensible rectitude, an impossible confidence, and a terrifying optimism. "You don't understand, Paul. They can do it. They can stop you now that they know where you are. You're facing the combined forces of the mightiest superpower in the world!"

Paul laughed. He leaned back on his knees, knuckles on hips, and let loose with a fiercely mocking roar that frightened her with its purity. He was that thirteen-year-old boy once more.

"Am I? Is it?" he asked with a piratical grin. "The whole government's against me? That would amuse a few senators whom I occasionally rent and an agency head I've leased with option to buy. It would bring a good laugh at CIA or FBI headquarters — they loathe the NSA *and* each other. And Space Command may ally with NASA now and then, but I know they would all love to see one another screw up."

He stroked her soft cheek and shook his head. "No, my love, I'm not facing a monolithic leviathan. I'm up against living, breathing human beings, each one a victim of his own dreams and fears, each one constructing his own little schemes for power. I can turn them against one another with equal doses of misinformation and truth, of bribe and threat. Why, I even know of one or two people still in NASA — still *alive* in NASA — who think what I'm doing will revitalize the agency by giving it a new space race in which it can compete. They think the UNITO monopoly would destroy what little incentive remains."

"People in NASA know... about you?"

His grin grew cocky. "Maybe a few. Maybe a little. Maybe enough to give *them* hope."

"Hope?" She sat up and began to dress. "The hope of a world can be destroyed by the actions of just a few."

He handed her a shoe. "If that were true, humanity would not have progressed beyond the cave. I've come to realize that the actions of a few — even of one — can realize the dreams of millions."

She reached for her other shoe. He playfully held it back. "I see now," he said, "why we chose the paths we did. We both made our choices out of fear. We both feared that NASA was too big to fight. You chose to join it rather than forsake Space. I chose to forsake Space rather than surrender. Neither choice was right because *fear* drove the decision. I saw that eventually. You'll see it soon."

"Now, though," she said, tapping a finger against the shuttle pin. "Right now they know where you are."

He ran a fingernail along the gold plating of the pin. "You think that knowledge of a single fact confers total awareness of a situation and galvanizes action. It might, in someone such as you or I. These people, though, these... pitiable vandals..." He shook his head and smiled in a lovingly didactic manner. "They can't act on their own initiative. They fear that most of all. Why else would they survive and thrive in a cumbersome bureaucracy? They won't act. They can't, not without creating a dozen contingency plans and developing ways to cover their own asses. And that takes time, something I'm not inclined to give them."

"If nobody in government can take action, wars wouldn't happen."

He stood. "Wars happen, my love, because they take action too late." He helped her up and slapped her bottom lightly. "If they could act decisively, without trying to second-guess what clandestine plots hidden agendas, and secret alliances obsess their superiors, there would be more assassinations and fewer wars. If they really wanted to stop *me*, they would not have sent *you*. They would have sent someone with a poison dart."

"What makes you think they haven't?"

"Not you. They don't trust you. That's why they're tracking your movements." He tapped at the pin. "This is a beacon *and* a leash. They fear you even more than they fear me."

She raised an eyebrow while buttoning her blouse. He slipped into his slacks and nodded with a wisdom she had never seen in him before, the wisdom she had sought vainly in others.

"I mean it," he said. "They trained you, they feel they created you, and they know that even so, you owe them no allegiance. I'm a cipher to them, something to be studied before they act. You they've observed for years and still they can't comprehend what makes you tick. They fear those who have the courage to sit on top of a gigantic bomb and ask them to light it up. They would not entrust their own lives to any such as they, and are baffled that you would. It scares them that you love Space enough to trust them to send you there. You confuse them. That's your strength."

"I can't betray them. I have a family. I don't know what danger they might be in..."

Volnos shrugged. "My family's safe. I can provide whatever level of protection—"

"I can't betray them because they may be right!" She turned away from him to look at the small orbital tug. Its ungainly shape, useful only outside the atmosphere of Earth, reminded her of illustrations from old space books, the books she devoured as a child, books filled with astounding predictions and heady optimism. She used to climb into small, tight spaces in closets and under tables to imagine what it must be like in the confines of a rocket ship. A claustrophile, that's what she was, though sometimes while flying she adjudged herself an agoraphile. An astronaut had to be a lot of both. Self-trained to be comfortable anywhere — including the lonely reaches of Space — she felt supremely ill at ease with the man she sought for years to destroy: the man she loved above all else.

"I always thought it was impossible to stand up to NASA."

Paul smiled. "Nothing is impossible to the man who has money *and* the will to use it constructively." He took her arm in a courtly fashion and walked her out of the storage mobile back to his office. "Okay. You remain the spy in our ranks." His tone remained confident, indulgent, very nearly condescending. "We'll let reality be the final arbiter. When we achieve orbit, I'll expect a formal apology and a change of allegiance. Deal?"

Tammy said nothing, more troubled than ever.

CHAPTER 40

I am fire and air; my other elements
I give to baser life.

— William Shakespeare

15 July

"Light off four rocket engines in the middle of South Bronx?" Sam Friedman stared at Davy Crockett as if he had been pole-axed. "You've gone nuts!"

Crockett gazed levelly at his friend. They sat in Davy's dorm room surrounded by Bernadette, Natasha, Hacker, and Penny. More by default than anything else, these six constituted the inner circle of the South Bronx conspiracy. Crockett knew more about orbital mechanics than the rest, and, as the only one who had ever flown anything, became the pilot by default. Friedman assumed the responsibilities of the fuel expert. Hacker — computer maven — programmed the ship's cybernetics, while Natasha designed the life support system. Penny, having nearly single-handedly assembled the ship, chose to serve as the all-around trouble-shooter. Bernadette learned everything she could about the diverse disciplines that astronautics comprised. She evolved into be the project manager.

They all sat around Crockett, shocked at his pronouncement.

"We've got to test fire the engines and the rotating seal on the centrifugal pump," he said. "Simple as that. And I suggest we do it just once, since the noise and fire will attract attention, which we don't want to do twice."

"And how in hell do you plan to do it?"

Davy smiled with a sly tilt.

▼ ▲ ▼

Sam stared at the massive steel stand bolted securely to the concrete floor and braced against the walls, a latticework of steel supporting the hub of the spacecraft's rotor. From its lower middle, two thick feed lines — wrapped in layer upon layer of heat resistant aluminized Mylar —

snaked across the floor toward two large tankers — still connected to the 18-wheeler rigs that brought them in — one of which shed cold mist from its frosty exterior. One tank was marked LOX and the other, originally marked KEROSENE, had been re-christened BAGELS in spray paint. Both were pressure fed by a third, smaller truck carrying a tank of liquid nitrogen, painted with the appellation CREAM CHEESE.

The four rocket engines, instead of being at the end of twenty-foot rotor blades, were each attached to stubby aluminum struts only three feet long and not at all aerodynamically designed. The tight array enabled the motors to direct their combined thrust outward without scorching the walls, while at the same time ensuring that the entire arrangement did not impart enough lift to wrench the assembly free of its moorings.

"This will never work," Friedman said to Crockett.

"Why? They can't lift up the whole building. If the bolts hold—"

"They'll hold," Giannini said.

"—the exhaust will dissipate sideways. Harmlessly. We run up the engines for a two hundred second burn, shut them down, hit the quick release on the stand, and haul the whole shebang back to the factory." He gazed at the others. "What could be simpler?"

Giannini agreed with Crockett's assessment. "The thrust needed to spin the blades on the real ship is small compared to a conventional rocket, so noise and exhaust will be way low. And the LOX will burn the kerosene completely so we won't have any smoke — just steam. And who'll notice a little extra humidity in the Bronx this time of year?"

Bernadette turned a wrench one more time to tighten down the videocam she had placed a few yards away from the engines. "And if the engines fly loose or the seal blows, we're far enough away from the factory that the ship isn't in any danger."

"Sure," Friedman muttered. "As if losing one of these parts wouldn't ground us just as effectively."

"Sam"—Davy clapped a hand around his friend's shoulder—"You've got to cheer up. I'm thinking of calling this Project *Que Sera Sera* in your honor. Remember — whatever doesn't destroy us makes us stronger!"

Friedman turned a gimlet eye toward his buckskinned friend. "And if this destroys us?"

Crockett smiled and gave Sam a couple of pats. "Then remember the Alamo." He raised both hands overhead and yelled, "All right people, it's show time! Initiate burn sequence start!"

" 'Remember the Alamo,' " Sam said to Natasha between status comments. "I'm remembering the July Fourth that I stood too close to a Piccolo Pete and set my hair on fire!"

Hacker keyed in the code to begin the countdown. "T-minus six minutes," he said calmly.

"Camera running?"

"Roger!" Bernadette confirmed.

"Telemetry?"

"Flowing," Hacker said.

Davy nodded and pulled a celphone from his necessaries bag and punched in a number. Someone instantly answered on the other end.

"Fire control," a woman's voice said. *"Receiving telemetry."*

"Great," Davy said. "Keep the line open." Then he called out, "APU's?"

"Ready for powerup." Hacker switched back and forth between half a dozen separate functions.

"Fuel and LOX?"

"Nominal," Sam said, looking at his own computer.

"Time?" Crockett asked.

"T-minus five minutes, twenty seconds," Hacker replied.

"All right," Davy said, looking around him. "Everybody run."

Relieved, the crew turned and raced from the building, out into the midnight streets. Crush 69 and other members of SBX-13 stood guard outside with chains, bats, and guns. They fit into the street scene far more reasonably than the scrambling post-grads, several in white lab coats like mad scientists, one in a faded army jacket carrying a wireless laptop computer, and the last one rustling out in fringed rawhide with a coonskin hat the tail of which bounced crazily against the back of his neck with every long, hasty stride.

"Pull out, guys!" he shouted to the guards, who swiftly joined the others in their retreat.

Everyone raced into another abandoned building diagonally across the street. Up five flights of stairs they ran. Each landing had been illuminated beforehand with more of Sam's glow-juice, the faint green light guiding their ascent. Breathless, they reached the roof and slid to a halt on the gravel-sprinkled tar. Over the waist-high cornice surrounding the rooftop, they leaned to peer at the test site.

The streets lay empty at that hour. The other gangs that roamed the borough kept their distance, too, by design of SBX-13, which had spread the rumor of a planned cop ambush. In the distance, police and ambulance sirens wailed their incessant song like cats in the heat. Locally, though, the avenue remained quiet and dark, lit only by two street lights at opposite ends of the street.

"T-minus two minutes," Hacker said.

The subsequent one hundred-twenty seconds consisted of a rapid-fire checklist conducted by computer and verbally confirmed by one of three sources: Hacker, Sam, or Carla Pulaski, the student on the other end of the celphone who sat in the safety and comfort of the dormitory watching the entire process on video and telemetry.

"T-minus ten," Hacker said. "Nine, eight—"

"Lines pressurized."

"Six, five—"

"Fire in the hole," Bernadette said, watching the video screen as igniters sent a cascade of sparks across each engine nozzle, white-hot points of light showering down to the concrete floor.

"Three, two, one, ignition!"

Outside the building, no one heard a sound at first, then the fuel flow rumbled like the sound of a distant waterfall. A dim glow radiated from the painted-over windows in the upper floors. At that instant, the night erupted with the hiss of a giant angry snake, augmented by an eerie whirring sound, as if a humongous Independence Day pinwheel had been lit off inside the abandoned hulk.

"We have ignition!" Sam and Bernadette screamed in unison, one staring at a string of numbers on a computer, the other watching the brilliant glow on a video screen.

An instant later, the video image tilted and went black as the exhaust tore the camera loose from its mount and flung it against a brick wall. Blinding white light glared through the windows an instant before shattering them completely to send thousands of shards glittering into the street. Steam erupted from inside, filling the streets with a dank, hot stench of burning fuel-oil.

"Cut it off!" Crockett shouted as the exhaust plumes sputtered out the doors and windows like geysers in a primordial hell.

Hacker's thumb frantically rolled over the small trackball, moving the cursor to a box that read ABORT IGNITION. His pinkie rammed against the enter key and just as suddenly the shrieking hiss reduced to a growl then to a sizzle as the fuel ceased to feed the ravening dervish. Slowly the throbbing whir of the rotor dropped in pitch and volume as the onlookers stood awestruck by the power of the array. Then Crockett shouted, "Pull the engines!" and the rescue team raced down the stairs and into the street.

The building housing the test stand radiated an eerie, dim orange glow that flickered through the blasted windows. Steam and smoke billowed from the rectangles like mist from a tomb. The echoes of their experiment dissipated by the time they reached the street, and the sound of car alarms and sirens reverberated through the night. From inside the test building crackled the distinctive sound of burning timber.

"We have less than five minutes to get everything to the factory," Davy yelled as he slipped on insulated Nomex gloves. "Roll out!"

He raced into the smoking building first, followed by Bernadette and the others, and checked out the engine test stand.

"Success," he said, gazing at the intact rotor and engines.

"Are your shoes warm?" Bernadette asked.

Davy looked down to see the soles of their shoes softening on the hot concrete near the test stand.

"Bring in the rig."

Bernadette trotted outside to where the engine-hauling semi waited.

The others joined Crockett at their own posts: Penny hopped into the cab of the fuel truck, Sam into the one carrying the oxidizer; Natasha disconnected the fuel lines and jumped into the nitrogen-tank truck to haul it away; Hacker gathered up the telemetry remotes, the ruined videocam, and miscellaneous equipment, threw them unceremoniously into the back of a pickup, and raced into the night, followed by Natasha and — with a tooth-jarring grinding of gears, a double-clutching Penny. None of the trucks had endured much damage, but the tires on each of them rolled with a sickeningly sticky sound as rubber peeled away from the hot concrete floor.

Bernadette backed her rig up to the edge of the test stand following Davy's hand signals, then waited with the engine running while he hooked up the winch. Unlatching the quick-connect bolts Penny had devised, he was able single-handedly to winch the rotor assembly onto the flatbed and secure the oblong test stand into matching bolts.

"All set," he shouted, jumping into the cab. "Burn rubber!"

Bernadette ground gears and the rig lurched slowly forward. Two loud bangs erupted from the rear of the flatbed.

"I didn't mean it literally!" Davy cried. "Damn. We got too close. The tires melted!"

"We'll make it," she replied, putting the pedal to the metal and lurching forward.

"We'd better," Crockett said, "before the fire department remembers there's a South Bronx."

▼ ▲ ▼

The fire department remembered. The following morning, Earl MacCray, chief arson investigator for the borough, arrived to see the engine company rolling up their hoses and securing their equipment. MacCray was a middle-aged, greying man of moderate height who carried himself with a stern pride in his Scots-Irish roots and a disinclination toward sloth. His uniform started out each morning spotless, though by the end of a good investigative day it might be sooty and water-stained. He was clean this morning, and he would stay that way.

He noted the shattered glass in the street and the minor smoke stains around the tops of the windows. Inside, morning sunlight angled in through only the uppermost openings to lend a misty, ethereal illumination. One of the other investigators peered at the floor.

"Something at the center of this warehouse burned hot enough to ignite those far walls," MacCray muttered, "yet it didn't warm up the very center."

"Backdraft?" somebody guessed.

"Too much heat for that. And look at these scorch patterns. Outward from the center, curving, as if someone had a flame thrower on a turntable."

"Illegal refuse," somebody else ventured. "The mob incinerating toxic waste?"

The chief rubbed his smooth-shaven chin. "Nope. HazMat would be dressing us in Saranex if that were the case. All I smell is kerosene." He shone the light all around the floor, muttering, "I don't think arson was the plan here, but I'll be damned if I can figure out what was." He kicked at the thick steel bolts protruding from the floor. "Something heavy and big. Something that needed to be held in place." He turned toward a husky lieutenant. "Bradley — how long did you say the noise lasted?"

"A couple of street guys said they heard a loud hiss or scream for a minute or so. DWM workers saw the glow from the fire and called. We had it out in twenty minutes."

"Earl!" someone hollered from the far corner of the building.

MacCray turned his head to shout back, "What?"

"Take a look!"

MacCray walked over to the wall, where one fire investigator pried the unmelted half of a New Jersey license plate from where it was stuck in the crumbling mortar.

MacCray held it up in the indirect glow of dawn. "Commercial truck. Registration tag number's burnt off, but we have half the plate's digits." He handed it to his stocky assistant. "Work on it."

Someone ran in to wheeze out the results of his foot sprint. "Followed the tire... melt marks pretty... distinctive... north to the... Bruckner onramp. Lost them from there."

MacCray nodded. "We've got some sort of professional operation going on here, but we'll find them."

▼▲▼

"Omigod!" Bernadette cried. "We made the morning news. We're screwed! It's over!"

Davy frowned and grasped Hacker's wrist TV to twist it away from Bernadette and toward him. Hacker continued to stare at the computer screen before him, reviewing the telemetry from the test. Davy took the earphone from Bernadette and listened.

"—lidated Edison denies that methane buildup was responsible for the mysterious fire that roared through a South Bronx warehouse last night —"

He handed the earphone back to her. "They haven't got a clue. Hacker — are you ready to upload the flight plan to the ship's computers for launch simulations?"

"Not yet. I need more software checks before I feel confident tha—"

"Just get it done quickly," Crockett said, walking over to the spacecraft. Its aircraft aluminum skin was almost entirely in place. The scorched engine test stand sat beside the vehicle while workers carefully removed each tip engine for examination and possible repair, and a second team craned the rotor into position between the propellant tank section and the crew module, which hung above the cylinder in a tangled mesh of nylon straps and bungee cords — a makeshift crane system devised by some engineering majors.

He climbed the scaffolding and entered the crew cabin to sit in one of the reclining seats, the same hard and narrow design as the ones for the Shuttle, and he gazed up through the trapezoidal polycarbonate window. The module lowered only an inch in response to the weight increase, the bungee web spreading the load to the nylon straps, which in turn distributed the load to scores of attachment points on the building's perimeter. Above him hung the flimsy rafters of the factory roof. He imagined the ceiling torn away to expose the sky and he and the others rocketing, gyroing — hell, *helicoptering* — upward into it. They could do it. It was possible. Then a cold dread gripped him, an unexpected emotion. This scheme might result in the sudden and startling end of his life at only twenty-four.

Davy Crockett was only twenty-seven when the Creek War broke out, he thought, *and he certainly faced death there.* He put his hands behind his head and pondered his ancestor and the frontier life. *Even with gunfire in the streets, people my age don't face death as often as people did then. Certainly not from disease or animals or exposure, and probably not from violence, either. Maybe that's why we're all slowly going crazy. Maybe guys like Crush are just frustrated pioneers, who can't fight nature so they fight one another. Davy risked his life numerous times, and ultimately lost it at the Alamo. How could I do or risk any less?*

"Davy?"

He shifted in his seat to see Bernadette, wearing a tight black jumpsuit with neon-pink trim and hash marks on the sleeves, climb into the cockpit. The small, truncated cone descended another inch, oscillated a tad, then stabilized.

"Howdy," he muttered. Outside, the sound of non-stop work carried through the thin skin of the spacecraft. Occasionally they both felt a tremor as the workers moving the rotor into place bumped into the crew module.

"What's wrong?" She slid into the seat next to his and leaned on her side to gaze at him with eyes that — thanks to tinted contact lenses — looked smoky grey, soft and adoring. "Are you worried, too?"

"Worried?"

"About blowing up."

Davy nodded. "Yep. Or the blades breaking off or burning away or the oxygen venting or—"

"We're all worried," she said, reaching out to touch his arm. "That won't stop us, though. We've got a great team building this thing, right?"

Crockett nodded and grasped her hand.

"And," she said, lacing her soft fingers with his, "they're building this ship out of nothing but pride of workmanship and pure love of the adventure, not out of some corporate hive mentality or desire to pull overtime pay by screwing up and redoing things. This thing has a better chance of launching on time safely than anything NASA has ever put up."

"I know that. In the rational part of my mind." He still looked troubled. "There's always that little part that I suppress, the part that says we're just a bunch of kids trying to put on a Broadway show in a barn."

She pulled close to him. "We're not kids, for God's sake. We're in our mid-twenties. That's what grad school does to people. Makes them think they're still teenagers. The whole damn' system's set up to keep us in perpetual childhood so we'll look to big daddy government for guidance and control." She put his hand to her breast. "I became an adult when I was twelve. That's simple biology. But no one wants to admit that anyone under forty can think for herself and take her own risks. I say let's do it and show them all! Let's just blast off—"

His sudden kiss changed the subject.

CHAPTER 41

There is no such thing as 'luck.' There is only adequate or inadequate preparation to cope with a statistical universe.

— Robert A. Heinlein

23 July

Hillary Kaye had spent weeks in one small valley in Somalia, yet she still felt like a tourist on a world cruise. She and Joseph Lester knew full well that they sat upon the *fin de siecle* story of the millennium.

And they could not tell anyone. Not yet. Not for weeks or months.

They both made up for that lack of an outlet by interviewing everyone they could, from local Somalis on the construction crew, to Reis, Franck, and the other flight crew members, all the way up to Haley, and Donahue and ultimately — finally — to Marcus Grant.

Kaye amassed hundreds of hours of video on her Canon DigiVid II, plus thousands of digital still images with her 64-bit Hasselblad. She tried to convince Grant to permit her to take everything with her into orbit.

"And I'll also need digital editing equipment."

"Forget it," Grant said. "Too much mass."

"How will Joe and I edit the documentary?" she demanded to know.

Grant — who seemed almost perversely cheerful of late, smiled and said, "It's all digital. All you need up in orbit is editing software to work on one of our computers. We'll store everything in a high-density memory system on the ground, you access what you want by satellite link, edit it in orbit, transmit it wherever you want." He picked up one of the camera's optical discs. "You'll only get to take up a couple of these. You can downlink the images Earthside whenever one disc is full. She travels fastest who travels lightest."

Kaye photographed every phase of construction, and — when done — conducted a tour with Lester through each of the crew and payload sections of the pods. Because all of the workers — in exchange for lucrative wages — agreed to live on site until their contracts expired after launch, (though most still labored in ignorance of that ultimate event), she decided early on to test the limits of their freedom to snoop. She and Lester discovered that none existed.

"What you see can hardly be called proprietary," Grant told her. "Even if I thought it was possible to 'classify' technology, I wouldn't. I want everyone to know how easy it is to get into Space. I want *customers*. And your coverage — when it's released — will net me plenty. The only reason for our isolation right now is that I don't want anyone to stop us."

When he said that, he glanced toward the simulator in which Tammy Reis practiced.

Lester interrupted them. "Come on. I want to shoot some inventory being sealed up for loading."

Under an open-sided tent fifty feet square, workers fiddled with goods and packing containers as if trying to solve three-dimensional puzzles. The goal was to pack as much into each container as possible without crushing anything. Accomplishing this required the sort of mind that could think in terms of shape and volume. One young local emerged as the most adept and became the head of the department, issuing rapid-fire orders to fellow countrymen in crisp Somali and to others only slightly slower in English.

The number of items being loaded varied impressively. Kaye attempted to compose artistic shots of the goods as workers packed them away, and managed to capture a few good ones of the souvenirs Haley intended to be their first line of profit: thousands of small postcard-sized schematics of Space Station *Volnos*, to be stamped in orbit with the date of the establishment of the first private space station and signed by each of the flight crew; dime-sized .999 fine gold medallions minted in South Africa with miniature versions of the same schematic; a mission patch depicting a silver-threaded S. S. *Volnos* in the center between Earth in the lower left quadrant and the Moon in the upper right, with the Sun radiating gold threads from the upper left quadrant.

The money-making commemoratives interested her less, though, than the items the crew of *Volnos* included in their own personal preference packets. Each of the twenty crew members could bring fifty pounds of personal property not considered relevant to work or survival. A husband and wife team of dentist/veterinarian and welder/metallurgist — Harry and Deanna Jakes — took along holiday decorations, including some Christmas lights, because they wanted to enable their six-year-old daughter Clarissa to enjoy her childhood even though she would spend it in an alien environment. Clarissa, for her part, insisted on bringing fifty pounds of toys, justifying her decision to Hillary by noting that she could play with them until she outgrew them, then pass them on to the other children certain to be born in the coming years. Billy Red Eagle, eight years old and the only other child on the flight, packed a Wrist-Rocket slingshot and a sack of buckshot-sized pellets composed of a variety of metals and metallic oxides; he hoped to create his own colorful meteoric displays for friends on the ground, though he admitted having no idea of the orbital mechanics involved. His parents, David and Janet Red Eagle, (chemist/ceramics and ecosystems/hydroponics) brought Cherokee and Navajo artwork and memorabilia, as well as an extensive collection of music and literature on disc.

Chad Haley showed off the bookplates he planned to sign and number in orbit, then send back to Earth to be affixed to copies of the book he intended to write about the project.

Marcus Grant refused to bring anything of his own. "I'm taking the whole space station," he told Lester, "which is a lot more mass than anyone else is allowed!"

Tammy Reis's personal preference payload interested Kaye most of all, consisting only of two items. She dangled a Flying A keychain before the camera and said, "I'm bringing this. It was a gift from the pilot who gave me my first flight. Her name was Winnie Mae and I only met her once, but I'll never forget her."

"And what's in the makeup case?" Kaye asked. It had been an object of speculation since arriving from Brazil by a circuitous route, under the watchful eye of a personal courier. Even in the summer heat of Kismayu, the brushed-aluminum container — slightly wider than a lunch box — remained cool to the touch, now and then releasing a puff of ice-cold mist.

Reis merely said, "It's a deferred decision."

Melissa Lundy, who brought one set of The Ark Society's cryogenically stored collections of genetic material, made the connection. "I'll bet she's got a bun in the freezer," she whispered to Adrienne Oakwood, the paramedic and fitness expert. "She and I met at the liquid nitrogen tank refilling our containers."

"That explains the tabloid chatter about what happened on *Constitution*," Oakwood whispered back. "But why would she freeze the fetus and take it with her?"

Melissa shrugged. "Sentimental notion of human rights?"

Lester asked crew members what he considered the most important question of all: Why leave Earth? He heard a different answer from everyone, yet each was, in a certain way, profoundly similar.

Ta'Shawn Wilks, a twenty-two year-old electrical engineer/computer hacker from Chicago, told the reporter, "Living a good, decent life on this planet has become so difficult that risking mine for a chance to leave sounds like a good deal. My parents are honest, hard-working people who stayed together through thick and thin. Do you think anyone wanted to ask them how they persevered for thirty-one years in the ghetto? No. Yet every time somebody got popped in a drive-by, news folk crawled all over us to uncover every detail of the blood and the anguish. That hammered into a lot of us the message that only violence gets noticed. The other message — that quietly *building* a life takes hard work and dedication — suffocated in the attention given to the brutal *end* of a life."

"I had become a money pimp for the university medical center," Dr. Joan McLaughlin said. "I grew more and more adept at writing grant proposals than at actual research. It reached the point where I'd be on the verge of a discovery only to shift gears and follow another tangent into some other field the government decided to fund more intensely. Research should be rewarded based upon *results*, not upon flashy proposals. Mr. Grant offered me freedom from those harpies. He didn't promise me success, just a chance to be left alone to *work*."

For Lester, every answer to his question conveyed an entire life story, a summing up of years, even decades, of frustrated hopes and ambushed dreams. For one, though, the dream seemed never to have been stymied. Jon Franck spoke with no bitterness of his life, perhaps because he always knew that somehow this would happen.

"It's always been my dream to live in Space. I don't think you can trace it to some early childhood experience. Some people are just born with the outward urge. It's a chance wiring of the head, you know? It's not genetic, it's not upbringing, it's... the way the neurons happened to connect while the brain's growing. Some people have neurons connected just right for playing the piano. Some people have the setup to handle higher mathematics. I wound up with the sort of wiring that when I first saw a picture of men on the Moon, said, '*that's* where I'm going!' If I'd been wired differently, I might have been perfectly happy working in a fast food restaurant, or fixing cars, or being a reporter. Instead, I became a pilot, then an astronaut. Now I'm an emigrant to the stars."

Tammy Reis gave Lester her cover story: "NASA betrayed its supporters and the American people," she said mechanically. "There were warnings, but no one heeded them: the way they handled setbacks, always blaming their critics and demanding more funding; the way management showed more interest in expanding the number of people under their command — that's how their salary was calculated, you know — than in streamlining information flow; the way they used the average American's respect and admiration for astronauts as a means to cover up their waste and outright lies."

Her tone grew less measured as she spoke of her friends and compatriots. "*Challenger* broke up on the day I joined the astronaut corps. My first introduction to the agency was to watch the managers run around obsessed with deflecting any blame from themselves. Every bit of truth that leaked out damned them as bureaucrats more interested in prestige than in progress, more dedicated to their executive jets than to our spacecraft, more concerned with expanding their expense accounts than fixing the Shuttle."

Tears welled in her eyes. She no longer spoke the lines mentally rehearsed for weeks and weeks. Something rose up from deeper within her to tell its own tale. "They put astronauts into *garbage cans.* Heroes... stuffed into trash bags and hauled out by truck. And I stayed with them." Tammy's fist clenched upon her thigh. "I stayed on and fought for NASA and did their dirty work because I thought I could make it better. I thought I could fix it from inside. I thought their goal was good and noble and I was honorable in sticking with it."

Hillary handed the camera to Joe in order to put her arm around Tammy, who seemed unaware of the gesture, lost in her own confession.

"I stuck with it through the worst. I saw what they sank to, to keep their budget. Sucking up to Congress. To Woolsey. A billion-dollar joy ride for that..." She shook her head. "And he cuts our budget anyway."

Tammy looked down at the floor, still shaking her head. "They kept doing the same old thing and it finally blew up in their face. In our face. In everyone's face. Two thousand dead. Because of a goddamned parenthesis. That's how complex they made it; a single parenthesis missing and everyone dies."

"And you think," Lester ventured, "that Marcus Grant can do better?"

She laughed weakly and ran a hand through her obsidian hair. "Marcus Grant does not respect his enemy. He has a double dose of the same sort of hubris that brings down every mad genius."

"So he underestimates NASA?"

"He has NASA pegged," she said with a grim smile. "He underestimates, however, what an unforgiving adversary Space can be. We'll make it to orbit, but I don't think we'll survive there very long."

It took Lester a moment to digest what she implied. "If you think this project is... doomed," he asked, "why are you in it?"

Reis gazed at the massive space vessel. "Because to trade death for even a minute in Space is preferable to spending a life in bondage to small minds and venal souls."

CHAPTER 42

There are some who think that those who oppose the space programme will doom mankind to extinction, or at least savagery. Therefore, they believe stifling, suppressing — even killing — opponents is Good...

— Samuel Edward Konkin III

23 July

"Is my hair falling out?"

Donahue looked at Haley and shook her head. "No, but I do note some grey."

Haley snorted. "And Grant looks as if he's getting blonder. What's up today?" He peered over her shoulder at a manifest.

"We're loading medical supplies, hydroponics, construction equipment, solar cells, reflective Mylar, the reentry pods for manufactured goods, and the rifles, pistols and ammo."

"Weapons?" Joseph Lester asked, walking up to them with Hillary in tow, her camera's red light glowing as she recorded the conversation. "That's a new item on the manifest."

"Absolutely," Haley said. "I don't think anyone should venture into a new frontier unarmed. Of course, that'll be for each crew member to decide. They'll be available if we need them. And they make cheap reaction devices for emergency maneuvering."

Lester looked relieved. "That solves a minor problem I've been meaning to ask about. I brought along a matched pair of hunting pistols. You wouldn't believe what I had to go through to smuggle past all those damned customs people."

"Really? What caliber?"

The two men wandered off, lost in weapons reverie, leaving Hillary with camera on shoulder and Joscelyn with hands on hips.

"Boys and their toys," Kaye muttered.

Donahue smiled crookedly and said, "So what caliber *are* they?"

The other woman turned her camera on Joscelyn to ask, "How soon do you estimate until launch day?"

"Oh, come on, Hill. Give it a rest!"

"It's July Twenty-Third. News out of California puts Laurence Poubelle's Daedalus Project at two months to launch. Freespace Orbital had a fire on the pad and is delayed indefinitely. Neither the Europeans nor the Japanese seem interested in developing a manned spacecraft and NASA teeters on the verge of mothballing its entire remaining fleet except for *Atlantis*, which relocated to Vandenberg. And no one's heard anything from the Russian space program in months. So you could be the first — and biggest — if you could just beat Poubelle. Are you going to try?"

"Hill, does a reporter ever take 'I don't know' as an answer? We have a schedule and we're moving along in a timely fashion. We're ahead in some places and behind in others. For all the talk about how NASA is a bunch of bureaucratic screwups, I'm really acquiring a respect for what they went through. Even without layers of paperwork and pleading for funding, mounting an effort such as this is stunningly difficult. I'm responsible — everyone involved is responsible — for twenty lives, including yours and mine. Not just to survive liftoff in an untested prototype spaceship, but to live and work in an incredibly unforgiving environment."

"Are you ready," Kaye asked, "to die trying?"

Donahue ran a hand through her auburn locks. "No. I'll never be ready to die. I'm ready, though, to set aside my fear of death in order to risk something important, something—"

The explosions outside caused the entire building to rattle as if an earthquake had hit it.

"Mortars!" Haley shouted, rushing inside with Lester at his heels. "Hit the deck!"

▼ ▲ ▼

One of the Somali workers translated the local news for Grant and the others. They stood listening to the radio under the tent while others checked the ring of pods for damage.

"They are blaming Bantu terrorists for the attack. I do not think it was directed at us. We were merely caught in the crossfire."

"It seemed more like a combination warning shot and test of our defenses."

"In response to the civil strife," the translator added, "the UN has authorized United States aircraft carrier to cruise the coastline and patrol by jet."

"All right," Grant said, glancing toward Haley. "You and Jo-Don in my office. The rest of you, back to work!"

As he turned to go, Tammy grasped his arm and whispered, "Now do you think they're so disorganized?"

Grant smiled coldly. "They missed us, didn't they?"

"Maybe they have a plan."

Grant's smile warmed. "Maybe they're as ambivalent about their orders as you are."

▼ ▲ ▼

Steven Milton displayed no ambivalence about his annoyance at the miscommunication, but such screwups often happened when orders filtered down from the top. He knew what he wanted to occur, but — in order to establish plausible deniability — he could only speak to his subordinate in vague, nebulous terms. His subordinate, though cagey at interpreting his desires, could only relay her interpretation of his orders with similar circumlocution. By the time the section agent in Somalia interfaced with one of the many revolutionary groups NSA maintained through its web of funding, the message had inevitably grown garbled.

The botched mortar attack would have to do... for now.

His intercom buzzed. "Yes?" he said.

"Monty Barron is here, sir."

"Why?"

"He's got Detleffsen's report, sir."

"Send him in."

Barron strode in carrying the tan-covered report. Milton immediately noticed that the man looked less husky, as if he had dropped ten or twenty pounds. He did not appreciate the leaner, hungrier look of the man.

"Why are you delivering Detleffsen's report?" he asked.

Barron smiled cheerfully. With a toss that sent the inch-thick binder slamming onto Milton's desk, he said, "Detleffsen quit."

"What?"

Barron's smile widened. "His report is great. He's managed to uncover hints toward a dozen clandestine space efforts worldwide. Even a theft of SS-18 boosters in Russia. Some colonel killed a bunch of UN and GRU people and disappeared. It's great reading." He sat down in the chair in front of Milton's desk and put his hands behind his head. "It's also pretty subversive. I'm immune to it, because I've got my own little space flivver in the garage. Detleffsen, though, he's another story. You assigned him because of his intense interest in space programs worldwide."

Milton nodded. "He was an expert. So?"

Barron examined the back of his hand. His voice held a mocking tone of intense amusement. "He became an expert because he was a fanatic. And when he uncovered so many tantalizing clues..." Barron dangled the sentence just long enough to see an annoyed frown build on Milton's small head, then concluded, "...he took it upon himself to disappear. I have no doubt he's seeking out one of the groups alluded to there."

"Impossible."

"We're hemorrhaging, Steve." He relished the way Milton squirmed at the thought of losing his own people to such a diffuse and diverse foe. "You should read what's happening at NASA. Workers, technicians, scientists, even management. Quitting, moving, emptying bank accounts, selling homes, vanishing without a word. I'm absolutely certain some of them will make a break for it sometime before the year is out, both to beat the Interplanetary Treaty deadline and to win that half billion. We can't find them and fight them on the ground. Once they launch, though, they'll be out in the open. Space Command can track them. *Huntress* can bring them down. All I need is enough black money to speed things up. I can't guarantee that I can—"

"Not a cent, Monty! I've got people in the field doing good, hard work on the subnational question. There are bigger problems afoot, like the party conventions."

Barron rolled his eyes. "Oh yes, the quadrennial drop-everything-and-spy-on-your-opponent circle jerk." He rose from the chair and tapped at the report. "Read it, Steve. These are people who don't bother to vote in a booth. They're voting with rockets. And if President Crane sucks up your time between now and November on bugging offices and sabotaging the opposition, I guarantee that you'll come trotting to me in December with a list of subnationals you need downed and maybe by then it won't be so easy." He smiled, gave Milton a three-fingered salute, and strode out of the office.

Milton flipped through the report. He was proficient enough an analyst to realize the thorough job Detleffsen had done, and realist enough to know that the worst time to distract politicians from their primary duty of seeking re-election was a leap year. Votes were a drug they mainlined with singular obsession.

He sighed and punched at his phone. "Get me Accounts," he said in a defeated tone. He would give Barron just enough rope to hang himself if he was wrong — or lasso the subnationals if he was right.

CHAPTER 43

All men should try to learn before they die
what they are running from, and to, and why.
— James Thurber

5 August

Barry Gibbon stopped walking for fifteen seconds, long enough to check his pulse. *Twenty-eight,* he thought, *times four is one hundred-twelve.* He resumed his stride across Washington Square toward the NYU campus. He stepped over a bum who stared upward with glazed eyes. *We're all in the gutter, but still gazing at the stars.*

Gibbon pondered a problem. Not merely his own personal problem, but a problem for all humanity.

Dean Everett Stevens suspected that an equipment-theft ring existed, fencing stolen lab articles, machinery, and computers. At his behest, Gibbon inspected the partial list of missing goods. In it, he saw a pattern, and that pattern disturbed him.

Every group requires a leader, every people a ruler. Despite his vocal appeals to democracy, Barry Gibbon knew that great deeds required great visionaries. He ruled his own National Organisation of Space Supporters with strong fist, albeit a fist hidden in the rafters, clutching the crux of many a marionette — his chosen means of operation.

When students organized, it required a ringleader. And half a century in academia served to hone his judgment until he could target the perpetrator with a hunter's accuracy.

It had to be Crockett, he thought. His type fit the pattern: intelligent, restless, scornful of authority, a tinker, charismatic, handsome.

He stopped to wheeze.

Gibbon's multitude of activities created a strain on his health. Still astonishingly spry for a man of his age, he knew that he must pace himself, hence the occasional pulse checks. *An old man's habit!* he mentally chided, for a spinoff of NASA research encircled one of his coronary arteries, constantly monitoring his blood pressure, pulse, and blood-oxygen level. It had been developed by one of the many students he had steered from space medicine into geriatrics by pointing out that what we learn on Earth prolonging lives now can only help space travelers thirty years from now.

Tomorrow he would board a plane to Edwards Air Force base to plead with the commander not to encourage Laurence Poubelle's publicity-grabbing stunt. After the record-setting test flight, the commander — an ex-test pilot — seemed of the opinion that a civilian test-pilot had as much right to use Rogers Dry Lake as anyone from NASA. Also near the Edwards and Vandenberg sites lurked a far more significant threat: Freespace Orbital and that pest who refused to fade away — Gerald Cooper.

Cooper presented a much greater threat than the grandstanding Poubelle, though the billionaire appeared likely to orbit his little toy first. Cooper possessed the vision of a complete space launch system and — worse — an overall plan for what to do with it. This business with Leora Thane and tourists. For the past three decades, Gibbon's various organizations continually fielded queries from the idle rich asking when routine tours would be available. The money was out there to fund Cooper's enterprise, money that Gibbon could not coax into NOSS's coffers.

A contingency plan arose in Gibbon's mind: if against all efforts Cooper succeeded, then perhaps a fifty percent tax on the ticket price of flights would bring in revenue that would otherwise be wasted on such foolish indulgences. He smiled. He would propose that to his good friend Senator Woolsey.

First, though, the problem of Davy Crockett and his buckskin brigade.

▼ ▲ ▼

Crockett flopped, exhausted, into the chair opposite Gibbon in the professor's cramped office, a sure sign of something in the works.

"Mr. Crockett," he said, pressing his palms together in a calculated gesture of pleasure. "How nice that we can at last meet without the distractions of a seminar."

Crockett drawled up his Tennessee accent, "You didn't tell me why you wanted me here, but if it's about my attendance, I've—"

"Not at all, David, not at all." He gazed at the younger man for a moment, sizing him up now that they sat near each other. His thin tongue licked quickly at his lips before he spoke. With a smile that bespoke an expansive and all-embracing friendliness, he said, "I know we've exchanged a few heated words in the master-pupil context, but I believe that is due more to a clash of superior intellects than a conflict of values."

"We believe what we choose to," Crockett said flatly.

"Yes... And I was so intrigued by your, shall we say, firm opinions that I was impelled to look at your scholastic record. You must trust me when I say it astonished me."

"I'm a trusting sort."

Gibbon eyed him and for just a moment a shade of annoyance scrunched his eyebrows. Recovering, he said, "Despite your, um, *extracurricular* activities, your grades are impeccable. I note, however, that you seem to lack direction in your field of endeavor. You have not yet specialized."

"Maybe I've got catholic interests." He punctuated the sentence with a wide grin and reached for a cheroot.

Gibbon nearly objected, then mentally bit his tongue and proceeded while Crockett lit up. "You've exhibited an interest in the space program, even if only to denounce it. As you know, The National Organisation of Space Supporters is actively involved in directing and influencing national — and now international — space policy. I think your obvious talent for rallying teamwork could produce results if you became part of NOSS. I foresee a future for you at the highest levels in Washington or even New York. Certainly, with the loss of *Constitution* and the Space Center, there is a crying need to reinvent NASA—"

Crockett stood. "Thank goodness this is a bribe. I thought you were going to discuss my grades." He blew an exquisite smoke ring that sailed directly toward Gibbon's face, framing it like the circle around a bullseye. "I can't be drawn into serving those I oppose." He rose to leave.

"It's a chance to change things for the better. To bend the program toward goals you think it should pursue."

"The only thing that would get bent," Crockett said at the door, "is my own moral backbone. Find yourself another dupe. You've got quite a pool to pick from."

The door closed quietly behind him. Gibbon stared at the frosted pane set in it and pondered the problem. *Perhaps more student outreach is called for.* There would be time for that. Gibbon was a busy man, and the next item on his agenda he considered a higher priority: Freespace Orbital and its damned Starblazer. Picking up the latest copy of *The Private Space Journal* — a magazine he would never admit to reading and that he subscribed to under an assumed name — he skimmed a report on the improvements made to the design, along with a proposed launch date within the next few days. He smiled wanly. He had stopped such upstarts before, and he would again. Cooper, however, was so close that personal intervention was called for.

Gibbon looked forward to a trip to the Mojave desert. He preferred dry heat to the dreadful humidity gripping Manhattan this time of year.

7 August

The knock at the door startled Cooper. Nearly midnight, the airport lay still and dead but for the occasional aircraft landing or taking off every hour or so. He saved the notes he had been dictating to the computer and walked to the outer office. In light of what happened to Larry Poubelle, Cooper now kept a loaded Astra Constable .380 autopistol with him while working nights. And most days, too. Hand on the grip, he switched on the outside lights to see the incongruous form of Barry Gibbon standing in the glowing golden beam, surrounded by darkness.

Puzzled, he released his hold on the weapon and hurried to unlock the door.

"Dr. Gibbon?" His voice possessed more than curiosity; it held an edgy foreboding aggravated by overwork and undersleep.

"Gerald, my dear boy, everyone else is at Vandenberg for your rocket's test day after tomorrow. Why did you make it so hard for me to find you?" He glided through the doorway and into the inner office. Mystified, Cooper locked the door and followed him, rubbing meditatively at the three-day growth of stubble on his chin.

"You look like simple hell, my friend, certainly not like someone about—"

"I was doing some last minute design rechecks. It's quiet out..." He peered at Gibbon with intense curiosity. "Why are you here?"

Gibbon sat in front of Cooper's desk in a posture he calculated to be of the necessary humility to make the pitch work. "Gerald, you've worked hard and long on the Starblazer design, and I've been so impressed by your work — as you know — that I've twisted some arms at NASA via some long-time NOSS members. They're poised to move into the management positions opened by the crash and have agreed in principle to test the Starblazer concept for use in the Advanced Light Lifter Unmanned Rocket Experiment."

Cooper sat behind the desk and leaned forward on one elbow, resting his head on his fingertips. In the corner of his eye he could see that the computer was still recording his words, making both a digital sound recording and a word-to-text transcription. It also picked up Gibbon's conversation, but even though he knew it hogged memory, he was too tired to switch the program off. "You'll have to pardon me," he said. "I've gone for three days straight without sleep."

Good, thought Gibbon. *The perfect time for poor decisions.* He nodded his head with restrained sympathy.

"What makes you think," Cooper said levelly, "that I care what anyone at NASA does?"

"Gerald, they are offering to fund your research and put all of their influence behind you. This could make Starblazer the satellite launch system of the next millennium!"

Cooper straightened up and placed his palms on the desk. "It will be that. And more, without NASA. With Leora Thane's backing—"

"Why are you wasting time with that shrewish ticket-hawker? Why demean yourself hauling about shiploads of idle gawking tourists when the Agency has satellites and planetary probes sitting waiting for lau—"

"I *want* to haul tourists!" Cooper said angrily. "Gawkers and pointers and wide-eyed kids who leave fingerprints and nose marks on the windows! I want to lift up workers and miners and settlers with callused hands who'll risk everything they own, who'll risk their lives just for the chance to live in a new world and make it theirs. I want to cram every ship to the bulkheads with the restless, the dissatisfied, the eager. I want to help everyone who's ever itched with the emigrant's urge to make a new start. For that, I don't need any so-called help from the Agency, or from you. I was tempted once to jump through your hoops, and I won't bother again. I don't need NASA."

"Yes, you do." Something altered in Gibbon's expression and his tone. His wan, humble smile did not alter, and his voice held the same tone, yet something about both seemed harder, less willing to maintain any pretense of civilized conduct. "You need NASA to stay out of your way. You need NASA not to use its influence in the aerospace community or in the military. You need NASA to sign off on your launch Friday—"

"They already have."

"A middle-management employee, if I'm not mistaken." Gibbon shook his head. "Some members of the press might look at that as your taking advantage of confusion stemming from a major tragedy. It appears so, shall we say, ruthlessly exploitative that it is certain to trigger congressional inquiry."

Cooper fumbled for a packet of cigarettes. "So what you're saying"— his hands trembled from weariness — "is that I've got to play along or you'll make it tough to conduct my business."

Gibbon, keenly observing every nuance of Cooper's body language — the tic under his left eye, the shaky hand, the nervous, darting gaze — adjudged the rocket designer to be very near a breakdown.

Instead of following his original intent of seducing Cooper into compromise, Gibbon suddenly decided to go for the kill.

"No, my friend. Whether you play along or not, I will make it *impossible* for you to conduct your business. And I will thereby be saving your life. Here's why." He leaned back in the chair, humble no more, speaking with a cool arrogance. "You would be *dead,* Gerald. Dead, because the military does not want and has never wanted a civilian presence in space. You think you've received roadblocks from NASA? Wait until the Pentagon sets its sights on you. You don't honestly believe that they simply forgot to inform you about the valve-frosting problem at Vandenberg, do you?"

Cooper stared. "How did you—?"

A crooked smile crossed Gibbon's thin lips. "I don't operate in a vacuum. I have an interest in knowing what all you subnationals are up to. That's the term we use to describe your kind. A little condescending, but then you play a fairly meager role in space, don't you? Nobody in the satellite community takes you seriously, not when they know that the military and NASA legally control all launches in the country and that all it takes is a little sabotage to scatter your spacecraft across the sky."

"They wouldn't do that!" Then he remembered Colonel Lundy's warning: *Range Safety is very important to monitor.*

"My boy, they have been doing it for years. Even the big players have had their share of mysterious failures. Strings of bad luck in recent years. Time-tested designs failing one after another. People who founded their own rocket companies — even seemingly acceptable people such as former intelligence agents and ex-astronauts — have turned up dead of brain tumors, or in traffic accidents."

"There was a company that didn't encounter any of that. I remember."

Gibbon smiled. "That was an aberration. NASA agreed to help because they never expected a winged, horizontally launched booster to work. They learned from that mistake." He shook his head pitifully. "No, my boy, whatever successes your little private efforts have had have all been at the mercy of a system designed to keep you earthbound. The ruling elite — and believe me, I have access to the highest levels, those who tell presidents and prime ministers what to do — will not permit access to space to hordes of commoners. The world's political economy is based upon scarcity. Space travel would disrupt that completely. Imagine what would happen if someone captured just one asteroid and fractioned out the metals it held. Prices and markets would collapse everywhere. And you can imagine how the military feels about anyone other than they capturing the high ground. Rather than see that happen, they would much prefer to invade an equatorial country on some pretext and disrupt a company's efforts, or blow up a spacecraft in the boost phase, or assassinate financial backers and company founders."

Cooper said nothing for a moment, his hand resting under his jacket on the grip of his handgun. After a long moment, he released it; when he spoke, his voice rasped. "This is not my country anymore."

Gibbon snorted. "It never was. This is the real world. Learn the rules."

As if in a dream, Cooper stood. "I have to go to Vandenberg. I have a launch in..." He looked at his watch. "In T-minus thirty-one hours."

"I promise you, Gerald, it will not go up. Something will cause it to fail. And if you persist in the matter, well..." He gazed at Cooper with eyes no longer limpid, but glinting like flint knives. "You don't have any children, but they know you have a wife."

"Get out," Cooper said, then he shouted, "I was an idiot ever to trust you!"

Gibbon rose to say, in a courtly tone, "And I saw that you remained a *living* idiot. Now that you've gained your new-found wisdom, I can do nothing more to protect you." He walked out of the office, turned at the door to smile and wave, then climbed into the limousine parked unobtrusively on the side of the hangar.

"Wait here a moment," Gibbon said to his driver.

After a few minutes, Cooper stormed out of his office, locked up, and jumped into his Corvette. The engine roared into life.

"Follow him," Gibbon muttered.

▼▲▼

The hot August air blew through the Mojave night with the languid force of a determined woman. Not moving fast enough to be overpowering, it was still a factor to be reckoned with.

Cooper wrenched the steering wheel of his vintage 1961 Corvette Stingray to the left, compensating for the incessant wind that sought to push him off the narrow Soledad Canyon Road. It served as a shortcut from the Antelope Valley Freeway to the 126 near Magic Mountain. The 126 turned into the Santa Paula Freeway, which led to Pierpont Bay and the 101. From there, his 'vette would take him down the Cabrillo Highway from Las Cruces to Lompoc, then down the 246 into Vandenberg. The trip would take less than three hours, especially if he could crank it up to eighty miles per hour most of the way.

The Corvette's headlights now and then illuminated a Joshua tree, causing Cooper to flinch at the sudden appearance of what looked like a standing figure. Every jerk pushed the steering wheel a fraction to one side or another, creating a swerve that he fought to correct.

He tried to think, to put the rush of emotion aside and simply deal with facts. He knew the science behind space travel. He spent his life studying engineering, astrophysics, chemistry, calculus, fluid dynamics. He knew that launching rockets involved a relatively simple process. Why, then had so many different groups encountered so many problems gaining a toehold in Space? With the swiftness of a sword, Gibbon had cut through all of Cooper's naivity and handed him the answer like his heart on a skewer. And that answer mixed tears of anguish with a sweat of terror to blur his view of the thin grey ribbon weaving left and right endlessly before him. He glanced at the rear-view mirror to see headlights behind him in the distance. He realized now that Thom Brodsky's paranoia was not merely horribly correct, it expressed pitiable optimism compared to the truth. He touched at his jacket's inside left pocket for reassurance. There, next to the stale victory cigar given him months ago by Larry Poubelle, rested his warning to mankind.

The headlights gained on him. His foot jammed down on the accelerator. Seventy, eighty, eighty-five, ninety. Swerve left, veer right. The smell of desert-dry earth choked his nostrils. Gravel flung from his tire treads knocked and rang against fiberglass and steel with the sound of bullets. Even above the roar of the Corvette's engine, Cooper's heart pounded in his rib cage like a trapped animal.

He thundered westward over the knife's edge of pavement, roaring past the town of Honby. The starry night sky battled with the full Moon for supremacy and lost. Even the Moon, though, faded in the lights that blazed down the road.

Cooper's breath raced. He slammed the accelerator all the way to the floor. Like a rocket, the Stingray surged forward. His arms ached to keep the wheel centered. Desert insects exploded against the windshield like meteorites.

The speeding man risked one more frantic glance into the rear view mirror. It proved to be his last voluntary act.

The Corvette screamed off the ribbon of earth and against the canyon wall. Momentum tossed it up the side and into the air.

Spiraling in space for an instant, Gerry Cooper's last vision was of the Moon — fat, white, and round — spinning madly out of his reach forever.

CHAPTER 44

Test pilots have a gruff saying which they like to use sometimes when they see a buddy going out to wring out a new airplane. 'Go blow up,' you tell him. It sounds cruel, but not to the other test pilot. He knows he may blow up anyway, and you're just using it as a little joke to help him relax. It usually works. On the morning when Al Shepard was going, and I was with him all the time, I had it in the back of my mind to say this to Al — just as he went up the elevator to crawl into the capsule. I knew he would have laughed, and it might have helped chase away the butterflies. But when the time came, I had a few butterflies myself. I couldn't say it.

— Virgil I. Grissom
We Seven

8 August

The four helicopters — one from the sheriff's department, one from Edwards AFB, and two from Los Angeles news outlets — continued to circle in an orderly fashion around the twisted remains of the Corvette. Early morning light glinted red as blood off the tortured metal and shredded Fiberglas.

Sherry Cooper, arriving with Thom Brodsky at the wheel of the company van, stared in mute shock at the remains of the car and at the yellow tarp covering the body a few dozen feet away.

The deputies were expecting her. One of them — a grizzled veteran of desert patrol — signaled for the van to stop. Thom set the brake and ran around to help Sherry step down into the culvert.

With few words, the deputy led Sherry over to the tarp. Brodsky held an arm around her as she identified her husband for the medical examiner.

"What we have here," the deputy said to Brodsky over the whine of the helicopters, "is a case of a high speed vehicle leaving the road at about a hundred-five. Mr. Cooper wasn't wearing his seat belt and was thrown clear but that didn't save him. This would have happened either way, I'm afraid."

Brodsky nodded. Sherry stood a few feet away, unsteady in the calm morning air, staring at the tarp and the shape described beneath it.

"Mrs. Cooper?" The medical examiner stepped up to her.

"Could you tell me what might be on this disk?" He held in his hand an evidence bag containing an optical computer disk and a fat, broken cigar.

She took it from him to examine, then shrugged listlessly. "Could have anything on it. We use them for ship design, for launch software, for manuals, journals, everything." She felt its lightness, knew the density of information it could hold. "We might need it for the launch tomorrow. May I keep it?"

"Not just yet, Mrs.—"

"Hank?" A husky deputy who was already sweating in the morning heat ran up to the medical examiner.

"Yes?"

"That second set of tracks? We found where they stopped. Ten yards beyond where the 'vette left the road. Then they make a U-turn and peel out."

Thom immediately said, "What tracks?"

The deputy said, "Long baseline car, wide track. American tires."

Sherry choked backed tears. "You think he was run off the road?"

The deputy shook his head. "No ma'am. But he was being followed, from the looks of it."

"I'll need to keep that disk, Mrs. Cooper," the medical examiner said.

"May I copy it in the van?"

He nodded agreement and Thom took her back to the van, where she slid the disk into the computer that Gerry had installed in the rear for on-site design changes. While it copied, she clicked the cursor on the file marked HEAR ME SHERRY.

Her eyes widened and she gasped as a tightness seized her chest upon hearing the digital recording of her husband's last words.

"Sherry my love, I hope you hear this in the event that anything happens to me. No time to explain. Everything Barry Gibbon just told me about tomorrow's flight is on this disk. Can't risk phoning you. Don't trust anyone but Thom and watch the range safety officer. *"I love you."*

She looked up at Thom, who peered over her shoulder as she erased — unretrieveably — the file from the original disk. "Gibbon."

"Gibbon killed him?"

She shook her head. "Gibbon told him the truth. The truth killed him."

The medical examiner knocked on the van's back door. "Mrs. Cooper?"

"Yes?"

He opened the door to say, "Did your husband own a gun? An Astra Constable three-eighty?" He held up another evidence bag with a dust-coated pistol inside. "We found this a few yards from the... from Mr. Cooper."

She nodded. "He bought several over the last few years. Here." She handed him the original disk. "It's the company's fax list. Nothing vital, but he would have wanted it for issuing a press release tomorrow if all went well."

The doctor accepted the disk.

"Are we free to go now?" Sherry asked coolly. "I have to make funeral arrangements."

"Yes, Mrs. Cooper. Thank you for your help. And I'm sorry." He eased the door shut.

She glanced outside the van toward the crash scene. "Let's get to Vandenberg."

"You're going through with the launch?"

She nodded. "Gerry had this dream of being a space pioneer. It was wild and romantic and in reality took years of hard, mundane work. He wanted to build new worlds on the Moon and in Space. How can I abandon him now? My frontier women ancestors rode the westward migration in covered wagons. Sometimes their men died on the wagon trail, but they pressed on. I can't do any less than that." She stared levelly at Brodsky. "You're going to help me."

He nodded. "I know."

▼ ▲ ▼

First, she pushed back the launch one week, but not for the reason anyone suspected. As the days passed, the guards and the launch pad personnel at Vandenberg grew accustomed to her coming and going at all permissible hours. With Brodsky's instruction, she grew fluent in all the necessary terminology of a rocket launch. Having worked closely with her husband, she already knew and understood the science, but those final few days of cramming allowed her the chance to learn more of what she needed to pull off her plan.

The pair ran launch simulations at the pad and further practice sessions at her hotel room in Casmalia. Brodsky doubted the chances of success and said so more than once.

"Can you think," she told him during their rehearsal, "of any other way to guarantee *Aurora*'s safety short of hauling it off of military land and building our own launch site? We're committed to using Vandenberg if only because we've reached the point where we can't afford to change plans."

"Can we afford to be shot?"

She dismissed the possibility with a wave of her hand. "Won't happen. GSN will be conducting a live feed to news bureaus around the world. Killing us would raise too many nasty questions, especially since this" — she held up a computer disk — "will be running onboard."

She gazed at him quietly and he saw in her eyes a steel-edged determination, tempered in the fire of her personal tragedy, that would risk disgrace and death to fulfill her husband's last and only dream.

9 August

If Larry Poubelle had a dream, it was that his mechanical arm would work flawlessly throughout the entire flight. RF insulation wrapped around it like a woolen sleeve. He tested it inside the cockpit with all instruments on and transmitting and the glitch failed to reappear.

He and Chemar ran hundreds of simulations of the proposed flight until they learned to handle every foreseeable contingency. The 747 mothership crew also worked in their own simulator, connected to the *Nomad* simulator, so that coordinated practice flights ran in real time. The crew's minds and muscles stored every step of the flight from launch at Mojave to landing at Edwards Air Force Base.

Poubelle grinned with delight every time he flew the simulator out of high-key over Edwards. Despite the best efforts of Senator Woolsey, the base commander granted permission to land on the dry lake bed. The billionaire discovered that he and the general shared a common trait: both had left a body part in Southeast Asia — the general, his right leg up to the thigh. They spent a good hour swapping cigars and war stories and showing off the abilities of their respective prosthetics. The general showed him a bizarre memento: the skeleton of his severed leg from the knee down, which an acid-stoned medic had boiled, picked clean, and presented to him as a souvenir of his stay. The general had mounted it on a plaque in his office with the slogan "*Fortes Fortuna Juvat*" engraved below it.

After a few rounds traded of stories about the peccadilloes of national politicians, the general offered Poubelle the use of the same strip of dirt used by shuttle orbiters for their landings. "Hell," he said, puffing on one of Poubelle's cigar, "I know that NASA won't be using it for years, and I doubt that *Atlantis* will launch out of Vandenberg any sooner."

With that approval in hand, Poubelle prepared to announce *Nomad*'s launch date. When he heard about Cooper's death, however, he visited the nearby hangar and found only a skeleton crew. Nearly everyone followed the Starblazer to Vandenberg, nursing *Aurora* through her final few days before her unmanned test flight.

"There's a widow who knows how to grieve," Chemar said as they walked back to the Daedalus hangar.

"You'd do that for me, wouldn't you?" Poubelle asked her.

She smiled inscrutably. "Before or after I put on my dancing shoes?"

▼ ▲ ▼

The announcement came that afternoon, in front of the assembled crew and volunteers plus a sizable turnout of newspeople. At least a dozen news teams arrived, including broadcast and satellite networks, local TV, and some newspapers. Many came to Mojave to cover the mysterious death of the lesser-known rocketman and welcomed the opportunity to form a companion piece with Poubelle's press conference.

Poubelle stood in front of *Nomad*'s blunt nose with D'Asaro at his side, she wearing the now-world-renowned flight suit (as seen in publicity photos and on the October page of the Daedalus Project Calendar). He made certain that he waved with his arm extended forward slightly for the benefit of the several 3-D HDTV cameras in the crowd.

"I'd like to take this opportunity," he said, "to thank our hard-working flight crew and volunteer team who have dedicated themselves these many months to preparing for this exciting adventure. And all of you out there who contributed to the Daedalus Project, here is the result." He patted the carbon-carbon nose ball of the spaceplane and said, "I'd also like to acknowledge the inadvertent inspiration given to this effort by Senator Woolsey and by the United Nations. Here is America's answer to the Interplanetary Treaty and to those who desire to extend their idea of one world government into Space. I, and the millions who support us, know that Space is too vast — hell, *Earth* is too vast — to be ruled by even the boldest imperialist, let alone the consensus-chasers in New York. I—"

A subtle elbow to his ribs served as Chemar's "shift rhetoric now!" signal.

"I therefore would like to announce that the maiden flight of *Nomad* will occur on September twenty-first, the last full day of summer and the birthday of H. G. Wells, which I think is entirely appropriate. We'll launch at dawn, orbit for a full twenty-four hours, then land at Edwards Air Force base on the Twenty-Second. Since no one else has announced a manned flight before then, I think my half-billion is going to stay where it belongs." He patted his thigh pocket. "Don't worry, though, since — in memory of our fallen colleague — I am endowing a Gerald Cooper School of Free Space Science and Philosophy at the University of Southern California, effective this fall semester."

Chemar stared at him. It was another impulsive act on his part, entirely unmentioned up to that instant. She wagered that even USC did not know about this.

"With this flight and that endowment, I throw down the gauntlet at the Interplanetary Treaty and UNITO!"

▼ ▲ ▼

Watching the live satellite feed in his Senate office, the elder Ludlow Woolsey smiled and said, "If you want to throw down the gauntlet, prepare to run the gantlet."

▼ ▲ ▼

At the same moment in Kismayu — under cover of darkness — Chad Haley directed the movement of tanker trucks marked as "fuel oil," containing (in actuality) liquid oxygen and liquid hydrogen. The local government officials, pleased to see such an advanced housing project in their nation, accepted with gracious equanimity the bribes that permitted the tanks to arrive without inspection.

Likewise for the crate marked "Lighting Fixtures" that really held something quite different.

"Stand back, everyone," Grant told the onlooking graveyard-shift workers. "This is going to be great!" He opened a side of the coffin-sized crate to withdraw a control box. In response to his manipulations, out stepped a machine that looked like a globe atop a cylinder sprouting six spidery legs; the legs, tucked in for travel, extended to a more stable position and walked it three legs at a time toward the toroid.

"Have to have a robot on a space station," Grant said in response to Tammy Reis's frown, maneuvering the machine via the control box. "It'll play well on the news and bring us a fortune in ancillary merchandising."

Tammy broke into the first unforced laugh she had experienced on her spy mission. She realized with sudden surprise and shame that was is her first genuine laughter in years. There was something *right* about these people, about this mission. Not just Paul and his rediscovered enthusiasm, but in every technician, engineer, and worker who lived, breathed, and ate Space. Some of the older ones, long retired from NASA, told her that this recalled the agency's very beginnings: immense vision, rampant optimism, utter dedication, and total faith.

Yet everything she *knew* about the contemporary world told her that this was wrong, that Paul and the entire project faced doom. Even if it *was* a feasible path to Space, it would not be permitted by those who ruled the skies.

Chad Haley — unaware of Reis's fears, or of her mission — certainly thought otherwise. He spent twenty-hour days reviewing every aspect of the project with anyone he could corral. Though flabbergasted by the mind-numbing size of the project, he had no doubt that they could pull it off if only he invested just a little more effort.

He gazed at Grant, boyishly maneuvering the robot into the crane to be lifted to the cargo area of Pod Eight, overseeing every aspect of construction in the hangers, taking brief times-out to run what remained of his world affairs via encrypted, scrambled computer uplinks. The man exuded total confidence in the scheme, even when faced with the complexities of running an enterprise as massive as any legitimate business.

There he went with that word again, *legitimate*. As much as he understood the theory and practice of counter-economics and parallel markets, he still held the impression — indoctrinated since childhood, and only forcibly altered by rigorously logical examination — that secrecy in and of itself denoted unsavory activity and that a secret business, hidden from the eyes of governments, could not possibly grow so huge without detection. Haley eyed the five of the sixteen giant intersecting spheres in his field of view and marveled.

He had watched with interest the way in which Grant and Donahue used government's paperwork as misdirection, either showing movement on paper while goods remained in one place or showing on paper that goods stood still while they actually traveled halfway around the world. It was nothing new or innovative on Grant's part — oil companies did the same thing to circumvent boycotts, embargoes, tariffs, and taxes. Manufacturers of all stripes — above-ground, perfectly "legitimate" producers of cars, computers, clothing, food — all engaged in various degrees of subterfuge in order to conduct their business and provide their wares in a world in which everything that was not mandatory was forbidden.

Marcus Grant offered a way out of all that as an unintended consequence of his quest for greater profits.

Only if the flying doughnut worked, though. Will it orbit? Will the thousands of tiny combustion chambers provide enough thrust to carry the structure upward? Will the welds hold? Will they pass Max-Q without breaking apart or encountering overpowering drag?

Haley constantly sought to assure himself that the computer simulations indicated the possibility — the slimmest chance — of achieving orbit with little or no fuel to spare. Once there, though, what?

Grant grew vague and evasive on that point, usually pointing to the publicity they would receive, sales of the memorabilia, the half-billion-dollar prize that Larry Poubelle *might* hand them, and some demonstrations of zero-G manufacturing on a somewhat larger scale than NASA had ever deigned to engage in. Most of the items on the manifest, though, consisted of material for research and experiments, not outright mass-scale manufacturing. Yet several large crates bore the non-descriptive designation "Misc. Machinery." What did Grant really plan to do with a space station and a score of crew members once they made it up there?

On that subject, Marcus Grant remained uncharacteristically mute.

▼ ▲ ▼

"Did you hear that?" Bernadette shouted. "Poubelle's going to launch in six weeks!"

"And Gerry Cooper's dead!" Sam added.

Davy put down the computer equipment and walked over to the TV set in shock. "What?"

"Cooper crashed in the desert last night. Poubelle says he's going to launch on September Twenty-First and turn over the prize money to USC."

Crockett turned his gaze toward the spacecraft in the center of the warehouse. It stood, nearly completed, like a great, gleaming white monument to the spirit of the man. The cross made by its Iconel-wrapped graphite fiber blades added to the image.

"He won't see his rocket go up," was all Davy said; something in his throat choked off any further words.

Bernadette put an arm around his waist.

"I don't think I'd feel this bad," he said, "if I'd just learned my own dad had died."

"Everyone else will see it go up, though," she said. "His widow plans to run a test flight of the rocket next week. Unmanned. What better legacy could he have left the world?"

"And we'll send this one," Friedman added, joining the pair. "This one is *our* legacy."

Crockett looked at them both. In his eyes glowed a sudden inspiration. "They might slip someone aboard *Aurora*, though. They could do it with that design. We've got to jump the gun. We've got to launch next week, too. But *before* they do! Sam" — he seized Friedman's arm — "what about the fuel?"

"The kerosene's arriving today. We can have the LOX delivered anytime."

Davy shifted his grip to Bernadette. "Crew?"

"We're all psyched and primed."

"Everyone listen up!" Crockett shouted. "There's been a slight change of plans. We launch this baby next week! I want final closeout no later than next Friday for a Saturday morning launch. You've done a great job so far and we can wrap this up in nine days!"

A cheer rose up from the crowd. For more than a year they labored in secrecy, scrounged equipment, begged money, and invested every spare minute of their own time and their parents' college funds in building the rocket, and now the culmination of their efforts approached. The cheer simmered down, followed by a profound silence as one by one they realized that their lives would soon change and change radically. Not just because their work on the spacecopter would cease, but because launching it would change history.

"Whoa!" Penny Giannini said when it hit her. "Mind blast!"

"All right!" Crockett said with a wave of his arm that set his the rawhide fringe on his sleeve whipping. "Let's git crackin'!"

The final few days passed in a storm of activity inside the factory. The hours blurred by for Bernadette, soldering iron in hand, installing the last of the electronics. Hacker uploaded the navigational information to the onboard computers.

Seemingly everyone at NYU pitched in, though this may have been an optical illusion caused by the hundred or so students actually involved trying to be in dozens of places at once. Burly male athletes sat at sewing machines under Natasha's guidance, stitching mission patches on the space suits and making final alterations. A Home Ec student cooked meals that a chem grad freeze-dried in his lab equipment and sealed in vacuum-pack bags.

Crockett oversaw the loading of supplies, using 3-D packing instructions devised by a math student who worked in fourth- and fifth-dimensional virtual space to guarantee that every piece of equipment fit into the lockers with minimal voids.

Natasha — also responsible for life-support — checked out the lithium hydroxide atmosphere scrubber using a gas spectrometer "borrowed" (as was nearly everything) from the university. Penny welded and welded and welded until — after five straight days and nights of the accelerated schedule — her lithe muscular arms felt just about ready to fall off.

13 August

Someone installed a large red digital clock next to the spacecopter. It read T-minus four days, seven hours, twenty-three minutes.

Crockett sat inside the spacecraft in the middle of the three seats installed side-by-side, in the style of the old Apollo command module, flipping through the pages of the original Davy Crockett's *Autobiography*. Bernadette sat a few inches away from him in her own narrow, uncushioned acceleration seat to his left. They both took the brief break to accustom themselves to the feel of the spacecraft. Their simulator had consisted of a computer at a desk, so their time in the cockpit was not quite idle time, nor was their conversation mere idle chatter.

"Suppose we make it to orbit," he said, book down and hands behind his head. "Suppose we win the prize money. Then what?"

"Who knows?" she said, arms folded. Her hair, dyed jet black once again and clipped into a coquettish French gamin style for the flight, matched her tight black Spandex pressure suit. She wore it constantly, claiming a need to get used to its fit. Davy suspected that she simply liked the way it looked on her. So did he, for that matter. "I thought we were going into Space just to prove it could be done. Just for the fun. The challenge. The fame. The money."

"We have to do more." Crockett's eyes gazed out the window to see beyond the rickety warehouse ceiling toward distant vistas. "We orbit Earth for a day and come back and what are we? Heroes? Or just crazy kids pinwheeling in and out of Space on a joyride? It's illegal to launch a spacecraft without a permit from the Department of Transportation. I looked it up. We'll be fugitives if they don't shoot us down first. We have to do more than just make the trip. We have to make ourselves immune to prosecution. Making jackasses of the world's only superpower isn't likely to help our case. We not only have to show how cheap and easy it is to use a rotorocket to achieve orbit, we have to be the ones to prove that there's a *reason* to go into Space. That we're not just screwballs. We've got to show that there's something in Space that Earth hasn't got—"

"Hard vacuum? Deadly solar winds? Meteors?"

"—something that will make ordinary people want to build spacecopters and *Nomad*s and *Aurora*s to join us up there. Something that makes what we do so unambiguously momentous that we'd *have* to be hailed as heroes when we return."

Bernadette gazed at him intently. "Why return at all?"

Crockett paused for a long moment. "What?"

"Why do we have to return to Earth? What if we could live in Space indefinitely? Why don't we just stay there?"

"You mean live there for the rest of our lives?"

She nodded, her jewelry chiming emphatically, pulling a dog-eared hard copy of *The Orbital Settlers' Guide* from the bag stowed beneath her seat. "This thing offers all sorts of ideas. We could convert the ship into a mini space station once we're in orbit. Power it with the solar panels and settle there. We could sell TV transmissions to networks on Earth showing our progress. No one could afford to come out just to arrest us or anything — and even if they tried, the public would be outraged. Attacking peaceful settlers and so on."

Listening to her, Crockett realized that Bernadette considered herself more than merely a co-conspirator in a hugely elaborate college prank. She shared with him a vision as overarching as his own.

There was reality to consider, though. "This thing's not built for long term potential. We *have* to come back in a few days. It's reusable, though. If there were a space station in orbit that we could service..." He shook his head. "We need fame right now. Notoriety. We've got to do this in such a way that anyone who denounces us also attacks American values. Maybe if we—"

"How," she asked, "could anyone denounce the great-great-great-great grandnephew of Davy Crockett for trying to tame a new wilderness?" Her eyes widened as she glanced at the book Davy was holding. "Play on that. That's our protection! You're not crazy. You're Davy Crockett — *King of the High Frontier*!"

A deep voice echoed inside the cabin. "And I thought you were building something innocuous, such as a drug lab."

Professor Barry Gibbon climbed unsteadily headfirst into the cockpit, staring at the pair with an unfathomable gaze. He seemed haggard and worn, showing every minute of his eighty-plus years. Something even darker lurked behind his eyes. Something, Bernadette judged, that lay beyond displeasure, beyond anger, beyond even hatred.

"I'd almost believe you could pull this madness off. Too bad you'll never know."

Bernadette began to speak but was cut off by Gibbon. "No, little lady. This is a bigger problem than you can imagine. Everett Stevens told me about his suspicions. I listened to some of the scuttlebutt among the grad students and asked around until I found someone timid enough to squeal."

"We can do it, Dr. Gibb—"

"Shut your mouth, boy! I offered you a chance to join up with the real program, but you thought you could steal your way to the stars. That won't happen. That will never happen. We're locking your kind out. If the American experience has taught us anything, it's that humans will ruin every ecosystem they invade, and I won't see you damaging the ecology of outer space with unregulated little tinpot vessels that you cobble togeth—"

"Space has no ecosystem," Crockett said, "except what we bring with us."

"Sure! Bring your air and your water, then start filling the universe up with your excrement and your babies and your mine tailings and your haphazard cities! It won't happen! I've spent my life keeping your kind earthbound, and I won't — *ow!*"

Gibbon fell suddenly quiet, silenced in mid-tirade by a sharp pain in his backside. Turning around to discover its cause, he saw Sam Friedman standing behind him in the hatchway, plunging the contents of a hypodermic syringe into Gibbon's wizened rump.

"I thought we'd probably need a full medical kit on the ship," Sam said, hefting a shaving-kit-sized bag onto the flight deck past Gibbon's wobbling legs. Smiling at the professor, he said, "Sleep well, doc."

Gibbon's eyelids drooped. "And to your list of crimes you may add kidna—"

"Great," Crockett said, seizing the professor's limp body before it fell out of the capsule. "What do we do with him?"

"Keep him out of circulation for a few days," Friedman said, heaving Gibbon out to the scaffolding with Davy's assistance. "No one will miss him. Have the guys release him after we've launched."

"No." Crockett stared at Gibbon's still form. "He'd have *them* arrested after he's released. I've got a better idea."

▼ ▲ ▼

Barry Gibbon awakened in a dorm room on a mattress set indecorously upon the floor and gazed drowsily around. The window and door had been bricked shut to hold him in complete isolation. The room contained only the mattress, a lamp, a TV set the size of a pack of cigarettes, a week's worth of water and freeze-dried food, a compact camp toilet lacking its legs, and a telephone handset.

Enduring a pounding headache from the drug, he groggily sat up to reach for the phone. A note taped to the handset read:

Dear Prof. Gibbon:

No one but we three know that you're in here. No one else is responsible. This phone will be activated at the outside junction box by a relay triggered at radio confirmation of our launch. You may call for help then. Enjoy your rest and watch the news for disproof of your theory.

Hugs & Kisses,
Bernadette, Sam, and Davy.

Gibbon tried the phone. It was indeed dead.

"Hello!" he screamed at the top of his lungs. *"Help!"* With what strength he could muster, he pounded at the walls, ceiling, and floor. No one responded. He listened for any sounds of outside activity. Many of the rooms stood empty during summer.

"And I'm sure," Gibbon hollered, "you've picked one surrounded by empty rooms on all six sides!"

He patted at his jacket. Of course, they had deprived him of his celphone. And he knew nothing about electronics that might have helped him convert the phone or the TV into some sort of miraculous transmitter. Rather than devoting years to studying the intricacies of human technology, he had spent his entire life learning how to short-circuit the human soul. He sat on the mattress and switched on the TV, determined not to spend any time pondering the wisdom of his career choice.

CHAPTER 45

Success is not the result of spontaneous combustion. You must set yourself on fire.

— Reggie Leach

17 August

It was a good day to leave Earth. The pre-dawn hour witnessed a scramble of activity inside and outside the factory. Outside, Crush 69 and his gang, dressed in their finest fringed black leather and carrying spanking-clean Uzis and Glocks in addition to their standard-issue baseball bats and knives, gently but firmly rousted street people and other squatters from all the rathole abandoned buildings within a five block radius. Video-communications majors set up a circle of rooftop cameras to capture the liftoff and fiddled with the satellite antenna intended to receive the spacecopter's telemetry and other transmissions.

Inside the factory, scores of students rushed purposefully this way and that. One crew used a cherry-picker crane filched from Con-Ed to dismantle the sagging roof of the building, careful lest the slightest piece of debris fall and damage the spaceship or its forty-foot-wide rotary wings. A ground crew hauled off the inflammable detritus, giving the fueling crew wide berth as they pumped jet-fuel grade kerosene and liquid oxygen into the waiting tanks from a succession of small tanker trucks. A thick blanket of cryogenic fog socked in much of the building like something out of a Victorian murder mystery.

▼ ▲ ▼

Fire Department Inspector MacCray did not usually spend his nights roaming through the South Bronx. Tonight, though — and for the past week — he played the detective, wandering the dark avenues and darker alleyways in plain clothes. So far, he had come up with nothing. Then he noticed two trucks lumbering down a deserted street. Two tanker trucks, both a little singed, one with a license plate missing.

Backtracking the trucks to the factory building, MacCray quietly observed the uncommon activity. Light streamed out of cracks in the painted windows. Young people came and went, obviously in a purposeful rush.

At first he presumed it to be a methamphetamine lab or some sort of gang headquarters. On silent feet he crept up to a rear window to peer inside. His angle of view encompassed the entire three-story-tall rotorocket and the remaining trucks that fueled it. The ceiling crew, having removed the beams and roofing material in a wide swath around the rocket, proceeded to cut and drop the remainder with less precision. Workers on the ground gave the activity wide berth.

No other equipment remained inside the factory but the giant white cylinder, cross, and cone of the spacecraft and the tankers. All the tools and machinery had been surreptitiously returned to their rightful owners. MacCray saw only an incredibly huge structure filling up with explosive liquids. After a moment of utter incomprehension, he raced away from the building to search for a phone.

▼▲▼

Bernadette and Sam — dressed in their skin-hugging black Spandex spacesuits — strode through the crowd of students. Each outfit bore custom-colored trim and hash marks on the arms, Bernadette's a retropunk neon pink, Sam's silver. One of the ground crew handed them a pair of armbands emblazoned with the official mission patch for the flight: planet Earth wearing a coonskin cap at a rakish angle, surrounded by the legend "Space or Bust!"

A mist of cold air flowed down the side of the fueling spacecraft over them. The greasy odor of kerosene mixed with the cool, fresh-air scent of oxygen in a combination that thrilled them with the threat of imminent danger. Smoke evacuators — courtesy of the NYU fire-suppression unit — dissipated the explosive mix to the outside air. A riot of colors in motion blurred the factory floor as students rushed about setting up the sacrificial cameras that would be incinerated after capturing the first few seconds of engine performance.

The two spacefarers approached the base of the gantry ladder. A war whoop drew their attention upward. After being repeated a few times, the rest of the crowd took notice and fell silent. The only sound was the creak and hiss of fuel tanks filling.

William David Crockett IV stood on the scaffolding at the hatch overhead, his ebon spacesuit and brassy trim barely visible beneath fringed buckskin pants and shirt. Atop his head sat his coonskin cap and from his belt hung his Bowie knife, powder horn, and necessaries pouch. He cradled in his arm an ancient flintlock rifle, flint carefully wrapped in Mylar to prevent an unintended spark.

"Thanks to all of *you*," he shouted toward the ground crew and cameras, "this spacecopter will be the first privately-built crewed vessel to achieve orbit. We kept a lot of you in the dark, working away from the factory, until tonight, but now that you're watching at the dorms and over there at Washington Heights, we've provided plenty of beer to make up for that."

Over the cheers, he shouted down to the video team. "Cameras ready?"

"Check!" came the hollered answer.

He turned his gaze to the tank crew. "Fuel?"

"Fully loaded!" one yelled, disconnecting the frost-encrusted hose with gloved hands.

The other two members of the flight crew climbed up the gantry ladder to join Davy.

"This is it, gang," he said quietly to his companions. "This is the moment we've been looking forward to and dreading. And either by coincidence, subconscious design, or divine intervention, today just happens to be the original Davy Crockett's birthday." He glanced at Friedman. "Swami Samesh, do you have a proper invocation?"

"God..." he said, gazing down twenty feet to the factory floor hidden in mist. "Please don't let us screw up."

Davy clapped him on the back. "Well said! I think you speak for us all. Climb aboard!"

▼ ▲ ▼

Outside, only a few blocks away, Inspector MacCray reached a phone booth. As with most phones in the South Bronx, this one had been completely vandalized. He spied another down the block. Running toward it, he heard footsteps from an alley.

"Well, well, well, oh me brother," Crush 69 said, flanked by two of his droogs from the SBX-13 gang. "Another stray. And this one doesn't look native."

▼ ▲ ▼

Graffiti covered one side of the spacecraft, applied by various students using a can of day-glo orange spray paint to sign their massive work of art. Bernadette — at the top of the gantry with the others — used the can to scrawl *Crockett's Rocket* next to the hatchway.

"I've been trying to avoid that little bit of poetry for the entire project," Davy said with a sneering mock grimace. Bernadette merely smiled warmly and presented him with a long, slow good-luck kiss. While they embraced, Sam elbowing past the pair to squeeze into his seat, Davy's hand reached blindly up to grasp a sheet of paper taped over the hatch. Removing it with a loud rip, he revealed the ship's true name in brilliant letters of gold and red. Breaking free from their liplock, Crockett turned her around to show her the name.

"*Bodacious Bernadette*?" she squeaked with a yelp of joy, nearly breaking his ribs with a hug and almost pitching him backward off the gantry when she kissed him a second, deeper time.

Crockett turned to face the grinning crowds below. "Everyone clear the area. Head back to NYU. Launch command is set up in the Physics dorm." He paused, one arm around Bernadette's waist, then raised his rifle and bellowed "Spaceward, *Ho!*"

The two followed Friedman inside to take their seats and strap in. They locked on their Air Force surplus helmets but left the visors up.

"Here goes somethin'," Davy said, switching on the flight computer. A synthetic female voice — adapted from Natasha's — began to read through the preflight checklist.

"T-minus forty-five minutes," it said. *"Seal crew cabin."*

"Check!" Bernadette confirmed. Sam pressed a key to signal the computer to move on.

"Attach and tighten five-point crew harnesses."

Each crew member in turn confirmed that they were indeed strapped in.

"Lower cabin pressure to eight PSI and flush with oxygen."

"Check," Bernadette again confirmed.

"You all went to the bathroom, I trust?"

"Hey! Who put that in?" Friedman shouted.

Davy Crockett snickered wickedly.

▼ ▲ ▼

MacCray — mugged and missing his pants — stumbled out of the alley toward another phone, discovered that it worked, and realized that he no longer possessed any change.

After a moment or two of angry rage, he realized that he could punch 911 for free. His finger jabbed at the buttons. The line connected. And encountered a busy signal.

▼ ▲ ▼

The dwindling crowd of students raced away from the factory in cars, vans, and on foot. The last tanker trucks rolled out. All that remained in the hollowed-out, cavernous building was the spacecopter, the engine-igniting pyrotechnics, and a trio of video cameras hooked to a small transmitter.

Back at the NYU physics dorm, scores of students and post-grads monitored the scene. Hacker and a dozen others watched the computers, Natasha stayed in radio contact with the spacecraft, a couple broadcast on ham radios telling their distant friends to "wait and see — you'll know what it was when it happens!" All in all, their tone sounded crisp and professional, yet nearly breathless with anticipation.

On the flight deck, the three finished their computerized checklist. Crockett's displayed guidance and navigation information and also tracked the airframe's structural integrity and dynamic stress. Friedman's showed the condition and functioning of the engines, fuel delivery, and electrical systems powering the torque-compensating anti-rotation motors. Bernadette kept her eye on the life support systems and tapped into NORAD's orbital debris management system to avoid encounters with any potentially dangerous space clutter.

The sixty-second countdown commenced. Prompted by the computer, Davy flipped a switch to send a piercing alarm wailing through the deserted section of the borough.

Almost deserted, but for MacCray — finally through to the police — shouting frantically over the sound of the alarm.

"Do you hear that?" he screamed, ducking and covering in his phone booth with a finger in one ear and the receiver pressed firmly against the other. "Get fire equipment over here, scramble the HazMat team, call out SWAT, and *alert the Air Force!*"

▼ ▲ ▼

"Oh God," Sam said as he watched the numbers descending on the computer screen along with a bewildering cascade of information on all aspects of the vehicle. "This is it!"

Bernadette turned to Davy. "I love you." She grasped his hand.

The computerized countdown cued up Holzt's "Mars" theme from *The Planets* on a portable CD player duct-taped to the bottom of the control panel.

"T-minus ten, nine, eight, seven, six — ignition sequence start — four..."

The cabin rumbled as fuel began to flow from the tanks into the rotor-blade feed-tubes and outward to the engine pods. A low, steady hiss commenced and grew louder as each of the four rotor-tip engines blazed simultaneously into life. The rotor began to spin, an eerie hum like a deep-throated bumblebee filling the air, reverberating throughout the empty city block. The computer adjusted the individual thrusts 20,000 times a second to compensate for torque and other flight variables. Lift increasing every second as the huge propeller sped up, the vessel rose up from the ground at a rate slower than the thrust of a true rocket but breathtakingly swifter than any other aircraft. An invisible, firm force pressed the three into their seats. Crockett noted the liftoff by observing the very edge of visibility at the bottom of his viewing port. Beyond the spinning circle of fire created by the tip engines, he saw movement.

"We've cleared the roof line!" he shouted. "I can see the Bronx!"

Two police helicopters racing toward the factory focused their spotlights on the cloud of billowing steam eerily illuminated by a fire within its depths.

Suddenly, a white, blunt conical shape erupted from the cloud as if thrust upward by a mighty hand. Out of the swirling cauldron of fire and mist whirled a flaming wheel that spun like a titan's fireworks. The choppers veered away from the hellish scene, their pilots reacting almost reflexively, their attention riveted on the brilliant meteor pinwheeling upward from the squalor like a halo of fire setting the entire night ablaze.

A video camera on a roof five blocks away caught the blastoff for the benefit of the students back at NYU. They watched the screen for a moment, then scrambled to windows for a real look. The few dedicated ones who sat by their monitors longed to experience the moment but stuck to their posts determined to lift the bird all the way to orbit.

The hiss and whir inside the spacecraft grew deafening as the rockets pushed the rotor to maximum lifting speed. The pressure of acceleration tapered off at their maximum rate of climb. As the engines burned fuel, however, the mass of the ship decreased, which meant they pulled two gravities and more.

After two minutes during which they shot upward aerodynamically to 45,000 feet, Crockett said, "Here comes the hard part — Mach One and transition to pure rocket power!"

"Roger, Davy," Natasha's voice came over the airwaves. *"We've all got our fingers crossed down here."*

The spacecopter, high enough in the troposphere so that the rotor was nearly useless, now also encountered minimal drag. The rotor sped up, which increased the centrifugal pump rate, throttling the engines up to full speed. The aerodynamic surfaces of the rotor blades had very little air to bite, so when the tips went supersonic — which on a helicopter would have meant control degradation, noise, and decreased efficiency — the entire spacecraft did, too.

The ship creaked, groaned, whirred, and clanged.

"Max-Q!" Crockett yelled. They passed through the most dangerous part of the flight, where aerodynamic stress on the ship increased to its greatest. If the ship held together, they would make it into Space. If not, they would never know.

"Still alive," Friedman said into his microphone. "Still alive."

The interior of the spacecraft shook violently passing through Max-Q. A cabinet popped open, spilling a load of freeze-dried food toward the rear of the cabin. Everyone gripped their arm rests as they rode the wildest thrill ride in the solar system.

Suddenly, the vibrations smoothed out and they experienced another increase in gees.

"Past Max-Q!" Penny yelled. "Eleven miles altitude, eight downrange. Four thousand FPS."

"Cabin pressure at eight PSI," Bernadette said. "Jalopy's holding together."

"Still alive," Sam repeated into his microphone. "Still alive."

"Roger that," Carla radioed to the voyagers. *"We appreciate it. Stay that way."*

The three spacefarers gritted their teeth under the ever-increasing force of the acceleration. As they rose higher and higher, as the air thinned out, and as they lost tons of mass in consumed fuel, the rockets imparted greater and greater acceleration per pound of thrust. The onboard computer altered the rotorocket's trajectory to an optimized pitch profile for insertion into a 100 nautical mile orbit.

At three gees for over seven minutes, they felt like human pancakes. Friedman nearly hyperventilated from anxiety, though Bernadette took it well; in fact, she experienced an odd tingle that spread through her body as the pressure and buffeting increased.

Crockett merely grinned. The acceleration dragged his grin down into a bizarre grimace, almost like a madman's.

▼ ▲ ▼

Closer to Earth, the police helicopters rattled in the corkscrewing wake of the ship's exhaust. The helical sound wave from the launch roared out in all directions, but even a few miles away the rotorocket could only be seen and not heard.

All of New York and New Jersey gazed up at this new star rising comet-like into the night sky. From Manhattan to Riverdale, from Newark to Hempstead, more and more people interrupted their individual lives to turn their heads up and see the gently whispering circle of light and smoke and wonder in the night.

Everett Stevens, walking across campus, saw and heard the liftoff. He also heard cheers from the dorm rooms. His worst fears more than realized, he rushed into the crowded building, shoving and wedging through the knots of students, a black thunderbolt of pure anger. On the third floor, he rammed through the clot of onlookers to burst in upon a makeshift mission control buzzing with activity, some of it beer-related, but most of it cool, sober, and efficacious.

"What in the name of Hell is going on here!" he bellowed. Then he saw hanging on one wall a rendition of the mission patch everyone now openly wore on armbands.

"Oh, my God," he uttered in a mixture of awe and horror. Someone laughed and stuck a beer can in his hand. Without taking his eyes off the video screen, he chugged a nerve-calming jolt of brew.

"I can still see it!" someone yelled at the window.

"This is the voice of NYU mission control," said Carla Pulaski, one of Bernadette's friends from the nuclear magnetic resonance lab. Her accent was pure unalloyed Brooklyn, but with a crisp efficiency that reflected how seriously she took being the voice now beamed via satellite uplink to the entire world. "After a successful launch from the South Bronx, a privately-owned and operated spacecraft is headed for Low Earth Orbit."

▼▲▼

A thousand miles away, Air Force General Harry Dorn elbowed his way into the NORAD-Space Command monitor room, followed by a dozen assistants of various lesser ranks. A man of average height and girth, he displayed a bulldog expression that glowered fiercely as he stared at a video screen in furious amazement. The screen — two stories tall, taking up half the wall of the huge room — showed a 3-D digital map of New York, canted to a nearly horizontal angle, with a red ascent trajectory rising out over the Atlantic. Tension was high.

"Any idea what it is?" Dorn demanded of the captain at his side.

"Radio reports intercepted from a couple police choppers in the vicinity mark it as a rocket of some sort. Ascent phase too slow for any missile design in the database, yet too fast for anything else except a jet climbing on afterburners. It's just shooting up like an elevator. Wait a sec." Capt. Lee pressed the earphone closer to his head. "Signal coming through RCA SatCom Eleven." He listened while others scrambled to make sense of the paucity of data.

"Trajectory and acceleration yield a mass of about twenty-five tons," someone said over the intercom. "Payload can't be more than a ton unless they're using composites, which the radar image suggests might be the—"

Capt. Lee interrupted with, "Verbal telemetry. Woman's voice." He gazed up at the screen with an expression of total disbelief. "NYU mission control?"

"Stay on it, Captain," Dorn said sharply, then barked an order to a lieutenant. "Get me that jackass at the NSA — Milton!"

"Online, sir," Lieutenant Kent said.

"Dorn here, Steve. What the hell are you doing out there?" He frowned upon hearing Milton's reply, his folds of flesh redoubling beyond bulldog wrinkles into something resembling a Shar Pei.

"Well," Dorn cut in, "the trajectory tells *us* that it's likely to go into orbit, *Mister* Milton, *sir*. So why don't you get on that little red phone and call Beijing before they get into a snit about this and decide to lob one in *our* direction!"

He turned toward Capt. Lee. "Bases on alert?"

"Yessir. DefCon Three."

"Downrange tracking?"

"From Arecibo to Farnborough, locked on."

"Any jets we can scramble for a looksee?"

Capt. Lee shook his head. "They got the jump on us."

▼ ▲ ▼

Back at the dorm, Dean Stevens seized a telephone and reached up to punch a number. No dial tone. Following the cord to the wall, he saw the plug lying on the floor, replaced by cords leading to the room's computer modems. Spying a girl on another phone, he pushed his way across the crowded room.

"Isn't it wild?" she gushed to a friend on the other end. As Stevens snatched the handset from her fingers, she shouted "Okay, 'bye, talk to you tomor—"

He punched 911. And got a busy signal. Before he could repunch, a student leaned on the cradle, saying "Sorry, Mr. Stevens. Incoming calls only tonight."

Stevens grasped the student's shirt, pulled him close, and hollered "You people are insane! Do you know in what danger you've put the city, yourselves, and the rest of the world?"

The other man shrugged. "They blasted off safely. The only risk now is to crew. Where's your spirit of adventure?"

"Where's your common sense?" Stevens asked. "What if some other country thinks we've launched a missile at them?"

Another student — shorter than the one in Stevens's hands and sporting more pens in his shirt pocket — said, "Their trajectory puts them into orbit before they cross any hostile nations. And we're broadcasting our peaceful intentions!"

Stevens looked around him, released the student, and shook his head. "You're all suspended," he muttered under the din before leaving the dorm in quest of another phone. "As if you cared."

▼ ▲ ▼

"Being tracked by NORAD," Bernadette calmly shouted to the others. "They've got our trajectory."

Davy added, "We're right on the beam to orbit — let 'em try and catch us!"

"We're using fuel faster than projected," Friedman said, "but still within parameters. Good APU's. All systems normal," he added, a look of continuing relief in his face.

The ship, still under acceleration, grew quieter despite the roar of the engines.

"We're beyond the atmosphere!" Bernadette cried in near spiritual ecstasy. "We made it!"

"We're halfway to anywhere," Davy Crockett said, putting his hands behind his head and feeling the exhilaration of the spacecraft's motion while Bernadette kept watch on the orbital plots on her screen.

The sky beyond the thick Lexan windows, long darkened from the orange-grey of a New York night, cleared even more as they left the stratosphere and entered the sharp, crisp, star-scattered obsidian hue of Space. The weight of acceleration grew less bothersome with each passing moment. It would soon depart them in an epiphany of release.

▼ ▲ ▼

"Sir." Lt. Kent handed the telephone to Gen. Dorn. Dorn identified himself, listened for a moment, then thanked the caller.

"That was the South Bronx Fire Department. It seems their arson investigator came upon a God-damned *rocket factory* in an abandoned building. Saw a bunch of God-damned *college kids* doing a pre-launch."

"Kids?" Capt. Lee asked, swiveling in his chair to stare up at the general.

Dorn stepped toward the huge monitor screen, glaring with troubled old eyes at the trajectory plot. "Yes, captain. We've got a God-damned *homebuilt* in orbit."

▼ ▲ ▼

Gibbon first gained knowledge of the launch when he felt more than heard it. The dorm room in which he had been sealed for three days began to vibrate, causing the wadded-up, empty bags of horrendously oily potato chips and other reprehensible post-adolescent food to rattle and buzz along the linoleum floor.

The telephone rang in the professor's prison. Picking it up anxiously, he heard Natasha's synthesized computer voice say, *"Launch is in progress. You are no longer a threat to NYU security. Your telephone is now enabled. Have a nice day."*

He punched 911 madly and waited for the call to connect. Seconds later, he slammed the handset down. "Damned busy signal!"

He next called Steven James Milton, Jr.

"Damn you, my dear," he said acidly to the woman on the other end. "If I had not been held captive for the last several days I would have received this week's courtesy code. 'Anthony Trollope' was last week's damned password and ought to be fresh enough to justify connecting me to Frederick, Chairman Milton's assistant who happens to be a member of my space organization and rather vindictive toward idiot subordinates!"

The call transferred instantaneously.

"Steven!" Gibbon's voice cracked. "It's three NYU postgrads in an single-stage orbital helicopter — I know it's all geek to you, but listen — cheap aircraft aluminum, not hardened against attack. It can be brought down with a LEAP or any variety of kinetic-kill device. Failing that, I say we unleash Montgomery Barron."

He snorted at Milton's stonewalling. "Did you think you could keep something like *Stark Fist* secret from *me,* Steven? Well, then you underestimate both my interest in subnationals and my influence in Washington."

He switched the handset off to regain the dial tone and punched in the number of campus security. That number, too, was busy. With a muffled curse, he entered the number of one of his graduate assistants.

"Cliff? Yes, it's me. I've been held prisoner in a dorm for three days! I don't know which one! The one that's bricked in! I know about the rocket! Stop staring at it like a slack-jawed bushman and come find me!"

He rung off and quickly punched in his home phone number, hoping that Evangeline had not gone into hysteria while he sat incommunicado. On top of everything else, he did not want to deal with an insane sister.

The phone rang once, then emitted an ear-piercing squeal.

"Hello?" he shouted. "Hello!"

The squeal stopped, followed by a click and his sister's level voice.

"Barrett? Is that you?"

"What in hell is going on there, Angie? Is someone messing with the computer modem?"

"Why, yes, Barrett. I am."

Gibbon felt an odd sinking sensation. Something in her tone had changed from the meek, self-effacing voice he knew. A cold malice tinged her speech.

"What the hell do you know about computers!"

"You'd be surprised at what I picked up the last few years while you gallivanted around for weeks at a time. I learned quite a bit about computers, wandering through The Net."

"Listen!" A growing panic seized him, a terror deepened by his sister's disturbing metamorphosis. "I've been held captive," he nearly whined. "I've got to get to the White House. Call—"

"I'm not calling anyone for you, dear brother. I've watched for too long your dreadful hypocrisy. Did you think I couldn't see what you were doing, what evil you enjoyed? I'm your sister, Barrett. I know you better than anyone. I know the lives you've destroyed. I put two and two together regarding Gerald Cooper." Her voice remained level, never rising, as if reciting facts from a history book. *"You always thought I was a dimwit because of my reticence. Still waters run deep, brother, deeper than you think."*

"Stop blathering and listen to—"

"Have you heard of a book called The Orbital Settlers' Guide*?"*

"No." Bile edged up from his gut to burn his throat.

"Oh, it's very popular on The Net. I've been posting it everywhere, and e-mailing it to every online member of NOSS. Not unlike self-publishing. Barrett, dear, do you know what a meme is?"

"Meme? That idiotic concept of infectious ideas?"

"Very good, brother. While you ignored me and harried me like a fishwife, I've unleashed a meme-plague upon UNITO."

Gibbon lost all trace of restraint. "You think a goddamned book *you* wrote could undo years—"

"Ideas matter, Barrett. You know that better than any. Why else have you battled to suppress the idea of Free Space? I've read everything you've ever written. I know you intimately. I wrote the Guide *to*

undercut every argument you've ever made. The djinn's out of the bottle, my brother. Witness the magic!"

▼ ▲ ▼

MacCray stood uneasily. Covered with wet soot and dirt, he stared up at the tiny pinpoint of flame heading nearly straight up and angling over the Atlantic. The knocked-down factory burned wanly as distant sirens grew louder. The two police helicopters returned to the area, circling around the blaze with spotlights illuminating the scene in a twisting cyclone of dust, smoke, and steam. News choppers joined in, some circling with the police birds, some hovering at a distance.

A larger helicopter — a UH-1H painted in military olive drab — arrived with the deep, stomach-thumping rumble of a transport, hovering low enough to disgorge a half-dozen lines from which troops descended like silkworms. They dispersed to secure the area, one of them taking a bead on MacCray, who had no pants to show, let alone his badge. Embarrassed and furious, MacCray raised his arms in surrender and shouted above the din, "I'm Chief Arson Investigator MacCray with the Bronx Fire Department! I can make a full report to your commanding officer!"

The private merely pointed his M-16 at the man in underwear, saying, "Please stay where you are, sir, until the area's secured."

MacCray kept his arms in the air and quietly fumed.

▼ ▲ ▼

Onboard *Bodacious Bernadette*, the computer voice announced that engine shutdown would occur in five seconds.

"Four, three, two, one, shutdown."

The engines cut off with an abrupt series of popping sounds, followed by the whir of the rotor bearings spinning freely. Though nearly frictionless, they would impart enough resistance to slow — probably over a period of hours — the rotation of the aerodynamically unimpeded blades. The weight crushing the spacefarers instantly ceased.

"Free fall!" Crockett shouted with a joyous war-whoop. "We're in orbit!"

Bernadette quickly checked her screen to confirm. "We sure are!"

"I think I'm going to be sick." Friedman turned five shades of green from the weightless sensation.

"Told you to go to Coney Island more often!" Crockett pulled a blister pack of pills from his spacesuit and floated it over to Friedman.

Sam frantically punched out a Bonine motion sickness tablet and chewed. Crockett turned to Bernadette. "Anyone else?"

For an instant she hesitated pridefully, then looked at Friedman, turned toward the buckskin medic and thrust out her gloved hand.

"What now?" she asked after washing the pill down with water from one of the drinking spigots. A droplet of clear liquid broke loose and drifted away from her in an undulating globule. She laughed.

Crockett pulled a tissue from his pocket and touched it against the blob. It attached to the paper like an attacking amoeba and instantly vanished into the fibers via capillary action.

"It's no time for dumb astronaut tricks, I can tell you that." Crockett called up a screen on his monitor. "We've probably put the fear of God in everyone down there. They may not believe Carla's ground-based transmission. By now, the Chinese may think the US is messing with fractional orbiting bomb systems again. Publicity will be our best defense against itchy trigger fingers."

Crockett flipped a few switches and the image of Carla Pulaski appeared. She sat at her post in flight control, where the party was going strong.

"Davy! I've got Davy, *guys!"* She turned back to the screen. *"We've gotten through to GSN and they just agreed to an exclusive patch. Ready to feed?"*

"Ready." Crockett tried to smooth his wayward hair. His cheekbones felt strange and his sinuses throbbed with an unfamiliar pressure. He stared seriously at the cigarette-sized videocam mounted over his control panel.

"People of Earth... *Greetings!*"

He broke into a wide grin. "I've always wanted to say that." Toning the grin down to a hearty, boyish smile, he said, "My name's Davy Crockett. I and two others have departed Earth in a spacecraft of our own construction. Our intentions are peaceful, and the rights to our story are available for a negotiable sum."

▼ ▲ ▼

Crockett's image overwhelmed the center NORAD screen.

"We hereby claim the half-billion dollar prize offered by the Experimental Spacecraft Association, deliverable upon our safe landing twenty-four hours from now."

The equally massive right-hand screen mapped the flight, now indicating the ship's orbital track. On the left screen appeared a growing number of small picture fields depicting news services worldwide as each picked up the story.

Gen. Dorn spoke on a red telephone handset. "Yes, Mr. President. The transmission really is emanating from Low Earth Orbit. This does not appear to be a hoax. You saw what it did to New York." After a long pause, he said, "No sir, we don't anticipate any military threat... well, that's NASA's problem, if I might say." He paused and mentally counted to ten. "No sir, we have no way of getting them down short of sending up a shuttle to retrieve them or shooting them out of the sky." Another pause to listen and fume. "Then I suggest, sir, that you speak to your campaign spin doctors to divine which response will win you more votes!" He slammed the handset back into its red cradle.

CHAPTER 46

An oppressed people are authorized whenever they can to rise and break their fetters.

— **Henry Clay**

18 August

It was the afternoon of the next day in Somalia, thanks to the international dateline, and someone's fist pounded on the door to Chad Haley's office. Haley stared blankly at weight-and-balance screens for Pod Sixteen, the last one to be closed out for launch preparedness.

Through the door burst Jon Franck. His intense agitation showed plainly.

"Chad!" he said breathlessly. "Somebody's launched!"

Haley sprang to his feet to demand, "Who? Where?"

"I saw it on TV in the break room. Launched from New York City!"

"New York?" Haley switched his computer screen to the menu, said, "Give me TV, satellite, GSN, news report, keyword 'rocket.' " The computer complied and the news popped up on the screen. As the story played, he buzzed Grant and Donahue.

"Meet the winners," he said as the other two raced into the office.

Grant watched only long enough to see the videotape of the liftoff.

"What the hell is that?" Joscelyn exclaimed. "A flying beanie-prop?"

"Jo-Don," Grant said, heading for the door. "Keep track of the fed's response. Tap into NORAD when you can. Chad — I want final inspections completed within twelve hours, everything secured for launch."

"What?"

He paused at the doorway long enough to say, "That launch just put every government on notice that they're not the only ones who can get a toehold in Space. If we don't launch now while they're still reeling from the surprise, they'll be ready for us." He raised a fist. "It's a one-two punch. And unless I've gravely underestimated him, Larry Poubelle will be aiming to launch today, too."

▼ ▲ ▼

Larry Poubelle lay in bed when the news arrived. Not asleep, though. Chemar groaned with annoyance as one of the arms wrapped tightly around her naked back warbled gently.

"If that thing has a fax shoot out of it I'll kill you," she whispered in his ear.

Without interrupting the rhythm of their lovemaking, he pressed a button on his arm and said sharply, "What?"

"Rocket launch from the South Bronx," said one of Poubelle's secretaries assigned full-time to monitoring news broadcasts and military communications. "Three college kids achieved orbit twenty minutes ago."

"Scramble the ground crew for launch prep." He switched off the phone and pulled Chemar closer to him. "Seems I may have to come up with five hundred million in real money."

"That's not all you have to come up with," she breathed into his ear.

"Vixen."

"I mean that you promised USC a bundle, too."

At a neuromuscular command, his robotic arm tingled ever so pleasantly with a mild galvanic charge. He traced a fingertip down her jawline, down her graceful sternocleidomastoid neck muscle, down to her breasts; he outlined her dark areolae, eliciting a gasp of electrified shock from her.

"I won't have any problem coming up with anything," he said, reaching lower still.

"Apparently not," she moaned. "*Mon dieu...!*"

▼ ▲ ▼

Colonel Vladimir Tuchapski had just finished lunch when he saw news of the liftoff. He performed a quick estimate of the spacecraft's orbital inclination, enough to realize that it posed no threat of rendezvous with *Mir*. The game, however, had just changed radically. The Americans were not as complacent as he had hoped.

Nor was GRU.

Hiding the missiles in the vast Russian deserts had been easy at first, but one could not hide from surveillance satellites forever. The purported high resolution of the Russian Soyuz Karta did not worry him as much as the known resolution of the sophisticated sensors onboard American and European craft such as Landsat-7 and SPOT. His only hope was that GRU would not be able to move through the financial and bureaucratic maze attached to enlisting foreign cooperation in tracking down the renegade colonel and his cumbersome pilferage.

He had taken the actions necessary to procure the missiles before their destruction by INERT or their seizure by this new monster, UNITO. He lacked any detailed plan beyond that. Stranded in the less-than-bucolic Rubcovsk, with his missiles erected inside a grain elevator, he now awaited word from Brajnikoff of their efforts to acquire the precious cargo vital to their reactivation of the Russian space station.

And to wait while watching the ultimate insult — *school children* orbiting a homemade space helicopter! He admired them, though, for hiding right under the noses of the ruling class. How daring to build a rocket in one of the most populous cities on Earth! Who would notice their comings and goings until too late?

Tuchapski lacked not for skepticism, however. His military mind immediately doubted the official version broadcast on the airwaves. Regardless, they announced the launch for some reason, if only as a backdoor to unraveling the Interplanetary Treaty.

"Colonel Tuchapski!" Capt. Brajnikoff crisply spoke upon entering the farmhouse that served as their secret headquarters. The younger man wore drab peasant clothing of coarse wool. He hefted tattered canvas shopping bags crammed full with anomalously sophisticated electronic devices.

"Sergei," the colonel said with greater relief than he dared admit. "Tell me you have it!"

The bags thumped victoriously to the kitchen table, joining the television set and ancient laptop computer. "We have latest navigation system software from Taiwan, Korean digital camera back, American artificial intelligence neural net for environmental control, and a jar of year-old beluga caviar to celebrate."

"Oxygen tanks?"

"Denkov is loading."

"Food other than caviar?"

Brajnikoff's smile faded. "Very little freeze-dried. Mostly canned borscht and vegetables. Some meat. Six month's supply at best."

Tuchapski sighed. "Canned is heavy. We'll have to leave behind some water bottles to compensate." He pointed toward the TV. "We'll not be alone."

Sergei stared wordlessly at the screen.

"GRU," Tuchapski said, "may be watching for us to launch now, rather than to export weapons to some foreign power. We may have to outrace our own anti-missile defenses."

"When do we launch?"

"Sooner than we expected, I fear."

▼ ▲ ▼

Sherry Cooper arose early that morning, working on final plans for *Aurora*'s launch. Delayed yet again from a Friday liftoff to the coming Monday, she took the opportunity to review her plans. Thom Brodsky pounded on the motel room door, startling her.

"They did it!" He whipped past her to switch on the TV.

Placing her hand on her sternum, she took a worried breath and said "Did what?"

"Orbited an SSTO! Listen."

The live broadcast from space showed a young man — his face high-cheeked and ruddy from the effects of weightlessness — dressed in raccoon-fur hat that refused to remain on his head and a buckskin jacket the fringes of which swayed this way and that like seaweed as he addressed the planet's billions.

"Our mission is peaceful. We only mean to orbit the Earth for a day, then return to a safe, powered landing. Our spacecopter was built entirely with volunteer labor, though we forthrightly admit that some of the components were... involuntarily lent to us by New York University and several other sources. And we lifted the orbital helicopter design entirely from other sources."

"Amazing," she whispered. "Space on a shoestring. Gerry would have been proud to know them."

Thom put an arm around her shoulder as she stood and stared at the screen, then at him. "Are you still prepared to go through with our plan?"

Brodsky nodded. He did not voice his main reason for agreeing to go through with her plan: that any fate they suffered as a result could be no worse than the price Gerry Cooper paid for his dreams.

"And Leora?"

He pursed his lips, then said, "I think she is one seriously disturbed travel agent, so I guess that means she's with us."

CHAPTER 47

The only thing that saves us from the bureaucracy is its inefficiency.

— Eugene McCarthy

17 August

"I don't have my damned White House pass with me," Barry Gibbon said through clenched teeth to the impassive guard at the rear gate to the presidential palace. "I have been held captive for three days and I have had no time to go to Langley to retrieve it. I'm the President's space science advisor and I need to be in on the decisions being made about that whirligig in orbit. I know who's behind it and Crane needs me, so get Steve Milton on the line and he'll authorize a temporary pass!"

"All such requests must go through the chief of staff," the guard said, then added coolly, "Sir."

Gibbon leaned close enough to the young woman that the corrupt stench of a long-neglected body hit her nostrils. "Then call!"

▼ ▲ ▼

In the White House Situation Room, NSA head Milton waited impatiently for President Nolan Crane to get off the phone. Other factions of the National Security Council listened in or conducted their own phone conversations with other hot spots. Crane — a vital, handsome man in his late forties — expressed constant irritation at the intrusive event diverting everyone's attention from the ongoing presidential campaign. His election advisors sat closer to him at the cluttered table than either the chairman of Joint Chiefs or Milton.

"And I don't care what it costs to redo the spot," President Crane said in a voice that would have been considered a petulant whine in anyone of lesser power. "I want to tie in with this future stuff." He listened, then said with extreme agitation, "You know what I mean. *Future stuff!*"

He slammed the phone down, saying, "Geez, what's it take to get a little vision from those wonks?" He turned to Milton. "What should we do?"

Milton looked up at his president and shrugged. "There are ways to bring them down."

"What exactly do you mean when you say 'bring them down'?"

"He means," Gibbon said, striding through the doors to the situation room, temporary pass clipped to his jacket pocket, cane wisping against the thick carpeting, "that we have got to knock them down at any cost."

The professor pointed to the TV monitors. On one, a woman newscaster described the launch of the spaceship, cutting away to spectacular videos patched in from NYU Flight Control, then to scenes around the campus. Police and news crews encircled the dorms, immobilizing the surrounding streets.

"This is a major crisis, Mr. President. The press is loving it. They're calling it SpaceCopter and Crockett-Rocket and Flibberty Belle and Bladerunner. As long as those kids are up there, they ridicule NASA, endanger UNITO , and pose a threat to national security. If they return safely, it only compounds that threat."

Milton, obviously in grim agreement, picked up a phone from the bank of dozens around the table and demanded a connection to NYU.

Crane rubbed the back of his neck. "Let's concentrate on priorities here. It's very important that our response not have a negative effect on the election. National security is all well and good, but if I'm not sitting here next January Twentieth, national security can go squat. They're just some college kids. I say ignore them. Hell, give them a medal and we'll pick up even more of the youth vote. Invite their grandparents and I'll talk about family val—"

"You can't slough them off that way, Nolan!" Gibbon spoke to the president as if scolding a pupil. "They built a spaceship in a run-down warehouse. A spaceship that NASA knew about and purposely avoided developing! If they stay safely in orbit for more than a few hours, every space case from San Diego to Atlantic City will try to shoot himself into the sky. Do *you* want to be the one who let a bunch of school kids make monkeys of the world's only remaining superpower?"

The chairman of the Joint Chiefs of Staff spoke. His accent betrayed his Georgian origin — European Georgia, that is — which still gave some of the older military men and women the willies.

"It is the opinion of the Pentagon that subnational ownership of spacecraft is as impermissible as subnational ownership of submarines, and for the same reason. The dominion of the United States is insufficient in both realms, and a subnational presence on either frontier is detrimental to our long-term interests."

"November Fifth is the longest term anyone here must consider," one of Crane's spin doctors declared. "Three kids hot-rodding in outer space is insignificant unless it impacts on the campaign! A hundred going up wouldn't matter if there were no foreseeable impact."

"What about the first one that *doesn't* make it to orbit?" asked a woman from the CIA. "Better to scare everyone out of it now by being firm than to see wreckage falling from here to India. That would be some impact for you."

"We can bring them down with an ASAT," Milton offered. "No one will know what happened. We can issue a statement that their ship probably broke up under stress and get Congress and the DOT to slap sanctions on all private rocket construction, for safety reasons, until the UN takes control. We ought to put a lid on it before you have a junior Buck Rogers land on the moon and start selling real estate."

"You people don't have any idea what this means," Gibbon said. "The actions of those kids completely undermines the integrity of the Interplanetary Treaty!"

The others stared at him as if he had dropped his pants.

"What," Crane asked, "does that have to do with anything? I know it's your baby and all, but—"

Gibbon stiffened. "The Treaty controls access to space in all signatory nations, and authorizes suppressive strikes against any non-signatory nations. Allowing those brats to stay up there would be the same as allowing homesteaders into Antarctica. It would violate the treaty and UNITO is authorized to use any means necessary to prevent private exploitation of resources that are the birthright of all."

The national economic advisor, Bret Wood, smirked. "A birthright no one can claim is no birthright at all."

Gibbon smirked right back. "The United States is bound by treaty to obey the United Nations."

"Not until January first," a small voice said from the far end of the table. The woman who spoke was not only physically small — shorter than the diminutive NSA chief Milton — her voice lilted softly in a high register. She was Helen Zylstra, the US ambassadress to the UN.

Gibbon glowered at her. She was the one who had abstained from a yea vote on IT. He said nothing, but tension seared between them.

She paused hesitantly for a moment, then said, "If you really want to be technical, UNITO doesn't have more than *token* power over space travel until 12:01 AM Greenwich Mean Time of January First next year. The next three and a half months could legally condone a sort of land rush — I mean, a *space rush* — for any government or subnational who wants to establish a living presence in Space. And I guess some people determined humanity's future important enough to search for a loophole and discovered one big enough to blast a rocket through."

She turned her petite blond head toward Gibbon and on her lips lay not a smirk but a warm and confidently beaming smile.

Milton offered the phone to Crane. "Be that as it may, Mr. President, think of the positive press if you can talk them down safely."

Crane took the handset. "This is the President of the United States. May I ask who I'm speaking to?"

"I'm Carla Pulaski, sir. NYU Flight Control."

"Well, good morning there. I'd like to speak to the pilot in command."

Carla patched his call through to Crockett. The president exchanged greetings with the spacefarers, then asked, in his most folksy re-election voice, "Well now, Davy Crockett, what the heck are you doing up there?" While he spoke, a constant stream of notes from Milton, Gibbon, and a half-dozen other advisors crossed in front of him. Some even tussled with others to convey their own instructions to the Commander-In-Chief.

Crockett grinned widely; it made his free fall-puffed face look expansive and caused his cheeks to bunch up like an older man's. *"Mr. President, I offer you greetings from New Alamo, an orbital allodial freehold."*

Crane covered the phone and said loudly, "What the hell is an 'allodial freehold'?"

Most shrugged. Gibbon said, "Ignore his babble. Just tell him what danger they're in. Scare them down."

Crane, though, read instead from a note handed him by one of his campaign staffers. "Thanks, Davy. You know, you've done your ancestor's memory well by putting that spaceship into orbit. Now that you've made your point, I think you'd better come down from there."

The image on the monitor kept its grin. *"And if we decide to stay, who can forbid us?"*

Another note, this one from Milton. "You can't simply just set up housekeeping up there," Crane read from the scrawl. "Space belongs to all mankind."

"Since we're part of mankind, it belongs to us, too," Crockett replied in his Tennessee drawl.

"Space exploration is the responsibility of the government." This note from Gibbon.

"Maybe yes, maybe no. Space has been explored plenty. It's time to settle here. And space migration *is an individual act."*

Crane, handed another piece of paper, changed his tack. "How can you even be sure you'll survive in orbit? NASA spends billions on—"

"You guys overprice everything. Watch us and see how it's done."

Crane covered the mouthpiece again to say, "He's enjoying this! Give me better notes!" He said into the phone, "Now, Davy, I know you're all wrapped up in the legends about your famous namesake, but..." he glanced down to read yet another note — this one again from Milton, "don't you know how many laws you're breaking? Illegal possession and use of unlicensed hazardous materials, operating an aircraft without a pilot's certificate, launch of a spacecraft from a facility not operated by NASA or approved by the Department of Transportation, reckless endangerment, failure to file a plan for flight through a positive control zone, arson, trespassing..." He paused to ad lib, "There's a lot more I could mention. Why, you could go to prison for a couple centuries for all this when you come home..." He looked up to see his chief of staff making a violent hand motion across his throat. "Not that you would!" he hastily added. "All we want is for you three kids to land safely and we'll pick you up wherever you splash down." That last caused him to think, never a good idea for Crane. "Do you kids even have passports?"

Crockett's expression collapsed into puzzled rage at the pettiness of the objections to his feat. *"Passports!"* he said in a growl. *"Passports? We don't need any stinkin' passports!"* A gloved finger jabbed toward the camera. *"We're leaving this crummy planet and settling a new one. Maybe not on this trial flight, but on the next! We've downloaded all our technical information onto The Net and every other computer bulletin board in the country, so anyone who wants to join us can build a ship to do so. Just don't try to stop us or — or..."* He reached behind him to unstrap his flintlock from its mounting place on the bulkhead. *"Or Ol' Betsy here will have something to say in the matter!"*

The President looked genuinely shocked. "You can't have a gun in outer space! That violates the treaty we signed with the — "

"We *didn't sign your damn' treaties. We're fed up with your jabberin' and jawin'. Y'all all can go to hell* — We're *going to the stars!"* With that paraphrase of the original Davy Crockett's most famous outburst, Crockett cut off communication and put the rifle away, then turned to his computer.

Friedman stared at Crockett, aghast. "I don't think it was such a good idea to antagonize a man who has ten thousand nuclear warheads at his disposal."

Crockett, all too cocky in his rage, said "What can they do — shoot us down with the whole world watching?"

▼ ▲ ▼

Somewhere in England, an F-15 painted grey with low-resolution ID roared down a runway and blazed upward into the afternoon sky on afterburners. Secured under its left wing hung a larger-than-usual missile.

▼ ▲ ▼

At NORAD, the jet's takeoff generated a radar blip on a skywatcher's personal radar screen. The computer readout next to the blip registered its rapid ascent. The skywatcher, Cpl. Maureen Loftus, punched a button and spoke into her headset.

Capt. Lee, standing by Gen. Dorn, responded to her call.

"What do you *mean* they won't confirm it?" He turned to Dorn. "Sir, we have a jet ascending over the Atlantic at high rate of climb. The C.O. at the air base denies it, stating no unusual activity—"

"Put it on the main screen," Dorn demanded. The red sine wave indicating the spacecraft's ground track and the blue line of the aircraft's trajectory did not seem to be heading toward intersection, but it was not the plane that was the problem. "ASAT," the general muttered with cool anger. "Somebody plans to blow those kids out of the sky." He picked up one of several red phones. "Get me the President."

At that moment, a civilian programmer for NORAD rushed up to Dorn with a handful of computer printouts in his hand. "General Dorn!" he said nervously. "Someone's tapping into our main data flow!"

▼ ▲ ▼

Bernadette saw the second line appear on her screen.

"We've got a bogey on an east-west ascent," she said. "NORAD's tracking it."

Friedman peered over at her screen. "Oh God," he said. "They're going to shoot us down!"

The image suddenly vanished, replaced by static.

Bernadette glanced up. "They've blocked our tap!"

Crockett's pulse quickened at the deadly turn the joyride just took. Then his resolve strengthened. Turning to the videocam, he switched to a second voice channel to ask, "Carla — are the media still listening?"

"What do you *think?"* she answered.

"Patch me in." After a pause to assume an outraged composure, he said, "Mr. President, People of Earth — Someone down there's about to take a potshot at our spacecopter from somewhere in England. We'll have further news on this atrocity as it develops. In the name of Free Space, we are not afraid to be martyred."

"I am so," Friedman muttered under his breath.

▼ ▲ ▼

The President shouted on the phone to Dorn. "Well, *I* didn't authorize it." He looked up at Milton. "Did *you* authorize it?"

Milton pursed his lips and shook his head. If he did, he would never admit to it anyway.

"Well, let's send it back to base," Crane told Dorn.

"No response, sir."

"Damn it! We can't shoot down a bunch of kids right after they announce it to the world."

"It certainly won't look like an accident," Milton said, "but maybe we can pin it on the Chinese."

"After he told the world it was launched from *England*?"

"Our old standby, then — terrorists."

Crane could barely control his anger. "What terrorist," he said through gritted teeth, "owns an anti-satellite missile and the jet to launch it?"

At NORAD, Gen. Dorn turned to Capt. Lee, his decision instantly formed. "Dispatch a jet to intercept that aircraft and bring it down."

"Too late!" Corporal Loftus shouted over the intercom. "He's launched!"

Up on the giant screen, an orange point of light branched away from the blue line.

Dorn, voice level and steely calm, reported this to the President.

After a moment of deliberation, Crane demanded to be reconnected with Crockett. Carla patched him through.

"Kids?" Crane's voice grew silkily gentle. "I know you won't hold me or the office of the presidency personally responsible for this, but it does seem as if there's been a... um, little breakdown in communication with one of our air bases in Great Britain. After all, you've got to expect, well, funny things to happen when you go around launching rockets without permission. Now, you must admit that was wrong, or at least very, very unwise."

Bernadette snidely said, *"If you all weren't so trigger happy, we wouldn't be in this mess—"* Davy laid a hand on her arm in an attempt to calm her.

"Well," Crane said, "be that as it may, I've just been informed that an F-15 has, well, it's sort of fired a missile at you. Now, we're not entirely to blame in this. After all, you *did* take us by surprise, and information flow is a problem this administration has been working on for some—"

"Is it an ASAT?" Crockett demanded.

"Why, yes it is. It's a kinetic kill device that's— "

"Launched at 100,000 feet altitude by an F-15, goes into orbit, explodes, and peppers the target with a load of buckshot-sized shrapnel."

"Why, that's right, I think. In any case, it's coming your way."

The three spacefarers stared mutely at one another for an instant, then broke into frantic activity. Bernadette switched her screen to onboard radar and told the others to seal their helmets and switch to personal oxygen. Friedman loudly worried about using fuel for evasive maneuvers while rotating the spacecraft into a correct attitude for escape.

"Stand by to fire engines!" Friedman cried.

Crockett interrupted the procedure. "We can't maneuver until the warhead has exploded, otherwise the missile can compensate and still intercept us. *After* the warhead explodes, all we need is one good kick to get us out of the buckshot's path."

"But we'd only have *seconds* to react!" Friedman appeared genuinely frightened.

Crockett smiled as he locked down his helmet. "Leave that to me."

"I was afraid you'd say that."

Crockett punched in orders for a three-second burn. Sam routed radar info and fire control to Crockett's console. His gloved finger hovered over the command key.

At an indicated distance of sixty-five miles and a combined approach velocity of 12 miles per second, the radar blip suddenly burst into a dimming cloud of smaller dots, each one denoting a possible spacecraft-killer.

With a karate-like shout of energy, Crockett jabbed his finger at the command button. The engines ignited with alarming bangs and the rotor whirred back up to speed, causing the ship to creak and pop. The force of acceleration rammed the trio back into their seats.

Davy clenched his jaw and whispered, like a prayer, "Remember the Alamo."

CHAPTER 48

Love does not consist in gazing at each other but in looking outward together in the same direction.
— Antoine de Saint-Exupery

18 August

Falling. Falling. This time from an impossible height. She was strapped spread-eagled in the center of the circular space station pinwheeling through the blackness of Space. The blues and browns of Earth careered around her. The sun flashed on and off. She felt the bite of atmosphere, heard the rush of wind in her ears, then screamed as the searing heat of reentry burned her flesh and bone. All that survived the flames was her shuttle pin, which grew larger and shinier until it was the size of the real shuttle. Larger, till it dominated the skies.

"Wake up." Marcus Grant crouched with one knee on Tammy Reis's bed.

"Paul?" she said groggily.

He sat on the bed to lay a hand on her shoulder. "It's time."

"I can't go yet," she murmured. "I have too much to—" She rubbed her neck and opened her eyes wider. "Paul? What..."

"We blast off today. Someone else made it to orbit and all eyes are on them. It's the perfect diversion."

Suddenly alert, Tammy sat up in bed, the covers slipping from her naked form. "This is it? We're leaving Earth?"

He nodded. "I've scrambled the ground crews. Everything's being stowed and locked down. The crew's boarding and making final preparations." He gazed at her intently, grave deliberation in his eyes. "I want your tracking pin."

Except for the Flying A keychain and the mysterious cryopack in her personal preference payload, it was the last remaining link to her past, and her only connection to NASA and the NSA. Without even stopping to consider the break this made with everything she once held holy, she said, “It’s on the dresser.” Then she reached out and touched his arm. “Paul...”

He gazed at her. She saw in him now a love as deep and wide and tall as she knew smoldered inside her own heart.

“We have to go now,” he said softly.

Her fingers clasped his arm and gently pulled him closer. “Then we have to say farewell to Earth.”

He seized her firmly and fell to the sheets. “Tammy,” he whispered, kissing her neck, her cheek, her lips. “If we die today...”

“If we die,” she said, rending his shirt from his shoulders and inhaling her lover’s sweet scent, “we’ll die together in the greatest adventure any two could ever share!”

They moved as one and she felt a familiar sensation overwhelm her, this time not with terror but with joy.

“I’m falling,” she whispered. “Falling.”

“Falling where?” he asked breathlessly.

“Into ecstasy. Into love. Into you, Paul. Into you.”

▼ ▲ ▼

“Where’s Marcus?” Donahue asked. She wore — as did most of the others — the official Grant Enterprises flight uniform over her matching skintight pressure suit. The much looser outer layer consisted of a maroon jumpsuit with grey piping and loads of cargo pockets. It was comfortable, utilitarian, and, on Joscelyn at least, sexy even to those who did not see the far more alluring outfit underneath. She had cut her long red hair short for the liftoff, as had many of the others. They gathered around her by the crane as the ground crew prepared the massive SSTO for liftoff.

Though early in the pre-dawn hours, everyone was awake and charged with the near-atomic thrill of anticipation. Haley gazed quickly around from his vantage on the cherry-picker, lifted four feet high to form an impromptu dais. Lights shone one the crew and on the lower sections of the pods, where tanker upon tanker pumped cryogenic fuel into the cavernous tanks of the space station. A cold mist flowed down the walls of the pods to form a fog in the humid night air. He shrugged. “Let’s proceed. I’m sure he’ll be coming soon.”

“All right, people!” Donahue called loudly. “I know this is extremely short notice, but you’ve all been briefed about the South Bronx launch. Mr. Grant feels that it’s now or never as far as the element of surprise goes. I want the flight crew to post themselves in front of their respective pods and wait for the lift to come to you.” Clipboard in hand, she began to check off names. Nearly everyone was present. "Where's Tammy Reis?" she asked.

"Present!" said a voice from the rear. Tammy — in uniform — edged her way to the flight crew section.

Joscelyn noticed that Grant, his grey hair shorn down to its sandy-blond roots, had arrived with Reis at the periphery and now strode through the crowd of nearly twenty to jump on the crane and climb up into the cherry-picker. She sensed something different in his demeanor and instantly knew where he had been. In a pained silence, she handed him her clipboard and stepped to the rear of the pallet.

Joseph Lester and Hillary Kaye — videocam on her shoulder — recorded the event for posterity. Lester had met his goal of weight loss and proudly wore his size 42-long jumpsuit as proof that he would not encumber the flight with any excess baggage. His cheeks glowed ruddily with excitement and heady expectation.

"Not much to say," Grant began. "We're all here — thanks, Joscelyn — and we're ready to go." He gazed at the expectant eyes watching him, at the faces of every kind that waited for some sort of benediction, some blessing for their leave-taking, their eagerness tempered only by the anxiety any emigrant feels at the point of imminent departure from one's lifelong home.

"We've practiced this a hundred times," Grant said. "And now that it's actually happening, I realize that we've never really done this before at all. No one has. Astronauts going to the Moon knew that they would return if all went well. Cosmonauts onboard *Mir* endured a short tour of duty by most earthly standards. I think we must assume the attitude of puritans and pilgrims: we're embarking on a one-way voyage fraught with danger and with promise. We'll only be two hundred nautical miles from home, but it will be as if a sea greater than any on Earth separates us from our former home.

"America was the New World for half a millennium. Now all of Earth is the Old World. Our new world will be just these sixteen enclosures — for a while, anyway — and we few settlers will be the entire population of this new frontier — for a short time, at least. We are a new community, bound not by nation, race, or class, but by one single, burning desire: to live and work in total freedom. To do that, though, requires the paradox that we confine ourselves to these tiny, fragile vessels under rules of conduct that would chafe even the most humble indentured servant. We do this because we know that freedom is not the measure of how large is your cage but how open is your future. On Earth, our futures are closed, constricted, and bleak. In Space, our futures loom as large as the Universe!" He glanced at his watch. "Everybody—"

"Before you dismiss us," Chad said quickly, "I'd like to introduce a couple who just arrived today who will be accompanying us on our trip. You may recognize him as the H. G. Wells of our age. He wrote the books that inspired us all our lives. Ladies and gentlemen, Rex Ivarson and his wife Grace!"

At the sound of thundering applause, Rex turned to wave lightly to the crowd, a little bewildered by the attention.

"They love you," Grace, squeezing his hand with warm tenderness.

"I'm just a writer," he whispered to her above the din. "The engineers who made this happen deserve the applause."

"They wouldn't have done this without your inspiration." She smiled at her husband's genuine humility, knowing it stemmed not from a deprecating self-effacement, but from an utter lack of self-obsession. This man was obsessed by science, by Space, by the future; he could not see his own greatness in his quest for such supreme goals, and that made him all the greater in her eyes.

A cheer arose from the crowd. Grant, surprised at his outpouring of passion and at his workers' emotional response, stepped backward, nearly losing his balance. Glancing at Joscelyn and Chad, then at Tammy, he nodded toward the toroid. "Let's go," he said quietly, then, to the crowd, "Flight crew — prepare to board!"

▼ ▲ ▼

In the next hour, all their planning became the template from which was drawn the chaotic reality of such a complex undertaking.

Tammy and Jon Franck conducted a walk-around check of the spacecraft, accompanied by the head of the ground crew. Each of the sixteen aerospike engines was given the once-over.

The trench had become a frigid, foggy pit due to the cryogenic fumes. Six large positive-displacement blowers labored relentlessly to draw off the dangerous hydrogen-oxygen mix and disperse it a few hundred yards away from the circular pit. Because of that, a constant, cold draft blew over the workers below.

The rest of the emigrants stowed their personal items onboard and sat and waited for their destiny in soft seats on the topmost deck. Some sat in pairs, others sat alone. In either case, the spacefarers were surrounded by the absolute maximum amount of cargo they could cram into the confines of the cabin and still expect to achieve orbit with reasonable certainty. For the next quarter-hour, the ground crew prepared the space station for blastoff, checking all electrical and fuel systems.

Tammy adjusted her five-point harness, verified that her helmet was strapped securely behind her seat, and slipped the Bose noise-canceling headphones over her ears. Unlike many in the crew, she had opted to leave her tresses intact. One woman, with medium length hair, had cut hers military-short, thinking it would save a pound or two of mass. At Tammy's suggestion, she weighed it, only to discover that the savings amounted to five ounces. "I'll keep my hair," Tammy told Grant, "and leave my pocket change behind."

Now — with the aid of Ta'Shawn Wilkes — she hacked her way into every global positioning satellite network around the world, enabling the onboard computer to calculate a collision-avoiding flight path into Low Earth Orbit.

"Begin flooding the moat," she read from the computerized checklist. Down below, workers hastily exited the trench and opened valves that drained the encampment's water tower into the circular excavation.

▼ ▲ ▼

"Tammy?"

"Yes, Paul?" She turned to see him in the cockpit doorway. With his dyed-grey hair replaced by short spikes of blond, he looked as young and eager as the teenager with whom she once dreamed of conquering Space. She never dreamed, though, that it would be this way, from this place, after such a life as she had led.

He smiled with a nonchalant self-satisfaction. "Before we light the fuses, I just thought I'd tell you that I've arranged a little demonstration for you."

She nodded to Franck. "Take it," she said.

"Don't get up," Volnos said. "Just switch your FMS screen to auxiliary."

The video screen, one of four set in the control panel, lit up with a radar image of the Arabian Sea with Sri Lanka at the far lower right and the Strait of Hormuz at the upper left. Dead smack center lay a bright blip executing a 180° turn from due west to due east.

"That's a remote-piloted airplane," Grant explained. "A surplus UAV we bought during Russia's going-out-of-business sale. It's outfitted with a radar multiplier so that its image is magnified to that of a C-130. It's also carrying your shuttle pin."

Tammy glanced up from the screen to gaze at his confident expression. She knew instantly what he planned to show her. "You think they'll fire blindly, without even confirming their target?"

He nodded. "Four minutes ago, I activated a solenoid that bent the wings up to activate the emergency signal."

From the upper left edge of the screen — somewhere in the Gulf of Oman — a startlingly swift radar image raced in an arc toward the UAV image.

"Submarine launch," he muttered. "They wanted to be sure they had something nearby."

The missile flight path overtook the UAV. Then both disappeared from the screen.

After a silent moment, Grant said, "Do you understand, finally, what your joining NASA meant to me?"

"I thought I could change it," she said without emotion. "Weed out the corruption."

Grant shook his head. "You can't weed evil out of evil ground. You can only abandon the desecrated earth and move on. And that's what we're doing." He reached past her to switch the screen back to its normal display. Pulling back, he paused long enough to touch his lips to hers. "Pilgrims leave their past behind them," he whispered, "and are born again in the new world."

"I love you, Paul."

He smiled as he eased out of the cockpit. "Then punch a hole in the sky."

▼ ▲ ▼

The onboard computer, with its powerful neural-net parallel processor, did most of the work that would otherwise have required dozens of technicians. Even so, the systems on each of the pods consisted of simple, non-redundant, do-or-die components. Everyone — except perhaps the two children onboard — knew what risks they ran. As the count approached zero, heartbeats soared.

At T-minus six minutes, the fuel and oxidizer tanks were topped off and sealed. Liquid nitrogen, heated by gaseous helium, pressurized the LOX tanks; in the LH_2 tanks, a similar system used helium and a separate vessel of hydrogen fed past a catalyst.

At T-minus three minutes, twenty seconds — as the ground crew withdrew far beyond the berms — Joscelyn Donahue's voice crackled over the airwaves.

"All hatches confirmed sealed. Cabin pressure on internal."

At T-minus two minutes, everyone locked on their helmets and checked their oxygen flow. It was more an act of faith than of safety. If any of the pods lost pressurization, the odds stood nearly at unity that a catastrophic breakup would follow.

"T-minus sixty seconds," the computer's voice announced. *"All systems autonomous."* From that point on, the sixteen pods — each containing 24,000 cubic feet of fuel and 8,000 cubic feet of oxidizer — were armed and ready for launch.

T-minus 55:

Haley sat alone in Pod Four, overcome with an attack of panic. Here he sat on the verge of everything he had ever dreamed and sacrificed for, and all he wanted was to be back in Long Beach in his cozy apartment, cruising The Net. *It was easier just dreaming,* he realized with a sickening drop in his stomach. *The hard part is to take action.*

He watched the constant stream of information cascade up his computer screen like a numerical geyser. He noted minor malfunctions here and there, then watched with nervous satisfaction as each one was corrected, bypassed, or noted and ignored by the computers or crew.

T-minus 45:

In Pod Seven, Melissa Lundy gazed upward through the polycarbonate of her helmet and the tiny window. She wished for all the world that Jack could have been here with her. He might have, too, if his devotion to NASA and his ardent love for the Shuttle had not taken him to his death. And what would her son Alan think when the crew introduces itself from Space? She gripped the hand rests and vowed to worry about it later.

T-minus 30:

Joscelyn, sitting beside Grant in Pod Three, concentrated totally on monitoring the fuel.

"Optimum pressure," she said over the intercom.

His fingers racing over the keyboard, Grant said, "Begin pre-heat fuel flow."

T-minus 20:

"All systems optimal," Haley noted. "We're go for liftoff."

"T-minus ten," Tammy said. "Igniters armed."

Hillary Kaye made one final adjustment to the videocam she had attached to the seat and pointed at Joseph Lester, the other occupant of Pod Two. Similar cigarette-sized cameras provided views of several other pod occupants, all feeding into her multiplexed digital 3-D HDTV recorder. This was one event she wanted to capture in its entirety. Her tense fingers gripped the hand rests as she stared straight ahead and held her breath.

Lester wanted nothing more than to close his eyes and pray, but he gazed at the minicam and spoke.

"This is it, ladies and gentlemen. The Universe... or nothing!"

T-minus 6:

Tons of liquid hydrogen flowed into the sixteen plug engines, feeding into each pod's 720 combustion chambers. There it mingled with tons of oxygen and flowed outward. Pyrotechnics ringing the edge of the moat generated a cascade of sparks, igniting the explosive mixture.

Tammy Reis felt the rumble of the fuel flow, then the thunder of the engines. For a moment, nothing more happened.

Outside, though, the engines blasted into the circular pit, exploding downward against the water with crushing force. The water absorbed the shock wave created by the downblast and converted the engines' exhaust into steam and scattered droplets. The water only survived for a few seconds. It was all that was needed.

"Three," Tammy counted. "Two." She watched the stream of commands the computer sent to the multitude of systems. "All engines running!" She took a deep breath.

"Blastoff!"

The engines throttled up to full power with the roar of a million thunderbolts. Tammy thrilled to the familiar elevator-up sensation that marked the first slow, gradual rise.

The ground crew watched in awe from several miles away as a flaming circle of fire arose from the desert valley. Steam, smoke, and dust billowed outward from below to choke the lungs and sting the flesh.

The toroid, as terrifying and stunningly beautiful as an avenging angel's haloed ascension, lifted straight up for a few seconds, then pitched eastward at a 1° angle, making a slow, graceful gravity turn as it climbed ever higher, arcing toward the dim colors of dawn. Behind it trailed a comet's tail of exhaust that high altitude winds immediately sheared this way and that as the first rays of the morning sun transformed the streak into broad brushstrokes of rainbow hues.

Tammy's blood pounded furiously in her ears. She welcomed the ever-mounting crush of acceleration as most women would embrace a lover. As she had embraced Paul. This was what she lived for. This was what she thought she would never experience again.

It did not take long for the flying ring to encounter Max-Q.

Metal groaned and shrieked under the unfamiliar aerodynamic pressures. Tammy kept watch on the computer screen, which depicted airflow around the outer rim and through the center of the ring. As the massive toroid approached transonic speeds, the airflow through the center constricted. The ride grew rougher, the atmosphere resisting the onslaught of the ever-accelerating ring. Tammy, a pilot in name only since the computer handled every aspect of thrust, attitude, and burn rate, watched the Mach number climb toward one as drag coefficient exceeded 1.1 and the flow-through hole narrowed to near nothing. A tremendous, low-frequency shudder reverberated through the vessel fighting mightily to maintain a steady ascent. A rosette pattern of shock waves began to form around the leading edge of the pods. Then — with a soul-shaking rumble — the entire five-and-a-half kiloton spaceship slammed through the sound barrier and roared upward through the dawn sky.

"Mach One," Tammy said through gritted teeth as the flight instantly smoothed out. "Airflow through center did not choke off. We're on our way."

At 261 seconds into the flight, the outer three rows of combustion chambers on each pod shut down. Though this further reduced the thrust — which declined steadily as propellant pressure and flow decreased — due to the aerospike engine design, this changed the area ratio of the exhaust bell, resulting in the increased fuel efficiency needed to achieve orbit.

Through the windshield that now seemed to be overhead, the deep blue-purple sky let Tammy know that she once again headed into Space. This time, though, it would be forever.

An ivory sphere rose over the limb of the turquoise planet just barely visible at the edge of the viewing port. Gibbous, bright, and achingly perfect, the Moon crossed the port for a moment, and Tammy Reis gazed at it with a joy and wonder underscored by the triumphant euphony of the rocket engines.

All the suffering of the last several years meant nothing now. As she rode on an arc of fire with her crew, she realized that nothing needed to be the way it had been. All the bitterness, the hatred, the betrayal — all of it — need never have happened.

She watched the monitors, her body and hands idle as the computer controlled the ascent of humanity's first pure, free, and permanent space settlement.

She was rising.

Rising!

▼ ▲ ▼

The pressure of acceleration continued to increase, mashing Paul Volnos into the seat. Never before had anything so simultaneously thrilling and terrifying overwhelmed his soul. Literally breathtaken, he wanted to yell, but his awestricken lungs lay paralyzed by the sensations surging within. At eighty miles altitude and 3 gees, he struggled to maintain consciousness while increasingly convinced that the dizzying acceleration would never cease. Just as panic began to overtake his rational processes, the incredible pressure ended suddenly and he became instantly weightless. No jolt, no forward lurch accompanied the change. Just pressure, then the incredible sensation of free fall.

The engines shut down safely and the colossal structure continued upward in silence on a ballistic trajectory into the blackness of Space. The life-or-death question was whether their trajectory would place them safely in orbit or take them back down to incineration in the atmosphere.

▼ ▲ ▼

The answer that appeared before Tammy's trained eye — displayed as a table of different orbital elements on the FMS screen — sent an electric jolt of alarm through her heart.

She fought the feeling of vertigo and nausea that accompanied weightlessness to ask Jon, "Are you seeing the numbers I'm seeing?"

"Yes." His voice lost any drawl it once had. "We didn't make it."

"We must have miscalculated payload mass." She looked over at him with a deadly serious expression. "Estimate time until orbital decay while I talk this out with Houst—" She froze. There was no Houston, no ground control, no team of scientists, technicians, or engineers to devote millions of man hours to rescuing them. They were utterly alone in the void.

"Paul?" she asked over the intercom.

"We made it!" he responded excitedly. *"We're in orbit!"*

"Not quite," she said. "We're in an orbit too low to maintain for long. We'll keep rubbing atmosphere at every perigee, which will slow us and drop us lower and lower until we deorbit. And this thing's not built for return trips."

"Can we raise it with a second engine burn?"

"Forget that," Franck said. "No more fuel."

"How about reaction rockets?"

"They're angled to impart a spin, not to provide axial thrust."

Franck's voice suddenly brightened. "Our orbit won't decay severely for at least a week. We can get out of this."

"How?"

Tammy gazed at the computer screen, thinking about the nineteen others whose fates depended upon the immutable physics of orbital mechanics. She felt no need to pray. Either their human ingenuity would save them or their destiny was sealed. No god she could have imagined would ever have tolerated idle whining.

Forcing her hands to the keyboard where gravity now absent would once have held them, she flexed her arm and wrist muscles in familiar old ways — space shuttle ways — as she pounded the keys in search of a solution.

Outside shone a harsh Sun amid velvet darkness.

CHAPTER 49

In this world there is always danger for those who are afraid of it.

— George Bernard Shaw

17 August

The pressure lifted from Crockett's chest immediately with the cessation of the rocket burn. He glanced at the other two.

"Still alive," he said, directing a grin at Friedman, then, with a whoop, addressed the world. "Hear that y'all? *Bodacious Bernadette* is still flyin'! Now if you could just rein in your posse, Mr. President, we'll be done with our little jaunt and down in time for breakfast tomorrow."

"Davy?"

"Yes, Carla?"

"If you don't have urgent ship's business, I've got about a gazillion news agencies on the line wanting to interview you."

"Oh?" He unlatched his helmet and gazed at the microcam, speaking suddenly in his most proper Bostonian. "Do I detect a renewed interest in Space among our esteemed members of the Fourth Estate?" With a wink at Bernadette, he said, "I don't want to play favorites, so we'll begin our interview with the highest bidder."

▼▲▼

"It missed!" Gen. Dorn shouted. The main floor of NORAD regained an outward calm under which simmered heart-pounding tension. No one had time to contemplate the importance of the momentous events transpiring upon their monitors.

Dorn did not know whether to feel relief or not. He had a grandson Crockett's age and wished the generation no ill. On the other hand, in Viet Nam, he had sent men Crockett's age to die in battle killing enemy troops Crockett's age. Never seriously having faced the question of a non-threatening subnational presence in orbit, he could formulate no opinion of whether Crockett and his crew constituted a true enemy. Unless the Pentagon or the President told him otherwise, he suspected that the best strategy would be to sit this one out.

Capt. Lee leaned over to say, "Another launch, sir. This time from Africa."

"Another one?"

"And it's *big,* sir!" the captain muttered. "Unless it's sixteen individual rockets flying an unbelievably tight pattern, we're showing it as a disc or circle of engines. Estimated GLOW is..." He stared up at the general. "Eleven million pounds!"

The ground track appeared on the screen, gently arcing up from Kismayu, passing over the Indian Ocean.

"Something coming through GSN," Cpl. Loftus said over the intercom. The huge right screen displayed the image to the entire cavernous room.

The man's face looked as if he had been up all night. Perhaps he had, but free fall contributed more to his appearance. His dark, curly hair attempted to keep its position, but drifted with his movements as he addressed the world.

"Good morning," Joseph Lester said, looking into the lens. Hillary monitored the camera image even though preoccupied with fighting her own battle against space sickness. *"Or good afternoon or good evening, depending on where you are watching this live broadcast from outer space. This is Joseph Lester for Global Satellite News, on assignment in Low Earth Orbit."*

"I am speaking to you from a seat onboard a revolutionary spacecraft — a single-stage-to-orbit space station that was launched fully assembled less than fifteen minutes ago. We are relieved to report that we have made it into orbit."

"Oh my God," Dorn said, flopping down in the nearest available chair. He instantly grasped the implications, turning to Capt. Lee to say, "We've lost the high ground."

"But to whom?" Lee pondered.

▼ ▲ ▼

President Crane watched his TV set shift the image of Davy Crockett to a small rectangle in the lower right portion of the screen, displaying the legend RAW SATELLITE FEED at its bottom. The main portion of the screen now showed Lester and the claustrophobic interior of the pod cabin.

"What is this?" he asked aloud. "Some kind of fad?"

"Mr. President." Gibbon intoned gravely now, his voice tinged with fear. Of anyone in the situation room, the old man possessed the greatest appreciation of the threat. "If this is not a hoax, this is the worst poss—"

One of the bank of red phones warbled. An aide picked up the receiver and handed it to Crane. "NORAD."

"General Dorn," the president said coolly. "Is this guy for real?"

"Yes, sir. We're tracking a circular object, two hundred feet in diameter, about sixty feet thick."

"Any weapons?"

"Sir, in something that large, they could carry enough warheads to carpet-nuke the eastern seaboard."

"Do you think they're carrying?"

There was a long pause. *"No, Mr. President, I do not."*

"I'd like to take a moment," Lester continued, *"to introduce you to the people who made this possible. And if you're wondering why you never heard about their efforts..."* The image switched to that of a camera mounted inside Pod Three, showing a man and a woman undoing their helmets and waving at the camera. *"...well, this man thought it best to keep a low profile. I'd like you to meet Marcus Grant of Grant Enterprises, builder of the world's first private space station!"*

Grant, hand cupped over an ear phone, spoke rapidly into his headset's boom mic. He glared at the red LED above the camera lens for an instant, then spoke.

"I'll be brief," he said, *"due to a little problem we've got here. I built this space station and launched it in secrecy because the United States government — in cahoots with other UN power blocs — would have stopped me if they had known. I have explicit proof in my case, and you've all seen what they've done to Larry Poubelle and Gerry Cooper. This space station — which could have been built thirty years ago, so that'll tell you something about NASA — is intended to be the first freeport in Space. Think of it as the ultimate empowerment zone.*

"Unfortunately, we were unable to calculate our ship's gross liftoff weight accurately, due to the pressures of time and all the skulking about we had to do to evade our enemy, the State. We're in a decaying orbit and desperately require a refueling flight. We're working on the numbers now. We won't need much, just enough to fire the engines every perigee until we're up to where we intended to be.

"I stress again that we are peaceful settlers, we carry no weapons that could harm anyone on Earth, and all we ask is for no interference with rescue efforts. How your governments respond to this request, friends, will reveal their true positions regarding human freedom and our future in Space. You've already seen them try to shoot down three

college kids. Wait till you see what they think of us!"

Lester's voice returned, this time over an image of another man and woman, working fast and furiously at keyboards, checking status lights, trying to find another way out of the emergency.

"That was Marcus Grant, obviously with a lot on his mind. Let's switch now to the pilot and co-pilot."

"Can't talk now," the woman crisply muttered. *"Jon, confirm the residual on pods seven through twelve."*

Back in the White House situation room, Barry Gibbon stared in dumb shock at the televised face and voice of Tamara Reis and felt the chill of stark existential terror lance through his bones.

▼ ▲ ▼

In the intensive care unit at Walter Reed, Garrick Madison sat by his comatose sister, quietly speaking to the motionless and frail lone survivor of *Constitution*. He spent every waking hour with her, talking to her, playing her favorite music, massaging her muscles and moving her limbs.

He described the image he saw on the TV screen. "The pilot looks like... my God, it's Tammy!" Then, as he had countless times before to the seemingly insensate form on the bed, he said, "Samantha, you've got to see this. Open your eyes and take a look! It's Tammy Reis, Samantha. She's in orbit! Listen to her! Open your eyes and look at Tammy!"

His request, just one of many over the last half year, had grown reflexive, automatic, literally unconscious. He did not bother to look down at her for a response. He missed the sudden flutter of her eyelids, their raising, the slow blink, the weak gaze upward.

His heart nearly stopped, though, when he heard her voice rasp "Tammy?"

▼ ▲ ▼

"That's Reis!" Gibbon cried in a voice trembling with dread. Her presence onboard the awesome spaceship was more than a personal insult; it marked the failure of his entire philosophy. If someone he had personally hand-crafted into the most ardent supporter of NASA could so utterly betray the agency, then...

Gibbon rushed to Steven Milton's side and bent down to whisper, "Project *Stark Fist*. Is it ready to fly?"

Milton looked up at him quizzically. "Never heard of it."

Gibbon seized the smaller man's arms and shook him once, then addressed him as if scolding a pupil.

"Don't play your coy little games with me! I have my own spies, you must know by now. It's absolutely vital that you bring down those spacecraft. All of them. Crockett's gang, too. No survivors, do you under—"

Milton shook off Gibbon's grip. "I don't take orders from cadavers. Piss off or you're out of here."

Looking stricken, Gibbon stepped back. His face hardened and he turned toward the president. "Sir, I urge you to—"

"Shush," Crane said, raising an authoritative hand.

"Okay, we're apparently in the midst of a crisis here," Lester said as the camera view switched back to him. *"We'll keep you informed about the rescue effort. Right now, I'd like to interview some of the other members of the crew. There are twenty of us in all, so let's see what we can get on the monitor."*

Lester paused, listening to something uttered by his assistant.

"Okay, most of the crew's experiencing their first taste of free fall and have their faces buried in airsick bags, so we'll just close for now with the reminder that this is a peaceful business effort and implore the governments of the world not to consider us in any way a threat to the peace and security of—" Lester began to look a little green. One hand darted swiftly to his mouth while the other waved a cutoff signal. The screen went black, quickly replaced by a GSN anchorman Tom McDermott.

"Let's go back to Davy Crockett on that other rocket that blasted into orbit this morning. Mr. Crockett, do you read me?"

Crockett's image filled the screen. He nodded.

"What do you think? It's getting pretty crowded up there."

"We all think it's great, Tom, and I'd say there's plenty of room up here for anyone who wants to come. We wish we could help ferry up some fuel for them, but this little spacecopter carries almost no payload, and we couldn't have built anything bigger to launch from the Bronx."

The anchor nodded, actually listening intently, not merely feigning interest. *"And that unprovoked attack?"*

"Let's be magnanimous and say someone made a hasty mistake and that I'm certain no government, least of all our own, would intend to harm us knowing that we're just youthful explorers on a carefree day trip."

"You've got to bring them down!" Gibbon shouted to the room.

"Yeah, right," Crane said. "Six weeks before the election and I'm going to shoot down civilians. Kids, no less!"

"Grant has already admitted to their spacecraft's failure," Gibbon said, advancing toward Crane with a sly expression. "If the whole thing just blew to bits, everyone would assume they broke up in the atmosphere, or that the vessel failed in some other fashion. You could comfort the families of the victims. You could pledge your support for continued space exploration through UNITO, for all mankind, as a tribute to their memory!"

Crane ignored the professor and turned to the chairman of the Joint Chiefs. "They mentioned a rescue. How about us? If we sent up the Shuttle from Vandenberg, we could offload Grant's crew and take them safely back to Earth. That would prove the Shuttle's superiority and make us the big heroes, right? Big fanfare, good photo op?" He turned to lift an inquiring eyebrow at his spin doctors.

"*Atlantis*," the chairman of Joint Chiefs grumbled, "cannot possibly be made ready on such short notice."

"Isn't it on the pad right now?"

The Air Force chief said, "Yes, sir, it is, but only for test-fitting. The launch complex has been in mothballs for more than a decade, and—"

"I'm not so young," Crane said to the older man, "that I don't remember the promises made when NASA sold the Shuttle to Congress. One hundred-sixty hour turnaround time. That's one week."

Gibbon cut in with a sarcastic snort. "NASA made up those numbers to snow Congress. They admitted as much, years ago. You couldn't get that white elephant to fly in a month. I say we take action *now*!"

Crane looked him up and down. "What do you mean 'we,' white man?"

Taken aback by the old rejoinder, Gibbon recovered quickly enough to say, "Every member of NOSS is a registered voter. And they'll vote for someone who backs the aims of UNITO."

It was Crane's turn to snort. "Like I need a hundred thousand space nerd votes. If I wanted voting blocks, I'd abolish gun laws and get four million votes from the NRA."

A campaign aide could not resist lecturing the professor. "No one wins," she said, "by attracting single-issue groups. They win by gaining the center. President Crane has to consider what is best for the majority of Americans."

"You drooling idiots!" Gibbon cried. "So obsessed with gaining the sanction of morons that you risk the very future of civilization! Can't you see that when these people leave Earth, they leave the State behind? You can't rule them from down here. Do you want a drug runner plying his trade from the high ground? Do you want nuclear power plants orbiting over your head? Do you want that cigar-chomping mountain boy to invite more of his ilk to join him?"

Crane shook his head. "Thank you for your input, Dr. Gibbon. Now please get the hell out of here."

At that cue, two Marine guards stepped over to Gibbon, quietly flanking the professor without touching him.

"Narrow-minded short-sighted nationalist bastards," he said icily. "The blood you'll have to spill to bring space back under our control will rise like a tide without ebb! A few drops now could avoid *oceans* later." He turned to leave, escorted by the guards.

Crane gazed at the commander of the Air Force. "I want *Atlantis* to fly a rescue mission. I want it launched within the week. And I don't want any screwups."

The general cracked his knuckles. "You want to risk another *Constitution*? Losing two shuttles, two crews, and two spaceports in the same year won't look good to the voters who paid for them."

Crane only hesitated a moment before saying, in a tone more commanding than either of them had expected, "That's why I said 'no screwups.' "

▼ ▲ ▼

Crockett switched off communication with the ground and addressed his companions. "We're safe now. We've had a long morning and I think we ought to get some... rest. Sam?"

The figure to his right said nothing. Eyes closed, Sam had fallen asleep in the unearthly free fall style: arms floating outward from his body, head bobbing lightly to the pulse in his carotid arteries.

"Bern?"

She gazed at him, an odd smile on her lips. "Yes, Cap'n?"

"Shall we perform a scientific experiment or three?"

With a flourish, she undid her straps and pulled herself over Davy.

"You utter cad," she said, pulling him close to remove his hat. She flung it away so that it spun — tail out — to hit the far bulkhead where it rested, hovering. She stripped the leather-fringe rawhide jacket from his shoulders — no mean feat in free fall — and whispered so as not to disturb the sleeping Sam, "You brought me down here to seduce me, didn't you?"

He ran his fingers through her ebon hair, smiling. "Purely in the interest of scientific research." Strong fingers unzipped and un-Velcroed her skintight Spandex pressure suit, unlatched the metal helmet collar encircling her throat, unlaced the long black gloves that ran up her forearms. She returned the favor until they floated before each other surrounded by an orbiting cloud of clothing, naked at the center in a lovers' embrace.

She reached down to caress him — or was it up? In free fall, there was no way to tell and that was just the way she desired it. He ran his hands over her breasts, watched them quiver sensually in the absence of gravity, then drew her close to him to feel the warmth of her body against his, inhale her sweet fragrance, and taste the passion on her lips, her mouth, her tongue.

▼ ▲ ▼

Chemar D'Asaro watched the monitor in utter fascination. "This is astounding."

All around her work station, volunteers and crew busied themselves with the final touches on *Nomad* and the airplane that would launch it. She alternated between glancing at the GSN broadcast and concentrating on re-checking *Nomad*'s flight software with the telepresent assistance of a systems analyst in Boulder, Colorado.

Larry Poubelle stood outside in the late morning sunlight conducting his own interviews with the press. He wore his pressure suit as if ready to take off at a moment's notice.

"All I can say is" — he cracked a wide grin — "it sure looks as if money can't buy everything, not even haste."

"So you don't mind that two different groups have launched before you're even ready?" one of the sweltering reporters asked.

"Hell no! That they whumped my tail makes me proud to be an American. A less wealthy American than I'd planned, but what's money except a way of keeping score? It's like manure — you've got to spread it around for it to do any good."

"So you'll still go through with it?"

Poubelle laughed. "Friends, I already set the final air record. I'm hitting Space purely for the adventure."

"What about the Woolsey congressional dynasty?" another reporter asked, his finger pressing against the receiver in his ear. "Father and son are on the Hill right now, promising to stop you."

Poubelle shrugged, spreading his hands in a gesture of mock resignation. "Since we began the Daedalus Project, the Experimental Spacecraft Association has grown on its own with almost no input from our end. There may be a hundred, a thousand others working on their own spaceships. The government — for whatever reasons they have — might be able to stop me, but they can't stop everyone. They can't lobotomize American ingenuity. They can't pith America's backbone."

▼ ▲ ▼

"We can only pray to almighty God," Ludlow Woolsey IV declaimed before the emergency joint session of Congress, "that when this criminal enterprise fails, when their insult to humanity crashes in flames, that it will not fall on innocent victims and cause even more devastation. My father, Senator Woolsey, served in these halls when Skylab dropped from the sky in the late 'Seventies. I remember well the fear we all endured as we wondered if the plummeting, burning metal would hit us. Imagine that smuggler's titanic monstrosity tumbling aflame through the sky, hitting Washington, Manhattan, Los Angeles!"

Woolsey's weeks in seclusion some months ago apparently had restored him to the peak of health. His handsome good looks imparted a harsh counterpoint to the outrage and indignation he displayed. His father, seated with the other senators, nodded approval of his son's speech.

This is good, the senior Woolsey thought. *He may have that shot at the Presidency that I never had.*

"You're all familiar with my father's blistering critique of the commercial space industry, with its reckless disregard for safety and its dismal launch record. And you know that I have been a tireless opponent of the manner in which NASA has conducted the entire *Constitution* inquiry. Now Marcus Grant — who many of you know from previous investigations is a smuggler, a black marketeer, and worse — is orbiting right over our heads claiming to be involved in harmless space manufacturing."

The congressman pulled a sheaf of papers from the briefcase on the podium and waved them in the air. "Ladies and gentlemen, I hold in my hand proof that Marcus Grant has transported into outer space over one hundred pounds of seeds, including those of the coca, opium, and marijuana plants, and the mycelium of the psilocybin mushroom!

"He's planning to turn that so-called space station into an orbital drug lab. And what's worse is that he can drop those poisons straight down on any part of the world he pleases and we can't stop him! He could rain death down upon our cities and we would be powerless to interdict it!"

He slammed the papers down on the podium, then leaned on it with his fists, glowering at his colleagues. "And now Mr. Poubelle pipes up, a man who has been before senate and congressional committees more than once. This arrogant fat cat whose wealth comes from another kind of poison — the radioactive kind — plans to hot-rod around the Earth." Rising as if buoyed by indignation, Woolsey mopped at his brow with a handkerchief and said, "I know he's packaged and marketed himself as some kind of Charles Lindbergh-type hero, but he's bought his prestige, he hasn't earned it. What has he got planned for outer space? Orbiting nuclear waste dumps, poisoning the ecology of space? He's familiar with risk assessment, yet he plans to launch a rocket plane — one that's never been taken to orbit — directly over the entire continental United States! If he cracked up, the pieces could fall on Las Vegas, Phoenix, Dallas, Shreveport, Savannah, or anywhere in between! We've seen the deadly consequences of a spacecraft disaster in the *Constitution* tragedy. We don't dare let that happen again!"

Leaning forward once more on the podium, he dabbed at his brow and said, "It is out of concern for America and Americans that I support the joint resolution forbidding Poubelle's irresponsible actions, and urge the president to order the Air Force to prevent tomorrow's flight.

"We don't need such perversion of American ideals. We don't want such corruption of the purity of space exploration. We cannot permit such a man to penetrate the sanctity of the heavens and plant the seed of exploitation and personal profit!"

Woolsey rubbed at his forehead. The other members of congress gazed at him curiously, and he noticed the twist of the lens on a C-SPAN videocam as it zoomed in on him. Suddenly, he grew flushed and agitated. They should be applauding such a fiery, inspirational speech, if only from knee-jerk courtesy. What went wrong?

He peered at a monitor on the floor. There, in the extreme closeup of his face, he saw the answer as it beamed around the world on orbiting TV satellites.

On his forehead, the capillary-rich scars from Tammy Reis's vicious attack on him had grown engorged with the blood of his excitement, spelling for all to see the damning confirmation he fought for months to suppress. Appearing as if writ by the hand of vengeful Providence, there burned Ludlow Woolsey's brand:

RAPEST

CHAPTER 50

A man's country is not a certain area of land, of mountains, rivers, and woods, but it is a principle; and patriotism is loyalty to that principle.

— George William Curtis

19 August

Dawn rose on a desert cut by the sounds of war jets circling over Mojave Airport. Sunshine illuminated the two F-16's for at least a quarter of an hour before it spilled into the high desert valley.

Larry Poubelle rolled a cigar in his robot hand, sensitive force-feedback circuitry sending impulses to the severed nerves at his shoulder, which in turn transmitted to his brain the sensations of a firm, crinkling cylinder of tobacco turning slowly in his fingers. He did not light up — *Nomad* sat fastened atop the 747 now, its fueling nearly finished. At a safe distance stood a swarm of reporters and onlookers, armed with a prodigious array of video and still cameras. One husband and wife pair stood hundreds of yards apart with two cameras set up for wide-parallax 3-D HDTV. All of them pointed their instruments toward one single object of attention. *Nomad*.

The sleek black upgraded X-15 A-2 rocket plane upon the highly-polished 747 looked like a shark hitching a ride on a whale. This shark, though, sprouted two fat hypersonic drop tanks. Both sported thin coats of frost — blessedly thin, thanks to the extremely low humidity of the mid-August desert air, the insulating properties of the spun-composite tanks, and the last-minute decision to borrow de-icing machinery from another airport occupant. Every pound of ice that coated either the external tanks or the mid-section of *Nomad* in which lay the internal tanks represented an extra pound of payload added and several pounds of fuel wasted. Poubelle dared not squander even an ounce.

Chemar strode out of the hangar to stand beside him. Cameras immediately turned to focus on her. She cut a stunning figure in her ebon space suit, helmet tucked under her left arm, right hand clutching the packet of personal items she planned to take with her. Her jet-black hair — styled short to be comfortable under the helmet and to survive the flight for the inevitable photo opportunities upon their return — framed her dark face and piercing golden eyes. She wore no makeup, for safety reasons, but on her it did not matter in the slightest.

Together they stood, watching through the frigid clouds of hydrogen and oxygen vapors that mixed so dangerously around the nonchalant ground crew. Several of them were old men, retired NASA and Air Force personnel who had worked on the original X-15 project thirty years before. They darted about prepping the spacecraft and mothership, spirited teenagers once more, with a universe of possibilities ahead of them.

An F-16 flew low over the airport, its weapon pods blatantly loaded with air-to-air missiles, and loudly cut in its afterburners to accelerate straight upward. It reached supersonic speed at five thousand feet, rattling the morning air with a loud sonic boom.

Poubelle shook his head. "Why don't they just pass at fifty feet and light the fumes? That would solve their problem."

"Do you really think they'll try to shoot us down?"

He turned his gaze toward the lifeless hangar where Freespace Orbital once buzzed with activity. "I don't know, kid. Absolute power engenders absolute arrogance."

A plain white sedan crept slowly to the edge of the hangar and stopped. The doors opened to disgorge six men in gas masks and bright yellow hazardous-material suits. They slowly advanced on Poubelle and D'Asaro. One of them carried a sheaf of paper as thick as a phone book.

"Laurence Poubelle?" the one carrying the papers asked.

The billionaire pointed his prosthetic thumb at the name embroidered in gold thread upon his breast. "You've got him."

"Thiel. State Department. We've met."

Poubelle nodded.

"This is a joint effort of the State, Commerce, Transportation, and Justice departments." Thiel waved the thick book. "This is our authority to seize all chattels real and personal including aircraft and hangars belonging to Laurence Poubelle, The Daedalus Project, Incorporated, American Atomic, Incorporated, and other persons identified in this finding."

The eight of them stood in the orange morning light, six yellow, two black, while curious press and public watched. They all noticed the side arms worn by four of the intruders.

"You know," Poubelle said, rolling the cigar in his titanium fingers, "that I'm not going to flop over and give up just because you wave around the eructations of a bunch of government attorneys who aren't competent to maintain a private practice." His eyes gazed into Thiel's with a disturbing mixture of aristocratic calm and hellish menace. "It's a funny thing about dawn over the desert. First there's no wind at all, then little gusts puff this way and that as patches of earth warm up to create thermals. Right now, I feel a slight breeze blowing the rocket propellant away from us. Then again, maybe I'm wrong and it's blowing fumes toward us."

He raised his arm and pointed the finger with its built-in cigar lighter toward the government agents. Smiling, he said, "Shall we find out which way the wind blows?"

Thiel shook his head and laughed, albeit nervously. "You wouldn't blow up you and your plane and your girl there."

"And you wouldn't dream of firing those guns in an explosive atmosphere, would you?" Poubelle turned to walk toward *Nomad*'s boarding ramp, D'Asaro in step with him.

Thiel snorted in annoyance. "Cuff 'em, guys."

The four gun-toting agents rushed forward. From out of the crowd flew a half-empty soda can, hitting one of them, causing him to stop and turn toward the onlookers.

Thiel raised his hands and waved them authoritatively at the throng. "This is an official government seizure under the RICO—"

A beer bottle clipped the mask over his ear. He reflexively wiped the brew from the rubber garment and jumped to dodge another missile.

Dozens of people, young and old, rushed under the perimeter rope and surrounded the six agents, yelling, spitting, and throwing snack foods.

One of the agents, hit in the back of the neck by an unopened beer can, slapped leather.

"No guns!" Thiel yelled shrilly, tearing his gas mask off to be heard above the din. "Let's go. He's been served." He stared up at the warbirds circling overhead. "Let's leave him to the big guns."

Taunted and jeered by the mob, the canary-colored crew silently climbed into their car and locked the doors, then cautiously backed away.

Poubelle and D'Asaro ascended the stairway leading up above the 747 to the cockpit of *Nomad*, seventy-five feet above the runway. From that vantage, they surveyed the skies.

The F-16's joined up and flew wingtip-to-wingtip down the runway fifty feet above the concrete. The noise was deafening.

"Nice air show, huh?" Poubelle yelled to the crowd after the roar died down.

"What are we going to do, Larry?" Chemar's voice lost some of its confidence.

"They won't intentionally collide with us, and I know Bischoff has enough nerve to fly the jet without letting them get to him. What someone might order them to do with those missiles— or what they might do under stress — is anybody's guess. In any case..." He gazed at the golden Sun in the east, at the vast blue sky laced lightly with high-flying cirrus, and then at his beautiful Chemar. "It's a good day to die."

Her aureate eyes widened as a fierce smile grew to efface all fear. "Let's go blow up," she said, putting an arm around his waist and waving the other at the crowd.

A cheer arose, then almost as suddenly fell silent. Everyone's attention shifted from the piggy-backed aircraft to the runway. Poubelle and D'Asaro turned to see what drew the crowd's interest.

The taxiways had become, in just a few minutes, a traffic-jam of airplanes all advancing toward the main runway. One by one, they made it to the runway, gunned their engines, and lifted off into the sky.

"We have an escort squadron!" Poubelle stared in astonishment at the procession. "There must be dozens of them!"

The drone of the aircraft taking flight, though, was quickly overwhelmed by something louder, vaster, and more encompassing. Poubelle and the others looked east, into the rising sun, and saw it darken.

From the east — and the north and south and west, for that matter — swarms of aircraft of all descriptions converged on Mojave like sea gulls on a locust hunt. Unable to maneuver at their high speed in such clogged airspace, the F-16's circled about inside the shrinking perimeter, then once more cut in their afterburners to roar straight upward, shooting out of the vortex at near-transonic speed.

Hundreds, perhaps thousands of aircraft filled the sky in a counter-clockwise flight pattern. General aircraft — Pipers, Cessnas, Beechcrafts, Northrops, Taylorcrafts — flew low and slow in their own particular circle. Farther out flew the powerful old warbirds: Spitfires, Zeros, P51-D's, Mustangs, Messerschmitts, and MiG's. Corporate jets formed a higher, wider shell: Learjets, Cessna Citations, Beech Starships. Even airliners including old DC-3's, DC-9's, MD-11's, Airbuses, 747's, and L-1011's — some chartered to view the event, others actually veering in from their flight paths for an unscheduled thrill — heeded the distress call broadcast the night before by ham radio, telephone tree, The Net, and other ways.

Helicopters hovered at the periphery: Bells, Sikorskies, Hueys.

Even homebuilts got into the act, displaying their bizarre designs and varying flight characteristics. Low-winged Lancairs, Zodiacs, Sonerais, KR2's, Zenairs, and Glasairs roared about. High-winged Avids, Wag-A-Bonds, Kitfoxes, RAN's, and Coyotes floated like butterflies. Seawind, Buccaneer, and Osprey amphibians looked like hyperthyroidal gooneybirds. Brand new Davis Gemini flying wings and venerable Long-EZ's buzzed and hummed, along with Cozys, Infinitys, Solaris, and other strangely shaped experimental planes. Velocity and Challenger and Quicksilver ultralights, Air Command, Ken Brock, Air & Space, and Barnett gyroplanes, Bensen Gyrocopters, Rotorway Executive and Cobra two-seat helicopters, Revolution one-seat eggbeaters, and nameless innovative abominations that creaked and shuddered.

One old and patched Vari E-Z carried a lean, henna-haired grandmother who piloted barefoot, but stayed in tight formation with the youngest and best of them, her face an ethereal mask of pleasure.

Biplanes existed in a class by themselves, bringing an anachronistic, barnstorming touch. Classic Nieuports, Jennies, a Sopwith, a pizza-financed team of aerobatic Stinsons, several Pitts Specials, and even a cherry-red Fokker Triplane buzzed in close with their engines chugging.

Fastening their five-point harnesses, Poubelle and Chemar locked on their helmets and ran the last check of their onboard computers. The fueling team down below gave them thumbs up and withdrew, other members of the ground crew retracting the gangway and unchocking the wheels of the 747.

"All right, Karl, talk to me." Poubelle cycled the canopy shut. Unlike the original X-15, it hinged in the front to minimize the chance of a catastrophic release. An integral part of the escape/reentry pod, it had to stay on no matter what.

The pilot of the Boeing, Karl William Bischoff, fired up each of the jet engines in turn once the cryogenic fuel tankers had pulled away to a safe distance. "Pipe down, Larry, and let me do my job," he said in that calm, dead-level voice cultivated by airline pilots. "Mojave Tower, this is Daedalus One, we are ready to taxi."

"Roger, Daedalus One," the tower replied. *"And watch out for that cloud of gnats out there. ATC has given up any hope of controlling them, and Edwards is just noting N-numbers of as many aircraft as it can for subsequent FAA action. Be advised you are flying in military-operation airspace if you exceed twelve hundred feet AGL."*

The 747 with its unrefulgently black companion slowly rolled away from the hangar. Cameras clicked, whirred, and hummed as the crowd — swelling larger minute by minute — grew ever more excited. The morning sun, high enough above the horizon to glow its familiar yellow-white, glinted off *Nomad*'s polycarbonate cockpit ports. Poubelle and D'Asaro gave one last wave to the throng and turned to focus total attention on their primary task: not blowing up.

▼ ▲ ▼

"Fly Swatter One to Fly Swatter Leader," one of the F-16 pilots radioed to his commander as he escaped from the tightening circle of civilian aircraft. "Be advised that maneuvering to pin down target impossible without significant collateral damage, over."

"Fly Swatter One, state target's position, over."

"Halfway down the runway, taking off."

"Fly Swatter One and Two, pull back and monitor the situation until target reaches flight level four hundred, over."

"Roger, Fly Swatter Leader."

Fly Swatter Leader circled overhead at 60,000 feet in a NASA U-2, taking in the big picture, but counting on the F-16 pilots to provide up-close information. From the greater-than-eagle's vantage, the U-2 pilot saw an unbelievable clutter of aircraft all around the Mojave Desert. Scanning the general aviation frequencies, he picked up at least a dozen near hits and what might have been two actual mid-airs. A low count considering the unprecedented congestion.

Fly Swatter One and Two stayed above the majority of aircraft that flew between 800 and 10,000 feet above ground level, watching and waiting.

The mothership rolled into takeoff attitude and after what seemed like eons broke free of her earthly bonds and rose into the sky. The bright 747 and her sleek black partner (midriff and drop tanks frosted white, which imparted a stretched-penguin look to it) performed a gradual left-handed climbing turn to enter the inner wall of the swirling vortex of aircraft.

"This is amazing," Chemar muttered into her headset.

"Yep," Poubelle said. "Looks like we got us a convoy. Imagine this many people with nothing else to do on a Monday."

"Cut the chatter, Nomad,*" Bischoff interjected, "and check propellant top-off."*

Poubelle winked at the pencil-sized flight recorder camera mounted atop his instrument panel. "Hey — what am I paying you for?"

Bischoff shot back with good-natured terseness, *"And what are you buying?"*

The cylindrical curtain of aircraft widened to give the 747 reasonable maneuvering space, yet hung in close enough to prevent a clear shot by any adversary. Chemar took a moment during a lull in her duties to scan the airwaves. On the general aviation frequencies, nearly all the pilots maintained silence, working furiously on their see-and-be-seen techniques. The frequencies used by the higher-flying airliners buzzed with more plane-to-plane discussion, especially concerning the parentage of the F-16 pilots and their superiors back in the District of Columbia.

As soon as the ungainly piggyback plane passed through 2000 feet above ground level, they entered Complex One-Alpha Military Operations Area. Their radios suddenly crackled with threats.

"All unidentified aircraft, this is Edwards RAPCON. You are ordered to return to point of origin and surrender to military personnel. You are in an MOA and subject to federal authority. Violation of this airspace will result in retaliatory action."

In a show of Gandhian aeronautical solidarity, none of the escort aircraft complied.

Chemar switched to one of the satellite news channels piped into *Nomad* from the 747's antenna array and discovered that one of the planes circling about them carried a reporter broadcasting live. He nearly prattled with excitement.

"Oh, people, I wish I could point this camera in every direction at once! Those of you with three-dee at home can see what I mean. We are literally swimming in a sea of airplanes. Look! Look! The Daedalus planes are overtaking us! There they go! Ooh, ooh, magnificent!"

"What is it about space flight, boss, that makes some people discuss it in orgasmic tones?"

Poubelle made a *tsk*ing sound. "A member of the Mile High Club needs to ask. When did you stop flying in your dreams?"

"Never. I still dream I'm falling, but just before I hit, I bounce back up and take off."

"Exactly," he said. "Most people lose those dreams when they pass through puberty. The true believers are still haunted — and driven — by that dream."

"Then explain airline pilots — they don't dream at all, I've heard."

"Hey," Bischoff protested. *"I resemble that remark! There's a big difference between us."*

"Such as?" Poubelle asked.

"Such as, I may be crazy enough to fly you up, but not enough to sit on ten tons of explosives and strike a match!"

▼▲▼

One of the monitors in the launch complex at Vandenberg displayed the aerial view of the scene over Mojave. Few of the personnel gave it more than a cursory glance. Too many other details commanded their attention.

Sherry Cooper darted from console to console observing the operations of Freespace Orbital personnel and the military and NASA employees. Behind her flapped the ends of the ankle-length turquoise knit sweater she wore unbuttoned almost like a cape. From beneath its folds trailed a long, coiled black cord connected to her headset. The intercom communicated with each of the four channels.

"Roger, Range Safety," she said on Channel One. "We'll have COLA for you shortly." The collision avoidance analysis came from Space Command Western Range and provided vital confirmation that *Aurora* would not hit any other orbiting object. From where she stood, she could see the range safety officer — once more Lt. Rollins — in charge of the flight termination system: the explosive charges that would blow *Aurora* to bits in the event of any deviation from her flight path.

Sherry gazed across the launch control room toward Thom Brodsky, whose nervous glance back at her confirmed that he stood ready to assist with her daring and dangerous plan.

Colonel Alan Shepard Lundy watched the proceedings from a vantage point near one of the computer banks. On the large wall screen that looked almost like a window, the squat, sky-blue rocket sat on its simple launch pad surrounded by cryogenic mist. The bright glow of morning illuminated its southeastern side to cast a long shadow across the concrete launch complex. In the distance, the space shuttle *Atlantis* stood huge and regal attached to its rust-colored ET and twin white SRB's amid drifting billows of light ocean mist and ground fog.

Lundy had fallen in love, though he would probably never use the term, with Vandenberg in his months commanding the base. The vision of it serving as a true, functioning spaceport filled him with a joyful anticipation constantly allayed by his awareness of the political and military realities he would witness on days such as today. He was about to watch another rocket company bite sea foam.

"COLA is clear," Lt. Rollins confirmed.

The launch director, once again Captain Fortney, spoke on Channel Four. "Confirm clear COLA, confirm downrange clear. Watching the situation over Mojave. Restart clock. T-minus ten minutes and counting."

Sherry leaned over the man in charge of monitoring tank pressure. "LOX tank full," he said. "Hydrogen tank at three-quarters."

The countdown proceeded flawlessly as Sherry's level of anxiety increased. She floated, almost, in a light-headed yet utterly aware state of intense consciousness.

"T-minus one minute," Fortney said on Channel Four.

Someone on Channel One said, "Uh, Captain, I have a mandatory abort on the command receivers."

Sherry, prepared for betrayal, put her plan into action. "No abort," she said in a husky voice over Channel One. "All systems go." She sidled over to the range safety officer.

Capt. Fortney, hearing the exchange not on his headset, but somewhere in the room, said, "Who's calling an abort, please?"

Lt. Rollins quickly responded — on Channel One — "Abort due to command transceiver call on Range Safety."

Hearing nothing over the intercom, Fortney repeated, "Who's calling abort?"

"No abort. It's just TM." Brodsky — on Channel Four — sounded calm and authoritative.

Confusion spread across the network and launch control. On one channel, all appeared well; on another, conflicting calls for an abort.

"T-minus thirty seconds," Sherry interjected. "All systems go for launch. Internal power. Pressure nominal. Telemetry flowing."

"We understand abort," a confused voice said on Channel Two.

Fortney covered up his boom mic and shouted, "Do we have an abort or not?"

Lt. Rollins began to shout his reply when something hard pressed against his spine at heart level. He heard the familiar snap of a thumb safety sliding to the decidedly unsafe position.

Sherry Cooper whispered to him with a voice as cold, fluid, and deadly as liquid hydrogen. "You can be a hero to your leaders by aborting the launch — and die not knowing it — or you can be a hero to the future by doing nothing — and live to see it."

Rollins sat frozen at the controls, his hand in place over the red FTS button.

"T-minus fifteen," Fortney announced. "Are we go?"

"We're go," said half a dozen voices over all four channels.

"No abort," Sherry said coolly.

"Range safety?" Fortney inquired.

Sherry pressed her late husband's Astra .380 more firmly against Rollins's back.

"Range safety says go," the lieutenant uttered hoarsely.

"T-minus ten, nine, eight..."

Sherry gazed up at the monitor. In the fascination of the moment, she still possessed the presence of mind to whisper into Rollins's ear, "Move your hand six inches away from the FTS switch. *Now*."

"Three seconds. Ignition sequence start."

"Valves open," a voice on Channel One said. *"Release clamps."*

"...two," Fortney continued, "one, ignition."

"LH flow one hundred percent—"

"Clamps away!" one of the Freespace people yelled.

Sherry stared breathlessly at the monitor as flames exploded out of the underside of *Aurora*. The orange flames and white smoke hid the robin's-egg spacecraft for an instant. Then, above the cloud, the graphite-grey tip of the spaceship poked upward.

"Liftoff!" Capt. Fortney said with a surge of enthusiasm. "Liftoff at twenty-nine minutes past the hour."

Everyone not intimately involved in monitoring the ship's systems stared at the wall screen with tense awe. Now the entire ship lifted clear of the smoke, rising on its fiery plume like a bolt into the blue. The camera angled to follow its ascent.

"Good burn," someone reported. *"Fuel flow nominal."*

Fortney glanced at the readout superimposed on his work station screen. "Altitude eight hundred feet. Go, baby!"

Rollins edged his hand toward the abort switch. An increase in spinal pressure let him know that Mrs. Cooper was not inordinately distracted by the splendor of the launch.

Colonel Lundy, observing the manner in which she leaned closely to Rollins and the way her right elbow extended backward under her long sweater, realized that she had taken his *sub rosa* advice and indeed was paying close attention to range safety. He smiled. His father would have been pleased, he believed, to see someone get results from the bureaucracy through such direct action.

▼ ▲ ▼

"Holy Chao!" Bischoff said, seeing the white plume rise out of the west. *"What's that?"*

Poubelle scanned the sky, saw the rocket's ascent, and instantly knew its origin. "That's Widow Cooper's *Aurora*."

"It's heading north," Chemar noted. "Doglegging to avoid us?"

"She's inserting it into a polar orbit, along the course a tour ship would take. Maximum ground track coverage. Maximum scenery."

"Ah."

Everyone onboard the two planes — except occasionally Bischoff — watched the arc of white topped by the bright point of light for as long as their climbing turn allowed, then waited impatiently for the scene to reappear in their left quadrant as they came about. By the time they saw it again, the ship ascended almost to invisibility.

"Good show," Poubelle said. Glancing at the altimeter, he added, "We're coming up on our own little moment of truth here."

At 12,500 feet altitude, many of the smaller aircraft had leveled off — open or unpressurized cockpits prevented many of them from flying higher without supplementary oxygen, though some hung in knowing that they had either half an hour or 1500 feet before oxygen became legally required. At 14,000 feet, those die-hards dropped out. When Daedalus One hit 18,000 feet and entered the positive control area, their escort consisted of corporate jets, airliners, and a few pressurized, turocharged piston planes. These scores of loyal fellow travelers tightened up their formation from a cylinder to a roughly spherical shape, most of them circling and climbing through the same altitude as the 747, some in a tighter turn far above and some mirroring the action farther below. The two F-16's orbited the protective shell, sometimes testing its integrity — and the pilots' nerves — by banking in closely and breaking away or rushing straight toward the equator of the sphere, pulling up on afterburners, and arching over in an outside loop. Then they power-dove down the other side, rotated 180°, and pulled an inside loop under the south pole region of the lowest aircraft. It kept everyone on their toes.

"Fly Swatter One and Two," the voice of their commander radioed. *"Shortly before launch, target will have to break away from the pack. At that time, you have authorization to paint the target, over."*

Not privy to the military-frequency communications, one airline pilot in the convoy kept up a running monologue for the benefit of his half-fascinated, half-terrified passengers.

"It makes you wonder," he said in that back-porch conversational tone some sky jockeys affected, "whether the government's so determined to keep Americans out of Space that they might try firing missiles in proximity to fully-loaded commercial aircraft." He did not realize that his comments — picked up by reporters with radio scanners — bounced the planet in real time via satellite news systems.

Leaving the Military Operation Area behind at Flight Level 180 — 18,000 feet — ended the stream of dire warnings from Edwards RAPCON. That tedious chore they handed over to the FAA.

"All unidentified aircraft, this is Lancaster Radio. You are in Positive Control Airspace without IFR flight plans or clearance. Those of you with transponders will be contacted for FAA action. Military authority has superseded and informed us you are subject to military response. That is all."

Lancaster Radio repeated the warning a few times before giving up. The two F-16s continued their maneuvers, emboldened by the diminution of the protective shell as more aircraft dropped away until only a fleet of corporate jets and a handful of airliners remained.

"Fly Swatter Leader, this is Fly Swatter One. We have transient windows of opportunity now. Do we have permission to lock on, over?"

"Negative, One. Hold off until target breaks free, over."

At FL 450, Bischoff leveled the 747 and brought it out of its extended turn at a heading of 90° — due east. The other aircraft cleared a path for it and fell into formation along its left and right wings at a safe distance of one-half mile. The airliners pulled away. Only a dozen jets remained of the thousands of airplanes that had joined in. These carried corporate executives and high-flying playboys (and a playgirl or two), all friends of the equally wealthy and flamboyant pilot of *Nomad*. Despite the presence of armed fighters, they treated the event as a champagne excursion. And now they awaited the grand finale.

"Well, Larry," Bischoff said jauntily. *"Here's where I bid you a fond farewell and haul my donkey back to base. Chemar — be prepared to lend him a hand... in case his fake one falls off!"*

"You slay me," she said in a deadpan tone. "Make sure your flying doesn't."

"All right, kids," Poubelle said, commanding the onboard computer to cycle its checklist. "Here's where we see whose rocket is faster. Top off tanks."

Pumps onboard the 747 fed more cryogenic propellant and oxidizer to the interior and exterior tanks to replace what boiled off during the ascent. The tanks sealed shut and the feed lines retracted, followed shortly by the external power connection.

"All power on internal," Chemar noted. "APU's operative. Drop-minus four minutes and counting."

While Poubelle and D'Asaro ran through their final countdown, Bischoff brought the 747 to its service ceiling and then exceeded the altitude by another 500 feet. *"Flight Level Four Fifty-Five and holding."*

At Drop-Minus one minute, he lowered the plane's nose to increase airspeed and allow for a positive separation.

"Nomad, *we are at five hundred-eighty knots passing through FL four-fifty."*

"Roger." Poubelle spoke in clipped, terse sentences now, his attention utterly concentrated on the spaceplane. "Drop-Minus thirty. Turbine lights green. Pressure green. Control surfaces functional."

"Six hundred knots, FL four-forty."

"Stand by for separation."

Poubelle's hands — real and robotic — tensed. His left lay poised near the ignition switch, his right on the control stick. Behind him, Chemar took a sudden breath loud enough to hear over the intercom.

"I love you," she whispered breathlessly.

"T-Minus zero," Poubelle said. "Drop."

A trio of gunshot-like explosions reverberated through the hull as explosive bolts severed the connections between *Nomad* and the 747. Poubelle edged back on the stick and the spaceplane pulled upward as the Boeing dove down and banked to the right.

"Clean separation," Bischoff radioed. *"Now give 'er the spur."*

Chemar watched her FMS screen, then cried out in sudden terror, "They've painted us!"

▼ ▲ ▼

Fly Swatter One acquired its target and locked its missile radar onto the black arrow. His thumb hovered over the firing switch as he decreased his angle of attack to gain airspeed and close in on his victim.

"Fly Swatter One," the voice of their leader radioed. *"Confirm you've engaged the enemy. Fire at will."*

He glanced up from the screen to peer through the canopy at the aircraft ahead. It lifted gracefully away from the 747, two fat fuel tanks attached to its underside. She was daughter to the X-15, all right, all grown up and more beautiful than her mom.

Inside his pilot's soul, somewhere deeper than his military training ever reached, lay the heart of a young boy who first saw the X-15 hanging high overhead in the Smithsonian and who gazed in awe at its singular beauty.

His killing thumb wavered.

▼ ▲ ▼

"I love you too, babe," Poubelle muttered to his co-pilot as he threw the switch forward.

The engine lit and — even at idle — crushed them with a two-gee acceleration. The computer took over and throttled the engine up to 100% rated thrust over the span of three seconds.

"God!" Chemar groaned as the g-forces mounted.

Poubelle said nothing as he fought to breathe, maintain consciousness, and perform what decision-making functions he needed to while software and hardware controlled their ascent.

▼ ▲ ▼

"Fly Swatter One, fire your missiles!" The order came through as a near-shriek.

"Sorry, Leader," the pilot replied, removing his thumb from the button. "Lost my radar."

Without a word, Fly Swatter Two locked on to the rapidly departing target and launched its missiles. Two ATAM's rocketed away from the F-16's weapons pylons and streaked toward the hot infrared source above and ahead of them. They accelerated to their maximum velocity, straining to gain on *Nomad*, which thundered through Machs one and two in its first twenty seconds of flight and now rose at a 45° angle through FL 700. At Mach 2.5, the engine sucked dry the contents of the hypersonic propellant tanks. Their job done, they separated with alarmingly loud clunks. Friction heating swiftly warmed them to furnace temperatures and tore them into chaff. That chaff collided with one of the missiles, detonating it in a spectacular high-atmospheric blast.

The other missile flamed out and drifted ballistically upward for a few thousand more feet before arcing ignominiously over to drop several hundred feet below its apex. Its self-destruct mechanism blew it to harmless scrap.

"Gee," Fly Swatter One radioed to his companion. "I guess it's catch-and-release day."

▼ ▲ ▼

Nomad's cockpit rattled and hummed, creaked and popped, shuddered like a mustang with the chills. When the hypersonic drop tanks cut loose, the thrust increased with yet another slam of acceleration.

"Mach four," Poubelle noted through gritted teeth. "Mach five."

"Fifty miles altitude. There's no atmosphere left," Chemar growled.

"All right! Two miles per second. APU warning light on two! Wait. It's OK now. Three miles per second. Three point five. Halfway there."

"Sixty miles!"

They spoke to each other as if they traveled alone, even though millions on the ground listened in, courtesy of the satellite news medium. No flight center with hundreds of employees existed on the ground to control the spacecraft; a single computer onboard handled attitude, trajectory, navigation, fuel management, and the thousand details relating to the furious energy that roared from the engine.

From the lower vantage of the 747, Bischoff and his co-pilot watched the pure white exhaust plume, the only visible indication of *Nomad*'s whereabouts. It curved upward into the big sky, far outpacing the slower airbreather. As had every other airliner pilot that day, though, Bischoff's thoughts wandered to the amazing feat of Marcus Grant. He marveled at the notion that one could build a full-sized space station on the ground and lob it into Space in a single piece. He wondered whether it would ever happen again... and if he could make the grade as pilot on one.

▼ ▲ ▼

The six-minute burn lasted for aeons. As the rocket ravenously consumed fuel and oxidizer and thus mass, the constant thrust on an ever-lighter spaceplane meant that the acceleration and g-forces crept upward with every second. Chemar had no idea how long the ton of sand had lain on her, but there had to be an end to it. The sensation, not painful or even particularly uncomfortable, nonetheless made for difficult breathing and laborious movements in her limbs. The most interesting and annoying sensation occurred in her breasts; even though she could not see over the bottom edge of her helmet, she felt as if some powerful lover's hands pressed them relentlessly against her ribs.

She gazed upward through the canopy and saw stars. Not the pale, twinkling, timid stars of an earthly night, but the stark, sharp, unwavering brilliance of starlight uninterrupted in its journey through the cosmos. The veil of air, veil of worldly tears and woe, pierced by the arrow that was *Nomad*, lay behind and below her as she raced away from all worry.

"Six miles per second!" Larry called out with difficulty. "Almost there! Fuel looks good. Attitude... good. Alpha and theta both on the mark. Six point five."

The groaning, creaking, popping sounds inside the cockpit abated as the ship's mass decreased. The roar of the engine a few yards behind them drowned out all other sounds.

Then, as if it had come loose and dropped away from them, the engine's roar muted until only the sound of the turbopump whining to a halt filled their ears. Their weight diminished to earthly proportions, then continued to decline. Chemar soon felt light-headed, dizzy. It was not a sensation of falling, but of not quite knowing which way was down.

"Burnout!" Poubelle announced. "Orbital velocity! We made it, babe!"

"Thank God," she whispered. Then she looked once more out of the canopy. The stars drifted from port to starboard. "Are we losing our yaw stability?"

He gazed at the stars, at the Sun, at the Earth. Then he glanced down at the flight management screen. "Hmm..." was all he said.

CHAPTER 51

Every great advance in natural knowledge has involved the absolute rejection of authority.

— Thomas Huxley

19 August

"I heartily suggest that you stand up and cheer."

Sherry Cooper pushed upward with the gun at Lt. Rollins's back. The lieutenant rose and clapped his hands along with the others in launch control. He applauded slowly, ironically.

Strobes flashed on the cameras of the handful of reporters present. Videocams focused in on her and she flashed a victory sign. Thom Brodsky stepped over to the range safety station to verify that the abort switch had been inactivated at the moment of *Aurora*'s safe insertion into orbit. To destroy the ship now would require a lengthy series of commands by several layers of management.

"Captain Fortney!" Rollins shouted.

Sherry secreted the pistol in her waistband holster.

"Yes, Lieutenant?"

"Sir, Mrs. Cooper interfered with my duties as range safety officer during the ascent phase."

Fortney gazed at Cooper, then at Rollins. "The ship made it into orbit safely, despite the confusion about an abort. What did she do?"

Rollins looked at the cameras, his mind racing to consider all the consequences of his outburst. He might ruin Freespace if he could have her arrested for carrying a gun onto military property. On the other hand, she would have plenty of opportunities to explain *why* she felt she needed to restrain his actions.

"Well, Mr. Rollins?"

"She... Sir, she told me that the abort command was in error because it was... on the wrong channel."

"Isn't that what happened?" Col. Lundy spoke up and looked about the room. "There wasn't any problem, was there? We can go over the TM and intercom transcripts, but from what I saw, Lt. Rollins correctly avoided an abort in the absence of any clear and present danger of the rocket straying from its flight path. I think the entire launch crew deserves an attaboy for a job well-done." He gave them all a thumbs up, most pointedly to Rollins, followed by a knowing one to Cooper.

▼ ▲ ▼

"Look at that!"

Davy Crockett struggled to keep his coonskin cap on. It floated above his head, rotating like the hat of a cartoon character caught by surprise. The finger of his other hand tapped at the screen displaying tracking data provided by a French lookdown-radar satellite. "Poubelle's made it up here with his X-15! And Freespace with their Starblazer, Grant Enterprises with an entire ready-to-go *space wheel!* Where do y'all have to go to get a little privacy?"

"We did pretty well a little while ago," Bernadette said with a lascivious smile.

Sam raised his hands in defeat. "I tell you, there goes the neighborhood. You move to the great outdoors and the next thing you know they're throwing up condos in your backyard."

"Guys," Bernadette said quietly, looking at the life support screen. "We've been up here longer than we planned to be." She turned a gimlet eye toward Crockett. "And burned up too much oxygen."

"I wasn't the only one breathing heavily," Davy said, pulling a cheroot from his jacket to perform zero-g tricks, such as attempting to balance his floppy hat on the end of the cigar with the other end resting against his fingertip.

"Well," Friedman said in a particularly persnickety tone. "If leadfoot over here hadn't altered our line of apsides, I wouldn't have to be running a new calculation—"

"And have you calculated," Bernadette asked, "exactly where we plan to set down?"

Crockett cleared his throat, pocketed the cheroot, and pulled his coonskin cap tightly down to his ears. The tail continued to sway, sometimes sticking up like a polecat's about to spray. "I admit we didn't give it much thought. We obviously can't return to the warehouse. Carla said it's ruined."

Bernadette nodded. "I suggest we aim for something wide and flat. Like the California desert."

"Even wider and flatter," Sam said. "How about Kansas?"

"No." Crockett gazed at his two crewmates. "Listen — we've got to make maximum use of the publicity machine we have here. Landing in the boonies is pointless. We want as many people as possible to see us and thrill to the landing the way they would an old-fashioned barnstormer."

"Oh, no," Friedman moaned. "Don't say what you're going to say!"

Crockett grinned, his eyes sparkling with mischief. "Yep. Central Park. Just before rush hour, so everyone leaving work can come and see."

"That's crazy!" Sam shouted, his glasses flying from his head. "Do you know what precision that would take?"

"Do you know that's how much faith I have in you? Besides" — Davy patted his friend's arm — "this spacecopter can land with pinpoint accuracy, even hover if it has to."

"I don't care where we land," Bernadette said, "as long as we do it within the next orbit. Have you two been holding it in the way I have?"

Guilty looks abounded. "I guess," Sam said, "the adult diaper idea sucked, huh?"

Bernadette nodded. "Royally."

▼ ▲ ▼

As they passed over the Indian Ocean, Sam issued the command to align and retro-fire the engines. The two minute burn set them irrevocably on the downward path toward the atmosphere. Less than half an hour later, the ship began to shudder. Helmets locked on, the three prepared for the most dangerous part of their adventure, which Carla downlinked and broadcast live on GSN and the network feeds.

"All right, Carla," Crockett transmitted. "We're biting air. Jettisoning the main fuel tanks... now."

Three explosive bolts detonated with startlingly loud bangs that *pangged* through the spaceship's hull. Through a rear-mounted fiberoptic video camera, the crew — and GSN viewers — watched the beer-can-shaped module separate with a puff of venting oxygen and kerosene. It began to tumble slowly away from the rear of the spacecopter, which now resembled an inverted cupcake with four popsicle sticks protruding from its wider end.

"Here's where it gets interesting," he said. "Now we'll rotate to an altitude only a tad higher than the Shuttle. We'll see if these student-built rotor blades stay on and don't embarrass us, or whether they burn off and... Whoa! A little pressure on our seats. Have they cleared Central Park yet?"

"Police have cordoned off the Great Lawn, but be warned they plan to bust you the moment you step out."

"I expect nothing less. How's Professor Gibbon?"

"I hear he got kicked out of the White House and retreated to Manhattan!"

"Then that makes our choice even tastier." A tremendous thump rattled the spacecraft. "Carla, we're about to begin aerobraking, so expect a possible loss of signal."

"Roger, Davy we'll stand by."

Something creaked, followed by a slowly increasing whir. Pressing his face against the viewing port, Crockett could see the outer few feet of the rotor tips as they began to rotate in the sparse air at ninety miles altitude.

The pressure on their seats increased as weightlessness was replaced by the more familiar sensation of weight; familiar, and just a bit unwelcome to some of them.

"We're aerobraking," Crockett broadcast to the world. "The blades are acting like the rotary wing on a gyroplane, imparting lift to slow our descent while providing drag for deceleration."

"Yeah!" Sam piped in, releasing nervous tension by babbling on about the rotorocket's unique features. "Our lifting re-entry keeps us up in the stratosphere longer, which reduces the heating rate *and* the maximum temperature on the ship. The blade's are heated on both sides, but that just increases the radiative area, and since they're rotating, the migrating stagnation point effect reduces the aver—"

"Sam!"

"What?"

"Shut up!" the other two cried in unison.

Davy regretted the end of the journey, though the demands of the moment prevented him from experiencing any emotion other than methodical attention to the myriad details involved in safely returning to Earth.

The suitcase-sized supercomputers borrowed from NYU performed the majority of the work during reentry. The crew, for the most part, nervously hoped for the best. Whereas the air friction during a normal spaceship re-entry would have enveloped them in a fireball of ionized plasma, *Bodacious Bernadette* decelerated at a prolonged and leisurely rate, descending almost invisibly across the North American afternoon sky, passing over Minneapolis, Milwaukee, and Detroit to its appearance over Passaic.

Then came the tensest part of the landing sequence. Descending now in a steep glide ratio of 8:1, the ship headed toward Manhattan only a bit more aerodynamically than a thrown stone. Over North Bergen, at an altitude of two thousand feet, Davy took control and — viewing the landing site via the aft-facing videocam, ignited the engines one last time to increase the rotor speed.

"We're hovering!" Bernadette shouted in amazement.

"We're on the mark," Sam noted. "Extend landing gear."

Using the GPS coordinates for Central Park and the guidance and navigation software, Davy piloted the ship at a descent rate of fifty feet per second, four landing gear pads extended like spindly feet.

All around New York City, people stopped and stared at the flaming marvel descending into the heart of their city. Construction workers a hundred stories high gazed in wonder at the blackened, fire-spewing pinwheel that dropped past them madly chopping air and continued downward into Central Park. The crowds surrounding the Great Lawn, kept at bay by riot cops and mounted police, heard the gentle hiss of the engines, the whir and throb of the rotor blades, and watched in awe. An immobile mass of spectators clogged the streets surrounding the park, especially between 81st and 86th Streets, rendering afternoon travel an exercise in futility. All eyes scanned the sky.

▼ ▲ ▼

From the window of his Central Park West apartment, Barry Gibbon watched the landing with a respectful awe. Something stirred within him, an emotion suppressed for years. Just as quickly as it welled up inside, he squelched it, recalling with gnawing rage the incomprehensible, gloating creature his sister had become. What hideous madness transformed her into the metaphysical saboteur now lurking in his own home?

Existential dread hit him square in the face. He no longer controlled the course of Man's steps to the stars. A multiplicity of feet now trod separate and divergent paths.

Barry Gibbon watched the flaming dervish descend into the center of the planet's most important city and saw a new paradigm for the aeon. And — realizing the power of its iconography — trembled.

▼ ▲ ▼

Davy and the others peered through their fogged helmets and scorched windows at the skyline of New York.

"World Trade Center!" Bernadette called out as the twin towers appeared at the bottom edge of her vision.

"Empire State Building!" Sam cried. "God, it's beautiful!"

"The Chrysler Building!"

"I think I saw Liberty!"

Davy's smile amid the buffeting of the engines suddenly faded. "We saw liberty up there. What we're coming back to, I can't predi—"

"Crossing Central Park West and Eighty-Second Street!"

A warning signal klaxoned in their ears. Two hundred feet over the great oval lawn just south of the huge reservoir, the computers could no longer rely on the accuracy of global positioning satellites. The piloting job fell totally into Crockett's firm grip.

With the aid of onboard radar, the computer, and the video image from a rear-facing camera, Crockett eased the spacecraft down toward the green.

"Fuel light," Sam said. "Forty seconds left."

"Easy," Davy muttered. "Easing down."

The hiss of the engines, reflected upward from the ground, grew louder through their helmets.

"Don't hit the Delacorte!" Sam yelled.

"Relax," Davy muttered. "Won't even singe it."

With languid grace, the spacecopter descended on the northern focal point of the elliptical clearing. NYPD sharpshooters from the Central Park Precinct lined the rooftops of the Delacorte Theater and Belvedere Castle, gaping in astonishment at a vision more Hollywood than Manhattan: a spaceship landing in their urban park. The spinning blades made the ship look uncannily like a semi-transparent flying saucer spewing fire from its edge.

Crockett throttled up just enough to hover a few feet above the lawn, then let the vehicle set down. The gentle bump of landing caught the spacefarers by surprise. It not only meant their safe return and the end of one adventure, it marked the beginning of a new one.

"Contact light!" Crockett whooped with joy and threw a series of switches. "Engines shut down! Rotor brake on. Shut fuel and oxidizer valves. Vent APU gases. Electrical system shutdown. We made it!"

Bernadette unstrapped and slid over to hug him while Sam just let out a deep breath.

"Welcome home weary voyagers," Carla Pulaski said in their earphones. *"I hear you'll be arrested shortly for illegal parking."*

"Among other charges," Davy radioed back. He unstrapped and joined the others in a scramble for the exit.

"You first, Davy," Sam said. "You were the guiding light."

Crockett smiled. "And there might be police snipers out there."

Sam clapped him on the back. "You know me too well."

Davy Crockett took a moment after cycling the hatch to remove his helmet and slip into his buckskin jacket and coonskin hat. He sat on the edge of the hatch listening to the descending pitch of the blades thwapping against thick and steamy August New York air until the rotor slowed to a stop. Removing Ol' Betsy from its place of honor duct-taped to a support stanchion beside the hatch, he slid down the side of the soot-streaked spacecopter and jumped five feet to the ground to wave at the camera crews racing toward him in Jeeps and vans, well ahead of the police, fire department, and military.

"Stay where you are!" boomed a voice from the heavens. A police helicopter or three circled the park, accompanied by more than a dozen news choppers. "You're all under arrest!"

From the periphery of the park came the sound of immense crowds booing and rendering Bronx cheers. From his vantage in the middle of the vast green, Crockett watched the mass of onlookers press unrelentingly against the police lines until here and there breaks occurred, allowing rivulets of humanity into the park. Within moments, the rivers became a flood, then a tsunami of cheering, jubilant well-wishers.

Davy took a deep breath. "New York, New York — I'd know that smell anywhere." He stared up at Bernadette and Sam. "Last one out locks up!" he shouted. "Remember, we're in Central Park!"

Laughing, Bernadette jumped from the hatch and into his waiting arms.

The crowd sprinted to reach the pair just a few seconds after a half-dozen cops tackled them. The civilians rent the pair from police custody and tossed them upon their shoulders as if they had just won the pennant for the Mets. Friedman stared at the mass of onlookers below him, grinned, and swan-dived into the crowd, who caught him and surfed him around the spacecraft. A massive triumphal march, which the police could only impotently observe at a distance, wended its way toward Washington Square.

CHAPTER 52

Security is mostly a superstition. It does not exist in nature, nor do the children of men as a whole experience it. Avoiding danger is no safer in the long run than outright exposure. Life is either a daring adventure, or nothing.

— Helen Keller

19 August

"Coming up on perigee," Tammy Reis said quietly. She addressed the other nineteen people onboard Space Station *Volnos*. Her words also crossed the vacuum of Space via radio, where a number of communications satellites rebroadcast it to Earth and to the other spacecraft orbiting the planet.

Volnos orbited in an attitude that put its longitudinal axis in line with its orbital trajectory so that the limb of a dazzlingly bright Earth lay just barely visible at the edge of every viewing port. Whether it was a top, side, or bottom edge depended on the pod which one occupied. Below the cockpit windows lay the endless blue of the Pacific. Above hung the trackless void of Space.

Tammy checked pressure in the fuel tanks while Franck said, "We'll burn it all down to fumes if we have to, but that won't leave us much for air and water."

"Let's do it," Tammy said, "in P-Minus five, four, three, two, one, *ignition!*"

Small amounts of hypergolic fuels in the engine igniters mixed and instantly burst into flames, lighting the hydrogen/oxygen mixture that weakly flowed into each of the thousands of tiny combustion chambers.

"Well, we know we can relight them," she said. "We're getting a good burn, but it's not adding up to much delta-*v*."

The onboard computer registered the change in velocity detected by the inertial navigation and guidance system, compared it to GPS signals, and displayed a running commentary on the outcome. Before any of the passengers detected the feeble effect the low-pressure engine burn had overcoming the massive space-ring's inertia, the sixteen engines sputtered and shut down one by one, like the flames of a gas range flickering out when deprived of fuel.

In Pod Three, Joscelyn Donahue's heart rate shot upward, as did Grant's. Their precious fuel had been used up; oxygen that would have provided the air for the space station, hydrogen that they would have combined in fuel cells to provide electricity and water. She kept her gaze riveted to the computer screen as the ship's software performed a quick estimate of the burn's effectiveness.

The slight increase in their orbital velocity ought to decrease the eccentricity of the orbit. The next apogee should be lower, and — they hoped — the next perigee should be higher. She gazed at the recalculation, knowing that Reis and Franck and Marcus and everyone else read the same information simultaneously.

"Not enough," Tammy's voice muttered on the intercom. The tension and disappointment in her voice mirrored the emotions of all onboard.

Grant nodded, running a hand over his short, sweat-soaked hair. Droplets clung to his forehead like a clear gel. "Are we in a more stable orbit? Something that could last a few weeks or months?"

"Yes. But you blew all your money putting this thing up. How can you pay for and build a refueling vessel in time to save us?"

"If I may interject a word?" came the soft Missourian tone of Rex Ivarson.

"You most certainly may, sir." Grant's tone, Donahue noted, was similar to that of a young man addressed by a grandfather whom he deeply respected.

"I admire your entrepreneurial spirit in building this amazing space station, and I thank you for bringing my wife and me up. However, it's obvious you have gone as far as you can on your own. As nice as rugged individualism is, sometimes you can achieve even more with a little cooperation. You might think about calling the Cooper widow and asking that she turn her next flight of Starblazer Aurora *into a fuel-ferrying one."*

▼ ▲ ▼

Joseph Lester kept up communication with GSN, acting as a temporary spokesman for S. S. *Volnos*. The newspeople on the ground, in return, kept him apprised of the status of the other adventurers. He signaled Tammy over the intercom.

"Aurora*'s in a high-inclination orbit,"* he said. "Nomad *made it up, and Crockett's spacecopter just landed safely in Central Park."*

"Yes," she replied in a drained voice. "The joint is jumping." In her mind lurked the image of Space Station *Volnos* breaking up, its crew incinerated or perhaps dying in agony as they plummeted in pieces toward the Earth. Falling, falling.

"There's no way either ship could reach us, is there?"

Tammy sighed. Even a science reporter such as Lester grasped little of the enormous complexity of space flight and the tremendous energy differences among the infinite variety of orbits possible. Once placed into a particular angle of inclination, at a particular altitude and eccentricity, a satellite or spacecraft required vast amounts of fuel to change its orbit significantly.

Her thoughts turned to Ace Roberts and she wondered what he must be thinking about two of his former helpers making it into Space while he still tinkered in his driveway. Maybe he felt far safer building something he only *intended* to fly, rather than actually ever flying it.

And forget the Shuttle, she thought acidly. Even if Vandenberg could launch *Atlantis* and it could dogleg far enough to achieve an equatorial orbit *and* still carry enough fuel to help them, neither Space Command nor NASA would actually lift a finger to help them.

Her thoughts shifted back to Freespace. She suspected that the only reason NASA helped them was that they probably expected *Aurora* to fail. Now the agency was trapped by the little upstart company's success. The same thing had happened a few years before with a commercial satellite launcher, whose unexpected non-failure backed NASA into a corner, forcing them to support subsequent flights. Maybe Ivarson had picked the right people to ask. Maybe the Starblazer *could* fly again. How, though, to avoid the prohibition on launching from Vandenberg over the entire continental United States?

Her eyes, so dark with meditation, brightened as she punched her intercom for a private line to Pod Three.

"Paul!" she said. "I have a way they can save us!"

"How?"

"Have them launch from Kennedy instead of Vandenberg!"

"Of course! I'll get right on it!"

▼ ▲ ▼

The message — relayed from orbit to Earth and back to orbit — had lost some meaning in the translation. Chemar frowned and said, "Boss, someone from GSN says that their reporter on Space Station *Volnos* said that Grant said he needed our help."

Wrinkling his nose at the tangled sentence, Poubelle said, "What can we do?"

"Loan Freespace our seven-four-seven to fly *Aurora* from Vandenberg to Cape Canaveral."

Poubelle grinned. "Of course. A refueling flight. A liftoff at KSC would allow them a low enough inclination to open up a fair-sized rendezvous launch window. You hear that, Karl?"

"Roger, big guy." Bischoff — now safely back at Mojave — acted as Earth-to-Space communicator for the Daedalus Project. *"Guess someone else will have to take the mic while I warm up old Susy."*

"Right. And make sure our own people handle the crane. They mounted it once before." He grinned over his shoulder at D'Asaro. "First day here and already the neighbors ask to borrow our tools!"

CHAPTER 53

I, for one, support all government space programs.
They give us some truly stupendous vehicles to hijack.
— Brad Linaweaver

20 August

Colonel Vladimir Tuchapski shook his head in wonderment and disbelief. While he struggled to evade KGB, and the military GRU, a gang of American capitalists, black marketeers, and school children soared into Space. It sickened the heart.

He hid such emotions from his cohorts, however, for to weaken now would prove the undoing of all his efforts. And to fail meant death. His government could never allow him to live after what he had done. Space presented his only escape route, *Mir* his only sanctuary. If he could reach it, he thought, all sins might be forgiven. If not, he would be beyond the reach of their vengeance.

The fat grain elevator in which crouched the bundle of rockets shimmered with summer heat. Inside, the stifling temperatures made work difficult and laborious, but still his men labored like Stakhanovites.

For Tuchapski, it did not matter whether they launched this week, next week, or next year. There *would* be a Russian presence in Space once more. Then — finally — the race would be on for the ultimate prize: Mars!

Mars, Ares, Red Planet; the names evoked images from his childhood. Americans could have Earth and Luna. Mars — the planet red as blood, the planet of the god of all warriors would be Russia's. Mars would be *his*.

▼ ▲ ▼

Montgomery Barron monitored the events of the past three days from his small office in Project *Stark Fist*'s hangar at Washington Naval Air Station. He had not heard word one from Milton or anyone else in that time. The college kids went up and came down, thus setting an example of success that others would surely imitate. That was bad enough, and Freespace's nearly flawless flight — if it ended in a safe landing at Vandenberg — set a regrettable precedent for coercing government cooperation in the future. Poubelle, though, thumbed his nose openly at NASA and the military, yet garnered an incomprehensible level of popular support and *ad hoc* defense.

Worst of all was the threat posed by Marcus Grant. A counter-economic space station, however primitive, presaged a danger to world economic and political dynamics that ought to be evident even to those rank fools warming seats on the Hill.

Yet no one sought to activate *Stark Fist* and unleash *Huntress*. Bureaucracies seldom handled radical change with ease. The Soviet collapse several years back paralyzed the West with indecision: support the old regime to maintain the intelligence community's beloved "stability"? Or make new alliances and risk stumbling into the unknown? Barron suspected that his superiors sat equally stunned by this new set of affairs. Stop Grant? Support him clandestinely? Or sit on hands with a wait-and-see attitude?

He had to act alone. On his own authority. The prospect thrilled and terrified him simultaneously. In order to protect and sustain his government, he would have to defy its rules. Not just its veneer of public laws, which the NSA violated routinely and with impunity, but its deeper, vehemently enforced code of obedience to the hierarchy.

If he presented them with a *fait accompli*, on the other hand, and gave them the results they desired along with tons of more-than-plausible deniability, he would be tacitly rewarded.

He gazed out the small office window at the sleek killing machine in the hangar. The fingers of his right hand drummed a light tattoo on the desktop. At the moment, the raptor sat clawless: the LEAP's with which it was to be armed foundered in the development phase, constantly falling in and out of congressional favor. Barron foresaw such a foulup; the interior weapons bay could also hold and launch two ASAT's. The hangar stored four prototypes from the defunct ASAT program.

He calmly picked up the phone and punched in the intercom number for the floor manager. "Joel," he said. "Load two ASAT's onboard *Huntress* and have her prepped for flight. We are *go* for operations."

His heart raced as sudden indecision gripped him. What if he misconstrued Grant's threat to the interests of the United States? What if Grant served some secret purpose of NSA to subvert UNITO? The Puzzle Palace, and certainly its rival, the CIA, constantly funded all manner of groups with seemingly contradictory aims, mostly as a way to monitor and control them. The old joke — that any subversive group with less than 50% CIA/NSA membership was not seriously subversive — held more than a grain of truth.

What if, by destroying the nascent space station, Barron destroyed a grand plan of one of his superiors?

The intelligence community, caught up for decades in spy-counterspy games, had evolved its own peculiar form of paranoia. Barron rose from his desk, refusing to surrender to such urges. Ultimately, an operative relied upon instinct, hunch, and a firm faith in the long-proven adaptability of the power elite. After centuries of turning every contingency into an opportunity to increase their power, even a screwup on Barron's part could be of some use somehow.

Barron, however, did not consider his action incorrect.

Bending over the console, he transferred information from Space Command and the Kettering Space Observatory Group concerning the orbit of Space Station *Volnos* into *Huntress*'s computer. Its equatorial orbital inclination meant that the planar window at Washington's nearly 39° latitude would be almost vanishingly short for an eastward launch. He would have to fly south first, chasing *Volnos*'s phase window, which was also quite narrow, but which he would have the computer calculate during the flight, then achieve orbit using the maximum amount of yaw steering designed into *Huntress* in order to realize a rendezvous. If he failed to enter at the proper phase point, he had the ability to wait in orbit for days if necessary to creep up on the target. The faster the better, though, as for any stalking assassin.

With a grunt, he straightened up, sucked in his gut, and strode purposefully to the locker near the office door. Like a matador dressing for a bullfight, he stripped his earthly clothes from his body and donned the heavy Kevlar-and-ceramic-armored pressure suit tailored to his frame and manufactured off-budget. No one knew; no one *would* know until he marched out onto the hangar floor.

He slid down the heavy helmet with the grey-green glass covering the eyes. It looked insectoid and utterly inscrutable. The helmet-mounted display provided all necessary information during air and space flight. In fact, the HMD replaced the actual view out of the cockpit with a high-quality computer simulation, yet relied only upon the spacecraft's own computers and information from Milstar and TDRS satellites, freeing Barron of any dependency on a ground-based guidance system.

He locked the helmet in place and breathed through the outside vents; the ship would provide him with its own oxygen once inside the cockpit.

Quickly he strode out the door and across the hangar floor toward the sleek, delta-winged aerospacecraft. White and menacing as death itself, it stood amid a swirling cloud of cryogenic mist from the fuels. Three men gripped the tow bar in front, ready to haul the killer spaceship onto the taxiway.

Charles Stansfield pounded over to him and hissed in a low tone, "What the hell are you doing?"

"Time to test her out," Barron replied in a voice muffled by the helmet. "See if she likes eating subnationals."

"Do we have authorization?" Stansfield sounded more than nervous.

"Chuck! Would I do anything without authorization?"

"Well... yes!"

Barron slapped Stansfield's behind and said, "Then you can have the joy of denouncing me to our superiors and moving up a pay level. See you in a day or two!"

The stout agent ascended the ladder with uncommon agility to lower his body into the narrow, lightly padded seat. Plugging in the fiber optic data lines to his helmet, he powered up the flight computer and watched as his dim view of the world around him vanished, replaced by a sharp, bright, 3-D simulation of the cockpit and surrounding hangar. Dozens of microcams provided the views, which the powerful, massively parallel neural net computer blended into the image. He grasped the controls and smiled.

He held the future in his hands.

Carefully rolled out onto the taxiway of Washington NAS, *Huntress* powered up her twin Pratt & Whitney jet engines. The startup team withdrew as the titanium virago rolled forward, its mission clear.

▼ ▲ ▼

The tower controller gazed at the blip on his ground-traffic radar, then reached for his binoculars to identify the unknown aircraft. What he saw caused his eyes to widen.

"What in God's name is *that*?"

A kid more pimple than Lieutenant JG peered through his own pair of binocs and whistled. "Some sort of delta-winged hypersonic plane. With a scramjet on its belly and six rocket nozzles up its ass!" He turned his head toward his superior. "It's like a miniature version of the old NASP!"

"The old what?" The controller reached for his microphone.

"The National Aerospace Plane. The runway-to-orbit spaceship that NASA would never admit was too big to fly. Someone's built it at its optimum size."

"Tower to unidentified aircraft taxiing toward runway, hold your position!"

A voice rasped over the radio speaker. *"Oh, don't worry. I'm just taking her up to wring her out a bit."*

The controller turned to the JG. "Get security on the ramp and stop him!" Then, into his mic: "Aircraft, you do not have clearance. Repeat, you are *not* cleared for takeoff."

The snowy spaceplane continued onward, the pilot unperturbed. *"Roger that,"* Barron radioed back. *"Clear for takeoff."*

"Negative, you son of a" — his eyes widened and his voice rose in alarm — "Plane on the runway! All aircraft abort landing and remain in pattern at eight hundred!"

The lieutenant JG grinned in delight to watch the bird fire up its mighty engines and roar down the runway. At the three-quarter point, it rolled, bit air, and jumped upward with an amazing agility. Afterburners ablaze, the anonymous flying wonder climbed away from the air station at a fifty degree angle with a rate of climb that would have made an F-111 pilot blink.

"Mach One," the kid said seconds later, viewing the event through his binoculars. At the moment the aircraft broke the sound barrier, a white, doughnut-shaped shock wave cloud appeared around the aircraft, courtesy of the humidity at the low altitude; the jet rammed right through it like William Tell's arrow.

The wide glass panels of the air station's tower (and every window for miles around) rattled suddenly as the sonic boom hit ground level.

Montgomery Barron blazed upward, bound for Space and ready for battle. He blacked out when the scramjets kicked in at Mach 4, throwing him back with nearly three gravities of acceleration. The onboard computer obligingly guided the spaceplane to fifty miles altitude and Mach 15, where the rocket engines took over from the scramjet to insert *Huntress* into her predetermined orbit.

Barron regained consciousness to see the Earth hanging above his head — the computer-generated version, complete with national boundaries and names — and rendezvous information ticking off distances and times. As he performed the operations learned by rote in the simulator, his mind raced jubilantly.

The game's afoot!

CHAPTER 54

My days are swifter than a weaver's shuttle.
— **Job 7: 6**

20 August

Sherry Cooper listened to the request beamed down from orbit. The man making the request was Marcus Grant. News reports had already re-identified him as one Paul Volnos, a former volunteer on Ace Roberts's shoestring project. That explained the name of his space station, at least.

"...then we have Laurence Poubelle's people mount it on his Seven-Four-Seven and fly it over to Kennedy Space Center for launch. After Joseph Lester plays it up on GSN, I expect everyone in the Experimental Spacecraft Association and a lot of others to flood NASA with demands to permit the launch from one of the smaller, functional pads."

"There's something in all this I don't understand," Sherry said. "*Aurora*'s still in a polar orbit. Why can't we simply land her at Kennedy and sidestep the whole airplane bit?"

A sheepish silence hung in the orbital void as Paul realized his failure to think in three dimensions. After a few seconds, he said, "Yes, that does sound less complicated."

▼ ▲ ▼

Vox populi, vox Dei is the purported philosophy of a democracy. Although America comprised fifty states united in a constitutional representative republic, the concept still held enormous power over the uninformed. Hundreds of thousands of calls clogged telephone trunks on Capitol Hill. The switchboard operators at the White House threatened to resign. Fax machines burned out under the stress of incoming pleas, petitions, and outright demands. Myriad voices bombarded radio and interactive-video call-in shows with almost unanimous approval for the mavericks.

President Crane, so close to being dumped by the electorate in November, threw his unqualified support behind what he called "the valiant New Frontierspersons" and issued an executive order compelling NASA, Space Command, and the FAA to render any and all assistance to Freespace Orbital in its landing at KSC and subsequent re-launch. The only help Sherry Cooper asked for, however, was that the sundry agencies stay out of her way.

Leora Thane awaited the return of *Aurora* with something more than a major investor's anticipation. Vandenberg prevented her from witnessing the spacecraft's launch due to certain indiscretions uncovered during her security check and also to her status as non-essential personnel. Kennedy Spaceflight Center, nominally civilian and suddenly under the harsh glare of scrutiny, allowed Freespace — and Thane — much more leeway. Her tourist-industry wealth had paid for the hasty renovation and upgrading of the modest block-house in which she stood, dressed in a white skirt, blue-striped blouse, and navy blazer, watching the orange dot in the sky grow brighter and larger as it seemed to fall straight toward the small pad that four decades earlier served to launch Redstone and Atlas rockets.

"Geez, here's a view you don't want to give the clients," she said. "Who wants to see tons of flaming machinery hurtling down at them?"

Her question bounced off deaf ears, since all in the blockhouse focused their attention on bringing the unmanned spacecraft down to a pinpoint landing. Throttling the fuel and oxidizer flow to the twenty aerospike motors, the software — nudged now and then by Thom Brodsky's commands — brought the reentry-scorched rocket to a hovering standstill ten feet above the concrete and fifty yards from the launch pad gantry.

Dust and steam billowed out from beneath the exhaust wash, hiding the ship. Bits of gravel hurled toward the wide, squat, and thick blockhouse windows. Using the glow of the rocket plume as his guide, Brodsky gradually decreased the thrust until the contact lights glowed green. Amid the cheers of his co-workers, he shut down the engines and the egg-shaped orbital semi-luxury liner eased to a rest upon its three landing gear pads.

Thane turned to Cooper and smiled broadly. "See? What did I say? If you had sent me up with twenty rubberneckers, we'd have some pocket change right now."

Sherry, releasing a sigh of relief at the landing, raised her eye-brows in a gesture of exhaustion and said, "Leora, you can go up with the flight *after* this next one and garner a load of free publicity."

Thane laughed. "Have you seen these nails? They normally don't do anything more strenuous than endorse checks. But I'll pitch in for the sake of the business."

"Great. Now let's see if this bird really does have a three-day turnaround time."

▼ ▲ ▼

"Damn," Poubelle muttered.

"What's wrong?" D'Asaro tried to peer over Poubelle's shoulder to see what was the problem, but the seat harness prevented any movement.

"My arm. I'm getting the same sort of transient loss of control I ran into on the first flight. The nerve feedback feels uncomfortably like a cramp."

"Will it interfere with reentry?"

She saw him shrug, saw his cybernetic arm twitch.

"I'll try to control it. You be ready to take over with the Dead Larry scenario."

"Very funny." Chemar resented the term more than Poubelle realized. Between their good-natured japes and their bedroom passion lay a calm center of love that neither took lightly. She knew he would give his life to save hers, and she to save his. Life without him was unthinkable to her. Live forever or die together was her motto. And she personally had no desire to die, so she intended that the Dead Larry scenario would remain just that — a scenario.

Nomad hurtled through Space backward at the moment, in preparation for retrofire. Backward and upside-down, so that the colorful expanse of Earth spread before their field of view, filling the cockpit with bright, soft light. She gazed down at her hands floating effortlessly in free fall. The diffuse glow that filled the cockpit — heavenly light from an earthly source — made her pressure suit seem a very light shade of black, almost a grey. The instruments and controls looked warm and otherworldly. She realized that she truly could live there forever, if he lived there with her. That thought, however, she deferred for later. Right then, her instruments displayed the countdown to retrofire.

"All right," Poubelle said. "Let's see if the engine turns over after a day."

"Sixteen days," she said, having counted the sunrises and sunsets they experienced every forty-five minutes, one each per ninety-minute orbit. Each one appeared or vanished with startling speed and breathtaking colors. She took a last glance at Earth, then turned her attention to co-piloting *Nomad*.

I'm coming back here, she thought. *No matter what, no matter how.*

"APU's are up to power," she said. "Tank pressure's optimal. Attitude is right on the numbers. Turbo's up to speed. Here it comes."

The blast of rocket power pushed them firmly against their seats, quickly throttling up to a full three gravities of deceleration. The spacecraft groaned and creaked, emitted loud clunks and high pings, shuddered and shook as if about to break apart. After a few moments that seemed to make the chronometer slow down its count, the engine throttled back.

"Good burn," Poubelle said, relief and amazement interleaved in his voice. His right arm jerked upward suddenly. "Damn it!"

"Okay," D'Asaro said, tapping carefully at the keyboard. "Taking over yaw and roll controls to orient us for airbraking."

A few gunshot-like firings jerked the Earth away from their view, replacing it with the sharp, star-studded velvet sky in which a furious Sun majestically rushed aftward. *Nomad* dropped Earthward nose up at a high angle of attack, though not quite as high as a shuttle orbiter on reentry.

"The arm's all right," he said. "I'll fly it in. Just be ready to take over now and again."

"Aye-aye, Cap'n. Sealing up port window." An exterior shield, designed to cover the left half of the canopy in order to prevent charring, slid backward and locked into place. It served as a last-chance maneuvering option, just in case the VR helmet gave out.

The black bolt, dropping into a lower orbit to compensate for its slower velocity, began to skirt the edges of the perceptible atmosphere. This translated into a series of jostling bumps as the spaceplane encountered variations in the thickness of the air at ninety miles altitude. At nearly five miles a second, differences of even a few molecules per cubic inch added up to an immense number of collisions on the belly of the spacecraft.

"Skin temp eight hundred," Chemar noted.

The altimeter proved worthless at such speed and altitudes, so readouts came from computer interpolation of GPS information. What Poubelle noticed caused him to bellow: "What the hell?"

Reentry and the subsequent airbraking created a sensation of increased weight downward in the seat and slightly forward. Both pilots detected a sudden decrease in both vector components concomitant with his outcry.

"We've Sängered!"

D'Asaro knew the term. Named after the German scientist Eugen Sänger, inventor of an X-15-like winged spaceplane, it meant skipping across the atmosphere the way a stone skips across a pond, done intentionally to extend a low-altitude flight. When unintentional, it meant missing one's landing mark by hundreds — perhaps thousands — of miles.

"We won't skip too far," Poubelle growled. "We're going to come down somewhere southeast of Mojave."

"How far southeast?"

"Way far!" He punched rapidly at the keyboard with his live hand. "I'm switching the FMS to energy management and tracking only. It's seat of the pants time!"

He edged the nose of the spaceplane lower, teasing at the line between Sängering upward and cutting too deeply into the atmosphere. Ramming back toward Earth at hypersonic velocities left little leeway for the middle ground. The blackness of Space faded, replaced by a purpling sky that glowed with the ionized plasma of superheated air. The FMS lost contact with the global positioning satellites during this period of reentry, relying on inertial navigation and guidance provided by its ring-laser gyros, the pilot's view in the VR goggles provided via the cameras, most of which remained sealed from the glare of plasma and the charring from bits of burning *Nomad*.

Poubelle made no sound for the next few minutes; no hummed tune, no meditative whistle, no unconscious trill escaped his lips. His entire being concentrated on easing the tons of metal and composites through its narrow, flaming corridor of unbelievably marginal safety back to terrestrial speeds and less heavenly altitudes. Every few seconds, the ship rocked with turbulence. Metal creaked, rivets strained, joints vibrated. From somewhere beneath their seats, wisps of smoke snaked up to cloud the cockpit's nitrogen atmosphere.

"Leading edge skin temp sixteen-fifty," Chemar said. "Approaching redline."

Poubelle said nothing but "Roger." Then his robot arm spasmed and he said, "Take over!" Chemar tightened her grip on the controls to continue the descent while he sought to regain management of his prosthetic.

The turbulence smoothed out, the superheated air around them cooled back to visibility, and the GPS signal returned.

"We're home," Poubelle said calmly. "I've got the stick."

"Where's home, though?" she asked, sliding aside the port protective shield for a non-VR look. "Is that the Grand Canyon?"

He opened the shields that covered the VR cameras and looked all around, then referred to his energy management system and GPS information. Immediately, he eased the stick and rudder into a hypersonic clockwise turn. "I can tell you this," he said. "We're not landing at Mojave. We'll be lucky to land it in California. No need to make hypersonic S-turns to bleed off airspeed, that's for sure."

The energy management system kept track of where the unpowered hypersonic glider could land by displaying an oval footprint on the digital map. The ellipse marked the maximum distance the ship could glide without hitting something hard and earthen. At forty miles altitude and Mach 4, the footprint covered a large area, but not large enough to include the Mojave desert. Its major axis just barely touched Palm Springs to the northwest and El Centro to the southeast.

"Can't make it to Palen or Ford." Both were dry salt lakes to the northeast. "Damn!" He kept tight control on the aircraft despite his outburst. "We just lost NAF El Centro. They've got a ninety-five hundred foot runway."

"Oasis is smack dab in the middle. Want to try for our own runway?"

"We'd be safer splashing down in Salton Sea. Hey! Palm Springs! Eighty-five hundred feet plus the overrun they added last year!"

"God knows we can use overrun," she muttered, examining the EMS footprint. "That's right at the northern edge, though, and it's not improving as we drop." The ship creaked and rumbled a bit. "We're at Mach three, altitude twenty-two miles."

He took a deep breath. "I can do it. Do we have any fuel left?" He turned his eyes toward that portion of the floating readout in the VR. "Hmm. About five seconds worth."

"What are you planning?"

Poubelle knew better than to keep secrets from his co-pilot. "We may need a final burst of power to get us home. The EMS will give us enough warning on that."

He checked the GPS locator, confirmed his course with the VORTAC beam from Thermal Flight Service Station, then switched the radio over to 121.5 to issue the warning that an unpowered supersonic spaceplane was headed in their direction.

Nomad dragged its cone of sonic thunder northeast of Superstition Mountains, rattling windows in Westmorland and Calipatria. He came in high over Salton Sea, so high that the vast date palm orchards were mere deep-green squares surrounding the deep blue body of water. He ignored angry transmissions from aircraft operating in the Kane MOA, preferring to maintain his heading and keep an eye on the EMS footprint. Angering them further, he actuated the explosive charge on the lower half of the ventral fin, blowing it off to provide clearance for the rear skids. The jettisoned chunk of burnt metal splashed into the briny depths of the inland sea. Palm Springs still hung just within or beyond the far end of the oval, sensitive to minor changes in Poubelle's input.

Off to his right — through his VR glasses, not the partially scorched viewing port — he saw the Desert Air Sky Ranch landing strip near the northeastern shore. Farther north, and smack on the coastline, lay his own too-short airfield. Off the left side of the plane — on the opposite shore — lay the town of Oasis.

Nomad shook with a sudden violence. "Under Mach One," he said. "Subsonic."

"That ought to please the people below us." Chemar said.

"Really? I've always loved sonic booms. Like knocking on the door to the future." He glanced once more at the display. As they closed in on Palm Springs, the terrain below them rose from the level of Salton Sea — 236 feet below sea level — to just about sea level at Indio, to Palms Springs's 462 above.

Poubelle used too much energy banking to get around the Thermal landing pattern. His destination now lay firmly outside the EMS footprint. Not normally a perspiring man, he began to drench his suit with a cold sweat.

"All right," he sighed. "Restart the turbine and let's light this candle again."

▼ ▲ ▼

Many of the citizens of La Quinta had heard about the spaceship dropping powerlessly in their direction. Inured to the savage summer heat, they stood outside with binoculars scanning the skies and radios tuned to the news.

"There it is!" someone yelled. All eyes turned toward the black spot at 10,000 feet.

All of a sudden a bright orange flame erupted from its tail and the swiftly moving rocket accelerated with startling speed. As suddenly as it began, the flame sputtered out. It provided enough thrust, though, to drive *Nomad* supersonic once more. Seconds later, the desert rumbled with the violence of its passage through the wall of sound.

▼ ▲ ▼

"That's got it!" Poubelle said, raising the nose in order to bleed off some of the speed in exchange for slowing the rate of descent. Returning once again to subsonic speeds while passing over the growing community of Palm Desert, the Palm Springs airport came into view. He vented what little fuel remained and dumped the peroxide from the exoatmospheric maneuvering rockets, then turned the radio to the control tower frequency, 119.7 mHz.

"Palm Springs tower, this is experimental spaceplane *Nomad* on heading three-ten approaching unpowered. Request clearance for emergency landing, over."

"Roger, Nomad, *you are expected. Be advised that FAA officials are present to oversee your arrest, over."*

"Roger that. Please advise them that my bloodsucking lawyers are on their way to throw my bail. Over."

Chemar gazed out the port window to see the series of small cities that created one long chain from Indian Wells to Palm Springs itself. The desert below the eastern foothills of the San Jacinto mountains consisted of an astonishing crazy-quilt of innumerable golf courses. One uninhabited fairway became the recipient of the jettisoned ventral fin section. Dropping through 3,000 feet, Chemar could make out a vast army of players on other greens and wondered how many interrupted their game to glance upward at the passing rocket plane.

No more time for sightseeing. Poubelle shouted "Take over!" as his robot arm malfunctioned in the clinch.

Chemar tightened her grip on the stick and placed her feet in contact with the rudder pedals.

"Runway in sight," she said. "Energy sufficient. May even need air brakes. Cycling gear." The two rear skids and the forward wheel dropped flawlessly with loud bangs that made the fuselage tremble. The greater drag caused a perceptible increase in the descent rate.

"Play her out," Poubelle urged. "Stretch it."

"Shut up, lover," she said with cool firmness.

Other aircraft circled above the landing pattern, avoiding the winged missile approaching the runway. Golf courses merged into a single green blur as *Nomad* dropped toward the surface with a 250 mph forward velocity.

She opened the air brake thirty per cent. The brake comprised two panels in the lower part of the dorsal fin, hinged on the leading edge and actuated by twin piston rams in the rear that shoved them into the air stream to bleed energy from the spacecraft. Their drop rate increased while their airspeed decreased.

Poubelle bit his tongue while D'Asaro maneuvered in toward the runway with consummate skill. His arm once more obeyed him, but he chose not to interrupt her efforts.

"Looking good," someone in the tower commented calmly.

Nomad descended in a nose-high attitude that made it impossible for her to see the runway. Lacking Poubelle's VR goggles, she relied entirely on the belly radar and the cumulative effects of her simulator training.

"One hundred feet," the radar said over her headset. She kept the nose up at the appropriate angle of attack. *"Fifty feet."* Her grip on the stick tightened.

The skids hit with a body-jarring slam to scream across the skillet-hot pavement.

"Contact!" the tower needlessly announced as the X-15 skidded down the runway in excess of 200 mph. Desert gulls shrieked and flapped out of the way, rodents skittered away to their holes, and snakes

soaking up a few extra calories of body heat slithered into hiding.

Immediately Chemar rammed the stick forward to push the nose wheel onto the ramp. On such a short — for them — runway, she dared not risk porpoising back into the air. The wheel hit, the tire squealed, and the spaceplane raced down the runway, now at the halfway point and still at triple-digit speeds. She opened the air brake to maximum.

"One-fifty," she read off. "One-forty."

"Uh, Nomad, *be advised you're eating up runway with about three thousand feet left."*

"Roger tower," she said, grunting with her effort to steer. "Be advised this thing has no brakes."

"We copy. Be advised you're headed straight for the Shell station beyond the runway."

"Down to ninety," she noted, all the while keeping the nose pointed straight down the runway. "Could you ask them to shut off their fuel pumps?"

"Already done," the voice from the tower noted. *"I suppose you're not interested in a brushless a wash, either?"*

"Roger that. We may need some detailing done, though." Her voice sounded calm, but her heart pounded audibly as the end of the runway still sped toward them at sixty miles an hour. The police had closed Ramon Road just in case, and it was probably a good idea.

"Oh God," Poubelle muttered. "Not again!"

Nomad skidded to the end of the runway, sliding onto the overrun at thirty miles per hour. The overrun consisted of grey-white gravel, into which the nose wheel sank and the skids bit. With a terrible lurch and crash of tearing metal and ripping composite, the wheel and rear skids sheared away from the fuselage. They skidded along the overrun, gravel shooting out from beneath them like a wake. Chemar strained to catch a glimpse of where they were headed, but she was not at an angle to see what lay straight ahead.

Then came another jarring impact that threw them down and forward. Scraping the asphalt overrun, the ventral fin dug in to act as an anchor. The stress proved too much for *Nomad*, which split in half at the belly, slamming the rear section to the ground and stopping all forward momentum with a sudden, final surge of forward-gees for the crew. The nose of *Nomad* touched and pierced the cyclone fence at the end of the property line.

Nomad lay halfway inside the airport perimeter and halfway out, bent and cracked in the middle like a bug with its back broken by a giant's thumb. Smoke leaked from the peroxide tanks and hydraulic fluid dripped onto the crisp white sidewalk paralleling Ramon Road. A small cloud of mist from the ruptured cryogenic tanks swiftly dissipated in the heat like ghosts vanishing at daybreak.

In an instant, sirens wailing, the crash unit and HazMat team arrived to drench the spaceplane in fire-suppressant foam. Police, FAA officials, and airport security followed, with the press bringing up the rear.

"Cheated death again!" Poubelle said cheerily.

"I wish to God you'd find something else to say whenever you land." Chemar watched the foam spatter the windshield. "I know that any landing you walk away from is a success," she said with a sigh, "but I have to say that this is the most embarrassing moment of my life."

Removing the useless VR goggles, Poubelle turned off the power switches, locked the fuel lines, and said, "Death is the only embarrassment you can't live down. You did what I couldn't, so don't sell yourself short. Now let's put on our best smiles. And don't forget to wave before we're handcuffed."

He opened the cockpit hatch and emerged, looking around at the gathering crowd and waving triumphantly. Chemar eased out of the cramped interior and turned to lock the compartment holding their mementos. The lawyers would retrieve them eventually.

The FAA official read them a short-form of charges while the police first seized Poubelle, then Chemar.

"Ooh," she said, gazing at the agent with her riveting golden eyes and playfully batting her lashes. "Real handcuffs, not plastic zip-ties!"

"Give me your arm," the officer said to Poubelle.

"Glad to oblige," he responded, undoing the seals on his suit, disconnecting his prosthetic at its shoulder bayonet connector, and handing the unit — still twitching — to the shocked policeman.

Chemar broke into uncontrollable laughter at the sight, relieved to be alive, their flight a success, and to know that an unquenchable joy for life still filled her man's heart.

Poubelle grinned at the FAA agent standing off to one side and asked, "So, how much do I tip the arresting officer?"

The skycop stared at him coolly and said, "A dollar more than you'll ever have."

CHAPTER 55

A strong body makes the mind strong. As to the species of exercise, I advise the gun. While this gives a moderate exercise to the Body, it gives boldness, enterprise, and independence to the mind. Games played with the ball, and others of that nature, are too violent for the body and stamp no character on the mind. Let your gun therefore be the constant companion of your walks.

— **Thomas Jefferson**

21 August

Col. Lundy faced a dilemma. Under orders to launch *Atlantis* on a rescue mission, he encountered competition from NASA for competent launch crew. President Crane had issued secret orders for the mission — to capture Space Station *Volnos* under the guise of saving its inhabitants — yet had also publicly announced his support for the private spaceship *Aurora* to land at Kennedy, refuel, and launch its own rescue flight. While he realized that perhaps Crane was playing a shrewd game of politics and public relations, he harbored the gnawing suspicion that the commander-in-chief merely possessed no idea at all of what to do.

Not that it mattered one bit. Orders or no, *Atlantis* headed nowhere fast. He held no doubt that *Aurora* could relaunch within 72 hours, barring sabotage. *Atlantis*, on the other hand, sat out on her never-used launch pad awaiting dozens of critical fixes and checks before she could lift off. Worse, in the past few days the steady attrition of technicians and engineers, which continually plagued both NASA and the military, grew to a hemorrhaging torrent as the surviving talent of the space agency and the Air Force headed for what they must have perceived as greener pastures — or blacker skies.

The shuttle was what it was because of a multitude of conflicting inputs. Congress dictated that each piece of it be manufactured in separate congressional districts: they made it a pie from which every congressman cut a slice. The Air Force, told that it would have to abandon expendable boosters and support the Shuttle, had demanded every conceivable bell and whistle, such as cross-range landing capability, which increased the orbiter's weight and decreased its utility. And NASA pursued its own agenda: to employ as many people as possible in order to swell each manager's salary, budget, and prestige. Timely access to Space played little or no part in their plans.

Due to decisions made a generation before, decisions based upon politics rather than science, bureaucratic interests rather than common sense, tax-funded profligacy rather than market-driven frugality, Colonel Alan Shepard Lundy gazed out his window at a white-and-rust-red Space Shuttle perched on its billion-dollar launch pad surrounded by a swarm of idle technicians impatiently awaiting parts cannibalized from *Discovery* and *Columbia* while an SSTO intended as a tourist vessel stood poised to make monkeys of them all.

Lundy smiled. He knew his father would have appreciated the irony. He might even have joined the river of expertise departing the space agency had those decades of short-sighted, treasury-plundering decisions not turned Spaceport, USA, into a funeral pyre for those who had burned with the dream.

▼ ▲ ▼

Barron knew that he could never achieve what would amount to a sneak attack. Though *Huntress* took advantage of some stealth technology, aerodynamic engineering demanded a sleek shape with few of the sharp edges seen in such aircraft as the F-117. Because of that, *Huntress* revealed its presence to ultra-wide-band ground radar and most down-looking radar satellites. And *everybody* was watching the skies these past few days.

His flight and ascent into orbit — public knowledge within seconds of igniting the spaceplane's six rocket engines — revealed nothing of his intent, however, and that offered him some element of surprise, but only if he acted swiftly and decisively.

The fastest approach would be along the path he now flew. The co-elliptic approach had cost him nearly all his fuel, since he had to dogleg and yaw steer in order to achieve the same orbital plane as the flying bracelet called *Volnos*. Being there, though, simplified the calculations of the relative motions involved. He would approach his targets from below and behind. When they reached a certain elevation above the horizon, they would be within range. His missiles would do the rest.

He dared not telegraph his plans by using radar. Optical tracking instruments alone would suffice until the final moments.

▼ ▲ ▼

"Yeah, I see it. Not too well, but it's there."

Grant peered at the onboard computer, which displayed a faint radar image of the unidentified spacecraft. Two pods over, Reis attempted to gain a visual image on the station's rear-mounted cameras.

"I'd wager it's coming for us, and I don't think we have to pose any friend-or-foe questions."

Grant nodded. "I wish now that I'd brought up a surplus Hawk missile I bought at a weapons bazaar in South Yemen. I left it behind because of its weight; I didn't want to sacrifice any other necessities."

"What else have we got?"

Another voice over the intercom said, *"I've got a solution. Maybe."*

The image of Joseph Lester appeared on Grant's screen. He held a dark walnut case in his hands. *"At what distance would an anti-satellite missile detonate?"*

"It depends. Anywhere from a few miles to a thousand yards," Grant said. "Instead of attacking head-on, the way they did with the Bronx kids, this one's making a co-elliptical rendezvous. The weapon won't be moving as fast. That might allow it to get closer."

Opening the lid, Lester withdrew one of the Wildey Survivor autopistols — with its 12-inch barrel attached and surmounted by a wide-aperture Gilmore Red Leader sight — and let it float in the air before him.

"I can bullseye a running coyote on a windy day at two hundred yards with this. The dot on the sight covers four minutes of arc. I don't have to worry about windage in a vacuum and the missile will be heading in on a steady course. The magazines hold six each, forty-five caliber Winchester Magnum rounds, plus one up the throat. Let me open up the airlock and I'll blast away until I hit something."

Grant's eyes brightened. "It's an idea, Joe. We've got shotguns, too. Maybe if everyone—"

"Shot won't impart enough energy per hit. That might ding it up, but we need a direct hit to cripple it or detonate it prematurely."

Tammy interjected, *"I think we need all the options we can muster, Joe. Can Hillary broadcast the shootout at the Volnos Corral over GSN?"*

Lester plucked the pistol from mid-air, spun it around his index finger, and snapped his fingers shut around the grip. *"No sweat."*

Grant nodded decisively. "Let's do it."

▼ ▲ ▼

Every pod had two shotguns stowed within reach of its occupants. Intended to repel human boarders rather than missile assaults, the No. 1 size shot in the shells would only disable the missile if several scored direct hits. A quick poll of the crew determined that sixteen members in twelve of the pods could engage in the firefight. They fastened their helmets, checked air packs, and snaked the short distance from their seats to the slender shafts through which they had entered. The tube-like air locks opened full-length inside. When closed and evacuated, the only way out was through the small hatch overhead.

Only one crew member could fit in each air lock at a time. That cut the number of artillery by four. They would serve as backup, but all knew that if the first fusillade failed, it would all be over by the time the second rank refilled the lock, climbed inside, evacuated, and eased out the hatch.

Tammy plucked a pump-action Mossberg 12 gauge from the arsenal, loaded it, and lanyarded it to her wrist as Lester had urged everyone to do; she picked up a length of safety line and hooked it to her belt with a carabiner. The other end she snapped around a u-bolt recessed in the deck of the shaft. Turning a simple valve, she voided the precious few cubic feet of air from the lock and opened the hatch to naked Space. Edging outward with the Mossberg leading the way, she pulled up to shoulder level and gazed around. Now came the hard part.

Since the hatchways faced forward along their orbital trajectory and the attack was approaching slowly from behind, the station defenders each had to make it from bow to midships in order to gain a clear line of fire.

Tammy had only done one EVA in her life as an astronaut. She wore a multi-layered NASA spacesuit and was clamped to the orbiter's mechanical arm. Here, she wore the minimum necessary to survive: a Spandex pressure suit that did nothing more than keep her skin from exploding, a helmet with a radio, and a breathing unit. The only thing keeping her from floating into the trackless void was an eighth of an inch thick length of braided aramid cord. She inhaled a deep breath of pure oxygen and stepped out into Space.

The equator of her pod lay just thirty feet away from her over the spherical forward half's tight horizon. Every three feet along the inner meridian rose a small loop welded to the surface — another place to clasp her carabiner. She chose to use them as fingerholds and pulled hand-over-hand across the dull aluminum surface. To her left and right, arching overhead, she saw the others climbing through the doughnut hole toward the interior equator of the toroid.

Twenty-three and a half feet to her left, Joseph Lester had lashed himself in a kneeling position, straining against the cord for tensioned steadiness. He yoyoed his pair of Wildeys on their lanyards, then got serious and assumed a hunched-over two-handed stance, alternating his sighting down left and right pistols.

To Tammy's right, Pod 16 — one of the two unmanned modules — sat with its hatch closed tight. Beyond that, a space-law specialist named Jay Thayerson, whom Chad had insisted on bringing along, stood at the ready in Pod 15. Janet Red Eagle, the hydroponics expert, defended her son Billy, who watched on the viewing screen of Pod 14 with wide, dark eyes. Next to them, Adrienne Oakwood — a paramedic and their would-be fitness coach — protested over the intercom that she had no shooting experience but would do what she could. Dentist-vet hyphenate Harry Jakes in Pod Ten swore that he could shoot hard enough to compensate for his wife and child remaining inside Pod 11.

Grace and Rex Ivarson, both seasoned sporting clay competitors, did not have to quarrel long over who took the honor of the first shots: Grace thoroughly trumped Rex's assertion that Man lived to defend Woman by calmly asking "Will the one who *hasn't* had brain surgery please put on her helmet?"

Ta'Shawn Wilkes and Dr. McLaughlin defended Pods Six and Five, respectively, while next to the doctor — in Pod Four — Chad Haley scanned the sky with binoculars pressed against his face plate, his head straining against the neckpiece to bring an eye close enough to focus. From Pod Three, Paul stared about in childlike wonderment undismayed by the danger they faced. Hillary secured her position at the viewing port in Pod Two, camera in hand. From there she could just barely take side-view images of the shootists on several of the farthest opposite pods. The rear cameras would be responsible for video of the onrushing attacker.

Tammy made it to the inner equator of the station. Facing aft, she clipped the carabiner on her front belt loop to the metal ring, and — belly to the hull — spread her legs wide, held the weapon with buttstock pressed firmly against her shoulder, sighted along the shotgun's barrel, and waited.

"All right, everyone." Tammy spoke slowly and clearly over the encrypted radio intercom. "Orbital motions are counter-intuitive to what we experience on Earth. When you fire at the missile — or whatever they may throw at us — you don't have to adjust for windage, but you will be compensating not only for gravity but for the fact that the buckshot will be dropping into a lower, faster orbit. The missile will come at us nearly dead-on, so you won't need to lead your target. Our goal is to put as much debris between it and us to disable or destroy it. Don't fire until told, then keep firing until you run out of ammo or until the missile passes. Do not fire after it passes or you might riddle the other pods with your misses. Stand by."

▼ ▲ ▼

Barron saw none of this activity in the surreal image on his HMD. He saw a blown-up display of the sixteen intersecting spheroids painted by the radar that he finally risked using. He locked the missiles on two pods opposite each other, figuring that secondary projectiles created by their destruction would pepper the other enclosures, rendering them useless if not immediately killing all onboard.

At six miles distance, closing at 20 feet per second, he activated the rotary missile-bay doors. The ASAT's locked into place, armed and ready to launch.

Barron's blood pulsed wildly in his veins. Sweat adhered tightly wherever it broke out on his flesh — in free fall it could flow nowhere else. His breathing quickened. With a feral grin he thumbed the firing switch and gloried in the hearty vibration of the killer birds' departure.

The missiles' exhaust plumes left in their wake a thin mist that glowed briefly in the flames of the solid-fuel motors.

▼ ▲ ▼

"Now!" Reis cried, firing the Mossberg at the twin rings of light suddenly flaring toward them. What on Earth would have been a deafening roar was barely audible as a vibration conducted through the shotgun to her bones. Nevertheless, a mule kick slammed Tammy's shoulder backward and the carabiner tugged violently at her belt loop.

The others experienced similar reactions, some of them gyrating uncontrollably. Only Lester, kneeling and using his recently uncovered musculature to absorb his pistol's kick, was positioned to deliver shot after shot from his Wildeys. One in either hand and both lanyarded to his belt, he alternated viewing through the pistol scopes, aiming through the right at the starboard missile, squeezing off a round, then — while his right arm and shoulder absorbed the recoil — switching his gaze to the left-hand scope to cover the portside missile with the targeting red dot. A shot from the left, then back to the right.

The missiles, rising to higher orbits from that of *Huntress*, slowed perceptibly as gravity worked its inexorable effect.

Lester quickly discovered that he was not hitting either missile. Windage may not have been a problem, but *orbitage* was. The bullets flew along paths that were not *quite* straight. They followed the curvature of the Earth in their own orbits.

Swiftly, he turned the windage and elevation knobs on the 32mm sights to compensate for his best estimate of how the bullets' trajectories would behave. Then he resumed his two-fisted shooting.

The feel of the pistols in free fall astounded him. Their weight meant nothing, yet the muscle power necessary to resist their recoiling momentum after each shot proved formidable. He fought back the fear that he might fail by mentally treating the onrushing missiles as nothing more than metal silhouette targets.

Rapidly approaching, murderously deadly targets.

Through his right-hand scope he saw an impact on the heat-seeking FLIR sensor in the starboard missile's nose. It may have been one of his shots, or it may have been a piece of buckshot. Whatever the case, he hoped it had some effect.

It did. The missile careened off course. He instantly shifted his efforts toward the other missile. It could not have been more than a mile away.

All the shooters turned their attention to the surviving missile. A fusillade of gunfire silently blazed away at the approaching killer.

Several shotgunners ran out of shells, leaving no time to reload. Two others suffered breech blasts as lubricants not intended for hard vacuum froze up and jammed the feeders. One of the exploding shotguns sent a blast of lead shot into Adrienne Oakwood's face, shattering her helmet and voiding her lifeblood into space. Screams died in the vacuum as lungs voided air and breathed nothing; her hands clawed at the polycarbonate shards, cutting open her fingers and only hastening her death. After a few minutes of thrashing and kicking like a rag doll on a rubber band, she grew limp. Governed now only by the laws of physics, her body gently expended the last of its kinetic energy in bumping first to one side then the other, pivoting around the carabiner attached to the eyelet.

Almost directly across from Oakwood, another disaster struck as Chad's own belt loop tore loose under the repeated stress. He drifted away from the hull, arms stretching frantically toward the cord. Tension recoiled it an inch too far away, and he stared dumbfounded at the hull dropping away from him like a ship departing a desert island. Without him. He watched as the others fought on. Without him.

The missile raced within seconds of killing range. Lester, down to one shot in his left pistol, released his right to float on its lanyard. Grasping the other Wildey with both hands, he coolly sighted in until the red dot covered the missile's warhead. He squeezed slowly and deliberately at the trigger.

The recoil battered his weary arm muscles one more time, slamming his sore back against the vessel. He lowered his aim to see the missile heading straight for him.

It did not explode. Inert, killed by Lester's final blow, slowed by the orbital mechanics of gravity, it sailed on ballistically to rip into the hull a few yards away from where he stood, tearing a hole in the aluminum-lithium alloy tank and venting a cloud of hydrogen gas — what little remained in the tank — into the vacuum.

With a sudden growl of vengeance, Lester cried, "Here's the one *I* want!"

He ejected from his left pistol the spent magazine — which sailed away into the void — rammed another home, released the slide to chamber a round, then retrieved his right-hand pistol to do the same.

The white spaceplane — a nameless, faceless attacker propelled by the inexorable laws of physics — drew closer to the circle of fusiliers without decelerating.

The universe swirled around Lester's consciousness as he gathered every ounce of concentration and channeled it into the hunter's feedback loop that runs from prey to eye to hand to weapon to prey. Then he uttered the prayer most appropriate to the situation.

"Eat lead, you son of a bitch!"

Both pistols fired at once, again and again as swiftly as he could squeeze the triggers. Blood thundered in his ears as the Universe contracted down into nothing other than shooter and target. Spent cartridges ejected outward to tumble away, twinkling in the sunlight like golden beads strung across the heavens.

▼ ▲ ▼

Huntress closed in on the catherine wheel of renegades without braking for rendezvous. Barron surveyed the damage on his approach. For all his effort, the missiles only punctured one sphere. Pitiably minor, easily repaired.

For an instant he considered ramming them, but he valued his spacecraft — not to mention his own life — too much to destroy either in what would be a decidedly Pyrrhic victory. Better to run away to fight again another—

The bright muzzle blasts from the lone standing subnat instantly caught his attention. *Huntress* possessed little in the way of armor. Low mass and high speed had been his only considerations. Nothing so primitive as guns for ship-to-ship dogfighting had entered his mind during the design phase. The next model — after a lessons-learned report — would undoubtedly have them. Montgomery Barron, though, would play no part in the construction of any descendent of *Huntress*.

Project *Stark Fist* ended with both a bang and a whimper. The bang came from the shattering impact of four copper-jacketed .45 Winchester Magnum slugs from the Wildeys. The cockpit canopy shattered as the nitrogen atmosphere exploded outward, sucking all sound with it. Barron felt, rather than heard, the fifth bullet pierce his shoulder. On Earth, hardly a fatal wound. In Space — harsher, vaster, and more desolate than any terrestrial wilderness — the ravenous void sucked at the bullet hole, drawing blood, vaporizing it, liberating gasses, and tugging at the torn flesh.

He gazed at the red mist in which he sat. His eyes focused beyond it, at the colossal structure into the center of which he shot like an arrow through a ring. Only as he threaded the eye of the needle in his rush toward death did he realize how *Volnos* dwarfed his own spacecraft, both in its size and in its purpose.

Every instant mattered now. *Look up!* The Earth hung overhead. Through the ragged frame of the blasted polycarbonate canopy, Barron gazed past the crimson haze of his own boiling lifeblood to see the deep greens and browns of Ecuador amid white swirls of cloud. The Sun glinted off the blue Pacific, then raced across the land, reflecting its image off of lakes, rivers, and irrigation ditches as if the Earth's surface were only a thin veil, behind which hid a dazzling god only occasionally glimpsed.

He realized that he would never make it back to Earth, that Project *Stark Fist* ended with him, and that he would die inside *Huntress*. Even so, he proved that he could build an SSTO, that it could intercept other spacecraft. Everything else simply constituted a failure of detail. He proved something else, too: to serve those in power required that he defy them. Through his individual force of will did he acquire the strength to overcome the inertia of the collective.

He wondered if similar revelations occurred to every dying soul. It no longer mattered. Life flowed out through his shoulder, allowing a numbing cold to spread across his chest. Only one option faced him now: to die in orbit, an eternal reminder of the glory that was Columbia, or to return to Earth in a fireball for all to see.

He chose. And as he chose another option appeared. A lone figure in a grey-and-maroon skintight pressure suit drifted a few hundred yards off his left wing.

Almost giddy with irony, Barron used his attitude jets to rotate about, then fired them on one side to shift over to the slowly moving figure. The side of the fuselage bumped up against the man, whose hand locked in a deathgrip on the open edge of the cockpit.

The engines on *Huntress* ignited gently under Barron's command, sending the crippled spaceplane back toward the space station at a meager four feet per second. The hunter stared at the hunted, no hatred in his eyes.

The man hitching a ride said something into his mic, then tensed his muscles and kicked away from *Huntress*. He scrabbled through the limitless void and his strategy became apparent: he hit one of the pods dead center. He bounced off, but inertia kept him moving aftward. Due to the curvature of the pod, he stayed in contact with the metal, sliding outward from his impact point and using the friction of contact to slow him down. Instead of heading toward the inner or outer part of the lumpy toroid, he managed to roll his slide toward the midline, wedging safely into the welded intersection of two spheres, where he remained to wait for a lifeline.

The engines of *Huntress* ignited once more, this time shoving Barron into his seat. He felt no pain. He existed beyond his body now, all intellect, all thought. He did not bother to rotate the ship around once more to place it in proper attitude for aerobraking. With its windshield shattered, the ship would have incinerated anyway. Instead, he gazed backward at a new constellation rapidly receding from him in the heavens: sixteen points of light that formed a perfect circle. As he deorbited and lost sight of its diminishing circumference over the horizon of Earth's curving limb, Barron realized that his age had ended and a new one had begun. Power would not be the goal of this new breed; the market had won. Slaves would not conquer the stars for their masters; free men would settle there for themselves.

The atmosphere of his home planet trembled against the stern, followed by a series of powerful shudders.

Montgomery Barron fought to stay conscious, to live to the very end of his body's physical existence. He wanted nothing more now than to die an astronaut's death. Like an honor roll he tried to remember all the names of the fallen: Grissom, Chaffee, White, Komarov, Volkov, Dobrovolsky, Patsayev, Scobee, Resnik, Smith, McNair, Onizuka, Jarvis, McAuliffe, Rader, Heinz, Taga—

Before he could finish naming the crew of *Constitution*, his thoughts were silenced as *Huntress* disintegrated into a hypersonic meteor of plasma and flaming debris. In the span of an instant he felt intense pain, then blackness, then nothing.

▼ ▲ ▼

To anyone in the Caribbean who happened to look west shortly after noontime, a bright orange-and-greenish-white fireball raced across half the sky. It left a trail that glowed for several seconds, even in the harsh light of day. More than a few awed children — young and old — made wishes upon it. For many of them, it was the loveliest light they had ever seen.

CHAPTER 56

O, Thomas, will a Race one day stand really tall
Across the Void, across the Universe and all?
And, measured out with rocket fire,
At last put Adam's finger forth...?

— **Ray Bradbury**

22 August

Sherry Cooper smiled with a confidence and relief she seldom experienced these days. The team of thirty ground personnel poring over *Aurora* completed their turnaround on the spacecraft in a little over fifty-four hours. Freespace stood ready to launch its second orbital flight less than a week after its first.

She sat in the blockhouse beside Thom, watching the countdown, which stood at T-minus two minutes. Her husband's Astra Constable .380 stayed behind in her hotel room; she would not need it today, she knew in her bones, what with the riot of reporters milling about the launch site. They covered this flight with a scrutiny unprecedented in the brief, spotty history of private space travel. After the spectacular success of Crockett's and Grant's secret launches, and the low-key downplaying of coverage on Poubelle's launch and *Aurora*'s maiden voyage, every news agency on the face of the globe realized that — this week — the history of the world had changed trajectory.

Nonetheless, she made certain that at least three news teams clustered around the range safety officer, recording his every movement.

The moment approached. Onboard the again-pilotless *Aurora*, in the payload section where one variant of the Starblazer design called for twenty seats intended for tourists, were instead two aluminum-lithium tanks, holding a combined total of 16,000 pounds of fuel and oxidizer above and beyond what it needed to achieve orbit.

All eyes turned toward the video screen at T-minus thirty seconds.

Sherry's heartbeat accelerated inside her; on the outside, perspiration prickled at her flesh. The first flight's success might have been a fluke. This second flight after rapid recycling of the spacecraft provided the true test of the entire Freespace launch system.

The future of her company, of private commercial spaceflight itself, rested on the events of the next ten minutes.

Deep inside *Aurora*, a computer command sent frigid liquid oxygen flowing trough pipes and valves to mix with liquid hydrogen in the twenty combustion chambers. Pyrotechnics, fed by the flow of oxidizer, ignited the fuel to unleash a powerful explosion of thrust.

"Liftoff!" the launch director said. "Liftoff of *Aurora*'s second flight, this time on a mercy mission to bring desperately needed fuel to Space Station *Volnos*."

Sherry Cooper nodded at Thom Brodsky, who tapped a few commands into his console. Television and radio audiences around the globe suddenly heard a familiar voice over their sets: the recorded voice of Barry Gibbon transmitted from onboard *Aurora*.

"The ruling elite — and believe me, I have access to the highest levels, those who tell presidents and prime ministers what to do — will not permit access to space to hordes of commoners. The world's political economy is based upon scarcity. Space travel would disrupt that completely."

"Who the hell is that?" someone said.

"Sounds like Barry Gibbon," Gen. Lundy answered, frowning. He turned to Mrs. Cooper. "What is this?"

"My husband recorded it just before he was murdered. Listen."

"... imagine how the military feels about anyone other than they capturing the high ground. Rather than see that happen, they would much prefer to invade an equatorial country on some pretext and disrupt a company's efforts, or blow up a spacecraft in the boost phase, or assassinate financial backers and company founders."

Sherry looked at Lundy, gravely grateful, and said, "Now, General, *everyone* will pay attention to Range Safety."

▼ ▲ ▼

At NORAD Space Command, General Dorn stayed awake for three days straight monitoring the events. Right now, he observed the orbital tracks of *Aurora* and S. S. *Volnos* approach rendezvous. Doubtless the refueling would proceed swiftly and safely. He came to expect that from this new breed of spacefarer. The fuel brought up by the ship was not much, but flight after flight would bring enough of it to make two engines useful. And Larry Poubelle just keeps routing those donations from Daedalus to the Ad Hoc Committee to Rescue *Volnos*.

Dorn looked as if he had spent a month living on the streets, and he felt like it, too. The full political, economic, and social impact of these space flights — the public ones and most especially the clandestine ones — were yet to hit. Short of outright attack — and he knew full well how Monty Barron had failed in that tactic — Space Station *Volnos* would continue to orbit the Earth with impunity, broadcasting whatever messages Grant wanted, manufacturing and deorbiting anything Grant possessed the raw materials to build or grow. And anyone who succeeded in launching a rocket into orbit — which now appeared simpler than ever — could resupply the station or, God forbid, lob up a second fully-built platform.

All this disturbed the general. A minuscule muscle under his left eye twitched incessantly. He knew more than nearly any other man about the theory and practice of war in Space. The one subject never dealt with in any seminar or think-tank piece was the absurd notion that government — the very concept of government — would be left behind by spacefarers in their exodus. That Space would become a frontier not in the sense of a new national border, but a frontier of unlimited wilderness, welcoming an unregulated, uncontrolled, possibly unconquerable horde of pioneers, settlers, and traders, separated by vast seas of Space, yet connected intimately by encrypted communications links and a shared distrust of all terrestrial authority.

"General..."

The voice broke his prognostic trance and he focused on Capt. Lee, who continued. "We have a confirmed rocket plume rising from Southern Russia. It's not from Plesetsk or Baikonur."

"Russia?" Dorn mused, looking upward at the huge screen. On it, a cherry-red curve rose from south of Rubcovsk. A 3-D rendering of the flight path predicted its insertion into an orbit very close to the 51.6° inclination of the ghost space station *Mir*.

Dorn's mind raced. A Russian presence in Space changed the recently upset power equation yet again. Though he expressed a low opinion of them otherwise, one thing he knew for certain was that no Russian could go for long without desiring some form of global domination. The possibility of exploiting this new factor expanded his options vastly.

Perhaps, he mused in silence, *the Space Cadets have not heard the last from us Grub Eaters*.

EPILOGUE

My interest is in the future because I am going to spend the rest of my life there.

— Charles F. Kettering

23 August

"I can see it!" Joscelyn Donahue cried out. Radar confirmed, hours before, that *Aurora* closed in on them via the optimal planar and phase windows. Something within her, though, refused to believe it until her own eyes gave witness.

The bright blue-white dot — crisp and sharp in the airless void — drifted slowly, almost imperceptibly slowly, below and behind them in its co-elliptic orbit. With thrust adjustments, it would be soft-docking with them within an hour.

She and the others waited, silently, almost breathlessly. Soon she, Chad Haley (none the worse for his startling side-trip) and a man she thought she knew, who now called himself Paul Volnos, would don their helmets, depressurize their air locks, and work their way across the outside of the space station to transfer fuel from the Starblazer to pods Five and Thirteen. More than the joy she felt at the imminence of their salvation, she thrilled at the power of the human mind: how a passion for the unknown brought her to the edge of Space, and how the compassion of strangers turned the complex laws of chemistry, metallurgy, physics, and mathematics into a successful orbital rescue.

Her gaze remained pinned on the approaching spaceship, as if losing sight of it would be a crime against their saviors, against all the efforts of man. *Aurora* became to her the symbol of everything decent, good, and honorable about humanity.

She no longer feared for the future of mankind. It could prevail against any adversity.

▼ ▲ ▼

Rex Ivarson could not sleep. While awaiting fuel for pods Five and Thirteen, the crew spent their time pumping the last wisps of hydrogen and oxygen in the other tanks into fuel cells for electricity and water. Then they flushed oxygen into the hydrogen tanks and opened everything up. In short order, the station had become a lot roomier.

Not until they had teased the wheel up to a stable orbit would they be able to give it the appropriate 3 rpm spin for pseudogravity. Until then, he and Grace enjoyed the unbearable lightness of being in free fall.

The view out of the thick window gripped his attention as surely as any earthly wonder. In his nearly nine decades of life, he had often imagined that he would someday live in Space. As the years trudged onward, though, and several false dawns teased him with promise then failed to deliver, he grew to believe that he would die on Earth. Now he gazed at the blues and greens and whites and tans of his home world and wondered — warmly, without nostalgia — if he would ever return. He withdrew the laptop computer from the pouch in front of him, pressed it securely to the Velcro fuzz on the lap section of his pressure suit, and switched it on.

MEMOIRS OF A TRAMP SPACER

I was born in a decade in which a hoofed mammal was the primary form of human transportation, and the airplane had only just been invented. I grew up in a town not far from where Mark Twain was born, and I shook his hand when he once visited, or so my mother said. I was two and he was seventy-five.

I am the world's oldest astronaut, yet I feel younger, more vital, lighter of heart, and more hopeful than I ever felt in my most callow youth.

Human ingenuity is the only true miracle, a thrilling marvel that puts to shame the meager boasts of priests and shamans.

Ivarson glanced over at his slumbering wife and smiled.

▼ ▲ ▼

The funeral was quick, simple, and inelegant. Adrienne Oakwood's body, wrapped in a sheet of gold-hued reflective Mylar, floated near the the hatchway to her pod, held lightly by Paul Volnos at her head and Chad Haley at her feet. The other defenders of the space station stood by their respective pods, while the rest watched from their view ports, mutely pensive.

Paul's voice sounded thin and worn inside his own helmet. "I didn't know Adrienne Oakwood too well," he said into the radio microphone, "but she proved her dedication to our cause by paying the ultimate..." His voice caught and paused as he gazed at the curving limb of Earth silhouetted against the black of Space. "It's so pointless," he said after a moment. "Why do they try to stop us from leaving? Don't they know we're no good to them staying where we don't want to be? Why attack us for following an urge older than society itself? What are they afraid of?"

He took another breath. "Adrienne died fighting to defend this puny toehold in Space against a power that envies and fears a free people. If her death has any meaning, it is to show the world that human beings still have backbones, and that there are some values worth fighting for, even to the end."

Paul released his grip. With a mighty shove in the anti-orbital direction, he and Chad propelled Adrienne's body away from the station. It drifted like a glittering charm lost from a bracelet. The others watched for a long while as they grew farther and farther apart. Sunlight danced on the funeral shroud until all the living could see was a sparkling pinpoint of golden brilliance.

▼ ▲ ▼

The crew of Earth's first genuine space station strapped in for a long-awaited full-length sleep period. The novices called it "night-time" even though the sky glowed with stars all day, too. One crew member, though, chose to sleep without straps that first night in Space.

Tammy Reis drifted in slumber inside the roomy hydrogen tank of Pod One. If it were not for the perforated decking that separated the tank into three levels, it would have been as large as a cathedral. It did not matter what size it was, she felt just as holy, just as blessed. Free of all restraint, she surrendered her conscious thoughts about her past and future to the eternal now of her dreams.

Paul Volnos, the only one not to turn in, took the first four hour watch. His heart still pounded from the excitement of viewing live GSN coverage of *Aurora*'s safe return to Kennedy and its subsequent preparation for another refueling flight. Sherry Cooper stated publicly that they had received investors' funding for the construction of another two Starblazers — one to be operated solely for Leora Thane's tours.

He maneuvered quietly through the holes cut to connect the spheres at each deck level. The pressure hatches would have to be shipped up on later Starblazer flights.

He hovered for a long time in Pod One — near Tammy, observing her sleep. In free fall her hair drifted loosely about her, undulating fluidly with her breaths. The pulse in her carotid arteries caused her head to bob up and down gently, as if nodding her approval. Her arms, unbound by gravity's pull, reached forward and outward from her body, like the open arms of a beckoning lover. Her face bore no evidence of the torturous path she had followed into Space. On it now lay the peaceful calm of one who has finally found her home.

She had served NASA in her passion for Space and received in return only a brief, painful taste of it. Rejecting her path, Paul had forsaken Space completely. Both actions, he realized now, gazing at the only woman he had ever loved, were mistakes. NASA was never really an enemy, simply an obstacle to overcome. No one, nothing outside of their own souls was ever the true enemy. The real foe, the most vicious betrayer, lurked only in their hearts, their minds, consisting entirely of fears, doubts, their sense of what life could or could not be.

Paul Volnos slowly drifted toward Tammy and tenderly took her into his arms, careful not to wake her from her slumber. Her warmth merged with his as — still in dreams — her arms closed about him.

She floated in the vast reaches of Space, naked before the splendor of the stars, and gazed at the planet below. Though she knew it to be Earth, it looked like no Earth in the waking world.

With carefree abandon, she dove toward the ocean covering a hemisphere and fell toward the rich blue sea, wind singing in her ears, the scent of salt and cool morning air filling her lungs. With a sudden surge of energy and motion, she rebounded into the sky, reaching upward, higher and higher, to embrace a pure white crescent Moon as she raced the Sun in its journey.

Tammy Reis touched the dawn of a new day.

The End

Acknowledgments

A writer is a sponge, and not just on the pocketbooks of friends and relatives. A writer absorbs information from many sources, processes it all through a particular world view, and creates something new and different. Below is only a partial list of those whose minds and works I have tapped for this novel.

Thanks to Ray Bradbury, for being an inspiration and for loving Space as much as I do, if not more.

Tom Brosz, erstwhile editor of *The Commercial Space Report*, for absolutely invaluable information about the various spacecraft used in this book and for providing me with contacts in the aerospace field. His artwork was also fundamental to my envisioning many of the spacecraft mentioned herein.

Bevin McKinney, for information about his Roton orbital helicopter.

Bruce H. Neuffer, for refining the concept of the fully assembled SSTO space station.

Oliver P. Harwood, for writing me about how the space bureaucracy suffers from the 'not invented here' syndrome.

Max Hunter, for having a truly revolutionary vision of single-stage-to-orbit spacecraft.

Gary Hudson, for hanging in there all these years. If Delos D. Harriman lives, it is within you.

Samuel Edward Konkin III, for his absolutely nail's-head analysis of the "Space Programme" and for all the wonderful quotes I had to choose from.

Tim Kyger, formerly of the office of Congressman Dana Rohrabacher, for filling me in on who truly controls NASA's fate.

Richard Kyle, for strategic ground support and owning the best bookstore in the world, bar none.

Gary Lane and Charles Mason for information about airmovers.

Roy Lavender for stories about the Apollo project and the glory that once was NASA.

Brad Linaweaver for promoting this book wherever and whenever he could, and for getting me and my daughter into movies as a diversion from my writing.

Ed Kramer, who pulled off this coup against all odds.

William O'Malley, whose Macintosh program Text Retriever recovered several pages of work that I thought were lost to a system crash and an unopenable file — bless you!

Jerry Pournelle, for all the wonderful information he has on his

GEnie® RoundTable, which helped immeasurably with the plotting of various conspirators' flights.

J. Neil Schulman, for seeing early on the importance of this novel and for inventing — and perfecting — the paperless books concept so that this novel could bypass the watchful dragons in American publishing.

Sherwood Smith, for providing valuable insight into the book's structure and hours of constructive criticism, for which I am extremely grateful.

Greg Benford, for the brains, talent and dedication to write about Space and the human heart.

Sean Sullivan, for letting me know what it was like to be at Kennedy Space Center that fateful day in January, 1986.

Aviation RT, Science-Fiction RT, Spaceport RT, Writers' RT — all on GEnie®, the erstwhile General Electric Information Network — Internet, and the World Wide Web, for enabling me to find answers to the most obscure aerospace questions.

Vincent Harper and Final Frontier Books, for appreciating this book enough to put their money where their minds were, and for possessing the technological savvy to put New York publishers to shame by taking the novel from electronic manuscript to finished book in less than two months! Thanks, too, to Output for the great look of the text.

Rob Prior, for working at James Bama-like speed and skill to create classic cover art.

My parents, Igor and Alexandra, and my sister Irene, for their support, encouragement, and understanding through all the years of my so-called writing "career."

Veronica — my love, my life, my best friend, my wife — you have been through so much and helped me so deeply and thoroughly that I cannot conceive of having gotten this far without you.

To all the men and women who have toiled relentlessly, lived and died so that we may someday — soon, I hope — live among the stars, this novel is for you. Through your Herculean efforts in the face of bureaucratic madness or boldfaced lies and coverup, you helped lift humanity to new heights.

And finally for my daughter, Vanessa, and my nephew, Justin, and all their generation, who are so young that the notion of men on the moon lays further in the past than it did in the future when I was their age. I hope you can reach and touch the planets that we so myopically let slip through our fingers.

AFTERWORD
by
Gregory Benford

In this big-hearted, sprawling novel Victor Koman takes on the quite near future — the toughest terrain in all fiction. Better, he tackles our rickety space program, hitting at soft targets. Reading it, I reflected back on my own involvement with space, from the freckled kid reading Willy Ley and Arthur Clarke describe how rockets worked, to a consultant for NASA and the Planetary Society. Somehow a lot of the zip has gone out of space for a lot of us, and for the public, too. Why? And what can we do about it?

We went wrong just after Apollo, I think. James Fletcher was NASA Administrator from 1971 to 1977, when the Shuttle was being proposed, designed and checked out — or rather, not checked out. He convinced Congress that this nifty little reusable rocket-cum-space-plane gadget would get magically cheaper and cheaper to fly, eventually delivering payloads to orbit for a few hundred dollars a pound.

The cost now is over $5000 a pound — a twenty-fold increase, allowing for inflation. The Nixon administration bequeathed to us an econo-ride Shuttle (and Jimmy Carter signed the appropriations bill for it). They also axed the remaining Apollo missions and the 1970s version of the space station, though these weren't vital. Their killing the long-range research for a Mars mission had great effects, however, because we now have no infrastructure developed for large deep space missions.

Then came the *Challenger* disaster, with Fletcher in charge again. In the *Challenger* commission report he allowed as how "Congress has provided excellent oversight and generous funding and in no way that I know of contributed to the accident." Except, of course, for consistent under-funding and pressure to attain goals set by people with little or no technical competence.

The shuttle is a spaceship designed by a committee of lawyers. "The fault was not with any single person or group but was NASA's fault," Fletcher went on, "and I include myself as a member of the NASA team." As Joe Haldeman sardonically remarked to me, "Most people would say he was more than just a member."

And we can't even buy shuttles in quantity. The Fletcher-Nixon vision saw a flight a week. That got scaled down to 24 a year, then 12. In 1989 there were 9, in 1990 six, with that abysmal prospect, a flight every few months, settling in as the normal routine until we begin building the Space Station in early 1999, when we will need many more.

Unmanned exploration was once the virtually unblemished, high-minded face of space. Now our failures accumulate. The wrong lens curvature of the Hubble telescope. The big antenna which won't deploy aboard Galileo as it limps toward Jupiter, years late; we could have sent it directly, on a Proton booster the Soviets offered us at bargain rates, but politics of the late 1980s ruled that out. The Titans that explode with billion-dollar packages aboard, the satellites which go awry. And the Mars Observer, lost to unknown error or just bad luck.

The repair of the Hubble Telescope lifted spirits a bit, but face facts: it was a repair job we should not have had to do at all. The Hubble mission was overloaded with tasks, and NASA elected to do them all with One Big Shot — a poor strategy when you're pushing the envelope in several different directions.

It wasn't always so. Voyager was a miracle. We caught the big brass ring on that one, beginning when an orbital specialist noted in 1963 that a Grand Tour could be won by looping a probe past several of the outer planets. The window for this orbital high wire act opens every 175 years, but the last time, when

Thomas Jefferson was President, we missed the chance. In 1972, when astronauts still tread the moon, we decided to go for the launch window in 1977.

I don't think NASA could do that today. Hell, it couldn't even decide to not do it that quickly. In just five years during the 1970s NASA invented and developed nuclear-power batteries which are still running, 16 years after launch. It assembled fail-safe computers and electronics that withstood the proton sleet of Jupiter, where a human would die of an houris exposure. Built to give us Jupiter and Saturn, they still forge outward after gliding past Uranus and Neptune as well.

The Voyagers keep sailing on just as they were, dutifully sending back reports to a society that has changed profoundly. Voyager is a legacy of the 1960s, a child of the hustling Space Age that wanted to do everything it could (and a few things it couldn't, like building a true space plane).

Gorbachev in 1987-88 sounded much like Khrushchev, talking up space. George Bush in 1989 resembled Kennedy, setting a goal: a manned Mars landing by the 50th anniversary of the Apollo landing, 2019. Both leaders sounded the charge. Both countries yawned and changed the subject. Shortly afterward, they changed the leaders, too.

What's different? The game has changed. It isn't national rivalry any more, and probably won't be for quite a while.

Bruce Murray, former director of the Jet Propulsion Lab and a professor at CalTech, pointed out to me many of these curious analogies and features of the Space Age, but his most striking analogy reached even further back.Once we had a distant, hostile goal, and men threw themselves at it, too: Antarctica. Early in this century, Scott and Amundsen raced for the South Pole with whole nations cheering them on. The Edwardian Englishman who tried to impose his own methods died. The savvy Norwegian who adapted to the hostile continent came through smoothly.

Others tried to follow. Shackleton made some progress, and then national rivalry became far more serious: World War I swallowed up the exploratory energies. Admiral Byrd and others made headway between the wars, but true, methodical Antarctic exploration did not resume in earnest until the International Geophysical Year, 1957.

The wars gave the International Geophysical Year teams cheap, reliable air and sea transport technology. (Scientists don't like to talk about it much, but modern war bequeaths science a feast of intriguing gadgets.) Military services were happy to assist, exercising their capabilities. International though the spirit was, national and territorial claims did not vanish; Argentina and Chile still mutter over their rights to turf. Indeed, perhaps the major reason nobody disturbs the present high-minded international air is that no serious resources seem to be at stake. Discover a rich field for mining or pumping and all bets are off.

Scott-Amundsen: Apollo. Shackleton and Byrd: Voyager and Galileo. The World Wars, in this analogy, are like our rising concern with domestic problems — not soaring nationalism, luckily, but at least a deflection of those energies to local concerns.

Bruce Murray pointed out, in a speech published in Space Policy, Feb. 1991, that a science fictional alternate world scenario could perhaps illuminate our predicament. Think what our world would be like, he said, if the two-term limit on the presidency had not been enacted in the late 1940s. Franklin

Roosevelt's four terms had provoked that change in the Constitution. The first president it applied to was Dwight Eisenhower. I remember how popular he was even in 1960. I'm pretty sure he could have beaten Kennedy; good grief, Nixon almost did.

Eisenhower would have presided over the whole early Space Age, 1957-64. He called space programs "pie in the sky," refused to fund research at a fast clip, and warned us against the "military-industrial complex".

In a parallel world with Eisenhower in office until 1964, we would have had no brave setting of the Apollo goal, no race to the moon. "It was that close," Bruce said.

He thinks that by 1990 we would probably have seen some US-USSR muscle-flexing in near Earth orbit and probably a few unmanned probes would have studied the moon. No Grand Tour trajectory for Voyager, probably no Mariner to Mars or any of the rest of it. George Bush's 1989 speech might have been a stalwart call for a manned moon landing before the turn of the millennium.

Not impossible. I can scarcely argue that such a plausible, sensible space program was unlikely. After all, I had once written a story in which Robert Taft got the nomination in 1952, not Eisenhower. (And Taft's private choice for the vice presidency was one Senator McCarthy of Wisconsin...)

The plausibility of this imaginary history tells us that we have been very lucky. We lived through dramatic times, Sputnik-Apollo-Voyager, which quite probably will be seen as like Columbus-Magellan-Drake. Maybe we are now getting back to normal. And normal means, alas, dull.

The trick in using analogies and scenarios is knowing when to stop. How does our predicament differ from the past? We must play to those differences if we are to steer a better course than Destiny would give us.

Large space projects have fed off nationalism. Kennedy sold fears of Soviet technology, with an attractive patina of worry over our science education. This worked well — and I directly benefited, being a senior in high school in 1959, from the special science courses rushed into the schools; in fact, I might well not be a scientist today, were it not for the sudden spotlight cast on lowly high school physics courses.

Gerard K. O'Neill tried to hook up his giant solar power collecting satellites to the energy "crisis" of the 1970s, but of course the price of oil fell well before any such gargantuan project could get under way. (I never really believed in the O'Neill designs or strategy, and spent an entire dinner in a pricey restaurant trying to argue him out of the approach. He was sure that eventually energy prices would prove him right. When he died in 1992 he was still rather wistfully pushing the project.)

The paranoia road is necessarily short. Fears abate. Enemies topple. So it's time to face "Space as a Place" — a terrain to be studied and used in its own right, not as a sideshow battleground for earthly concerns.

We must also face the fact that we've done the easy things. Putting a pressurized Huygens probe on Titan, amid chilly winds and with many more light-minutes of delay in getting radio orders through, will be a much tougher job than was landing Viking on Mars.

There are some signs of intelligent management, though. In January 1994 NASA launched Clementine, a bargain basement mission. It rose on a Titan IIG rocket, recycled after spending 25 years in an Arkansas ICBM silo. It is a light, low-cost probe, using (and testing) sensors developed by the Ballistic Missile Defense Organization, the heir to the Strategic Defense Initiative, a.k.a. "Star Wars." Clementine was state of the art with a powerful laser-ranging device which mapped our moon completely for the first time.

Contrasting with the billion dollar Mars Observer, Clementine cost a mere 75 million. Plans for a second mission which will rendezvous with an asteroid and study it come in at about 30 million dollars. A small team put Clementine together in two years. Such savings point to the hard-nosed, realistic program we need.

Space must be made cheaper.

The reality of the late 1990s seems to be that the Shuttle will remain a time bomb in the belly of NASA. Its own internal studies show that the odds are about one in 80 of a major accident, every time it flies. I served on a study group assessing the Shuttle in the 1970s, and we calculated the odds rather higher — about 4%, or one flight in twenty-five. Regrettably, *Challenger* was right on the money. Then NASA became obsessed with hand-tuning every bolt on the craft, and now the odds are better.

But they will never be good. Rockets are not safe, period. The Titan failure rate is about 3%, and the Russian Protons do about the same. No rocket has ever done better over the long haul.

The schoolteachers-in-shuttles agenda, sold the public for so long, came out of wanting to project the Eisenhower perspective—a go-slow Space Age, elbows tucked in, chin down, making no mistakes. How can we counter that?

First, appeal to the frontier. Young people, not just Americans, want to believe in an expansive sense of the future. More than consumerism and the Beavis & Butthead worldview. Our time needs heroes rather desperately. Notice how the media seize on the merest sign of character, such as Attorney General Janet Reno's accepting some blame for the errors of her underlings. Political leaders are tuned to sense this better than scientists. That's why the emphasis on manned space, which scientists like James Van Allen deplore because, after all, it is pricey and returns little for research folk to study. Man-in-space is a political event.

Actually, the general risk of rocketry plays to this. Danger equals drama. It would be a breath of fresh air if the President would simply tell the public that every launch is much more like a test pilot run, with casualties expected. No schoolteachers riding a bus into orbit. Instead, gutsy men and women on a wing and a prayer. As in The Right Stuff, "No Buck Rogers, no bucks."

We'll probably have a shuttle blowup before this decade is out, a fiery finish with grieving widows, and we might as well be prepared. Indeed, the deeper lesson we should drive home is that space will never be safe. Adventures aren't.

Second, we should have a clear set of cost-conscious reasons for every single project. Here the Antarctica analogy helps.

There are still solid national reasons for space. Nobody thought that there were good scientific uses to Antarctica when Scott and Amundsen raced across it. We didn't see that chilly clime as a laboratory peculiarly sensitive to the whole planetary system.

Now the 'ozone hole' is a major diagnostic of our planetary health, an early indicator of the depletion which is hard to measure globally, but gives itself away among the frozen crystals floating high above the poles.

The space analogy to this is "comparative planetology." We can learn basic information about how our system works by seeing the variants played out on Mars, Venus and elsewhere. These places can teach us much about the sensitivity of planets to the sun, to chemical components in their atmospheres, and much else. Clearly there is some connection between solar activity and climate, but we know little of how it works, much less how to make predictions. Mankind arose during the last great inter-glacial time, and another may be coming. What should we do about it?

The Martian polar caps contain layers going back to the Ice Ages of Earth. Was the main cause external to both planets—the sun? Or is there something more complicated going on, involving the atmospheres as primary players?

These questions are best answered by robots. They send back reams of data, grist for the scientists' mill—for people like me, who explore the solar system in their mind's eye. What about manned flight?

An old siren song might work here: leadership in aerospace. Control of how to get into orbit. This novel imagines a single-stage-to-orbit approach. I favor two stages, getting a rocket plane to 60,000 feet using reliable jet plane methods, an ensemble that could take off from any large airport.

No matter; both approaches should be tried. On the larger horizon, many space advocates have regrouped around a clear, seemingly inevitable goal: Mars. Mostly, I suspect, for its romance, mystery and the classic: because it's there. And it's also the one goal which can quicken the pulse of the multitude.

I don't think anything on the space menu can satisfy a public longing for action with meaning nearly as well as Mars. It will be expensive and dangerous and we can all go, via TV.

But to even propose such a thing, as George Bush did, pushes quite a few problems to the top of any space agenda. Current blue-sky planning for Mars exploration assumes that we will use liquid rockets and take about a year each way. This means problems of human deterioration in zero g become major: calcium leaches from bones, muscles atrophy. Obviously (to nearly everybody but NASA) we should study people inside spinning cans, to see if centrifugal effects will duplicate gravity in the physiological sense?

Or perhaps we should look beyond chemical rockets. To fast ships which can get a small payload, of people plus a few weeks' rations, to Mars within a month. Their supplies could be pre-positioned, waiting in orbit at Mars. Nobody needs to leave until all their support gear is in place and working. Here the "Mars Direct" plan outlined in Robert Zubrin's *The Case for Mars* has compelling logic.

All these are policy decisions, but they must be made in light of what humanity as a whole wants to see in space. Drama. People. Mystery. Wonder.

Perhaps manned presence should be seen now as intrinsically international, because we desperately need goals as big as the human prospect. The world needs lofty aims. Space buffs love their iconography — the drama of liftoff, of horizons brimming with the unknown, of Voyagers serenely gliding above alien landscapes. As well, they have an answer to those who say that these are simply the distractions of a high culture, perched atop a seething, oppressed mass.

The industrial nations have about twenty percent of the world's population. The bulk of humanity labors long and hard for little. Not because the advanced nations steal their wealth — that same twenty percent produces two thirds of the world's output, including agriculture — but because most of the world has never learned the many social and intellectual abilities which produce wealth.

We will probably have no real peace in the world until most of humanity is somewhat prosperous, or at least has solid hope of becoming so. But if they pursue the agenda of the industrial nations, the strain on raw resources will be vast. So, too, will be the pollution from more mining, metal smelting, fossil fuel burning, irrigation and the like. The planet simply can't support it, not with present technology.

The energy and mass needed for uplifting humanity must come from elsewhere—space. And it is quite foolish, in the long run, for us to do messy, polluting things in this thin shell of vulnerable air and water which gave birth to us all.

We're fouling our nest. But a smart bird learns to fly.

June 20, 1998